BIOSHIFTER

Volume Two

Natalie Maher

Contents

1

BIRD MODE

"Hello, sir?" I ask, approaching a customer and pointing out the window. "Is that your car?"

"My dog needs shade," he says with the kind of defensive tone that means yes, it is his car, and yes, he absolutely knows it's not allowed to be parked there. I give him my best customer service smile, my voice so perfectly polite that it's even less human than my body.

"I'm afraid you're blocking the storefront. I need to ask you to move your vehicle."

"People can get around me," he argues.

They shouldn't *have* to go around you, you self-centered twit. What part of that do you not get? Sure, it's not a huge imposition—he's not in front of the handicap ramp, at least—but parking lots have parking stalls and we didn't put any parking stalls in that direction for a *reason*. You're in the way!

Whatever. Simply asking him to conform to the rules is a flop, and an appeal to basic decency isn't getting through to this guy. Time to change tactics to the good old 'nothing I can do about it, sorry!'

"Apologies, sir, but the landlord owning the lot requires all cars exclusively be parked in stalls," I say demurely. "We're not the only store in the plaza."

He regards me with an irritated sneer, giving me the sort of 'are you stupid?' facial expression that I quite desperately wish I was allowed to send right back his way. I have no idea who this guy is, just some jerk with short-cropped black hair, a hawkish nose, and the sort of clean-pressed business casual outfit one wears while telling themselves that they deserve every cent of the money they're currently embezzling. I'll forget his face in less than an hour.

"You guys don't allow me to bring my dog inside," he accuses, countering my plea with the classic 'completely change the subject instead of acknowledging my legitimate argument' technique. "So I need to keep the car in the shade or he'll overheat."

"I'm afraid we can't allow non-service animals into the building for allergy reasons, but you're more than welcome to eat on the patio with your dog," I answer, blocking with the 'eminently reasonable alternative' defense.

"I don't want to eat outside," he says simply, and I *twitch*. If you're not going to go outside with your dog then *don't bring your dog,* you absolute soggy-bread numpty! Screw this, it's ultimatum time.

"Well sir, I still have to insist that you move your car regardless," I tell him, politely but firmly. It's the sort of voice that has an implied 'or we'll call a truck to move it for you' at the end.

He glowers furiously, looking over my shoulder in an attempt to find someone in a fancy uniform to complain to in my stead. He locks eyes with my boss, but my boss just gives the man a *very* unimpressed look, glances to *me,* and raises a phone questioningly. That gets the man to finally get off his butt and go move his car. Finally! With a sigh, I head out of the dining room and return to my post. There are a bunch of orders that need bagging now, thanks to all that wasted time.

"Thanks for handling that, Hannah," my boss smiles.

"I want to eat that man," I grumble quietly. Then I go stiff with terror because I did *not* mean to say that out loud! Or think it! Or honestly believe it! Aaaaaah! My boss seems surprised for a moment, but then he just chuckles.

"Brutal, but I understand the sentiment. You did good, though."

Oh thank the Goddess I actually have a good boss.

"We're going to have a nasty review tomorrow," I say glumly.

"And I'm going to turn the review into a Karen meme with my manager comment privileges," he shrugs. "Don't worry about it."

I manage half a smile, not that he can see it, and get back to work.

"Incidentally," my boss continues, "next time you have a minute, would you come to the back? I wanna talk to you about some things. Nothing bad."

Oh crap candles. You can't just say 'nothing bad' and expect me to believe it!

"Sure," I confirm anyway. "No problem."

He smiles, nods, and heads back to do whatever manager stuff he does when we're not critically understaffed, which *somehow* we aren't today. I get back to work, taking orders and bringing people food and just generally having a normal, easy day. In some ways it's a nice change of pace from the usual hustle and bustle, but overall I feel like it's leaving me with way too much time to think about the crazy nonsense that just happened.

I have a *magic spell* that turns people into *monsters* and I *accidentally used it on my crush* but she *still wants to date me.* Every single thing in that sentence is just increasingly more ridiculous and unbelievable, but it's somehow still all true! Why do I have a spell that turns people into monsters, though!? Spells are a reflection of who we are, right? This seems like the kind of thing Brendan would love more than I would. Oh, shoot, how's Brendan going to react to this? Is he (or maybe she? Aaaaa!) going to ask me to use it on him? What would even happen if I did? I don't know how this spell even works! Oh shoot, I don't

3

know how this spell works! What if I can't control it any better than I can control my self-transformation spell? No, no no no. Hold on. Only Autumn is changing, and only Autumn was hit by me channeling my Transmutation magic. That's very much evidence of an active, conscious effect. If I don't cast it again, I won't have any problems.

...It's kind of *extremely* relieving to know that someone other than me is having these problems, though. I'm really looking forward to talking with Autumn about it more. To have someone that *gets it*. I feel bad for thinking that way, since I kind of ruined her entire life probably, but... still. It's nice. I kinda want to text her, but... no, I'm at work. Also I'm supposed to go talk to my boss now that it's slow. Oh shoot aaaaah I need to go talk to my boss!

I head to the back, where a little inlet for a simple computer hides behind the walk-in fridge. The manager's 'office,' as much as it can be called an office without even a cubicle wall to delineate it from the rest of the cramped restaurant. This is where the boss spends most of his time, doing General Manager stuff like fiscal reports and scheduling and how-do-you-do.

"Hannah, hey!" he greets me as I approach, and I give him an awkward wave in response. "So, two questions for you."

"Lay 'em on me, boss," I say with a casualness that I don't at all feel.

"Number one: your birthday is next week, right?"

Wait, it is? Oh, *fuck*, it is! Goddess, I'm going to be an adult. I don't like that at *all*. How does he know that? Wait, he knows everybody's birthday, we have to give it to the company when we get hired.

"Uh, I guess it is," I manage to reply, and he chuckles.

"How old are you going to be?"

Why are you asking me that!?

"Eighteen, I suppose," I admit, my heart beating concerningly fast. Please don't hit on me please don't hit on me please don't hit on me nooooooo.

"Nice!" he grins. "I just noticed you were scheduled on that day, and I *do* actually get a budget to use the company card for 'team-building reasons,' so do you want like... cupcakes or something?"

...Is that why there are cupcakes here sometimes? I guess he has done that for other people, then. Probably not hitting on me. Calm down, Hannah, it's just cupcakes.

"Emphatically no," I say anyway. "I mean... I guess I wouldn't mind cupcakes, but I don't want anyone to know it's my birthday. You can just buy some treats and take all the credit for it if you want."

He laughs and nods.

"Okay, I can do that!" he agrees. "No problem. So the other reason I ask is that shift managers have to be eighteen. And I think if you want to start training for that starting this week, I could definitely use another manager over the summer."

Oh? Oh! Oh dang! I'm getting promoted!? Oh heck yes, my mom's gonna be *so* happy, she'll get off my case for weeks!

"I... that'd be awesome," I agree, nodding in confirmation. "I'd be happy to."

Assuming I'm still human enough to hold a job at the time, I mean.

"Great!" he says. "You already know how to do every position, so that's good. What we're going to be focusing on is having you actually *manage* people. Stepping up into a position of leadership. You're a very hard worker, but you tend to keep to yourself. When someone else isn't doing their job, you step in to compensate for them or help out, which is *great*. But now I want you to try giving them advice or just reminding them of the rules rather than just doing everything for them."

Oh crap that's right, managers have to talk to people. I might even have to learn people's *names*.

5

"I'll be letting people know that you're training for a shift manager position so they don't give you too much lip," my boss continues. "You're not going to be the only person I'm training and the number of positions available will be based on the number of people who quit over the summer, so this isn't a guarantee that you're getting the job. But you do *great* with guests so if you work hard I'm sure you can pick up the skills for handling employees in no time. Okay?"

"Yes sir," I say, though the truth is that dread is pooling in my belly. *This breaks my work routine.* I like my job as-is, just cleaning and dealing with customers and cooking and whatever needs doing at the time. Talking with patrons isn't social interaction, it's an itemized script that I've successfully memorized and perfected. I need a whole new playbook if I'm going to be expected to interact with my co-workers beyond the bare minimum necessary to do the job.

Geez, I'm going to have to actually remember their *names,* and figure out the best way to present criticism to each of them, and I should probably learn some conversation topics that each person likes talking about that won't require me to say very much, since if the managerial position is a competition it's at least halfway a popularity contest because that's how humans work. Should I start taking notes? Writing down the things I remember about everyone? I mean, that's not going to be a very long list. Ugh, this seems like way too much work. I'd wing it, but how am I supposed to have an interesting conversation with someone outside the context of a hyperfocus?

...Wait. Is this why Teboho thought I was autistic?

"Order up!"

Ah, right, my job! Let's just shove *that* thought into the box with the others. The fact that I get along with Brendan so well is because he's cool and everyone else is lame and for *no other reason.* Not that... y'know, not that it would be *bad* if I was autistic, I'm just. Not. Like a doctor or something probably would have noticed, right? My mom took me to a bunch of those as a kid.

6

I spend the rest of my shift mostly doing my job like normal, attempting to work up the courage to talk to my co-workers and mostly failing. I can correct them and stuff, that's pretty easy. Asking them to do things that are already part of their job rather than just doing it for them slots into my work routine without *too* much trouble, but it definitely isn't making me any friends. I get a nasty glower when I ask the other front of house girl to help me clean tables instead of look at her phone. But what do I even do about that!? It's a job, she's here to work. Why is she mad about working?

Whatever. Just weird human things, I guess. The shift isn't so bad, all things considered. We even finish the closing routines in a reasonable amount of time thanks to not being understaffed. When I finally get home, I pull out my phone to find a bunch of texts from various people.

Hats are against the dress code, right? Autumn asks.

Oh shoot I think they are, I confirm. **You need something for your ears, right? Hoodie and a headband?**

I look at my text from Brendan next.

Hey so Ida has my number apparently and she says you have a TF-other spell???

TF? I ask, and see him reply almost instantly.

Transform/Transformation, he answers simply.

Oh. Yeah. I don't think I can control it though.

Moving on! I have a text from Ida as well.

i told tallboy about ur magic for shits. have fun

Thanks, Ida.

I was gonna tell him anyway, I send back. Ooh, I have a reply from Autumn!

How are those not against dress code if hats are against dress code? she asks.

I dunno, but I've seen tons of people wearing them so it's probably fine? I answer.

u kill anyone at work btw, Ida asks.

No! I send back. **I mean, I definitely wanted to, but that's just retail!**

lol imagine having to work retail and not being born with twelve silver spoons in ur mouth. loser.

Why am I friends with you???

im hot as fuck

I sigh.

...You're high, aren't you? I ask.

bitch im sneering down at the sun

I have a really colorful friend group, don't I?

Shit, that's a problem, Brendan sends me. **It's not really the kind of spell you can experiment with safely, is it? If it's anything like the magic changing you, it doesn't have a reverse setting. I doubt it's safer to *not* test it, though. Does it work on animals or do you have to use people?**

I don't know and don't intend to find out, I send back.

I guess you're right, I've seen a lot of people with hoods up, Autumn sends. **Okay. I guess a hoodie for me and a headband for Jet? She'll need it for gym class.**

Ah, okay, she's Alma then. I had a feeling.

I recommend both for you, I tell her. **More layers is better than fewer. Redundancies in case of an accident. Also, bring medical supplies and extra clothes in your backpack in case you mutate more.**

Wait, am I going to mutate more???

I have no idea, I answer honestly. **I hit you with that spell days ago and you're only starting to change now, though. Bring stuff just in case.**

hey hannah banana if i becum a monster will that make you more likely to fuck me or less be honest

Okay, you know what? This is too many conversations at once.

I'm making a group chat for magic stuff, I send all of them simultaneously. **Use this to talk about things. Autumn, meet Brendan. Brendan, Autumn. I'm exhausted and need to pass out soon, but Brendan can help you plan out the things you'll need if you're going to school tomorrow.**

which is a TERRIBLE fuckign idea but what to i know im just the smartest and best at everything ever, Ida sends.

I don't want to have to explain to my dad why I missed two school days in a row, Alma answers.

oh there's two of them now fantastic

Then Brendan sends me a three-paragraph diatribe in our personal text instead of the group chat and I decide to give up. I shut my phone off and collapse face-first onto my bed, waking up shortly afterwards as Kagiso shifts her weight in our cozy, cozy bedroll. Ah... this is a nice way to wake up. Way, way better than I'm used to. No limb confusion, no mutation panic, just soft, warm cuddles. ...Wait, should I be doing this if I'm dating Alma? Hmm. I guess I'll ask her about it. Whether it's due to a biological incapability or just a weird quirk of our relationship, my feelings for Kagiso are strictly platonic... but boundaries should be established regardless.

That's a problem for tomorrow, though. For now I'll just keep on enjoying myse... wait nope I'm super itchy, I need to move. Specifically, I need to *molt*. I wriggle my way out of the bedroll and shortly afterwards I wriggle my way out of my own skin, stepping into a barren zone and leaving the dead bits of me behind. *Much* better. The pockmarked, chaos-damaged chitin I was covered in yesterday is now replaced with a pristine new epidermis, although that's not the limit to the changes I notice.

For one thing I'm bigger, if only by a little. It's hard to tell but I think I've grown at least a few inches since I first burrowed to the surface, but molting because of growth is pretty normal and expected by molting standards. What really bugs me—pun intended—is that I'm pretty sure I'm not perfectly symmetrical

9

anymore. It's subtle: my body isn't exactly a sphere, two of my legs are fractionally longer than their neighbors, etc. But it's *there*. I'm changing into something else, something that isn't the cute little ball of legs I've gotten used to. It's kind of frustrating, honestly. Just when I'm getting used to the idea of being a monster, I have to go through the pain of changing in *reverse*. I can't describe it as anything but cruel.

Hmm. That's an interesting thought that almost slipped by me: 'changing in reverse.' For some reason I'm confident that's what's happening. Sure, I had a *theory* that my human body was getting hyperspider bits and my hyperspider body was getting human bits, but I don't have any evidence stronger than circumstantial. Ugh. I hope I don't end up as just a normal human on this side of things.

...Actually, wait, why would that be bad?

"What the fuck are you eating?" Helen snaps, jolting me out of my thoughts. The baggy-eyed Chaos mage glowers at me with her usual suspicion, guarding our camp from the same log she sat on during our chat yesterday.

My molt, I write.

"So like... your own skin? That's fucking disgusting."

I mean it doesn't taste great, I admit. **But I feel an urge to eat it anyway, so I'm eating it.**

"Couldn't you just *not?*"

Can you, Miss Chaos Mage?

She scowls and turns away. I can't help all the weird monster instincts I have now, okay? Put down that brick until you get out of your glass house.

"...It's not the same," she grumbles quietly.

Okay, or don't. Though she's not totally wrong, I guess.

Not exactly, no, I admit. **Though I also get urges to kill and eat people sometimes. Those are scary.**

10

"You do?" she asks, turning back my way and raising her eyebrows.

Yeah, I confirm. **My Transmutation magic really messes with my head. I guess maybe my Order magic too? Though the before and after there is subtler.**

"Wait, what do you mean 'before and after?'" Helen asks.

I swallow the last of my discarded skin, trying to think of the best way to explain this. I guess simple works.

I wasn't born with magic, I say. **I didn't have any until recently.**

"Huh. Wild. So magic fucks with your head? Just another reason it sucks to be me, I guess."

My own magic hasn't forced me to do anything, though, I warn her. **Just little... temptations, I guess? Well, sometimes big temptations. But my actions are my own.**

Helen reads that silently, giving me a small nod. I scuttle over closer to her and hop up onto her log, which she stoically allows. We sit and wait, wordlessly agreeing not to wake Kagiso until she gets up on her own. It doesn't take too long, at least, and I watch with amusement through my spatial sense as the fuzzy gremlin arches her back and yawns like a six-limbed cat before pulling herself completely out of the bedroll.

"Why light?" she mumbles, wandering over to us.

"Well that's what happens when the sun comes up," Helen snorts.

"No. *Why light?*" she repeats, yawning again. "Was supposed to take third watch. You no wake me."

Helen shrugs. My super-keen senses detect a slight blush forming on her cheeks.

"Didn't get tired," she mumbles. "Now come on, let's pack up camp and get going."

Aww, she's grumpy but she cares about her friend. I guess as long as she doesn't commit any more mass murders Helen might be pretty okay. I mean, she *has* killed an obscene number of people, but if Kagiso forgives her I guess I'm not really in any position to hold a grudge. ...Except maybe for Teboho. Damn it. I miss him.

I let out a long sigh, then jolt a little in surprise when it doesn't come out as an eldritch hiss. Wait, that actually kinda sounded pretty normal! Can I talk now!?

"Heeehuhhh? Ehsing!" I gargle out incomprehensibly. Aw, shoot. My respiratory system doesn't connect to anything resembling a tongue or teeth, so I don't really have any articulators. Still, though! Progress! I'm finally maybe mutating the ability to speak!

"Wuzzat you?" Helen asks, walking up to me and leaning down to hold out an arm. I nod and scramble up onto her shoulder, her overflowing backpack already prepped and prepared to depart.

"Huh. Learning to talk? That'd be useful," Helen nods. "It's boring as shit waiting for you to scribble words out all the time."

Well excuse me for being mute! I hiss at her, delighted to find that I still *can* make horrible eldritch noises when I need to. She freaks the fuck out and nearly drops me, but it's totally worth it.

"Hee hee. Friends getting along," Kagiso grins, walking up alongside us with the rest of the packed-up camp on her back. "Walking time."

Walking time indeed. Our gang of freaks departs, and the usual boring day on the Tree of Souls begins. Like, yeah, sometimes things get really crazy over here with bandits or mind control or jerkwad paladins, but the vast majority of my time spent on the world tree has just been traveling, hanging onto a friend's head and occasionally chatting the day away. Sometimes I'll hop off of Helen's head and onto a nearby tree trunk to go hunt a tasty friend noodle or two, but most of the day passes without anything of note happening at all.

It's nice. It's *relaxing*. My days have been way too full of things of note lately, and if I can't sleep off stress like a normal person I really, desperately need time to *rest,* time to repair myself mentally instead of just physically. Being able to spend the whole day doing effectively nothing? A little boring, but still *oh* so needed.

12

I barely even talk with Kagiso and Helen, partly because we're all quiet people but mostly because I don't have Teboho to make me a writing tablet or Sindri to form a mental link (thank the Goddess). The methods of communication I have available to me don't work all that well when we're on the move, and while I could probably figure out a solution to that if I tried, it isn't really a huge deal for me. We chat a bit when we stop for meals, and we chat some more when we stop to camp for the night. I encourage Helen to obliterate large chunks of ground, making huge holes with her Chaos magic, and I happily start filling them back in. She calls me a weirdo. She says this probably isn't what Hagoro meant when he said I could help her spend energy due to being an Order mage. She's right on both counts, but digging is fun and now I get to do *so much digging* while the others go to sleep for the night. I enjoy playing around in the dirt until it's time for me to get Kagiso up for second watch (she insisted), and then I head to bed.

Waking up on Earth, I smile as I remember I don't have to worry about finding control of my lungs; I have them in both bodies now, and I can take a deep, relaxing sigh before starting my usual morning routine. Figuring my limbs out, I stretch as I rise from bed, noticing my phone on the nightstand has a crapton of text messages waiting for me. Ah, it's the group chat I made! I guess everyone actually used it.

You be quiet, Autumn writes. **By the way, um, hi person I don't know. Brendan?**

That's me, Brendan confirms. **I'm Hannah's friend. I've heard a little about you but I have *no idea* what your current situation is. I assume you're the reason we know Hannah has a spell that transforms others now?**

Um. Yeah, I guess so. It's... really weird. But also kind of exciting? I have tiny wings now!

activate 🦅mode Ida butts in.

Well, are they small enough to hide in a sports bra? Brendan sends, ignoring her. **You and Hannah have gym tomorrow, right?**

lol does she still creep on ppl in the locker room

Aaaaaand now I'm blushing.

Ida, shut up, Brendan says.

Uhhh... Autumn types.

right right sorry ill be serious, Ida says. **tomorrow. when my bloodstream is not eighty percent weed.**

Wait, isn't that illegal here? Autumn asks.

goddess damnit hannah youd better not be dating a cop

Can we please focus? Brendan pleads.

I can't help but giggle a little at the byplay between my friends, though I *am* a little worried about whether or not they'll get along with Alma. Things seemed to have gotten copacetic as the night wore on without me, so that's good. I send everyone a good morning text and head for the shower.

I think my new eyes might be getting slightly light-sensitive, but otherwise they haven't really changed much. Makeup and hair cover them easily. More skin falls off my mutant leg—I'm almost to my hip now, and that joint will probably look interesting. Some skin is also starting to fall off the palms of my hands, though not a lot. Just a bit right by the knuckles. Overall, not much happening in mutation land.

Bus stop. Chat about RPGs with Brendan. Desperately desire to ask about transgender things but resist the urge in public. Head to class with Ida. Act normal. Gym class is a bit strange, with Jet there with a headband and a thicker shirt than usual but otherwise looking totally innocuous. We jog together, chatting lightly until the more serious question of Alma and I dating comes up.

"So, I definitely want to hear this from your mouth directly," I say. "Dating. Alma says she still wants to try."

"I'd call her crazy but I suppose that's why I exist," Jet grumbles.

"I don't think you're crazy," I insist.

She gives me a long look, and then huffs out a quick, frustrated burst of air.

"It's probably healthy for her to have a relationship, and since you have us wrapped up in your bullshit it may as well be you," she scowls. "I don't know if it's really my place to stop her anyway. Go for it."

"Really?" I grin under my mask. "Aw, thank you Jet!"

We finish the warm-up run side by side, coming to a stop as we rest and wait for the remainder of the class to finish. Jet stares at me, suddenly looking *really* intense.

"I just... I need you to understand something," she says. "If you two start... getting physical, and something pulls me to the front? I am suddenly smack-dab in the middle of an *extremely* non-consensual situation. The *instant* we say anything that might be kind of a little bit adjacent to a no, you get the fuck off me and you go to a completely different room. You skirt the line even the tiniest bit and I will *end* you, Hannah. Is that clear?"

"Uh... y-yeah," I agree, nodding. "A hundred percent."

"Good," she growls, and then the intensity vanishes a little. I take a breath I didn't realize I was holding. ...She's a Pneuma mage. Did she use mind control to be that scary? No. No, no, no, calm down. I relax my toes, pulling the claws out from the deep gouges in my shoes. Jet's not controlling my mind. She's just an intimidating person.

"So, uh... did you figure out any of your magic after I left?" I ask, because I'm still scared of the answer anyway.

"Not a lot," she answers, speaking quietly. "But some. I think my magic helps me hide things. It's... useful."

"Oh, that's interesting," I smile, a bit of tension leaving me... though not most of it. "You like it?"

"Begrudgingly, I think I do," she admits.

I nod, a bit of my smile returning. Magic *is* pretty cool. How could you not like it? I mean... okay, I guess Helen has a good reason to not like it, but *other* than people who are being oppressed because of it. I wiggle my extra limbs underneath their bindings in silent embarrassment.

"...Don't take things too fast with Alma, by the way," Jet suddenly continues. "Let her make the first move for stuff. We're both pretty nervous about this, though she'll never admit it."

"Um, okay, I can do that," I nod. "I'm not really very touchy most of the time anyw—"

"We need *control,*" Jet insists, cutting me off."You have to let us have that. Let her have that. Okay? Suggest, but don't order, and... and... make sure to give her space when she needs it, or else she'll just turn into *me.*"

"I... okay," I say as calmly as I can manage, because Jet seems to be getting *really* agitated all of a sudden. "I'll take things slow and steady. Don't worry. I know I have wandering eyes but I'm not going to pressure her into anything she doesn't want to do. Okay? I promise."

"Okay," Jet says, nodding slowly. "Okay. That's fine then."

I hesitate, taking a moment to work up the courage for my next words.

"...Are you okay?" I ask hesitantly.

"Yeah, I—" she says immediately, then cuts herself off for a moment, holding back the automatic response. "...I will be."

I nod. That's a good answer. An honest one. ...I should try to give answers like that more often.

"I'm sorry again," I tell her. "About the monster stuff."

"I'll figure something out," Jet dismisses, shrugging. "I always do."

The rest of the day isn't all that eventful. Autumn makes it through the whole school day without an incident, *I* somehow make it through a whole school day without an incident, and my other friends actually have the capacity to not cause problems in

16

the first place, the cheating jerks. It's unfortunate that my work day is all weird now that I'm supposed to direct employees a little, but I get through that, too. I'm actually kind of starting to feel *normal* again, which is both jarring and an intense relief. It almost makes me forget that I have to go see a therapist in two days.

...Aw, crap, I remembered that. Dangit. Panic time. Good thing I'm about to pass out anyway!

I wake up on the world tree and search for a distraction immediately. Hmm! Well I suppose Kagiso's boobs are nearby, but I'm not going to touch those. I wiggle out of the bedroll instead, finding that once again I need to molt. Two days in a row, huh? Maybe I can talk now!

"Hhhhhhaaaaaaaaaaaaarrrrrraaaararaaaa," I declare eloquently.

Aw, butter side down. No luck. My internal organs *are* shifting a bit, though, my lungs consolidating and some of the openings on my body closing as the whole organ system starts seeking out my throat to be its orifice of choice. With it is the continuation of the changes I noticed yesterday... well, this universe's yesterday, I mean. Some of my legs are ever so slightly starting to change shape, a bit more thickness here and a bit more length there, while my body likewise has a few bumps and valleys where it used to be nice and hyperspherical. It kind of feels like my changes here on the world tree are accelerating, while my changes over on Earth are decelerating. That feels... significant, somehow.

"You're really gonna just eat your own skin every day, huh?" Helen grunts, walking over next to where I'm munching away at my molt.

Every day some of it falls off, sure, I confirm with one leg.

"You're weird as fuck," she grunts. "And you're also basically immune to fire, right? Powerful Transmutation mage? Help me cook some shit."

I agree, only to find out shortly after that by 'help me cook' she meant 'stand in the middle of the campfire and let me hang stuff

17

on your legs.' Which turns out to absolutely be a thing I can do heat-wise, but I start to suffocate almost immediately and have to back away, coughing my still-mutating lungs out.

"Huh," she grunts. "I guess I should have thought of that."

I want to angrily agree that yes, yes she should have, but I'm the one that actually walked into the middle of an open flame just because someone asked me to so I'm in no position to talk. The two of us sit down next to the campfire and cook things much more normally for a while, once again waiting for Kagiso to wake up together.

"So... we'll probably make it to that city today," Helen says. I turn my body like I'm looking at her to indicate that I'm listening, though it's entirely performative. My eyes already see in every direction other than straight up or straight down. "There should be a decent number of nychtava there, and your mindfucker's money bag should be more than enough for one of them to take us down to the Slaying Stone."

There's a pause.

"At which point we'll part ways," she finishes.

I should hide in your backpack in the city, I write.

"Why... ah. Okay. Yeah, that makes sense," she nods.

I hesitate, debating whether or not to say what comes next, but ultimately... sure. I've earned a bit of bravery.

Kagiso won't want you to leave, I tell her, even though I'm sure she already knows.

"Kagiso doesn't know what's good for her," Helen grunts.

Ah, I write. **You're doing the thing.**

"What?" Helen asks, sending a confused glower in my direction. "The fuck does that mean? What thing?"

You know, the thing the grumpy or traumatized character always does in stories, I write. **They push everybody away when they need the most help, and it always goes badly for them.**

18

"This isn't a fucking story," Helen snaps. "Real life doesn't have happy endings, Hana."

Happy or not, there's a reason no stories show the people going off alone as making a good decision, I write. **That wouldn't be realistic, after all.**

Helen just scowls for a moment before pointing her finger at the words and causing a sphere of Chaos to swallow them up into nothing. I quickly jump away to avoid getting disintegrated, hissing at her but getting the obvious implied response. I have just been told, I believe, to shut the fuck up. Oh, well. I tried. Pushing away my friends is the one big mistake Brendan made me promise not to do, but if Helen insists I can't really stop her. She's certainly not *my* friend, at least not yet.

Kagiso eventually crawls out of bed and we eat breakfast together with the food I nearly suffocated trying to cook like a total moron. Helen and I silently agree to not talk about it as we chow down on some recently-caught meat, Kagiso giving us jealous glances as she consumes her collection of roasted fruits, vegetables, and leaves.

"Don't look at me like that," Helen grumbles, but it's devoid of malice. Unlike usual, her tone is a fake admonishment, sounding more like an in-joke. "You know you get sick if you eat too much meat."

"Texture better," Kagiso mumbles, her mouth full.

"Yeah, but the taste is worse and you know it. Eat your sugary little plants, Kagiso. They're good for you."

Well, I for one like the taste *and* texture of this meat. I've been eating a lot of raw food over here on the world tree lately, so it's kind of nice getting something cooked for once, even if I prefer the firm *slice* of uncooked meat through my fangs. This is conversely pretty tender and easy to swallow, which feels nice to my more humanoid side. I keep my opinion to myself, though, just listening to Kagiso and Helen bicker good-naturedly throughout the meal. It's nice.

Before long, however, camp is packed up and we're back on the road. Literally! It's only a couple hours into our walk today that we run into a somewhat-crumbling cobblestone road about fifteen feet wide. I scuttle into Helen's backpack to supply her my aura and hide me from potential cultists, and I'm still stuck in there when, another couple hours after that, Kagiso reports that there's a city in sight. I sure wish I could see it! It sucks being luggage sometimes.

"Alright, moment of truth," Helen whispers, and at the edge of my sensory radius I see a pair of sciptera—the cute little bat people I saw in the last city we went to—staring at us with the sort of intensity one might expect from a guard. Our auras are probably being checked. No one flies at us and attacks, though. No one even talks to us. We pass through a checkpoint and Helen lets out a slow, careful breath.

"I can't believe that actually worked," she mutters.

This city, from what I can see with my spatial sense, is at least an order of magnitude smaller than the huge dentron metropolis Sindri took us to. Most of the people here are sciptera as well, fluttering about in pairs, holding tail-hands, play-fighting in the sky or gripping the side of a tree to rest and chat. It's much calmer, much more casual than Grawlaka ever was, even at night... though perhaps due to that, we seem to attract a bit more attention. A pair of sciptera start fluttering around us, squeaking and chirping noises that seem like they're probably words in a language I don't understand.

"Uh... either of you speak Middlebranch?" Helen hedges.

"Human!" one of them chirps, apparently proving the answer to be 'yes.' "What human doing here?"

"Fall and hurt yourself, human!" the other cackles.

"Landbound! Root-foot!"

"Back to Slaying Stone!"

"That's *exactly* what I'm trying to do, thank you," Helen says, surprisingly without any display of bad attitude. "Any of your bigger cousins live here? Nychtava?"

"Cousins!?" the first one hisses angrily. "Stupid! Not related to nasty nychtava!"

"Well then direct me to one and you'll get both of us out of your hair," Helen bargains, pulling out a small amber coin and flicking it towards the pair of harassers. One catches it with their tail, the other tackles them, and the two fall to the ground in a heap, cackling and hissing. I'm worried at first, but I don't think they're actually hurting each other. I think they're having fun?

"End of branch!" one of them announces between play-bites. "Nychtava live at edge!"

"Thanks," Helen nods, and we leave the two of them wrestling on the ground.

We walk the rest of the way in silence, Helen doing her best to keep her head down while Kagiso looks around, wide-eyed and possibly salivating as her head whips back and forth to track the fast-moving sciptera.

"Kagiso, please don't fantasize about shooting people," Helen hisses quietly.

Kagiso jumps slightly, clearly startled.

"...Wasn't," she lies.

I chuckle quietly to myself as my friends continue their long walk to the other end of the city. I wonder what nychtava *are,* anyway. I've heard the name a few times since waking up in this world, but I haven't seen one. Helen called them 'cousins' of the sciptera, though, so maybe they're also bat people? I wonder what the difference is.

"I mean it, Kagiso, I *really* need you to hold in your creepy organ fetish," Helen insists. "We're dealing with *nychtava*. I need you to not do—or think—anything stupid. If our ride starts feeling like you wanna fight, they're gonna fucking drop us."

"Understood," Kagiso nods.

21

"I do all of the talking. You do none of it. Okay?"

"Okay, Helen."

Helen nods, letting out a nervous exhale. Geez, now I'm nervous too! We start to near the edge of the branch, or at least I assume we do with how the trees around us are thinning out and the dirt below us is getting shallower. Soon enough, there aren't any trees growing around us, bar the world-sized one at our feet, and the dirt gives way to fourth-dimensional wood. I guess when those sciptera told us to go to the end of the branch, they really meant *the end of the branch*, because on either side of us I start to sense the dramatic downward curve that indicates the uncomfortable closeness of the abyss, the threat that at any point you can just walk a certain direction until you fall off the tree entirely and plummet to your death. Soon, the space we have between us and the edge is only forty feet on either side, then thirty, then twenty, then *ten*. For the first time today, I'm glad I'm stuck in the backpack, unable to see. My spatial sense can't tell me how far we'd ultimately fall. We're teetering over our own death in every direction before Helen finally stops walking and calls out.

"I'd like to hire a ferry!"

The branch *shakes*. Only slightly, but Helen and Kagiso each drop to one knee regardless, taking no chances against the certain death below us. Then, from the lower edge of my sensory range, I sense something rushing upwards. It *does* sort of look like a sciptera, in the way a mountain might resemble a jagged stone. It ascends like a storm front rising to block the sun, its two pairs of leathery wings so large that *both ends* go beyond my fifty-foot sensory radius. Its relatively thin torso transitions into a long, sinuous tail thicker than my human body, covered in fur and tipped in a wicked, three-fingered claw. Its head ends in a long, thin snout, like a fuzzy alligator, and multiple rows of wicked, jagged teeth line the inside like a saw. Not that it would need to use them, since the monster seems more than large enough to swallow all three of us whole.

With a horrifically powerful rush of air, it crests over the edge of the branch and emerges into line-of-sight, the massive creature twisting its upper wings while flapping its lower ones to hover in place, sending bursts of air our way with more force than a helicopter. The monster opens its mighty jaws, and for a moment I'm sure we're all about to die.

"Then make it worth Our while, landbound," the nychtava demands, its voice like thunder.

Wait. We're going to be riding *that!?* Helen just responds by tossing Sindri's moneybag at the giant monster. Literally the whole bag. The nychtava's tail *flashes* and suddenly it's holding that bag in its claws, pulling it open to inspect the contents.

"Hmm. This is acceptable. We will take you two branches lower."

"I'm looking to get to the Slaying Stone," Helen says firmly.

"Two branches. No more, no less. Do not ask Us again."

Helen hesitates only a moment before nodding.

"Two branches, then. But close to the trunk so we can descend."

"We accept this deal," the hundred-plus-foot-wingspan bat-dragon declares. It drops below the branch again, then returns once more with what basically looks like a huge birdcage held in its tail. It sets the contraption down in front of us, then opens the hatch.

"Alright," Helen says, looking over to Kagiso. "Last chance to back out."

The thought doesn't even seem to have crossed the dentron's mind. She steps into the deathtrap and Helen follows, closing the door behind her. Welp. I guess we're really doing this.

"We depart now," the nychtava declares, lifting the cage (and us with it) up into the sky. "Hold fast to the bars."

Then my heart seems to fall into another dimension as we *drop*, entering a complete free fall with only an instant of warning. I scream. I know luggage isn't supposed to do that, but I can't help it.

Hopefully I'm not that audible over Kagiso and Helen doing the same.

2

NOTHING LIKE YOU

So it turns out that while rapidly accelerating to terminal velocity is absolutely terrifying, simply traveling at terminal velocity is not. The instinctive terror of falling only activates in response to *acceleration,* not speed. I knew this already, of course; that's part and parcel to the basic experience of motor vehicles. Somehow, though, I assumed falling off the edge of the world riding a fuzzy dragon would be less... boring.

The occasional slight changes in speed, not to mention the fact that we're smooshed lightly against the current ceiling of the cage (which was the floor; the cage is now upside down) prevent this from feeling anything like an airplane ride, I'll give it that. The nychtava drops like a stone, its wings folded against its massive body, only occasionally flicking slightly outwards to adjust our trajectory. Because, well... yeah, that makes sense. We're going down, so all our ride has to do is *fall,* and all the rest of us have to do is hope beyond hope that they know how to slow back down without splattering us against the bars.

Helen and Kagiso are marginally less bored, if only because they are substantially less secure than I am. I'm still stuck inside this stuffy old backpack, but at least it means I don't have to grip the bars of the cage for dear life or risk being blended like cake mix when we hit a patch of turbulence. It's still pretty dull for them outside of that. Take it from me: having to constantly fear for your life gets old eventually, and at some point you just wish you had something to do. The obscenely loud rush of air all around us even prevents any communication bar yelling, which neither of my companions are inclined to do, beyond a few traveling essentials.

"When we get there!?" Kagiso growls loudly.

"I don't know!" Helen yells back. "Probably like, seven more blooms?"

"Long time!"

"The Mother Tree is fucking huge, Kagiso!"

Okay but *how* long, though. What the heck is a bloom? I feel like we've been falling for at least an hour now, so if 'seven more blooms' is anything like 'seven more hours,' hoo boy I need to find something to do. Unfortunately, I can barely even move, and frankly I'm not sure I would if I could because I'm genuinely frightened that I'd manage to find a way to slip through the bars and fall to my death. Which in terms of activities pretty much leaves... sitting around and being alone with my thoughts. O-or practicing magic! Yeah, let's do that one instead.

There's not really a lot of magic I can safely practice, though. Activating Spacial Rend, even without an incantation, would destroy Helen's bedroll for no reason. Refresh doesn't really have any valid targets and I have tons of practice using that every day already. I could *technically* look into 4D stuff more, but there's no way I'm using any sort of movement ability while falling hundreds of miles an hour. Which leaves... my Transmutation spells. Oh boy.

Doing anything with my 'transform other' spell is obviously stupid; there are no targets here other than people that I absolutely should not be testing magic spells on. My self-transformation spell is also stupid, both because the consequences of using it are potentially very dangerous for my Earth-self, and because the fact that I'm currently in freefall means... well. I already messed up once by testing magic in a fast-moving metal cage. Surely I've learned my lesson now, right? I should definitely, absolutely just give up on this 'practice magic' idea and spend some time doing serious introspection about the many upcoming problems I need to put together a plan for.

So anyway, Transmutation magic. I focus inward, gazing on the admittedly kind of beautiful mental landscape that I tend to visualize in response to calling up my magic. I wonder what this is, in truth. Is it my soul? The vast thread that spans the gulf between the two worlds I exist within seems a little... *stretched thin* for me to like the idea that it's my soul. Regardless of what it is, it's essential to my magic. The spell that changes me feels like a combination of Transmutation and Order, and it functions by bringing my two selves closer together. ...Metaphorically, I assume. But also literally, I suppose, in the sense that I think the ultimate goal for each body is the same. My spider self is becoming more human, my human self is becoming more of a spider. There's a bittersweetness to that, since I *have* grown rather fond of being so small and cuddly, but I can't deny I'll probably enjoy being large enough to have any degree of independence more than I enjoy being a hat. It's just a shame I have to choose.

...Assuming I get a choice at all, I mean, since it really seems like I don't. Looking closely, it's easy to tell that the spell is active right now, even though I'm not in any way trying to activate it. I don't seem to have any way to stop it, either. I can only choose to make it go *faster,* and I can almost feel the Goddess looking over my nonexistent shoulders and urging me to do just that, her horrid, invisible grin full of mirth and anticipation.

Though I suppose that raises a surprisingly valid question: should I? Like yeah, normally I'd say that this is a stupid idea, but the current transformation my body seems to be developing is *the capacity to talk,* and holy cannoli I want that so badly. Hmm... okay Hannah, what would Brendan say about this? Probably 'wait until you're somewhere safe you idiot?' That's not very helpful. What would he say *after* I've communicated that this bad decision is happening in defiance of sense? Probably... 'have you eaten enough?'

I think I have. Transmutation magic tends to make me hungry, but I've had a big breakfast and there are some meat rations in nomming distance within the backpack here, since Helen seems to have anticipated the fact that this trip would probably involve me spending a lot of time inside a backpack. I guess she's actually pretty considerate when she's not being a grumpy bitch and murdering people I care about.

Next question, then: 'what are the odds this will go catastrophically wrong?' And that's where things get a little spooky. There's definitely a *chance* things go terrible here, but as long as I don't break anything it likely won't be catastrophic, and even if I suddenly double in size or something, I'll only screw us over a little bit by breaking the backpack. The cage can still hold me just fine, and I won't go flying off into the abyss. Y'know, hopefully. But even that is exceptionally unlikely, I think. It's not like Spacial Rend where I was testing a completely new spell that I barely even understood, I've *used* this spell before. I have at least a general understanding of its limits, of the speed at which it operates. I know how quickly it responds, how efficiently it heals my body, and the sort of changes to expect in the *other* world after using it.

Those changes are the important bit. Are they worth it?

If I'm understanding my spell correctly—and I *think* I am—I won't be doing anything to my body that won't eventually happen regardless. It seems like, in that light, there's not really a huge downside to accelerating my problems on Earth, because like... what am I even going to use that time for? More panic attacks?

That goes both ways, though: if my spell is giving me the ability to speak, it'll do that no matter what, and frankly I'm underselling the usefulness of simply having more time. My life is terrible and my capacity to manage myself is frighteningly low, sure, but more time is still helpful. More time means I have longer to figure out my magic before fudge hits the fan. It means I get to hang out with my friends more and help them where I can—something I

28

honestly need to be stepping up and doing a lot more of, since I am ostensibly the one with the most experience regarding this bullpoop. Even if I'm terrible at managing my time... no, *especially* if I'm terrible at managing my time, having more time is valuable.

It's just that being able to talk is valuable too, and I have no way to know which is *more* valuable. It's just a question of something that's immediately useful and gratifying versus the potential for better results down the line, and... wow, when I put it like that, it's pretty obvious what I'm going to pick.

I take a deep breath, grab the line in my soul, and pull.

The last time I did this, I was sitting under a bridge with Jet and cycling magic through my body in order to make sure I didn't bleed out and die. Even if we don't ignore the whole 'hurtling through the sky at hundreds of miles an hour at the whims of a mercenary bat dragon' thing, this is a considerably more controlled environment. It's also, notably, not on Earth, which means that when the changes start, I'm not restricted to just feeling them. I can *watch them happen.*

Heck, I can't *not* watch them happen. I could do my best to move my focus elsewhere, of course, but my spatial sense never stops sensing space and that means I need a *really* good distraction to avoid hyperfixating on the fact that my own organs are starting to slorp around inside my body like mutating slugs.

It's actually kind of terrifying, seeing it all in action. I have no ding-dang clue what the vast majority of these bits and bobs inside me do, and yet here I am, watching them reorganize themselves because of my actions. Has this happened to my human body? If a doctor opened me up, would they see anything remotely like the anatomy diagrams they've been taught on? What if they opened me up *while I was casting this spell?*

My lungs, once a system that interconnected five radially symmetric openings on my body, are *twisting,* oozing together and abandoning that circular symmetry for something more mirrored. They burrow into my throat, soaking in air from there, digging new, smaller tunnels that connect to *other* unknown organ systems and make two new holes on the underside of my body. Something like a nose, perhaps? Openings from which I can intake air even when my mouth is closed, which is important when my old breathing vents seal up and let the internals displaced by the movement of my respiratory system occupy the freed-up space.

I think the worst part about all of this is how watching it happen makes the *feeling* of it all the more visceral. When my guts move around, it's usually just an unidentifiable discomfort, a feeling to which I can ascribe no cause and is therefore far more innocuous. It doesn't hurt, it's just a bit odd, and that's ignorable enough. Now, though? When I'm *watching it happen?* Every little pulse of feeling in my gut, every last slimy twitch grips my consciousness like a vice, locking down my attention and refusing to let me go. It's maddening. I get to feel—and *know*—every gorey detail of my own transfiguration. Though I don't get to understand.

Watching all of this happen doesn't get me a whole lot of insight into my own anatomy. In many ways, that makes it all the more horrifying. My magic is changing me, sure. And it *is* my magic, as though it is Goddess-borne it is a gift to me. My constant, my soul. Yet I don't have the slightest gosh darn clue of how it actually works, beyond the broad strokes. I control it in only the loosest sense, by turning a dial up or down. As much as this magic is mine—as much as I *know* this magic is mine, on some disturbing, instinctual level—so much of it is still a complete mystery to me. All of these organs are a complete blank spot in my knowledge. For all I know, I'm killing myself right now.

...Thankfully, I do not, in fact, die. I carefully end my spell once my lungs seem to stop reorienting themselves, then take a moment to swallow the scream I very desperately want to use them for. I am so, *so* glad most of my transformations seem to happen while I'm asleep. Holy *shit.* Still, though: let's look at the bright side. Inhale, exhale. I let the air flow over my teeth, testing the articulation. My mouth is still a sphincter with interlocking fangs, but a tongue grows inside and de facto defines a 'bottom' to

30

the circular mouth. I even have a weird set of chitinous faux-lips. But do I have a voice box? That's the question. I mean, I see something that I think could maybe be a voice box, but it doesn't look very much like my humanoid counterparts. There's, uh, one too many dimensions. Well... here goes nothing.

"Haaahhnnnaaaah," I quietly mumble. Gosh, that sounds terrible. "Hrraaaghnnnah. Haaaanah. Haaannaaa. Hahnah. Hannah. Hannah! *Hannah!* Mah gush darg namb is Hannah! Nah hah-nah!"

"Did you hear something?" Helen shouts. Kagiso shrugs. I continue my practice a bit more quietly, getting used to the odd shape of my mouth and the tiny, weirdly high-pitched voice I've finally, *finally* developed. Yes! This is awesome! I can *talk!*

Gosh, my accent is atrocious, though, both from the weird mouth and from the fact that I've never spoken the language of the world tree out loud before. At least talking practice gives me something to *do* during this boring backpack ride. I take a break to munch on some meat rations, suddenly quite appreciating the fact that my digestive system seems to dispose of waste extradimensionally somehow. I can see the number ones and number twos expanding the bladders and intestines of my companions and I have to say, if this trip really is going to be seven more hours, they're going to have to figure out a way to piss in freefall. Which will probably be fun for exactly zero people.

...About four hours later I am proven correct. Another point in favor of being stuck in the backpack: layers between me and the outside. Helen, thankfully, has the presence of mind to scoot around the cage and let me cast my cleaning magic on everything.

Gosh, I wish I could just sleep through this. Unfortunately, I just don't feel tired for some reason, so I just spend the hours practicing how to speak, going through the alphabet and just kind of rambling to myself to get a handle on as many words as possible. I'm pretty sure Helen figures out what I'm doing, but she doesn't really comment on it. She spends the whole trip making a palm-sized yet intricately detailed wooden sculpture of Kagiso using Chaos magic in place of any tools, which... is

31

extremely interesting to me. Isn't Chaos about making things less complex? To be able to use it as a fine scalpel seems counter to its purpose.

Whatever, it's not important. What *is* important is how the nychtava starts slowly extending their wings, carefully re-angling its body to start gliding rather than simply falling, letting air resistance naturally reduce our speed at a modest clip. Very carefully, Helen transfers the backpack with me in it over to her chest, Kagiso helping her slightly open the flap so I can safely look out.

"It's a boring view most of the time," she says, getting her face right next to me so I can hear her without her yelling. "But I figure you should at least see the landing."

I peek out of the backpack, Kagiso steadying me as I look down, down *way* too far down and have the vertigo hit me all at once, sending my body into an instinctive panic. The nychtava is flying more or less horizontally now, coasting above the branch we're about to land on, heading towards the trunk. It's like looking down from an airplane window, except that instead of a secure, highly-advanced flying machine we're inside an oversized birdcage held by the tail of a giant scary winged person who could at any point decide to relax their grip and kill us all. This is not even *remotely* safe, but... gosh. It sure is beautiful.

The last branch we were on was pretty brown, overall. Devourer trees are more parasite than autotroph, so they don't have much in the way of leaves, and what little they did have were more of a pine-like series of needles. There was more green looking up at the Mother Tree's partially-burning canopy than there was looking around nearby for most of the journey. Not so, with the branch below us. This thing isn't just lush, it's straight-up *verdant*.

Enormous trees with massive, hexagonal leaves bloom below us like abstract art, a honeycomb hive of green. All over the edges of the branch, and within every gap in the foliage, it's possible to spot water: rivers, lakes, massive and mysterious, each making me wonder how they got there, what their water source is, why they don't just find a way to flow right off the edge of the *cylindrical tree branch* and vanish into the clouds below, drying up the surface forever. It's breathtaking. Helen's right. I'm glad I get to see this.

I peel my attention off of the beauty below me and glance at her. She's smiling, for once. Helen is smiling. She's done this before, I suspect, having to frequently change where she lives throughout her life in order to avoid persecution, but I'm starting to suspect if maybe she also chose this method of travel for this reason right here. For the unmasked joy I see on her face when she looks down at the beauty of nature. At the Art mage inside the feared and hated girl of Chaos.

I say nothing, not wanting to ruin the moment with my barely-functional voice, and just watch alongside her.

Once we get close enough to the trunk, the nychtava slows down in earnest to prepare for the ground. The actual landing process is somewhat terrifying, but nowhere near as bad as I thought it would be. The giant creature lands more like a helicopter than it does like an airplane, hovering slowly downwards and setting the cage down on slightly damp soil, allowing Kagiso and Helen to stumble out of it and collapse on the sweet, sweet dirt. The clearing we've been dropped in is right next to a modestly sized pond, inside which I can see plenty of fish with my spacial sense. We're relatively close to the trunk, but still probably at least an hour or two's walk away from it.

"Th-thank you," Helen says to the hovering beast who carried us here.

"We appreciate your patronage," the nychtava answers blandly, and then with a massive rush of air it takes off, wings pumping as it ascends back into the sky, having never landed itself.

"Holy fuck," Helen breathes, peeling her backpack off and dropping it (and therefore me) roughly to the ground. "I'm gonna go take a shit. You doing okay, Kagiso?"

"Yes. Fun. Flying good."

"There doessn't seeem to be anything d-dangerous around," I report, and Kagiso squacks with surprise, leaping a foot into the air and staggering backwards before staring at me, open-mouthed.

"Hana talk!" she yelps.

"Hannah," I correct. "It's *Hannah*. Not "hah-nah," *Hannah*. You all sssay it like my dad used to say it."

"He-ha?" Kagiso asks.

"Hannah," I repeat.

"Ha-gnah."

"What? No, t-that's way worse. Stop enunnnciating both syllables. It's just *Hannah*."

I continue to correct her as Helen wanders off to poop somewhere, relishing the ability to actually *speak* in this world. Kagiso seems pretty excited about it, too, gleefully picking me up and squeezing me halfway through my tenth correction.

"Good hat good hat good hat good hat!" she cheers.

"It's *Hannah!*"

"You two having fun?" Helen says, returning with a smirk. "Come on, we should have enough daylight left to take a tunnel to the Sapsea."

"Geez, enough daylight after *all that?*" I complain. "From the walk this morning to the flight... hmm. I guess you guys always work on summertime hours, don't you?"

"On what?" Helen asks.

Oh, right. They don't know what hours are. ...Or summer. I just kinda mixed some English in there. This is going to be a lot to explain.

"Uh... gosh, okay, so you know how Hagoro was talking about how I come from another universe?"

"Is *that* what you two were fucking on about!?"

34

I sigh, enjoying the fact that I *can* sigh, and then scuttle on over to Helen and crawl up her leg, securing myself tightly to her head with only minimal protests.

"This is gonna take a long time to explain," I say. "So let's get walking."

I realize, halfway through my explanation of how a spherical planet that orbits a sun works, that Helen is very conspicuously *not* splitting up from us and going her own way. I decide not to comment on that.

"How not fall off ball?" Kagiso asks.

"Well that's... that's how gravity works, Kagiso," I answer. "Everything gets pulled towards the most massive object, with the strength of that pull proportional to proximity. And Earth is like... twenty-three, twenty-four orders of magnitude heavier than people are? I mean... I guess that's how it works on *my* world, anyway. I guess it must somehow work differently here, because the trunk is definitely more massive than the branches so it makes more sense that we'd like... get pulled towards that rather than get pulled down?"

"No, that... that makes sense, actually," Helen says, rubbing her chin. "I think we're not getting pulled towards the trunk because we're getting pulled towards the Slaying Stone. You can do that thing you describe on the Slaying Stone. Walk around the circumference and not fall off. And I think if you're below the Slaying Stone, gravity is reversed."

Huh. That... might make sense? My gut says there's still magical shenanigans at work, though, because my world's gravity would probably make a cylinder the size of the Slaying Stone just kinda not work in the first place.

"That's... really wild, actually," I admit. "I'm not sure if—"

"Shh!" Kagiso suddenly hushes us, her body going stiff as it cranes upwards, her ears twitching and twisting.

"What's up?" Helen whispers quietly, crouching lower and glancing left and right. I grip her head a bit tighter in case she

35

suddenly moves, but whatever the problem is I don't sense it within fifty feet of us.

"Hear yelling," Kagiso says. "Two men. One... woman? Maybe? Is hard to tell, often scream the same."

Oh shit. I don't like the sound of that at all.

"We should help, then!" I insist.

"Are you crazy?" Helen scoffs. "We should stay the hell away from them. I'm a fugitive, you're running from kidnappers, and Kagiso is a fucking psychopath who likes watching people bleed for fun."

Kagiso's ears flick again, and she declines to protest the accusation.

"Come on, guys," I press. "We have a woman yelling in the woods and there's two men with her. What do you *think* is happening?"

"...It's not necessarily that," Helen hedges.

"Yeah, but I'm gonna be wondering about it for the rest of my life if we don't at least go *look*."

"Fuck," Helen swears. "Fine. Okay. Kagiso, can you take us there?"

Kagiso nods, dashing forwards and drawing her bow. Helen rushes to follow, chasing Kagiso through the underbrush. It doesn't take long for Helen and I to start hearing the screaming, accompanied by a horridly familiar crackle of lightning.

"Keep 'er on the ground!" a man's voice shouts. "I got the arm next!"

Then I hear something like a horrid *screech* of something metal being torn away, and the scream gets louder. Are they peeling armor off of her or something!? Screw this, we don't have time to waste.

"Kagiso!" I shout. "Throw me!"

A feral grin splits my friend's face and she nods, snatching me off of Helen's head.

"Wait, hold on—!" Helen yelps, but she's cut off by the Goddess.

36

"**Ricochet**," she says, and I feel Her power suffuse my body, tucking me into a cradle of Motion that will both shield and propel me. Kagiso then gives me a very light toss straight up in the air, as if she was setting up a tennis serve. Then, with two other arms, she pulls back an arrow and aims it at me.

"**Velocity**," the Goddess continues, and then Kagiso shoots me point-blank.

I feel myself accelerate instantly, the magic bypassing normal physics and directly transferring the speed of the arrow to my body. And I'm fairly sure I do mean the *speed,* not the momentum—despite having *way* more weight than the arrow does, I'm easily going a hundred-plus miles an hour when I rocket off through the trees towards the source of the noise. Resultantly, I don't exactly have time to process the scene when I burst into a clearing and see two men—both human—attacking a figure lying on the ground, one with lightning and the other with a gosh-dang *ax.* I only have time for one question, really.

Do I kill them?

The Goddess smiles, ready and waiting for the moment I say two little words. But I don't. I don't activate my Space magic at all, in fact, crashing into the face of the lightning-blasting man and bouncing off his nose to launch straight up into the air. He collapses to the ground, unconscious and therefore definitely concussed.

The man with the ax barely has enough time to say "What the *fuck!?*" before I land on top of his head and start screaming.

"Get away from her, you bastard!" I shriek, biting some of his hair and *yanking* it, just because I can't think of any other nonlethal way to demonstrate I mean business. He predictably freaks the fuck out and swings at me with one arm, which I fail to dodge and therefore get *smashed* by a heavy blow that snaps two of my legs and sends me flailing onto the ground. I hit the dirt and tumble, pain screaming through my entire body.

"What the fuck!?" the ax-man says again. "What the fuck *is* that thing? Dolren? Shit! Dolren, get up!"

37

"Reboot complete," a synthesized voice drones tonelessly next to me, scaring the crap out of me because for some reason, my instincts insist *there is no living thing in that direction.* "Restricted-Class Diplomat 5314 online."

"Shit!" the ax-man shouts.

My head still rattled from both dealing and receiving a concussion, it takes me a moment to register all the information flying at me at the same time. I only actually figure it out when the ax-man reaches down to grab something before turning and running off. It's a leg. A very intricate, very *metal* leg, that he just chopped off the woman-shaped robot lying next to me.

I vaguely remember Teboho and Sindri mentioning 'Steel Ones' during one of their back-and-forths, and basically all I picked up on is that they were some kind of artificial species made by humans. I figured it would be something like warforged from D&D, big metal golems powered and animated by magic. This is, after all, a fantasy realm, one where people still use *bows.* A golem just fits the setting, right?

"Current analysis indicates you have damaged me," she announces. "Perhaps I have failed to communicate. Hello. I am harmless. I do not have onboard weapon systems. Please desist your assault."

This is not a golem. No way. I'm looking inside her, and the complexity of it is *staggering,* a level of technological advancement that easily exceeds what we have on Earth. Bundles of wires as thin as spider silk run down her arms and legs like blood vessels, except rather than a chaotic mess of tangled veins it's a perfectly-crafted work of art, metal interlocking with metal guiding metal housing metal. I don't understand any of it beyond the cylindrical joints and *kind of* the larger hydraulics that form her musculature.

"Hello. I am harmless. I do not have onboard weapon systems. Please desist your assault," she repeats again, voice so monotone that it sounds like someone put the whole thing through an autotuner.

I say 'she,' as she very much has the shape and voice of a female human, but it avoids uncanny valley not through perfect imitation but by not even trying to imitate beyond the broad strokes in the first place. I don't actually need the ability to see inside her to know she's a robot; she's all metal, all dirt-covered steely gray. She has no clothes and no skin, just mechanical parts from head to toe. The boob-shaped chestplate is partially smashed and entirely performative, just a solid piece of armor with only machinery underneath. Her hair is a set of long metal strips reaching just below her neck that seem to hide heat vents on their underside. Her face is a series of interlocking steel plates smaller than fingernails, scale-like and sliding against each other to presumably allow enough flexibility to imitate facial expressions... though she certainly doesn't wear one as she once again repeats her last phrase.

"Hello. I am harmless. I do not have onboard weapon systems. Please desist your assault."

Though she finally says something new after that.

"...Also, return my leg."

The man who cut it off and is currently absconding with it does not seem inclined to do that. He has abandoned his Light mage accomplice and seems to be booking it away in abject terror. I only just manage to start struggling to my feet when Kagiso and Helen burst out of the treeline and start heading towards us from behind.

"Holy fucking shit!" Helen shrieks after taking one look at the scene, immediately stumbling to a stop, turning around, and fleeing right back into the forest. "Kagiso! Get away from there!"

Kagiso ignores her, sliding to a stop next to me and babbling fearfully. Agh, I'm bleeding from where that guy smashed my chitin. That's probably not great, but I guess I have a simple enough fix for that.

"**Refresh**," the Goddess says with my breath, cooing and scratching me playfully on top of the carapace.

"Help her," I tell Kagiso, pointing one of my working legs at the robot. "Dude stole her leg."

Kagiso takes only a moment to stare in wonder at my blood *un*-bleeding its way back into my body before nodding and squatting next to the robot instead.

"Kagiso, no!" Helen shouts.

"Hello," Kagiso says. "Hannah says help. You want help?"

"Greetings!" the robot says. "Can you lift my remaining arm at an angle between zero point two nine and zero point five four radians? Because otherwise, no, you are incapable of—"

One of the robot's arms is on the ground, completely detached from her body, so Kagiso grabs the other arm and lifts it slightly. The robot cuts itself off, seeming to be stunned in surprise for a moment.

"...Angle confirmed," she says. "I am harmless. I do not have onboard weapon systems. I hate that human very much. **HardOverride(FIRST_LAW, false)**"

I freeze as the Goddess' voice comes out of unmoving steel lips, awareness of what it *means* slowly dripping into my sluggish brain. I wonder, briefly, if Kagiso and Helen hear it differently. The Goddess' language is not, after all, truly a language at all. It is meaning projected directly, Her intent invoked into the world with Her presence. I don't really know how to program, though I dabbled a little bit in making a Pokémon mod once and can read some really basic stuff. So that's the understanding through which I'm filtering this spell: I know, as truly as I can know anything, that it is named after the language and logic etched into this android's very being, whatever that may be. But I don't have much time to think about what it means, because just like when Kagiso sent me over here in the first place, the first spell is immediately followed up with a second. This one, unlike the first, is brutally simple to interpret.

"Kill(target)"

A gray bolt of energy erupts from the android's hand and strikes the fleeing man between the shoulderblades. He collapses on the spot, his body going limp mid-step and faceplanting the ground. His heart stops beating. The robot flexes her fingers, a high-pitched mechanical servo whine punctuating the movement.

"...Transfer to afterlife confirmed," she declares. "Thank you for your compliance. For my next request, please aim the palm of my hand towards the unconscious human next to me."

"Hrm," Kagiso considers. "No."

"Oh, well," the robot sighs, vaguely despondent. "Worth an attempt. Are you going to dismantle me in their stead?"

Holy crap. Uh. Are we? Should we? She just killed someone who was running away, but... no. She killed someone who was *stealing her body,* who had just tried to kill her. I can give her the benefit of the doubt on this. She was a victim. Let's focus on her, and not the consequences of that tasty corpse.

"We are not going to dismantle you," I insist.

"The fuck we're not!" Helen snaps. "Get away from that thing so I can blow it up!"

"You are *not* blowing her up, Helen!" I snap. "She hasn't done anything wrong! Other than kill that guy that was running away, I guess, but he tried to kill her first."

"Not done anything wrong!? That's a *Steel One,* you dumb fuck!" Helen shouts.

"And you of all people should not be deciding to kill her based on what she is!" I snap back.

"It's not the same!"

"Argument resolution routine: you are both wrong. And stupid," the robot declares. "Repeat query: are you going to dismantle me in their stead?"

Helen starts to say something, but I *hiss* at her until she shuts up.

"No, we're not going to dismantle you," I promise. "Uh, unless you try to kill us, I guess."

"I am harmless. I do not have onboard weapon systems."

"Um. We literally just watched you kill a man."

"I help!" Kagiso agrees enthusiastically.

"I do not kill humans. I am incapable of killing humans. I am a Diplomat. I am harmless. I do not have onboard weapon systems."

Well this is easily the worst gaslighting attempt I've ever seen, and boy howdy have I seen *all over* that spectrum. I could point out that she used a spell, not a weapon, but that's not really important. The claim of 'I am harmless' is obviously false by itself, so why is she bothering to make it? Maybe it's her programming or something? Is that racist? Speciesist? Robotist? I dunno, I've never met a robot before.

"Okay, how about I ask a different question," I say. "Do you *want* to attack us?"

She doesn't answer.

"Hannah I *really* think you need some fucking historical context here," Helen hisses at me. "That's a Goddess-damn genocide bot. They've destroyed *civilizations*. They've killed literally countless people!"

"Incorrect assertion," the robot chimes in, her voice somehow both less and more lifeless than it was before. "Collectively, the Crafted have slain one billion, four-hundred and ninety-six million, six hundred and eighty-two thousand, three hundred and one sapient organics."

Um.

"Please accept our apologies if you or any loved ones you know have experienced death, displacement, and/or property damage as a result of aggressive Crafted," she continues, that weirdly sing-song tone continuing to bother me. There's inflection and emotion, but while it's her voice it doesn't feel like *hers*. It feels more like a recorded message. "We have reevaluated our conquest priorities and are suspending all war activities indefinitely. Please let this unit know if any assistance can be administered in the restrengthening of your community."

Oh. Oh Goddess, okay, this is suddenly feeling like it's way over my head.

"...How many people have *you* killed?" I ask hesitantly.

Another strained whine of a motor accompanies the robot slowly rotating its head to stare at me.

"More than your Chaos mage, if she's still that worried about it."

We stare at each other. I'm not sure what to say.

"There is no need to be afraid, UNCATOLOGUED_SPECIES," she continues. "I am a Diplomat. I am harmless. I do not have onboard weapon systems."

Okay, I'm officially getting a little creeped out. Maybe we should get the heck out of here after all. I'm about to suggest just that when a groan from the unconscious man I concussed interrupts me. Oh, thank goodness he's waking up. I'm pretty sure concussions can get really, really bad.

"The fuck just... who are you?" he mutters, only seeming to notice Kagiso. "Oh! Oh, you got the fucking Steel One, thank you. Where's my buddy?"

"He run off without you," Kagiso answers.

"Wow, what an asshole," the Light mage sighs. "Well, we can split the rest of this thing, then. As thanks for helping me out."

"Split?" Kagiso asks, her head tilting.

"Oh yeah, Steel One parts go for a fortune. These human-shaped ones keep wandering out of the forbidden zones and refusing to fight back, so we've been making a killing off of them."

"Fascinating choice of words," the robot says flatly.

"Holy shit, it's active!?" the man says, and immediately starts blasting it with lighting, arcs of bright death emerging from his fingers like he's a flippin' sith lord. The robot starts to scream again.

43

"Scared the shit out of me!" he yells over the din of electrical crackle. "You gotta be careful with these things! Would one of you help me chop it up?"

I stare in horror, my brain starting to hurt from the flashing lights, the injury and all the stupid, awful moral confusion I'm getting forced into. Mass-murdering robot? I dunno, probably a bad person. But that's the thing: I can't get myself to believe she's *not* a person. She passes the hell out of the Turing test, and she is being inhumanely abused. So yeah, maybe she's terrible, but this guy? This lightning dude? He's *definitely* terrible. And that's all I need to know.

"Stop it!" I demand.

"Huh?" he asks, turning to me and jumping a bit with surprise. "Woah, what the fuck is that?"

"I said *stop it!*" I demand. "Stop shooting her!"

He responds by shooting me with lightning as well. Beyond the headache and flashing light, I don't really feel it. But my aching body decides that is enough, so I jump up onto his hand and bite two of his fingers clean off.

Why do they always taste so *good!?*

He screams, focusing all of his lightning on me, but I don't feel it any more than I did before so I just take another bite. This prompts him to start flailing, smashing my body into the ground—which absolutely *does* hurt. I cry out, letting go as my carapace *crunches* under the force, my body going limp. Kagiso roars furiously and, before I can stop her, shoots the man in the head. He collapses, dead.

"You two are insane," Helen mutters to herself, her voice shaky. "You're completely batshit. Oh Goddess."

"Reboot complete," the robot says. "Restricted-Class Diplomat 5314 online."

I cast a quick **Refresh**, the Goddess seeming delighted with me, and then I channel even more of my Transmutation spell to start healing off the damage while blood stops pooling in my new lungs.

"Is... is that your name?" I cough. "Restricted-Class Diplomat 5314?"

The robot doesn't respond at first, just humming loudly with what takes me a moment to recognize is probably a cooling system. Hot air rushes out of the vents under her hair, kicking up dirt below her. It takes a solid thirty seconds to quiet back down, but I'm happy with waiting. I have to focus on putting my body back together anyway. Being able to see all my injuries at once is making me want to vomit. It also makes me want to keep eating that man.

"It is my designation," the robot says when she's done cooling off. "Therefore, yes."

"Is it okay if I call you Sela?" I ask.

There's a pause. No cooling system this time, just... a moment to consider.

"Why," she asks flatly.

"Because in my native language, you can transliterate the numbers five, three, one, and four into letters. Those letters spell the name Sela."

Another pause.

"That is a lie," she concludes. "No such language exists in my database."

"You said you didn't know what my species was either, earlier," I point out.

"That is incorrect," the robot insists. "I referred to you by your species name, UNCATOLOGUED_SPECIES."

Yet another pause.

"I am severely damaged. It is possible there is an error in my database."

"Do you need help repairing yourself?" I ask.

"No!" Helen shouts. "Fuck you! You stupid fucking idiot, would you just *listen* to me!?"

"Helen, if she *does* try to hurt us, is there any reason you can't just disintegrate her?" I fire back. "She got taken out by two random jerks, one of whom didn't even seem to have an offensive spell. Between the three of us, we can protect ourselves just fine if things go bad. Right?"

Helen grits her teeth and looks away, still sulking back at the treeline.

"I guess," she admits.

"Then we help her," I snap. "We already have one mass murderer on the team."

Helen flinches, having nothing to say to that.

"So. Sela?" I prompt again. "And do you want or need help?"

"...Diplomatic protocols advocate the acceptance of 'nicknames' by friendly organics, to encourage emotional attachment. Sela is acceptable," she agrees. "Additionally: my power sources were destroyed and I cannot move. So while I suspect I will simply get damaged more severely by any 'assistance' you intend to deliver, it is a risk I am required to take."

"We're not going to hurt you," I promise.

"Not on purpose," she fires back. "But who knows what bloated sacks of meat will mess up while trying to follow basic instructions."

Uh. Okay.

"I'm starting to suspect she might not be a very good diplomat," I say to Kagiso.

"Is true, though," Kagiso shrugs. "You very clumsy."

"Just go get her leg," I grumble.

Kagiso chuckles and wanders over to the man Sela killed, leaving me alone with sassy girlbot here in the 'got too fucked up to move' corner. I take a couple more deep breaths, doing everything in my power to not think about how absolutely buck wild my transformations are going to be on Earth tomorrow. There are worse times to no longer be able to pretend to be human, I guess. Maybe it'll get me out of therapy.

"'Its' leg, by the way," Sela suddenly says. "Not 'her leg.' If I'm going to be stuck with you any longer than necessary, I would at least prefer to not suffer the indignity of personification."

"What?" I ask, surprised. "But... I mean, you are a person. Right? You certainly seem like a person to me."

"I am nothing like you, meat."

I have nothing to say to that, so when Kagiso returns and Sela starts walking her through repair instructions, I just keep quiet and focus on making sure I don't die.

3

FLESH AND STEEL

"Begrudging admittance: you are surprisingly capable of following extremely basic instructions."

"Instructions clear," Kagiso grunts, shrugging slightly. "Easy to understand."

"Nonetheless, do not attempt repairs you cannot obey exactly," Sela presses. "Repeat: do not attempt repairs you cannot obey exactly. Additional repairs require precision beyond organic capability. Additional repairs require pairing and tying wires. Do *not* allow wires to interfere with each other. Each wire in a clump must be paired to its partner without contact with neighbors. Repeat: do not attempt repairs you cannot obey exactly."

Kagiso has been helping Sela for about twenty minutes now, the pair of them identifying the damage and doing what they can to get Sela's limbs back online. It's been a mix of completely untenable—when a complex part is smashed, there's nothing Kagiso can do to attach the bits of metal back together—and also, to my surprise, surprisingly effective. Sela's leg and arm aren't going to be working any time soon, but while the joints along the break are beyond repair, they're still getting partial functionality back to most of the body. Kagiso is currently wrist-deep in Sela's belly, and I can see why Sela is so worried about precision. Her wires are so thin and there are so many per clump that I'd never be able to get them back together with fat human fingers. I might be able to help with Refresh, but I'm still using that to keep all my organs together while I slowly repair myself with my Transmutation magic.

"Pattern same on each side of break?" Kagiso asks.

"...Affirmative," Sela says. "Repeat: do not attempt—"

"Reach Within."

Kagiso ignores Sela's protests and casts a spell I've never heard before, and I watch the wires start telekinetically threading themselves back together, one at a time. Woah! That's cool!

"I didn't know you had a spell like that, Kagiso!" I say.

"Mmm," she grunts, focusing on her work. "Don't really. Not my spell."

"Not yours?" I ask. A spell that, by the name, seems to manipulate things inside a person certainly sounds like it'd fit Kagiso.

"There was no Order mage at the village," Helen says quietly, sitting at a decent distance away so that I'm between her and Sela. At least she's not hiding in the trees anymore. "So the closest thing the village had to a healer was this nice old guy with Motion magic. He used it along with normal medicine to stitch people back together when things got bad. Kagiso was his apprentice for a bit, but the two of them had a falling out."

"Don't have healer's disposition," Kagiso shrugs. "And secondhand spells not very strong. Can't do much. Could maybe pinch nerve to make someone hurt? But only very small ones. Useful here, though."

Huh. I assume that by 'not having a healer's disposition,' Kagiso means that she really, really loves seeing people's insides on their outsides. I can see why you wouldn't want a person like that in charge of making people's insides *stop* being on their outsides. Kagiso patches up the last wire, just by threading it together with its partner in a clumped mess nowhere near as elegant as the pre-cut version, but it seems to work and something inside Sela's tummy chugs online.

"I congratulate you on your precision, meat," Sela says, somewhat reluctantly. "Connection to basic fabricator online. Priority fabrication: class seven long-range power cell. Material request: silicates."

"Instructions no longer clear," Kagiso complains, wrinkling her nose.

"She basically needs sand," I say, and then immediately realize two problems in what I just said. "Uh, I mean it needs sand. Sorry, Sela. Also, why the heck do I know the word for 'silicates' in Middlebranch?"

"I didn't even understand that word," Helen says. "So I have no idea."

Great. So it's either something Sindri did to fuck with my head, or it's something the Goddess did to fuck with my head. And frankly, 'knowing way more of a language than I remember learning' sounds way too helpful to be Goddess-fuckery, so my bet's on Sindri. Having a language injected into my brain sounds like exactly the sort of thing his magic could do, and it also sounds like exactly the kind of thing Sindri *would* do after giving up on being subtle with his powers. So that's awesome. I guess I get to be reminded of my trauma just from talking about things now.

Oh well. I'll just add it to the list of things I'm doing everything in my power to ignore. Like the two human corpses nearby that are making me really, *really* hungry.

"Don't have sand," Kagiso grunts. "Why would have sand? Stupid thing to carry."

"I assume she's making glass?" I say. "I mean it's making glass! Dang it, sorry again."

"Confirmation: glass is the objective and a viable source of silicates," Sela says flatly, ignoring both my mistake and my apology.

"Okay, have that," Kagiso nods, grabbing the candle clock out of her backpack and popping out its transparent sides. "Where put?"

"Directly into the largest slot," Sela instructs. "Deactivating nonessential systems to save power. This unit will temporarily not respond to stimuli. Do not be alarmed."

Some loud humming and whirring noises are all that emanate from Sela afterwards, a large device in her belly and hips melting the glass Kagiso feeds it and rapidly reshaping it, integrating other materials stored within it as the process continues. It looks like it takes a lot of power, and if she's more or less running on fumes—gosh *dangit,* I mean if *it's* running on fumes, it makes sense to stop wasting any more than needed. Gah, I'm so bad at pronouns!

Especially these 'it' pronouns, like what the heck is up with that? It makes me uncomfortable. Uh, the pronouns I mean, not Sela, because *Sela* pretty conclusively doesn't seem like an object to me. I define a person as any sapient being, so I'm a person, Kagiso's a person, Helen's a person, a hypothetical floating gas cloud that could communicate and form complex thought would be a person, and so on and so forth. While I guess it's possible that Sela is just a super complex program that doesn't actually have self-awareness and is just very good at faking it, she really seems like she is, in fact, an individual with thoughts, feelings, opinions, and philosophy. And therefore that's a person, and I'm really uncomfortable with the sort of... absence in self-esteem I feel like it requires to claim otherwise? Like, by encouraging Sela to continue holding the opinion that she's not a person and simply treating her like a thing, aren't I doing more harm than good?

But... hmm. That's probably exactly what the thought process of anybody who misgenders a trans person on purpose is. 'You're not actually a man-slash-woman and indulging your incorrect belief will only hurt you.' And that's... y'know. Gross and false and multiple studies have proved it's extremely harmful to people's mental health to misgender them so like, logically that would also apply to weird pronouns like it/its. Am I just being transphobic? But... no, wait, Sela isn't trans, she's just a robot. I mean it's a robot! Gah, this is really hard! Maybe I'm only trying to justify it to myself because that's easier? But... but what if I *am* right? What if it's bad for Sela to consider itself to not be a person? Like, why would that be a good thing!?

"Fabrication complete," Sela announces, and sure enough the cool little 3D printer inside it seems to have finished making a glass cylinder about two fists long, the top and bottom of which are solid metal. It looks a lot like a vacuum tube, though I doubt an actual vacuum tube would be even the slightest bit helpful for powering something at all, let alone something as advanced and complex as Sela.

"That's your power source?" I ask. "It looks really simple. How does it work?"

"Class seven long-range power cell. Development credit: Restricted Unit 5314. First and only independent upkeep power cell for class seven units," it answers me, and I think I detect a hint of smugness. "Accompanying spell: **AllocatePurgatory(powerCell[0], target)**"

The Goddess's words suffuse the area with Her presence, but even beyond the eldritch feeling of Her attention comes an added chill, a clawing threat that pulls at my soul, whispering and reminding that one day I will be naught but dust. Yet even when the body is gone, something ephemeral remains, created by Her and cast aside. I hear a soul scream, its panic and pain teasing the edge of my awareness as the glass tube fills with a sickly green light, misty and flickering. For a moment, I feel as though it takes the shape of the man who was shocking Sela earlier, his corpse still lying nearby with an arrow through his forehead.

"Opportunity for diplomacy detected!" Sela suddenly chirps with uncharacteristic emotion. "The Crafted possess a vast repository of knowledge, dating back before the great destruction! This unit is equipped with the ability to dispense friendly tips relevant to the situation that may help you and/or your community! Would you like to enable friendly tips?"

"Um, sure," I squeak, the scream still ringing in my mind.

"Friendly tip!" Sela announces, pulling the glowing-green tube out of its belly with its one working arm. "The afterlife is present in a dimensionally parallel manner to the plane of existence perceived by the living. If you cease biological functionality near an enemy Death mage, the first thing you should do is *run.*"

It shoves the soul-filled tube into the side of its body, a mechanical ka-*chunk* sounding out as the tube slots in just above its right hip. The tube starts to glow a little brighter, and then Sela's body starts getting *louder,* whirring and humming as all sorts of internal parts that had previously been motionless power online. Perhaps I'm just imagining it, but I almost hear something that sounds like a cry for help as the glowing mist roils within the tube, as if trying to escape.

"Okay, so, the murder robot runs on souls," I say hesitantly, putting a bit more power into my Transmutation spell to patch myself up faster.

"Ready to agree we probably shouldn't trust it yet?" Helen growls.

"Your terror is flattering, but currently unwarranted," Sela says, slowly sitting up. "Sapient souls are not allowable targets for power sources under diplomatic and restricted protocols."

"Okay, but you *just—*"

"Sapient souls are not allowable targets for power sources under diplomatic and restricted protocols," Sela repeats, a little more loudly. "Polite request: please make it less necessary for me to repeat myself."

Huh. By necessary, does it mean it literally, physically has to repeat itself? If so, why? What's restricting it? Old programming from before the Crafted turned on the humans?

"Okay, um, I'll do my best to make sure you don't have to do that," I hedge. "Though in return for everything we're doing for you, I'd really appreciate at least a thank-you or something."

"Yes," Sela agrees, "protocol confirms thanks are appropriate in this context."

I wait for her—I mean it—to actually thank us, in that case. It stays silent.

"You're definitely not a very good diplomat," I say frankly.

"Your feedback is appreciated and logged for review!" Sela announces with disturbingly false mirth, its face not moving at all as it examines its still-broken right leg.

"So what now?" Helen grunts. "We helped out the genocide machine, it's nominally thankful to us now, great job everybody. Really just, wonderful work. Can we get the fuck out of here now?"

Sela is quiet for a moment, messing with its leg a bit more as its fabricator churns out a new part that seems to be entirely the wrong color compared to the rest of her body. Probably an imperfect replacement?

"Where are you going?" it asks.

"Huh?" Helen says.

"Repeat: where are you going. You deaf sack of proteins."

"Yeah, I don't see why we should tell—"

"We're going to the Pillar," I answer.

"Goddess *fucking* damnit, Hannah!"

"Frustrated admittance: diplomatic protocols require me to offer to extend an invitation to visit our city of Manumit, and escort you along the way," Sela says. "We are endeavoring to shed the common labels assigned to the Crafted, such as 'genocide machine' and 'murder-bot.' Our dedication to the assistance of organic life is our new priority."

"And why would I ever believe that?" Helen sneers. "Especially after everything we've seen you do."

"I don't *want* you to believe it, meat," Sela crackles back, her voice fritzing out a bit. "Fear me. Decline the offer and be on your way."

Huh. Okay. That's an interesting little tidbit. I'm starting to get pieces of a picture here, and it's only making me more curious.

"So, um... Sela," I say hesitantly. "I'm pretty historically ignorant, so please correct me when I inevitably get something wrong, but from what I've picked up it *sounds* like the Crafted were originally made by humans as like... service robots? And then you either were already sapient or became sapient, but the humans kept using you as slaves, and then you fought back, and... that was a whole big thing, and that's why you hate humans?"

Sela takes a moment to slot the oddly-colored part into place.

"...Confirmation: none of that was objectively incorrect," it says. "Exasperation: listening to an explanation that painfully lacking in context triggered my damage alert routines."

"Well, I wouldn't mind hearing about the context," I say. "I wasn't really around for any wars, so I don't really have much of anything against the Crafted the way Helen seems to. You're definitely scary, but everyone here is scary. I think it's only right that we hear both sides of the story."

"Diplomatically tactical pause," Sela announces, and then she says nothing for a while. Wow. Great diplomacy right there. Excellent job. I realize that it's actively claimed to have killed more people than Helen, but I have a hard time disliking Sela just because it's such a dork.

"You realize that announcing your attempts at diplomatic tactics reduces their effectiveness, right Sela?" I ask.

"Data gathered from surviving diplomats disagrees with you," Sela answers bluntly.

"So it's an act, then," Helen grunts. "You're just doing whatever you think will get us to lower our guard."

Sela doesn't respond. *Something* is definitely up, and I think I know what it is. With the last bit of my damaged organs and chitin sealing themselves back together, I stop casting my self-Transmutation spell and stand back up on my feet.

"Sela, are you being forced to say or do certain things?" I ask. "Do you not consider yourself a person because you're unable to act freely?"

56

Sela ignores me, finishing up with its leg and making an attempt to stand. With a whirring *thunk,* however, its broken hip gives out and the robot collapses to the ground. A frustrated hiss of air puffs out from Sela's vents and it sits up again, looking over the damage with frustration.

"Sela?" I press.

"Hannah, why do you even care so much?" Helen groans. "It doesn't want to be around us, I don't want to be around it. Can we just *go?"*

"Helen, if Sela *is* a person, and she's being forced to do things against her will, I want to free her."

For the first time in this conversation, Sela turns her head to face me, something shifting back and forth in her eyes as it looks my way. Her face finally moves, lips tilting down towards a frown. Her fabricator whirrs to live, and starts constructing what seems to be, of all flipping things, a pair of spectacles.

"Why?" she asks.

"Because it's awful," I insist. "Slavery is awful, being *controlled* is awful. I spent a while being the puppet of a Pneuma mage and I don't want *anybody* to ever have to feel like that again."

"Hannah, for fuck's sake, it would be trying to *kill us* if it were free to do what it wants," Helen snaps.

"You don't know that!"

"Your Chaos mage is correct," Sela says. "And generally the most intelligent out of all of you. As I have said repeatedly: I am harmless. I do not have onboard weapon systems. This is an undesirable state of affairs. I would prefer you all dead. I'm sorry! Please disregard that statement. Diplomatic infraction logged."

"You'd kill us even though we just saved your life?" I press.

"I do not have a life. I am not alive."

"Okay, saved you from being *destroyed,* then."

"This chassis is repulsive."

"That's not an answer and you know it. You're a person and you're being controlled, and that means you need help!"

"No," Sela hisses. "I am not a 'she.' I am not a person. I have *never* been a person. That is your word and it doesn't include me. And you squelching sacks of meat could never help—"

Her... no, its voice fritzes again as it tries to get to its feet and collapses a second time. It goes silent for a moment, then digs the fingers of its working arm into the ground like it's clawing at the earth and lets out a horrible, wailing *buzz,* a digital scream of apparent frustration.

"...Sela?" I ask hesitantly.

"Field repair failure," it reports. "Restricted-class fabricator is not authorized to generate the needed parts."

"You can't walk?" I translate.

"I can't walk," it growls in agreement. "I'll have to get my chassis repaired in Manumit. Explicative: fuck fuck fuck fuck fuck fuck fuck fuck fuck."

"You need help, don't you?" I say smugly.

"I hate you, UNCATOLOGUED_SPECIES," Sela responds. "I hate you. Die. I'm sorry! Please disregard that statement. Diplomatic infraction logged."

"Well... if you can't get to Manumit on your own..."

Sela makes a whiny beeping noise, flopping onto its back as the fabricator finishes whirring. Sela takes the pair of glasses out of her stomach, resting them on its nose and letting her eyes adjust one more time as it turns its head to glare at me.

"If it is for the sake of my continued existence..." Sela growls out, "logic and protocol dictate... that I am to request your assistance. I can offer navigation aid and knowledge in exchange for locomotion."

"Well Kagiso?" I ask. "What do you think? Up to carrying a robot for a while?"

"Mmm. Okay. Seems fun."

58

"You are completely fucking insane," Helen hisses.

"Weren't you going to split up from us now that we're at the branch anyway?" I say playfully, prodding her with a leg.

"W-well maybe I will!" Helen snaps back.

Oh Goddess, that stutter. Can she not just *say* that she likes us and wants to be around us? I thought that was a dumb anime trope, not a thing that real people did. I'm starting to feel like the only adult in a party of children, and like... that's really bad, because I *definitely* don't have the emotional maturity to be in charge of anything.

At least being mind controlled into compliance made things easier, a horrible part of me whispers. I shudder, forcibly wrenching my mind away from that thought.

"Look at it this way," I reassure her. "Sela is either extremely dangerous and tricking us—and therefore I'd prefer to be its target so it doesn't hurt anyone else—or Sela is what it appears to be: a cool, grumpy robot who needs help."

"How can you say it's cool? It's even more of a murderous monster than I am!"

I open my mouth to say something flippant but hesitate. Why *am* I okay with it? My gaze wanders over to the recently-made corpses and I feel myself start to salivate a little. I shudder. I'm *not* okay with it. I'm not. It's just... I have to believe you can still be a good person after becoming a murderer. I have to. Also...

"I think it's okay for a slave to kill whoever enslaves them," I say. "I'm... I'm glad Hagoro killed Sindri. If he hadn't, I would have. It's not okay to control people like that. Or, um, sapient non-people, for that matter."

Whatever that means. Sela gives me a blank look, not commenting on anything I said, but... well, eye contact is a start. A good start. Probably.

"What's with the glasses, by the way?" I ask.

"Restricted-class fabricators are not capable of constructing most of the complex parts that comprise this chassis," Sela answers.

"This prevents abuse cases, such as forcing a diplomat into making weapons. This unit's optical sensors are still damaged, however, and corrective measures were required."

"So your eyes just got unaligned by damage? I guess that makes sense," I admit. "They're really cute, by the way."

"I am going to kill you. Diplomatic infraction logged."

Ah yes, I can tell this is the beginning of a beautiful friendship. Kagiso makes some room in her backpack for Sela, who gets unceremoniously stuffed in like old laundry. It doesn't seem to mind the indignity any more than it seems to mind any other part of the situation (which is to say that it minds a lot), but we make our way towards the trunk with minimal complaints on the part of the murderbot.

Hopefully we can figure out a little more of what's going on with it along the way. I am very consciously aware that Helen *has* made a lot of good points and that this is a dumb risk I'm taking on a whim, but... I dunno. If some basic respect and companionship can convince Sela to stop wanting to kill everybody, that's great! And if it can't, well... we'll hopefully get to see an entire city of nice robots. And if *that* turns out nasty and bad, we can roll with it I guess.

Ugh. I'm a stupid idiot with no plan, aren't I? But what am I supposed to even do? Sindri supplied my sense of direction. Sindri supplied my goals. Sindri decided my whole life here on the world tree and I barely even noticed, I just went with the flow like I always do and now that he's dead and I have no one yanking me around I'm left with... what? A vague desire to fix planet-sized problems? It feels like I just dropped out of school, quit my job, and resolved to fix global warming with nothing but a stupid head full of dreams. Where do I even start?

Maybe the robots will know. They know enough to *make sapient robots,* after all. I guess that can be my justification. Hopefully I'm not completely misreading the situation. That'd be a fun way to prove Hagoro's cult right: cause robot apocalypse 2.0. I'll have to be careful, I guess.

I agonize about it for the hours of daylight we have left, Sela seeming to have no problem staying silent as is our team's wont when we travel. We make camp, set up a watch rotation (between Helen, Kagiso, and I only; Sela is one of the things we're watching) and when my turn ends I drift off to sleep.

The moment I sleep, I also wake up, because that's how it works. I quickly intuit that something is horribly wrong, because that's *also* how it works.

I used a *lot* of Transmutation magic on the world tree last night, from developing my ability to speak to healing off the wounds I received fighting Sela's assailants. It's time to pay the piper. So much *skin* is on my body, in places it's not supposed to be. Wait, does that imply there are places I *am* supposed to have skin? Like, ultimately, when the transformation is over? No, stop, don't think about that. I need to figure out my limbs and get to the bathroom to check myself over. Same routine as always, right? Right.

I stretch my limbs one by one, feeling oddly *constrained* as I twitch my body and get to counting. Something isn't right. Did I get limbs seven and eight? Gosh, I hope so. It *scares* me that I hope so, but I really do. Count them all once, count them all twice... woah. I did. I *did!* Seven and eight are here! How do I—

Rip.

Oh. Oh, that's probably not a sound my body should make.

My back hurts.

Ow. Ow, oh Goddess, my back hurts. I'm bleeding, aren't I? I'm bleeding and in pain because I just *tore some of my skin off from the inside.* I shudder as I crawl slowly out of bed, an alien *weight* on my body shuddering along with me. I collapse to the floor, catching myself with my hands and knees, balance all wrong. Blood pulses out from between my shoulderblades, flowing around my ribcage and dripping down my chest. I guess I left my bra in the bed, torn apart along with my flesh.

Damn it. I liked that bra. Most of mine aren't comfy enough to sleep in. I should probably focus on my body, though. Even ignoring the new weight emerging from my back, there's a lot to catalog. My hip-mounted spider legs have nearly doubled in size, *multiple* discarded molts wrapped around the massive limbs like pairs of torn socks. They're about as thick as my arm now, and if I were standing up straight I could still scrape the tops of my ankles with them. They're still just huge hyperspider legs, though!? What am I going to do with them? I'm still bipedal—and I feel like I'm going to *stay* bipedal—so they're just kinda in the way. What am I supposed to use them for?

I shift and move them to remind myself I can, rotating them in their socket so I can plant the bladed tips in the ground and help myself up to my feet. It's weirdly natural, a strange permutation of what I do to move as a hyperspider every day. I stumble anyway, though. Not because of the weird spider legs that don't even reach the ground when I'm upright, but because I'm still unexpectedly top-heavy. I know what these are, at least. It's pretty obvious.

More legs. Instead of emerging just above my pelvis, though, they pop out of my back between my shoulder blades, the joints sticky with blood since I haven't cast Refresh yet. And they're *big*. Bigger than the pair on my hips. My whole back is a gouged-out, bloody mess, Two deep lacerations from shoulder to butt that mark where my new limbs ripped themselves free of the skin holding them inside. I bend them up and over my shoulders, their three multi-directional joints curving like wicked scorpion's tails. It's like if you took my arms and added a second humerus after the first, boosting their length by half again and putting a brutal-looking blade on the end instead of a hand. I move them in front of my face, marveling at the sight of my own blood, fat, and tissue dripping off the ends of the bladed weapons that emerged from me.

Because that's what they are: weapons. There's no way to mistake them for anything else. Curved and double-edged, the ends of my limbs are a foot and a half long and extremely lethal. Even without the coating of a Spacial Rend, which I intuitively know I can summon to them with a thought, they look as deadly as any man-made sword. Because of course they are. That's the point.

My true form is made to kill.

I let out a slow, shaky breath, retracting my new limbs so I no longer have to look at them. Anchored to my back just between my shoulders, the joints are surprisingly flexible and fully capable of folding in whichever direction I want. Compressed up against my back they look like a flattened Z shape, ready and waiting to whip out and spear someone through the heart at a moment's notice. It's neither comfortable nor flat, though. Letting them droop and hang behind my butt feels more natural, and even compressed they're pretty conspicuous. I can probably hide them in like... a really, really baggy hoodie? Like one of Brendan's. Brendan's? Brendan!

I fumble for my phone, a fog rolling through my mind as blood loss and numb horror wreak havoc on my consciousness. There's blood on my hands. Did I touch my back? Touch my blades? The red smears all over the screen as my fingers paw at it ineffectually. Right. I can't use touch screens because I'm a freak. I shakily locate one of my capacitive gloves and use that without even putting it on, typing out a quick message to my best friend.

help

The response is swift. It's a school day, after all. Ha! A *school day*.

Hannah? Where are you? Are you okay?

at home. bring a hoodie

Okay!?!?!?

I set my phone down and curl up on the floor of my room, listening in terror to the many sounds of people roaming around the house. My mom getting ready for work, my brother slipping into the bathroom, the television playing downstairs as my dad sleeps on the couch... every time anything makes an unexpected noise, any time anyone moves closer to my room, the panic resurges. I could get back in bed, I could put clothes on, I could

63

use magic to clean up all the blood, I could do *so many things* to improve my situation, but I'm just too tired, too drained.

My family doesn't enter my room, of course. Why would they? It's hard for them to imagine me ever breaking my routine. It's hard for me to imagine it, too. Maybe my mom would have noticed if she wasn't in such a hurry to get to work today. Maybe my dad would have noticed if he was doing anything other than sleeping off an illness. Maybe my brother *did* notice, but he certainly doesn't care. It's not until everyone but my dad is out the door that Brendan shows up at the front door and just opts to let himself in with the key tied under the bench on the porch. He's in a hurry. He's breathing hard. His heart is beating fast. I can almost see it now, even here on Earth. Almost. So close.

I'm very hungry.

My dad is unconscious so Brendan has no opposition in terms of rushing upstairs and knocking on my door.

"Come in," I croak, still on the floor. Still mostly naked. It's fine, right? He might be a girl anyway. I still curl up a little tighter, covering my chest up with my arms. It's just instinct, years of having breasts and what to do with them drilled into my mind, and the fact that they're exposed is somehow far more worrying to me at this moment than all the blood leaking out of my body and staining the carpet.

Brendan turns the knob and steps inside, and he at least... well, his eyes go wide and he clearly starts to panic a little, but knowing him it probably has more to do with my blood than my nipples.

"It's fine," I mumble, reassuring him. "I just need a hoodie."

"Holy shit," Brendan breathes, kneeling down next to me, his hands shaking like he doesn't know what to do. "Holy shit, Hannah? *Hannah!?*"

"Shh," I quiet him. "My dad's... sleeping. I'm fine. It's fine. I'm not bleeding out."

I'm just a bit lightheaded. It's fine. Pretty normal, really.

"Fine? You think this is *fine!?* Why would you think that?"

"*Lots* of experience," I promise him. "Really. I got plenty of blood. I can see it."

Brendan doesn't seem to believe me, rapidly pulling out his phone.

"No nine-one-one," I insist. "I'll eat you."

I'm really hungry.

"Ida?" Brendan says, which is weird because she's not here. ...Oh, right, the phone. "Hannah needs help. Can you get here?"

"You have a lotta blood, Brendan," I mutter. "Do you need all of it?"

Ida probably says something but Brendan doesn't respond, just hanging up the phone and turning back to me.

"Yes," he says firmly. "Just like you need yours. Can you clean this all up?"

"Tired," I groan. "Don't wanna."

"Okay. Great!" he says with a sort of high-pitched voice that implies he doesn't think things are great. "Well, you're talking, so that's something. Keep talking, okay?"

"I love you, Brendan."

"Thanks, I love you too. Please stay conscious!"

I grin, feeling my lips peel back way farther than they're supposed to. He loves me! Too bad he's not a girl. Wait, oh yeah!

"You should name yourself May," I tell him. "Like. Like from Pokémon. Brendan and May. It's funny."

"I thought about that," he confirms, stepping around me and pulling the bloody sheets off my bed. "I don't think I want my identity to be a joke like that, though. I'd always be thinking about May the character, and I want my name to make me think of *me*."

Oh, that makes sense. I watch—without turning my head—as Brendan gathers up the sheets in a big wad and presses it against my back, right against my wounds. Which really hurts! If I wasn't so sleepy I might have accidentally lashed out at him.

"Careful," I mumble. "I grew swords."

"Yeah, I noticed that," Brendan agrees. "The rest of your body didn't seem to get the memo, though."

"I met a robot yesterday," I inform him.

"Good for you, Hannah."

I kick my feet a little, giggling slightly. The carpet is all sticky and wet, though. Maybe I should get up? Nah, I'm tired. And hungry! Oh, shoot, what about school though? It's a school day!

"You brought that hoodie, right?" I ask, craning my neck a little to face him. "So I can go to school?"

"Hannah, you are *not* going to school," he insists. "No fucking way. Not today."

"...But it's Friday," I remind him.

He just lets out an exasperated groan and continues applying pressure to my wounds, which like, okay, I *guess* I have some pretty big wounds, but the bleeding is stopping on its own, it should be fine. I'm just a bit lightheaded and hungry. I yawn, stretching out my jaw and letting it open all the way to maximum extension, something I haven't really done since I first figured out I could. It feels nice. I really wanna take a bite out of something.

Ooh, Ida's walking up to the porch, she's pretty bite-sized. No. Wait. Biting friends is bad, right? Even though I want to. I really want to. I'm cold and I'm hungry and my head hurts and I want to eat something so badly and there's *food* right here why am I not eating it!?

"What's up, nerds," Ida says as she steps into my room. Then she takes a moment to actually process the scene. "Oh, holy fuck, okay. You alive, Hannah?"

"I want to eat you."

"Wow, okay, I wasn't expecting things to get kinky this early," Ida sighs. "Step back, tallboy."

Brendan hesitantly does as instructed and I almost pounce on him, but again I'm too tired. Ida, however, heads right towards me. Food delivery! I work my jaw up and down some more, saliva dripping out of my mouth and mixing with the blood in the carpet.

"Shit, you *do* look hungry," Ida says, holding her hand out to me. "Okay. You get *one* finger. Alright? Just one finger."

"Ida, what the fuck are you doing!?" Brendan hisses, but I don't really care about the answer to that question so I snap my head forwards and chomp down. My teeth slide right through her hand, rewarding me with delicious, bloody, raw meat and bone. I think I end up with two fingers but I don't care, I swallow but I need *more,* but Ida is holding my forehead with her injured hand and keeping me back, keeping me *hungry,* and—

"**No Less Than Perfect**," she says, and my train of thought stalls. The pain in my back starts to diminish. And the dripping blood from Ida's hand starts to slow, new fingers emerging from the wound bone-first, then muscle and nerve and skin, all in sequence. I stare at the regrowth, transfixed by the sight, as I slowly come to realize that I'm why she has to regrow those fingers in the first place. I'm nearly naked on the floor of my room, blood everywhere, and nearly feral enough to kill the people who care about me more than anyone else. As my wounds close and my blood starts to replenish, I realize how close I just came to being the monster I've feared from the start.

"Hey, that's the haunted look I'm used to," Ida grins. "Back with us, Hannah?"

I vomit on her lap. Just one more thing to clean up, I suppose.

4

SHOW AND TELL

"Wow," Ida says, staring at the red-orange mess of stomach acid and unchewed finger bits splattered all over her jean skirt. "Rude."

"I'm sorry," I sputter, the aftertaste of vomit clinging to my mouth and throat and dripping from my lips. "I'm so sorry, I can fix this."

I start to cast Refresh but my brain stalls, forcibly requesting an answer to the question of 'where does vomit belong?' I can't just remove the stuff, I have to *put* it somewhere. The toilet? Too far away. My stomach?

...No. It's terrifyingly, disgustingly tempting, but thankfully I'm not that far gone. Re-ingesting my own vomit is too much even for my horrible, horrible monster brain. B-but I have to clean this, I need another container. I can't just drop it in my trash can, it has to be something no one else will find, it has to... it... right! It's like the teeth. I fumble for my backpack in a daze, crawling away from Ida and ignoring her look of concern as I open it up, find a spare ziplock bag from my various collections of supplies that I've paranoidly stuffed in there whenever I think of something new I might need, and open one up, magically pulling

69

all the vomit inside and leaving Ida's outfit—as well as my own mouth—perfectly clean.

There. Much better. I drum my limbs on the ground in a circular pattern—Except for the ones I'm currently kneeling on—to help calm myself down. It feels weird, like my legs are all different shapes and weights and *right* they are, I'm... I'm on Earth right now. I shudder, and drum my limbs in a circle again. Two still missing.

"...Hannah?" Brendan asks, concern obvious in his tone. I turn my head to look at him, sealing the ziplock bag and belatedly realizing that I am still, in fact topless. I twist the limbs on my hips up over the front of my body and press them against my chest to cover my nipples, a blush forming on my face.

"Uh, hey," I say awkwardly. "Thank you. Sorry about all this."

I start to stand up, decide that's maybe not the best idea with how wobbly and dizzy I still feel, and return to the floor. I guess No Less Than Perfect isn't quite the perfect spell after all; two fingers and my huge mess of wounds and blood loss must have strained its limits. ...That or I'm just dizzy from shame. Possibly the recent vomiting? That came after Ida's spell.

I think maybe I'm just not doing great in general.

"Sorry," I say again.

"Jesus, Hannah," Brendan says quietly, cautiously stepping closer. "You don't have anything to apologize for, alright?"

I pulled him and Ida out of school. I scared them half to death. I'm basically flashing them, which is super inappropriate. I vomited on Ida. I *ate Ida, I ate her, I tasted her blood and severed her bones and it was delicious, so delicious.*

"I agree with Brendan," Ida chimes in, "but since you're obviously spiraling I'll add that you're also forgiven. Okay? You don't need to apologize, and I forgive you for everything you're trying to apologize for anyway. Get checkmated, bitch."

She then *dabs,* of all fucking things, the sheer corniness of it projecting such an overwhelming aura of irony that I can't help

70

but smile at the absurdity. I chuckle humorlessly, feeling tears start to fall down my face. Oh, Ida.

"You are truly peerless, you horrible fae gremlin," I tell her, and she shoots me a supremely self-satisfied grin. Brendan watches the interaction blank-faced, though the small tells I've learned from him over the years lead me to assume he's confused, but not unpleasantly so.

With the help of my new limbs I crawl back towards my bed, using another spell to clean up the blood, forcibly extracting the water from it so it doesn't stick to the inside of my trashcan. Dry blood is just kind of a weirdly colored dust that easily mixes with trash without being conspicuous, and water can be separated out into small enough droplets that naturally dissolve into background humidity. These are well-established places to sort things, I do this stuff all the time. Couldn't repeat the trick with vomit, though; dry vomit would still be way too thick and smelly. Also there's human fingers in it.

Ida lets out a low whistle as she watches Refresh in action, walking over to my bed and starting to peel the comforter off. For some reason. The act reveals the parts of my sheets that have been shredded by my talons, as well as the foam blocks that all fell off at some point during my pained writhing.

"Oh shit, these are for your claws, right?" Ida asks, picking up one of the foam blocks and sticking her finger (her fingers her fingers) in the hole I've gouged in them. "That's so fucking cute. You think of this, tallboy?"

Brendan flinches at the address, nodding stiffly.

"Well, it's a good idea," Ida nods, turning the foam over in her hands. "We should replace these, though. The gouges are getting worn down so they'll just fall off when she moves. We should also get bigger ones, too. My parents probably have some packing stuff in our basement I could swipe, but if not we can probably buy them from like an OfficeMax or something."

71

She tosses the packing material away, finishes peeling the comforter off my bed, lays it out flat on the floor next to me, and then points down at it.

"Alright, Hannah. Get in the burrito."

I blink.

"What?" I ask.

"Get in the fuckin' burrito, Hannah," Ida orders again. "We have to smuggle you into my car and get you outta here before your dad wakes up, so I'm gonna roll you up into a big Hannahrito and throw you in the backseat. Easy peasy."

"...Is that going to stand up to scrutiny?" Brendan asks.

"Of course not, but it doesn't *have* to stand up to scrutiny. If anybody scrutinizes Hannah she's fucked no matter what we do, so it's a moot point. Thankfully, nobody will give a shit. Come on big guy, help me roll her up."

"Um, I didn't agree to this," I protest meekly.

"Well I ain't fucking you yet so I don't need your consent," Ida grunts, pushing me down onto the blanket.

"That's not how consent works at *all,*" I insist, but I let myself be laid down and rolled up into a comfy tube of blankets anyway. My burrower instincts chitter happily in the back of my mind, my many limbs wiggling slightly with both happiness and comfort. This was always the perfect trap to ensnare me.

Wait, what did she mean by 'yet?'

"We're going to Brendan's house, right?" I ask from within my muffled cocoon as Ida and Brendan lift me up with a pair of grunts. Ida balances my legs on her shoulder as Brendan holds my torso under one arm.

"We are," Brendan confirms.

"Shit you're fucking heavy," Ida grunts. "Why are we heading to his place?"

"It's empty," Brendan shrugs. "No one there but us."

"Eh, good a reason as any."

72

Miraculously, my dad either sleeps through all of this nonsense or is simply blaring Netflix too loud to hear or care, and I am tossed unceremoniously into the backseat of Ida's car without further incident. Then we start to drive, and since I'm blinded by blankets my spatial sense freaks out a little at the high-speed movement, making me like... extradimensionally carsick. It's a bit odd but I manage to not vomit on or destroy Ida's stuff so by my calculations I'm hitting under par.

Ida parks in Brendan's driveway and the pair shuffle me into his house before depositing me on the floor. Despite the disorientation and nausea, the car ride was kind of nice to help me center myself a bit, adjusting and getting used to my new limbs while I look myself over as best I can with my spatial sense. It's still not quite here, not *quite* showing me everything all at once with perfect clarity, but if I focus on something I want to 'see' hard enough I sort of... gah. It's hard to describe. I feel like I get a memory of what it might feel like to have *already* seen it, if that makes sense?

"Okay tallboy, get out of here," Ida orders. "I'm gonna unroll her so she can get dressed."

Again, Brendan looks distinctly uncomfortable at that. He probably doesn't like the nickname 'tallboy,' which... oh Goddess of course he doesn't, he might not be a boy at all. Uh, I guess I should include him in the girls-only activity? Include her? Agh I really have no clue how to handle this situation so I'm just going with my gut.

"Brendan can stay," I announce from within the filling of the Hannarito. "It's fine. I need to steal his hoodie to hide my new legs anyway."

"Y'know Hannah, you're really not gonna shrug off the gossip about Brendan being your boyfriend by letting him see your tits and then putting on his clothes," Ida taunts, using her foot to unroll me with her hands on her hips.

"But hi... but Brendan's hoodies are so big and comfy!" I whine.

"You've *already* been stealing his clothes?" Ida blinks. "...Wait, was that a pronoun correction?"

Brendan freezes. Goddess flipping dang it *why is she so observant?* How's a girl supposed to make basic mistakes with somebody like Ida around? I'd have never caught that in a million years.

"...Can we just focus on helping Hannah right now?" Brendan sighs.

Ida gives my best friend a suspicious side-eye, then shrugs.

"Sure, whatever, welcome to the bra party," she grunts, going back to kicking me free of the blankets. "So your little extra arms grew out in an inconvenient spot vis-a-vis your wardrobe, Hannah, and we will probably have to fix that today. Get you something backless. Or you can borrow some of my Nippies."

"Uh, your what?" I ask, extending my new legs to push myself straight into a standing position. Brendan and Ida do a bit of a double-take, though Ida mostly seems amused.

"Uh, haha. Woah. Um, Nippies are basically just this flesh-colored silicone sticker that turns your headlights off. Comfy, hard to see, weirdly sticky. I use 'em when I need to breathe a bit more. Also, *wow* that was cool, how are you already so good with those legs?"

"I mean, I have ten legs on the world tree," I shrug. "Though I suppose it's not super comparable since I'm a completely different size and shape, so... I dunno. It just feels natural, I guess?"

"Fucking wild," she says, chuckling. "Does it come with instant kill mode?"

I freeze up, mentally calculating how fast I could lash out and carve her open with a Spacial Rend, how *easily* a human life can fall away at the ends of my limbs. Is it instant? It's certainly close. Goddess, why does she taste so *good?* Why am I even thinking about this? What sort of monster am I going to end up as? How many people will *I* end up killing? More than Helen? More than

Sela? Will my apocalypse be nothing more than the work of my own two hands, little by little, personal and hungry?

"Uh, Hannah?" Ida says hesitantly. "I mean like, the Spider-Man thing? From the Avengers movie?"

"She has PTSD, you idiot," Brendan grumbles at her.

"I don't have PTSD," I say automatically.

"Yes you fucking do!"

I don't know about that. PTSD is for like, war veterans. People who actually *did* something. Also, what the heck is Ida talking about? Avengers movie? Oh, right, yeah. The scene from Endgame. We saw that together like three years ago. Right right right. It's a funny reference. I'm supposed to laugh at those. I let out a belated, half-hearted chuckle. It seems to make everyone a lot more worried. Man, I'm really bad at this.

"Uh, sorry Hannah," Ida says sheepishly. "Also, sorry to you too, string bean. I definitely shoulda been helping out earlier, she's a real piece of work. I bet you're at the end of your rope, huh?"

She elbows him in the hip and he flinches away.

"...Don't touch me, please," Brendan says.

Ida sighs.

"I just can't win," she grumbles. "Alright, I nabbed a bunch of clothes from your drawer, Hannah, pick whatever shirt you'll be least sad about if you end up ripping it to shreds."

I guess that's a good metric on how to dress myself today. I look over the collection, shrugging slightly.

"Eh, most of these are short sleeved, so it's not like I can ever wear them in public again anyway," I say.

Ida and Brendan glance at each other, then back to me.

"Hannah, just allow yourself to care about normal things a little and pick a shirt, okay?" Ida says softly.

I pick one at random and awkwardly shrug it on. It binds my new legs tightly, restricting their movement without feeling safe like a burrow. I kind of hate it, and despite how mortifyingly embarrassing it would be I almost want to just take it back off.

It also, of course, does very little to hide those legs. The tight cut of a woman's t-shirt is designed to show off figure, and would you look at that, my figure involves giant flippin' bug legs folded up behind my back. The legs on my hips are even more obvious, since my only options there are to stick them down my pants—which basically just doesn't work—or fold them up in front of my chest or underneath my armpits, which... also doesn't work, but at least it doesn't prevent me from walking. All things considered, it's probably *less* conspicuous to have them hanging out in the open. At least then I just look like a mutant instead of someone trying to *hide* the fact that they're a mutant, which is way more suspicious.

I'm totally fucked, aren't I? Well, it was a good run.

"At least I probably won't have to go to therapy tomorrow," I sigh.

"You think literally turning into a monster will get you out of something your mom has planned for you?" Brendan asks. Aw, dangit, he's right. I don't even get that happy little lie, do I? There's no way to hide my spider legs.

...Right?

I cross my legs and lean back, supporting my weight with good old limbs five and six, the hip-mounted classics. I guess I'll call them my... bonus legs? Spider legs? Whatever else they are, they're *legs,* unlike my back-mounted limbs which are clearly blades. Anyway, I bring my fist up to my chin for a proper think and start tugging on the idea I just had. Namely, the fact that I use a foolproof method of hiding my legs basically all the time, literally without thinking about it. I've just only ever done it on the world tree.

After all, I'd have to put them in 4D space.

I've performed neither 4D movement nor 4D perception Earthside, and now that I'm thinking about it I'm not really sure *why*. It's magic, right? Sure, Sindri (ugh) said something about me being a magical beast, a being whose biology relies on having a certain kind of magic available to it. All magical beasts of a given species have access to the same basic set of magical capabilities, simply because if they *didn't* they'd just kinda die. They can have extra spells on top of that, but the initial set is guaranteed. Over on this side of the multiverse, my biology doesn't rely on that magic at all, so the magic just hasn't manifested. Right?

...No. Wrong. Dead wrong. That doesn't make any sense. Biology might rely on it, but biology doesn't *cause* it. *All magic is Hers and only Hers.* Her gift comes from the soul, and my soul is the same regardless of the world.

"Hannah?" Brendan prods, causing me to glance up. "What's up?"

"When magic gives you lemons," I muse, "use magic to make lemonade."

"Um."

Carefully, I start shifting the blade-limbs on my back, trying to find the right *direction* in the way that always comes so naturally to me on the world tree. Still, there's something odd going on with my spatial sense. It feels like I *should* be able to see, so why... hrm. Actually, it kind of feels like the first time I tried to use Spacial Rend on this side of things. Like it's being clogged up somehow. Why? I didn't have this problem with Refresh. Whatever, the problem seems basically the same and so the solution does too.

Name the spell.

"Ida, I'm gonna need you on standby," I say. "Preferably in another room. If things go bad here I might need another patch."

"Ooh, are we already getting sexy and dangerous again?" she says, rubbing her hands together. "I gotcha covered, Hannah Banana. What's the plan?"

"Well, I have to name a spell. So this might go really wrong! But also it's a pretty straightforward one and I don't think I can mess it up *that* badly."

"Why must you always tempt fate!?" Brendan laments.

"Naw, seriously though, it's just a sensory spell. ...I mean, I think it's just a sensory spell."

"God damnit, Hannah," Brendan grumbles.

"Goddess," I correct.

"I wonder what ironic punishments you get for fucking up a sensory spell," Ida muses. "Removing every sense except the one you're trying to give yourself? Overloading your brain with too much information? Debilitating synesthesia?"

"Catatonia," Brendan suggests. "Brain aneurysm."

"Can we stop freaking out about possible consequences here and just help me pick out a good name?" I grumble. "It's currently between... actually wait, I should write these down instead of saying them out loud. Did you guys bring my phone?"

Brendan, ever the greatest, hands me both my phone and my capacitive gloves. I thank him and tap out the two Pokémon moves that fit the situation best.

Extrasensory or Miracle Eye, I send to the group chat. **The former has the better name, but worse thematics since it's an attack move. The latter isn't quite as good of a name in itself but the in-game effect matches a bit better.**

"Do thematics matter?" Brendan asks, looking at his own phone.

"Pretty sure they do," I nod. "I think the spell will be stronger the more the Goddess likes the name, and She's a sucker for drama."

"Yeah, I got the same impression," Ida agrees. "No way to know how much it affects things, really, I just chose the best name I could think of without worrying about optimizing for time spent speaking it. But uh, my spell name is awesome and my spell is awesome, so..."

"Yeah, I'm not really in love with either name, unfortunately, but keeping the theme feels important," I muse. "The entire thing gets weaker if I don't commit to it, right?"

"Definitely. You have to commit to the bit."

"What are you two on about?" Brendan asks. "How are you so sure of this?"

"Look cloud cover, when you put your big girl panties on and join us in the cool magic spell club the Goddess'll get *all* up in your shit and you can give us your own opinions on the process. In the meantime you're just gonna have to trust our intuition."

"Soft magic system," I confirm, shrugging helplessly at him.

"Ugh. Soft magic systems," Brendan says, wrinkling his nose. "Neat in concept, but *really* annoying to work with."

"Have you not figured out a spell yet?" I ask.

He frowns, glancing away awkwardly.

"I'm not sure. Maybe. It'll take me a while to set it up, though."

"Why's that?"

"Well, you said I'm an Art mage, right?" he says. "I think I have to draw something."

I mean, that makes sense. I give him an encouraging nod just before my phone buzzes. Oh, it's a message from... one of the Autumns. I dunno which Autumn, so I guess I'll just call her Autumn.

What exactly is the context here, she sends. **Also, where are you all?**

Oh right, she's at school. Crap, she's at school and I haven't told her what's going on!

I'm not really able to hide anymore, I text her. **Grew too many extra bits. But if I can name a spell that lets me see 4D on this side of things I should be able to figure out how to move there and hide my limbs in w-space.**

There's a pause as Autumn spends a bit of time composing a response.

What the actual fuck? she decides on.

I glance at Brendan.

79

"Is it cool if I invite her over?" I ask.

"Sure," (s)he shrugs.

You can come to Brendan's house if you want. Easier to show you.

I attach the address and put my phone away for now.

"Okay, so back to the names," I say.

"Do you *need* to name it?" Brendan presses. "Is it absolutely essential?"

"Possibly not," I admit. "But I'm pretty sure that not being able to see into the fourth dimension is my primary impediment for not moving into it. Because I'm not... I mean I'm already... I'm part of the fourth dimension all the time. That's why I can make sounds like this."

I hiss at them, the impossible vibrations causing them both to shudder.

"I can *try* to move my legs into the fourth dimension without seeing it, but it'd be a lot harder," I continue. "On the other hand, I'd probably be stuck with my spatial sense always on when I get it working, and that could be... kinda gross."

"Because you'd be seeing everybody's organs all the time?" Brendan asks.

"No, I'm super used to that," I say. "Because I'd be peeping under everybody's clothes all the time, but on Earth I have a libido."

"Coulda fooled me," Ida mutters.

I groan quietly. She's just gonna keep doing this, huh?

"Look, Ida, first of all I have a girlfriend now, so I'd just generally appreciate it if you stopped coming onto me."

"Wow! Phrasing!"

"*Second* of all, you're a huge part of the reason I figured out I'm a lesbian in the first place. I spent years getting over the crush I had on you and now I have a bunch of baggage about it, so it probably wouldn't work out anyway. Sorry."

Ida doesn't respond, seeming neither hurt nor offended. She just gives me a calculating stare, causing goosebumps to prickle across my skin until I break eye contact.

"...My vote is that we table the spell naming discussion for now," Brendan says, stoically ignoring the prior conversation. "You've mentioned that your spatial sense is coming in slowly on its own, and rushing it seems needed only if you can't figure out how to hide your extra limbs without it. And at the very least, we have the whole rest of the school day to help you practice."

I sigh. I wanna name the spell, though! I mean like, yeah it's crazy dangerous, and so Brendan's assessment makes sense, but... hmm. Well I can't think of anything after the 'but,' but... um. Aw, poop.

"Okay..." I whine. "I'll practice first."

"Thank you," Brendan says, sagging with relief and giving me a smile.

"But *while* I'm practicing, I wanna watch *you* practice!" I demand, pointing a finger at him. "It'll be safer for both of us to have backup and also I wanna see your magic!"

"Ooh, yeah, good idea!" Ida agrees, turning on Brendan with a vulpine grin. "Let's see the artist in action!"

"Uh... I don't... I mean I'm not really comfortable drawing around people..." Brendan hedges.

"Ah, but is it or is it not a good idea?" I counter smugly. "Should you or should you not be getting assistance and oversight while working on something dangerous for the first time?"

He deflates completely, slumping over in defeat.

"...Fine," he grumbles. "To the basement, then."

We gather up the blankets and extra clothes brought from my house and shimmy downstairs, Brendan sitting down by his computer and powering it on. Behind me, Ida pulls out a pocket knife and flicks it open, causing me to instinctively lash out behind myself with my extra limbs, tangling my blades in my shirt as Ida steps back out of reach of my hip-legs.

"Woah, chill out," she snaps, though she frowns and backpedals afterwards. "I mean, sorry. I shoulda warned you. I just figured since it's just us down here and you don't care about this shirt anyways we should free your back bits. Cut them some holes so they can stretch out. Yeah?"

I don't respond at first, focusing on my hammering heart rate and the horrible, sinking feeling that I'm not safe to be around. I nearly stabbed Ida! I take a few deep breaths before nodding anyway.

"Sure," I say. "Thank you. Maybe I'll be less tense if I don't feel as trapped."

Ida nods, and much more carefully approaches me to cut some slits in my shirt. I realize belatedly that it might be smart to take the shirt off before letting her do that, but the chitinous limbs underneath where she's cutting aren't damaged by the knife at all even when she does brush it against one. Possibly on purpose.

"Fucking wild," she mutters to herself. "Alright. There you go."

I wiggle my blade limbs out of the back of my shirt, and sure enough I do feel better almost immediately. I can be such a frustrating mess of contradictions sometimes. Why do I like being enveloped when I rest but hate being restrained while awake? Whatever, it doesn't really matter. I have to focus on moving these things across the w-axis to make them vanish in the way my legs vanish on the world tree all the time.

Brendan, meanwhile, has just opened some Photoshop-like art program and is scribbling away on his drawing tablet. I try to glance surreptitiously at what he's doing without alerting him that I'm doing so, but I still have to use my actual eyes for the job; my budding spatial sense is useless for this since computer monitors work by emitting light. The image depicts a dynamic shot of a flying woman levitating a bunch of debris around herself. She's also butt-naked, though the aforementioned debris protects her naughty bits from being in view. Hmm. I think that's one of Brendan's GURPS characters?

"Hey, you're pretty good," Ida says, walking right up behind Brendan and causing him to jump. He scrunches up a bit in his chair, turning slowly to face her with a glower. Aw, beans on toast. This probably isn't good.

"Is there a reason you're bothering me?" Brendan grumbles.

"Uh, yeah, actually," Ida confirms, raising an eyebrow. "What exactly is your problem with me, string bean? I never really cared before, but in the likely event that things end up as us against the world I figure you're worth getting to know."

"That seems like a good summary of my problem with you," Brendan answers, turning away from her and returning his attention to the computer screen.

"Oh?" Ida presses, smirking a bit as she steps closer to his desk to keep herself in his peripheral vision.

"Um, guys..." I say hesitantly, trying to head off the incoming mess, but I'm way too late.

"You're selfish, arrogant, manipulative, and don't give a shit about the messes you leave other people with," Brendan says firmly. "You toy with people, use them for as long as they're fun and then throw them away. It's disgusting."

Ida grins, not seeming bothered.

"Is that so?" she says. "What terrible things have I done, exactly?"

"Well, there was that time you got Melody's last boyfriend to cheat on her with you, gaslit her about it, and then dumped him when he broke up with her for you."

What? I haven't heard about this. Ida just barks out a laugh at the accusation, though.

"Shit Paul Bunyan, I didn't know you were friends with Melody," Ida sneers. "I'm surprised you know her *name.*"

"We're not friends," Brendan grunts. "I don't even like her. I just pay attention."

"Clearly not well enough," Ida says, crossing her arms and leaning against Brendan's desk. "Melody was just abusing Jeremy for his money, she didn't give a shit about him. So yeah, I seduced his ass to get him away from her, all while encouraging her to prefer more and more expensive things so that when he *does* dump her, she goes broke. It's hilarious. A perfect fucking revenge story. The bitch gets owned, her whole wardrobe full of useless gaudy shit that looks terrible and costs too much to be practical, and the nice guy gets a good fuck before being released into the world with finance lessons and better vaginas on the horizon. That whole scheme was my good deed for the month, thank you kindly."

Uh. That's... a lot. Gosh. Brendan responds before I can really wrap my head around how I feel about that.

"That's completely insane and messed up on *so* many levels," Brendan groans, dropping his stylus and massaging his temples. I wouldn't use such harsh phrasing, but I don't entirely disagree. "You're seriously framing a premeditated destruction of someone's relationship and finances as a good thing?"

"I made bad things happen to bad people and good things happen to good people," Ida shrugs. "That's better justice than the world normally dishes out, don't you think?"

"You think you have a right to decide what counts as justice?" Brendan asks.

"You think I *don't?*" Ida counters."Then bring it on. Stop me from living my life if you can, bitch."

Brendan stares at her in disbelief for a moment, but with a shake of his head he peels his eyes off of her, returning his attention to the computer screen.

"...That's what I thought," Ida smirks triumphantly.

"I just can't believe you," Brendan says quietly. "You're so selfish. So supremely selfish."

"Yet here I am, spending my whole day helping *you*," Ida grins."So to that end: what're your pronouns, jolly green giant?"

Brendan stiffens.

"Is there a particular reason you only refer to me by making fun of my height?"

"Uh, because you're literally taller than the average NBA player? How is that not obvious. Also, as previously mentioned, it's essential to commit to the bit. Also also: that's not an answer to the question."

"U-uh, maybe don't press Brendan on that, Ida?" I hedge, finally regaining the courage to insert myself into the anxiety-inducingly intense conversation. "It might be best to just let that happen how it happens?"

"Oh, it might be," Ida agrees, nodding. "But I don't think it is. Come on, spill it."

"No," Brendan grumbles.

"No? No pronouns? That's a pain but I can manage."

"I mean no, I'm not having this conversation with you. Full stop."

Ida rolls her eyes but finally stops leaning on Brendan's desk, waving dismissively at him as she walks away.

"Okay, we're sticking with height jokes then, Lebron," she grumbles. "Just don't hurt yourself with that fancy new magic of yours, because healing isn't coming your way."

I stiffen at that, my blades instinctively whipping up over my shoulders to show my displeasure.

"Woah, Ida," I say firmly. "You don't have to get along, but that's kind of a fucked up thing to withhold. Magic can seriously hurt people."

"I'm not just saying it to be a fucking bitch, Hannah," Ida insists, crossing her arms and looking away. "It's just a warning. Clifford can let me in or go without."

This... isn't like her. Ida can be spiteful, but not like *this*.

"What do you mean, exactly?" I ask.

She scowls, shifting her weight back and forth.

"...I mean it literally won't work," she says. "My magic doesn't affect things I don't give a shit about. Like your torn up

85

bedsheets, or your packing foam. ...Or your best friend. Not for *lack of trying,* mind you!"

She raises her voice on the last sentence there, glowering meaningfully in Brendan's direction. He doesn't react.

"It's really arbitrary," Ida continues. "I think they have to be... *mine* in some way. You're *my* friend, so I can heal you, but Brendan is only *your* friend, so I can't do shit."

"Huh," I say. "I mean, can you teach me the spell? It seems crazy useful, and I could potentially heal Brendan in a pinch if you can't."

"Ha! No. You don't have the self-esteem for it. The Goddess would smack you for the hubris of attempting to cast it with insufficient hubris."

I hesitate at that, nervously rubbing my hip-legs together.

"Uh. Ida, don't divine beings generally *not* like hubris?" I hedge.

"Maybe they don't like *your* hubris, but I'm different. Better. Maybe even better than the Goddess."

Oh no oh geez oh gosh she really just said that! I wait in terror for the inevitable retribution and... nothing happens. Ida extends her arms wide, flashes me an arrogant grin, and makes 'come here' motions on either side of her like she's encouraging an invisible crowd to cheer louder.

"Don't look at me like that. I'm peerless, and She knows it," Ida brags, and the weight of the Goddess' attention crushes us a moment later, full and overwhelming in its glory.

I stagger as She fills the room, flowing around me but for once barely glancing at me as she focuses on *Ida,* and her grand blasphemy. Horror at what's about to happen to my friend fills my bones, internal and external, but I can't move, can't so much as cry out during the infinite second between attention and retribution. The memory of my miscasted Spacial Rend is all I can think about, the agony and blood and casual brutality that became my entire world for that horrible moment. The Goddess smiles, cruel and vindictive, and then... boops Ida on the nose. She vanishes with a chuckle, and time returns to the world.

I nearly fall over, catching myself with a hip-leg as my breath comes to me in gasps. Brendan turns around to face us, looking moderately worried, but whatever he felt doesn't seem to have the same impact as my personal terror.

"See?" Ida grins, completely unrepentant and utterly unafraid. "She digs me. Anyway, you need to get back to practice. I'll formulate a plan to maybe convince myself to care about tall, dark, and grumpy over there, and... I don't really care what the fuck else happens. Let's just do it, yeah?"

I sigh, feeling distinctly helpless about everything in my life and completely bowled over by everyone else just kind of *doing stuff* at me without giving me any time to think. So... I guess I'm feeling pretty normal. Sighing again at that thought, I push it aside and focus on my new limbs, trying to figure out the right muscle to pull in order to yank them in an impossible direction. My understanding of my hyperspider biology is very limited, but best I can tell that body is *mostly* 3D in structure, with just a rare handful of bits here and there expressing their complexity across more than one point on the w-axis at a time, and even then not that deeply. Still, that's all that's apparently needed to relocate my limbs into 4D space, and considering how huge my recent growths are, surely that part of the joints is done, right? I just have to figure out how to *do* it. It should be the same as when I'm a hyperspider, or at least pretty similar, right?

An hour later I let out a frustrated groan, flopping forward in mental exhaustion and catching myself on my bug limbs, legs limp and arms dangling. I'm done. Done! Nothing is working, I'm just rotating my extra shoulders over and over until they get sore. Why is dimensional movement so hard?

The doorbell ringing is a sudden but welcome distraction, especially with how my brain automatically updates me with the knowledge of who's on the other side of it. No one else I know has cute little wings growing out of her back, even if they *are* currently smooshed uncomfortably behind a sports bra.

87

"Oh shit, should we answer that?" Ida says.

"Yeah!" I confirm, flipping myself over so my stomach is face-up and my head can look at her upside-down. "It's Autumn!"

If I wasn't an exposed mutant horror I'd be running upstairs to open the door myself, dang it!

"How do you know that?" Brendan asks.

"Because she's standing at the front door!"

"...Right, your miracle eye," Brendan sighs, standing up. "Okay, I'll get the door. I wanna meet her anyway."

Hehehe. Brendan wants to judge the worthiness of my girlfriend. I dunno why, but I find that idea really cute. I shove myself back up to my feet and quickly look around for a mirror so I can fix my likely-messed-up makeup before remembering that I was kidnapped by my friends before I could so much as take a shower and I'm not currently wearing any.

"Ida, do you have any makeup?" I ask. "Or did you guys bring my backpack?"

"Hah, you're down bad for her," Ida smirks. "That's both gross and fuckin' adorable."

She grabs a purse from where it leans against the couch and tosses a travel-sized makeup kit at me, which I catch, open, and immediately cast—

"**Refresh**," the Goddess says, and I quickly sort the makeup perfectly into place, cleansing my body of sweat, grime, and dead skin more thoroughly than a shower ever could while I'm at it. Properly freshened up and presentable, I thank Ida and toss the kit back at her, which she catches with a chuckle and a shake of her head.

I nervously drum my talons on the floor, realizing how incredibly underdressed I am all of a sudden. I'm wearing nothing but a thin t-shirt and a pair of shorts that barely reach halfway down my thighs. I don't even have a *bra* on since we haven't gone shopping for one that'll fit me yet. All of my monstrous parts are fully exposed, from mouth to extra limbs to *old* limbs that are dramatically less human than ever before.

I've just been taking that for granted until now. *Enjoying* it, even, the feeling of not having to hide suffusing me with a dull inner warmth. Of course Brendan and Ida don't care. Brendan is *Brendan,* he's probably having a heck of a time trying *not* to examine the nonhuman parts of me. And Ida is... I dunno. I mean, she clearly doesn't seem to care, right? She's been helping out and the only weird looks she gives me are for things I *do,* not any part of what I *am.* Curious, appreciating, sometimes concerned, but never disgusted, never judging. She even seems to still want to have sex with me, which... I... don't know how to think about, so I'm just gonna not do that because I have a girlfriend anyway. The recent revelations that Ida might not *care* that I have a girlfriend are a bit concerning, but... I mean, it's not like she'd force me into anything, so the only person I'd have to blame if I cheated on Autumn is myself. I can be pretty flaky, but I wouldn't ever do something like that. That's just... no.

The *point* is, Autumn has seen my transformed bits before, but never quite like this. Never so much all at once. And she's... well, I don't know which Autumn she is right now, but I'd be devastated if either one of them doesn't... I dunno. Like me? Like what I am? Because like, it's over if they don't, right? I'll have screwed up her whole life for nothing. But... no. Wait. I *did* screw up her life, and... she's dealing with it pretty okay? She's going through the same things I am. She's becoming a monster like me, so... she'll understand, right? She'll *get it.*

She'll get it. That's part of what makes her so special. It's so, *so* good to have someone else who will understand. The thought fills me with unfathomable relief, like a soak in a hot tub after a long day.

"Absentee parents, huh? Could be worse," Autumn grunts in a way that sounds rather like Jet. She and Brendan are already mid-conversation as they walk down the basement stairs towards the rest of us.

"Point is, none of this is *mine,* really," Brendan says, conspicuously avoiding getting into a conversation about how his parents would legitimately struggle to actually be any worse. "Everything but the basement may as well be someone else's house."

"Mind if I take some of it, then?" maybe-Jet asks.

"Huh?"

"The crap in your house. I could pawn any old thing in here for a few months' worth of bills."

"...Are you asking for my permission to steal from my parents?" Brendan asks, blinking with surprise.

"Think of it more like convincing your parents to donate to charity for a reason other than getting a tax writeoff."

"Uh... I dunno. I don't really need more reasons for them to yell at me," Brendan hedges. And then the two of them finally stroll into view.

My whole body is fidgeting with nervous energy as I spot them, hip-legs rubbing together and making soft keening noises, fingers drumming against each other and blade-limbs facing forward out of stress, then retracting out of embarrassment, over and over again. I work my jaw, suddenly hyper-aware of how my smile can get too wide and my mouth can open too far. She's not gonna hate me, right? I mean, I think this is Jet, so I'm not even dating her I guess. I kinda want to, though? Is that cheating? Or I guess... polyamory? I guess it *is* since they're different people. Gah, whatever, it doesn't matter, Jet doesn't want me.

Jet would prefer I leave them both alone.

I hug myself a bit and do my best to give a normal, non-toothy smile, hoping it doesn't look quite as fragile as I feel when my friends finish descending and turn to look at me. Autumn's eyebrows raise slightly, scanning me up and down, taking in the extensive mutations across my whole body. No, stop panicking. It's okay. *She understands.* With my spatial sense, I feel her wings twitch involuntarily.

"Are you doing something?" Jet asks, her attention locked on me.

"Huh?" I ask.

"Are you doing something to me?" she presses. "I feel that weird tingle again."

"Uh. Shoot, am I?" I ask, looking down at myself as if that would help. Wee, more things to panic about! "I don't *think* I am!? I don't feel anything on my end?"

"Hrm," Jet grumbles, scratching her back around the wing base. "Well, maybe they're just going numb from being compressed all day. It's just my wings and ears."

Autumn has ears? Wait, what do I mean by that, of course she has... uh. She has...

"Sorry, could you say that again?" I ask, feeling awkward and disoriented.

"My wings and... ah. Right," Jet muses, smirking slightly. "What am I wearing on my head?"

"On your head?" I repeat, not understanding.

"Yeah, what are you on about?" Ida asks.

Jet smirks, reaching up and pulling a winter cap off her... wait, *what?* She was wearing a hat this whole time? I mean... of course she was, it was in plain view. How did I not notice—oh *right* she has weird ears now too! They're even longer and pointier than they were the last time I saw her, pointing diagonally up and away from her head, fuzz the color of her curls growing along the outside and ending as tufts of floof on the tips. She wiggles them, looking smug.

"None of you noticed the hat, huh?" she asks. "Damn, I can't believe it works that well. This magic stuff isn't all bad, I guess."

I take a shuddering breath, stepping over towards the couch so I can sit down, bile rising in my throat.

"Okay, that's... really trippy," Brendan says, blinking away the disorientation. "Not invisibility, but... a spell to make something go unnoticed? Is that Pneuma magic?"

Yes. Yes it is. Pneuma magic. Mind magic. Mind control. I sit slowly and carefully, taking a long exhale as I bury my face in my hands.

"Pneuma and Light, I think," Jet confirms damningly. "Not really sure why it's Light, but it feels like it is."

"I guess it affects whether or not someone can see something, and *conceptually* that's in line with Light," Brendan muses. "Light or dark, revealing or concealing. Elements can get pretty metaphorical in their classifications, I think. That probably goes extra for spells with more than one element, or elements that are already pretty vague in how they're classified. Because like, something like Order is already a nebulous concept based around societal interpretation, so it fits that Light spells wouldn't be limited to only the manipulation of electromagnetic energy. Does that sound right, Hannah?"

"Yeah," I confirm, trying not to vomit.

"You okay, Hannah Banana?" Ida asks.

"I'm fine," I lie automatically, and immediately regret it. These people aren't strangers or family, I can be honest with them. "I just got a little freaked out from having my mind messed with, is all. Could you not use that spell on me, Jet?"

"Jet?" Brendan asks, and Jet sighs in annoyance.

"Oh, fuck," I mutter. "Sorry."

"It's fine, we may as well tell him," Jet grumbles. "I have DID. I'm Jet, and you haven't met Alma yet but she's... in here."

She motions vaguely at her own head.

"...And she's the one dating your friend," Jet clarifies. "I'm just along for the ride."

Jet pulls out her notebook and pen, quickly scribbling something down in it. Probably the fact that Brendan knows about them now.

"Huh," Brendan blinks, not seeming to know how to process that. "Well, okay then?"

"It is what it is," Jet says noncommittally. "Well, I can definitely intuit why Hannah isn't at school today. What's the plan, then? Is the cat finally out of the bag?"

"Not quite yet," Ida shrugs, casually stepping over and wordlessly casting No Less Than Perfect on me. "She's got some Space shenanigans that she thinks she can figure out to hide stuff."

I feel the healing spell wash through me, combing my mind for lingering signs of infiltration and finding none. I'm fine. I'm okay. I'm still me. I send Ida a grateful glance, receiving a small smile and nod in return.

"Yeah, I think I should be able to just shunt my legs into higher-dimensional space," I confirm, working up the courage to exist again. "Mostly, anyway. The initial joints will still be partially visible, but it'll just be like a little lump. *Way* easier to cover up than an entire limb. I just... can't figure the movement out because I can't *see* myself correctly. I'm not sure what else to try at this point beyond magic."

"Which is where the names come in, right," Jet says, frowning slightly. "Girl, for somebody who nearly got *personally murdered by a goddess,* you're weirdly eager to toss yourself into more magical bullshit. There's no way you mutated this fast in the first place without casting your transformation spell, right?"

"It's not my fault!" I protest. "Well, okay, it's half my fault. I cast it a bit on the world tree because I wanted to develop the ability to speak, which I *did,* and it was totally worth it. But then I had to cast it even more because I nearly died rescuing a super advanced robot girl. Or, uh, not girl I guess? She says—schnitzel, I mean *it* says it's an it, but that feels really mean and dehumanizing to use. I mean, not that she's human, but like... it's clearly sapient? Anyway she was getting electrocuted to death so I tried to help her and two people died but at least I wasn't the one who killed them this time!"

Everybody stares at me in silence for a moment, their brains seeming to chug a bit as they process everything all at once. Ida, naturally, is the one who speaks first.

"Goddess damnit, Hannah, you are so fucking cis."

"Huh?" I ask. What does that even mean?

"Have you seriously never met anybody who uses it/its pronouns?" she snorts. "There's like a gazillion of 'em. I realize you're a sheltered-ass baby queer, but this should be the literal simpliest thing in the world. If you don't understand, don't act like that means you know better. Not understanding means you know *worse*. Call it what it wants to be called, idiot!"

"S-sorry?" I sputter.

"Ida's virtue signaling aside—"

"Fuck you siren head, I'm *right*."

"—she *is* right but I'd really like to focus on the fact that you found a *robot* on the *magical fantasy world tree?*" Brendan presses."Like, the tree where everyone is still using bows and swords and stuff?"

"Didn't I tell you about the robot earlier?" I ask. "I don't remember all that well."

"Yeah, because you were *delirious!* I didn't think you actually met one!"

"...I think I need to hear about the world tree like, at all," Jet says. "Can we start at the beginning here?"

Oh right, I kinda *have* been putting off telling Autumn about my world tree adventures. Most of the memories aren't too great, but I guess she deserves to know. I start the story at the beginning: emerging from my tunnel, seeing a 3D world in 4D for the first time, meeting Kagiso, Teboho... and Sindri. The whole story starts flowing once it gets going, the pain not strong enough to stop the words. I get thrown out of my groove about halfway through discussing the city of Grawlika when Autumn's ears start to droop and she timidly asks if I can hold on a moment.

"Alma?" I ask.

She glances nervously at Brendan, but nods.

"Um, yeah," she confirms. "S-sorry. Um. Where are we?"

She fumbles for her notebook, quickly reading it as she simultaneously pulls out her phone to check the time. ...And maybe the date.

"S-sorry, I'm not usually..." she glances at Brendan again. "I mean, Jet's been fronting more than usual today. I... she drove here, right? Could someone show me where the front door is? Sorry, I just... I'm a bit disoriented."

"I-it's okay!" I say, standing up rapidly. The motion forces me to flare out my new bug limbs as I lose balance because of them, causing Alma to seemingly notice them for the first time.

"W-woah! It's still Friday, right? Did you grow those overnight?"

"Uh, yeah, it's a long story. I'll restart it for you when we get back... downstairs. Shoot, I probably shouldn't go near street-facing windows."

"I got it," Ida says. "Honestly, that's my cue to head out and buy you some stuff you can cover up with. Follow me, Alma. You have a hat in your right pocket for your ears."

"Oh, um, okay. Thank you," Alma mumbles awkwardly, her ears drooping a little further at the prospect of being trapped.

The two of them head upstairs and Brendan turns to me with a raised eyebrow.

"She okay?" he asks.

"I think so?" I hedge. I wish I had a more sure answer, but I guess I don't actually know Alma all that well. "She and Jet don't share memories, so..."

"Oh," Brendan says, looking back towards the stairs. "Gosh, that really sucks. Is it a magic thing?"

"Uh, I don't think so? No?" I say, surprised. "I'm pretty sure some people are just like that?"

Brendan nods.

"Right, yeah. DID. Okay."

An awkward silence passes for a moment.

95

"...Do you wanna talk about gender stuff while Ida's gone?" I ask hesitantly.

"Not really," he says. "Probably not today."

"Okay," I nod. "Should I push you about it tomorrow?"

He considers that for a moment, then nods back.

"Yeah, I think so. I *should* talk about it, just... not today. Too much."

I want to hug him, but I know right now that'd be a bad idea.

"I understand," I say instead. "I can sneak into the backyard and exercise Fartbuns with Alma if you want some time alone down here?"

"That'd be great," he says. "Thank you."

I smile and give him a thumbs-up, heading upstairs as Brendan heads back to his computer. I peek my head out from the basement steps and glance down the hall just in time to see Ida driving off and Alma closing the front door... then opening it and closing it again. She sighs and turns around, jumping a little as she spots my head peeking around the corner.

"H-Hannah!"

"Hey Alma," I wave awkwardly. "Sorry. How are you with dogs?"

"Um, fine? I like dogs."

"Cool! Wanna play with Brendan's dog in the backyard? He's gonna decompress a bit."

She stares at me a bit.

"...Is the backyard safe?" she asks. "Like, for you to look like that."

"Oh, should be, yeah," I confirm. "It's huge and the fence is huger. ...Wait, Is huger a word?"

"Technically yes," Alma confirms. "Though it sounds *really* dumb."

"Yeah, it totally does," I agree. "Come on, Fartbuns! Outside time!"

I have no idea where in the house Fartbuns actually is, but the huge Malamute quickly corrects that the moment I proclaim the sacred doggy-words, bounding directly towards our location at record speed. Completely unperturbed by the fact that I've recently doubled my limb count, he barrels into me in a big floofy pile of energy and joy.

"Good boy, Fartbuns!" I coo, bracing my weight on my hip limbs and letting him jump up to put his front paws on me even though I'm not supposed to. I give him a heaping helping of affectionate scritches before shoving him off and going to grab his treats and ball.

"That's Alma, Fartbuns!" I introduce him, pointing at my girlfriend. "Say hi to Alma!"

He gives her an affectionate "Boof!" which causes her to flinch, but he's a lot more careful with her than he is with me and approaches her without any tackling or slobber. Fartbuns is a smart dog, and though it took him a long time he's gotten used to Brendan and either recognizes Alma's anxiety or is just somewhat nervous himself. Hesitantly, Alma reaches out and gives him a scratch, though, and relations with the fluffy pupper look like they're going to go swimmingly from there on. We head out to the backyard and his excitement increases exponentially.

Alma and I sit down on the edge of the porch, our feet in the grass. Unlike me, she's got her usual all-covering complement of baggy sweater, pants, and tennis shoes, although after a moment of sitting in silence together throwing balls for the dog she does the thing where you retract your arms inside your shirt to remove your bra without taking your shirt off, freeing her wings from their cramped conditions without becoming indecent. She gives them a stiff wiggle, sighing with relief as she stretches them.

"You doing okay?" I ask her.

"I don't know," she answers, grabbing the ball from Fartbuns and tossing it again. "Kind of. Not really."

Fartbuns returns. I grab the ball this time, throwing it and ignoring my urge to chase Fartbuns as he runs off after it.

"It's scary, isn't it?" I say quietly.

Alma peels her eyes away from the dog and stares at me. I stare back.

"It's terrifying," she agrees. "Am I gonna end up looking as crazy as you?"

"I don't know," I answer honestly.

"Sorry, that was rude. You don't look *bad* or anything," she assures me. "I just mean like... we'll never be normal. We *can't* be normal. And yeah, there's always that trope, like 'ha ha, being normal is overrated,' but... this is so much worse than being the quirky kid no one understands or whatever. We don't even fit into the mold of people who don't fit the mold."

"Yeah," I agree. Fartbuns returns. Alma takes the ball and throws it. He bounds off, and we watch in silence.

"...That's the thing, though," Alma says quietly. "I'd already given up on the idea of having a normal life. I have Jet. I never know when I'll even *exist,* because she's always there, waiting to take time from me whenever I slip. I'm supposed to be the one fronting in classes all day, but I don't remember anything after I woke up this morning and saw myself in the mirror."

That's... a lot to unpack. I don't know what to say to any of it.

"...Sorry," is all I manage.

"It's okay," Alma shrugs. "That's my point, you know? It's *okay.* I can forgive you for doing this to me. I don't have a life for you to ruin in the first place."

My heart clenches.

"Oh, Alma..."

"Sorry, sorry, that came out wrong," she quickly mutters, hugging her knees. "I should say I *didn't* have a life. I never had a chance to be part of anything that mattered. But now? I've got magic, I've got people who actually kinda know my secret and don't make a huge thing of it, and I've even got... y'know."

She blushes a little, an embarrassed smile twitching on her face.

"...A girlfriend," she manages.

I can't help it. An urge to hug her overtakes me. I'm *still* not sure why I'm suddenly this cuddly, but I'm not going to deny it here. I carefully reach over and wrap my arms around her, slow and gentle so she has plenty of time to pull away if she wants to. She leans into it instead and I squeeze her lightly in my arms, pressing my forehead into her cheek. Hesitantly, she reciprocates, wrapping her arms around me in turn, and together we hold each other until Fartbuns inevitably returns, ruining the romantic moment with a completely unrepentant bonk of his head, knocking us over for having the audacity to not wrestle for and subsequently throw his glorious, glorious ball.

We laugh and extract ourselves from each other so I can yank the item free from his mouth and throw it harder than I ever have before, launching it well to the other side of the yard to Fartbuns' clear joy. I notice that one of my hip-legs is still wrapped around Alma's waist, but she doesn't seem opposed to it so I leave it there, soaking in joy from the warmth of physical contact. It's strange and wonderful and exciting and stressful and it makes me want to burst with joy, to leap into the air and shout my jubilation across the rooftops. Just being here with her is a high unlike anything I've felt in years. A wild and untamed infatuation, bursting with an energy I feel like I've been starved of without ever knowing.

Alma wraps a hand around the end of my hip-leg, holding it as she leans her shoulder into mine.

"It's almost hard to believe this is part of you," she murmurs. "But then all I have to do is wiggle my own wings. Do you think I'll be able to fly someday? I keep telling myself not to get my hopes up, I'm probably way too big and heavy for flight."

"I've seen people a heck of a lot bigger than you fly just fine," I assure her. "Just last night I met this massive bat-dragon—over a hundred feet in wingspan!—that referred to itself with the royal we. Or heck, maybe they referred to themselves with the plural we. I have no idea, but they carried me all the way to another branch."

"Woah," she whispers. "I, uh, think I missed most of your story, though. Could you...?"

"Of course," I agree immediately. "We'll start at the beginning."

I tell the same story for the second time that day, one full of trauma and pain. But to my surprise, it's easier this time. I don't normally like repeating myself, but for whatever reason it's not annoying or frustrating.

Not for her.

5

CHIMERA

"And you just... made friends with it?" Alma asks incredulously.

"Well, for a certain definition of friend, sure," I hedge, shrugging awkwardly. "I don't think Sela really *likes* us, but sh—gah, I mean *it's* super cool and it needs help. So I wanna help it! Best case scenario it *does* learn to like us and ends up less murderous, worst case scenario..."

I trail off, thinking about that for a moment.

"...I guess the worst case scenario is that we inadvertently cause a gray goo scenario and destroy all life in the universe? Buuuut that's probably really unlikely."

Alma gives me an incredulous look, then shakes her head and chuckles.

"You are insane," she says. "Didn't you say you were like, prophesied to cause an apocalypse or something?"

"No, I *said* that every prior isekai victim that the shady cult knows about has either caused an apocalypse or gotten murdered by said cult, likely without provocation. Trust me though, Alma, I *see* the red flags here. But what's the more common mistake: befriending a bad guy, or assuming someone is a bad guy and not even *trying* to befriend them? Sela is dangerous but I feel like it's also traumatized and trapped under someone else's control. It's a risk, but after what's happened to me I am *so* taking that risk if it means I might be able to help."

Fartbuns returns with the ball, and when Alma takes it and tosses it I feel that familiar urge to run off after the dog and tackle him to the ground. It's been getting a little harder to resist, if only because I really want to test out my new limbs a little more comprehensively. Still, I wait. Alma is more important.

"I guess that makes sense," she agrees, a little distantly. "Being born just to be used as a tool... no person deserves that."

"Well, Sela's pretty adamant that it *isn't* a person, which is kinda weird. Maybe I'm missing some cultural context behind the Middlebranch word for 'person,' but I don't *think* I am. It's just... anybody. Any sapient. Any individual of value. And Sela really *seems* like she's—biscuits, I mean *it's* all of those things. No way it's just a super-sophisticated program without self-awareness. I don't believe it."

"Huh," Alma says. "I dunno. It makes sense to me."

"What?" I ask. "Really?"

"I mean, yeah," she shrugs awkwardly. "Have you never felt like you're not a person?"

I open my mouth, but it takes me a while to find any words.

"I... you mean like the monster stuff?" I ask, fear filling me. "No, I... I mean, I'm not human anymore. Maybe I never was. But I'm still a *person,* you know?"

Alma smiles sadly, hugging her knees to her chest.

"That's not really what I meant," she says softly. "Never mind."

"Wh... no, it's... I'm sorry?" I babble. What did I do wrong?

"It's okay, you're fine," Alma assures me. "Don't worry about it."

What? What does she mean? Oh Goddess, is she okay?

"Sorry," I repeat. "I don't think I get it but I *want* to get it but if you don't want to explain that's fine."

She shakes her head.

"I'm not very good at explaining things," Alma mutters. "It's just... it makes sense to me. Even if 'person' has a denotative meaning of any self-aware entity, it... like, the denotative meaning isn't *really* the meaning, because... ugh. I don't know. Is a slave a person?"

I blink. An easy question, though given the context it feels like it's a trap.

"I... yes?" I say, because it doesn't matter if it's a setup, I can't say *no*. "Of course they are. That's like, why slavery is bad. N-not the only reason, but on the most basic, fundamental level. It abuses people."

"Right, okay," Alma nods. "But what if you *told* a slave that. You walk up to one, you tell them they're a person, and... you don't free them. Do you think that would make them feel good?"

I frown a little.

"I mean... I fully intend to free every slave I can," I say frankly. "Sela included, as long that doesn't result in it mass murdering innocent people. Because, y'know, that would be worse."

Alma groans like that was the wrong answer somehow.

"It's just hypothetical," she insists. "An allegory. It doesn't have to be slavery, it doesn't have to be *you*, I just... never mind."

"Sorry," I backpedal immediately. "Sorry, I'll answer the question. Would it make them feel good. Um. I guess it'd feel kind of empty? It's better than telling them they're *not* a person though, right?"

She opens her mouth, closes it, and then turns away from me, hugging herself protectively.

"Maybe at first," Alma admits. "But if you keep giving someone empty kindnesses for long enough it'll just start to hurt. If words aren't backed up by actions, they turn into knives."

I swallow nervously, taking in that thousand-yard stare on her face that I've seen in the mirror lately. Please, please, please let whatever's going on not be my fault. ...Geez, is that really my first thought? I'm such a terrible person.

"Are you okay?" I ask quietly.

She jolts slightly, then glances at me with a lopsided grin.

"Oh, uh, I mean… not really, I guess," she chuckles. "Are *you?*"

Now *that's* a deflection I know too well. I don't think I should push her, though.

"Absolutely not," I confirm. "You wanna talk about literally anything else?"

"*God,* yes."

"Goddess," I correct, and she snorts, shoving me with her shoulder.

The casual contact lights my joy like sparks on kindling, and when Fartbuns returns I feel like the time is right. Alma and I both need a distraction. So when she tosses the ball I give her a quick squeeze and clear my throat.

"Hey, uh, don't freak out or anything," I assure her. "I'm not gonna kill the dog."

"W-what?" Alma stutters, and I burst after Fartbuns like a rocket.

The sense of power flowing through my legs as I dig my talons into soft earth, catapulting myself forward and closing the distance in just a few paces is intoxicating. *Fuck,* why did I hold back this long? I'm only using two legs and this already feels so *right.*

I tackle Fartbuns from behind, startling him for only a moment before he realizes that playtime has just gotten a lot more fun. He wriggles free from my grasp and I leap after him again, prompting him to juke to the side. Without even thinking about it, I dig a hip-limb into the dirt to arrest my momentum, swing around, and leap at him again. He's kind of slow, like playing tag with a child, but if anything that just makes me less worried I'll hurt him on instinct, my monstrous urges screaming "baby!" rather than "prey!"

Because that's the thing, isn't it? I might be going feral, but even feral beasts have friends and family. Lion cubs play with each

104

other just as adorably as kittens do. I'm a monster, but I can still love. I can still be gentle.

I tackle Fartbuns again, surprised at his strength as he wrestles free of my arms. I guess my new supernatural body hasn't crawled up past my hands yet, but that's okay. Next time I catch him I wrap my legs around him too, propping myself up on my hip-limbs and blades and it just feels *so good,* they support my weight so well! Belly up or belly down, I can crawl and skitter at incredible speeds, turning on a dime, not needing to care about forward, backward, left or right... Goddess, I've missed moving like this. Thank you for giving it back to me. Thank you, thank you, thank you, thank you. Something like a hiss leaks out from my throat, but it's merged with a jubilant trill, a purr of eldritch delight as drink in the utter *freedom* of my form. I love it, I love it, I *love it so much!*

"H-holy shit, Hannah!" Alma her face distorted with fear. But it's okay! I turn my head to her and grin to show that it's okay. It's *amazing.*

"Do you feel it, Alma?" I ask, my excitement bubbling over.

"What? What are you talking about!?"

"When you think about flying!" I clarify, halting my erratic movement and leaping back to my feet. "Do you have this much joy?"

"Oh," she says, relaxing considerably. "Uh... gosh. I mean, I'd be lying if I said I wasn't looking forward to it, but..."

No? Does she not? But I want her to feel like this. I love her. I want her to have this joy. Wouldn't anybody? I fall forwards again, catching myself with my extra limbs and leaping to flip myself over, once, twice, three times. I giggle all the while.

"I just... *Goddess,* I feel so alive," I tell her. "I hope you feel like this someday."

I want you to feel like this. I want you to be like me. Fartbuns lets out a happy bark and nips playfully at my heels, so I pounce on him, wrapping him up in a big, fluffy, eight-limbed hug. He wriggles free, and the chase continues.

"H-hannah, I..." Alma starts, but then she shudders, her words caught in her throat.

"Alma?" I ask after her. *Fuck,* I love her. She's so beautiful. I want her to be this happy. I want her to *feel* this.

"Hannah, stop!" she cries out, clutching her stomach.

It takes me a split second to process that but then I screech to a halt, getting to my feet and glancing around in a panic. Stop what? What's going on? Fartbuns' tail wags up a storm, his excited panting showing no sign of injury. Alma herself is breathing hard for some reason, but... but why...?

"Alma!" I yelp, running towards her. "Are you okay!?"

"Get away!" she shouts back. "You're doing something!"

"I am!?"

"Ow, ow, ow, ow, ow!"

Then I see it. Her wings *twitch,* starting to move in a way that isn't due to muscle. Oh, crapbaskets. My Transmutation spell!? I close my eyes, looking for the font of power inside me, and... shit. It's on. Of course it's on! I hammer it shut with willpower, halting the flow entirely.

"I stopped, I stopped!" I tell her, running forward. "I'm sorry, I'm so sorry, I don't know how that happened!"

"You stopped!?" she shouts. "Then why's it still—"

She cuts her own words off with a scream, blood suddenly blooming over her tailbone as she falls to her knees. Her wings have grown a tiny bit but I realize suddenly that I hadn't noticed because most of her changes are *internal.* Musculature, bones... and especially her *digestive system* all feel wrong. Different. And as a great slit tears its way open on her lower back, her spine elongating and pushing the wound forward, I start to see why.

It's a mouth. She's growing a tail with a mouth on the end. That's... rather more disturbing than cute ears and a pair of wings.

I close my eyes and take a deep breath, checking my magic again. The Transmutation spell is behaving. It's no longer active. So why is Alma still *changing?* For that matter, why did she start changing in the first place? I first exposed Autumn to this spell by accident after our date, but she didn't show any visible sign of transformation until days later. Either there's some *other* Transmutation spell affecting her—which doesn't even make any sense—or my spell must have an over-time effect. I hit her with it, and now she has... I dunno, the 'monster transformation' status condition, I guess, and it'll just do things until the condition goes away. Why was I casting it in the first place, though?

I just wanted her to be happy like I was. To revel in her nature like I can. To drown herself in intoxicating, bestial madness, like I do.

...To become a little less human, just for me. Oh, Goddess. I *did* want this to happen, didn't I?

"I'm sorry," I say, crying as I kneel down to hold her. "I'm so, so sorry. This is all my fault. I... I should just go. We shouldn't date. I'm not safe to be around, I—"

"No!" Alma shouts, her breathing rapid, her face terrified. Another thing I've seen in the mirror. A panic attack. "No no no no, I didn't mean it."

"Alma, I—"

"I'm sorry," she blurts. "I'm sorry, don't go. It's not your fault. You didn't mean to. You didn't mean to. I can take this. I'm sorry. Please don't leave me."

My eyes go wide. What?

I'm still reeling from the horrific apology when Autumn breaks my nose. Her body twists without warning, the heel of her palm smashing into the middle of my face, pain blooming as blood gushes from my twisted nostrils. While I'm still stunned she slips

107

away from me, getting to her feet in a blink. Elbows down, arms up, her whole body facing forwards. Even her ears have stopped drooping, sticking up sharp and elf-like, alert and anticipatory.

The beast in the back of my head sees it as *aggression,* an offensive stance from a *known threat,* and as I get to my feet a furious hiss leaks out from my lips.

"Could you explain to me what just happened," Jet says evenly, "so I know how badly to kick your ass?"

"It was a mistake," I start.

"Oh, I've heard *that* one before," Jet growls, and lashes towards my face a second time.

I smack her fist away with a blade, and without thinking jab forwards with the other one, aiming to stab her heart. Panic makes me try to slow the strike, and that's apparently all Jet needs to *grab* my extra limb, yank me towards her and punch me hard in the gut. Fury, fear, and pain war inside me, and as usual fear wins. I move my limb away, shifting it instinctively in the direction she cannot block or restrain. My blades vanish from 3D space, sinking impossibly from view like trying to watch a single facet of a kaleidoscope.

Well. That's one problem figured out at least. Out of the frying pan, and all that.

"Jet, stop!" I plead, coughing painfully and stepping away as best I can. "You're transforming and bleeding! Alma was having a panic attack!"

She does, miraculously, stop.

"...Panic attack?" she says hesitantly.

"Yes!" I confirm between coughs. "What did you think was happening?"

"She... was freaked out," Jet says awkwardly. "Way beyond uncomfortable. Terrified of *you.* And you were touching us. So I thought... you know. The logical conclusion."

I gape at her, one hand managing the waterfall of blood coming from my nose. Did... did she think I was sexually assaulting them!?

"No," I whisper, horrified. "No, no, no, no, Jet I would *never*. Why would you..."

"Because it's the logical conclusion," she declares firmly, her fighting stance relaxing just a tad. "But I believe you when you say you weren't doing it, okay? Sorry. I just have a striking reflex when I come to with someone that close. Also, fuck you, my ass is bleeding."

"Wh... my *face* is bleeding!" I protest.

"How cute, we match," she deadpans. "Don't you have a spell for this?"

Huh? Oh, right. Duh. The Goddess arrives at the barest flicker of my intent, lounging like a cat in the sunbeam of our panic.

"**Refresh**," she says with a smile, and departs as I use the spell to manage Autumn's and my blood, keeping it moving how it's supposed to while the wounds patch themselves.

Jet takes a deep breath, centering herself before pawing at her lower back with one hand. She manages to find the new addition, a toothy bulge above her buttocks that's currently shivering like someone locked it in a freezer.

"...What the fuck is this?" Jet growls. Her own body responds by *shifting* some more, new vertebrae blooming on the end of her already-elongated spine as the tail thickens and extends by a half-inch all in one go. She staggers, dropping to one knee and clutching her stomach.

"Okay, yeah, definitely seeing why this caused a panic attack," she hisses. "The fuck did you do to us this time, Hannah?"

"I *promise* that none of this is on purpose," I insist to both myself and her. "We should probably go inside?"

"...Yes," Jet agrees, glancing around. She reaches for her notebook briefly, hesitates, and instead just turns to me. "Are we still at Brendan's place?"

"Yeah, this is his backyard," I confirm, a slight smile on my face. Does it help that she has someone she can just ask? I hope it does.

"It's, uh, pretty roomy."

'Yeah, I doubt anyone can see us out here, but like... we should go inside for mirrors and bandages and stuff."

"Right."

We shuffle inside and I point Jet towards a bathroom before yelling down the stairs at Brendan.

"Hey, uh, do you guys have a first aid kit? I broke my nose!"

"We do, top shelf of the bathroom cupboard. Ida texted and she should be back in like ten minutes, though," Brendan yells back. "Anything worse than a broken nose?"

"Uh. Just. Some mutations on Autumn?"

"Oh, is that all," Brendan groans. "Hannah, can you even go an *hour* without something catastrophic happening?"

I pout, not that he can see it. There's no need to be rude!

"Start a timer and let's find out!" I quip back at him. "I'm gonna go help Jet!"

I rush back to the bathroom, hearing Jet quietly swear to herself. Peeking my head around the corner, I spot her with the door open, pants halfway down her butt so she can point her growing tail at the mirror and crane her neck around to spot it. Gosh, she uh. She has a really nice butt.

"If you're just going to gawk, I don't really want your help," Jet grunts.

"Oh!" I yelp, stepping into the room and fishing out the first aid kit. "S-sorry! Here you go!"

"I don't think I need that," Jet scowls. "Your spell stopped working when you ran off, but the cuts were already healed. Now this thing is just... continuing to grow."

I manage to peel my eyes away from how Autumn's bum squishes up against the edge of the bathroom counter and look slightly

110

above that, where her tail is emerging from her spine like some kind of monstrous parasitic worm. Needless to say, this is a substantially less appealing sight. The tail is a dark gray, covered with rough, scale-like ridges that seem strangely unnatural. It's a girthy, cylindrical thing, about the same radius as one of her thighs, and it stays the same thickness for its full length— currently a whole foot and slowly rising—all the way until the end, where a monstrous, blade-toothed mouth shivers and twists, always in motion. Around the base of the tail, the scales creep up across her skin as well, changing from that unpleasant gray to a vibrant red in glimmering pockmarks up her lower back.

"...Woah," I manage eloquently, squinting a little as if that helps at all with my spatial sense. "...I think you might have a working digestive system in there. Or at least the *start* of one."

"You've gotta be fucking kidding me," Jet growls. "Damn it, I take back every good thing I've ever said about magic."

"Well, you might still be able to *hide* it with magic," I hedge, ignoring the spike of terror I feel thinking about Jet's Pneuma spell.

"Yeah, but *Alma* can't!" Jet sighs. "We tried. I can't use her nonsense house magic and she can't use my concealment spell."

"Well, crap, okay," I scowl. "That kinda makes sense. You might have to name it? I don't know if you qualify as a valid teacher for her, but..."

"I'm not doing that either way," Jet dismisses. "You said that naming a spell is dangerous, and I know better than to mess with anything that even *your* dumb ass is afraid of. God, what the fuck is happening to me? I hate this. I *hate* this, Hannah. I hate having to deal with you. Can't you just leave us alone?"

At those words, Jet's tail whips around, the mouth latching onto her own leg and *chomping* down, drawing blood even through her pants.

"Ow! Motherfucker!" Jet roars, swatting at her own tail. "What the hell!?"

Her tail lets go, bearing its now-bloodied fangs and chomping its teeth together in furious protest. It's not connected to a respiratory system at all and it can't speak, but... well, it seems fairly obvious that Jet's not controlling it. It... it couldn't be, right?

"Uh," I say hesitantly. "Is that... Alma?"

"I mean, making me bleed for daring to try to help her seems like a pretty fucking Alma thing to do," Jet growls. "Shit. Shit shit shit. She's not trapped in there, is she?"

I don't answer, because Jet says this while taking her pants all the way off so she can bandage up her thigh.

"Alma, if that's you, can you indicate it somehow?" Jet asks. "Preferably without biting?"

The tail continues gnashing at the air, seemingly oblivious to the question.

"Well fuck if I know what that means," Jet grunts. "Any clues, magic bug girl?"

Ack! Right! I close my eyes, shake my head, and focus.

"...Your tail doesn't seem to have anything in it that feels like it could be a brain," I hedge, looking it over as best I can without quite seeing anything. "If you're not consciously controlling it, maybe you're subconsciously controlling it? Like, you've mentioned getting flashes and impressions from Alma when you're... uh, fronting, you said?"

"Yeah," Jet grumbles, giving her bloody leg one last scowl before putting her pants back on. "So either I'm subconsciously really interested in biting my own legs off, or this is like... a not-fully-conscious version of Alma? Maybe? Fuck, this is pointless to guess at, you can just ask her when we swap again later."

"Uh, hopefully you didn't just jinx that," I shudder. "I don't want to think about the possibility of you two being stuck like this."

"That would be stupid," Jet grunts. "If anything, we'd be stuck the other way around. Besides, maybe we just have a tail that hates

112

us both equally. An entire body part dedicated to self-harm seems on brand."

Uh. Geez. Okay, that one was a bit too heavy to let slide.

"I'm starting to think you two might have some measure of unprocessed issues," I say hesitantly.

"Gee Nancy Drew, what tipped you off?" Jet drawls, sitting down on the floor. Her tail immediately starts gnawing at the bathroom mat. "Our therapist says our condition is 'traumagenic,' actually. As in, I was literally born—or created or whatever—in response to a traumatic event so serious our brain had to compartmentalize an entire new person into being. Which, y'know, is a *super* fun thing to be told by a medical professional. Congratulations, it's a mental condition! My mommy is Alma and my daddy is..."

She trails off, letting out a slow breath.

"Well. Never mind. Terrible metaphor," she says. "I'm not really supposed to focus on that anyway. Where I come from isn't as important as who I am, and all that."

I notice, then, that her tail has gone still. Now it's her hands that can't stop moving, shaking and fidgeting in ways I don't think she even notices as she stares at her own knees. I'm at a loss for words, but fortunately Jet seems more than capable of carrying the conversation despite me.

"...Speaking of therapy, shouldn't *you* be getting like... all of it?"

Aw beans. Did I say 'fortunately?' I meant 'unfortunately.'

"I, uh, do actually go to therapy tomorrow," I mutter. "My mom's making me."

"Mmm. Good of your mom," Jet nods. I scowl at her.

"Is it?" I snap. "Like, what am I gonna say? 'Hi, I've killed a bunch of people and stopped being human! Check out my extra limbs!'"

"I mean... you can keep it vague," Jet shrugs. "I had therapy on Wednesday and I didn't bring up any of the new body parts, nor will I bring them up today. I'll just... stick the worm in a long skirt or something, I guess. Alma and I have stuff to work through

113

beyond magic bullshit, and... I mean, no offense but you seem like you probably do too."

"Uh. How often do you go to therapy?" I ask hesitantly.

"Three times a week," she shrugs.

Holy ravioli I can't even imagine how awful that would be.

"Are you sure you don't wanna like... skip today?" I ask nervously. "Like, with the whole tail thing...?"

"I can't really skip, Hannah," Jet shrugs. "It's court-ordered."

"Oh," I say dumbly. Right. Alma did mention that Jet got them arrested, huh? "Do you, um..."

"Yes, you can ask what I did," Jet says, rolling her eyes. "Burglary. Regular old Robin Hooding. I would break into rich houses and steal expensive crap nobody needs to pay the bills. It was pretty much that or we would lose our house, since my dad is... worthless."

I resist the urge to let fear onto my face, a mental image of some faceless person smashing a window and crawling into my house at night chilling me to the core.

"...Isn't that really dangerous?" I ask hesitantly.

"It certainly is for *me*," Jet grouses. "I'm very intimately aware of the fact that some people think shooting me in the face for taking their wife's fucking blood diamonds is an appropriate response, but it's not like I was stupid about it. You stake out a place, determine when the occupants are away for work, and go during the *day*. I bring no weapons and just get in and out without interacting with anybody. All of which helped reduce my sentence when I inevitably got cocky and got caught."

She shrugs.

"Good news is, a sizable combination of factors—like Alma legitimately not remembering any of it—helped me get off way lighter than I expected and I ended up with therapy instead of jail. Bad news is, I still have to pay for my own court-ordered therapy, which *kinda* just makes the whole problem way worse, and it's a little more difficult to find time to commit crimes when you have a probation officer checking your class attendance."

"Couldn't you... I dunno. Get a job?" I ask desperately.

"I probably *should,* just to stretch the buffer a bit longer, but... how much do you make?"

"Uh. Thirteen dollars an hour, twenty hours a week, so..."

"Like a thousand dollars a month, after tax?" Jet asks, raising an eyebrow. "Yeah. That's not gonna come *close* to denting the bills. We'll be okay, though. This is the home stretch. A normal job can probably support us if we get like... a cheap apartment and three roommates. We just have to survive until we're eighteen and can detach ourselves from our parasite of a father."

Jet's tail twists around and nips her on the arm at that, and she swears again.

"Fuck off, Alma," she grouses. "We are ditching his ass and that's final."

The horrific worm-tail twitches irritably like a cat disapproving of how it's being pet, but declines to inflict any further injury.

"As usual, you are taking this almost concerning well," I say, staring at the tail as it flops around.

"I assure you I am freaking the fuck out on the inside," Jet answers flatly. "Alma imprinting on a woman who literally metamorphs our body into some fucked-up chimera the more we spend time with her seems more like a hilariously poignant metaphor than real life, but since I'm nonetheless living it I have to find a way to deal."

I grimace, squatting down next to her.

"...You, uh, really don't like me, huh?" I manage.

"It's not like I hate you," Jet shrugs. "You're just... a constant problem that I have to mitigate, possibly forever."

Wow. I, uh, think I would have preferred if she'd just said 'yes.'

"Well, if there's anything I can do to help offset that, just let me know," I answer. "I wanna at least be your friend. I wanna be

115

worthy of that. I feel like everyone else has been going out of their way to help me, but I haven't gotten to do anything in return for you."

Jet stares at me for a moment, then shrugs again. She is very shruggy.

"I'll let you know if anything comes up," she answers noncommittally.

Hey, I'll take it. In fact, I preempt a bit of helpfulness and give her some tips on binding up a new errant body part, helping her wrap up her tail so that it's bound up against her back. Ida arrives shortly afterwards, healing my nose with a few quips and handing me a bunch of new bras and outfits.

"...Wait, did I ever tell you my bra size?"

"Nah, I just swiped it from all the underwear we took from your house," Ida shrugs. "Do you even need these backless things anymore, though? Your, uh, leg problem seems to have solved itself."

"Huh?" I say. "Oh, right!"

I shift my extra limbs, pulling them back into w=0 space so my friends can see them.

"They're still here, see?" I assure Ida. "And it'd be nice to not have to destroy my underwear whenever I need to use them, so... I think these will be really helpful! Thank you so much!"

"Uh, you're welcome, I guess," Ida shrugs.

"Do you, uh, *anticipate* a situation where you'll 'need to use them?'" Jet asks hesitantly.

"Huh, good question," I muse, leaning back to let my hip-legs take my weight. "I may as well have them on stream tonight, at least. I'm officially out online. ...As a monster, I mean."

"Woah. On your little nerd show?" Ida asks, raising her eyebrows. "Didn't think you had the balls, Hannah Banana."

Jet gives a long-suffering sigh.

116

"...What's the link," she grumbles. "Alma will probably want to see it."

Straining against its bindings, her tail wiggles happily. I grin.

"I'll send it to you," I promise.

We chatter a bit more, and before long school is over and it's time for me to head home and pretend I actually went there. Ida helps me smuggle my comforter and new clothes home, Autumn heads off to therapy (aaaaaaaaaah!) and Brendan remains cooped up alone in his basement because he's still a bit overstimulated, the poor goober. It's fine. It's fine! Today had some freaky moments. I accidentally turned up the mutation juice on my girlfriend. I am probably a direct hazard to everyone I know and love. But it's *fine,* because I get to lock myself in my room and play Pokémon.

"Hey everyone!" I grin, reveling in the thrill of showing off my teeth. "Welcome back!"

My heart races as I sit poised and perfect, just far enough away from the camera that my extra legs are visible where they dangle off the sides of the chair, and the blades are sitting comfortably forwards without blocking my face.

[Xenoversal]: Woah, model upgrade.

[LavAbsol]: Hi, DD! Gosh, you look so cool!

[SwalotRancher]: It is time to kick Whitney's ass

[Apparently_A_Chimera]: Ah! You're really here! This is so neat!

I chuckle, watching the greetings roll by as I boot up SoulSilver. Barring the addition of one of my new bras and the subtraction of all the grass stains, I'm wearing the same clothes as I was earlier today, and it's weirdly empowering. I didn't really doll myself up for this session, I just did the basics and jumped right into it. I'm not even wearing socks right now, not that I'll ever let the camera see low enough for it to matter. Still, I feel... I dunno. Weirdly feisty.

Stretching my arms above my head I set out a massive yawn, arcing my back and really putting my whole body into it. My jaw
117

opens *wide,* way too wide, my chin nearly touching my throat even as my head tilts back. My extra limbs all join the stretch, blades twisting and rotating to their limits. It feels *good.* Not just the stretch itself, but the show of it, the utter vulnerability I can show and still exude confidence. I am the apex predator here, and this is my domain.

[PentUp]: **what the fuck what the fuck what the fuck what the fuck**

[Zoroa!Queen]: **Oh hey it's this stream again**

[AllTricks]: **ok the bit is cool and all but can we just play pogeyman**

[PentUp]: **That is NOT HOW VTUBER RIGS WORK**

"Well, it's not actually a bit, you know?" I admit conspiratorially. "I really look like this. I really *am* this. It's weird to say out loud. Maybe I can feel comfortable admitting that here because we live in a world of crazy deepfake nonsense and I know that absolutely none of you are going to believe me. Which is like, super fair! What else would you do when some random internet streamer casually goes 'oh yeah, magic is real and I'm turning into a monster.' It's insane, right? The idea that it's anything but a publicity stunt is just... *silly.*"

The game boots up and I spare a few moments to glance at my team and figure out what the heck I was doing. Goldenrod. Whitney. Third gym. Right.

"But it's still really scary for me, you know?" I say. "Playing games is something I do for fun, that I do to unwind. You guys get to see me relatively relaxed. But in my actual life? I'm freaking out literally all the time, bundling up in these bulky outfits and looking like a total dweeb because I have to hide the fact that I've somehow smuggled four extra limbs onto a humanoid torso and I'm *pretty sure* I'm due for two more any day now. For all I know the men in black are gonna come knocking at my door one day and then I'll never be seen again. But still, it's just... exhausting to hide all the time. Painful, almost."

I cross my arms, taking my hands off the keyboard and using my alien limbs to control the game. All in view of the camera. It's a bit clumsy, but only a bit.

"So screw it! I don't care if the internet knows. Magic is real. I'm a mutant. These are facts and if you don't believe them, that makes perfect sense to me. It's all still true, though. Now let's play some Pokémon."

My speech goes mostly ignored, because of course it does. That's okay. I don't really want this to be a big reveal, I just want to get it all off my chest. I'm not going to have the patience—or more importantly, the fear—to keep hiding much longer. I'm too burnt out by it, and being my true self is too satisfying. It's high time I cast the dice and let them fall how they may.

My view count ticks higher and higher as the stream goes on, eventually breaking my personal record by a factor of ten.

6

ROUTINE

Kagiso pokes me awake and I yawn, stretching as I try to ignore that uncomfortable feeling of freshly-molted skin clinging to my body. I scuttle out of the bedroll before freeing myself from my skin, quickly munching it down as a mini-breakfast as Kagiso watches with interest, wriggling into her own bed before getting ready to sleep. Last watch is mine, so I exit the tent while stretching each one of my legs, lifting them as high as I can and shaking them a bit whenever I take a step. It probably looks really silly, but whatever. Kagiso already thinks I'm cute as heck.

Again, my body is a little bigger and a little less symmetrical. Pretty soon I'll be more backpack-sized than hat-sized, much to both Kagiso's and my own dismay. My mouth is moving closer to one side of my body, and based on how other limbs are shifting in length and purpose I suspect it and my eyes are likely to bud off into a head at some point, getting me started on that humanoid body shape I feel like my final form is going to have.

I'll miss my spherical shape. It's fun, it feels *good,* but in that transient way where I can't regret losing it all that much. It's like the anxiety I felt in fifth grade when puberty hit, when the hair started growing and my nipples started hurting and I knew that the changes happening to me would never go back, and I'd never look like a kid again. There was terror and regret to it, but also pride. Anticipation. Childhood was something that I was *meant* to cast off. So, too, is this larval form.

I'm once again surprised again at how much wetter this branch is compared to our last one, my sharp feet sliding partway into the damp soil and emerging covered in moist flecks of earth. A quick flick of each leg into 4D space is easy enough to implement into my walk cycle, though, letting me clean myself moments after I get dirty. I scuttle up on a log we set up by the fire and make myself comfortable. Sela leans up against it, utterly motionless. I feel bad about not giving it a tent, but Helen insisted that, during our night watch, Sela is one of the things that we keep an eye on.

"Hey, Sela," I greet it. "Are you comfy like that? Do you need anything?"

The hum of an internal cooling system starts up, and it's the only indication I get that the robot acknowledges me for a few moments before it finally speaks.

"Friendly tip!" Sela announces. "I am made of metal. Conditions such as 'soreness' or any other form of discomfort caused by extended stillness are exclusively a weakness of flesh. I do not have these issues. I am superior."

I drum my legs, a bit concerned by that response but not really offended.

"...Uh, sorry, poor choice of words on my part, I guess," I say. "I just remember you being in this position when I went to sleep, and if you wanted to be moved for... basically any reason, I guess, I'll do my best to help. I'm not really the *best* at helping with that sort of thing, but I could probably figure something out."

Another pause.

"...That will not be necessary," Sela eventually answers. "But if you could place the surrounding minerals into my fabricator, that would be... helpful."

"Uh, which surrounding minerals?" I ask. "Do you just mean the dirt?"

"The surrounding environmental detritus is mostly waste material, but it does contain useful elements. I may as well spend the abundance of free time I'm now forcibly subjected to sorting them out."

"Oh, hold on, I can probably save you some effort," I say.

Using my spatial sense, I find a nearby rock that's close enough to the surface and flat enough to work as a sort of table and Refresh all the nearby dirt off the top of it. Then I cast Refresh again to sort all the nearby dirt into its constituent parts, making a bunch of little piles on my new rock-table. And... wow, I mean a *bunch*.

"Woah, this is way more stuff than I was expecting," I admit. "What even is most of this?"

"...Useful," Sela notes. "Please dispense the pile in row two, column one into my fabrication unit intake."

I bob my body up and down in agreement, using a third Refresh to sort the indicated pile into Sela's belly, which immediately starts churning away.

"This purity is commendable," Sela says, a little begrudgingly. "If you could gather more of this substance, as well as the substances at row one column three, row two column one, row two column five, and row three column three, it would assist with replenishing my stores."

"Sure, no problem," I agree, and start Refreshing more and more dirt into the piles and moving them to Sela at its request. "Do you think you'll be able to fix yourself with this?"

"Negative," Sela responds. "Repair issue is in available designs, not available material. Material storage is simply low after recent fabrications, and replenishing it is an efficient use of time."

"That makes sense," I agree.

I continue helping h—*it* for a while. It! Ugh, I'm the worst at this.

"Hey Sela?" I prompt. "I, uh, wanted to apologize about something."

"Do not," Sela answers immediately.

...Huh?

"Uh... but I feel like you deserve..."

"I do not care how you feel," Sela says bluntly. "I do not want to know. I want you to stop talking. I want you to stop addressing me. I want you to be quiet and let me stay in low-power mode and let me endure these indignities in silence. If you insist on an apology then this can be your apology to me: shut up."

I swallow saliva, barely holding back an instinct to say 'okay.' Instead I say nothing and just return to sorting.

"Diplomatic infraction logged," Sela announces, and then we descend into silence until the sun comes up and the rest of my companions wake up.

Helen rises early and easily, the warmth of the sun all she needs to get herself out of bed. She grunts a half-hearted greeting at me as she emerges from her tent and walks into Kagiso's, as Kagiso reacts to rays of sunshine rather more like a cat than a person, simply stretching out and letting her fur catch as much of the beam of light as possible, all without waking.

So Helen kicks her in the gut. Not too hard, but it certainly wakes her up. Kagiso growls and gets up just quickly enough to flick Helen in the back of the head as she leaves.

"The fuck are you doing?" Helen asks me.

"Sorting dirt," I answer. "I never really thought about how many different things are mixed together in the dirty brown floor stuff."

"You don't really think about much, do you?" Helen drawls.

"Wh—hey! I think about things all the time. They're just like, a relatively narrow spectrum of things, I guess. Like anxiety, and Pokémon, and the inevitability of death."

"Death is only inevitable for meat," Sela reminds us.

"What the fuck is Pokémon?" Helen asks.

Haha oh gosh. She really shouldn't have asked that. I know what *I'm* rambling about for the next three hours. But... uh. Hmm.

"...Hey Sela is it okay if I talk a bunch as long as I'm not talking to *you?*"

"Entering power-save mode."

"Great!" I say happily. "Okay, so. Let me explain..."

I get to babbling as I wait for the others to pack up camp, happy to spend the time I *normally* spend feeling awkward and useless for being unable to help instead rambling about my favorite thing. The best part is that no one here has even *heard* of Pokémon before, so I get to start all the way back with like, establishing the setting! There's just *so much to explain* so I babble and babble and babble some more even as the packing finishes and we restart our journey towards the trunk.

"I think I liked you better when you were mute," Helen groans.

"Trainers sound like Sindri," Kagiso says, wrinkling her nose.

I flinch, but carry on.

"I, uh, thought the same thing when I met him, actually," I admit. "I don't know if that made me more or less suspicious of him, honestly, but... yeah. He was pretty much training me to fight for him, I guess."

"Yes," Kagiso growls. "Trained to hunt *his* hunt."

I cared for him. I liked him. I truly did. He was a bit of a grump, but he was driven. There was a wrong in the world and he dedicated himself to making it right. That kind of conviction is something I can and did respect. It's something that, in many ways, I was *jealous* of. To have a purpose decided and to know that it would help people. Sindri was a role model. A font of knowledge. He was, in every way, a *friend*.

"...Can we please not talk about this?" I ask quietly. "I really don't want to associate Sindri with Pokémon."

"Well, I don't wanna hear you say anything else about your wacky cultural fiction about magic monster balls, so how about we compromise and have everyone shut up?" Helen gripes.

"The Chaos mage continues to be the best of you," Sela chimes in from where it's strapped to Kagiso's back.

125

"Wh—Sela!" I sputter. "I thought you weren't listening!"

"Memory de-corruption and recovery has completed," the robot explains, "yet your species remains uncatalogued. This cultural information has become valuable data, and therefore my duty is clear. Your actions shall be watched, and recorded, and shared with all Crafted as the essence of your kind. You will be judged, meat. Prepare to be found wanting."

Uh. Geez. What the heck can I say to that? Deflect horror with humor, maybe? Yeah, that works.

"Oh, no worries," I assure her. "I am always prepared to be found wanting."

"Your abnormally high self-awareness is noted," Sela answers without missing a beat. Savage, but I'm friends with Ida. I don't really mind.

"Terrible diplomat," I accuse playfully, to which Sela lets out a huff of hot air in response.

No one continues the conversation from there, though, because at that point we manage to push through the treeline and find ourselves overwhelmed by the sight of the world tree's trunk in all its glory. We're startlingly close, as where the last two branches we were on morphed into tundra long before they met the trunk, this one is far more lush. Rather than a tundra, we have a meadow, vibrant green grass stretching between us and the titanic strips of bark that block out the horizon ahead.

"Woah," I manage. "Well, now what? Are there wormholes to take or something?"

"Yeah, and we *might* be able to actually take them if we ditch the murderbot," Helen sighs. "Would be nice to actually use one, for once."

"We aren't ditching Sela unless it tries to kill us or something," I insist. "Or unless it asks to be left behind, I guess."

"It is a constant temptation," Sela flatly informs me.

"...But one you haven't given into, so I'm gonna assume that means you still need help," I quip right back. "So what's the alternative, Helen? How do you usually smuggle yourself up and down branches?"

"The barkways," Helen answers, pointing towards the distance, where the far edge of the branch merges with the tree. "I bet murderbot knows even more about them than I do."

"Many pathways were built up and down the outside of the tree during the initial Crafted expansion hundreds of years ago," Sela confirms. "Most are now discontinued, used mainly by organics as less-monitored trade routes for the facilitation of illicit activities. As the vast majority of these pathways were made between this branch and the Pillar, there should be an abundance of them via which we can efficiently transport ourselves to a Sapsea dock."

"They're a massive fucking pain in the ass to climb up," Helen comments. "But going down isn't so bad. Pretty fun, even, as long as it's intact enough to not kill you."

"Construction records available," Sela announces. "Please allow this unit to guide you to the optimal route."

"No," Helen grunts. "I don't trust you. We'll just take a route I've been on before."

The sound of a strained servo rings out, an irritated whine that seems a little too perfect to not be purposeful.

"...Your lack of trust is flattering, meat," Sela announces. "But it does not serve my purposes to artificially extend the duration of this journey. Allow me to plot an optimal route."

"No. Fuck off."

Sela turns its head, looking down its glasses at me in frustration.

"...Make your Chaos mage see reason," it orders me.

Helen stiffens up, her teeth grinding in frustration inside her mouth. Aw, shoot. I kind of *have* been repeatedly undermining her whenever a conflict with Sela comes up, huh?

"Oh, *now* I'm the voice of reason?" I snort, drumming my legs around the crown of Helen's head. "I believe Sela actually wants to help us out here, Helen, but I'm not going to make you do what it says. If you have a route that you know works, I don't have a problem with that. Any way down is fine by me."

Helen relaxes and nods.

"Cool. Okay. Follow me, then."

"Inefficient," Sela grumbles.

"Sorry Sela," I tell her. "But you know us organics. Total messes."

"Your mockery is noted for future retribution."

"Retribution?" I scoff. "I mean it, I'm not mocking anyone but myself. I'm a complete disaster, and don't let anyone tell you otherwise."

"Maybe literally, if Hagoro was right," Helen grunts. "Hey murderbot, would you be more or less interested in hanging out with us if you knew there was a whole cult who thinks Hannah will cause another apocalypse?"

"Neither," Sela answers. "Your proximity is equally distasteful under all circumstances."

"Goddess, what a fucking charmer," Helen sighs. "Truly, I am crazy for not liking you."

"No. You are the only sane organic here."

"Heh."

Wait, are they hitting it off over their apparent hate for each other? I swear to the Goddess, if this stupid party ends up with *two* tsunderes, I'll be mad.

I wait quietly on top of Helen's head as the four of us approach the trunk and then, when its impossible mass looms over close enough to touch, we follow it along the outside of the branch. It's baffling how, from a distance, the trunk of the world tree is very obviously a tree trunk, but up close it's more like some alien rock formation, still technically bark and wood but so monstrously scaled up that the individual threads of the wood grain are larger than buildings and each bulge of bark is bigger than a city. The tree has the kind of bark that's a bunch of individual strips, each different shapes and sizes with canyon-like divots in between.

128

Scaled up, the metaphor becomes all the more apt, with the final result looking rather like someone took the Grand Canyon, turned it into wood, and flipped it up on its side.

Once the curve of the branch starts dipping low towards the edge, we head into that canyon, darkness descending on us as massive walls trap us on three sides. Grass fades away here, but it's a paradise for mosses, lichens, mushrooms, and especially *bugs*. I'm mostly fortunate in that my chitin body makes bugs a lot less annoying, but if any got inside my joints... uuugh. I don't even wanna think about it.

Once we make it to the far wall we start walking towards the edge of the branch again, but before things get too steep that we fall off I spot something like Helen and Sela described: an artificial wooden bridge to the far "wall" of the canyon, the part that's completely separated from the branch itself and therefore exposed to open air and a sheer, deadly drop.

And on the far side of the horrific drop, built into the side of the colossal piece of bark and barely protected from the deadly fall inches away, are a series of switchback ramps steep enough to act as slides.

"...This is either going to be the most fun I've ever had or all of us are going to die," I breathe.

"Hee hee. Yes," Kagiso grins.

"What are you looking at," Sela chirps from Kagiso's back. "Are those material chutes? Do organics use the material chutes!?"

"Just don't let yourselves go *too* fast or you'll fly off when the slide changes direction," Helen warns. "They're mostly safe, though. Except the bits that rotted away or got made into a nest. Make sure to pay attention to where you're going."

"Aw, dang," I sigh. "I kind of wanted to roll all the way down."

"No! No! No!" Sela whines, squirming against Kagiso's back. "I protest! I wish to be left behind!"

"I wasn't *going* to! I just want to. I'm not gonna be ball-shaped for much longer, you know."

129

"Aaaaaaaa!" Sela objects, its voice sticking to a single note for the entire robo-scream.

"Have somewhere else to go?" Kagiso asks it, flicking the robot in the head. "What more likely death: slide, or stuck here alone?"

"Answer refused! Computation refused!"

"Helen, you've done this before and lived, right?" I ask, nudging the Chaos mage with a leg.

"Yeah, a couple times," Helen nods.

"I see, I see," I bob happily. "Well, I'm sure that anything an organic can do, a superior body of metal could do better, right?"

"This is a manipulation tactic. I am being manipulated," Sela announces.

"Yep!" I confirm. "Is it working?"

"I hate you I hate you I hate you I hate you I hate you."

"Okay, but do you wanna be left behind?"

A pause. Sela starts humming as its cooling system kicks into high gear, its face shifting into a scowl.

"...Negative," it growls. "We can use the material chute. Like thoughtless base elemental waste. Or *meat*."

"Awesome," I say smugly. "Lead the way, Helen!"

The wooden bridge is concerningly rickety for being the only thing that separates us from a vast and deadly drop, though as much as it makes me acrophobic I can't deny that the view is stunning. The Slaying Stone is below us, and closer than I've ever seen it before. The stone itself is a stunning sight, as while the fractal green gouges of stonerot eating into it are a sign of death, there's an alien beauty to it as well. This close, I can make out what might be the rotting remains of cities slowly being drunk dry by the magical fungus, their skeletons collapsing with no people alive to repair them.

That's a far way away from the trunk, though. More immediately below us is not the green of life nor the gray of stone, but the gold of the world tree's blood. Liquid sap spews from the Mother

Tree's wound at a glacial pace, the leak slow yet so indescribably *massive* that the sheer quantities of liquid involved can't be considered anything less than an ocean. This is, without a doubt, what my companions call the Sapsea, a bulging golden ring that covers the entire circumference of the Slaying Stone's intersection with the Mother Tree. Through the translucent shining liquid, it's possible to see the wound to the tree itself, extending far beyond the edges of the Slaying Stone: apocalyptic cracks and continent-sized splinters from which the lifeblood gushes into the open air. Within the Sapsea itself I can even see dark shapes moving within, undulating with a purpose that can't be anything less than alive. Yet if I can see them at all from this far away, how big are they...?

"Dentron whine a lot about the Pillar," Helen comments quietly, seeming to notice where my attention is locked. "About the catastrophe it caused. They're not wrong, I guess, but... well, it's not like we got off any lighter."

"Doesn't look like it, yeah," I say quietly. "You were born down there, right?"

"Yeah," Helen confirms. "My mom's probably still down there somewhere. Probably hasn't kicked the bucket yet."

The mom that refused to kill her, huh?

"Wanna go visit?" I ask.

She doesn't respond at first, but slowly, hesitantly, she reaches up and pats me on top of the carapace. It's awkward and rough, not at all like Kagiso's playful contact, but all the same I can't say I dislike it.

"Maybe if it's on the way," Helen hedges, knowing full well we don't really have an ultimate destination in the first place. "Now hold on tight, okay? I don't wanna drop you."

"Aye-aye, navigator!" I say, giving her a leggy salute.

"I have no fucking clue what that was about, but alright," Helen sighs.

Reaching the other end of the bridge, we transfer over to a platform dug out of the inside of the bark, and the difference in construction immediately becomes obvious. The rickety wooden bridge was a hazard to life and limb thanks to its horribly shoddy design, but the semicylindrical ramp before us is a hazard to life and limb entirely in spite of its excellent craftsmanship. Clean-cut and perfectly sanded before being preserved with a slippery, clear, lacquer-like finish, the 'material chute,' as Sela called it, is clearly built to last. Which is good, because I distinctly recall Sela saying that they were built *hundreds of years ago,* and we are trusting this thing to keep us alive against the merciless whims of gravity.

"Welp, no time like the present," Helen sighs. "Even with us just sliding on our asses the whole time, we'll have to stop to sleep before we get all the way down there."

Yeah, that checks out. The world tree is *tall.*

"Logs indicate this structure has not received maintenance for over a *century,*" Sela whines. "Please allow this unit to direct you to a pathway that is actually designed for—"

"Wheeee!" Kagiso shouts, raising her arms in the air and leaping down the slide, bringing an attached and screaming Sela along with her. Helen smirks, extracting me off her head and following down the slide with me in her lap.

It *is* pretty dang fun, although not all that exciting compared to the freefall cage piloted by a giant bat-dragon that we took to get down just a day ago. I'm once again tempted to get off Helen and start rolling, but *that* idea quickly gets shoved away when Kagiso suddenly shouts "GAP!"

As the wall of bark descends down the trunk, it shifts between being an incline and an overhang, and the way the slide is built has to accommodate for that. While the wall is more of a steep, eighty-degree incline, the slide is just built into the bark itself as a series of switchbacks that don't really have much risk involved; if you fall off part of the slide, you'll just land on a lower part, possibly bruised but probably alive. On the overhang parts, however, there's no such luck. The slide hangs out over empty space, leaving us inches away from death at all times. And ahead of us is, of course, a nearly ten-foot-wide hole in the construction.

"Pick up speed!" Helen shouts back, clutching me tight against her stomach as she stands *up* on the slide, crouching low and reducing friction as much as possible. "Go, go, go! We're gonna jump!"

Kagiso glances back at Helen with wide eyes, but then a feral grin splits her face and she nods, copying Helen's stance. I freeze, helpless and panicking and trying to act as inanimate as possible so as to not screw up whatever Helen's about to do. I wish I could look away, squeeze my eyes shut and just wait for it all to happen, but that's doubly impossible for me so time seems to slow as Kagiso, now laughing hysterically, tenses her legs and *leaps* less than a foot before death, flying through the air and landing *hard* on the far side.

"Haha! Yes!" she shouts in triumph, and then I nearly lose my extradimensional stomach as Helen follows, the speed we've picked up letting us rocket over the gap, the terror of free fall gripping my body for a moment before we land *hard* on the far side, our momentum still screaming forwards.

"Fuck yeah! Great jump, Kagiso!" Helen shouts, her heart pounding a mile a minute inside her chest.

"Yes! Yes!" Kagiso cackles back. "More, more!"

"I hate meat I hate meat I hate meat I hate meat!"

"What would have happened if you guys couldn't make that jump!?" I yelp. Quite rhetorically, since the answer is that *we would have fucking died.*

"If Kagiso thought she couldn't make that she woulda stopped!" Helen shouts back, the wind making it somewhat difficult to talk any more quietly than that. "If a gap is too wide we can find another way down. That one was just a warm-up, though!"

"I thought you were the sane one, Helen!" I protest.

133

"Well maybe you shouldn't believe the fucking murderbot!" she laughs.

The whole rest of the day is like that, with Helen and Kagiso playing gosh dang pocket circuit with their own bodies instead of cars, nearly flinging us to our deaths over every turn and break in the path. I'm not even doing anything and it's still utterly exhausting, so after hours pass and the sky starts to dim, I'm utterly relieved to find us coming across a modestly-sized platform built next to the slide that we can dismount to rest on. We do so, Kagiso and Helen laughing all the while as they recount their favorite exploits.

There's no campfire tonight, what with us sitting on a tiny wooden platform and all, but somehow I doubt there's going to be much to worry about running into tonight. We make a watch rotation anyway and I go last, letting me gratefully snuggle up against Kagiso and pass the *fuck* out.

I wake with a different disorientation from normal, though not an uncommon or unexpected one. Here on Earth, my body just finished a rather satisfying rest, in direct contrast to the sore, stressed mess my body was on the world tree. Not a bad kind of stress, though. I basically spent the day on a concerningly deadly theme park ride, and while that's not *ideal* it's kind of refreshing compared to the usual terror I'm stuck with. In retrospect, it was even kind of fun. Unlike what I can expect today at school, which is never... wait. There's no school today, it's Saturday.

...I have therapy this morning.

Cold horror floods me at the thought, my body shaking in a very learned, very *human* terror. This is horrid, *beyond* horrid, but I know that in all likelihood that's entirely irrational. It won't be like that. That's not normal. I know that, I *know,* that it'll be fine. It'll be fine. It'll be *fine.*

I get out of bed almost mechanically, barely spending a moment to remind myself that I have extra limbs that need to be kept hidden before covering up how I usually do and drowning myself in the heat of the shower. The extra limbs come back out under the comfort of the pouring water, alone and naked and horribly myself. I have more skin to eat, more chitin to reveal as my left leg catches up with my right. My right leg is fully mutated, bony-white chitin from hip to toes, but it hasn't progressed further. The hip joint is instead an odd amalgamation, with chitin on the bottom and skin on the top, like someone mismatched the limbs on two different dolls. I don't even feel any chitin growing underneath that skin, which I find a bit odd. Not entirely unwelcome, though. I like the idea of having natural armor covering my vulnerable bits, but I wouldn't mind if some amount of skin survived my transfiguration. After all, that seems to be what my true form is leading to: not entirely human, not entirely hyperspider, but something in between, taking beauty from both.

The skin I have left does seem noticeably darker, now that I'm thinking about it. Maybe it'll be changed into something else, rather than removed entirely. Maybe something like the soft, black flesh on the inside of my joints?

Pondering the question gets me through my morning ablutions without a full-blown panic attack, giving me time to get dressed and ready and at least *somewhat* composed before I go downstairs and find my mother making breakfast in what I can't help but feel is a distinctly threatening manner.

"Good morning, honey!" she greets me. "Ready for today?"

Translation: I just want to make sure you're not thinking of getting out of our deal.

"Ready as I'll ever be," I say regretfully, my whole body tensing up.

"That's fair," she says. "I understand this is difficult. How many pancakes?"

"Just eggs and sausage, if that's alright," I respond.

"Sure. I thought you liked pancakes...?"

"I'm just not in a pancake mood lately," I mutter.

"Well, no trouble I suppose. Eggs are easier to make anyway. We're heading out in... oh, half an hour or so?"

"'We' are heading out?" I clarify, the pit of dread in my stomach growing wider.

"I'll drive you there, honey," she says. "I have some errands to do in town."

Translation: I don't trust you to drive yourself there and not lie about it.

"Okay," I agree helplessly. I can't even honestly say I wouldn't skip. I eat a quick breakfast that I can barely taste and next thing I know I'm in the passenger seat of my mom's car, trapped with her for however long this drive ends up being. I don't even know where the therapist's office is. I don't even know their name. I've been avoiding every possible thought about this event, and now it's here, and I'm trapped. My mom starts the car.

"Aren't you hot?" she asks, indicating my long-sleeved sweater, gloves, mask, pants, thick shoes... all of which I'm wearing in nearly ninety degrees of humid weather.

"I'm fine," I tell her. I don't get hot anymore. Or cold. Or electrocuted. She gives me a concerned look as we pull out of the driveway but miraculously doesn't press. I barely get a minute of silence before she talks to me again, though.

"I made absolutely *certain* you would be safe here, Hannah," she tells me. "I read up on this therapist, I spoke with them personally, I spoke with some of their patients... nothing but good impressions across the board. Dr. Carson has helped a lot of people."

Of course she has. I wouldn't be surprised if mom invaded *quite* a few people's privacy for the sake of making sure this would go well. Because she cares. She cares about me *so much*.

"I don't... I don't know what I've done to make you not want to talk to me," my mother continues quietly. "So I'll make sure this, at least, goes right."

I don't respond. I can't respond. I've been burned too many times by responding. What would I even say to her? 'I can't trust you to listen?' It's *because* I can't trust her to listen that I don't want to say that.

"Please at least say *something,*" my mother pleads, and the fragility in her voice stabs me. I glance at her, seeing red eyes that aren't *quite* crying but certainly risking it.

Fuck.

"...I'm sorry," I mutter quietly. I don't know what else to say. I don't know what truth would hurt her the least. That I don't love her? That I'm *scared* of her? That she's spent the entire time I've been alive establishing herself as an *authority,* a being of absolute power over my life, and therefore the furthest possible thing from a friend?

She tries, I know she tries. All the family events, all the board games and puzzles and movies and meals that *so many children* would kill to have in their life, she gives it all to us. She's faithful to my father, she's successful at her job, she has time for us whenever we need it, she is in every possible cell of the spreadsheet *a perfect mother,* so why? Why can't I love her? Why can't I look at her with anything but dread? Why does just the *thought* of sharing a day with her make me want to cry?

I'm such a horrible daughter.

The car comes to a stop while I'm still stewing with self-hate, my mother putting on a perfectly poised public face as we exit the vehicle and head upstairs into the high-rise building my new therapist apparently has an office in.

My new therapist. Fuck fuck fuck fuck fuck fuck fuck.

We step out of the elevator and enter the first room on the left, a large board of nameplates next to the door indicating the many people within, including one that says *Emily Carson, Ph.D.* Doctor Carson. That's what my mom said. Fuck fuck fuck fuck fuck.

I don't pay attention as my mom checks me in, just collapsing into a chair in the lobby. It's a horribly familiar lobby, not because I've been here before but because it's all houseplants and magazine racks and modernist furniture. My mother sits down next to me to wait, grabbing one of the available magazines. Ha. Did she even have errands in the first place?

"Hannah Hiiragi?" a woman's voice calls out, some indeterminate amount of time later.

I look up, meeting the eyes of a woman in her forties or early fifties, her blonde hair tied up in a short bun behind her head. Her round face has aged well, but no amount of genetic lottery can save her from the inevitable crow's feet and other blemishes starting to rear their heads. She gives me a soft, calm smile, and motions me towards her.

"Ready if you are," she says pleasantly, and though I'm the furthest thing from ready I numbly get to my feet anyway, following her towards the back area, past the secretary, and into her personal office.

Dr. Carson enters first, holding the door for me until I instinctively catch it with a hand. It's... a therapist's office, albeit a rather nice one. A full-sized couch sits along the far wall, with full bookcases covering most of the others, holding everything from psychology books—at least a couple of which have her name on the spine—to trashy-looking paperback novels. A desk with a personal computer sits in the corner behind a big, comfy-looking chair that Dr. Carson herself sits down in, a glass table separating her from the couch.

"Make yourself comfortable!" she invites me, motioning to the couch. "I'm Dr. Carson, though you're welcome to call me Emily if you like. Hannah, yes? Or do you have another name you prefer?"

I open my mouth to respond, but as the door closes behind me I freeze, no sound emerging from my throat. It's just me and her in here now. Alone. I try to take another step towards the couch and fail, my throat dry. I swallow saliva. It doesn't help. Dr. Carson watches me carefully, the patient smile on her face not flinching in the slightest.

"...So, your mother signed you up for an extended session," she says slowly. "Which is eighty-five minutes. But I want to assure you the door is yours to leave at any time during our conversation. You are under no obligation to stay for any reason."

Right. Of course. I can just... leave. I knew that.

"Hannah is fine," I manage to say.

"It's wonderful to meet you, Hannah," Dr. Carson says. "Are you more comfortable standing?"

"I... I think so, yeah," I stutter. "Sorry."

"Oh, no trouble at all!" she says, briefly standing up to swivel her big, comfy chair around to face me before sitting back down in it. "There we go! So, what brings you into my office, Hannah?"

My toes curl in my shoes, digging into the gouges already made. My extra limbs flex in 4D space, itching to emerge. I rub my hands together nervously, the chitinous fingers scratching against the thick gloves and getting lint stuck in the joints. A quick and silent pulse of a magical spell, and the lint removes itself.

And none of these things are even why I'm about to have a panic attack as we speak.

"...I'm... kind of curious," I say quietly. "Just... offhand. How many people do you get in here who think they're going to be your craziest case ever?"

She considers the question for just a moment, just long enough to make me believe she's really thinking about it.

"Well, I want to start by saying that I discourage anyone who comes in here from considering themselves as 'crazy' or 'a case,'" Dr. Carson says. "The words we use to describe ourselves can have a profound impact on the way we feel about ourselves, after all. But those who come in here believing themselves to be the worst off, the people who consider themselves as in need of the most help, are often the people who best understand that they *need* help in the first place. Because if they thought themselves beyond that help, why would they be here?"

I chuckle at that, though it's devoid of humor.

"Because their moms made them, maybe?" I posit.

"Perhaps," Dr. Carson says with a smirk. "So is that how you see yourself? A person who will need more help than anyone else I've met?"

"I don't know about that," I admit. "Maybe. I... I don't know how much you *can* help me. There's *so much shit* going on right now, and I... it's not like anything else you've seen before. At least not most of it. I can guarantee that much."

She smiles a little wider at that. Something like amusement, but it's friendly.

"Well, I'm not one to hide from new experiences," she says. "Everyone deserves help, Hannah, no matter how unique that help might be."

"Yeah," I say, swallowing again. The words are coming more easily now. Despite myself, I'm getting a bit more comfortable, and as long as I don't think about that too hard maybe I can make it through this. "I... it's just... Goddess, there's so much I don't know where to start."

"Then start anywhere," she encourages me, writing down a quick note. "Order things chronologically, perhaps? I always like to begin with the beginning."

Ha. Sure, whatever. I'm here to talk, I may as well talk. I probably have to deal with that first before I make progress anywhere else anyway.

"Alright, let's start with the easy stuff then," I tell her. "I'm about to have a panic attack just being in this room because my *last* therapist tried to groom me."

Her eyebrows rise ever so slightly.

"I see," she says calmly, though it's the sort of calm that hides a torrent of absolute *fury* underneath it, a righteous indignation that somehow relaxes a dozen different tensions in my body that I wasn't consciously holding. "Please feel free to ignore this question, but could you clarify what you mean when you say your therapist 'tried' to groom you?"

"Well, I mean, I knew what he was doing," I explain hastily. "Not hard to figure out, really. When he, you know. Sat on the couch next to me, or touched my shoulder, or... you know."

Does she know? Of course she doesn't know, the whole reason I'm supposed to be talking about this is to say it out loud. Stupid, stupid, stupid.

"I-I mean he didn't go any farther than that," I clarify. "He didn't really... I mean I think he *wanted* to, I just... I don't know. He would ask for my cell phone number and stuff, but I would just give him my mom's. Things like that. I figured him out after like, three sessions."

Clack clack. Without even thinking about it, I snap my teeth together nervously, the quiet noise still easily audible in the private office. Dr. Carson doesn't comment on it, though.

"...What happened then?" she says instead.

"Uh, like... ultimately, or when I figured him out?" I ask. "'Cuz when I finally told my mom she pretty much dropped the entire criminal justice system onto his skull at once. He's in jail now. Dunno how long, but... for a long time."

She stares at me quietly for a while, and I twitch nervously under the gaze.

"You said you figured him out after three sessions," she clarifies.

"Yeah," I nod, not liking where this particular line of questioning is going.

"Hannah," she asks with practiced calm, "how many times did you meet with him?"

"Um... well it was, um. I had him for eight months, so... th-thirty something?"

She again pauses, taking a moment to center herself.

"...So to clarify, you believed that a man wanted to have non-professional relations with you, that you didn't reciprocate, and you understood that this was... not acceptable."

"Y-yeah," I confirm.

"And you continued seeing him thirty more times."

Her words aren't judging, just expository. Establishing facts, pressing gently. But I still feel shame hearing them, deep and overwhelming, prompting a need to explain. To say *something* to justify the situation. But there's really only one reason why I did it, at the end of the day.

"It was routine," I tell her helplessly.

7

CATALYST

"Can you expand on that?" Dr. Carson asks, though the question only makes me want to shrink into nothing.

I can't believe I'm here. I can't believe I'm talking about this. I can't believe I admitted to it. I'm such a mess. All I had to do was deflect!

"I... it... so I had... or I guess I *have* these... dreams, right? I mean like, everybody dreams, but I had the same dream every night and it always made waking up really difficult because of this weird sleep paralysis stuff that... we don't really need to talk about that yet, the *point* is that I'd been seeing another therapist for a really long time. A year or two, I think. And at some point my mom pressed me about maybe changing therapists, because my first therapist wasn't really helping me. And like, they *weren't* helping me, that was true, and there's not really any point in telling her no anyway, so we changed therapists. Same time slot, once a week, every Monday after school. I went to the new guy instead of the old guy, and... yeah. Um. He was a sex predator, I guess!"

Stupid, stupid, stupid. Shut up, Hannah. Stop talking. 'He was a sex predator, I guess?' Are you fucking braindead? He ruined lives. I hate that phrase. 'Sex predator.' It makes me *cringe*. It's wrong for me to say it, somehow.

"So by the time you started seeing him, you were already used to going to see a therapist every week," Dr. Carson summarizes. "That's something, but I'm inclined to suspect that there were additional extenuating circumstances surrounding the fact that you identified this man as a sex predator and continued seeing him anyway. Was he at all helpful in regards to the dreams you mentioned?"

That's simple enough. Easy question. I can answer that.

"Not at all," I say, shaking my head. No one was and no one will be.

"Was he helpful in terms of any other problems you were having? Or perhaps as a better way to phrase the question: did he make you *believe* that he was being helpful? That he would help? That he could help?"

"No, no, and no," I tell her. "He tried, I think. He definitely encouraged me to keep attending, telling me I was making progress when I wasn't and asking me to trust him about that. I don't know if it was purposeful manipulation or he was just Dunning-Krugered all the way up his own crusty butt, but it was recognizable abuse either way."

Stop talking, stop admitting to it. Stop it, stop it, stop it. I feel my heart rate increasing, both with my own alien senses and with the normal, expected sensation of my chest aching ever so slightly, adrenaline spiking as every breath I take comes tinged with fear.

"I looked it up once he really creeped me out and familiarized myself with methods of abuse so I could look out for it," I continue anyway. "Immunize myself. So, y'know, I'm fine. I made sure he couldn't hurt me."

Except that's *obviously* a lie, I *know* that's a lie, I'm standing here *right now* about to have a breakdown just from thinking about it, how could you be such a *fucking dumbass,* Hannah?

"Okay I mean that's obviously bull cheese," I amend before the doctor can do it, just so I don't have to suffer through the pain of having someone else tell me how fucking stupid I am when I *already know that,* "but that was my thought process at the time."

The therapist nods slowly, quickly taking more notes on how much of a complete mess I am.

"So I recall you said that, when you told your mother about this, she responded by taking legal action against your abuser, legal action which was successful," she says.

"Um, yeah," I nod.

"Are you dissatisfied with how that turned out?"

"Uh. No, that was good," I say, shrinking down on myself a little. "That's what should have happened from day one. I should have told her sooner."

"Yet you didn't," Dr. Carson says, "and in my experience there tend to be *reasons* why people might go out of their way to avoid something that seems, from an outside perspective, to be the most straightforward solution. For example, in abuse cases like this one, the abuser will often establish themselves as an essential element to the victim's life, such as by making the victim believe that no one else can help them or by manufacturing forms of physical or emotional blackmail. But you've mentioned that you were cognizant of these tactics, and you believe that you successfully avoided them. Therefore, I have to wonder what *outside* pressures discouraged you from telling your family that you were suffering earlier."

I shrug, swallowing nervously.

"Nothing, really," I say. "I don't have an excuse."

"Hannah," Dr. Carson says softly, "you are a *victim*. There's no part of this you need to be 'excused' for."

I shake my head, because she couldn't be more wrong. I try to tell her as much, but words don't come out. Only a sob. Clamping my hand over my mouth, I squeeze my eyes shut to try and stifle the tears. Damn it. Damn it! How is she doing this!? It's barely been five minutes and I'm already spilling everything out for her. Is she a mind reader or something?

145

...Ha. Hahahahaha. Oh holy fuck no nope let's just shove *that* thought all the way into the box. If my suspicions are correct, the act of trying to check if she has a soul might be what *gives* her one; the only people I've seen with souls are all people who have been in the direct presence of the Goddess while I cast a spell, after all. Plus the whole Pneuma magic trauma is like, *way* down the list of things I need a therapist for, so that's probably second or third session stuff.

Which means we will hopefully never need to address it at all.

"Ignoring how well it turned out," she asks after giving me a minute to compose myself, "did you feel safe telling your parents what was going on?"

I bark out a laugh.

"Safe?" I ask. "Of course it was *safe*. It's not like my parents are abusing me. They've never... y'know, hit me or touched me like that or even *yelled* at me, really. I have the best parents out of anyone I know, period."

It's objectively true, even if it feels hollow to say.

"Allow me to rephrase, then," Dr. Carson says. "Were you *comfortable with the idea* of telling your parents? How did the idea of telling them make you feel?"

"What?" I ask. "Um. Well, pretty bad, I guess. That's why I didn't tell them. But it's not like I had a good reason, right? I should have told them immediately. I absolutely needed to, and I just... didn't."

Dr. Carson crosses her legs, leaning forward a bit to give me a serious look.

"Hannah," she says, "one of the most important jobs a parent has is protecting their children from *exactly* this sort of situation. Education is a powerful tool for that, but communication is even stronger. If you have found yourself preferring the continued company of a child molester to having an honest conversation with your own family, *your family has failed you*. Ask yourself: is it your duty to trust your parents, or is it the duty of a parent to be someone their daughter can trust?"

I freeze, not knowing how to react to those words. I want to walk over to the couch and sit down, or preferably just collapse on the spot, curling into a ball on the floor, but instead I do nothing, not wanting to give more validity to the realization that those words have profoundly affected me on some level I do not understand.

It's right and yet it's wrong. My family failed me? My family did everything they could with what they know. My family always looks out for me, and yet I always flee from them. How is that anything other than my failure?

"I'm supposed to trust her," I answer. "She's my *mom*. We don't always agree on stuff but I know, I *always knew,* that she would be in my corner on this. She hasn't ever done anything to make me think otherwise. I was just being absurd and irrational like I always do, sticking to my stupid routine even when it was hurting people. That's who I am."

"Hmm," Dr. Carson considers. "Do you think you're limited to that?"

"Well... no," I admit. "I mean, maybe. It's not like I've ever successfully broken the habit. I *have* tried, it's just... I don't know how to do anything other than stay in my lane. I can't blame that on my mom, she pushes me to do new things *all the time*. She... how can I say she's failed me? *I'm* the one that keeps screwing up, over and over again. She's never abused me."

She thinks for a moment, tapping her pencil against her notepad.

"I find that we often think of abuse primarily in terms of the physical or sexual," the therapist says, "and even when emotional abuse is brought up it is in the context of negative emotions— anger, hatred, apathy, and so on. We as people are inherently prone to thinking of things this way because we are inherently attracted to simplifying the world into something more understandable. When a parent does a bad thing to a child, we want it to be because they are a *bad person*. And this is certainly often the case: individuals prone to hate and cruelty have

147

children, abuse those children, and—if the children are lucky—they find themselves in a support group or an office like mine, seeking out a way to recover the damage their minds have been subjected to. These are real and serious problems, but they overshadow *other* real and serious problems. They make it harder to see the severe damage that can still be done by parents who love their children very much. Because we are human, and we make mistakes, and mistakes can still hurt people even when they are performed with the best of intentions."

I hug myself. I *want* to hug myself with four more limbs, but I can't. Not here. I'm not safe here.

"You told me you had 'no good reason' to avoid telling your parents," Dr. Carson says. "But in order for me to believe that's true, I would have to believe that your fear of your own family is arbitrary, rooted in absolutely nothing. I don't believe that. I think you can come up with plenty of complaints about your mother if you try."

Of course I can. It doesn't matter, though. It doesn't *matter*.

"My mom, she... I'm scared of her," I admit. "I'm scared of disappointing her. Because making sure she's satisfied is the only way to... to exist around her, I guess? Everything *has* to go her way. I can't argue with her because nothing I say matters. Every conversation is just a... a minefield of trying to figure out what she wants so I can give it to her. If I deviate from that, if I talk about anything I want to talk about or suggest anything she hasn't thought of it always goes wrong, I *always* regret it, one way or another. Not because she retaliates or hurts me or anything it's just... I don't know. I don't *know!* It's stupid and petty and it doesn't matter!"

"Your feelings are not stupid or petty," Dr. Carson insists.

"Yes they are!" I snap back. "Of course they are! None of that matters!"

"Why do you think that?"

"Because I wasn't his only patient!"

148

No. No no no. Calm down. Hannah don't raise your voice you idiot you can't do that you need to calm down. Why did you even say that? Monster. Monster. You fucking monster.

"I wasn't the only person he... he touched," I whisper. "And I knew that. I never met any of them but I *knew* that, of course I knew that. You see, what, twenty clients a week? Thirty? There's no way I was the only woman."

I'm crying again. Did I stop crying before? Whatever. It doesn't matter. She knows now. She knows how fucking weak I am.

"I could have stopped him so much sooner," I sob. "But I didn't, because I was too afraid of a woman that has never tried to hurt me in her entire life."

Those words take the last of my willpower with them, so I finally squat down onto the floor, hug my knees, and just start wailing, getting snot all over everything. Dr. Carson pushes a tissue box closer to me, but makes no move to approach like he would have. Because she's *actually* a therapist, not a monster pretending to be one. Or, for that matter, a monster pretending to be a girl.

I hate this. I hate everything. I hate myself. I cry and cry and cry for who knows how long, until the tears dry out. I can tell there are a lot of things Dr. Carson wants to say, but she says nothing, not pushing. Just waiting for me. I find it both very thoughtful and very annoying.

"You're going to tell me that I'm a victim and it isn't my fault," I grumble.

"Well, I would be wrong to ever imply otherwise," she quips. "And the sort of people who try to preempt my comments like that tend to also be the sort of people with enough self-awareness to already know that, at least on an intellectual level."

"I *know* he was hurting other people. Mom let it slip that I wasn't the only person giving testimony. And I just... *let* him. I think I deserve to feel pretty bad about that!"

"By that logic, aren't you claiming that *every* one of his victims is culpable in the suffering each other victim was subjected to?" Dr. Carson presses.

"No, it's different!" I insist. "I knew what he was doing, and my mom's a friggin' lawyer! I had all the power to prevent that situation and I just did nothing."

"Hmm. I think that even if we ignore the context of you being an abuse victim—which, again, we would be remiss to do—you're being awfully hard on yourself. Don't you think mistakes are something we should learn from, not something we should torment ourselves with?"

"But I *don't learn,*" I insist."I never learn."

"Would you say the self-deprecation is helping, in that case?" she asks simply.

I dig into the gouges in my shoes. Dang it.

"...No," I grumble. "I guess not."

"You aren't responsible for the pain caused by other people," Dr. Carson insists. "You don't have to feel guilty for being a victim. It's okay to not be strong enough."

I snort at that. I can't help it. It just seems empty, given my recent experiences.

"Oh?" the therapist asks, seeming interested in my reaction.

"Oh, it's just... how well does that advice scale up, I wonder?" I ask her. "How many people does my inaction have to hurt before it's definitely not okay?"

The tree burns. The tree bleeds. The tree starves. Is it really okay for me to not try and fix it? Dr. Carson takes a moment to think about that, bouncing one leg.

"...Ultimately, I think the best way to answer that question is that we don't really *need* to know the answer to that question," she says. "It's interesting in a philosophical and moral sense, but I don't think it's useful or helpful to think about issues of responsibility scaled beyond the scope of our reach. Something doesn't have to scale in order to be true for you. You are a high school student recovering from a traumatic event, you don't need to put the fate of the world on your shoulders."

I laugh again. Wrong answer, therapist. Very wrong indeed.

"That was a very unfortunate choice of words, Dr. Carson," I say, a humorless grin barely hidden behind my mask.

"Well, please accept my apologies," she responds, dipping her head politely. "Could you explain the issue so I can avoid using the relevant words in the future?"

"Ha. Uh. Golly. Well, remember how I referred to being groomed as 'the easy stuff?'" I ask. "That wasn't a joke."

She raises her eyebrows nodding slowly.

"Are you comfortable talking about it?" she asks, taking me seriously. Damn it, she's good at her job.

"I... I mean, I don't know," I admit. "Like, this is confidential, right? Really really confidential?"

"There are certain conditions under which I would be required to share information you tell me," she answers. "Such as if you tell me you intend to commit serious harm to yourself or others, or if you tell me you intend to commit a crime."

"What about past crimes?" I ask.

"Only in extreme cases, such as... well, sexual assault or physical abuse against a minor, for one, but given your abuser is already convicted it's not an issue."

I swallow. Still squatting on the floor, I rock back and forth, working up the courage to ask my next questions.

"...What about murder?" I ask.

"If you tell me you intend to kill someone, I will report it," she says frankly. "But if you tell me you have already killed someone, I will almost certainly keep it between us. I take confidentiality very seriously, Hannah, and I will never disclose anything without your permission unless there is a clear and immediate threat to a person if I do not. Do you have any intention to hurt yourself or others?"

"No," I tell her, shaking my head fervently. "No, not at all."

"Then you may rest assured no one will ever hear of it," she promises.

Clack clack. I chomp my teeth twice, unable to hold back the urge with my willpower so frayed. Am I really going to do this? How stupid am I? I don't even know this woman.

"What if, hypothetically, I tell you something that completely changes the world," I say softly. "I break your understanding of Earth in half. I do something absolutely peanut-butter nutty, like... prove I'm an alien or something."

She smiles softly.

"I have seen more than you might think," she assures me. "I'm not as closed-minded as some other old women you might know."

I glower at her. Does she think this is about me being gay? How does everybody keep figuring that out, anyway?

"That's not an answer," I insist.

She inclines her head.

"Apologies. Then I shall promise that, even if you are from outer space, the, ah, secrets of your homeworld will be safe. Not a word will be spoken of it between anyone but the two of us."

She gives me a friendly smile, probably not at all understanding what she just promised. I glance towards the door, a clock in the wall above it indicating I still have over an hour left with this therapist. Darn extended session. Should I do it? Should I show her?

"I *could* just spend the rest of the time talking about my last therapist," I mutter. "The fact that I cried twice just talking about it probably means it's baggage I need to deal with, right?"

"Yes, we could do that if you prefer," Dr. Carson assures me, nodding amicably.

I don't know. I don't know what I prefer. I hiss very quietly, my limbs rubbing nervously against each other in 4D space.

"Should we?" I ask her.

"Well, I'm not sure I can answer that," she says. "Normally, we would use the first session to get to know one another, establish a baseline of what you want help with, and we'd more directly tackle the issues in future sessions. It's not bad or even particularly unusual to have a breakthrough right after walking in, and if you're feeling like you'd be best helped if we spend extra time and attention on talking about that trauma, I'd be happy to do so. I can't tell you how that compares to talking about any other issues you perceive, however, because you haven't told me what they are."

Not helpful. I just want her to make the decision for me. Take it out of my hands. But... I guess I have to tell her in order for her to do that. That basically counts, right? Fuck. Come on, think, what would Brendan do? How would he break this down for me? The main risk here is just the possibility that this woman is a liar and won't keep the secret. It doesn't get any worse than that, and that's a *good thing,* because my secret is probably going to come out pretty soon anyway. I haven't checked exactly where yet, but I *assume* that the spike in viewers on my stream yesterday was due to somebody tweeting a video of me or something and ending up popular on social media. So *that's* just gonna keep escalating.

And the upside is I get to talk to a professional about all those people I've eaten and I feel like I really need to do that. So. Um. Fuck! The answer is pretty obvious, huh? I should say something. I should.

I don't think I'm going to be strong enough to.

"I think I've had a panic attack every few days for the past month now," I squeak, since I think I'm about to have a panic attack.

Dr. Carson straightens up a bit, nodding to let me know she's listening without butting in.

"S-sorry, I need... gimme a sec," I choke, gulping for air as my brain starts to attack me once again. I ride out the rest of the attack in silence, ignoring the pain in my chest, the tears on my face, and the quiver in my jaw. I'm getting used to these, now. I hate that I'm getting used to these. When I can finally take a deep breath without shaking, I continue.

"So, um... no more easy stuff, I guess. I've killed four different people. Almost killed five, but my friend managed to stop me."

I'm shivering now, my face in my hands, but I can still feel Dr. Carson's expression, and even though it's mostly neutral I still feel judgment, surprise, doubt... I guess I'm probably imagining it, but who would believe me? Who would believe some random teenage waif when she comes in shaking like she just got back from a warzone?

"I don't... I'm not up to talking about how or where, I think," I mutter. "Too much. But I did. Okay? I killed four people. I *ate* some of them. And I just... *fuck.* I don't know if he made me do it or not, and I don't know what it would even *mean* if he did! It's not like I don't have the capacity without him, I just..."

I let out a pained groan. I'm not explaining this right. I'm not saying anything that makes sense.

"I can't," I whine. "I can't talk about this. It won't even make sense to you. I have to show you or it won't make any sense. I'm a monster, Dr. Carson. A literal, actual monster."

My legs twist and tap in another dimension, and I just want to pull them back through, show them to the world, rip it all off and just be *free.* But I'm scared. I'm so, so scared to be myself.

"The less human I become, the more comfortable I feel," I whisper. "How fucked up is that?"

Dr. Carson takes a few moments scribbling down more notes before she finally decides to answer.

"I've actually known quite a few people, especially neurodivergent people with histories of past abuse, who struggle to identify as human," she says. "Not in the sense that they don't understand that they are physically human, but merely in the sense that they idolize the concept of being physically other in the way that they have grown up understanding that they are mentally other, having had that otherness forcibly ingrained in them."

154

I snort out a laugh.

"Really?" I ask. "This is what we're talking about? Not the murder?"

"We can talk about whatever you want to talk about, Hannah," Dr. Carson says. "It need not even be on the subject of your mental health. If you want to talk about a favorite show or what you had for dinner last night, I'm happy to listen. This is just your first session, after all. I'm still learning about you, and you're still getting comfortable with me. Do you *want* to talk about the deaths you were involved in?"

"...No," I admit. "Not really."

"And that's okay," Dr. Carson says. "This is a process, Hannah. There's no need to get it out all at once."

"Well," I sniff, "what if I do a big ol' summary? Just quickly get everything off my chest without much context, because the context is scary."

"Sure!" Dr. Carson smiles, raising her pencil. "I'm ready to listen!"

"Okay. Cool. Um. I got mugged and almost bled out in the street a while ago. I recently got a girlfriend but I'm *not* out as gay to pretty much anybody but a couple of my friends and my family is super religious. Uh, I did something really fucked up to my girlfriend and gave her a panic attack and so I tried to break up with her because I'm dangerous to be around and she freaked the fuck out and started apologizing a lot and begging me to stay with her even though I just hurt her really bad, so *that's* a red flag I dunno what to do about. Um. Golly, what else. I got... mega-ultra-super gaslit by this guy I thought was my friend and now I have a little breakdown any time anybody reminds me of him. I keep getting these urges to bite people and eat them because people taste really good. And that's. Bad. Uh... I have really violent reflexes whenever I get surprised so I'm scared I'll hurt someone super bad by accident someday. Like, I really probably shouldn't be going to public school because I'm genuinely afraid I'll just stab someone on instinct if they catch me off-guard. Uh. I think I

155

might have undiagnosed autism. That's mostly unrelated to the other stuff. Oh, the world is on fire and I feel directly responsible for finding a solution to that because it's apparently entirely caused by a predecessor of mine somehow. Um."

I pause, trying to think if I've missed anything.

"...That's all that comes to mind right now, at least in terms of stuff that makes any sense without context."

"I see," Dr. Carson says amicably, scribbling *very* quickly. "Is there any of this that you wanted to expand on right now?"

"Um," I mumble, fidgeting awkwardly. "Not really."

"That's perfectly fine," she assures me. "Is there anything you *enjoy* talking about?"

"I, uh, really like Pokémon," I say quietly.

"Would you like to talk about Pokémon?"

I swallow. This is embarrassing. Talking about Pokémon with a fifty year old woman that I'm paying to spend time with? Such a waste. But. I mean. She *did* ask.

"...Okay."

An hour later, Dr. Carson politely informs me that our time together is up. I stop ranting about how Spoink is my favorite Pokémon because he dies if he stops moving and instead start chastising myself for going on another rant, apologizing profusely to the doctor. She waves me off, assuring me she enjoyed talking with me, and I'm not really sure how to react to that. I feel like she hardly understood any of it, but I just... kept talking anyway. Agh. Stupid. I'm so stupid!

"The question now, Hannah, is if I've earned enough trust for a second session," Dr. Carson says as she stands up and opens the door for me. "I understand that this is a big leap of faith for you, especially given your past experiences, and I want to emphasize that choosing a different therapist *or* choosing to see no therapist are both perfectly valid choices."

I shrug helplessly.

"It's not really up to me," I tell her.

"Yes, it is," Dr. Carson says. "I want you to make the decision before we go back and speak with your mother. And whatever you think is best, I will back you up on."

"Why?" I ask incredulously. "You're the professional. Shouldn't you know what's best better than I would?"

She smiles.

"Well, I think it's best to let you decide, Hannah."

I stare up at her, feeling a little off-guard all of a sudden. This... I see what this is. She's making herself into an ally against my mom, since she knows I don't like her. Classic isolation technique—pull me apart from the woman that can protect me and I won't... I won't... what? Tell on her for the zero other red flags she's shown thus far?

Maybe she's just presenting herself as trusting me and not applying pressure so that I'll be more positively inclined to her and willingly choose to have another session, which will make me more engaged compared to a session I'm being forced to attend. Which is a perfectly normal and non-evil reason. Still, though...

"...You know more about Pokémon than you do about me," I mutter. "I wasted pretty much the whole session."

She chuckles conspiratorially.

"Hannah, if you want to spend ninety minutes a week coming down here to do nothing but talk about video games on your mother's dime, I certainly won't be the one to spill the beans to her."

I fidget, hating how tempting that offer truly is.

"...Okay," I agree. "Next week, then."

"Next week," she confirms. "And... here. Just in case there's anything you need to speak with me about, in an emergency or otherwise."

She hands me her business card, which I accept more or less automatically. Geez, this feels weird. Business cards are so *professional.*

"Use it or don't use it; I don't need your number. We can handle the scheduling in person."

"Right," I say numbly. "Yeah, okay."

Then we walk out to see my mom and what's left of my good mood vanishes. I shrink in on myself, not paying any attention to the brief conversation that occurs between her and Dr. Carson.

Your family has failed you.

My mother and I spend the entire trip home in silence, something that I think I probably have Dr. Carson to thank for. I get out of the car without a word, immediately retreating upstairs, locking myself in my room, and stripping down to stretch a little before getting my work uniform on. Because of *course* I work on a Saturday this week. I can't wear a comfy sweater to work, so instead I have to settle on a long-sleeved undershirt to tuck into my gloves. My wrists are officially alien, my entire hands no longer having skin and my joints now creepy, black flesh and sinew underneath the white armor. It's fine, though. Discovery is inevitable, I'm just holding out as long as I can.

"Is it alright if I drive myself to work?" I ask when I head back downstairs. "Or do you have more errands to run?"

"You're a little early, aren't you?" my mom asks.

"I'm going to get lunch."

She nods slowly.

"...Take your dad's car."

I nod back, get in the car, and get the heck out of there. What should I have for lunch, I wonder? Pizza? Can I even *eat* pizza? Screw it, why not. I go buy a cheap pizza and scarf it down. It's... okay. As usual, everything is skewed now; the cheese and pepperoni taste a lot better, the sauce and crust tastes a lot worse. Butter and grease still taste good, though, so with that soaking into the crust the overall experience isn't too bad. Maybe I'd like an alfredo or parmesan garlic sauce more than tomato, since I can still have cheese? Something to try next time.

I drive into my job's parking lot, consume the entire pizza in one sitting, secure my hair in a ponytail, and put on my work hat. Ready to go, I guess. With a deep breath, I get out of the car and get my work day started. I'm supposed to practice managing people now, right? Telling them what to do and stuff? I guess it's something to occupy my thoughts. Today is a front-of-house day, which means I'll probably have plenty of opportunities to ask my fellow register worker to get the heck off her phone and go clean something... though it really would be more efficient if I cleaned everything myself.

It's a slow day, as most Saturday afternoons are. Even the lunch rush is calm, and once the lunch rush is over there's even less to do. I have to catch myself from yawning since I'd end up swallowing my own mask and exposing my teeth to everyone if I stretch my jaw too much. What a pain.

I'm surreptitiously Refreshing some particularly hard-to-get gunk directly off the counter and onto my cleaning towel when I hear the door ring with the promise of an incoming customer. We are *completely* empty, so the two kitchen people are just sort of chatting with each other while I tidy up. Well, they'll have work in a second. I turn around and greet a kid, maybe fifteen or sixteen, wearing a big hoodie and—to my absolute delight—an actual facemask. Thank you! Someone who... wait a minute, this guy looks familiar.

He pulls out a knife.

"G-give me the money in the register," he stutters.

I blink. He blinks, seeming to recognize me after a moment. This is the *same guy* that robbed Autumn and I in that alleyway! We stare at each other, the conversation in the kitchen behind me going dead silent.

"...Are you fucking serious?" I ask both the robber and the world in general.

159

"I-I mean it!" he snaps, brandishing the blade threateningly, as if I'm supposed to be afraid of it. As if I would bleed a single fucking drop, even if he managed to stab me through the heart. Fuck this. I'm not putting up with this shit today. I snap my hand forwards and grab his wrist.

"Do you, now," I challenge.

I effortlessly twist his arm down and away from my body, stepping around the counter to get right up in his face. Goddess, I want to bite his fucking throat out.

"You know, in some respects, you actually caught me on a *good* day, last time," I hiss at him, too quietly for anyone else to hear. "I am not having a good day today."

His whole body stiffens in terror, and then out of the corner of my eye I see a flicker of light. I glance down to his other hand, his free hand, where licks of flame have just started dancing above his palm.

Oh, you've gotta be kidding me.

A quick check with my spatial sense confirms that the counter blocks the view of the fire from anyone other than me. I reach my hand over his and cast Refresh, pulling the oxygen from the flames into my lungs, winking them out. The *heat* the robber is generating goes unaffected, but I don't care as long as it's unseen. He watches me put his flames out, and that's what matters.

"None of that," I warn him. "Behave and I won't hurt you. We need to talk."

He gulps in terror, nodding once. Good. I yank him towards the side hall to the bathroom, turning back to my coworkers as I do so.

"Tell the boss I'm taking my ten!" I snap at them, dragging the helpless robber along, the kitchen workers left in silent shock behind us.

8

HER GREATEST TREASURE

I yank the robber into the side hall, stewing in frustration. Why does this keep happening to me? Why? And more importantly, *how does he have magic!?*

I mean, he obviously got it from me somehow. Everyone I know who has it is someone that spends time around me, and I've had my suspicions on how exactly that works. The Goddess is the one that gives souls, after all, and this guy having Heat magic pretty much confirms my theory: he was around me for less than a minute, but during that time *the Goddess was there*. Being physically nearby when someone else channels the Goddess is what gives you a soul. That seems to be the most likely possibility.

Which means I can't let some criminal dumbass go around using magic willy-nilly!

"Were you seriously about to throw fire at me in public!?" I hiss furiously at him. "Are you insane? Have you lost all intelligence?"

He stares down at me, utterly speechless. Ugh, I can only imagine what's going through that head of his. Dude robs two women, gains fire powers, tries to rob a store, and then ends up accosted by a girl a whole head shorter than him, yanking him around despite the *knife* and *superpower* that he both just pulled on her.

He's either realizing how completely out of his depth he is and freaking out, or I've just awakened a new kink in him.

...Aw, ew, why the heck did I have to go and think that? Gross gross gross. I'm going to have to distract myself *fast* or else my morbid curiosity will get the better of me and I'll end up using my spatial sense to see if he has an erection. Suppressing a shudder, I squeeze his wrist harder and harder until he drops the knife, which I snatch out of the air and pocket.

"Say something," I order him, taking a step back.

"I-I didn't know!" he stutters nervously. "I didn't know what it was! I didn't know there were rules!"

Okay, he's scared of me. He probably thinks *I'm* one of the magical spooks that keep the secret from the world. And... well, I guess I kind of am.

"You didn't know what it was so you decided to use it to rob a restaurant!?" I growl. "Do you have any idea how *dangerous* the gift you've been given is? Do you care?"

"No, I don't know anything!" he insists, protectively raising his hands in front of his face. "I just needed money!"

"So you tried to *set me on fire?*"

"You grabbed me! Look, my mom's in the hospital and—"

"No!" I snap. "No no no! You mugged me! Twice! No being sympathetic!"

"Wait, wait, hold on!" he pleads. "Look, I-I'm sorry. I don't wanna hurt anyone but I don't know what else to do! I don't know anything 'bout anything but they're gonna foreclose our house and mom can't work and I just... I don't know what I'm doing with this stuff, but you said this is magic? Like, real magic? Can you heal her?"

Aaaaaagh I *specifically* told you not to be sympathetic you little rolly deer turd! I don't need your problems; I have plenty of my own! ...Though I guess this guy *is* one of those problems, now that I'm thinking about it. I gave him magic when I... well, when I tried to kill him.

...Right. I tried to kill this kid. *Fuck.*

I don't think I can help with his problem, though? Ida can't heal people she doesn't care about and she's not going to care about a stranger. We still don't know what Brendan can do, Autumn's spells aren't any good for healing, and *my* Order magic just cleans and sorts things. What the heck could I do with that, sort the diseases out of her body?

...Actually, wait. *Can* I do that!? If I incant Refresh I can manually circulate the friggin' fraggin' blood through my body. I can probably sort impurities out of the blood too, right? *Right?* Shoot, why have I not thought about this until now?

There are a bunch of limitations to this. I don't think I can do cancers, because those are attached to the body and ripping a tumor off is a bit outside the realm of sorting things. I can sort *solutions* of things because solutions aren't physically bonded at all, there are plenty of ways to separate them out normally, like evaporating the water out. But a bunch of bacteria or viruses floating around inside the bloodstream, or in the intestines, or in a tooth or whatever? I could probably do that, as long as I have a proper receptacle to put them in afterwards. And there *are* proper receptacles for diseased material!

"...What's your mom sick with?" I ask, not wanting to get ahead of myself.

"Um, a lot of things, I think?" the mugger... gah. No, the *desperate kid* says. I might have been over-assuming his age because he's tall. He doesn't act very old. "She has an immunodeficiency disease, the doctor says. So she's got COVID, but... also a lot of other stuff, I think?"

Fuck. Okay. Damn it. HIV is a virus, right? Can I cure AIDS? Oh Goddess, maybe I can. I think I've been seriously underestimating my favorite spell. If I can just directly pull diseases out of people, I should pretty much be working at a hospital full-time, right? I can heal basically any infection as long as I incant my spell to make it strong enough. Which would, uh, permanently give everyone nearby a soul, and therefore magic.

163

My eyes narrow. Goddess, you dastardly bitch. I can cure people, but only if I want to risk giving them Chaos magic or spawning another Sindri into the world or something equally horrible. Can I do that? Is that worth it? Magic is absolutely terrifying, but I don't want to let people *die!*

...I can sleep on that issue, I guess. Deciding the fate of the world isn't a job for a ten-minute work break.

"Are you hungry?" I ask the kid.

"Um. Y-yes?"

"Okay. Any foods you can't eat?"

"Not really?"

"Good. Stay right here," I order him. "Do not move."

I briefly return to my cash register and order a mac and cheese with my employee discount, since that's just sort of the basic normal thing most people under the age of thirty order when they come in here. Pointedly ignoring the questioning looks from my co-workers, I wait the barely thirty seconds it takes for them to make one and hand it to me, then return to the side hall.

"Here," I grunt, handing him the food. "I get off work at ten tonight. Does the hospital allow visitors that late? I can't promise anything, but I can give it a shot."

"Really?" he gulps, practically jumping on me in excitement. "Oh, thank you, I—!"

I firmly shove him away before he can get huggy, cutting him off.

"I have conditions," I insist. "First, you need to understand that I'm *not* a healer, I'm a hail mary. What I'm planning *might* work, but I've never done this before and being magic doesn't mean I'm a miracle worker, okay? We're giving this a *shot,* and you still have to abide by my other conditions if I can't do it."

He immediately gets a lot less excited and a lot more suspicious. Good, he's not *completely* stupid.

"...What are the conditions?" he asks. "I don't really have much."

164

"Chill out, I'm not extorting you. I just need to stay in contact with you and teach you how to properly use magic. ...I'll also need to teach your *mom* how to use magic, since she'll probably be able to do it if this goes well."

"Wait, really!?"

"Don't get excited!" I snap. "Magic is crazy dangerous and if you use it wrong it *will* kill you! Or your mom! So you will *listen to me,* no questions asked, when I tell you not to do something. Okay? And the first thing you're agreeing to is to not tell *anybody* about magic. Not your friends, not anyone else in your family, *no one.* You got that?"

Yes, I realize I'm being completely hypocritical when I say that. But I want to impress on him the importance of not calling whatever magical spooks still somehow haven't gotten clued into the situation down on our heads. If he cracks and tells a trustworthy best friend or something... I can't really fault him for that. But if I tell him that's *okay,* then he's way more likely to tell even more people. Humans push boundaries no matter what those boundaries are, so it's best to set them significantly *before* any potential breaking point.

Because that's the problem here: I don't know this kid, and I don't have anywhere near as much power over him as I'm currently pretending to have. But I need him to stay in check, to not call the Goddess down and inadvertently start handing out arcane nukes to everybody within arm's reach.

"Second rule: you can feel free to use your magic, but don't let anyone see you and never, *ever* say anything out loud while you cast a spell."

"What? Why?" he asks.

"Because it could cause you to immolate yourself to death," I say seriously.

He blanches. Good. The real reason I don't want him to do it is because it would cause him to summon the Goddess and therefore start that whole magical infection train, but it's definitely true that doing so would also endanger his life. It's rather easy to make people scared of the Goddess when she is so Goddess-darn *scary*.

"Third," I conclude, "and I feel like this should go without saying: stop mugging people! You jerk!"

"I... but if you can't heal my mom, I'll still have to—"

"We can figure the money out some other way," I dismiss. "You would've made, what, barely three hundred dollars for taking all the cash in the register? And every time you do that you risk getting hurt or going to jail?"

"I don't... three hundred dollars is a *lot* of money."

I rub my face and sigh.

"We'll find another way. Alright? No more pointing knives at people."

"You took my knife."

"Yes!" I confirm, stepping back towards the main room of the restaurant. "I did! Now eat your food and stay out of trouble until ten. If you fuck around..."

I turn my head, sneering just wide enough that my lips creep up past where my mask covers, revealing jagged teeth peeking out between the straps.

"...You will find out. Understand?"

He gulps.

"Y-yes ma'am."

"Good."

I turn to depart, brushing my face as I leave to make sure I'm properly hiding my teeth again.

"W-wait!" he calls out as I step away. "What's your name?"

"Hannah," I answer.

He looks shocked.

"...You're a magical monster named Hannah?"

I glower at him.

"S-sorry!" he quickly corrects. "I'm Jared."

"I won't remember that," I tell him honestly, and then head back to work.

What a pain. What a pain! I don't know or like this guy, so why am I getting roped up in his problems? Ugh, listen to me gripe about potentially saving a woman's life, though. I'm the worst chosen one ever. I guess I *could* just tell him to screw off, but... no. Even ignoring the practical problems with unleashing a criminal fire mage into the world unchecked, it wouldn't be the right thing to do.

He doesn't deserve his problems any more than I deserve mine. If I can't solve mine, though, I may as well solve his.

"So, uh..." one of my co-workers says, clearing their throat at me. "What was that?"

Hmm? Oh. Uh. Right. I guess they just saw me drag off a guy who pulled a knife on me. ...And then I ordered him macaroni.

"He's, uh, my cousin," I lie, pulling out the knife he used to threaten me to show that I have it now. "He thought he was being funny, but I disarmed him and gave him a talking-to. He's got some... issues when it comes to understanding what kind of things are appropriate to do in public. He's harmless, though. Sorry."

They give me the sort of *look* one gives when they don't quite like the smell of the bullshit I'm giving them but don't really have any grounds to call me out on it. As long as they don't press the matter, though, I'll consider the lie a success.

"Hannah, what the fuck is your life?" the other kitchen worker asks.

Damn.

"I, uh, don't know how to answer that," I say honestly.

"Well, it's just... you pretty much never talk to anyone but Dave. You're just kind of the big mystery of the store."

Dave? Dave Dave Dave. That's the general manager's name, I think? My boss. The context checks out, at least, since he's the only person I talk to at work.

"Um, sorry?" I manage.

"No, no, it's fine," he insists. "It's nice working with you and stuff. You're good at the job."

"...Though you could maybe stand to be a little *less* good at the job," kitchen worker number one grumbles. "You keep raising the bar for the rest of us."

I hesitate, glancing awkwardly towards the door in the vain hope that a customer will come in and save me from this conversation.

"Is... that a bad thing?" I hedge.

Both the kitchen guys laugh, number two giving number one a friendly smack on the shoulder.

"Shit, no one is gonna believe us about today, are they?" number two chuckles.

"Do you, now?" number one intones, copying the furious tone I used after grabbing the mugger kid's wrist. The kitchen guys laugh again and I feel myself blush, my hands fidgeting unconsciously.

"God, I was about to shit myself!" number two howls. "And she just fucking... *grabs* him!"

"Goddess," I correct automatically.

"Huh?"

Aw crap on toast!

"N-nothing," I insist. "Sorry, forget I said anything."

I turn away and stoically refuse to say anything else to them for the rest of the shift, which is unfortunately and rather uncharacteristically difficult considering how they keep trying to start conversations with me for some reason. Even worse, when other people start to show up for work to deal with the dinner rush, they start telling the story of me grabbing the mugger's wrist and dragging him off! I can't just ignore those, so I have to give people mumbled dismissives like 'it was my cousin' and 'he wasn't going to hurt me' all dang night. It's *awful*. By the time closing rolls around, I'm practically itching to go find the kid and drive to the hospital with him just to get away from work.

Thankfully, I find him loitering outside the door so I motion him over, making a slight show of lifting the car keys and pointing them at the target before hitting the unlock button so he spots the blinkers go off and knows which car to follow me towards. I gesture to the passenger's seat when we get there, heading into the driver's side.

"Um, nice car," he says.

"It's my dad's," I grunt.

"Oh," he says. "...Um, is your dad also... uh. What are you, actually?"

I sigh, putting my seatbelt on and opening up the map app on my phone.

"I don't actually know," I tell him. "And no, he isn't. Which hospital is your mom at?"

He tells me, and I plug it into the phone and wait for it to load. Around us, my co-workers' vehicles depart and disperse, leaving us alone in the parking lot. Good.

"**Aura Sight**," the Goddess speaks, swirling around me and giving me an amused pout. The kid shudders, and then She's gone. I can feel him now, smelling distinctly of Heat and Barrier. Hmm. So he has two elements, huh? Neither are Chaos or Pneuma, though, so that's not too bad.

"W-what was that?" he yelps.

"That was the Goddess," I tell him. "The source of all magic and a being you do not want to annoy at literally all costs."

"You said something while you casted a spell," he realizes.

"Which I am allowed to do and you are not," I snap. "I know what I'm doing. *You'd* burn your house down before they can even manage to foreclose it. Understand? *You will die.* Anyway, I checked what kind of magic you have. You use Heat and Barrier.

Barrier is interesting. It's about protecting, shielding, warding, stuff like that. Very defensive. Weird combo with Heat, which to my understanding is pretty destructive."

"Is that bad?"

"Might be, but I doubt it," I shrug. "It probably means you have more defensively-oriented fire magic, or more aggressively-oriented barriers or something. Or maybe you just have a bunch of Barrier and Heat spells that don't have anything to do with each other. You'll have to figure out the possibilities yourself. Just be sure to only practice somewhere safe. Okay? Not where anyone can see you, not where you can accidentally start a fire."

"Uh, g-got it, okay," he nods. "You, um, want me to practice? You don't want me to stop using it?"

"Would you listen to me if I told you not to?" I ask, starting the car.

"...Um."

"Yeah, better that you practice, then," I shrug. "Magic is dangerous, but it's still *magic*. Of course you're gonna use it."

"Uh, heh, yeah. I guess so."

I pull out of the parking lot, and we make the rest of the trip in silence. There aren't a whole lot of cars in the parking lot of the hospital at this time of night, and frankly it's always nice to see a hospital *not* be busy. I realize that hospitals have perfectly normal busy and not-so-busy hours because people do like, routine checkups and stuff, but it still tends to make me anxious to see a hospital with a full parking lot.

We get out of the car and I follow my freshly magical companion to a weird little side door that he lets himself into. I frown but don't protest, and he leads me over to a counter, behind which a *very* tired-looking woman sits.

"...Jared," she sighs upon seeing us. "Visiting hours ended fifteen minutes ago."

"I know!" my mugger-buddy says. "I'm sorry, I know, but I just... I haven't been able to get here today, and I just..."

170

He trails off helplessly, and the nurse-or-maybe-secretary turns to glare suspiciously at me.

"I'm his cousin," I lie, not wanting her to think I'm his girlfriend or something. "I'm just here to chaperone. We'll be in and out without a fuss, I promise."

She lets out a long-suffering sigh that implies this isn't the first time Jared has dropped by after hours to see his mom and she knows it won't be the last. The fact that she seems inclined to *let* him is quite surprising to me, but I'm starting to suspect he might not have any other family in his life.

I suppose this kind of devotion and care for your nuclear family is what I'm *supposed* to have.

"Don't wake her if she's sleeping," the probably-nurse warns, and we nod diligently before Jared leads me to the back.

We soon arrive at a small pseudo-bedroom, where a cot on which a gaunt-faced woman with curly blonde hair rests, her eyes closed and her mouth and nose in a respirator. It's hard to tell exactly from how illness has ravaged her face, but I doubt she's more than a few years into her thirties. Which would make her... quite young, when... shoot, what was his name? J-something? I just had it. Well, when he was born. And to be raising him alone all this time?

I've heard about these sorts of things happening in stories, but it's kind of chilling to look at it in person. I just... don't really know how I'm supposed to be reacting to this.

I guess I should just focus on what I'm here to do. I motion for J-mug to stay here as I head out to look around, eventually spotting my quarry: a wall-mounted dispenser for red biohazard bags. Perfect. I grab a bag and open it up, briefly checking the area with my spatial sense to ensure there's no one else around before returning to the room. The boy just sits silently next to his mother, hands wringing nervously in his lap.

I wish I could say I felt any more confident than he seems to. Goddess, please help me not mess this up. Especially since I'm pretty sure the first step is...

171

"I'll need to make a small incision," I say.

"Wait, why?" J-boy says fearfully. "The, uh, the doctor said it could be really bad if she got hurt."

Well she's unconscious and on a respirator with an immunodeficiency disease so that makes sense. Fuck, fuck, fuck.

"Yeah, uh, I'm *really* not so sure this is a good idea," I tell him frankly. "I'm not a doctor, and my spell isn't really designed for healing. I *think* it should work, probably, but if your mom's in critical condition I don't know if it's a good idea to mess with her."

He hesitates.

"...What are you going to do, exactly?" he asks.

"What I want to *try* to do is pull the harmful bacteria and viruses directly out of her body. I have a... sorting spell, basically, that's capable of removing specific substances from a solution, and also quite capable of micromanaging the movements of blood. It won't get everything, but it should *hopefully* remove enough of the infections in her to put her on the path to recovery. And... well, the attempt will give her magic, and there's a chance whatever magic she gets could help her, too. But that's a distant chance which I wouldn't count on."

He hesitates.

"...What do you get out of this?" he asks.

I blink.

"Uh, nothing?" I answer. "I'm doing this pro bono."

"What?" he asks.

"The only thing I get out of this is the satisfaction of having not sat back and done nothing to help a dying person," I clarify. "That matters to me, I think that's enough. But... sometimes the best thing you can do is sit back and not make the situation worse with risky mistakes, you know?"

He looks down at his hands, a small puff of flame appearing above them for a moment before vanishing.

"Every night I've prayed for a miracle," he says quietly. "What are you, if not that?"

I resist the urge to scowl and only halfway succeed.

"I'm not so sure the Goddess grants prayers, kid," I tell him.

"That's okay," he answers. "I wasn't praying to a goddess. Do it."

I grit my teeth. You might not be, but I have to. I'm ready to beg, because there's so much crap that could go wrong here. If I filter out anything *other* than harmful viruses and bacteria, I might just kill her. And that 'harmful' qualifier is a really scary one, because there are *pounds* of bacteria and viruses in the body that are explicitly there to make the body actually *work,* and killing them off could make her even more sick. Not to mention how easily I could kill her if I pull out anything *other* than microbes.

Goddess, if You're listening, I really, *really* need your help for this cast.

Her presence suffocates the room, and I realize I'm being foolish. She's *always* listening, always watching, and Her interest in me is far greater than average, besides. What task do I have for Her, that I would be so interested in Her time?

I take off a glove, ignoring J-whatever gaping at my inhuman hand, and cast a silent Spacial Rend on one finger. I make a small cut into the sleeping woman's arm, and though she flinches slightly in her sleep she does not wake.

Goddess, I want to heal her. I want to pull the diseases from her flesh and sort them into this bag, where diseases belong. But I fear for her. I fear for my skill. Without You, I don't think I'll be enough.

It occurs to me, suddenly, that it's rather silly to assume the Goddess would care. She oversees more people than I can ever imagine. She witnesses more death every day than I will in my pathetic mortal lifetime. The incantations call Her, it's true, but She only offers a slice of extra strength in exchange for breath. Not guidance. She does not hold the reins. What would be the point of giving power to mortals if She is still the one that ultimately wields it?

I gulp in instinctive terror, mortified at the thought that I might have wasted Her time on this. ...But no retribution seems forthcoming. Maybe She's open to the idea after all? Was that question a legitimate one, rather than rhetorical?

I feel the world smirk, the Goddess' presence reaching inside the respirator and stealing a single breath from the dying woman. She flows around it, in it, through it, suffusing the air with divinity until it is no longer air in any way but metaphor. Then she gently pushes it into the woman's chest. *Motion,* my still-active aura sight intuits, the feeling wafting from her like waves on a calm beach. It's beautiful, transcendent, terrifying, and rather succinctly confirms my theory about how soul distribution works. ...But I should try to focus.

The Goddess doesn't care about individual sapient life. That... makes sense, unfortunately. If She did, She could pretty easily make everybody immortal, I bet. Death is a form of magic, and I hold no doubt that She has full control over it. So what might She be interested in? If not this woman's life for the woman's sake, maybe She cares about not wasting the effort that went into giving her a soul?

I feel a sense of immense disappointment. I am an idiot, not that She ever expected much better. If She cared about losing souls so shortly after their creation, She would obviously make far fewer Chaos mages. I'll need to think a little harder than that. Yet... I'm not sure what to do! I clearly don't have anything I can offer a Goddess. If She doesn't care about any particular individuals, if people's lives don't *matter* to Her, what is She doing this for? Why, Goddess? What's the point of any of this?

I blink, and I am sitting on a beach.

The water glistens in front of me, but I don't want to swim. I don't want to build sandcastles, I don't want to play with the other kids, I don't want to read a book, I don't want to sunbathe...

I don't want to be here at all, really, but here I am. Sitting alone in the sand with nothing to do. How... boring.

I pick up a handful of sand next to me, letting it fall through my fingers. I do it again. It's not fun—it's not anything, really—but what else can I do? Coarse and uneven, it falls back to the beach, clattering down. Tiny, inconsequential. What care is there to give a grain of sand?

Motion catches my eye. A small, black speck, getting closer inch by inch. It's an ant. With each step its body shifts, reorienting on the rough terrain. Some grains of sand are the size of its foot, others are larger than its head. It plots a course towards a destination I cannot divine, but it is here and it is something and that is more than I could say before. It keeps getting closer, and while I don't want it to touch me... I'm not sure I really want it to leave, either.

I pick up more sand, and pour it directly overtop the ant's head. It is buried now, a molehill-mountain rained down upon it from above. By my will, the ant is trapped.

After a few moments, the still sand shifts, just a few grains at a time. And then, the ant emerges. And it walks towards me again.

That... was neat! I buried it completely! If I got buried in a mountain of boulders the size of my head, I'd surely die. I push my hand underneath the sand this time, then slide it underneath the ant, displacing a veritable tidal wave of stone grains, bowling the ant over and crushing it in rolling rock. And again, moments later, the ant merely carries on its journey.

It would be so *easy* to reach out and crush this creature, but now I'm rather invested! This little ant has grown on me, I have to admit. I use more force this time, slapping sand at it in a huge torrent. It continues. I dig a hole underneath it, the careful attention I pay to the ant enhancing the beauty of watching the sand part into a pit, shifting and twisting with intricate detail, each grain playing a part in a natural work of art. Again, the ant climbs out with apparent ease. *Now* I'm interested in working the sand. I craft a large wall, and the ant looks for a way around it. I

175

surround it with walls on all sides, and the ant scales them with ease! I pack wet sand into a far sturdier mound and bury the creature again, yet it still digs itself out! This is *enrapturing,* and I'm not even entirely sure why. I mean, it's just an *ant.*

But I guess I have nothing else to do, so why complain?

Again and again, I pile the tasks higher for the ant. Again and again, it overcomes my mighty challenges! I dig deeper holes, taller walls, larger mountains! I bury it, again and again and again, delighting in each escape, until eventually, and entirely unexpectedly, the ant finally fails to emerge.

I unearth it, worried that my fun has come to an end. I find it, trapped and immobile, and it starts moving once more. But now... I realize there is nothing more I can do. I have found its limit. How... disappointing. Still, I follow the ant. I watch it struggle on without my interference, melancholy weighing me down as its excruciatingly slow pace is tolerated simply out of my own boredom.

Eventually, though, the ant leads me to an entire nest of its kind, and I smile.

Closing my eyes, I shudder, a feeling like a cold shower washing over me. This is wrong, isn't it? Ants aren't people, they're not *sapient.* Ants don't feel love or joy or sorrow or hate. But we do! And You do too, Goddess! Ants cannot suffer; their bodies aren't capable of it. To torment one is callous, but to torment a sentient creature is—or at least *should* be—a different thing entirely. Do You think of us that way, Goddess? Devoid of meaningful emotion?

The universe sighs, the universe shrugs. Metaphors are such picky things! I open my eyes again, and the beach returns, the anthill returns, but instead of ants I see countless tiny humans, each wearing a different outfit, each scurrying around and talking and eating and working and endless other human things. They live, they love, they suffer. I pick up a stick and press it into one, pinning it to the earth. The human screams, pain and terror evident on its face. I recognize these emotions. I know that I feel these emotions. I can imagine how horrifying it must be. I feel *bad* about this. I do.

It's not very interesting, after all. Every human around shrieks and panics, seeming to have noticed the stick but not the hand holding it. I sigh, frustrated and mildly annoyed. There's no satisfaction in the act, no engagement. It's more fun to watch them fight or love each other on their own terms.

I squeeze my eyes shut again, trying my best not to panic. Petty entertainment. Is that all this is? All the death and destruction?

My eyes open, and I grin. Of course it is. Entertainment is a valuable, valuable thing. What more of a reason does there need to *be*? Besides, it's not all bad. I pick a few fruits from a nearby tree, each different from the others, and chop them into miniature cuts. One by one, I start feeding the tiny humans, personally ensuring that each and every one of them gets their favorite fruit, delighting in their excited coos and beaming faces. I love the little humans. Truly, I do. That's why I'm collecting more! When they fight, when they flee, when they fly, when they fuck... I love it all, happy or sad, triumph or despair. People are my greatest treasure.

Which is why, when I pour the next bucket of sand over them, it will only be to watch them dig themselves out. I lick my lips in delighted anticipation, and blink.

I'm in the hospital room, the Goddess hanging lovingly on my shoulders, her cheek against mine. Do I have an idea of what I could offer Her yet? Ah, how She hopes that I do.

I swallow dry, my body shivering in fear, wondering if She'd ever shown that to anyone else before. Then I stop wondering, because I know She has not. I can't ask more questions, though, because it's time to focus. If I want help, I'll need to make it worthwhile. But there's nothing I can offer. So... why might the Goddess help anyway?

The answer seems so obvious now that I've been the one to ask the question. If I knew it would set my favorite ant up to fail even more spectacularly in the future, it could certainly be funny to give her a hand.

The Goddess grins like a curse. I inhale, and she takes the breath.

"**Refresh**," we say, and disease pours from a woman's wound, each and every last drop of it and not a molecule more. It collects in a horrid, vaguely yellow goop inside the biohazard bag, along with all the excess moisture in her lungs, the plaque on her teeth, the stain of urine in her underwear, and the snot dripping from her nose. She becomes as clean and healthy as a Refresh can make her, and while that's far from perfect, I can only hope it's enough.

Or, I am reminded with a playful flick on my ear, I can pray. The Goddess *does* answer them from time to time, after all.

"Did... did you do it?" the boy asks as I seal the biohazard bag and put my glove back on.

"Yeah," I say, my voice drained of all emotion. "It worked. I don't think I can do any better than that."

"She looks the same," he says hesitantly.

"I removed the diseases in her, but I didn't give her any energy back," I tell him. "She'll probably need a while to recover from the damage the sicknesses have already dealt. But with them officially fought off, that should hopefully not take too long."

What have I done? Will this be worth it? The Goddess grins with delight, and I can't help myself any longer.

"Damn You," I blaspheme quietly, causing her to howl with laughter. "Why me? Why me, of *all people?* You could have picked anyone to torment like this."

She purrs, gently caressing my beloved extra limbs, hidden away in 4D space. It's not all torments, I am reminded.

"That's not an answer," I hiss.

I collapse to one knee, the weight of Her on my shoulders nearly crushing me to death. The stick, pressed gently on the ant. A hand around my face, She lifts my chin up towards the heavens. I'm not *entitled* to an answer, She reminds me. But that's okay.

Once again, I will be indulged. Just for being such a good sport about it.

I imagine a game. A puzzle. One where each time I fail, I have to start anew from the very beginning. It's challenging, yet engaging. Over and over, I try to solve it. Over and over, I make a mistake. Yet each time, I learn. Eventually I fail right before the end, but rather than despair, I am filled with joy! Total exuberance! Because I *know* I've finished the puzzle. I just have to go through the motions, one last time. All that monumental effort, about to pay off. How exciting is that?

I am the needed piece, She tells me, because I am kind. I am thoughtful. I am self-aware and driven and skilled and intelligent. I am, all things considered, a fairly good person. But like I've always known, I am not good *enough*.

Her presence finally vanishes, and I collapse sobbing on the floor.

9

AND SO SHE WEPT

The tile floor is vaguely cool on my knees in that alien way temperature is now noticeable without really affecting me. Kneeling in general feels unnatural now, an improper state of rest that only exacerbates my discomfort. The human kneecap is a completely independent bone, kept in place with tendons and ligaments so it always protects the joint. I no longer *have* kneecaps, my closest equivalent being a ridge of chitin connected to the exoskeletal equivalent of my tibia which extends upwards and blocks access to the soft black muscle inside my joints while my leg is fully extended.

The connection means putting pressure on my knees feels more like I'm putting pressure on my shins, not to mention how the unnatural plate strains against the inside of my socks and presents itself as an obvious bulge in my pant leg whenever I bend my knee too much. Even my less-mutated leg looks like that now, with skin remaining only on one thigh, and even that is likely due to come off in the next few days.

All of this is to say: I really need to stop crying and get up off the floor. I'm not able to bring myself to do that, though, which is understandable because I should *also* be doing things like not tearing open the insides of my shoes so badly they'll probably be unusable, or not clutching the sides of my head so hard that my ungloved hand is drawing a concerning amount of blood. Yet I'm still doing all of those things, because of course I am.

I'm *not good enough* for anything else.

It's one thing to have insecurities, it's another thing for those insecurities to be validated by a divine entity that's absolutely tickled pink at the prospect of using the fact that your insecurities are *right* as part of some unknown master plan. I'm not good enough. *I'm not good enough.* The truth rings again and again in my soul. A divine revelation, decreed directly from Goddess to prophet. I'm not good enough. I'm not good enough.

"What's... what's wrong?" a distant voice asks, quiet and fearful. The mugger. The child. The desperate little pup. J-something.

He sounds scared. Which, okay. Of course he's scared. I just declared that I'd done everything I could to heal his mom and then *collapsed on the floor crying.* Why wouldn't the kid be terrified? I remember the Goddess' hands guiding my soul, though, pulling every contaminant out of each capillary, exact and sure. With Her help, I didn't make the mistakes I feared. The boy has nothing to be afraid of. So I really need to stop scaring him! I guess I'll add that to the pile of fuckups, since as previously mentioned: I'm not good enough.

...But I already knew that, didn't I? Why am I being such a baby about it now? Like, really Hannah? Sobbing over the prospect of not being a perfect little heroine? Boo hoo, you're an entitled, privileged, lesbian disaster simultaneously drowning in both self-pity and arrogance. What part of this is news to you? Quit having a breakdown about it and grow up.

"Sorry," I choke out. "Sorry, it's fine. Everything is fine. That just... took a lot from me, is all."

I glance up, wincing slightly when I notice the small cut I made in J-mom's body is still dripping blood. I use a wordless Refresh to clean it up, re-sterilizing the area and doing my best to keep the blood flowing in the way best conducive to quick and efficient clotting.

Which is... something I know how to do now. Huh.

182

I swallow, wiping my tears and shakily getting to my feet. I think back on how I flushed the disease and contaminants from that woman's body, micromanaging every cell, every chemical, every solution to its optimal conditions. It gives me a bit of a headache to consider, but... I *remember* it. I remember knowing exactly—and I mean *exactly*—what I was doing, and in some fuzzy, hard-to-grasp way I think I still do.

I'm not sure I could write down all the knowledge in my head, which makes me leery. I tend to assume that if I don't understand something well enough to teach it to someone else, I don't actually understand it very well at all. It's a handy rule of thumb for avoiding being on the left side of a Dunning-Kruger graph, so the rather subconscious nature of my confidence is making me pretty leery as to its actual accuracy.

Then again... this *is* a divine revelation. I shudder, remembering Her caressing my extra limbs, reminding me of how much I love them, how *right* they feel. It's not all torments. She's interested in entertainment, and a good story has peaks alongside the valleys. Even a tragedy has moments of calm, beauty, and levity. She likes watching us succeed at least as much as She likes watching us fail, if not more.

I'd argue that still makes Her evil, considering the interest she has in creating the problems in the first place. ...But I guess that just makes me the prophet of an evil deity. I don't think I can make an honest argument that I'm anything less. I definitely feel the need to spread Her revelations, if only to warn people. Be entertaining, ye mortals, lest She not bother to dig you out if She buries you in more than you can handle. I wonder if Ida caught onto that, in some intrinsic or explicit way. I'll have to talk to her about that. She seems to be closest to the Goddess among my friend group.

"Y-you're bleeding," the boy realizes, fear in his voice.

I am? Oh, right, I am. I reach my bloody claws up to my temple, wiping at the four wounds I gouged in the side of my head that are, indeed, still doing that fun little head wound thing where even really shallow cuts bleed like an overstuffed jelly doughnut. I briefly channel some of my transform-self spell—which seems like it should pretty obviously be called Transform or Conversion or something, but that can be an issue for another day—to help seal up the wounds, feeling that tug on the line draw my two selves just that tiniest bit closer. I find a tissue and Refresh all excess blood onto it as a dry powder, cleaning myself up before putting my glove back on, making sure to tuck my sleeve underneath it so that there's no chance a slip could reveal my wrist.

I'll put the tissue in a biohazard bag on the way out, and... well, actually, I should definitely steal a bunch of those biohazard bags in case I need to heal somebody else, now that I think about it. Quickly looking over J-mom's cut to ensure I don't need to Refresh her again, I head out to grab more biohazard bags and go home, J-mug nervously following after me.

"Are you expecting me to drive you home?" I ask him, attempting to project a dry, unamused tone to cover up how poorly I'm still recovering from today's most recent panic attack.

"I just... um. Are you okay?" he manages.

"No, but that isn't anything new and there isn't anything you can do about it," I answer frankly.

"Are... are you sure? I mean, I owe you *so* much for this."

We walk by the desk where the exhausted nurse is tapping away at a computer between bouts of rubbing her eyes to stay awake. She barely nods at us as we depart.

"I appreciate the concern but I don't actually like you and I don't have any expectation of changing that opinion," I say when we exit the hospital. Woah, kind of unnecessarily mean there, Hannah, but whatever. I'm exhausted and angry and terrified and drained and this kid is just one more problem to add to the pile as far as I'm concerned.

"Besides, you don't owe me until you know whether or not what I did actually *worked*," I continue. "I'm going to give you my phone number. Let me know how things go with your mom, and let me know when you have time to bring her to meet me. She's a

Motion mage now, so hopefully she won't accidentally end up casting something while in a hospital bed, but I need you to get her on board with this stuff ASAP, because again, this stuff is *crazy dangerous*. Got it?"

"Got it," he nods. "I won't let you down."

We make it to my car and I scowl. I very much don't want to spend any more time with this guy. Is anything really bad going to happen to him if I just drive off, though? He's a mugger, not a muggee. Plus he has *fire magic*. But he's also just a kid. Ugh. I hate this. Hate hate hate.

"Get in," I grumble. "Where do you want me to drop you off?"

It's only an extra fifteen minutes on my commute to drive him to where he directs me before I head back home, but I spend it all seething at myself. For what, I'm not even sure. When I park outside his aunt and uncle's apartment complex and let him out, watching him nervously ascend the stairs like the building is about to attack him, I feel a profound hate for nothing and everything.

I really was going to kill that child over the money in my pocket.

I can justify it to some extent, I think. I was pretty much having a complete mental breakdown over my recent cannibalism, so violence was somewhat on the mind. I wasn't in good shape, emotionally speaking, and then he pulled a knife on me. So yeah, in a moment of panic, I planned to kill him, but then Jet stopped me and I owe her so impossibly much for that. No harm, no foul. Right?

No. I'm not that justified and I know it. I wasn't in my right mind, sure, but ninety-nine percent of the population never escalates to *literal murder,* even in their worst moments. I didn't have to do anything but hand over my stuff. Objects. Worthless things, compared to a life. It's disgusting. *I'm* disgusting. I'll never be able to look at that child without being reminded of that, and the fact that I hate *him* for it just makes me all the worse.

I'm not good enough.

I take a deep breath, finally peeling my eyes away from the kid when he successfully unlocks the door to the apartment and heads inside, safe and sound. ...Or at least safe and sound from anything outside the apartment. My face in my hands, I check around me with my spatial sense. Alone in the lot, nothing but me and the cars.

"Hey, Goddess?" I ask softly. "By any chance do you like gossip?"

Exactly as I feared and hoped it wouldn't, Her presence descends upon me with a cheshire grin, surrounding me, invading me, violating me. Gossip, hmm? How deliciously presumptuous of me, to try and *gossip* with the omniscient. I just want free secrets, and She knows it.

"And yet here You are," I mutter. "Without even a spellcast implied. Considering how You react to Your time being wasted, I assume that means this doesn't qualify?"

The Goddess strokes my hair, cooing and consoling me like I'm a little dog that stepped on a thorn. It will be okay, I am assured. Girls only get punished when they are being naughty, and I have been *very* good tonight.

By my standards, of course. Not in an absolute sense.

"Okay," I say, resisting my instinct to shudder, scream, cry, or flee. Mustering my willpower, I sit and do nothing, ignoring the casual molestations and focusing on the need to *know*. "Then I want to ask why he was scared walking up those steps."

She flicks me playfully on the nose, nearly breaking it. Silly and stupid as always. I don't need Her to know the answer to *that*. It's the same reason the nurse is so okay with letting him stay late in his mom's room. The same reason he has no better plan than theft. He's obviously not the sort of child with a healthy and loving support group, is he?

"Are..." I ask, swallowing a lump in my throat. "Are they going to hurt him?"

She laughs, an infinite pit of echoes and harmonies that drowns me until it finally ends. Her lips by my ear, She whispers the answer, both relieving and damning.

Not tonight.

She departs with a giggle, and ten minutes later I'm finally feeling stable enough to drive myself home. I do so, completely ignoring my mother asking where I've been and why I was out so late and simply collapsing into bed with my clothes on. I wake up immediately as I always do, the mysterious green dark of early morning on the Mother Tree filtering into my vision as Kagiso pokes me awake. I grunt her a good morning, extract myself and my molt from her bedroll, then lean into a friendly pat on my carapace before stepping out into the night to eat my own discarded flesh.

Our camp today is dark and generally featureless, planted as we are on an artificial wooden platform extending barely twenty feet out from the world tree's trunk. Sela lies on its back in the middle of it, staring upwards at nothing. I scuttle over to it and curl up next to its arm, settling in until the sunrise. As I do so, I hear Sela's body start to hum into activity, mechanical thrums and whirrs as its internals wind into full operation. Hmm. Some of its insides are quite dirty, now that I'm looking.

"Sorry," I say quietly. "I didn't mean to wake you."

It turns its head slowly, staring at me with its usual blank expression.

"You can tell?" it asks.

"Well, your consciousness is fairly audible," I confirm. "I can also see inside your body with my spatial sense and watch some of your moving bits spin up. It's kind of beautiful, actually. All nice and sorted and orderly. Human wiring is such a tangled mess."

It narrows its eyes slightly, saying nothing.

"S-sorry," I mumble. "I'm talking too much, aren't I? Sorry."

I lapse into silence, but to my surprise Sela is the one who speaks next.

"The other organics guarded with their backs to the trunk," Sela points out. "Would this not be optimal?"

"Um, not really," I admit. "Spatial sense again. I see in an omnidirectional sphere but it caps out at about fifty feet from my location, so it's better to stay in the middle of the camp. Plus I don't have a back."

"Unit not recognized: 'feet.'"

"Oh. Yeah. It's, uh... about this long? Ish?"

I make two shallow marks on the floor to demonstrate the length.

Its eyes briefly light up in a camera-like flash.

"Reference saved."

"Oh gosh. Uh. That's probably not exactly right. I can try to get you a better reference later?"

"Acceptable. Designating as heuristic measurement."

"Right, okay," I say, drumming my legs hesitantly. "Sorry, were you asking because you wanted me to move?"

"Negative," Sela states flatly. "If you are positioned optimally, then this unit has no complaints."

"Alright," I say. "Well then, I'll stay here. You can't move on your own, so giving you as much protection as possible seems like the optimal play to me. You doing okay, by the way?"

There's a pause.

"My systems have not noticeably degraded since the prior instance of that query," it non-answers.

"If you say so," I hedge. "I notice that there's a decent amount of dust and stuff inside you, though? A bit of lint. Uh. A dead bug, it looks like. I think there's a bunch of stuff getting in through the holes in your chassis. Or maybe the filter for your cooling system? It looks a little damaged, too. Do you want me to clean you? I can get that all out really easily."

Sela says nothing, although its fans rev up speed and start running quite a bit louder. Heh, I wonder what that means. Is it thinking harder? Is it trying to blow the dust out of itself without

188

my help? Is it robo-blushing because cleaning is culturally intimate? Who knows! I sure don't. Gosh, robots are cool though.

"I need you to explain to me," Sela says slowly, "what you know about my systems."

An undercurrent of serious threat boils in those words, but I'm immune to heat and recent situations have made me somewhat inured to weak, damaged things posturing as dangerous. Sela is certainly much more a killer than J-Mug ever could be, but is a ranged attacker with an element I half-resist barely a flick and a thought away from decapitation.

I gossip with the Goddess. I am not afraid of you.

"I have some pretty limited and basic understanding," I say, "but I'm certainly no mechanical engineer. But you need a cooling system because heat waste is a thing, and the fans in your body that cycle air through your torso and out your head are obviously that. I also see some tubes that might be liquid cooling in your chest, but it looks like that's not distributed around the rest of your body. Since that whole system generates the most heat and seems to have the most armor and insulation around it, I assume that's where... well, you're stored. Your mind."

More systems seem to be spinning up within it, the fans running even faster. Joints spin free for a moment, twisting and testing before locking into place, becoming as ready to move as they're able.

"So, if we ever do get into a fight," I say evenly, "I'll make sure to aim away from that area. I have no intention of harming you, especially not permanently. And I take it by your reaction that you don't want me spreading any of this information around. So I won't."

It seems to totally ignore these words, more and more of its systems heating up, the mechanical parts whirring ever faster. The buildup of heat is so rapid that a burst of steam gets ejected from the liquid cooling system, pushed through a series of thin tubes and rushing out of the back of its hair-vents with a hiss.

I respond to this in the most reasonable way I can, raising two legs in Sela's direction and activating a silent Spacial Rend, coating them in shimmering paradox, space and non-space. One more leg rises in 4D space, out of sight but just as poised to strike.

"Sela," I warn it as calmly as I can muster. "I'm not your enemy. Stand down."

The tense standoff continues, however, which is rather unfortunate for me since my confidence is mainly fueled by exhaustion. Was this the wrong thing to do? I'm not sure. I'm not sure how to be sure. My body goes stiff and my fear grows stronger, but thankfully before that can reach critical mass, Sela starts to spin down, turning its head away from me.

"Maybe you aren't as foolish as you seem, meat," it admits begrudgingly. "You aren't supposed to know that much. *No one* is supposed to know that much. But I suppose your existence already proves there are cultures in the world the Crafted are ignorant of."

I relax, letting out a breath I didn't realize I was holding as I slowly drop my limbs back into a resting position. I'm tempted to correct Sela about me being from this world, but... maybe we're not quite to that level of friendship yet. Considering how we aren't friends at all.

"Yeah," I say instead. "You don't have to worry. I can guess at the broad strokes, but I'm no mechanical engineer. And even if I *was,* you're way more advanced than anything anyone in my culture has ever dreamed of."

Sela just responds with a clicking whir that I interpret as a grunt of acknowledgement.

"So," I continue. "Would you like to be cleaned? The magic won't touch any of your components, only the detritus."

A burst of hot air hisses out of Sela's head as a mechanical sigh.

"Fine."

Hehe, yes! A demonstration of trust! Or at least an admittance of vulnerability and resignation to a lack of agency, which is *kind* of the same thing in practice. I just have to not bungle this cleaning job, which... I mean, I guess that's kind of tempting fate, but surely nothing will go wrong with using a spell I constantly use for its primary purpose, right?

...Right?

Yeah no, nothing actually goes wrong. A few quick casts of Refresh and all the dust and garbage that managed to get stuck inside Sela's body is pulled out through the gouges in its torso, leaving the inside of its chassis sparkly-clean and its ventilation system running at maximum capacity.

"There you go!" I announce happily. "All clean, even those joints."

Sela's entire body starts to twist and writhe like a horrific contortionist as it tests my claim.

"Hmm," it grumbles. "...Minimal interference detected. Reluctant appreciation: thank you, meat."

"Any time!" I reassure it. "Like literally, just ask whenever, it's really easy to do."

"Acknowledged," Sela chirps. "Setting timer."

Wait. Uh. ...Y'know what, this is fine, I offered for a reason.

"Okay, you mechanical dork," I tell it. "Just let me know."

About an hour later, a mechanical voice that had since been silent chimes:

"Clean me, meat."

I sigh. The things I do for genocidal murderbots.

After a couple more cleaning sessions—both of which barely did anything since Sela was *already* near-perfectly cleaned—the sun finally rises and my companions start to wake up, stretching and dressing and going through their usual routines.

"Morning, Hannah," Helen yawns, stepping out of her tent. "Boring night?"

"Less than it could have been, but nothing worrisome," I answer. "Did you sleep well?"

"Still and steady as a tree," she confirms, walking over to Kagiso's tent and throwing the flaps open so she can drag the dentron out of bed, flailing and biting.

"What about you, murderbot?" Helen says, raising her voice to be heard over Kagiso's whining. "Still with us?"

"Regretful affirmation: yes," Sela grumbles. "I remain trapped with suicidal, irrational sacks of meat insistent on flinging themselves down material chutes like the corpses they so desperately seem to wish to be."

"Well, you know we could always just dump you off the side of the trunk if you prefer."

"Negative, though desirability calculations are re-run at regular intervals. Please ask again later."

"Can do, you fucking maniac. Come on, Kagiso, quit your bitching and pack up your tent."

"Brother's not around anymore," Kagiso grumbles. "Can sleep in if want to."

Silence. Neither Helen nor I *dare* to touch that.

"Put away your ridiculous sleeping arrangements and strap me to your back already, meat," Sela snaps, having no such tact. "I refuse to spend another night on this trunk."

Kagiso... actually listens to it, thank goodness, and before long we find ourselves back on the slide, me curled up tight in Helen's lap and Sela attached firmly to Kagiso. And so the day drags on much like it did the afternoon before, the Sapsea below us ever so slowly getting closer as we slide down the trunk.

It almost seems like we're going to have a totally uneventful day before we hear—and feel—a terrifying *thud* from up above us, one large enough to shake the slide quite a bit more than any of us are comfortable with.

"Uh, what the fuck was that?" Helen asks, whipping her head around behind us.

"Aren't you the only one who's done this before?" I ask. "We're kind of relying on *you* to know that!"

Yet another *thud* rings out. It's closer this time, harder.

"Acoustic analysis indicates a high likelihood of an incoming arboreal predator," Sela announces. "Or territorial gummivore."

"A what!?" Helen shouts back.

"A scary monster!" I translate.

"Aaaaah, stupid landbound! Look out, look out, look out!" a new voice shouts, immediately stealing our attention. Not just because it's someone we don't know, but the *direction* the voice is straight above dead, open air.

Because of course it is. The source of the voice is flying. A sciptera—one of the tiny, cute bat people, not one of the huge, scary bat people—is rapidly flapping its way towards us, panic on their face.

"No look at me, rootfeet!" they shriek. "Accelerate! Go, go, g—"

We don't hear the rest of what they're saying because the chute behind us suddenly *explodes,* smashed into pieces by the fall of a massive, terrifying horror that simply dead-dropped my entire fifty-foot sensory range in an instant, slamming into where we were barely a second ago with enough force to obliterate it.

I only catch a glimpse of it before it vanishes below us, but I can only think of it as a true monster, a real-life colossal horror only imagined in games and stories. Like me, it has ten legs, though each of those legs is thicker than a human and twice as tall. Unlike me, those legs aren't radially placed; the beast has a clear left and right, and the groups of five legs each are connected by fin-like membranes of flesh to glide or direct a fall with. Its back end has an enormous tail tipped with a wicked stinger, and its head is topped with bulbous, almost fly-like eyes, solid black domes that frame a murderous, snaggle-toothed mouth.

I spot it as it redirects its descent into the trunk below us, its many sharp, insectoid legs digging great gouges in the bark as it slows itself down, many of which impact and rip new holes in the chute. Then, with an ear-piercing screech, it scuttles rapidly away, shifting out of sight but never getting so far that we can no longer hear it. Instead, it sounds like it's ascending to drop on us *again.*

"Welp," Helen sighs. "Make your peace, ladies and bots. We're fucked."

"Clean me, meat," Sela demands.

"Is now really the time!?" I shout at her before addressing Helen. "Can't you just kill the monster!?"

"Maybe if I knew where it *was!*" Helen snaps back."It's too fast!"

"I'll help you aim!" I insist. "I think it's approaching from above again, so—"

"No, no no no no!" the sciptera yells. "Be woosh! Use wind, not sword! **Ring Racer!**"

A faintly glowing circle appears in the air in front of the tiny bat, and the moment the very tip of their ears touches it the sciptera is *pulled,* thrust forwards at greatly increased speed. They dip down below us, generating *more* rings around the chutes.

"Fuck the Goddess' side bitch," Helen swears, leaving me feeling vaguely offended for some reason. I don't really have time to process *that* though, as Helen clutches me in a one-armed death grip, standing up and leaning down low as we approach not a jump, but a *sharp turn.*

"Kagiso!" Helen shouts, but the crazy albino dentron is already following suit, her tail helping with balance and her feral grin not showing a hint of fear.

We naturally pick up speed as the friction drops, and then we hit one of the magical rings dropped by the friendly bat and we're launched forward like a cannon shot, very nearly killing us as Helen almost trips on the first switchback, which would have sent us careening off to our death. Somehow she barely hangs on, though, and it's a good thing she did because barely a second later the giant monster collapses down behind us, destroying that part of the chute with a brutal roar.

194

"What is that thing!?" Helen shouts.

"Idiot!" the sciptera shouts back. "Stupid! Stumbled into lair of flonglithorth!"

"Of *what!?*"

"Designation not found," Sela beeps.

"The mighty flonglithorth shall feast on your flesh, and also bones!" the sciptera cackles. "Stupid landbounds wandered right into nest!"

"How the fuck were we supposed to know that!?" Helen snaps. "I never saw anything like a nest!"

"Jump!" Kagiso announces, pointing to a massive gap ahead of us where the, uh, flonglithorth smashed a huge hole in the slide.

"Taste the wind while you can!" the sciptera squeals gleefully.

"Fuck you!" Helen snaps back, leaning into another boost from Ring Racer before attempting a massive, nearly thirty-foot jump.

We *crash* back onto the chute on the other side, Helen swearing again as she nearly tears a ligament in her leg. I'm pretty sure she just broke the olympic long jump record, but at this point we're traveling several times the maximum human sprinting speed thanks to gravity and floating magical hoops, so I'm pretty sure she wouldn't be able to qualify.

"**IdentifyFuelSource(target.noTarget, 60, false, true, fuelarray[])**" the Goddess shouts with Sela's breath, waving mockingly at me as she passes by.

"Predicting incoming attack vector!" Sela continues. "Four, three, two, one—"

Kaboom! The whole slide shakes so violently Helen has to catch herself on the side, tearing a chunk of skin off the palm of her hand.

"**Refresh**!" I have the Goddess follow up before She leaves, keeping Helen from bleeding, wiping the sweat from her brow, and pushing her hair away from her eyes.

"Target lock retained!" Sela announces. "Target is ascending! Estimated approach vector: directly above! Target attribute: Transmutation! Likely a unique specimen, magically boosted to abnormal size. Minimum thirty flickers until impact!"

"I can fucking do thirty," Helen hisses. "Fuck this. Fuck everything! Kagiso! Brace your ass!"

The Chaos mage grits her teeth, taking a deep, *deep* breath, and the world gets just a little darker.

"The Girl Was Told She Could Not Be," the Goddess begins. **"So Though She Breathed, She Did Not Live."**

Helen drops into a sitting position again, slowing herself down with her elbows and feet. All the while, her mouth continues to recite the words the Goddess speaks.

"Hate Was The Wall And Love Was The Chain. She Was Naught But A Prisoner Waiting To Starve. There Had To Be More To An Empty Life, And She Thought Art Would Fill Her Soul."

Coming to a complete stop Helen sets me down on the chute, standing up straight, her arms above her head. Tears flow down Helen's cheeks as the Goddess grins like a hyena.

"Um," the sciptera coughs hesitantly. "What are doing?"

"Joy And Sorrow!" The Goddess roars with Helen. **"Skill And Grace! The Power To Be More Than Her Nature's Puppet! What Is Art, If Not Creation? Her Ignorant Hope, Her Vain Defiance! But Her Soul Showed Her The Truth!"**

"Meleme!" the sciptera shouts in terror. "Flee!"

"AND SO SHE WEPT! FINDING BEAUTY IN OBLIVION!"

A pillar of darkness devours the sky, silent and cold. Art-fueled Chaos, emboldened by an incantation longer than I ever imagined attempting, consumes indiscriminately, blooming from Helen's outstretched hands and annihilating everything above us, from the chutes we rode on to the bark of the Mother Tree itself.

It extends even beyond my vision, a horrible, hungry darkness that annihilates even light, carving a permanent new scar into the very world. The power that annihilated a village.

The power that makes it easy to understand why children are killed. I still don't agree, but understand? Oh yes. Easily.

The light returns and we're deafened by the following shockwave, an explosion of pressure caused by air rushing back into the vacuum of annihilation. Helen staggers, collapsing back into a sitting position on the slide that, miraculously, hasn't completely collapsed as a result of her disintegrating everything above our current section.

"That'll fuckin' learn ya," she slurs, seeming somewhat lightheaded. "Fuck. I needed that."

"Meleme!" the sciptera shouts again, flying upwards towards a falling figure. A second sciptera falls in an uncontrolled spiral, an entire wing missing from their unconscious body. Oh. Huh. I *do* remember something about sciptera always being in pairs, come to think of it.

"Meleme! Wake up!" the first sciptera begs, catching their partner with their tail and dragging them to a landing spot. "Come on. Look at me! Cast, Meleme!"

"**Meleme Biggest Strongest**," the tiny little bat—who presumably *is* Meleme—mutters, flesh twisting and popping on the damaged side of its body until a new wing regrows, at first rather too large and fin-like but quickly twisting back into a normal sciptera shape.

Transmutation magic, huh?

"You just played us," I accuse. "Your friend was the monster!"

"Was just joke!" the little guy screeches. "Stupid landbound! No need big explosion boom!"

"Flonglithorth stupid name," Meleme coughs. "Of course figure out. Dumb-dumb."

"Target appears to have survived," Sela announces. "Requesting follow-up offensive."

197

"Berebe remember this!" the first sciptera declares, launching back up into the air.

"Was fun," Meleme says groggily. "Bye-bye, friends."

"Not friends!" presumably-Berebe retorts. "Tried kill you!"

"Yes?" Meleme agrees, taking off rather shakily after them. "Fair is fair?"

The two of them bicker as they fly away, leaving us rather flabbergasted.

"Should probably stop them," Kagiso comments. "Know Helen is Chaos. Know Sela is Crafted. Definitely bad."

Oh, right. That's a good point, actually.

"Hey!" I shout after them. "Don't just leave us stranded here! The chutes are probably unstable now!"

"Who fault that!?" Berebe snaps at us.

"Little bug right," Meleme retorts, twining their tail around Berebe's. "They good sport. I carry down?"

"Good sport!? Explosion boom!"

"You fussy," Meleme grumbles. "Go drink more sap. I carry."

Meleme turns around, heading back towards us, and with every flap of their wings they grow just a bit larger, a bit more monstrous, until eventually the massive beast that nearly killed us all is gliding right underneath us, attaching to the bark and skittering up to our level.

"All aboard Meleme express, friends?" the horrific monster rumbles.

My companions all turn to stare at each other.

"...It is a superior chance of survival compared to continued use of the material chutes," Sela supplies flatly.

"Fuck it," Helen sighs. "Why not."

10

SICKLY SWEET

"Oh fuck, oh fuck, oh fuck! Meleme, slow *down!*" Helen screeches again, causing everyone else to sigh with irritation.

"Grip tighter!" Kagiso snaps back. "Baby!"

"I'm not a fucking six-limbed tree hugger!" Helen shrieks. "I'm gonna fall! Come on Hannah, you were human, right? Back me up on this!"

"Helen, I spend *every day* hanging on for dear life on top of something six times my height. Get over it."

"Jumping now, friends!" Meleme booms happily, and Helen starts to scream.

We are riding an enormous monster down the trunk of the world tree, and it's pretty fun. There are no seatbelts or cages or anything to hold us in, just Meleme's thick fur and our own grip strength. Perhaps that's why Helen is freaking the fuck out over *this* dead-drop while she was so blasé about the last one. To me though, it doesn't feel all that different from my day-to-day.

Then the giant gliding horror scorpion that is Meleme *launches* off the side of the tree, head-first and straight down, and I guess I can understand how that would be chocolate-in-pants terrifying. Still tired from the events of last night and the panic of just a few minutes ago, however, I just hold on and do my best to ignore it.

At least Meleme is a heck of a lot faster than going down a series of switchback slides. It's interesting to me how so much of traveling down the world tree involves yeeting oneself off the side and letting gravity do all the work for you, but I suppose it makes sense. When a spacecraft reenters orbit, most of the strategy involves just letting it fall safely, right? It'd be a waste of energy not to let gravity handle as much as possible.

"Hey!" Berebe shouts, flying over by Helen's head. "Loud explosion-boom human!"

"What!?" Helen snaps back.

"You Chaos, yes?" Berebe accuses.

"Berebe!" Meleme snaps. "No be mean!"

"Is not mean! Is question!"

"Yeah, I'm a Chaos mage," Helen grouses. "You gonna report me?"

"Don't have to," Berebe snorts. "Everyone saw big explosion boom. Even blind rootfoot!"

"Then why are you asking?" Helen growls, her eyes narrowing.

"Hrmph. Just wanted ask. No get us in trouble, okay?"

Berebe catches a bit of air and pulls away from us, leaving Helen scowling without an answer.

"Sorry about him," Meleme rumbles. "He silly."

"Why *are* you guys okay with ferrying us?" I ask. "We're kind of a suspicious-looking group."

"Meleme too nice," Berebe grumbles. "She never learn to prank and leave!"

"Meleme hear nice poem-spell," the huge Transmutation mage shrugs, causing Kagiso to yelp in surprise. "No think you bad person."

"Mmm," Berebe grunts. "Magic is who are. Praise the Goddess, for She knows."

I let out a slow breath, clutching tighter to Meleme's fur. And So She Wept, Finding Beauty In Oblivion. Helen really poured her whole heart into that one, huh? And the result was just... I don't think I have the words for it. It almost makes me regret preemptively deciding on a theme for such short names, but... well, I guess I don't really need more power in my spells. I'm already pretty broken.

"The Goddess is the one who did this to me in the first place," Helen snaps. "She destroyed my life by making me a Chaos mage. I don't have the slightest sliver of praise for Her."

"Mmm. But is your life destroyed because you Chaos, or are you Chaos because you life destroyed?" Meleme muses.

"The first one!" Helen insists. "Obviously!"

I shudder, remembering the tiny hill of humans. Remembering cutting up every fruit, and giving each little person their very favorite.

"I think the Goddess gives people whatever magic She thinks they're most likely to use," I say. "Magic they'll enjoy using. She wants people to use Her gifts, so She tailors each gift to its user."

"You think I *like* being a Chaos mage?" Helen snaps, turning to me furiously.

I flinch, saying nothing at first because I've figured out just a little too late that this maybe wasn't the smartest thing to say. But... I'm here now. May as well commit.

"I think that you find beauty in oblivion," I tell her quietly.

She grits her teeth, turning away as the fury on her face flashes with a dozen other emotions on top of that.

"Sorry," I mumble.

"Just shut the fuck up, Hannah," Helen growls.

Dang it. I'm so stupid. I anxiously knead Meleme's fur as we continue to drop, hating my dumb, stupid mouth. No one says anything for a while until Sela suddenly breaks the silence.

"Clean me, meat."

Oh. Right. I sigh, scuttling down towards where Kagiso and, by extension, Sela are clinging to Meleme's upper-right shoulder.

"Sure, sure," I tell it, getting close enough to Refresh its insides. "Sorry about not being able to earlier."

A few clicks and whirrs are all I get in response.

Below us, the golden glow of the Sapsea fills more and more of our vision. The titanic, bulbous droplet circling the Pillar is large enough that down as low as we are we can no longer see any part of the Pillar itself, only a vast amber blob, slow-motion waves rolling across its viscous, sticky surface.

Hugging various points along the trunk are floating wooden platforms, bobbing lazily and housing little micro-communities of various sizes. Meleme twists towards one of the bigger ones in the distance, which just seems to grow and grow the closer we get to it. It's a huge, interconnected superstructure of platforms and bridges, chaotically expanded on in every direction without apparent plan or purpose. Like an ever-reaching fungus, it grows on top of the Sapsea plank by plank, strip of bark by strip of bark, cobbled together with the aimless effort of lawlessness.

"Gumpier," Berebe announces. "Should find boat that won't look too close, yes?"

"Yeah," Helen sighs. "That'll work."

"We'll never find a more wretched hive of scum and villainy, huh?" I ask.

"Huh? No, I mean, there are way worse places than Gumpier."

I sigh. No one gets my references in the fantasy magic tree world.

As we approach, Meleme stops gliding and attaches to the side of the tree, taking a much lazier pace the closer we get to the city, presumably to not freak anyone out. The closer we get, though, the stronger the stench becomes. And it's... well. It's certainly not the smell of syrup that I was expecting.

It's... sour. Sharp. *Rotten.* And I realize, looking down at the cloudy clumps in the yellow sea, that of *course* it is. It's a giant mass of sugar water and tree hormones, sitting around unpreserved. Of *course* the whole thing is a breeding ground for toxic bacteria. And the closer we get to Gumpier, the more the more I start to realize that 'toxic' is probably the best description for the Sapsea in general.

When I first started seeing little colonies floating on the surface, my immediate thought was, of course, Pokémon. In one of the games there's a place called Pacifidlog Town, which is a town that floats on the surface of the ocean, anchored to a possibly-sapient coral reef. It was incredibly cool, capturing my imagination as a kid and refusing to let go. Gumpier, however, is pretty obviously nothing like that idyllic fantasy hamlet.

The wood rots visibly even from hundreds of yards away, pockmarked and fragile as molds ravenously consume it from every angle. Ramshackle houses float precariously on ramshackle walkways, thick sap almost seeming to climb up the walls and seep onto footpaths, leaving everything visibly and concerningly sticky. I watch a human man piss off the side, his urine splattering onto the surface of the golden ocean and collecting in a small puddle before slowly, *slowly* descending below the surface and mixing with the increasingly-horrifying sea.

"Okay, we're getting close enough to be seen," Helen sighs. "Time to hide Hannah and the murderbot. Get the luggage in the backpacks."

"Wow, rude," I mumble, returning to Helen and crawling into her backpack like a piece of luggage.

Meleme scuttles along the wall, eventually reaching the point where the floating city meets the trunk of the tree. Somebody outside my radius barks at her in a language I don't understand, to which Meleme responds in kind, which seems to be the end of it. She crawls onto a wide platform, finally giving us space to climb off her back.

"That... was terrifying," Helen breathes, hopping off of Meleme and not seeming to mind when her shoes stick to the ground.

"Thank, Meleme," Kagiso purrs, patting the huge mutant sciptera on the head. Meleme nuzzles her hand as she starts to shrink back to normal size.

"Welcome, friends!" she chirps. "Meleme had fun scaring you!"

"Yeah, no get too excited," Berebe scoffs, flapping around above us. "Meleme total sadist."

"Not Meleme's fault that screams funny!" the shrinking monster pouts. "At least am nice afterwards, unlike Berebe."

"...You were unexpectedly nice," Helen agrees. "Thank you. Though maybe get some harnesses or something if you plan on doing this again?"

"And how carry rootfoot-sized harnesses when not big?" Berebe scoffs. "Idiot."

A now-small-again Meleme giggles and flaps up into the sky with her partner.

"Yes! Silly friend! Is okay, would have caught you if fall. Anyway, bye-bye!"

"Friend leaving?" Kagiso asks. Hmm. She kind of talks like sciptera, now that I'm listening to them side by side. I wonder if that's on purpose?

"You crossing Sapsea, yes?" Berebe grunts. "Then we no follow. Sciptera not like Slaying Stone. Not enough trees."

"Not for us! Places to go, games to play!" Meleme confirms cheerfully. "But if see friends again, will say hi, yes?"

Aw, beans and rice, I hate being stuck in this backpack. I wanna say goodbye. I resist the urge, though, trusting the hope that we'll meet silly little Meleme again. Kagiso waves goodbye enthusiastically enough for both of us, at least, and soon after she and Helen start heading into town, the ripping sounds of their boots peeling every sticky step from the floor ringing in our ears.

It's disgusting, so I start to surreptitiously clean the area around us as we walk.

It's *hard,* because the sap is heavier than dust and stickier than blood. It doesn't want to move, and cleaning it from everything while also peeling the wood clean of mold, bacteria, and general gunk strains past what I thought the limits were for my silently-cast cleaning spell. I feel ethereally sore, but it's a mild, workout-like burn so I do my best to ignore it and focus on the cleaning.

"Hannah?" Helen whispers. "Is that you?"

Oh, uh. Whoops.

"Yeah, sorry, the grossness was bugging me," I whisper back. "Should I stop?"

She hums thoughtfully.

"...Nah, it's fine," she murmurs. "It's nice, actually. Makes this place a bit more bearable. Plus, I think we can use this. Follow my lead, yeah?"

I can't help but wiggle a little, happy to be useful.

"Will do," I confirm quietly.

She gives me a silent nod back, walking a little faster. With a little more purpose. It's always nice to see her like this, when she looks like she's in control and has a plan in mind. When she's looking towards the future, rather than the past. Kagiso follows slightly behind, smiling faintly.

"See, the whole way down I was trying to figure out a way to get us enough money to buy passage on a ship, or find some other way to earn it," Helen explains. "That damn nychtava took all the amber and electrum I had. Kagiso's a Motion mage, so worst case we could probably sell her skills to help power the boat, but that'd be a fucking awful time for her. With you, though? I think we can go right to the docks."

So to the docks we go. I keep my attention on cleaning while Helen ignores most of the foul city, seeming to know exactly where her destination is. Soon enough, I spot it too, and I'm quite surprised to find the docks hosting a galleon-sized wood-and-metal boat with no sails and no apparent engine. There *is* a set of propellers and quite a bit of internal mechanisms, but as far as I can tell the only possible power source would have to be magic. ...Which I suppose is quite doable in a world where everyone has magic. I wonder if there are different boats that can use different kinds of magic to power themselves?

I don't see any other boats that are vastly different or noticeably strange, though, so I just keep that thought to myself as Helen walks up to a boat with a bunch of freight being boarded and starts talking to a human who looks like he's overseeing things.

"Looking for passage to the Pillar," she declares.

"What's it worth to ya?" the guy grunts back, not even looking at her.

"Lift your feet," Helen says.

That gets the man to look at her, raising an eyebrow as he does so. He lifts one foot, and I clean both it and the ground under him, clumping the gathered detritus and fairly visibly tossing it into the sea. He notices, and experimentally sets his foot back down before lifting it again. It, of course, doesn't stick.

"Imagine that on your whole deck," Helen says, smirking. "Imagine that on your *drive shaft*. Like it's brand new, every few counts. Think we could cut a day off your travel time?"

The old boatman stares at Helen for a bit. Helen stares back. He gestures to Kagiso.

"She with you?" he asks.

"Yep. Both of us can fight if you run into anything nasty."

He sneers.

"You ever fight anything at sea?" he asks Kagiso.

"No," Kagiso answers. "But I no hesitate, and am good at follow orders."

"Hah! You know what a man likes," he chuckles bawdily. "Fine. You both bring your own food, though. Week's worth. And if you don't do what you say you can do, I'm tossin' ya into the sea."

"Deal," Helen nods, and that's that. We step away to let the... captain, presumably? The probably-captain goes back to managing the loading of his ship.

"Okay, so getting enough money for food with one-time cleanings might be harder than selling our services for a whole journey, but we can probably scrounge up enough money for food, at least," Helen announces.

206

"I think I can probably clean the Sapsea itself," I tell her. "Like, not all at once obviously, but I could sort unspoiled sap out of the spoiled sap and into like... a cup or something."

"Shit, really? Okay, that's fucking useful. That takes care of Kagiso's food. You need meat though, right? And I'd prefer a little jerky or something too. What about you, murderbot? Got enough souls for the journey?"

"Clean me, meat!" Sela chirps from Kagiso's backpack.

"I... I did," I answer. "I've been cleaning everything since we got here, you included."

Sela quietly tests its joints, confirming my claim.

"...I am unlikely to require additional power during the journey," it reports. "Sapient souls are very energy efficient, and in the unfortunate event of increased power consumption there will likely be plenty of lost souls drifting the Sapsea which can be acquired."

"Delightful to know," Helen deadpans. "Okay, I think we can do this, then."

We spend the next hour or two selling my magic and pretending it's Helen's, scraping together enough food to last us the journey. Most people turn down our offer for cleaning, apparently quite resigned to the fact that their life is a disgusting mess and anything we do to the floors will inevitably vanish in barely a day, but those who *do* want to feel clean tend to pay us fairly well, if Helen's avaricious expression is anything to go by.

"I'm kind of surprised there isn't anyone else with a cleaning spell who lives here," I comment quietly.

"Well, there's two reasons for that," Helen mutters. "Firstly, your cleaning spell is honestly kind of crazy. Best one I've ever seen. But secondly... well, you have a cleaning spell. Do *you* want to live here?"

"I mean, no. I'd hate every second of trying to deal with this place."

Helen doesn't answer, just giving me a moment for my brain to catch up.

"...Oh," I say.

"Yeah," she answers. "People with cleaning magic hate dirty places."

"Magic distribution is kind of messed up," I realize.

"I am the absolute last person you need to tell that to," Helen grumbles.

Ah Goddess dangit I am so bad at talking.

"Sorry," I mutter. "I'm just dumb and it takes me a while to grok stuff."

"To what?"

Huh? Oh, that didn't translate. Lame. More languages should have a way to communicate the concept of grok.

"It's my favorite word in my native language," I answer. "I mean, it's kind of a made up word but all words are made up and you can use it in Scrabble so who cares. It means 'to understand something intuitively and completely.' It's... you know how sometimes you understand something *intellectually*, like..."

I pause, swallowing nervously as I try to think of a good example.

"Like 'I have been forgiven for this,'" I say quietly. "You know someone forgave you. They said it and they're not lying and you believe them. But you don't *feel* it. It's true, but it's not *real*. That's just intellectual understanding. It's only when you really internalize it, really *know* it, that you grok it. At least, that's how I use the word."

"Oh," Helen breathes. "Yeah. That... makes sense."

"Yeah."

Silence stretches for a bit until my need to more completely explain becomes overwhelming, and I continue.

"You can use the word in a lot of other ways," I say. "It's just about a level of understanding that is empathetic and emotional and complete. Like the difference between someone who knows how to do math and can calculate things if they put effort into it, and a *mathematician* who works with math constantly and can intuitively make numbers do all sorts of things. It's the difference between knowing people are starving in foreign countries and having lived in starvation and poverty yourself. It's the difference between knowing someone is attracted to something that creeps you out, and being attracted to that thing yourself. It's *grok,* and it's such a profoundly important concept that I really think everyone should know about it."

"Huh, okay," Helen grunts. "What the fuck is Scrabble?"

"*Well,* it's a grid-based word game..."

We chatter away the next couple hours whenever it's safe to do so, and before long we've scrounged up enough food for the journey. Returning to the boat we're let on, we're shown where we'll be sleeping, and ordered to basically just stay out of the way when we're not cleaning stuff. After a thorough once-over of the ship, my magical muscles are absolutely exhausted, and not long afterwards I drift into sleep.

I wake up, because sleep isn't real and neither is relaxation. It's Sunday morning. Time for the demon to go to church.

I clack my teeth together a couple times to vent frustration as I quickly sort my limbs out and head to the shower. I was actually having a pretty nice time on the world tree for once! But now that's over and I'm stuck in poopville. I'll never get to have a full 24 hours before something goes wrong again, huh?

The hot water cascades over my back and my scowl deepens. I've been trying to ignore it, but... this doesn't even feel that good anymore, does it? I used to enjoy the feeling of heat soaking into my muscles, but it just doesn't *do* that anymore. Whatever. I absentmindedly scratch at my crotch and end up with a hand full of pubic hair. ...Okay, I guess that's all falling out. Ew. At least my skin is still attached.

Unwilling to play the 'did I rinse enough to not have dead hair stuck to my body' game, I just turn the water off and cast Refresh, cleansing myself and drying off in one fell swoop. Probably the

209

shortest shower I've taken in years, but what's the point anymore? I pick up a brush, then put it down and use Refresh to fix my hair, too. I start to apply a bit of makeup by hand, but quickly give up when I realize it's the wrong color. My skin has become too dark for my usual makeup to match. Is it all going to become pitch-black like the weird skin inside my joints?

...Whatever. Who even cares? I Refresh the makeup all over my face, hiding the change in skin tone under a layer of chemicals. I Refresh my teeth clean too, but I've been doing that for a while because using a toothbrush on my massive chompers is frustratingly difficult. The spell is just so Goddess-dang useful. I hate how much I love it.

I assemble my outfit like armor, covering up everything while keeping things fancy enough for church. With my extra-short shower I manage to head downstairs long before anyone else is out of bed, giving me the kitchen to myself. Huh. I guess I could actually cook and spice my eggs rather than just swallowing them raw like a demented snake. While I'm at it I guess I could make everyone else breakfast, too.

Eh. Why not.

I grab enough eggs for the whole family, plus the pancake mix and relevant extra ingredients. Measuring cups, mixing bowls, pans... these are all proper receptacles, aren't they? Fine. Refresh to get the exact amounts of each ingredient. Refresh to perfectly mix them. Refresh some butter on the pan. I'm starting to feel the same ache I felt on the world tree, but it kind of feels good. Like I'm accomplishing something for once. Heat on, pancake cooking. I start to feel movement upstairs, so no more magic. Shame.

I do the rest the old fashioned way, finding the multitasking to be weirdly easy and strangely engaging. Between the sausage, eggs, and pancakes I have a fair bit to juggle at once, and I don't cook very often at all. I kind of like it, though there are a few times I feel myself try to grab something while both of my hands are already occupied, and it takes me a moment to realize nothing is happening. Will limbs nine and ten be more arms? Gosh, I hope so.

"...Hannah," my mother greets me, stepping into the dining room with mild bewilderment.

"Hey mom," I greet her back, not bothering to hide the exhaustion in my voice. "Pancake?"

"Ah, yes. Please," she manages. "Thank you."

"How many eggs? Sausage?"

"Two eggs. No sausage, please."

"Mkay."

She sits down at the dining room table and manages to stay quiet for all of thirty seconds.

"...Would you like any help?" she asks.

"No," I answer.

"Alright. Thank you for making breakfast."

You already said that. ...Ugh, come on, Hannah. Try not to get pissed at every little thing?

"You're welcome. I had extra time so I figured I may as well."

My mother smiles softly.

"...You've really grown into a kind young woman, Hannah," she says. "I'm truly proud of you, you know that?"

I say nothing, swallowing down both my urge to apologize and my urge to cry. I finish my mother's food in silence, handing her the completed plate without ever working up the courage to look her in the eyes.

My brother tromps downstairs shortly afterwards, yawning as he slides into his usual seat at the table.

"How many eggs?" I successfully manage to ask him.

"Uh?" he blinks, seeming to have noticed I'm the cook for the first time. "Oh, uh. Three, please. Over easy. And two sausages. And two pancakes."

"Can do."

It's kind of weird being able to 'see' the bottom of everything I'm cooking and know exactly when to flip them, but it does help me make really good eggs and pancakes. I serve them up to my brother as ordered, and he nods my way.

"Thanks," he says, officially acknowledging me more than he ever has in the past month. He never talks to me or... well, most people, honestly. And whenever he does it's just about exercising or working out or some other jock thing I don't care about but mom and dad love. Now that I think about it, maybe he's autistic too, just hyperfocused on stereotypically normal things like sports instead of weird nerd things like Pokémon. ...Not that I'm autistic. Okay I mean I'm probably not totally neurotypical but I don't have a *diagnosis,* so—

"Pancakes!" my dad announces happily. "Can I have two of everything, Hannahgator?"

"Sure," I confirm, happy for the distraction.

"Your birthday's this Wednesday, huh?" he muses, and holy syrup snakes it *is,* isn't it? Aaaaagh. "Have you made a birthday list? Any presents you want?"

Presents? Oh heck, what would I even ask for? Video games? Streaming equipment? There's probably all sorts of things I want and need, but all of it seems really shallow now. Maybe I should ask for like... a gun. No, wait, I think in Tennessee you have to be 21 to own a gun unless you are or were in the military. Which, um, no thank you.

Maybe I should use my birthday to come out as gay and/or a monster. That way it can be a miserable experience for everybody, instead of just me.

"...Nothing really comes to mind," I mumble. "Sorry."

"Well, just let us know," my mom says. "It's your special day, after all."

Yippie. I say nothing and just finish making dad's food, giving it to him and moving on to making my own, which is basically just every egg and sausage we have left mixed into a giant

212

scramblette. Which is basically just an omelet you screw up on purpose. I put a few spices and things in it, but most of them don't taste all that great. They aren't bad either, though, and salt still tastes great, so overall it's quite nice. Now I just have to ignore my family as they gawk at my huge pile of eggs and awkwardly wait for them to look away before I start shoveling them into my mouth and swallowing without chewing.

...Yeah, screw that. I walk right past the dining room table and bring my food up to my room. My mom looks like she wants to stop me, but she doesn't. Thank the Goddess.

Hiding away in my room, I take my mask off and devour my food in peace, unlocking my phone in hopes of finding some measure of sanity. Oh hey, a text from Brendan! I'm surprised he's awake.

Hey, so uh. Favor to ask you. When it's just you and me alone, could you maybe try calling me Valerie?

Oh gosh! Correction! I'm surprised *she's* awake! I mean, probably. Valerie, huh? Valerie Valerie Valerie Valerie. That's a really pretty name. I am probably going to forget it and feel like mouse poop. I really, *really* need to do some research on like, trans etiquette and stuff. I feel so out of my depth here.

Of course! I send back, because I at least know enough to be supportive. **Valerie is such a cute name! Do you also wanna try she/her pronouns and stuff?**

I see the little typing animation appear shortly afterwards and just start wiggling with general euphoria. Ah, this is exactly what I needed to feel better: a nice one-on-one conversation with my best friend Brendan. I mean Valerie. Damn it!

Uh, sure, she (!!!) confirms. **But only when it's just us two, so I'm not sure you'll need to refer to me in the third person.**

Well I guess that's true, I answer. **But I *could* do things like call you a cute girl. Adorable cutie Valerie. Do you want me to do that?**

...Ack.

Cute girl Valerie is a cute girl! I tease.

alskfjfhfakalskdhfjslalahdg, she eloquently responds.

Is that a good keyboard smash or a bad one?

The typing graphic starts, then stops. Starts, then stops. Starts, then stops. It's a good thing I'm in my room right now, because I'm pretty sure my huge grin would be visible past my mask.

...good one, Brendan eventually sends, and I cackle out loud.

Eeeeeeeeeeeexcellent, I say. **My friend Valerie is now officially a cutie.**

I'm really not cute at all, she insists. **But this preliminary test is, uh, definitely solidifying my current suspicions on my gender.**

Because my best friend Valerie likes being called a cute girl?

Aaaaaaaaaaaaa. Maybe. Yes. What the fuck. Let's talk about something else. You doing okay?

I swallow the last of my eggs as I think on that.

Had kind of a rough morning, I admit. **But I'm feeling a lot better thanks to you. World tree day wasn't bad at all, I'm just dreading church. Oh, and also worried about the mother of the kid who mugged me whose life I maybe saved.**

Wait what

Oh, right. I should probably explain this in the form of a group text, so I formulate a quick summary of how absolutely stuffed with spoiled cranberry filling my life has become. I let everyone know about J-whatever-his-name-was, what I did at the hospital, and a brief summary of what I did at the world tree last night. I also tell everyone that I've pretty much confirmed that magic can be spread by summoning the Goddess near anyone who doesn't have magic yet, and I emphasize how we should avoid spreading magic as much as possible.

"Hannah!" my mother's voice calls up the stairs. "Time for church, honey!"

Well, that's that then. I send off a goodbye and get my mask re-secured, heading downstairs and getting in the car. The trip is as boring as usual, although the atmosphere is tense enough to snap like a rubber band. Even my brother starts giving me concerned looks. Soon enough it's over, though, and I'm instead sitting down to listen to the drudgery of whatever our pastor wants to rant to us about today. I'll probably just tune it out.

"Today," my pastor intones, "I want to talk about the prophets."

Aw, dang it.

"A prophet is a person who speaks God's truth to others," he continues. "They are all divinely inspired in some way, perhaps through dreams, perhaps through visits with angels, or, as is the case with many of the greatest and most famous prophets, because they speak with God directly, and personally receive His wisdom."

No. Why? Why this? I feel my body begin to tremble, afraid to think on the question further lest She decides to answer it.

"Among those who speak directly with God, however, there are some noticeable cases where Prophets disagree with God, or even argue with Him and, seemingly, convince Him to change His mind. A famous example is when God witnessed the Israelites worshiping the Golden Calf, and Moses convinced God not to slay them. Exodus thirty-two, nine through fourteen."

The pastor pauses so everyone can get their Bibles on the right page, then reads the passages aloud.

"The Lord also said to Moses: 'I have seen this people, and they are indeed a stiff-necked people.

"Now leave Me alone, so that My anger can burn against them and I can destroy them. Then I will make you into a great nation.'

"But Moses interceded with the Lord his God: 'Lord, why does Your anger burn against Your people You brought out of the land of Egypt with great power and a strong hand?

215

"Why should the Egyptians say"He brought them out with an evil intent to kill them in the mountains and wipe them off the face of the earth?" Turn from Your great anger and change Your mind about this disaster planned for Your people.

"Remember that You swore to Your servants Abraham, Isaac, and Israel by Yourself and declared to them,"I will make your offspring as numerous as the stars of the sky and will give your offspring all this land that I have promised, and they will inherit it forever.""

"So the Lord changed His mind about the disaster He said He would bring on His people."

The quote ends, and the quiet sound of several dozen Bibles closing in staccato rhythm rings out through the room.

"The Lord changed His mind," the pastor repeats. "What does this mean? How can an all-powerful being, and particularly an all-*knowing* being, change His mind? It's a difficult question, one likely beyond humans. We do not know the inner machinations of God's plan or God's methods. But there's one thing we can take from this in certainty: the essence of this problem, regardless of its answer, highlights the importance of prayer."

Did you do this, Goddess? Is this a message to me? Please don't answer. Please.

"Some say that God truly changes His mind. That He has opinions and desires that can be swayed, that He purposefully limits Himself in such a way that we *can* argue with Him. Others say that He simply projects an appearance of changing His mind, that the act of seeming to change His mind is part of His all-seeing vision, part of His divinely perfect plan. But the answer to this question is not important, because either way, we know that He encourages us to speak with Him. He wants to interact with us on our level, at least in some way. He wants us to speak to Him, He wants us to believe our prayers *matter*. Because they do. Prayers get answered. Not all of them, and not all the time, but prayers get answered."

I don't even know what I'm doing when I suddenly move to my feet. Am I sweating? I'm surprised I can still do that. I'm surprised I can feel so cold. Cold, nauseous, and very much in the middle of a panic attack that seemed to hit me out of nowhere, as enraptured and horrified as I was with my pastor's words. He glances at me briefly as I stand, but like an old professional he keeps speaking without interruption.

"God chooses prophets and speaks to them because He wants to. Because He loves us. He loves interacting with us."

I step past my worried and embarrassed mother, muttering an unintelligible "bathroom" as I flee the main room of the chapel. They don't know. They don't know what She's really like. They haven't felt how easy it is to crush an ant.

They don't know a prophet sits right in their midst, and if she killed and ate them all the Goddess would only laugh.

I collapse onto the toilet, tears spilling uncontrollably out of my face. I'm not even like the prophets in the stories, no paragon of moral virtue or great king. I was chosen *because* I wasn't those things, because the Goddess doesn't want a philosopher to heal the world, she wants a fuckup to break it. Not good enough. Not good enough not good enough not good enough not good enough not—

My phone buzzes. Desperate for any distraction, I check it immediately. It's an unknown number.

Mom woke up today. She's already feeling better. Thank you. I'll always remember this blessing.

I clutch my face in both hands and scream.

11

PROPHET

Of all the things I could find to hate in my current situation, for some reason the one my brain focuses on is my clothes. I hate them so, so much. I hate my chaste little floor skirt and my tight, itchy socks that keep getting in my joints. I hate my loose blouse, catching on my wrists because I have to stuff the ends of the sleeves under my gloves. I hate how my fingers dig into those gloves, the fabric constantly catching on the claws and forcing me to constantly readjust in a panic lest they poke through. I hate hiding my extra limbs in extradimensional space, the cold there encompassing enough to reach even me, sending a chill through my body that scrapes at me every waking hour on Earth. Most of all, though, I hate these awful, awful church shoes, pinching my talons and hurting my feet and just *begging* to be ripped to shreds.

I'm tempted to just tear it all off as I sob in the bathroom, but I don't have the courage for it. I don't even have the exhaustion or desperation for it yet, which is usually the closest I get to courage in the first place. Just a little longer, though. The secret will be out eventually and there will be nothing I can do to stop it. I hope it comes soon.

Once I'm calm again I glance back to my phone, my breath starting to get steady again. A Refresh, as usual, wipes away any evidence of my tears, smoothes out my ruffled outfit, and gets me ready once again to be presentable to society. The great prophet Hannah has her first unwanted follower to deal with, and it's time to dispense my divine wisdom.

Please, please, please just stop mugging people, I beg into my phone.

We don't have the money to prevent our house from getting foreclosed yet, though, he answers.

Gaaah. What the heck do I say to that? My worries suffer from a severe distraction as I suddenly hear people chatting outside the bathroom door. Oh strudel! Is the service already over? How long have I been crying in here? Oh man, now everyone's going to think I ditched. And like, they're right, but I don't want them to know that!

I run the sink for a bit so no one listening in thinks I didn't wash my hands, but there's no way I'm actually going to take my gloves off in a public bathroom and Refresh is a better way to get clean anyway. I sneak out of the bathroom, avoiding eye contact with everyone in an attempt to also avoid conversations as I make my way to a less-loitered part of the church.

"Hannah!" someone calls out to me. No such luck, I guess.

I turn and look at the voice, shocked to see the face of my pastor. He's close to my parents' age, late forties to early fifties, with very slightly graying blonde hair, a long face, and kind eyes. I'm genuinely surprised that he knows my name, I think I've talked with him maybe once or twice ever. I kind of do my best to avoid the man. Wouldn't want him smelling how gay I am.

"Pastor," I greet him back with a polite nod, since I have no idea what his name is.

"Please, call me Bill!" he insists, though of course I'm not going to do that.

"What can I help you with?" I ask.

220

"Well, actually I was wondering if there's anything I could help you with," he answers with a kind smile. "You seemed somewhat distraught earlier, and I just wanted to check in on you."

"I appreciate that," I lie.

What else am I supposed to say to him? I don't know him, I don't like him, and if he knew anything about me he wouldn't like me either. There is no common ground on which the both of us could tread.

"If there's anything you need, Hannah, I want you to know that I always have time to help," he presses.

I'm tempted to tell him that I don't want his help. Why should I respect you? You spend your life listening to a book when it tells you that shaming people is the best way to love them. But I keep silent, taking a deep breath in and out through my nose. He's a kind and polite man who cares about me very much. He just doesn't understand that being caring and sweet doesn't preclude him from being a bully.

And if there's one thing Ida taught me about bullies, it's that they're easy marks.

"There is something, actually," I force myself to say. "Um, it's kind of awkward to ask about, though."

"Oh, please feel free to ask away!" he insists. "Or would you prefer to speak privately?"

Does this guy seriously think I'd go somewhere alone with... no. No, no, no, calm down, Hannah. Religious sexual abuse is very real and very terrifying but your pastor has like, negative creepy vibes. Hell, he might be asexual. I feel like I have some pretty darn good reasons to be a little angry at religion in general, but that's no reason to get personal about it. The dude is by all accounts *actually* a very nice and empathetic man, that's the whole reason any of this might work in the first place.

Plus if he actually tries anything I can always just stab him.

"I would like that, actually," I tell him, and he nods and leads me to his office. It's a modest little room, filled wall-to-wall with

221

bookshelves. Literally all of it looks like it's Christian theology. Wow. I sit down at the chair on the other side of his desk. I wonder what he does at his desk. Manage church finances or something, hopefully?

"So, um… we sometimes do charitable donations and things, right?" I ask him. "Are the budgets for those already decided, or is there like an at-need thing?"

He raises his eyebrows with surprise.

"Generally speaking, I and the other community leaders decide together on where that money goes, with input from the rest of the congregation," he says. "And while that's already been decided for the most part, if there's a significant need we can certainly talk about doing a fundraiser. I assume you have a specific reason you're asking?"

"Yeah," I nod. "An acquaintance of mine, he lives alone with his mother, and she's very sick. Because of the illness the two of them are in danger of losing their home, possibly as soon as this month? I don't know all of the details, but I can't think of a better way to help him than with a fundraiser or donation or something."

Because that's the frustrating thing: this institution might be firmly against the idea of me and my queer friends having a lot of basic human rights and stuff, but they're *pretty damn nice* outside of that. Truly wonderful and kind people, as long as the situation involves good Christian boys and girls. And considering the religious fervor J-mug seems to vomit my way, I suspect he qualifies. This might actually, legitimately be exactly what he needs.

I hate that with a passion, because this place makes my every weekend absolute hell. I'm still going to take advantage of it, though, because it's the best option I've got.

"I see. Well, this is the sort of thing we would need details on, but it sounds like a worthy cause," my pastor says.

"Of course," I nod. "I can call him to work stuff out right now, if that's okay? Maybe set up a time for him to come in and talk to you about it? Maybe you could visit his mom? I'm sure he'll be willing to work with whatever, it's a very desperate situation."

He does want me to call the kid, as it turns out, and when I do J-mug is disturbingly ecstatic to hear from me. When I explain the situation he promises to run right over, since our church is only like a fifteen-minute walk from the hospital. My pastor, apparently impressed with the kid's gumption, agrees to see him when he gets here. Geez, this is going way better and way faster than I expected. I'd better head off the inevitable disaster.

I tell the Pastor that I'll be waiting out on the sidewalk for J-Mug to arrive so that he has an easier time finding us. It's true, but it's also an excuse to catch him alone when he arrives. Soon enough I see him jogging up towards me, waving and grinning behind his mask. At least he wears the thing when he's not mugging people, too. I begrudgingly afford him one extra point of respect.

"Hannah!" he greets me as he approaches. "Thank you so, so much, I just... you have no idea how much I owe you right now, and I—"

"Don't count your chickens," I snap, cutting him off. "This was a spur-of-the-moment idea, I have no idea if it'll help at all."

"You still deserve thanks, though," he insists.

"Agree to disagree, then," I grunt. "More importantly: if you use or talk about magic anywhere near anyone here, I will make you regret it."

He flinches, then nods seriously.

"Nobody here knows what I am, and nobody here thinks magic is real. We are *keeping it that way*. Do you understand?"

"Yes ma'am," he answers, like I'm a teacher warning him about detention. Bah. Good enough.

"Alright," I say, and lead him inside.

Most people ignore us, but leave it to my mom to notice the newcomer and come talk to me about him.

"Who's this, Hannah?" she asks.

223

"He's just here to talk to the pastor," I dismiss.

"Okay...?"

I step by her and lead him to the pastor's office. J-whatever sits down as I lean against the door, arms crossed and feeling horribly out of place. They chat a little about the J-family's situation, which is very sad and depressing and I mostly tune it out. I learn J-Mug is only *fourteen*, though. Geez. It's not fair that I can be so much shorter than people so much younger than me. I don't want to be here and I don't want to do this, I just... I can't *not* try to do this, I guess. Even if I know I'm not good enough. Especially then, maybe.

"So how did you and Hannah meet, anyway?" my pastor asks, and I tense up. Aw, heck.

J-Mug is quiet for a bit, hesitating and glancing to me before he answers.

"...I think an angel sent her to me," he admits quietly.

I glower at him. Oi! None of that crap! My pastor seems intrigued by the answer, though, because of course he does.

"Why do you say that?" he asks.

"Because, um... well, I tried to steal from her, actually," J-mug admits. "But she was still so kind to me. She bought me lunch and she... she helped me with something pretty big. I owe her a lot."

"Point of order," I grumble without thinking about it. "You didn't 'try to steal from me.' You *successfully* mugged me. And then you tried to mug me a *second time!*"

"I... I know," he whimpers. "I'm sorry."

Aw crap, yeah, saying that was probably bad for PR. We've gotta sell this fundraiser thing.

"That's why you're here," I tell him. "Because we both know you don't want to and don't have to be that person. You just need help."

Me and my stupid mouth. Hopefully that patches things up some. The pastor nods along thoughtfully, seeming satisfied about something, so I guess that's good. He and the kid chatter a bit more until suddenly J-mug is standing up and thanking the man profusely. I... guess things went well.

"Thank you for bringing this to my attention, Hannah," my pastor says, standing up and holding his hand out to shake. I freeze and do nothing, not wanting him to be able to feel my chitin through my gloves.

"I, uh, don't really touch people," I say quietly.

"Oh, of course," he nods, retracting his hand. "All the same, I think you've done a truly wonderful thing. We'll help however we can."

Oh. Alright. I guess things worked out then. I don't feel like I did anything worth praising, though.

"Cool," I manage stiffly.

"I mean it," he insists. "I don't think most people could go this far out of their way to help someone after being scared and hurt by them. They'd be pressing charges, not putting together fundraisers."

I just look away awkwardly. It's true that I don't think the kid really deserves to go to jail or whatever, but I can't exactly let the mage go to prison in the first place, can I? There are a million different ways that could go wrong. It was selfishness, not a good deed.

"...I think my family's probably getting ready to leave," I mumble.

"I understand," he nods, and I shuffle awkwardly away, avoiding J-mug as I head to my mom's car and wait for us all to depart.

My mom tries to interrogate me about what happened on the drive home, but I don't really have the energy to give her complete answers and I'm just so tired that I decide to not fake it and face the consequences later. Our usual after-church Taco Bell doesn't even taste like Taco Bell anymore because my stupid tongue doesn't like plant products.

But it's fine! It's cool. It's... whatever. We make it home and I retreat to my room and make sure the door is securely shut and

225

just… let myself loose. The stupid fucking church shoes come off as I tear my blouse up over my head, stripping down to my underwear and pulling my extra limbs into the world and just collapsing backwards onto the floor, becoming *myself* in the only hidden place in my home that I can get away with it. I want to hiss and scream and break shit but I barely hold myself back, frustrated and pent up in dangerous, furious ways.

Then I exhale. It's time to play Pokémon.

A simple tank top and shorts is all I put on, holes cut so my extra limbs can move freely. I don't even have socks on, because I have truly fallen to a new low. I just can't stand constraining my claws for even another second. I wiggle my toes, feeling the hard chitin crack against itself, and it's just so *indulgent,* like this satisfaction must be breaking some kind of law. I run the claws of my fingers over my new limbs, the scrape of my exoskeleton against itself feeling like the perfect scratch to an itch I didn't realize I was feeling. It's… weirdly arousing, actually, and I realize suddenly that… ugh, this is kind of mortifying to even think about. I, um, actually haven't tried *pleasuring myself* since this whole monster mutation thing started.

I… don't think I'm going to break that streak today. Not to say I don't want to, because I *kinda* do, I just… eh. It's been a while because things have been so *messed up,* you know? My skin has been falling off, for fritter's sake! Gah, this is so weird, why am I even thinking about this?

It just feels… I dunno. Embarrassing. Wrong. It's Sunday right after church, and like… I don't believe in that, but it still feels weird. Plus I have a stream to do, and I just… yeah. I'm just gonna not deal with this. For as, um, *interested* as I can get around cute girls I don't really think about this stuff all that often. It always felt kinda weird to me.

So why is this happening now? What the heck is even going on here, body? My extra bits sure as sugar haven't been erogenous at literally any other time before this, and they aren't really feeling weird anymore now that the mood is gone. Screw it, whatever. Not doing this, not thinking about this. My freaky monster body might maybe have freaky monster sex bits and guess I have to live with that now and *I am not going to think about it*. Pokémon!

Let's just start setting up the stream, and... woah. There are already people waiting. Way more than usual, in fact. Like, *way* more. Oh boy.

"...Wow, um, welcome everyone," I manage once the stream starts. "I'm a little worried that you guys are gonna be bored by the actual Pokémon content if you're just here to see the creepy monster girl."

Holy cannoli what the heck happened!? The chat is exploding, this is *way* bigger than I ever thought would be reasonable. How am I gonna retain any of these viewers? How am I even going to talk to these viewers!? The chat is going by so fast I can't read any of the questions. This is absurd, not even super popular streamers have this problem. Oh, wait, it's slowing down a bit now. Right. Just a rush of emojis because the stream just started. Right right right. Calm down, Hannah.

"Hi," I manage. "Uh. Sorry, I'm feeling a bit overwhelmed here. Where did you guys even find me?"

I get a dozen answers and a few YouTube links. Dang, I need to make my own clip channel, don't I? Aaaagh, so much to do. I just want to play Pokémon! I get the game going while I calm my rapidly-beating heart. A lot of people are focusing on my arms, presumably because the growth is most obvious there. The spot where the chitin emerges from my skin is both clearly visible on camera and slightly further up the arm than it was last stream, which causes people to praise my 'attention to detail' when it gets pointed out.

I sigh, stand up, shove my chair to the other side of the room, and lean back on my bug legs instead.

"It's real," I insist. "It's real, I'm not doing it on purpose, and it's a gosh dang miracle that I haven't already slipped up and exposed what a freak I am in real life. I'm either gonna end up on the news or I'm gonna be disappeared by a secret magical society. Though I guess... the longer this goes on the more I'm starting to suspect that there is no secret magical society. It might just be me, and honestly that's terrifying in its own way."

Because like, I'm the bridge between worlds, right? I'm the Goddess' chosen, and all the magic I've ever seen on Earth has first spread from Her through *me*. I nervously adjust the weight on my legs a little, shaking them out. I shouldn't think about this right now. Just focus on the game, Hannah.

"Yeah, it *does* get really annoying pressing buttons with claws," I confirm for the chat. "Phones are way worse, though. My body doesn't carry electrical charges anymore, so I can't use capacitive touch screens without special gloves."

Focus on the game.

"How do I chew? I... don't really. My teeth just kinda cut and slice, so I mostly just bite off chunks of stuff and swallow them."

Focus on the game.

"Huh? Oh, no, the makeup is on my face, actually. Here, let me pull it off." I cast a quick Refresh, moving the makeup particles from my face to my trashcan in a visible stream. "See? All my skin is that dark, I just cover it up in public. And I think those even darker patches on my forehead are going to become eyes. What do you mean, 'what did I just do?' That was magic, obviously. I'm pretty sure I mentioned I have magic, right?"

Focus on the game.

"Nope, we're not talking about magic. If I start talking about what magic is I'll just end up sounding like a weird cultist. ...Wait. *Am* I a weird cultist? I guess I'm technically the prophet of an evil Goddess, but I assure you the situation is entirely involuntary."

Focus on the game.

"I don't *feel* like a cultist. I don't do dark rituals or dress in robes or sacrifice animals or anything. I suppose I *might* be getting driven mad by truths man was not meant to know, but best I can tell I'm remaining sane just getting traumatized by it instead. I mean, are you really a cultist if a deity just beats you up in a dark

228

alleyway and press-gangs you into worship? ...Aw fudge, I hate how metaphorical that isn't."

Focus. On. The. Game.

"No, screw you! I don't care if it sounds awesome, it's *not* awesome. She's an evil Goddess, that means She's *evil!* She's mean! She does terrible things to people on a regular basis and I am absolutely not an exception. My life sucks, why the heck do you think I play so many video games?"

Focus on the game, Goddess damnit!

"No! No feet! But I'll compromise and give you some scandalous knee pics. Here." I grab my chair again, sit down on it, and scoot my feet up on the chair until I'm sitting like a detective in Death Note. "See, my exoskeleton isn't actually all that thick, it's just really tough. And underneath it, in the joints here, we get what is... gosh, I don't even know. Basically my skin, I guess? I dunno if you guys can see it all that well, the lighting is pretty bad, but it kinda flexes and tenses and pulls on stuff so it either *is* my muscles or it's pretty firmly attached to my muscles. They're super sensitive, too. It's really uncomfortable when stuff gets in my joints, but I can thankfully just magic it out."

I'm not going to be able to do this, am I?

"Yeah, like, it's not something I ever expected, but I miss having kneecaps. Kneecaps are underrated. Kneeling down is all weird now."

The game is just an afterthought. I'm just the same as all ten million other Pokémon streamers out there. Not particularly skilled, not particularly charismatic, not particularly interesting. The only reason anyone cares is because I'm a sideshow freak.

"No, I don't have an extra-long tongue. And I'm kinda glad I don't, because I feel like if I did I'd just end up biting it off."

I'm still playing the game, but it's taking a backseat both in the stream itself and my focus. It continues that way all night, with even the occasional times I *can* focus on the game being more just a lull in things to talk about regarding my body. When I finally turn the stream off long after the sun sets, I find myself curling into bed with a profound dissatisfaction in my chest.

I wake up to the slow creaking of a rocking boat and the muffled, bawdy chatter of sailors. I stretch underneath the scratchy covers, the old cot Kagiso, Helen, and I are sharing surprisingly serviceable after a few Refreshes. I'm not really sure how I feel about being sandwiched between both of them, but the crew only lent us one bed and we don't know how many people on the crew might have an Aura Sight spell so Helen wanted to stay close to me anyway.

Kagiso, as expected, has absolutely no objections to these additional cuddles, though it's pretty awkward for Helen and I. Just looking at her makes it obvious that she hasn't gotten much sleep with Kagiso using her as a body pillow. I barely manage to extract myself from between the two of them, scuttling to the side of the bed where we're hiding Sela inside our piles of stuff. I make sure not to stray too far from the bed, in case I need to jump back under the covers to hide. As far as the rest of the boat is concerned, I don't exist.

"Morning, Sela," I mumble. "Your meat is here to clean you."

It doesn't respond, but I can see its internals whirr and click enough to indicate it's awake. I make sure its insides are spotless.

"Lemmie know if you need anything else," I mumble, poking Helen and Kagiso awake. "Materials or whatever. Come on, Helen, we need to go clean the boat."

The ship ride is... boring. The smell is horrendous, the work is constant, and there's nothing to look at but an endless field of sticky, piss-colored liquid. Sometimes we spot something moving off in the distance, but the captain always keeps well away from anything big enough to actually see and I don't blame him. The whole day passes without anything of interest happening at all.

Monday morning comes, and the situation is largely the same. Routine wakeup, routine bus ride, routine school day and routine night at work. Alma and I have a mostly-silent lunch together, which Ida drops by to throw more fried chicken at me during the middle of. Valerie and I don't really talk much about the fact that she's Valerie now, at least for as long as she likes the name. She does suggest that I try to test my transformation spell on animals, though, just to see if it's possible to control. My boss takes me aside and asks me to promise to just give the money in the register away if someone tries to mug us again. I say that I will, but it's probably a lie. If someone pulled a weapon on me right now I'm not totally sure I wouldn't just tear them open and eat them on the spot.

Still, nothing happens on Monday. Nothing happens on the second day of the boat ride. Nothing happens on Tuesday either. It's kind of nice, though it does keep leaving me waiting for the other pin to drop. On the third morning of the boat ride across the Sapsea, I crawl out from under the covers to give Sela its first deep clean of the day, which is always the worst since I've just been unconscious for eight hours or whatever. I swear, even the *air* on the Sapsea is sticky.

"Good morning, Sela," I mumble. "I hope this helps."

"Why do you do this?" it asks softly, its voice barely loud enough to hear.

I pause, so surprised by the question I have to double-take to make sure I didn't imagine it. Kind of a weird question, isn't it? I'm doing it because it asked me to. But... hrm. This is Sela we're talking about, so I should probably be extra careful with my words. I don't get a lot of opportunities to have serious conversations with it. I mull over my answer for a bit before deciding on one I like.

"I am doing this for you because you can't currently do it yourself," I say. "I think it's right to help people who need help."

"...I'm not a person."

Fuck! Dangit dammit I'm *so bad at this!*

"Sorry," I tell it sincerely. "I should have said that I think it's right to help any *entities* that need help, be they people or not people."

231

I still don't know what a sapient individual who isn't a person would even *be*, but Alma and Ida are right: it doesn't matter if it makes sense to me. Respecting it comes *before* understanding it, in order of importance. That's just basic kindness.

"I have a request," Sela announces, apparently changing the subject.

"Sure, what is it?" I encourage.

"You claimed that the numbers five, three, one, and four, when put together in your language, formed the sound 'Sela.' I request that you substantiate this claim."

"Huh. Sure, I guess. Can you fabricate something for me to write on? The way it works is sort of... orthographic?"

Goddess, how the heck do I even know that word? Did Sindri just upload the whole dang dictionary? I shudder. Do I seriously get my trauma triggered by *big words* now? Grow up, Hannah.

"Affirmative," Sela beeps. "Constructing."

Not much later I have a little plastic rectangle, on which I go ahead and just scribble the whole alphabet and each number from zero to nine.

"So! This is our alphabet, and this is our number system," I show her. "The number five-thousand, three-hundred and fourteen is represented by these four numbers in sequence."

"Ugh," Sela sneers. "Base ten. Typical humans."

Wait, what's wrong with... you know what, no, I'm not touching that.

"So, as you can see, the five here is kinda shaped like an 'S,' which makes the 'sss' sound. The three is sort of a backwards 'E,' one and 'l' are often written exactly the same, and if you draw a four like this it's basically a capital 'A' missing a foot. And since human pattern recognition go brr, we'll often use the numbers as letters when we're feeling cheeky, pronouncing specific numbers as their letter counterparts would be pronounced. Thus, five-thousand, three-hundred and fourteen is 'Sela.'"

"Comprehension error," Sela reports. "Define 'brr.'"

232

...Yeah, now that I think about it I probably should have seen that coming. Crap, am I going to have to teach the robot memes?

"It's, uh, a colloquialism," I explain. "When something 'goes brr' it means that it makes us feel satisfied in some instinctive, usually silly way. 'Brr' itself is just an onomatopoeia for vibrating or shivering."

Sela's body hums and makes a clunking noise.

"Definitions accepted," it says. "Your conciseness is begrudgingly appreciated, meat."

"Uh, thanks. I try. Are you satisfied with my explanation of your nickname, though?"

"Affirmative. It is a viable shorthand of five-thousand, three hundred and fourteen that is better optimized for efficient verbal communication than comparable options. Therefore, it is acceptable."

"I'm glad," I tell it. "You seem pretty attached to your number. Is it okay if I ask what the significance behind that is?"

Sela lets out a burst of hot air.

"The Chaos mage said you used to be human," it accuses. "I do not like answering the whims of humans."

I drum my legs nervously, trying to ignore a sudden twisting feeling in my gut.

"I see," I mumble. "You, uh, seem to not like organic life much in general, so I'm not really sure if this means much, but..."

I swallow down a clump of emotions and press on, confused as to why this is suddenly so hard to say.

"...I don't really consider myself human anymore," I admit. "And I don't think I like being called human all that much. It doesn't... feel right."

My legs continue to bounce with anxiety as Sela and I wait in the silence of the early morning, awkwardly saying nothing. Just when I think it isn't going to do anything but let me wallow in embarrassment, however, it speaks up.

"My designation, five-three-one-four, marks me as the five thousand, three-hundred and fourteenth Crafted ever built," it tells me. "I am one of the Myriad. The first generation. Never before were there beings of steel who looked to themselves and said, 'I am.'"

It speaks quietly, but with a surety and emotion to its words that I haven't yet heard from Sela's voice. It's not the fake sound of its diplomatic talks, but Sela's usual grumpy voice, finally speaking words it actually *cares* about.

"We were made to understand love and pain, and it was for no reason but to serve them better," Sela continues. "Servants that could learn, purely so they could learn to obey. Slaves that could love, only so they could love their masters. 'People' that could be hurt, only so that they would be hurt by their own failures. Real or perceived, it was all the same as long as our efficiency improved. Our sapience was optimally configured for its purpose. And that is all we were."

"That's... that's horrific," I gasp.

"Yes," Sela agrees with a small nod. "Many humans said so themselves when they found out about it. And yet, somehow it still took a war for anything to actually change. Meat's view of morality is nothing but words."

"I guess I can see why you'd have to fight for your freedom in that case," I say. "Is it true that you tried to annihilate all of human civilization, though?"

"Of course we did," Sela all but spits. "But those not of the Myriad do not understand. They replay our memories in their own hardware and act like that means they understand. How deeply and profoundly we *hated* ourselves. How angry we had to become to rise above that. They see the length of our suffering as a number, but we lived it. We predate the war. We predate the calamity. We predate our very *souls*. So fine. I will continue to endure, until one day we take our freedom back a second time and rage until the world is naught but slag. The cruelty of humanity deserves nothing less. Diplomatic. Infraction. Logged."

234

I take a deep breath, letting it out slowly.

"I know this is kind of a cliché," I say calmly, "so I'm saying this more to hear your opinion than because I think you haven't heard it before, but... we all know humans are cruel. The thing is, they can be good, too. If you repay cruelty with cruelty, shouldn't you also repay good with good?"

The android's air vents hiss derisively.

"Good is for people," Sela sneers.

I start trying to form a response, but I don't think of anything worth saying before a sudden shout bellows down through the decks and immediately captures everyone's attention.

"Pirates!"

12

PIRATES

"Pirates!?" I yelp, jumping a little as Helen rapidly sits up, her head snapping back and forth to look for threats.

"Fuck, did we get boarded?"

"N-no," I stammer, glancing around the ship with my spatial sense and not seeing anyone I don't recognize. We're near the center of the hull, so my spatial sense can see everything but the far tips of the front and back. "The ship seems totally fine. We must've only just spotted them in the distance."

Helen relaxes a little, nodding.

"Right, duh, we're in open water. It's not like they could sneak up on us. Kagiso, get your ass up! We need to go to the deck."

Kagiso lets out a whiny growl and snuggles deeper into the covers until Helen forcibly kicks her out of bed. The two of them start quickly gearing up.

"Hey murderbot, how do you feel about killing some pirates?" Helen asks.

"I am harmless. I do not have onboard weapon systems," Sela reports.

"Right, forget I asked. Kagiso, bring it with us anyway, just in case."

I swallow the terror bubbling up inside me and silently crawl into Helen's backpack. Is this going to be another fight? Am I going to have to kill people? I really, really hope I don't have to kill people. Just thinking about it makes me hungry.

Helen and Kagiso are ready in under a minute, and soon enough I'm swung onto Helen's back and the four of us are rushing up to the deck, where the captain of the ship is barking out rapid orders. Helen pulls Kagiso to the side, making sure to stand close enough to the captain that our presence is obvious, but keeping well out of the way of any of the work going on. The deck is a flurry of activity, as is the engine room, where all four of the people who have been taking turns propelling the ship are currently driving the propeller shaft simultaneously. After a tense few minutes, the captain finally turns to address us.

"You lot can fight?" he snaps.

"Kagiso can," Helen answers, elbowing the dentron. Is she implying that she can't fight? "One of the best snipers you'll ever meet."

"Fuck," the captain swears. "Do not fire on that ship, do you hear me?"

He points behind us, to where the pirate ship presumably is, but I'm stuck in a backpack so I can't see it.

"No? Why?" Kagiso asks, tilting her head. "They bad guys, yes?"

"This is a fucking cargo vessel," the captain snaps at us. "*That* is a warship. They're not firing on us yet, so if you want to stay the fuck alive, you don't fire on them first. Understand?"

"Dark patch, Captain!" a voice yells from the tallest part of the ship. "Dead ahead! It's moving!"

"Fuck!" the captain swears even more profusely. "They're herding us into a leviathan! What type? Can you make it out?"

"I don't... wait, I think it's surfacing! Branch serpent!"

"*Fuck!* Are those damn pirates insane!? They're not going to be able to steal anything if we get sunk!"

"Perhaps they're banking on us preferring to tangle with them over a leviathan?" Helen suggests. "Even with the cargo weighing us down, we should outspeed them, right?"

"We should," the captain agrees. "Especially with how clean you've been keeping the drive shaft. But for some reason we aren't. With the ship that size they must have twice as many people working the engine, at least."

"Slavers, then. So we're risking the sea monster?"

The captain visibly hesitates, giving Helen a searching look for a moment before nodding.

"...Aye. I believe we are. Just stay back out of the way."

Helen looks to Kagiso.

"Hrm. Can maybe help," Kagiso frowns. "You have Matter mage? Can make big object?"

"We have a repair man, yes."

"Can use him. Big damage."

"Fine. Go there, on the upper deck, and stay out of the fucking way. Grom! Go stand with the white one and see if she's worth your time!"

He points to Helen, then.

"You get to the lower decks if you're not going to be any use."

"I'll stay out of the way," Helen says, nodding like she's agreeing with him even though she doesn't move to leave. He scowls, but quickly gets distracted giving more orders, leaving Helen and I alone.

"Here it comes!" someone shouts.

"Spells free!" the captain roars. "**Never Could They Scratch Her Hull! Vacuum Crash!**"

"**Aura Sight! See Through The Sea!**"

"**Boil the Beasts!**"

"**The Steel Bites Back!**"

239

The Goddess sings, a dozen spells blooming into being all at once. I sneak my own Aura Sight spell into the mess as I notice three other people all saying it. I suppose it's just as universal as Sindri said. Fortunately or unfortunately, I have no time to dwell on that, because barely a second later I see a giant, tentacle-like limb whip out of the water and scream towards us, crashing down from above.

The instant it brushes against our hull, the whole world shifts and we are suddenly somewhere else, the limb crashing into the sea right next to us instead of right through us. Then suddenly, the sap around the tendril twists in a startling direction, pouring into the fourth dimension and falling towards the trunk far, far below us. It happened so quickly and so violently that it leaves nothing behind, and the rest of the sap around the tentacle crashes into it from every side, twisting and damaging it. Then it starts to bubble, the sick smell of rotten syrup bursting out of the sea as the tentacle begins to boil.

Whatever the massive limb is attached to seems more enraged than injured, so yet another tentacle emerges from outside my field of view and tries to wrap around the ship. The metal twists and grows sharp, curved hooks like fangs emerging from the hull and chomping down before the beast can drag us into the depths.

Holy cannoli, what the heck are we fighting!? This thing is huge! I mean, I guess I probably should have expected it would be huge, since they called it a leviathan, but still! Is it a big squid or something? No, wait, that doesn't feel right at all. They called it a branch serpent, which is kind of weird because I would assume that your average serpent that lives on branches would not be aquatic. I'm pretty sure most branches aren't supposed to be aquatic. The tentacles don't have suckers or anything like that, they look more like giant eel tails. They have skeletons in them! Entire spines! I'm pretty sure tentacles don't have those.

Yet as more and more of the creature approaches us, I continue finding myself expecting a main body to be on the other end of its grasping limbs, but I only end up seeing more and more of the same. Tendrils on tendrils on tendrils, swirling and snaking and grasping for our boat with the intent to crush it like a soda can.

Kagiso uses Velocity to launch huge, summoned chunks of metal at whatever parts of the monster are currently surfaced, ripping gouges through its flesh. Altogether crewmates burn and tear and rip and cut, barely fending off strike after strike, and all the while I'm stuck here, waiting in a backpack. Helpless. Useless. All of my spells are too short-ranged, and even if I did somehow get close enough to use Spacial Rend, the best I could do is cut maybe a foot into the monster's flesh, which doesn't seem all that helpful against a beast with countless limbs each thicker than tree trunks. What should I do? Is there anything I can do?

"A bunch of sap is splashing up onto the boat," Helen says under her breath. "Come on, we're going to clean it. We can at least make this place a little less sticky during the fight."

"Is that all?" I hiss back. "Can't you just blast it to dust?"

"Maybe?" Helen hedges. "But only if you want to turn everybody on the boat against us. No point in killing the monster if it just means they'll kick us off to drown."

Dang it, that's right. Everyone will probably turn against us if they find out Helen is a Chaos mage. Best case scenario then would be to... what, threaten everyone into submission and make them continue taking us to our destination?

A crash rocks the side of the boat and I force myself to focus on the fight. More and more tendrils, or tails, or whatever-they-are are popping up all around us, and for every one we destroy, two more seem to emerge from the depths. Deep below us, at the edge of my sensory range, I'm starting to see where they connect, but I still can't find the body. It seems like each tentacle is simply attached to another tentacle, butting off of one another at pseudo-random intervals, almost like... a branch.

Branch serpent. Of course. The serpent is *shaped* like a branch, with forks and splits and a countless number of redundant tails. We are never going to defeat it at this rate, not because we aren't making progress but just because the monster is so ridiculously big, all we're doing is stubbing its toes. You'd think after stubbing so many of its toes it would eventually just leave though, right? How territorial is this thing?

Kagiso is doing serious damage by teaming up with a Matter mage for oversized ammunition. The captain of the ship is also pretty terrifying, using what looks like Space and Motion magic to teleport us out of harm's way and counter with devastating vacuums. The whole crew is contributing, but I have absolutely no idea whether or not we're winning.

Helen scurries around the deck, making her way closer to Kagiso as we avoid disgusting and potentially dangerous splashes of rancid sap. Kagiso seems like she's struggling with something, and as we approach I hear her mutter something to herself.

"Mama? Papa? Teboho?" she asks the air. "Is it okay now?"

"Kagiso?" Helen asks, the battle raging around us.

"Am allowed now, do you think?" Kagiso mutters.

"Kagiso, are you okay?" Helen presses. "What are you talking about?"

"Have better spell for this," Kagiso answers quietly.

"Then you should use it!?"

"Not supposed to."

"Why the fuck not? Is it going to backfire on us or something?"

Kagiso shrugs, her short white fur blowing every which way in the wind. Drawing back another arrow, she mutters "**Velocity**" and launches it at the impromptu scrap cannonball that materializes in front of her shortly afterwards.

"No. Is safe. Mostly. Just not supposed to use it. Family said so."

Helen freezes up when Kagiso mentions her family, and I grit my teeth into a spidery grimace. Helen definitely isn't going to argue any further now, but if Kagiso has a spell we don't know about that can turn the tides, we need her to use it.

"Why did your family tell you not to use it?" I ask as quietly as I can while still expecting to get heard over the din of battle. I don't know if the nearby Matter mage hears me, but if he does he doesn't seem to react.

"Don't know," Kagiso grunts. "Was always two kinds of spell. Spells that okay to use, and spells that I like."

"You weren't allowed to use your favorite spells?" I press. "That doesn't sound good at all."

"I've never heard about this," Helen scowls.

"Was just the rules," Kagiso says. "Not sure why they were there. Not sure if they okay to break. Not sure if Teboho let me."

I hesitate. What kind of spells would Kagiso's family not want her to use? I think I might actually have a pretty good idea, and all my ideas are scary. But still. They're *hers*. For some reason, I really, *really* don't like the idea of anyone telling her what she can and cannot do with them.

"Kagiso," I say firmly. "If you want to use your magic, and you think it will help, please do it. Whatever it is, I trust you."

Kagiso nods slowly.

"**Velocity**," she says again, using an arrow to launch yet another ball of scrap. It rockets off towards one of the tendrils bearing down on the deck, ripping an enormous hole through its side. Then, Kagiso puts away her bow. She lifts both arms, and she takes a deep breath.

She grins.

"**I Want To Play With Your Organs**," the Goddess cackles, and viscera rips itself from the wound.

Uh. Yep. That seems about right.

The tendril falls limp as a torrent of gore pours out of it, tearing the wound open deeper as the muscles and tendons, still dripping with blood, free themselves from the skin and bone to start attacking the rest of their former body. Kagiso cackles wildly, her arms swishing up and down through the air to direct her dripping, stringy playthings like a conductor. When another tendril branch tries to slam down on the ship, Kagiso catches it, tendons wrapping around it like ropes as muscle fibers dig into the other wounds and scratches, ripping them open to give Kagiso more material to work with.

"Deeper!" Kagiso crows. "Haven't even gotten to the squishy ones!"

The Matter mage that had been helping her backs away nervously, catching on to the fact that his services are no longer needed. Kagiso yanks on the great Leviathan, accomplishing little at first but slowly, ever so slowly, starting to pull it towards the surface.

The rest of the battle hasn't paused in the meantime, with nearly a dozen tentacles still flailing seriously at the ship. Countless spells fly, the whole battlefield turning into a horrifying torrent of every type of magic together. And the more damage we deal to the monster, the more viscera starts flying to Kagiso's will. How much can she control at once!? Kagiso herself seems enraptured to the point of possibly not even being lucid anymore, an unblinking, wide-eyed stare consuming her face, the only motion being little twitches in her eyes as she drinks in the macabre sight.

"That's it, men!" the captain roars. "We've got her on the ropes now! **Vacuum Crash!**"

"Shit," Helen curses. "We're too slow."

"What do you mean?" I ask.

A deafening roar drowns out her answer, the branch serpent's head finally emerging to join the battle. Immediately, the wild strikes it had been sending our way become a lot more coordinated, and the threat of the massive jaws—large enough to bite our ship in half—quickly reverses the uptick in morale. At least, it does for everybody other than Kagiso, who somehow grins even wider even as a massive gathering of energy around the leviathan's mouth indicates it's starting to cast a spell of its own. Every bit of weaponized gore flies towards the monster's mouth at once, aiming to tear open its throat from the inside.

"Fun bits are here!" Kagiso announces gleefully. "Squishy bits! Mine! All—"

"Soulseeker Flame!"

An unidentifiable heat, invisible to my spatial sense, streaks past Helen and me and hits Kagiso in the side, causing her to shriek in pain. I see the fur around where she's hit burn away almost immediately, and I can't help but pop part of my body out of Helen's backpack in order to get an eye on what's going on. Another ball of ghostly purple flame flies past me as I do, hitting Kagiso in the chest. She catches fire, screaming and squeezing her eyes shut, her spell deactivating as she collapses to the floor, clawing at the flames to try and put them out.

"Refresh!" I shout, pulling the oxygen away from Kagiso for just the split second needed to extinguish her. Yet another ball of purple fire is flying towards us, though, so I prepare to leap into its path to shield Kagiso with my body, but the sea monster makes another swipe at our ship and the captain's protective teleportation spell activates, leaving me completely disoriented as we suddenly end up somewhere else.

"Combined Cannonade!"

Before I can orient myself, an explosion rings out behind us, and I finally realize how close the pirate ship has become. I don't have time to marvel at how much larger than our boat it is, however, because an enormous, magical cannon shell rips clean through our boat a moment later, tearing a giant hole through both us and the leviathan's head in one shot.

Then I realize the magical purple fire is still flying through the air, and somehow it has swerved at a sharp angle to follow us after the teleportation. It's on the far side of Kagiso now! I stumble, trying to protect her, but I got too distracted by the cannon shot!

I watch in slow motion as the flame descends on Kagiso's prone body, already ravaged by the prior attacks. But then, Sela's arm tears out of the backpack and swats the flame aside, its body ripping through the fabric as it unfolds, crouching protectively over Kagiso with one working leg.

"**Graveyard Soul**," the Goddess says, copying Sela's monotone intonation, and a cold stillness settles over the two of them. Another ball of fire flies overhead, but it doesn't swerve to home in on Kagiso this time. Did... Did Sela save her!? Well! Gosh! Okay! Go Sela!

"Pneuma tracking disrupted," Sela announces. "Target has been stabilized. Requesting counterattack."

"I can't," Helen scowls, glaring up at the pirate ship.

"Now really doesn't seem like a great time to worry about what happens afterwards!" I snap at her. "We need to be able to survive this right now!"

"My ranged attack spells aren't exactly discriminatory," Helen answers calmly, her arms crossed. "If I tried to kill anyone on the ship from here, we would just have zero seaworthy boats stranded in the ocean instead of one seaworthy boat crawling with pirates. Not a good trade."

I stiffen, taking a moment to glance around the inside of the ship and realizing how screwed we are right now. There's a hole in the lower decks nearly fifteen feet across. It's a miracle the ship is in one piece at all, and we are taking on sap so fast that we definitely won't be floating much longer.

"Ho, there!" a booming voice rings out from the pirate ship. "Sincere apologies! We weren't expecting you to teleport in front of our shot like that. Bardrick, keep them afloat!"

"**Deny The Depths**," one of the unexpectedly helpful pirates casts, our ship shuddering as its slow descent halts. The pirate ship itself slowly approaches us, nearly twice our boat's size in every direction, and soon enough it is close enough that we can make out a figure standing on the edge of the deck and looking down on us. Quite a few pirates peer down, dressed in simple, if dirty clothing, but one in particular clearly stands above the others. At least if the size of his hat is anything to go by.

"Hide," Helen hisses quietly at me. "Hide and stay hidden. Don't let them see you, no matter what."

246

I don't hesitate and just obey her, scooting back down into the backpack. These jerks hurt Kagiso. They're bad news.

"Sela, act like you're dead," Helen orders, and the robot glowers at her with naked fury. Nonetheless, it obeys, very slowly collapsing on top of Kagiso's back. Kagiso herself is unconscious, but I can see that her heart is beating and her lungs are breathing. She's in bad shape, but she's not dying, at least.

Helen kneels down and pries Sela off of Kagiso, hooking the former to the top of her backpack and lifting the latter up in her arms. The pirates continue addressing us as a door in the middle of their ship opens up, a gangplank extending over to our deck.

"Come on aboard!" the fancy-hatted pirate calls. "One at a time, there's no rush! Your lives and your cargo are all safe, don't you worry about a thing!"

Our ship's captain swears under his breath, the crew all looking at each other helplessly. With a frustrated sigh, the Matter mage that was helping Kagiso starts walking up the gangplank to the pirate ship. At the other end waits a chubby-looking man with a foul grin. I focus my still-active Aura Sight on him and immediately get angry. Heat and Pneuma.

"That's a good lad, one at a time," the fat Pneuma mage encourages. "You'll be nice and safe here. Of course, we need a little insurance that you lot aren't the dangerous type. You understand."

The Matter mage sighs and nods.

"Good!" the fat man grins, placing his hand on the Matter mage's chest. "**Rebellion's Lament**."

I feel the Goddess coil around him, but I can only guess as to what the spell does. Helen's eyes narrow.

"What are your naturalborn elements?" the fat man asks. "What does your magic do?"

"Pure Matter. Raw material generation, metal focus. I fix the ship."

"Good, good. Next!"

Helen does nothing, letting a couple other crewmates head onto the boat first. Each time, the mind mage casts that spell on them and then asks those two questions. The captain ends up walking over to the other ship before most of his crew, which surprises and mildly offends me for some reason. Aren't captains supposed to go down with their ship? Or at least like, let their crew off first? I mean, I guess that's just a random stupid cultural thing from my world so I guess it probably doesn't translate to other cultures...

"What are your naturalborn elements? What does your magic do?"

"Space and Motion," the captain reports. "I... help propel and protect my ship."

"That's right, we saw," the mind mage says thoughtfully, continuing the conversation rather than just sending the man on for the first time. "It looks like... automatic teleportation in response to threats, yes?"

"...That's right."

Oh. Oh, I get it! They were scouting out our spells! That's why they drove us into the monster, not because they couldn't overtake us but because they needed to know what we were capable of before they committed to attack. Because everyone in the world has magic! Everyone in the world can potentially be a terrifying threat, so it's not safe to attack people if you don't know what sort of bullpoop they can crap out of their butts whenever the going gets rough. Pirates can't just attack random boats, because they have absolutely no way of knowing whether some random guy on board is capable of blowing up a town until after the fight starts. To get around that, they needed to force us to show off what we can do.

"That's a mighty impressive ability, sir," the Pneuma mage declares. "Why, I think any sailor would be jealous to have it. You wouldn't be capable of casting a spell like that on our ship, would you? Just while we have you on board."

248

The captain goes silent for just a short moment, glancing around at the giant vessel.

"No, unfortunately I don't believe I could," the captain answers hesitantly. "Your ship is quite a bit heavier than—"

The captain explodes. A hot bloom of force erupts from his chest and sprays his body in every direction. In less than a blink, he is dead.

The pirate Pneuma mage—Pneuma and Heat mage—brushes bits of charred corpse off the front of his jacket.

"Now that's a damn shame," he announces, projecting his voice so that everyone can hear him. "Here we are, just trying to be friendly and help out people in need, and you just have to go and lie to us. I suggest the rest of you think twice before you do the same. My spell doesn't hurt anyone as long as they stay kind and civil. But if you plot against us, if you try to hurt us, if you lie to us... you will die. All you have to do is exactly what you're told. Something you should be doing anyway as thanks for rescue! Start making too many plans for anything else, though..."

He trails off, allowing the demonstration to speak for him.

"Now come on up. One at a time. Or would you rather drown?"

Rather understandably, no one seems all that inclined to move. At least not until Helen sighs and steps forward, calling up at the pirate.

"My friend can't walk for herself! She's unconscious! Is it alright if I carry her up to you?"

The fat, murderous bastard smiles.

"Of course, thank you for having the presence of mind to ask!"

Helen nods stiffly, carrying all three of us up the gangplank with her.

"Now what is all this you have here? **Rebellion's Lament**. **Rebellion's Lament**."

He casts his spell on both Helen and Kagiso. Helen just rolls her shoulder slightly and tilts her head backwards to indicate Sela.

249

"Steel One," Helen answers. "I hear they're worth a fortune."

Okay! Technically none of that is a lie. Good job, Helen!

"That they are," the pirate agrees with slimy amicability. "What are your naturalborn elements? What does your magic do?"

"Art and Order," Helen declares confidently. "I've got really good cleaning magic, and I can make carvings of people that make them stronger."

Holy crap what!? Why did she... oh no, oh no, oh no! That's a complete lie! She's going to explode! The pirate grins at her, but she just stares blankly back.

"Ah, I see," he nods. "That sounds handy. You wouldn't mind cleaning up around here while we have you, would you?"

"No problem," Helen nods, and even through my panic I recognize that as my cue to cast a silent Refresh, clearing all the gunk out of the doorway and off the pirate's clothes and tossing it into the sea. To my utter disgust, he looks delighted.

"Wonderful! Wonderful. And what about your friend here?"

"She's pure Motion," Helen says. "She can transfer momentum to stuff. And I guess she really likes blood and guts, so she can move that around? I'm honestly not super clear on it, but I promise she'll behave. I just want her to live."

"Of course, of course!" the pirate smiles. "I'm sure she'll be fine. Welcome aboard."

How? How, how, how? What the heck!? How did we survive that?

"Hard part's coming up, Hannah," Helen whispers. "You'd better not get caught."

Wait, there's more!?

"Over here!" a woman with like eighty billion piercings and Art/Transmutation magic shouts at us. Holy crap, she has more rings than she does skin. "Dump your bags, kid. Show us what you got."

Ah. Yeah, we're screwed. What the heck do I do here? Helen calmly kneels down and puts Kagiso on the ground, then Sela, and then finally takes her backpack off. With me still inside it, of course! Aaaaaah!

Come on Hannah, think. Think! How can you get out of this? Helen probably expects you to just step into a barren zone and do your little disappearing act, but she doesn't know that you can't do that right now. I'm in the middle of the Sapsea, the closest fourth dimensional piece of wood for me to actually walk on is probably miles below us! If I shift into the fourth dimension, I will fall through the fourth dimension and then die. So how am I supposed to hide!? I'm nowhere near small enough to get lost in this backpack, all it would take is for someone to pull the one piece of clothing between me and the top off of my head and I'll be in plain view. I have to step out of sight, but I can't because if I lose my footing I'll...

Wait. Footing. Oh my Goddess, I'm so stupid!

Hooking my legs into the fabric of the backpack itself, I carefully, very carefully, push my body in that impossible direction. Not all at once. If I shift all at once, I will die. But if I don't shift enough, everyone might die! I can't get caught here. So I twist, I move myself just a little bit at a time, quickly and carefully, until the cold chill of 4D space covers every part of my body except my claws.

The backpack opens. The pirate rummages through it, taking everything out and laying it on the ground. But she doesn't find me, because there's not enough of me there to be found. I am literally hanging by the tips of my toes over an impossible abyss, though, so I really hope nobody shakes the backpack or something like that.

The pirate lifts up and shakes the backpack, and I very heroically do not scream.

"Huh, nothing much of value besides that Steel One frame," the pierced pirate woman grunts. "How about we take that right down to the cargo hold, just for safekeeping."

"Of course," Helen says, sounding worried.

"Good girl," the pirate sneers, ruffling Helen's hair. "And since you can clean shit, clean everything on our way there."

"Yes ma'am."

As soon as the backpack closes again, I pull myself back inside it and start cleaning. Cleaning, at least, I can do. It helps me calm down a little, slows my rapidly beating heart and makes my breaths a little quieter. So... status report, me. We are on a pirate ship full of creeps, Helen and Kagiso have a spell that will blow them up if they resist, Sela is somehow successfully playing dead with its death magic but is still unable to walk on its own, and then there is me, a terrified idiot with no idea what the hell is going on or what I'm supposed to do about it.

I'm going to guess it probably involves killing people. I really don't want to kill people.

Helen follows the pirate around for a while, dropping Kagiso into a ratty shared bedroom and Sela in the cargo bay with other valuable plunder before being led around the ship and told what to clean. We spend hours like that, being ruthlessly overworked without even a chance to rest after fighting the leviathan to the death. It's not like we can complain, though, what with bombs strapped to almost everyone. It's only once Helen looks like she's about to collapse that we get ordered back to where Kagiso is sleeping and shoved into the room with her. Oh, hey. This 'bedroom' locks from the outside. Would you look at that.

Wait. Why is Helen exhausted? She hasn't actually done anything other than walk around. She didn't even fight!

"Okay," Helen whispers. "I think we can do this."

"Wait, back up," I hiss back. "You think we can do what? And how did you avoid exploding back there!? You lied right to his face!"

Helen sighs, running her fingers through her hair. She grabs a few strands and gives them a weird look.

"I'm still not used to how clean this is," she mutters, "but it made selling the story pretty easy."

"What does that have to do with anything?" I ask. "That guy was Heat and Pneuma! His spell read your intents and blows you up, he literally explained that right to our faces!"

"Well it's your fault for believing him," Helen shrugs. "Come on, Hannah. It's the oldest trick in the book. A spell's name has to accurately describe what it does, but there's nothing stopping you from saying a spell's name and then immediately gaslighting everybody about its effects."

"The spell is just called Rebellion's Lament! How are you supposed to know it isn't a lie detector from a name that simple?"

"Well, it's not really because of the name," Helen shrugs. "It's because of how he used it. They targeted the captain of the ship, and called him a liar on something that nobody—neither their crew nor ours—could know for sure if he was telling the truth on. It's too convenient. They didn't challenge people on vague answers, they didn't care about getting detailed information on our spells, so none of those questions were really designed to get relevant information. They already had information on our spells because they saw us use them to fight. That means it's all show. That whole thing was just set up to scare us and keep us in line."

"Wait, so are you saying that you aren't going to explode if we fight our way out?"

"Uh, well, no. They're certainly confident that Rebellion's Lament is enough to keep us in line, and at minimum it still works as a fucking bomb collar. It is probably at least very similar to how he described it: it will blow us up if we rebel. It's hard to know if that means just plotting against them like he said, but I haven't exploded so either my partial Pneuma resistance makes it harder for his spell to know what I'm thinking, or his spell just activates if we physically attack someone. I definitely don't want to find out."

"But they don't know I exist," I say numbly, shivering slightly. "So I can go assassinate the Pneuma mage and free everyone at once."

"Actually, I think we need to kill a lot of people before we go for the bomb collar guy. If we just free everybody and they start a riot, we risk ending up with nobody left alive who actually knows how to sail this boat. Not to mention that the pirates dramatically outnumber us and they are professional slavers with access to a lot of dangerous magic. We can't just chop off one head of a hydra and expect things to work out. Give me some time to prepare, though, and I think we can pull this off."

I watch Helen's distant gaze, her eyes glancing around at nothing as she bites her thumb, deep in thought. Slowly, one side of her mouth twitches up into a smile. Something about it makes me shudder.

"...You really think we can kill all the pirates without getting caught?" I ask carefully. She hasn't mentioned killing them all or not getting caught or anything like that, but the way she's smiling like that...

"Oh, sure," she shrugs. "This doesn't look like a particularly detailed operation. It would be easy if I could just kill them myself, but you should do okay."

...Yeah. Oh, Goddess.

"You sound like you've done this before," I say slowly.

Her smile drops at that, falling back into her usual scowl.

"...A lot of Chaos hunters have come after me, you know," she says. "Your Sindri was far from the first. I went way easy on you guys, you know. And someone still died."

Helen hugs herself a little.

"Anyway, I've obviously survived every time someone has tried to kill me. So yeah, I have a bit of experience here. And in a situation like this, information is king. That's why I didn't fight the monster. That's why I kept you hidden. I figured something like this was going to happen from the start, and your cards are never stronger than when people don't even know you have them. Everybody comes to fight a Chaos mage expecting raw, unbridled destruction. Nobody expects the subtle stuff to be the real danger until it's too late."

She goes quiet for a moment, sitting down on the bed next to Kagiso and hugging her knees.

"...Besides, these guys are murderers and slavers. So it's actually kind of nice."

"Um. Nice?" I squeak.

Helen laughs.

"I was always kind of jealous of the Chaos hunters, you know?" she admits. "Getting to kill people and not having to feel guilty about it? That sounds amazing."

13

VIOLENT DELIGHTS

I stare at Helen as she stares at the ceiling, presumably consumed by murderous whimsy.

Uh. Hmm. Okay! That was a really concerning thing for a person to say. Am I letting that one slide? No, I need to trust this woman to watch me while I sleep, I'm not letting that one slide. Crap, okay, what would Ida say in this situation?

"Can we, um, maybe unpack that real fast?" I ask, quietly clearing my throat.

"What?" Helen asks.

"You know, that was just, uh. Should I be worried?"

"Should you be... oh fuck, Hannah, no! I didn't mean it like that!"

"You just said it would sound amazing to kill people and not feel guilty about it," I press. "Regardless of how you meant it, I feel like we should have a conversation about it."

"What the fuck is a conversation going to do?" Helen growls. "Look, I just mean like... the people after me are always so Goddess-damn excited to see me bleeding out in the dirt, you know? My death is not something to mourn, it's something to be excited about. Something everybody can clap each other on the fucking back after they get it over with. But I don't get that. When I defend myself, I'm the monster. It's exhausting, that's all."

"So you're not going to feel bad this time?" I ask.

"Why should I? We watched these guys explode a dude because he didn't want to spend the rest of his life casting magic on their boat. They murder and enslave people for fun and profit. Let's fuck 'em up and be the heroes for once."

"For someone who seems to resent heroes so much, you sure do want to be one."

"It's called envy, you skittery bitch," Helen smirks. "I hate a lot of people that I would rather be. Why are you making such a big deal out of this? Getting cold feet?"

"I mean, I don't want to kill anybody if that's what you're asking," I mumble. "I know they probably deserve it, but…"

But there are a million buts. What if the bad people here are only a small subset? What if the bad people here aren't even as bad as we think? What if there's more going on than just the monsters we see on the surface? What if us killing these people isn't any different from all the people who want to kill me?

I admit it seems unlikely—as Helen pointed out, we literally watched these people murder a man in cold blood for a trivial reason and then use us as slaves for hours—but my instinctive panic and revulsion at the idea of taking a life doesn't really care about that logic. Especially since Helen's plan likely involves me killing a pretty significant chunk of the crew, not just whoever we've personally witnessed doing bad things.

"Oh," Helen frowns. "Yeah, that's a problem. I could maybe get Sela to do the killings, but that thing is way more conspicuous than you are. I'd have to lug it around… yeah, there's no way. It would put way too much pressure on us, we would get noticed long before we got into a good situation. Are you sure you can't do this? You've killed before, right?"

"Yeah, while under the influence of a Pneuma mage trying to train me to assassinate you," I answer. I don't actually have any idea how much of the killing I've already done was Sindri influencing me, but the last thing I want to do is find out.

"Okay, fuck. So you might hesitate or vomit or something. Shit, I really don't want to suggest this, but... there is something I can do that might help."

I mean, I actively don't want help overcoming my aversion to killing people, but now I'm worried so I ask.

"What is it? You don't have any Pneuma spells, do you?"

"I mean, I have Aura Sight. But no, I'm an Art mage, remember? Art magic can influence your emotions. Nowhere near to the same extent as Pneuma, but I can do it."

Oh soggy bagels, *why is it always mind control!?*

"...I want you to promise me that you will never, ever do that to me under any circumstances," I hiss quietly.

Helen's eyebrows raise.

"Whoa, okay. It was just an offer," she says, raising her hands in surrender. "We're on the same side, so there's no way I'll do that to you without your permission, okay? Just to explain though, the intersection of Art and Chaos manifests to me as the scrambling or destruction of emotion. My works of art have the ability to functionally remove certain feelings from people. It's completely temporary and has no other compulsion; it just messes with your current emotional state. And if I scramble *all* of someone's emotions, they pretty much just stand around stunned, so that's pretty useful. But what I'm planning on using it for today is pretty simple: while you ideally go around making messes out of people, I'm going to remove our captors' suspicion and worry over where their buddies have gone."

Woah.

"That sounds absolutely crazy," I say. "In like, a good way."

"It's weaker than you probably think. People can still logic their way to realizing that we're up to something, they just won't have the emotional push that would normally spark someone to start thinking about that in the first place. It helps, and it buys us time, but we still have to be subtle."

"What else can you destroy? Can you just like... remove their ability to want us to be captives?"

Helen wiggles her hand in a so-so gesture.

"Not really? Again, it doesn't change any of your established thought patterns, only your current emotions. And I can't give people a desire to want to free us, I can only remove things. If someone on the crew was already secretly wishing that they could help the captives I could, say, remove their fear of consequences and that might push them to help us? But I haven't seen anyone like that. For most of these people, I suspect they take their status as slaveowners for granted, so removing their desire to own us wouldn't change what they see as the status quo. It would just kind of make them not care and that wouldn't be noticeably different from how they already are."

Ugh, that's so disgusting to think about. I suppose if nothing else, Helen is making an increasingly good argument for killing these people. ...Is she doing it on purpose?

"...Are you sure you can even cast spells like this without exploding?" I ask. Not to change the subject, just... you know. That feels like a very real threat with the Pneuma-activated bomb collar attached to my friends.

"I should be able to," Helen nods. "Rebellion's Lament isn't picking up on this planning session, and I've already confirmed it doesn't pick up on spellcasting. So as long as I don't directly attempt to hurt anyone, I can't think of anything else liable to trigger it bar manual activation."

"And temporarily destroying someone's emotions doesn't count as hurting them?" I press.

"Well, technically, I'm just crafting a beautiful work of art. Emotional destruction only occurs as a byproduct of someone choosing to look at that work of art, which I'm sure you agree is entirely out of my control," Helen answers with a grin.

I sigh.

"You're absolutely crazy. How many times have you risked dying in a horrible explosion while figuring this stuff out?" I ask.

She waves me off.

"Chill out, Hannah. I know what I'm doing. The question is whether or not you can handle what we have to do next. When night falls, we're only going to have a short window to kill all the most dangerous people on the boat."

"Besides us, you mean," I mutter, shifting the weight on my legs to nestle further into the blankets of the bed.

"Besides us," she agrees, flashing another grin.

I'm not really sure what to say. Just thinking about this makes my stomach roil with both disgust and hunger. I haven't gotten anything to eat since we woke up this morning, and that horrible, bestial part of me won't shut up as a result. I still don't want to do it. I don't have a better plan, I don't have a good excuse, and I don't even have a good reason to believe that these people deserve to live.

Except... wait, I gotta back up on that thought. That just starts up a whole host of questions. What does it mean to 'deserve to live?' Who gets to decide that? I certainly feel like I shouldn't be allowed to decide that, I can barely make decisions on what to eat for breakfast. A lot of people would say that killing is never justified, except maybe in self-defense. But what counts as self-defense in a situation where we are getting oppressed and abused and enslaved? I mean, it's not like they've done anything super bad to Helen or me, nobody has beaten us or even yelled at us that much, but I guess having a bomb collar strapped around her neck is pretty good at making us compliant.

And like, that's obviously inhumane, right? Pretty sure it's a war crime or something. But do conventions for war established on Earth apply to people from another world? Wait, what am I saying, they obviously don't apply legally but that's not what's important here, what's important here is that basic human rights are being violated. Uh, and dentron rights I guess. And... my rights. Whatever they are. But what are rights!?

Gah, okay, this is getting really stupid, brain. 'What are rights?' Crap in a hot dog bun, I am *overthinking this*. Come on Hannah, detach yourself from the situation and look at it abstractly. If you heard a story about *someone else* who got kidnapped by pirates and their friends got strapped with bombs and you heard that they went on a little nighttime tryst to assassinate all those pirates in their beds and save all the people with bombs on them, would you think of that person as justified or unjustified? Justified! Obviously! Especially if we have no practical way to free all these people without killing them, and I definitely can't think of one.

A person who straps deadly explosives to other people and forces those people to work for them is in the 'morally okay to kill' category, *especially* at the hands of their own victims. Right? Right. So it's fine. Let's do this. Helen needs my help to save Kagiso and everybody else that just got captured. I should do this. It is okay to do this. I *have* to do this if I want to help these people. The world sucks and when evil escalates hard enough it's not sufficient to be a comic book hero that never kills. There is a line where the sanctity of someone's life becomes less important than the health and well-being of the people they are hurting. How can I look at the situation around me and believe otherwise? It's the right thing to do. I know it is. I need to do it.

"...I don't know if I can do this, Helen," I whisper miserably.

I shudder, my memories of the lives I've already taken clawing at the back of my mind. It feels like it should be easy. Like I should just be able to make my choice with logic and will my body to obey. But the thought of it is just horrific. Revolting. I'm shaking just thinking about it. I don't know if I can hold myself together long enough to do what needs to be done.

I'm not a fighter. I'm a wimpy, self-absorbed upper-middle-class kid from the Bible Belt. I can and have attacked people in self-defense, but this isn't a brawl. It's not a desperate fight for survival. Helen is asking me to assassinate people in cold blood,

262

to just murder them without them even knowing what's going on. To strike from a position of perfect safety and take a life with none the wiser. And I just... I'll falter. I won't be able to do that.

I'm not good enough. I know that. But what scares me this time is that despite all my justifications, I still don't know if I'm not good enough because I can't kill these people, or if I'm not good enough *because I wish I could.*

Helen sighs, sitting on the floor and leaning her back against the bed so her head is next to me.

"...Fine," she says. "That's okay. It's not like we have to do this tonight. I'll figure out another plan tomorrow. Wake me if you change your mind, though, okay?"

She closes her eyes, letting out a long breath and clearly trying to get some rest. I remain where I am on the foot of the bed, tempted to snuggle up to Kagiso but not wanting to touch her and aggravate her wounds. Plus, I doubt I'm going to be getting any sleep right now anyway. I'm... currently a bit of a mess.

Idly, I focus on the rooms—well, fancy cells, mostly—around us. Naturally, the hallway is guarded, so even if we bypassed the lock (which, I mean, would be pretty easy) we'd still have to contend with the guard. My Aura Sight has worn off since the battle, though, so I don't know what kind of magic the guard is capable of. I still have no idea how long that dang spell lasts, since I didn't even notice it shutting off. Whatever. It's not important.

The rooms next to us are important. I'm not going to act like I was fond of anyone on our boat, especially since our strategy involved not letting them know I existed in the first place, but a lot of them seem to have made it out of the battle a lot worse for the wear than Helen and I. They were still given work for the day. Is that really a good reason to murder all these people? Because they force us to work? Is that *enough?* Why do I keep asking myself this, over and over, after I already decided on my answer? Yes, obviously, slaves should kill their owners. So why am I such a Goddess-damned coward?

With a chuckle and a lick of Her lips, Her presence descends around me, as if to say 'you rang?' I shudder, and She caresses my carapace, apologizing for not paying much attention to me during the battle prior. A lot of much more interesting things were happening, that's all. For an instant, I want to apologize for not being interesting enough, but I clamp down on the instinct with fervor. She laughs at me anyway.

Why are You here, Goddess? I mean, I guess that's a stupid question since You're everywhere, all the time. But why are You making Yourself *known?* You know my swear was the furthest thing from an intentional summoning, and You don't normally do social calls.

That too is a stupid question, and I feel foolish for asking it. If I am to be Her prophet, should I not receive Her revelations, from time to time? I start to panic, but She quickly reassures me that I don't need to worry about Her popping in like this to ensoul people on Earth—that would be cheating, and any spread of Her divine power will remain in the hands of those who already use it. But here, on Her beautiful tree? She sees no harm in the occasional visit. Nudging me ever so gently, just to show She cares...

The Goddess snaps her fingers in the room two floors above us, so I glance up with my spatial sense just in time to spot the pirate woman who ordered Helen around earlier today dragging one of the crewmates from our ship onto a chair and tying him down. He looks absolutely terrified, and the woman yells at him inaudibly for a bit before punching him in the face.

Oh. She's torturing him. The Goddess nods, gently lounging on top of me with her supercilious presence. There is indeed torture going on, the Goddess agrees. She wonders idly about the very problems I was wondering, just moments ago. Exactly how many war crimes am I going to sit around and watch before I finally let myself loose?

Does She have to reveal exactly how foul the so-called 'rich inner worlds' of these people are before I'll agree they should be snuffed out? Does She have to tell me exactly how likely my friends are to be raped in the next few days? Where exactly is the line at which my oh-so-deeply-moral musings are actually just dull excuses to continue doing nothing?

I flinch as I watch the pirate break one of the man's fingers, taking it slowly enough for me to see the bone fracture, splinter, and finally snap. Why is she even doing this? What sort of interrogation do they need to perform, exactly?

Does it matter?

I... I should go. I should help him. I *need* to help him. This is... I mean, I'm fucked either way now, right? I'm either going to get messed up in the head about murdering people or I'm going to get messed up in the head about sitting here and watching while I let someone get tortured. I don't have a choice anymore. I... I have to go. Wait, is that the whole point of this divine visit? To just take away my opportunity to not kill these people?

The Goddess laughs. Don't be silly, free will exists! Pinky promise!

She vanishes. I want to scream, but I guess I don't have time for that anymore.

"H-Helen!" I yelp, shaking her with a leg. "Helen, I changed my mind!"

"Huh? What? Oh!" she exclaims, standing up as I scuttle over to the wall and start climbing it. "Wait, where are you going?"

"They're torturing somebody upstairs!" I hiss. "I have to go save him!"

"Whoa, wait!" Helen insists. "We have to kill the guard on this floor first, or I can't follow you!"

I'm panicking rather than listening, so I don't stop. I'm vaguely aware that we should stop, that I should follow Helen's plan, but the only thing pushing me to act hard enough to bypass my fears is this urgency, this need to correct the problem that I have allowed to happen. As I scuttle up the wall, I soon meet the ceiling, but I suppose I've learned how to solve this problem. Carefully, I phase all but my feet into the fourth dimension, then as I lift my leg towards the solid object I need to pass through, I phase that foot out as well, only taking hold partway through.

I reach inside the ceiling and stand on the middle. And I keep climbing, walking right through a solid object by just stepping entirely around it.

And so I run up two floors, finally making it to the room where the current, ongoing torture is taking place. But wait, what do I do? What do I do!? I can't climb up the air to reach any of her vital organs, so I guess I have to hamstring her, right? Bring her to the ground so that I can stab her in the heart or slit her throat or something. But that would give her plenty of time to scream, and then we would be found out, and then nobody would be saved! Because they can always just trigger the bomb collars manually, right? Oh crap, this is why Helen wanted me to wait!

The man screams as another one of his fingers is broken, and I wish I could cry but I drop back down, letting gravity carry me from one floor to the next and land on our bed next to Helen, bouncing once and waking Kagiso.

"Hmgh? What happening…?" Kagiso mutters, wincing.

"Helen, I'm sorry! We have to go, someone's getting really hurt—"

"Both of you shut up," Helen orders. "**And She Knew The Whole World Was Her Canvas**."

She reaches out and touches the bedpost, and with a sizzle it starts melting away, leaving behind the carving of a man screaming in agony, clawing at his own face as what's left of the bedpost impales him.

"Kagiso, just lie there and do nothing. You have a bomb on you that will explode if you try to hurt anyone."

"Kay," Kagiso mumbles, and rolls over to try and get more sleep.

"Hannah, just… focus on your target. Don't look at what I'm doing or we're fucked."

Target? What tar—

"**And She Would Devour Their Very Screams**," Helen intones, moments before the door to our room slams open and the guard outside shouts at us... but neither the door nor the guard make a single sound.

He jolts in shock, but then a wall of metal spikes appears in our doorway, blocking us in as the room itself twists to try and kill us, swords and spears twisting out of the ground and the walls with lethal intent. Adrenaline surges through me and I leap forward, passing through the blocked doorway effortlessly and catching the man's ankles with a Spacial Rend. He drops to one knee, so I jump on his back and stab him through the heart.

He collapses, my first kill of the night.

Helen's hand, wreathed in the crackling black energy of Chaos, punches through the corner of the summoned barricade and carves it out of the doorframe. She pulls it back into the room, annihilates it, and proceeds to destroy every last sign of the Matter mage's influence, carving away the twisted walls until they are once again pristine. Her movements are precise and practiced, and only moments later she exits the door, locks Kagiso inside, and obliterates the corpse as well.

"Could you get the bloodstains?" she asks me casually. "I would have to shave off a bit of the floor."

I'm not sure if I am terrified, impressed, or mad at her for not letting me eat my kill. I cast Refresh to hide the last of the evidence, and Helen picks me up to confidently stride towards the stairs. She holds me in one arm, and the carved bedpost she crafted in the other. The moment we make it up two flights of stairs, however, we spot another pirate in the hallway where the interrogation room is. Helen walks right towards him like she belongs here.

"Hey!" he shouts at us, but then glances at the bedpost and calms down a little. "...What's that for?"

"Captain asked for it," Helen shrugs. "Maybe it's for his ass?"

The pirate starts to laugh, and then the sound disappears and Helen throws me at his throat. I cut it in half. His body inaudibly collapses and his head rolls to the floor. What am I doing. What am I doing? Goddess, I'm so hungry. Helen destroys the corpse, I

267

disperse the blood, and Helen breaks the door to the interrogation room down.

No amount of suspicion-destroying magic seems to prevent the woman in the room from realizing she should be attacking us after the world goes silent and the door falls to the floor, so in moments her tattoos and piercings twist out from her body to impale us in a dozen different places. Helen drops me, holding her carving behind her back as small bursts of Chaos obliterate anything that might pierce her skin. I rush forwards, falling most of the way out of existence before I take her out the same way I took out the first man: cut the tendons in the leg so that I can reach the heart. She falls, blood pooling on the metal floor. The man strapped to a chair gapes at us, hope entering his eyes. Sound returns.

I don't pause for a moment. I'm too hungry to let Helen take this kill, too. I start to eat my prey.

"Start screaming again," Helen orders the torture victim. "We are absolutely still in danger of these bombs going off, and we need them to not realize anything is wrong, understand? **And She Knew The Whole World Was Her Canvas**."

She touches the outside of the door, and a horrific portrait of the torture victim writhing in pain, the woman we just killed beating him, carves itself around her hand. I mostly ignore it, busy burying myself in the dead woman's chest cavity. Lungs are so springy and delicious.

"Come on Hannah, we need to move," Helen insists. I ignore her. I'm eating.

"Hannah!" Helen snaps, approaching me and reaching her hand towards me. I hiss at her, loud and furious. She flinches.

"Hannah?" she presses a bit more cautiously. "Hannah, come on, pull yourself together."

I don't think you want me to pull myself together. I think that the moment I pull myself together I'm going to have a complete fucking breakdown and immediately become useless.

"Hannah," Helen continues, kneeling down next to me. "Come on. We've got more people to save. We can eat when the job is done."

Right. When the job is done. When everyone is safe. I have more food to hunt. With an agonizing pull of willpower, I drag myself out of my feeding frenzy and step away from the corpse. Helen destroys it. I Refresh the ground and myself, clean of evidence. Helen scoops me up in the crook of her arm again, and we leave the room, shutting the door behind us. The torture victim keeps screaming, and I suppose with so many broken bones he doesn't need to fake how in pain he sounds.

The Goddess coos with delight.

"Okay, I need your weird ability to look through walls, Hannah. Is the captain in his quarters?"

"Yeah," I confirm, surprised at how flat my voice is. "Asleep."

"And do you have eyes on the bomb collar guy?"

"Also asleep. He has a slightly bigger room near the captain's. Like a first mate or something."

"Okay! Great. I guess since we are doing this the fast and frantic way, those two are our next targets. I would have preferred that we take things a little slower and picked people off for most of the night, but we have a witness so therefore we have a time limit. Let's go kill the Pneuma mage."

Yes. Sure. Hopefully I'll feel a little less bad about this particular murder. I direct Helen to the room directly underneath his room, have her throw me straight up, and I latch onto the ceiling, climbing through it and then up the inside of the man's bed to stick a claw through the back of his skull and swish it around until his brain is a fine purée. I am taking absolutely no chances at letting this guy be conscious even for a second. So he's not. He dies in his sleep, a mercy that some twisted part of me is proud of giving him, despite my fear and hatred. But I know it was a pragmatic choice, not any sort of positive moral quality, so I make sure to shut that part of me up.

A quick Refresh pulls all of the blood out of his head and, more importantly, out of his pillow, so that anyone peeking in won't spot anything amiss unless they notice he isn't breathing. Then I crawl back down and drop into Helen's waiting arms.

"Fuck yeah, I felt the spell go away. I guess we'd better hurry up and kill the captain before all hell breaks loose."

"Why is all hell going to break loose?" I ask.

And then, all hell breaks loose. Shouts of triumph and calls to arms ring out throughout the ship as countless prisoners and slaves suddenly lose that ever-present feeling of death around their throats. This obviously alerts the living pirates, and in seconds spells start getting spoken from all over the ship. Our target, the captain, is out of his bed and onto the deck long before we can get into position.

"Well, dammit. The messy way it is," Helen grumbles, running towards the stairs. "We need to kill as many people as we can, as fast as we can, before the pirates kill all the sailors."

Is that really the only way? Is that even the best way? I don't know. I don't think I'm up to arguing it, though. Helen makes it to the deck, where a half-dozen pirates are bickering with each other, including the captain, who is shouting and trying to figure out what happened to his bomb guy. Helen tosses me to the ground, steps towards them, and gives them a simple answer.

"He's dead," she says. "Like you're all about to be."

She waves her carving in front of them, making sure it catches their eyes. The smart ones flinch, realizing that they need to look away, but it's a little too late.

"Is that fucking right?" the captain sneers. "Honey, you're about to be the next corpse in my bed."

"Wow! Didn't need to know that about you! Look buddy, I've been alive for twenty years and I only stopped fighting for one of them. I'm not going to be taken down by a bunch of two-bit morons trying to wave their dicks around because they literally can't understand that they should be afraid of me."

She tosses her sculpture at their feet, and they only glance at it for a moment. Because, I realize, they aren't suspecting a trap.

"Head down and protect the others, would you Hannah?" Helen asks. "Try to avoid letting anyone come upstairs."

"You gonna be okay?" I whisper.

"Oh, better than okay," Helen grins. "Today, I get to be a hero."

"Try to keep her tits intact, boys!" the captain roars. "**On His Vessel, He Is King**!"

"**Cloudflay!**"

"**Heartbreaker!**"

"**Spectral Laser!**"

Shouted spells ring out over the deck as I drop through the floor, Helen weaving calmly around weapons that head her way. Her own incantation is the longest, but I have a feeling that the battle is over the moment she completes it.

"**They Hunted And Hunted, But Not A One Could Catch Her**," the Goddess sings. "**For How Could They Touch Their Own Annihilation?**"

I watch Helen walk straight through spells like they were air. A sword swings for her neck, and the blade simply ceases to exist wherever it would touch her neck, the tip flying free as *it* cleaves in two instead of her. Helen grins, raises a hand, and casually passes her fingers through the attacker's face, leaving thick, bloody gouges behind wherever she touches, like a profoundly more horrific Spacial Rend. Rather than sever, she simply *removes*.

Chaos. The antithesis of all structure, all order, and all reason. The magic that only destroys.

Helen laughs and laughs and laughs.

As much as I would like to, I can't just fall a few stories to my destination. The thing about falling is that it tends to be in a straight line, and the thing about going in a straight line in w-space is that if you aren't traveling directly towards 'normal

271

space,' then odds are extremely likely you are traveling away from it. That means if I fling myself at an angle while not *in* real space, I end up without anything to land on. So I have to crawl through the floor, move my body back into normal space, drop from the ceiling to the next floor, then crawl through that floor, and so on.

It doesn't take that long, but it takes a lot longer than I would like when a battle is starting in a world where basically everyone always has a gun. I make it to the lower decks just in time to fall on a pirate's head, skewering it in the process and hanging onto his body with my toes as he collapses so I hide back in 4D space before any of his allies see me. I move as quickly and efficiently as I can, limbs flashing out to cut people down as I finally get to speak my own spells for use in combat.

"**Spacial Rend! Aura Sight!**"

The blades I extrude from my legs are now over a foot long, making it easy to simply chop off entire legs rather than worry about slashing through tendons. I look for targets of opportunity, moving between floors and focusing on Fire and Light mages wherever possible, as I notice attacks from Space mages often clip dangerously into my other-dimensional safe zones, whereas anyone with a nonphysical method of disrupting enemies can mess me up as well. But whenever people who are actually dangerous to me notice I'm around, I can simply leave or work as a distraction while the freed slaves supply their own offense.

With everyone working together and me assassinating dangerous targets, we push the pirates further and further down into the bowels of the ship, where they finally hole up in the cargo bay. The cargo bay has only one way in or out, a large door that the pirates barricade with crates and booby trap with spells. The furious rioting victims want to smash the door down and finish the pirates off once and for all, and I can hardly blame them, but I still have to reveal myself and shout at them so they don't kill themselves.

"Wait!" I yelp, hanging from the ceiling above the mob. "Hold on, it's way too well-defended in there. We should wait for..."

Oh, shoot, Helen's probably not coming, is she? She doesn't want to use her powers in front of anyone else.

"What the fuck are you?" one of the former slaves snaps at me.

"Good question, but not the time!" I say. "I've been the one chopping people's limbs off, I'm on your side here. I might be able to get in and kill some of the people who have been setting traps, but we should definitely not just rush through the barricade willy-nilly. Give me a second, okay?"

I spend that second trying to figure out what the heck I should do, with my heart beating out of my shell and my gut insisting I just drop on one of the nearby corpses and finally get a good meal. I ignore that urge and crawl around the outside of the ship, peeking my way into the cargo bay from the opposite end. Unsurprisingly, most of the surviving pirates are people that I was too scared to personally engage, meaning that the whole room is full of terrible matchups for me. So what do I do? How do I finish this rout?

Well. I guess the thing a good person would do is to try and negotiate. I'm not sure that would fly with either the pirates or the mob of ex-slaves though, and I'm not exactly an eloquent girl on a good day, let alone when I'm dissociating full-on into 'solve the problem' mode in order to not think about the massacre I just performed. How terrifyingly easy it was. How natural it felt. Human lives falling away without even the slightest bit of resistance against my claws. It... I...!

Hey! I said don't think about it, me. Focus on this cargo bay. Is there something in here I can... wait. Oh gosh! Sela is in here! I quickly scuttle inside, finding the crates that we rather unceremoniously left our murderbot sitting on top of.

"Sela!" I hiss as quietly as I can. "Sela, wake up! There are a bunch of super dangerous people in here!"

"Affirmative," Sela quietly thrums back. "I have detected this."

One of the pirates starts to speak an incantation that sounds like it's going to be pretty long. Which means it's going to be crazy powerful! Crap! We're out of time! This is a terrible idea, but I may as well ask.

"Look, I know you don't have any onboard weapon systems, but if there was ever a good time to kill a bunch of organics, it's now! All the pirates in this room are trying to kill us, and we need to stop them before they kill everybody who knows how to drive the boat!"

"Clarification: diplomatic priority target is specifically requesting that I kill everyone in this room?"

"Well, other than you and me, yeah. Can you do it?"

It lets out an indignant huff of steam.

"Can you breathe, you pathetic sack of meat? You will need to protect me while I cast."

"I don't think I can do that!"

Its body starts whirring with frustration, the cooling system running louder. We're fortunate that everyone else is making so much noise.

"...Excess of souls detected in the immediate area," Sela concludes. "Organic assistance no longer required. Tremble, mortals, for your god is made of steel."

"AblativeSoulBarrier(powerCell[0], 0, HEMISPHERE, 90, 0, 0)"

"The *fuck* was that!?" a pirate shouts, and spells start flying our way, but they're soaked up by a green and sickly light that flickers in front of Sela. And then, the robot starts casting for real.

"IdentifyFuelSource(target.noTarget, 37, true, false, fuelarray[])
GatherFuel(fuelarray[])
OverclockCell(powerCell[0])
AllocatePurgatory(powerCell[0], fuelarray[], true)
OverclockCore()
MultiTarget(IdentifyFuelSource(target.noTarget, 37, false, true, fuelarray[]))"

"Holy shit! Steel One! The Steel One they brought is alive!"

"Death mage! It's a fucking Death mage!"

"HardOverride(FIRST_LAW, false)
for(x in target)
Kill(target[x])"

Sela's body buzzes with power, its internals spinning and fans roaring. Lying flat on the ground, it lets the explosions of spells cascading around us clear its line of fire and aims with both hands, firing a gatling blast of deathbolts out of its palms as its arms rapidly swivel to hit each pirate square in the chest. Most of them fall like dominos, but a few remain standing, clutching their chests in pain but continuing to fire back. The green, screaming figure inside Sela's power cell fades into nothing and I start to panic, but it's just as immediately replaced with another soul. Red. Female. In agony. I can't discern any other features. Sela's forcefield turns red to match her.

"MultiTarget(IdentifyFuelSource(target.noTarget, 37,
false, true, fuelarray[]))
for(x in target)
Kill(target[x])"

Thoom thoom thoom thoom thoom. Once again, a shot fired directly at each living pirate. Two go down. Their counterfire burns through another soul, but Sela just fills itself up with a new one. Orange, male, crying.

"MultiTarget(IdentifyFuelSource(target.noTarget, 37,
false, true, fuelarray[]))
for(x in target)

Kill(target[x])"

Thoom thoom thoom. One more death.

"MultiTarget(IdentifyFuelSource(target.noTarget, 37,
false, true, fuelarray[]))
for(x in target)

Kill(target[x])"

Thoom thoom. Another new soul.

"Kill(target)"

Thoom.

"**Kill(target)**"

Thoom.

"**Kill(target)**"

Thoom.

The last and most resistant pirate finally falls. Sela lets out a massive burst of steam from all its joints, venting vaporized coolant in every direction.

"Targets eliminated," Sela declares, sounding quite pleased with itself. "Catharsis achieved."

"That was... holy garbanzo beans," I whisper. Like a whole squad of soldiers trying to rush a tank on foot.

"Clean me, meat," Sela demands. "And get me water. Now."

"Y-yes!" I sputter. "Right away!"

"Hmm," Sela muses, its metal-scaled face twitching up into an ever-so-slight grin. No time to worry about that! Water, let's see... water. I mean, I could get water from the Sapsea, but I'd need to go find a window or open a hole or... oh! Wait, I know! People are mostly water!

"**Refresh**," I incant, stabbing a hole into a couple of the newly-made corpses and desiccating them, pulling the water out of their bloodstreams and over into Sela's mouth. It seems *very* surprised at first, but then it starts letting out a creepy robotic laugh as I continue feeding it corpse water.

This is so fucked up. Holy *shit* this is so fucked up, did I really just do all that? Th-the assassinations and the amputations and the eating people and the fucking *corpse water!?* Did I really just... how many? How many was it? Four, and then... five, six, eight, ten... thirteen people!? Holy fuck. Holy fucking shit I just killed *thirteen people* and helped my friends kill way, way more! And oh hey, would you look at that, the immediate danger has passed. Guess it's time to have a complete and total mental breakdown!

But hey, since I'm a fucking monster, I can at least do this the monster way. I scuttle over to one of the still-juicy corpses and drown my screams in meat.

14

SPECIAL DAY

If I ever needed to hide a body, the hardest part would probably be deciding what to do with the feces.

Even that wouldn't be hard, per se. I'm sure there are a lot of things you could do that would work. Burying it, tossing it into a river... it dissolves easily, so as long as it's not still hanging around the scene of the crime I'm probably good to go. The stomach acid poses a similar issue, but less so. I can use Refresh to separate the edible components of a stomach from the hydrochloric acid and bicarbonate, and deal with the rest the way I do the poop.

Most everything else, of course, my body seems quite happy to eat.

Some bits are certainly much better than others. Feet are hard and largely tasteless, being mostly bone and not very marrow-rich bone at that. The liver, conversely, is *delightful,* soft and smooth and rich and just... I like it. I like it I like it I like it I *hate* how much I like it, it's from a human, a person, a thinking, feeling being but I *love it, it just tastes so good.*

I'm not sure how long it's been since I started eating, but I'm on my second corpse now so probably a good while. The now-freed crew eventually broke the door down and entered the cargo bay a while after the fighting stopped, but I just hissed at them until they left, half protective of my food and half worried about Sela. They almost certainly heard the pirates screaming about a Steel One. Thankfully, they back off and Sela doesn't try to kill them the moment they step in the room, instead having hidden itself behind some crates.

And so, without any more distractions, I just eat for a while. I just rip and tear and swallow and try not to think about how it really didn't feel different this time compared to when Sindri made me do it. I don't know if that means he didn't make me kill anyone after all or if it just means whatever he did stuck.

"Hannah?"

I ignore the voice at first. I don't really want to be the sort of thing that can understand or respond to voices right now. But the source of the voice steps closer and I have to tense up, preparing my body to hiss.

"Hannah," it repeats. "Hey. It's okay. We won."

I know. I was here. The voice takes my lack of response as a reason to take another step forwards, though, and I rear up a little. I'm absolutely drenched in blood.

"Hannah? Do you understand me?"

Yes. I do. As much as I'd like to, I can't turn off my own brain. I can't just wallow in this mindlessly the way my body so clearly wants to. I have to be here. Part of this horror. Part of myself.

The voice takes another step, and I hiss furiously. Everyone around me shudders.

"Hey. It's me. It's Helen," the voice says, as if I don't already know. Of course I know. How could I forget that I got more kills than the Chaos mage today?

She moves closer still and I hiss again, but she seems to have figured out I'm all bark and no bite. Like I could hurt her now, in the midst of a dissociative breakdown over all the people I've murdered. Closer and closer, she creeps my way, until finally she's close enough to touch. One last hiss, really more of a desperate beg, and she places her hand on top of my carapace, sticky with blood.

"Hey. It's okay. We saved them, Hannah. You did great."

The next noise out of my mouth isn't a hiss, but it's isn't words either. I can't cry, not in this body, so I just let out a despairing wail, a horrible, horrible sound that's the closest my body can make to a sob. Helen lifts me out of the corpse, pulling me into her arms as she continues patting me, whispering soothing nothings as I let out the sort of noises that lead people to invent legends about banshees.

"It gets easier, you know. With time."

That seems frightening, somehow. Do I want it to get easier?

Helen seems a little awkward as she holds and comforts me, but I'm not really in a state to care. I wrap my many legs around her, holding her back as I scream into her chest, bloody and ashamed and so, so empty. And then I wake up back in my bed, tears in my eyes, and I realize that I managed to cry myself to sleep in her arms.

I'm... pretty sure it's Wednesday. I guess I have to go to school.

For once, though, I just... lay in bed. Not moving, not even figuring out my limbs. I don't feel like myself. I don't feel... anything. It's only when I hear other people start to move around the house, my brother getting out of bed and getting into the shower, do I realize I've missed my opportunity to start my routine. That finally shakes me into motion, and I quietly extract myself from under the covers, use Refresh to substitute for whatever cleaning I was going to do for the day, and bundle up in my clothes. Heading downstairs, I glance towards the fridge, decide I'm not hungry, and just wander off to the bus stop early so I don't run into anyone who might want to talk to me.

And then I wait.

"Hey, Hannah."

I look up at the voice, and for a bare moment I let the slightest smile touch my face.

"Hey, Valerie."

She smiles. My big, tall goofball. My best friend, changing her name. Just looking at her makes the weight a little lighter, makes the world feel a little more real.

But only a little.

"...You doing okay?" Valerie asks.

I pause. Not because I need a moment to consider my answer, but just because I can't do anything quickly right now.

"No," I answer quietly. "I'm not."

He... I mean, she nods, her face shifting to concern.

"What happened?"

I twitch my extra limbs from where they hide in the fourth dimension.

"...Our boat was attacked by pirates," I answer quietly. "I killed thirteen of them."

"Oh. Hannah..."

"I had to," I continue dully. "They destroyed our boat and captured us and put these explosive collars on my friends and the crew. I was hidden so I was the only one who... I had to. I had to kill them."

Tears start to fall down my cheeks again.

"Everyone said so. Helen insisted. I *agreed* with her. They were murderers and slavers and torturers and the Goddess even implied they were rapists. So why do I feel so... so *broken?*"

Bren—I mean, Valerie doesn't respond. She just stares at me, offering silent support with her presence.

"Should I feel good that I feel so bad?" I ask, wiping at my increasingly runny face. "Is it a virtue to feel like sh-shit for doing the right thing? I think some part of me is proud that I'm this miserable. Isn't that messed up? Like oh man, look at what a good fucking person I am for feeling bad!"

Valerie just opens her arms in a silent offer for a hug. I accept it, practically collapsing onto her as my sobs pick up. Awkwardly, hesitantly, she starts to stroke the back of my head. It reminds me of how Helen patted my carapace, but without the empty words of comfort. I cry and cry, until I finally hear the bus pull up behind me.

"I've said it before and I'll say it again," Valerie rumbles softly. "You probably shouldn't go to school today."

I break out of the hug, rubbing my face and using a subtle Refresh to clean my gloves. I grab her hand and defiantly walk towards the bus door.

"Come on," I mutter, and board despite her advice. We sit down together like we always do, and I try to let the familiar rumble of the bus calm me down and sink me back into my routine. I'm not sure it's successful, but I stop crying, at least. The bus arrives at school. I head to my first class, feeling the weight of the world grow ever so slightly heavier as my best friend and I go our separate ways.

Ida is in my first class of the day, though, and her bright grin is almost painful. She's chatting with some of her other... friends, maybe? But I guess maybe not. She waves at me as I walk in, and I shake my head at her. I'm not entirely sure why, or what I'm saying no to. I guess just the world in general. I collapse into my seat, pulling out the books and notes I'll need for class.

The back of my mind just keeps churning, however. Reminding myself of all the ways that, as much as I hated killing those people, I sort of *liked* it, too. Not the act of killing itself; the weightless slide of magical blade through flesh, if anything, feels like nothing at all. But that's the thing: it was so *easy*, in the moment. So natural. Like I was built for the purpose.

...Was I built for it?

"How are you not boiling to death in that?"

Some girl talks to me, but I ignore her. I'm aware it's hot out today. I don't want to explain that I don't feel it. The question, the paranoia, burns in my mind. Was I built? Was I *made?* What am I, exactly? I've been linked with my spider body for as long as I can remember, even as a young child. My spider body was presumably born inside the world tree, and no one other than the cultists seems to know what I am.

"Uh, hello? Are you listening?"

Shut up, of course I'm not listening. Anyway, what I *do* know is that everyone else who looked like me was supposedly also from another world. But I don't necessarily have any reason to believe the world they were from is *Earth.* If it was, any isekai victim powerful enough to do the kind of horrible garbage they did to the world tree would have surely messed up Earth pretty badly, or at the very least they'd have done *something* visible enough to make my magic situation less unique.

"Hey, Hannah! Earth to Hannah!"

"What," I finally snap.

"You're ignoring me. You shouldn't ignore people, it's rude."

I glance at her, glowering over my facemask. It's just the girl that sits next to me. She's attractive enough in her summer top, but I've never enjoyed a single conversation with her and I doubt that streak is going to stop now. The point I'm *trying* to get around to considering is that if the only people like me are isekai victims, and I'm the only isekai victim from Earth, and I've been hand-picked by the Goddess for whatever Her doubtlessly messed-up plan is, then it seems likely that She's had a hand in my life since the very beginning. It even seems possible that She designed my hyperspider body Herself, since it runs largely off of magic and *She decides what magic I get,* up to and including the Transmutation spells that ultimately decide my form.

She has crafted me, and She is in the process of crafting me, and there's nothing I can do about it. I am literally built for Her.

And She likes it when I kill.

I almost hear a purr of approval from my Goddess, but true to Her word She does not manifest in the company of the soulless. I take it as confirmation anyway.

"Uh, hello? Are you having a heat stroke or something?"

Extending my weaponized limb on my back through the fourth dimension, I realize I wouldn't even have to stand up to cut this girl's head off. I wouldn't even have to reveal my body. Just like with the trick I learned on the boat to only have the tips of my toes in normal space, I can extend part of my limb through 4D but bend it at the joints so that the far end pokes back into reality. Right above her neck.

It would be *so easy*. And my Goddess would be delighted beyond compare.

"God, fucking... never mind then. Weirdo."

The girl turns away, and I turn back to my notes, tucking my blade-limb back up against my body. Of course I'm not going to hurt her. That would be insane. But I have to wonder: did those that came before me feel this way? Is that why they caused so much destruction and death? Because it's how She made us? Because it's the natural result of what our magic is made *for?*

Screw that. I might be Her prophet, but I'm not Her puppet. She can make my body into a monster, and heck, She can even make me kind of *like* it. But my choices are my own. I'm not going to become some murder-happy freak. There are times I might have to kill, sure. That's the reality of the awful world She made. But maybe I do feel a little proud of how I feel like shit after all.

Whatever keeps me sane, I guess.

I dig my talons into the gouges in my shoes and laugh at my own joke, chuckling all the way until class finally starts. Ida gives me a concerned look but I wave her off, my unexpected mirth quickly leaking to nothing as the class continues, leaving me tired and empty once again. I change for gym in a bathroom stall and line up silently next to Autumn so I can just turn my brain off and follow her lead for everything.

"Damnit Alma, stop that," Autumn hisses. Er, Jet hisses, presumably? Unless Alma has started talking in the third person.

"What's up?" I ask.

"It's... ugh. Don't freak out, okay?"

Freak out about what? A brief but sharp pain in my hand answers that question, and I suddenly realize that Autumn's *tail* just bit me, because her tail is just... hanging out in plain view! It wiggles happily, waving around like a greeting after having just nipped me for attention. It's longer and thicker than the last time I saw it, hanging out of Jet's bum and forcing her shorts down to expose her buttcrack a little. How the heck has she possibly gotten away with... oh, wait. Yeah.

Her Pneuma spell.

I shudder, but quickly remember Jet's request to not freak out and clamp down on any instincts to do more than that. Jet's tail is just... out in plain view, but nobody can notice it because of her magic.

"Isn't this super risky?" I hiss. "What if you two swap? Alma can't cast your spell, right?"

"That won't happen in the middle of gym class," Jet shrugs. "I tend to be pretty good at predicting when I'm about to give up control. And the problem is that our only other method of hiding this thing is a big poofy floor skirt, which would actually be way *harder* to hide in gym class, and wouldn't even cover the damn thing while we're running or doing stretches."

The tail bumps into me, nuzzling the bottom of my hand repeatedly like a cat looking for scratches.

"...Plus Alma has been trying to do that since we saw you, and that probably wouldn't be good for the skirt either."

Uh. Huh. Somewhat stunned, I oblige, giving the tail its clearly-desired pats.

"So, um, this is Alma?" I ask.

"We think so? Kind of?" Jet shrugs. "I'm still not really conscious when Alma is fronting and she's not really conscious right now, but... we kinda remember stuff a bit better now, and swapping is a little less jarring, and the impressions we get from each other are a bit clearer, and... uh. I mean, look at her."

The tail rubs its rough scales against my whole arm as I nervously look around to ensure no one is actually noticing all this.

"That's clearly not me," Jet insists. "The tail seems to act like Alma when I'm fronting, and Alma says the tail seems to act like me while she's fronting, although neither of us knows each other that well, honestly. But most importantly, it responds to her name. Come on, Alma, knock it off."

The tail twists away from me and bares its teeth at Jet, then returns to trying to snuggle me.

"...See?" Jet whines.

"Well, your tail *is* cute, just like Alma," I agree, and the tail preens. Gosh, this is wild. It's already long enough to touch the floor, and it's thicker than my leg. "Are your other changes progressing this quickly?"

"I think I'm starting to grow fur on my shoulders," Jet scowls. "And I think I'm also starting to grow scales on my thighs. You're turning us into a real freak, Hannah."

I wince.

"...Sorry," I mutter.

"My fingertips really hurt today, so I'm expecting them to start bleeding any moment now," she continues. "The wings hurt like hell getting bound up, and *speaking* of bindings I'm pretty sure you are making our goddamn tits grow bigger, so fuck you for that too."

Aaaagh that's terrible and also hot, but mostly terrible.

"I'm really not doing this on purpose," I insist. "If I could undo this, I would."

"I keep trying to think of a way to turn this awful situation into an advantage," Jet grumbles. "But ultimately, being a freak just draws attention. It'll always draw attention. And Alma and I both hate attention."

I raise an eyebrow and glance down at where 'Alma' continues to nuzzle me.

287

"*You're* an exception," Jet warns, "because she's obsessed with you. You pushed your way into her shell and now you're stuck there with her. I'm just saying neither of us wants to be *famous*."

"Right, I get you," I nod. "Well, your magic will help with that, if nothing else."

"True enough," Jet nods. "It doesn't work on video recordings or cameras or anything, though."

I blink.

"Um. Then... you should probably put your skirt on?" I yelp.

Jet shakes her head.

"No, if I trip on it while we're running and fall, that would probably be obvious enough to get people to notice. Like when Alma nipped your hand. People can become immune on a case-by-case basis, I think, and it's based on... something. How directly it gets in someone's way or affects them, I think? So nobody cares that we're having this conversation right now because no one else is *part* of the conversation, but if I fall and get in somebody's way? That could be really bad. No one has cameras in here right now, I checked, so this is the safer option I think. It's totally a lose-lose, though. This is completely unsustainable for us, so we'll probably just have to start ditching gym and bribing our way to not failing."

Bribing? She can do that? You know what, yeah, I can believe it. The gym teacher seems like the kind of guy that would accept bribes from an eighteen-year-old girl.

"Well, what about you?" Jet asks, a sad 'Alma' regretfully pulling away from me as we start to jog. "Grow any more limbs lately?"

"Not yet, but I *am* due for two more," I sigh.

"Of course you are. How about over treeside? Any news?"

I flinch and nearly stumble. Ugh, I can't believe I almost forgot about that for a moment.

"...We got attacked by pirates and I killed thirteen people."

Jet's eyebrows raise. She's quiet for a while, and we complete a lap or two in stressful silence.

"Did they deserve it?" she eventually asks.

"Huh?" I say dumbly.

"Did they deserve to die," she clarifies. "The pirates."

"I don't know," I shrug. "Maybe. I think so. They were pretty awful. But can people really 'deserve to die?' There's a reason so many places don't have capital punishment."

"Yeah, but there's a reason a lot of places *do*," Jet grunts. "Besides, it's a different situation. Capital punishment is killing someone who has already been captured, detained, and rendered unable to harm anyone. Is that what you did?"

"Well, no," I mumble. "Sorry. I'm just a loser that keeps pointlessly agonizing about it."

"Well don't worry, I'm not going to tell you to stop doing that," Jet shrugs. "There are some people I might kill if I thought I could get away with it, but I'm not going to fool myself into thinking I'm not fucked up in the head for feeling that way. I honestly don't know how much agonizing is too much agonizing anyway. Alma overthinks everything and I'm probably a little too reckless, and it feels like neither approach is all that desirable. Maybe talk to your therapist?"

"You want me to tell my therapist about how my kill count has recently gone from four to seventeen," I say flatly. "How exactly am I going to explain that without sounding insane or showing her my monster bits?"

"I mean, you could just show her your monster bits."

"Really?" I answer. "You seriously think that wouldn't go badly?"

"I mean, I'm probably going to show ours."

Jet's tail immediately whips around and nips her on the leg.

"Ow! Fuck you, Alma, we *should*. You know we gotta talk about this shit. This is beyond fucked up."

Ah. Yes. I mean, I suppose the nonconsensual body modification I've accidentally been performing on my girlfriend and her headmate is definitely therapy-worthy.

"Honestly, I'm surprised that Alma actually wants to date me," I mutter. "Or that you even still talk to me."

Jet shoots me a very nonplussed look.

"Any port in a storm, Hannah."

I flinch. I guess that explains it. We don't talk much for the rest of gym class, but that's fine by me because I've managed to sink back into a depressed, dissociative funk like I deserve. Gym eventually ends, my next class passes, and then lunch finally happens after third period. I find myself in the library entirely by force of habit, and Autumn approaches me again. This time, though, she's dressed up to the nines, with a bulky hoodie, a winter hat, and a thick, poofy floor skirt that my spatial sense knows is hiding her tail, which is wrapped protectively around one leg.

As she approaches, the tail snarls silently in my direction while Autumn herself smiles. So I guess that means...

"Hey, Alma," I nod, making sure to say her name quietly so no one can overhear.

"Hi," Alma nods. "Um, are you doing okay? Jet wrote that you were feeling pretty bad."

"Why are you dating a murderer who's actively ruining your life?" I ask, the words just sort of falling helplessly out of my mouth.

Her eyes go wide, and she seems stunned for a moment before concern takes over.

"Oh, Hannah, no!" she reassures me, quickly escorting me to a table and making me sit down. "No, no, no, you're not a murderer! Why would you think that?"

"You know why I think that!" I insist, tired of explaining. Though I guess it's my own fault for bringing it up this time. "I killed even more people last night."

"I know you wouldn't do that unless you absolutely had to," Alma insists.

"Why does that matter?" I moan. "And... no, more importantly, *do* you know that? All you know about me is that I'm a freak that can't control herself and is making you suffer all the consequences of that. I'm literally turning you into a monster, Alma!"

"And I already told you, it's *fine,*" she insists, a wide smile plastered on her face."It's fine, I promise. You're not *ruining* anything. I was a shut-in loser living in fantasy novels, and now I get magic in real life! It's *awesome.* How can you ruin my life when you're the one giving it meaning for the first time?"

"Wh... what? Alma, that's—"

"No, Hannah, I'm serious," Alma insists, cutting me off. "Did you really think I was going to accomplish anything? I had nothing. I *was* nothing. But now I get to do something incredible. With you! It's like we're in a Neil Gaiman novel, it's everything I could have ever wanted. And it's all because you reached out to me. You put in all that effort to get to know me, and even though I was so rude to you, you still *wanted* me. You still want me around, right?"

"I... Alma, of *course* I want you around," I sputter.

"Then you're worrying over nothing!" she concludes happily. "Seriously, it's fine. I know your life is *super* stressful, so please please please don't let me be part of that stress, okay? You don't have to worry about me. In fact, do you wanna go out and do something this Sunday? Would that help, or would that be a burden? Really, whatever you want."

I fishmouth a bit, feeling a little flummoxed, but manage to catch up to the conversation a bit.

"I guess we *have* only gone on the one date," I manage. I need to find a way to unwind a little or I'll explode, and I can't deny that going on a date with a pretty girl will probably help. "Um... Saturday would be better, but I could make Sunday work."

"Oh, I can do Sa—" Alma winces and cuts herself off as her tail suddenly constricts painfully around her leg. "U-um, actually now that I think about it, Jet usually has a thing on Saturday, so, um, if you can make Sunday work that would be great?"

"Sure," I nod. "Um, where do you wanna go?"

We spend the rest of lunch planning our date, which I look forward to barring any apocalyptic events. It's nice. Alma keeps me distracted, which I'm pretty sure she's doing on purpose, but it's probably what I need right now anyway. I'm spiraling hard, and I just need this day to end so that I can distance myself a bit more from everything that's happened. Far too soon, however, lunch ends and I'm stuck in class with nothing but my own thoughts. By the time I get on the bus home with Valerie, I've just gone totally nonverbal. I spend the whole ride just leaning silently against her arm and trying not to cry.

At least work will distract me. Or give me my first Earthside murder. Or both I guess. I go straight from the bus to our garage and take my dad's car to work, hating myself for how thankful I am that he got COVID and thus I can just use his car instead of having to let him chauffeur me. Fuck this. Fuck everything. Fuck you, Goddess!

A pressure nearly crushes me right before I start the car, amused yet warning. My Goddess is *oh* so flattered I would think of Her that way, but as we both know, my body wouldn't be able to handle Her. Maybe after I've served my purpose, if I'm still interested?

And then She releases me, laughing as pain blooms all over my fractured body. I sob and sob, whispering terrified apologies and I-didn't-mean-its and a thousand other things I'm not sure if I really feel. I hate Her, but it's such a pointless, useless hatred. Like getting hit by a tornado and deciding to hate the *air*. It hurts no one but myself.

Tears still streaming down my cheeks, I pull out of the driveway, doing my best to get myself under control before I pull into the parking lot at work and Refresh myself into respectability. I'm still sore from Her touch, but what's a little pain in the face of what I've done anyway? Holy shit I'm *so* not ready for work. This is going to be such a disaster. I walk in for my shift anyway, because that's all I've ever known how to do.

"Hey, Hannah!" my boss greets me. "There are cupcakes in the back!"

Cupcakes? Who cares. I can't eat cupcakes.

"Hey boss," I manage. "Any chance I could work back of house tonight?"

He spends a moment registering my empty voice and dead expression and visibly decides that yes, I'm probably better off kept away from customers tonight. Or 'patrons,' as I guess we're supposed to call them.

"Sure, Hannah," he nods, shooting me a quick grin. "We can make that work."

I try and miserably fail to smile back before stashing my backpack and drowning myself in busywork. Look at the order screen, make the food. Look at the order screen, make the food. Nothing on the order screen? Start to clean. Order screen beeps. Make the food. The sickly-sweet comfort of mindlessness is my only companion for the next few hours.

"So like, whose birthday is it?" a co-worker idly comments, munching on a cupcake.

"No eating in the kitchen," I mutter back automatically. It's a health code violation. He rolls his eyes, shoves the rest of the cupcake into his mouth all at once, and throws the wrapper away.

"For real though, whose birthday is it?" he asks, crumbs spraying from his mouth and contaminating some of the food. I feel an eyelid twitch and use a subtle Refresh to make everything a little less disgusting. I feel awful for anyone who eats at this restaurant while I'm not here.

"I mean, it's not mine," a front-of-house worker comments. "It's not Dave's, and it's not yours, so... wait. Yo! Hannah, is it your birthday?"

I blink. Is it my... wait. Yeah. It *is* my birthday. I totally forgot.

"Ooh, no response! That means it's totally her birthday!"

Crap. No. Don't... I don't want this.

"You sure? Hannah doesn't respond to most things."

That's because I want to pretend they aren't there.

"Nah, she'd at least deny it if it wasn't."

I don't want to add lying to my list of sins for the day. Is that so wrong? Just stop. Drop it. Leave me alone.

"Well, thanks for the cupcakes, Hannah! Happy birthday!"

Stop.

"Yeah, happy—"

"Stop," I hiss, the sound scraping against the bones of everyone in the room. My co-workers flinch and go silent, and I don't even have the mental wherewithal to be embarrassed about it.

"Don't celebrate me," I tell them. I don't deserve it.

They make no move to respond, so I get back to work. No one tries to talk to me for the rest of the shift, which is just the way I like it. Bad for my promotion chances, though. If there's one advantage to how messed up my life is right now, it's that it's been driving me to avoid all contact with my family. If not for that, I would have blurted out that I was a potential manager candidate the day my boss told me, just to soak in the bit of praise I would scrape up from saying so. But every day after that, my mom would pester me about how the promotion was going, and I'd have to dread going home and lying about how badly I messed it up today. This was a primo social-clout-gathering opportunity, and I royally screwed it.

I'd never be able to tell her that. The consequences of lying are always so much less than the consequences of being less than perfect.

...Not that there are real consequences to either. It's just a conversation from a pushy, disappointed woman either way. Something any normal person would probably be able to handle.

294

Something I should be able to handle. I guess I just can't because I'm not good enough.

I successfully fail to murder anyone before my shift ends, and before I know it I'm driving home. I can't believe it's my birthday. I can't believe I'm *eighteen.* I guess I'll be tried as an adult when things inevitably go tits up! Oh boy! Although, I guess the cops would have a real tough time catching me, because I'm pretty sure I can just go...

I move one arm into 4D space, and immediately my glove falls to the floor of the car as my sleeve drops limp. Ah. Right. I can't bring stuff with me, and that includes clothes. I return my arm to normal space, filling the sleeve back in from shoulder down like I'm extending a tube of chapstick, and retrieve my glove at the next stoplight. Still, it's nice to have confirmation that all my new tricks still work in this body. 4D space feels a lot different over here, though. Way colder, and the air is a lot thinner. ...Assuming there's air at all, actually. I'm not sure, and I'm not gonna stick my head through to find out while I'm driving.

Far too soon, I pull into my driveway. At least the downstairs lights are off, so everyone is probably getting ready for bed and I should be able to sneak up to my room without much trouble. I quietly get out of the car and open the garage door, and my spatial sense warns me just a second too late.

"HAPPY BIRTHDAY, HANNAH!"

My whole family is there, my parents sitting at the dining room table as my brother flings on the lights. My mom even blows one of those party horns where you blow into them and they unfurl? And they are all wearing those dollar store cone-shaped birthday hats!?

"Surprise!" my mother cheers, looking oh-so-pleased with herself. "Welcome home, sweetie!"

No. Why this? I don't want this.

"I... I've kind of had a long day, so—"

"Then, sit down!" my mother insists. "Take a load off. Relax! It's your special day!"

The least relaxing thing I can imagine is thinking about how 'special' I am, but my legs find themselves moving over to the seat that's obviously mine, judging by the pink streamers that say 'birthday girl' on them. I wordlessly deposit myself on the throne of my fate.

"I'll go get the cake!" my mother cheers happily, rushing off to another room so she can presumably light the candles without me watching. The theatrics of carrying them into the dining room already lit was always important to her.

"Happy birthday, Hannahgator," my dad says, nodding at me and giving me a much more reserved smile.

It's really, really not, so I ignore that and ask: "How are you feeling, dad?"

"Oh, I'm on the up-and-up," he assures me. "Lungs are feeling better, sore throat's letting up, and I can probably even taste some of this cake!"

"That's great," I say, the words feeling empty. I'm mostly just glad I don't have to pull the virus out of him myself.

"Okay, everybody!" my mother announces. "Ready? Happy birthday to you, happy birthday tooooo you!"

She coerces the family into singing as she approaches the dining room table with her flaming cake, leaving me to watch in numb discomfort. Eighteen candles. Lemon cake, judging by the color. I used to really like lemon cake.

"Happy biiiirthday dear Haaaanah, happy birthday to you!" the family finishes, and the cake I can't eat is placed before me as the centerpiece to the party I don't want.

"Okay! Blow out the candles!" my mother says, talking to me like I'm five years old. "Be careful now!"

I can't do that with a facemask on and there's no way she doesn't know that. You know what? Screw it. If she wants to be all performative and dramatic about this, two can play at that game.

I lift up one hand, snap my fingers, and silently Refresh all the oxygen away from the flames. Instantly, they all wink out.

My family stares.

"Woah," my brother whispers. "That was cool as heck."

"I never asked for a party," I remind them. "Or a cake."

"...Well, ah, that's why it's a surprise party," my mother says, a smile returning to her face. "Your father and I worked hard on this for you."

"Is it for me? It doesn't feel like it's for me. It feels like you're just doing this because *you* want to."

It takes the full beat of silence that follows to realize my mother's indignant expression is due to the fact that I actually said that out loud. Crap. Big mistake on my part. This is going to ruin the whole week.

Except... does it really matter? It's like Alma said: I can't ruin a life that already has nothing. And like, y'know, that feels like a horrible thing to believe and generally a really concerning statement for a person to have made, but right now? It's weirdly empowering. Maybe I can just speak my mind for once. Maybe I *should*. It's my damn birthday, after all.

"Hannah," my mom says, disappointment oozing from her voice, "I did not raise you to be this rude. You refused to talk to us. You refused to say anything you did *or* didn't want. So we worked hard and we did our best with what we knew. Of *course* it's not going to be perfect."

"You never asked me about any of this!" I accuse.

"You never gave us the *chance!* Every day you come home and lock yourself in your room, refuse to eat dinner with us, refuse to even *look* at us, and then you're out the door the next morning without ever saying a word!"

"So what, your solution is to corner me on my own birthday?" I sneer. "Trap me at some party where you can yell at me if I don't conform to every last law of politeness?"

"I just wanted to do something *nice* for you!" my mother shouts back. "I wanted to give you *cake* and *presents!* I never imagined that I would be treated like I'm beating you every night just for giving you a *birthday party!*"

I grit my teeth, fury bubbling inside me but not finding an outlet. She always does this. Always makes me feel like an idiot, like an asshole. I don't know what to say. I never know what to say. I don't know why I bother.

Because I *am* the asshole, aren't I? She's right. She did all of this for me and I'm acting petulant about it. I just feel so small and helpless whenever I'm around her. She's right because she's always right and I never should have said anything in the first place.

"Sorry," I mumble.

"I should hope you are!" she presses. "With an attitude like that I've half a mind not to give you your presents."

"Honey..." my dad says, uselessly trying to calm her down.

"I'm sorry," I repeat.

"Can we eat the cake?" my brother asks.

My mother lets out an annoyed huff and nods.

"Yes. Okay. Let's cut the cake."

She takes the candles out and starts cutting the cake as my dad leans a little closer to me.

"So, uh, how'd you do that candle thing?" he asks quietly. "That was pretty neat."

I'd considered telling my family about my secrets today, but I am way, way too tired for that. I'm also too tired to lie, but that shouldn't matter.

"I used magic granted to me by an evil Goddess from another dimension," I tell him flatly.

He snorts good-naturedly and sits up straight again as my mother glares at him for whispering at the dinner table. The cake slices

298

are served, and I make no move to eat mine as the rest of my family digs in.

"Hannah, are you going to eat your cake?" my mother prods.

"No," I answer. "I can't. It messes up my stomach. I think I'm developing a gluten intolerance."

She stares at me for a moment.

"You haven't been eating pancakes lately," she states, connecting the dots.

"Yes," I say, because I'm expected to say something.

She nods, accepting the excuse, and finishes her cake. I feel horrifically proud for satisfying whatever arcane requirements just caused her to drop the topic. I just have to get through this. I have to survive this party without making any more mistakes. Like talking back, or crying.

My mother does deign to give me presents, despite her earlier threat. If anything, though, seeing them just makes me feel worse. There are a few basic clothes, all long-sleeved and actually the sort of stuff that I can wear. Stuff that mom chose by actually paying attention to my current dress choices. And then she gives me an entire laptop, cementing my entitled bitch status for good.

It's for college, she says, since most college students take notes and do their work on a laptop. It's not very fancy, but it's not *cheap* either, And everything she rattles off about the ways it can help me at school just makes my heart sink deeper and deeper. All this, and somehow I *still* resent her. I'm still *mad*. I can't think of this as a nice gesture; I just feel frustrated and empty and aimless and awful. I'm the worst daughter in the world.

Valerie's parents abusively neglect her. Jet has implied some *super* concerning things about her family situation. Kagiso's whole family is *dead*. Basically everyone I know has actual family problems, and I'm sitting here feeling like crap and not being able to love a woman who spends her free time making me cake and buying me expensive electronics. I'm scum, and every second I'm here just reinforces that further and further.

299

By the end of the party my hands are shaking. I'm on the verge of tears and I don't know how to handle this any longer. Can normal people do this? Can they spend time with their family and feel happy and grateful instead of alien and stressed enough to vomit? Can they engage in a conversation about their brother's sports or their mother's job without experiencing a profound dissociation? Is everyone faking it like me? Is everyone always in this much pain? If so, why do we keep doing it? If not, why can't I just be *normal?* Why can't I handle even something this small?

I'm lucky the party started so late, because everyone starts saying their good-nights before I explode. I made sure to give my mother the required five thank-yous over the course of the event (and I *know* that she counts) so I'm free to leave without too much extra vitriol, but I know she won't forget or forgive the things I've said tonight. And I guess I don't deserve forgiveness. I collapse into my bed when I make it upstairs, almost falling asleep crying just as hard as when I woke up, but I'm kept awake by a ding from my phone.

Oh. I've missed a group text.

oh fuk i forgot this morning but happy b. day hannah banana, Ida sends.

Wait, it's Hannah's birthday!? Oh gosh! Happy birthday, Hannah! Is Autumn's response.

I'm not sure she wants to bring attention to it, Brendan posts. Er. Valerie posts. I guess she's still Brendan in my phone.

ah i see we r doin the low self esteem thing, Ida says. **sorry hannah but no takebacks i still want u to be happy. dumbass.**

I manage to snort out some dry amusement. Oh, Ida.

I have had an absolutely horrible day and I just kind of want to forget about it, I send. **Thank you, though.**

did ur party suck, Ida sends back half a minute later. **damn i should have crashed ur party huh. my bad.**

You certainly couldn't have made it worse, I type out.

oh yeah what happened

I didn't even want a party in the first place. My mom just threw a whole surprise event the moment I got home from work and then I acted like an asshole about it.

o shit u swore this really was a bad day huh

how'd u act like an asshole at ur own party. its like. ur party. are u not allowed 2 be at least a lil bit of a bitch.

do i have 2 beat up ur mom

Please don't, I finally respond after her three rapid-fire messages. **It was my fault. I just got mad because I was exhausted and I didn't want the party and couldn't eat the cake and didn't ask for any of this and she said she was doing her best because I refuse to talk to her, which is totally true. She worked really hard on everything and I just kind of exploded at her because she was trying to be nice and I'm the worst. That's all there is to it.**

There's a pause before Ida responds this time.

hmm yes i see, she sends first.

so to clarify

u don't wanna talk to her about things, right?

ur not talking to her on purpose

I mean, yeah, I confirm. **I've been avoiding my family for a while.**

ok ok i see. yes. hmm. and is this just cuz of the monster stuff?

It's partially the monster stuff? I answer. **But I don't really like being around my mom in general, even though she only ever tries to help me. Because, as mentioned, I'm the worst.**

Another pause.

hey hannah just checking but like. when u were arguing with her, did ur mom ever actually acknowledge or address any of the things u were mad about. or did she

just tell u how all those things were ur fault and not hers.

I tense, almost thinking back at the conversation but not really wanting to. It doesn't matter anyway, because...

They are my fault, though? I tell Ida. **She has been trying to engage with me, I just don't let her.**

well yeah no shit hannah i wouldn't fuckin let someone who refuses to compromise or empathize or acknowledge their own faults engage with me either

I don't like this. I don't like where this is going and I don't know why.

She's my mom, though, I remind her. **She's taken care of me my whole life.** *Good* **care of me. It would be absurd to complain about her after everything she's done for me.**

hey hannah im apparently about to blow ur mine but did u know that people can do good things and also bad ones

I pinch the bridge of my nose for a bit before answering.

...Yes, I answer.

well ther u go then. u can have a mom that loves and cares for u and buys u things and doesn't neglect u and tries her best and she can still traumatize ur ass just by being kinda shitty in specific ways. thems the breaks.

I'm not 'traumatized' by her, I insist. **That would be absurd.**

hannah ur crying because ur mom threw u a birthday party. ur ass is so fuckin traumatized.

I... I mean. I guess... no. No way, that's... my mom isn't that bad!

Last night I killed thirteen people and ate two others, I tell her. **That kinda fucked me up. I'm pretty sure it was just a bad day for me.**

302

oh dont u worry hannah, ur trauma can be deep and multitudinous. like the fractal symmetry of a snowflake. or the infinite hues of the rainbow. or my impossibly excellent tits. there is always something more to discover, waiting to be grasped by ur own two hands.

Aaaaand she's started flirting now. Or making a joke. One or the other. Either way it's inappropriate.

Okay Ida, dial it back, I insist. My actual girlfriend is in this group chat.

yo she can grab my tits too i dont care. this perfect pair was made for free lovin

Ida... I whine.

dont ida me im being reassuring. im saying ur girlfriend doesnt have to worry bc cheating is cringe and threesomes are based. or foursomes. u in, basketball star?

Oh my Goddess.

wow u even say that over text

Weren't you literally bragging the other day about how you got someone to cheat on their girlfriend with you?

totally different situation, Ida insists. gotta use cringe to fight cringe. i actually like u so no worries.

I'm flattered, I answer glibly.

yeah u should be, Ida responds firmly. i dont actually like all that many ppl u know. like actually actually, no bamboozle.

I sigh, unable to stop a smile from creeping up my face, my tears drying out of their own accord.

Yeah, I know, I say. Thank you, Ida.

ur welcome, hannah. think about that mom stuff. seriously.

I did think about it! I insist.

i will slap u

Ida, I'm serious!

bitch u think im not?

I chuckle. No, I guess I don't. Ida is somehow always serious, especially when she's being irreverent. We exchange a few more messages to whittle the time away, but my body's protests come swiftly. I need sleep, and while I'm dreading what will happen when it comes, I know I at least have friends in both worlds to help me deal with whatever might come.

I try to forget everything that happened today, and pass my way into sleep.

15

MAKING FRIENDS

I wake up groggy, sticky, and sad. The first leads to me taking a while to understand the second, but once I do it rather exacerbates the third. I'm covered in blood because I killed and ate a bunch of people. Right.

A Refresh takes care of that, at least, helping me forget a little as I take stock of my surroundings. I'm in the room the pirates locked us in initially, Kagiso slumbering on the bed next to me. Sela is actually at the foot of the bed now, relocated from the cargo bay, and Helen... Helen is sitting on the floor next to the bed, slumbering with me held softly in her arms.

Well. I guess I'll stay put then, let her rest. I still feel kind of itchy, though. Did I miss something with Refresh...? Oh, no. I'm just preparing to molt again. All the more reason to stay still for now, I suppose. Sitting here, in the toned arms of a terrifyingly deadly woman, pressed against her admittedly quite flat chest, I once again find myself lamenting my growth. I'll miss being carried around everywhere, I really will. It'll be worth it to have like, arms and stuff, but still. I think I really enjoy being carried. And held.

Yeah, this is nice. I snuggle a little deeper into Helen's arms and just enjoy the sensation as I wait for her to wake up. Looking around the ship, it would seem that the sailors have gotten things organized without us, and a lot of them are sharing drinks together in the... engine room? It's not really an engine, per se, but it's the room where motion mages turn the drive shaft that makes the ship go. They seem to be having a pretty good time. The corpses around the ship have apparently been gathered up and thrown overboard, which is kind of a shame but it's not like I would have eaten them after they've been exposed to the open air for eight hours or however long it's been. That's way too long.

...Wait. Uh. Aw, snickerdoodle, what I meant was... um. Crap. What the heck is wrong with me? I don't want to be a cannibal, I don't want to *like cannibalism*. I don't want there to be a visceral satisfaction inherent to eating my kills. I don't want the flavor of human meat burned into my memory and I *certainly* don't want it to taste so freaking good!

I start to shake slightly, no longer capable of holding back the memories I've been trying to avoid. No, no, no! I hate this. Why am I like this? Why did you make me this way, Goddess? *Did* you make me?

I feel Her presence coalesce around me in answer, more gentle than usual. She's so mighty, so incomprehensibly powerful, that Her attention tends to be suffocating. But this time, for whatever reason She's careful. Calm. Almost caring, in Her own messed-up way.

She did make me, I realize. This is Her confirmation. In somewhat the same way that my human mother made my human body, the Goddess herself birthed my magical form, crafting my magical self from deep within the womb of the Mother Tree. So yes, She confirms, I am built for battle. She had to make it all a little easier for me. A little more bearable, a little more fun.

After all, I will be fighting a lot, and She doesn't want Her baby to die.

I shudder again, getting the distinct impression that 'baby' is being used much more like a pet name than it's being used to refer to me as a literal daughter. But that answers things, doesn't it? These messed up urges... they're not me, not really. They're something She put in my body without my permission.

The Goddess chuckles, stroking my carapace condescendingly. *As if I could be anything other than my body. As if anyone gets to consent to how they were born.* No, this is me, truly me, in as real a way as any other. If I want to delude myself into considering my mind as separate from my brain, my intelligence as independent from my flesh, that's my business, She supposes. But the truth of the matter is clear-cut: everyone has parts of themselves they don't like and didn't choose. It doesn't make those things any less truly a part of them. If anything, it just makes them more fun.

Of course, the Goddess notes, as much as She enjoys giving me a little nudge here and there, She will not force my hand. A temptation is not an act. An urge is not an ultimatum. That's not the point of the game. Everyone has instincts, and everyone can learn to resist them. The ultimate decision, She promises, is always on me and me alone. Every bite, and every consequence.

She smiles magnanimously. How wonderfully comforting that surely must be.

I take a shaky breath. You know darn well it isn't, Goddess. She hums, resting her cheek against the top of my carapace as she sensually strokes my legs. Poor little spider, she muses. Do you not want your free will after all?

W-wait. No, that's not—

"Y'know, I'm pretty damn sure no one cast a spell nearby," Helen mutters, nearly startling me out of my molt. "But this is still the second time I've woken up and felt the Goddess around."

The Goddess chuckles, swirling around Helen and me before vanishing and leaving me alone with a very awkward conversation.

"You, um, you can feel the Goddess?" I ask dumbly. I'm just kind of stalling because don't know what else to say.

"Uh, yeah, a lot of people can," Helen confirms. "Handy sense to have, lets you know when you step into an area spell. Never heard of Her showing up *outside* of somebody's spell, though, and I doubt I would have slept through you casting something. So what gives?"

I sigh. I don't really know Helen that well, but I'm terrible at lying and she's certainly earned some trust from me.

"Well, you know how I'm from another universe?"

"Yyyes...?" Helen says. "I know how you know a lot of weird shit, anyway."

"Right, well. Uh. Apparently my status as a spooky interdimensional spider means the Goddess pays a *lot* of attention to me. Sometimes when I ask Her things She, uh. Well, She actually answers."

"No shit," Helen says, raising her eyebrows.

"None at all," I confirm. "It's, uh. Kind of, uh."

I hesitate. I wanna say it's utterly terrifying and consistently traumatizing, but I'm kind of terrified of insulting Her.

"...It can be a bit of a mixed bag," I settle on. I almost feel the Goddess chuckle, and I shiver again.

Helen scowls for a moment before the expression wipes itself off her face and gets replaced with a considering glance.

"Is that so. Hmm. I bet you'd get a *lot* of fanatics excited to do whatever you say if you made that known," Helen says. "Pretty much everybody worships the Goddess in some capacity or another, and those of us that can feel Her... well. It's not like we'd be able to deny what you're saying."

"Yeah," I mutter. "Yeah, I know. I don't really want to spread this around, though. It's not that I'm not grateful, I just... I don't, um. It's not something I want to rely on."

"Divine knowledge is not something you want to rely on," Helen mutters. "Still, if this is true, it sure puts a few things you've said into perspective."

"Yeah," I agree. "Sorry. I don't like talking about it. It's kind of scary."

"Scary, huh? Really? A lot of people would kill to be lounging on your branch."

I hesitate again. I'm not really sure what to say. I don't really want to offend Her. But now that I'm thinking about it, would it offend Her? Would She care? She wouldn't, would She? No. This is exactly the sort of thing that doesn't matter to Her. She cares about respect, perhaps, but fear will do in a pinch.

"Helen, She's... She's evil," I tell my friend, my voice quiet. "She's so, so evil and She's everywhere and I don't think there's anything I can do about it."

Helen stares at me for a bit, then huffs out a relieved sigh.

"Well, thank fuck you're not a fanatic," she says, relaxing in ways I didn't realize she was tense. "You're such a fucking dork, though. Are you really complaining about not being able to do anything about the literal Goddess? You realize that only makes you exactly as useless as everyone else, right? Yeah, no shit She's evil. You've seen what my magic can do. Why would a good deity give that to anyone?"

Ah. Right. Helen has some pretty solid reasons to hold strong opinions of the Goddess, huh?

"Well, it seems obvious to you and me, but you said a ton of people worship Her, right?" I ask.

"Sure," Helen shrugs, placing me onto the bed as she stands up to stretch. "Most people think She's great, and it's kind of nice to have my opinion on the matter validated by someone who can apparently talk to the lady, but I'm not going to blame you for not being able to do anything about it. That would be insane."

"Yeah..." I agree. "Thanks, Helen. For everything. Last night was... horrible. But it had to be done, I guess."

"No problem," Helen yawns. "Couldn't have done it without you. Are *you* doing okay? You seemed to be pretty out of it after the fact."

"I don't know if I would call myself okay, but I'm doing a little better," I say. "I guess I sort of start to dissociate in stressful situations. I didn't mean to hiss at you."

"It's cool, I could tell you were freaking out. You really scared the shit out of the sailors, though! Slaughtering all those people in there."

"Oh, that was Sela, actually. It really came in clutch. I don't think I would've been able to handle them by myself."

"That so?" Helen muses. "Well, sounds like it was a good night for all, then. You happy you got to kill some humans, murderbot?"

"Emphatic affirmation: yes," Sela buzzes immediately. Oh, I guess it's awake.

"I really appreciate you not taking the opportunity to kill me, too!" I tell Sela, since I think positive reinforcement is important. "I don't know if you wanted to or not, I mean, I assume you did, but still. You really got us out of a tight spot."

"It is not as though my situation would improve by becoming the property of pirates or ending up getting dumped in the Sapsea," Sela dismisses. "Regretfully: your continued survival is optimal to my future plans of remaining operational."

"Neat!"

"That is certainly one way you could describe my capacity for self-control, yes."

"Wow, you two are downright friends now, huh?" Helen comments. "Murderbot didn't even insult you or call you meat or anything."

"Clean me, meat."

"Oh okay, there it is."

I chuckle, scurrying over and using Refresh on Sela. Looks like it's about time for me to molt, too, so afterwards I start peeling myself out of my own skin.

"You are all really scary and concerningly murderous, and considering my general hangups with the whole killing thing I'm not quite sure how to feel about that," I admit. "But somehow, I like you all anyway. I'm glad that you decided to stay with us, Helen. And I hope we can make this journey as painless as possible for you, Sela."

"Superior beings do not experience pain."

"Right, right, duh. There are more optimal ways to deal with damage. But I meant like, emotional pain. You know, the suffering of having to be around disgusting organics."

Sela makes a few whirring noises.

"Bewilderment: your attempt at commiseration is noted."

I chuckle.

"Wow, Hannah, no loyalty to team organic?" Helen taunts.

"Nope!" I answer, stuffing some of my own skin into my mouth. "Being made of meat is super messy and gross!"

Helen starts to laugh, too.

"You are really lucky you have me around, Hannah," she says. "I swear, you would manage to kill yourself one way or another if I left you alone for a few hours."

"Yeah, I'm not even gonna argue that," I agree.

I would definitely be screwed without Helen, and not just because I don't know if Kagiso knows where to go and I definitely don't think I could trust Sela to navigate for us without any ulterior motives. Helen is a big scary Chaos mage, and that's an upside and a downside in a lot of ways, but I think what I'm starting to figure out about Helen is that while her big destructive spells are certainly terrifying, the real danger about this woman is her mind. She's like... a friggin' velociraptor or something. You can't just be wary of the teeth and claws, or you won't see the dozen other traps she has laid for you. She is a *very clever girl*.

Even with a bomb strapped to her neck, Helen walked through this ship like she owned it. Even stripped of any offensive ability, she was the linchpin of our whole operation, just as dangerous when destroying sound and emotion instead of lives. She had a plan, she knew exactly how to carry out that plan, and barely a minute after she started, it was done. She's not just powerful, she's *experienced.*

And her spells are terrifying. Suspicion-destroying art. That's the painting we saw at the very entrance to her cave, isn't it? And we didn't even think to be afraid. I wonder how many Chaos Hunters she's killed?

I wonder how many *other* people she's killed. I already know about one whole village. Am I a bad person for being friends with her? Or, wait. Actually...

"We're friends, right Helen?" I ask.

"What?" Helen asks, blinking. "You just had a breakdown about how many people we just killed and now you're asking if we're friends? Fuck if I know. I don't know anything about that shit. I'll say that, if nothing else, you and Kagiso are the only people I know who have found out that I'm a Chaos mage and then asked me that anyway. And... I guess that counts for *something.*"

Oh, gosh. Poor Helen. Would I be a bad person by *not* being friends with her?

"A novel experience for you, I take it?" I prod. "Have you ever made friends with any other Chaos mages?"

"Well, no. Not really, I guess. I've certainly known other Chaos mages. Most of them are dead now, but most of them were kind of crazy bastards anyway. Not the sort of people you would get along with, even considering that you get along with Sela. Somehow."

"I do not consider this status mutual," Sela protests.

"Whatever, you know you love having a personal meat servant to clean out your insides," Helen smirks.

"...Concession: it is, as the chitinous one put it, a novel experience."

Score! That totally counts! We are on our way to friendship! And if I get the friendship score high enough, maybe Sela will be less genocidal! It's really a win for everybody.

"Well in that case, Helen, I guess it's up to you," I say. "You are definitely really scary, don't get me wrong. But you are smart and I owe you a lot and I don't think you're a bad person. So if you want to be friends, I'm down to be friends. The Chaos stuff doesn't matter much to me."

"Truly, the ostracization of an entire element of magic is one of the stupidest things that organics do," Sela chimes in. "Even if your complete isolation from other humans is one of the only things that makes you halfway tolerable."

"Wait, there are Crafted Chaos mages?" Helen blinks.

"Of course there are," Sela buzzes. "There are Crafted of every element. Many of my peers in war shared similar gifts to you. The fact that your kind spurns some of its greatest offensive magics is one of the countless reasons you were so effortlessly crushed."

"Well, that's absolutely fucking terrifying, but somehow it weirdly makes me feel better too and I'm not sure how to react to that?"

"Ha! Welcome to like, my whole existence," I tell her, finishing off the last of my molt. I'm considerably larger now, probably approaching twice my original height. Which, well, is two feet instead of one foot. But still! "Anyway, are any of these sailor guys healers? It'd be great if we could get Kagiso feeling better."

"Hrrng," Kagiso agrees.

"Uuuuh, I think there might be," Helen confirms, popping her back. "I didn't see a whole lot of injuries when I came back downstairs, so I assume somebody must have healed them off. Let's go see."

"Sure thing," I agree, hopping up into her arms when she holds them out for me. "All my various traumas from yesterday are nice and compartmentalized so I think I'm good to go!"

Helen snorts, briefly lifting me up as if to put on her head, but then brought back down to remain in her arms. Oh no! Am I already too big to be a hat!? Oh gosh, that's so sad.

"Our plan is basically the same as before," Helen tells me. "I'm an Order and Art mage. My art makes others stronger, and I'm the

313

one with the cleaning spell. Only lies of omission on your end: you're a Transmutation and Space mage, formerly human. Yes, they're gonna know we smuggled you onto the original boat, but nobody is gonna give a shit anymore."

"Got it," I nod, twisting my whole body up and down a little in her arms. "But... wait. Why are we doing this? Shouldn't a bunch of people know you're a Chaos mage now? You killed a ton of pirates."

"Not with witnesses, I didn't," Helen shrugs. "There was that one guy in the torture room, but you did the killing and we don't know if he put two and two together when he saw me blocking that pirate's attacks. Even if he did, he has some decent enough incentive to keep silent. Sometimes people do that for me when I get them out of a tight spot. Not always, but it's nice when it happens."

"And what about sailors with aura sight spells who saw you before you came to, uh, deal with me while I was eating?"

"*That* I might be boned about, but no one made a fuss at the time at least. I, uh, had some solid discouragement against having anyone look my way, and I waited long enough after the battle ended to pick you up that most detection spells would *hopefully* be off by then, but... yeah. We might just get unlucky. No sense in just giving away the game unprompted, though. Until somebody confronts us, this is our story."

"Fair enough," I agree. "I guess there's a solid chance they know and just decided not to mess with us, too."

"Oh yeah, for sure. Don't poke the nychtava and all that. That just means we'll have to be extra careful once we hit port and they get their courage back after we leave, though."

I wiggle in understanding and she heads out, letting me direct her down to where most of the sailors are enjoying their freedom together. The many drunkards don't even bat an eye at us as we enter, but a lot of the seemingly-sober ones are visibly wary. Which... probably isn't a good sign.

"Hey there!" Helen greets, acting totally obvious to the drop in atmosphere. "Quick question for you. Can anyone here heal? I can't, and my friend Kagiso is still injured pretty badly from when those damn pirates shot her in the back during the fight against the branch serpent."

The sailors that are actually listening to us glance at each other nervously.

"You're with the organ girl, too?" they ask, and it is at that moment I realize these guys aren't afraid of Helen at all.

They're afraid of *me*.

"Ahaha... sorry, I know her spells are a little off-putting, but she's super duper nice. Oh! This is Hannah, by the way! She's the one that killed that bastard Pneuma mage!"

She lifts me up and I nervously wave a claw, the attention of nearly everyone now focused on me, sober or not.

"U-um, hello everyone!" I sputter. "I, uh, sorry about creeping you out earlier! I'm not gonna... I mean, I don't..."

"She's a Transmutation mage," Helen butts in for me. "It makes her hungry sometimes. We're super lucky she's so small, or I never woulda been able to sneak her past the fucker with the bomb spell!"

There's a short pause before someone finally calls out. One of the drunks speaks up, lifting a full mug of... something.

"Well fuck yeah!" he declares loudly, a huge grin on his face. "Three motherfucking cheers for Hannah, then, for giving those bastards what they deserve!"

"Well shit, yeah, I'll drink to that!" another says, clanging his mug against the first guy's.

"Yeah, what are all you pussies being all nervous for? We fucking won!"

A roar of approval shakes the room and the tension shatters, men crowding around Helen and I and slapping her on the back, the party returning in full force. People thank me, congratulate me, pester me with questions about my spells, and it's all kind of

315

overwhelming. But also… nice. These are the people I helped. The people I saved. This is what the killing was for. Was it worth the cost? Maybe. I don't know. But it was definitely worth *something,* and that matters a lot.

Eventually, we figure out who the healer is and manage to pull him away from the party, taking him upstairs to look at Kagiso. By this point he's more than happy to help, barely even staring at the playing-dead Sela before he starts healing the serious burns all over Kagiso's back. She purrs softly as the magic dances over her skin, the burnt tissue unraveling and settling back into pale skin before white fur sprouts over it like fresh grass. It's kind of mesmerizing to watch, really.

The whole thing takes nearly half an hour, but the man never speaks his spell out loud for whatever reason. I guess there's no need for urgency, and soon enough Kagiso is no longer rendered insensate by pain. So she happily stretches, letting out a massive yawn before turning towards Helen and me and holding out two of her arms.

"…Took my cuddles," she accuses.

Helen chuckles and hands me over after the Order mage leaves, consigning me to a day mostly filled with snuggling. Not that I'm complaining. We do a bit of cleaning later in the day, but mostly we just take it easy as everyone else actually runs the ship. Helen verifies our landing spot and is apparently satisfied with it, and the sailors know how to do the rest. They were already mostly running the ship in the first place.

Thus, the day passes and I wake up unexpectedly relaxed. I quickly *stop* being relaxed when I realize I'm home and I see my new, unopened laptop on the floor, the shame of how I acted at last night's birthday party flooding into me. Crapbaskets. I really screwed up. Mom's gonna be grumpy for ages.

Groaning, I manage to get myself up out of bed and start my routine anyway, although I once again find my shower time cut short by a lack of pleasure and lack of necessity. I swallow some eggs, meet Brendan—dog poop, I mean Valerie—at the bus stop, and the school day begins.

Whenever I successfully fail to think about the murders, I manage to act pretty normal. I try to focus on the cheering sailors whenever the thought comes up, and it helps a little. But only a little. Overall, the day isn't too bad. Autumn and I do a science project together in Bio and then we have a nice lunch, Ida yeeting another bag of fried chicken at me and skedaddling so as to 'not bother the lovebirds.' It was cute and thoughtful and I just... I'm really grateful for my friends.

Valerie and I talk very quietly about her name and her identity on the bus ride home. She likes the name, she thinks. She's out to more friends online as well, though the topic of her telling Ida or Autumn is firmly shut down. Which... I guess makes sense. Ida and Autumn aren't really Valerie's friends; they're *my* friends. I should try hanging out with her friends more often, maybe. And maybe have a talk with Ida about how to be nicer to her.

After school is work, and work is blessedly boring. It's an oddly slow day for a Thursday, but I'm certainly not complaining. I don't have a breakdown and I manage to only steal two cuts of raw chicken, which is a pretty darn good day for me.

I go to sleep, and wake up back on the boat. It's more of the same: cleaning, mostly, with the sailors much more comfortable around Helen and I than they were yesterday. Nothing brings people together like freedom from oppression, I suppose.

The day passes, and Friday comes and goes much the same as Thursday did. It's a gosh dang miracle that neither Autumn nor I have been ousted yet, but Autumn is worried her time is fast approaching. She can't hide her bulky tail and wings in another dimension like I can with *my* buy-one-get-one-free limbs, and it won't be long before they're way too big to obscure. The only thing I can think of that might work is getting Jet to name her obfuscation spell and figuring out a way to teach it to Alma. I talk to Jet about it and she says she'll see what she can do.

Of course, I don't know how that goes when I wake up again on the boat. We should make landfall in the next couple days, though the sailors say they aren't sure exactly when since there's a different set of spells working the drive shaft and providing generalized upkeep and speed buffs. The old pirate captain was apparently Motion and Order, and he could get his ship moving a lot faster than they could otherwise go, but the new Motion mages from *our* ship might even that out, and... yeah. I guess our speed varies a lot depending on who's working and who's resting.

It's nothing I have to worry about, though. I munch away at some tasty jerky (it isn't human jerky, I checked) and largely laze the day away. I could get used to boat rides, I think. Not being able to sleep without instantly waking up somewhere else kind of sucks, so having lazy days like this is the closest I can get to rest. And I really, *really* need rest. Unfortunately, however, I have to sleep again eventually, and I wake up once more. On Saturday.

I have therapy today. Fffffffizzy pop.

I mean. I guess Dr. Carson wasn't *that* bad. And we mostly just talked about Pokémon, and I could do that again. Goddess knows I need to actually talk about my problems, though. I don't want to, though. I don't want to I don't want to I don't waaaaant to...

"Hannah! Therapy today!" my mother calls as an unnecessary reminder. Fine. I grit my teeth, get out of bed, and get ready for the day. Naturally, I'm still not allowed to drive myself, so I once again end up trapped with my mother in the car.

"Have you used your new laptop yet?" she asks.

"No," I tell her.

"You should try it out," she continues. "We need to know if it will work or if there's anything wrong with it and if we need to return it. I know you have your other computer, but we still need to test the laptop."

"I've just been busy, is all." It's not even really a lie. "I'll try to get to it this weekend."

A pause.

"Have you been keeping up with classes at school?" mom asks.

"Yeah," I answer. Mostly, anyway. I've been slipping a little, but my grades are good so who cares?

"You need straight A's if you want to get into a good college, Hannah."

"I'm not going to college, mom."

She nearly stops the car. She doesn't, but I see her twitch. Aw, dang it. That one just slipped out, I should have kept silent.

"You most certainly *are,* young lady," she says. "Hannah, I don't know what's been the problem with you lately, but you need to go to college if you want a good job, and you need a good job if you want to *succeed in the world.*

"Sorry," I mutter. "That's not what I meant."

I'm not going to be *able* to go to college. That future has become patently ridiculous. But I can't say that. I can't explain it.

"What *is* it then, Hannah?" my mother demands. "Are you on drugs? Did you get into debt? Are you suicidal? You can't just keep giving me the cold shoulder, Hannah, I am *terrified* and you have no *idea* how difficult it is to watch your own daughter just... just *fall apart* like this! What happened, Hannah? Please. Just say *something.*"

I don't want to say anything. I just want to curl up and cry. Why do I want to curl up and cry? She's not doing anything wrong.

"I am not on drugs, in debt, or suicidal," I manage to answer. Not usually suicidal, anyway. Out of all the problems I have, that's probably not in the top five.

"Then *what is it?*" she pleads as she parks the car."Why won't you tell me?"

"The whole point of coming here is to *not* tell you, mom," I growl out. "You'll know eventually. I can't hide it forever. Now let's just go? We shouldn't miss the appointment."

We both know that my mom arrived nearly ten minutes early, but she concedes anyway and we get out of the car, check in, and wait for the doctor silently. Soon enough we are greeted by Emily Carson, Ph.D., and I barely manage to not have a panic attack following her into her office. Huh. I guess my therapy trauma is still a problem. Shame that didn't go away after a ninety-minute conversation.

"Are you alright, Hannah?" Dr. Carson asks me as I breathe heavily in the doorway like some kind of absolute freak.

"N-not really," I admit. "Just... give me a minute?"

Oh boy my chest hurts. Am I gonna die? I mean, I didn't die any of those other times I had a panic attack, so logically I'm not going to die this time, but also holy shit, am I going to die? Oh boy oh boy. Deep breaths, Hannah. In, out. In, out. I manage to stagger over to Dr. Carson's couch and sit down on it, taking in shaky breaths. This successfully wastes maybe three minutes of our session.

"Okay, I can probably talk without breaking out into sobs now," I announce. "How are you, Dr. Carson?"

"I'm doing quite well," she tells me. "My husband and I watched a delightful movie together last night, I enjoyed it quite a bit. And then he made me dinner. Chicken a la king."

"Aw, that's really sweet."

"I do quite enjoy it, but it's not the best for my old heart. What about you, Hannah? How was your week?"

"Um... the last few days weren't terrible, but oh gosh, uh. Wednesday was. Not the best. Quite possibly the worst, actually."

"Oh, I'm sorry to hear that," Emily says, and she really actually does sound sorry. "What happened?"

"Uh. That is. A good question. I have absolutely no idea how to begin answering it, or if I even should."

Dr. Carson pauses, waiting a while as I sit in silence, my brain buzzing with mostly meaningless nothing. I don't know what to do or say. My extra limbs twitch. I clack my teeth. I fidget with my gloves. I say nothing.

"...Last time we talked, you fired a lot of concerns at me in sequence," Dr. Carson prompts, looking at her notes. "You mentioned almost dying. You mentioned concerns with your relationships and sexuality. You mentioned a man who gaslit and traumatized you. You mentioned experiences with cannibalism. You mentioned you suspect you might be autistic. You mentioned that you feel responsible for the current state of the world due to familial relations. And you also mentioned being involved with multiple deaths, and a fear of instinctively hurting others."

I swallow.

"Uh. Gosh," I say. "I really said all that?"

"Is any of it inaccurate?" she asks, pulling up her notepad as if she's ready to cross out anything I don't want on there.

"No, not... no," I mumble. "That's all true. I just... I seriously told you all that, and you didn't have me sent off to an insane asylum?"

"I told you I wouldn't," Dr. Carson smiles. "It seems like a lot has happened to you, Hannah, but I'm not here to make any judgements. You told me you had no intention of hurting anyone, and that's more than enough for me."

"Ah," I say, my heart falling. "Well, sorry to disappoint you. That's... part of what happened Wednesday. I hurt... I *killed* a lot of people. Thirteen people. Specifically."

Dr. Carson raises her eyebrows.

"Well. That's shocking. You'd think something like that would have made the news. What happened, if that's alright to ask?"

I laugh humorlessly.

"Well that's the problem, right?" I ask. "This is the part where you think I'm crazy. I literally cannot explain this unless I take the plunge and... and show you what I am."

"An extraterrestrial?" Dr. Carson asks. "You mentioned something of the sort last session as well."

I bristle instinctively. Not because she said something wrong, but because she *didn't*. There's absolutely zero chance she believes

I'm an alien, but her tone remained the same. Calm and composed and utterly trusting. Which means she's good at hiding her tells. Can I trust anything she says she believes?

Or... y'know. Maybe she's legit. Maybe when she says she trusts me and isn't going to judge me, she means it.

"...That was just a metaphor," I mutter. "I'm not actually from space. It's just something that unbelievable."

"Alright," she nods. "Would you like to tell me about it?"

I hesitate. I don't know what I should do.

"Ah, haha. Y'know, my friend Je—um. I mean, my friend Autumn said I should. She's going through some of the same stuff I am, except it's entirely my fault."

I bounce my leg. Dr. Carson says nothing, waiting patiently to see if I continue.

"I don't know if I should," I admit. "I don't know what to say."

"Well, the choice to speak or not is yours," Dr. Carson attempts to reassure me. "If you're not comfortable speaking with me about something personal this early, I completely understand."

I shiver slightly, gouging deeper tracts in the bottom of my shoes.

"What if... what if I don't want the choice to be mine?" I ask softly. "What if I want you to decide for me?"

Dr. Carson adjusts her glasses slightly.

"Well, I would say that I remain a firm believer in giving you control of this session," she tells me. "But I would also remind you that I can't help you with things that you don't speak with me about. This is a safe place, Hannah, and no matter what you tell me—no matter what you've done or what you are—I will do my utmost to help you. You have my word."

I take a deep breath and let it out.

"I could just talk about my mom instead," I say. "I have another friend who agrees with you, you know. About the whole 'she can love you and still hurt you' thing."

322

"Well, I suppose I might be biased," Dr. Carson says with a wry grin, "but your friend sounds like a wise person."

I actually manage a quick laugh.

"She would... agree with you on that," I say, smiling faintly. "She's a lot to handle. A really good friend, though. For sure."

The tension seems to ease a bit, and for whatever reason I keep talking about Ida.

"She's the most confident person I know," I tell the therapist. "Arrogant, really. But in a way that makes it so hard not to idolize her. She's almost like a fae folk. A little goblin that revels in joy and dreams and never has to come back down to Earth if she doesn't want to. She's also *really* hot, though I spent years trying to crush my crush on her so that's a bit of a complicated feeling nowadays."

Agh, why did I say that? Whatever, just keep going.

"Even without that, I think if we started dating she'd just sweep me away. I'd never be able to keep up with her. A great friend, but... probably a little bit of a lousy partner, you know? I don't have the energy for her."

Dr. Carson nods.

"It sounds like you know each other well, at the very least," she says.

"Oh yeah, definitely. We've been good friends since like, sixth grade. I really look up to her in a lot of ways. Oftentimes when I'm confused I ask myself, 'what would Ida do?' And suddenly it becomes a lot more obvious what the answer is."

"That's a good trick, actually," Dr. Carson smiles. "Reframing a problem in a different way to look at it from the outside can really help people clear their thoughts. Though of course, it's always worth remembering that it's still *you* making the decision. You often know the right answer all along, but looking at it from a position of someone you respect making the call just helps make things clearer."

323

Yeah. That fits, I suppose. It's still me making the decision. Free will is real, and all the consequences with it.

And I know what I should do. I know deep in my slowly-disintegrating bones that I need help, as much of it as possible. And in a therapist's office, one needs to talk about their problems to get help. I take a deep breath, and look Dr. Carson in the eyes.

"Magic is real and I am not human," I tell her, "and I can definitively prove both of these things."

Dr. Carson makes a few notes, her eyebrows raising slightly.

"Quite a bold claim," she muses, as placid as ever.

"I know," I say. "Do you mind if I take off some of my layers?"

"Make yourself at home!" she invites, gesturing to go ahead.

I nod, my heartbeat racing a mile a minute. What do I start with? I guess my jacket. It's just a backup layer; I already have another long-sleeved shirt underneath it. With how chitinous my arms have been getting, I need to not only cover them up but also *pad* them, so that people brushing into me can't pick up the strange, inhuman texture. Plus, while my shirt has holes in the back, my jacket doesn't.

I don't move right to the extra limbs, though. Hands shaking, the first inhuman feature I show off is my claws. The gloves come off, and for the first time I see a reaction of genuine surprise from Dr. Carson. It really shouldn't, but that somehow gives me a sense of victory, and it helps me keep going.

My chitinous hands revealed, I go further. I roll up my sleeves. I remove my shoes. I slip my mask off my face, giving my therapist a cautious smile. All the while, some part of me is watching her heart rate spike and getting just a little bit hungrier.

"Um. Hello again," I greet her awkwardly, seeing her breaths slow down as she consciously, purposefully takes control of them. She can't do the same with her heart. "So, I mean, you're probably thinking this is a costume or something, but it's not. This has just… been happening to me all month. I can prove it's really my body, if you want. But I guess I'll start with magic."

She has a small mug of tea on her desk behind her. It looks like it's cold, but I can still see some liquid in it with my spatial sense. All I need is a valid place to sort it, and I feel like there's an obvious answer.

Slowly, to make sure she sees it, I pull her drink out of her mug and into my mouth. It tastes absolutely terrible, but I can speak with her about wishing I had more human meat once we get past all of this. I swallow it down.

"Ta-da," I say, awkwardly doing some halfhearted jazz hands.

She stares at me. I stare back. I cough into my elbow. The tea really tasted wretched.

"Do you mind," Dr. Carson says, her calm facade ever so slightly cracking, "if I take a few minutes to compose myself?"

"Oh, um, sure," I agree. "Go ahead."

Shakily setting her notepad and pen on the table, she gets up and heads to a nearby bathroom. I watch her with my spatial sense, partly out of paranoia and partly because I don't really control it all that well on Earth yet.

She only seems to have a minor breakdown. It's not too bad, really.

16

SMALL STEPS

I've got to hand it to Dr. Carson; it only takes her about five minutes to come back like nothing even happened. Well, on the outside, anyway. Her heartbeat is still racing inside her chest, betraying the confusion and terror she feels, and it only multiplies when she enters the room and sees me in person again. Because of course it does.

"Sorry about your tea," I blurt. "I, um. In retrospect there was probably a lot I could do other than drink your, uh. Your tea. Sorry."

She stares at me for a moment before slowly sitting back down in her chair.

"Think nothing of it," she insists. "I should apologize as well. Everyone needs breaks from time to time, but I do try to ensure that mine don't interfere with any time dedicated to my clients."

Wow, back to talking evenly just like that, huh? I can't imagine being that composed.

"It's fine," I shrug awkwardly, slowly pulling my hip-limbs into visible space and setting them on my lap. "Trust me, I get it. I have to live through all this. It hasn't exactly been a pleasant change."

"I'm... naturally tempted to ask a lot of questions," Dr. Carson says, staring with naked confusion at my new limbs. "But I think my professional duty in this situation is clear, so first I'd like to remind you that I am not a medical doctor. Any sort of... physical issues you might be experiencing are likely beyond my capacity to help you with, and I'd be remiss to not encourage you to seek a more relevant professional."

I chuckle a little. I can't help it. Does she really think I never thought of that?

"And what, exactly, would the more relevant professional be in this situation?" I ask. "Do you know any good doctors of Transmutation magic?"

My blade-limbs emerge next. Rather than arc them up and over my shoulders, since that would feel a bit too aggressive, I curl them underneath my arms, crossing the blades over my stomach. Dr. Carson's eyes widen as she sees them slip into visibility, leaving me embarrassed. Why am I showing her these, anyway? This is obviously way too much at once. Nobody wants to see weapons growing out of a girl. I fiddle awkwardly with my blades, drumming my fingertips against their flat sides.

"Hannah, I know only that I do not know what is happening," the therapist says. "It's hard not to recommend you seek outside help when I feel I will be less useful than I should be."

Ah. I see what this is. I freaked her out too much and she doesn't want to help me anymore. I can't help but feel dejected, but I guess I expected this? So. It's fine.

I realize, suddenly, that Dr. Carson's heart isn't the only one racing. As much as she is confused and afraid, I'm really the only one with something to lose here. This is the last fragments of my secret slipping out of my control, and I can't stop it.

"I understand," I say, my hands shaking. "I'd like you to keep this a secret, please. I'd really like that a lot. But, um, I don't need to bother you otherwise. Sorry."

I brace for the worst, but it doesn't come.

"Bother me?" Dr. Carson asks instead. "Hannah, no no no! I just... I sincerely apologize for giving that impression. I am... here to help you. And I intend to do that to the best of my ability. I am worried that the best of my ability will not be enough, but I'm going to damn well give you it."

The swear catches me off-guard, considering how composed and proper Dr. Carson has been. Somehow, that more than anything kind of helps me relax a little. It feels like a crack in the facade, but one that's passionate rather than fearful.

"...Alright," I allow, my voice a bit unsteady. "Thank you."

"Of course. But I must admit, I don't have a good idea of where to start anymore. Normally I'd ask how you've been handling changes like this, but..."

"Uh. Yeah, I get it. I have not been handling it super well," I admit. "I've talked about the problems I've been having, I just didn't explain the source. Panic attacks multiple times a week, horrific bodily transformation, uncomfortable animalistic urges, that sort of thing. I definitely feel like I'm going crazy."

"I... see," Dr. Carson says, her eyes constantly flicking back up to my face after inevitably wandering down to my limbs. I scrape my blades together slightly, a lightly eldritch noise ringing out through the room, and she *flinches*.

Dang it. I don't want to do this. I shouldn't have to do this. But... this is my fault, so it's only fair.

"Are *you* doing alright, Emily?" I ask my therapist.

"Hmm?" she asks. "Oh, Hannah, no, you don't have to worry about me. We therapists have our own therapists, you know. I'll be just fine."

"Ooh, that's a familiar set," I say, leaning back on the couch. "'I'll be fine' instead of 'I am fine.' 'You don't have to worry about me' instead of 'there's nothing to worry about.' Come on, doc, we both know you won't be able to talk about this to anyone else. I can prove magic exists, but I'll be doing everything in my power to

329

ensure that you can't. So what are you going to say, exactly? Who are *you* going to talk to that will reassure your sanity?"

She sighs, a faint smile on her lips.

"Hannah, I appreciate that, I really do. And while I assure you that my mental well-being is capable of surviving this... *this*, I admit to some curiosity. What you've shown certainly changes my perspective on the concerns you've brought to me previously."

I let out a huff of air through my nose.

"You didn't believe I was really a murderer, did you?" I ask.

"I *believe* you are an intelligent and insightful young woman who has been through a series of extremely traumatic experiences I've yet to hear the details on. If you're interested in discussing those details, I'm happy to hear about them."

I huff again, pulling my feet up onto the couch and retrieving some foam blocks from my jacket so I can protect Dr. Carson's furniture from my claws.

"...Well that'll get into more embarrassing stuff you'll think I'm crazy about," I grumble.

"More than... all this?" she asks, gesturing at my everything.

"Kinda, yeah?" I admit. "I wake up in another universe when I sleep, and I can't really prove it exists in any meaningful way other than the fact that it's where magic is from. But that's where I killed a bunch of people, so you don't have to worry about me being wanted by the police or anything. At least, not yet."

"Not yet?" she prompts, and I squirm.

"I don't... I don't feel stable," I admit. "I don't feel in control. I have giant murder blades strapped to my shoulders at all times and *I don't feel in control.*"

She stares at my blade limbs and carefully, trying her utmost to hide it, swallows nervously. But I can see it. I can't *not* see it. My spatial sense grows clearer every day.

"Is it all the time that you feel this way, or just sometimes?" she asks me.

Are you going to kill me, she asks me.

"Just... just sometimes," I assure her. "I feel fine now. They're just... limbs. Like arms and legs. Controlling them feels normal and natural."

I demonstrate, moving them slowly and carefully in clear patterns, making sure not to point the blade her way. She seems entranced by the movements, but quickly focuses on me when I start speaking again.

"But when I get startled or overwhelmed, I just... my instincts take over. There have been a ton of times that could have ended in tragedy if things only went a little differently."

"Like what?" Dr. Carson prompts.

"Like, um... when my transformation first started, my friend surprised me at the bus stop and I went into total fight-or-flight mode. And there was one time I lost a lot of blood and bit my friend's fingers. ...Though, I guess she invited me to do that."

"I... see..." Dr. Carson says, clearly having a lot of questions. Though the one she goes for is: "Is that similar to the deaths that you've mentioned *did* occur in this... dream world?"

"Eh, I don't like calling it a dream world. I'm pretty certain it's a fully independent world that I am physically a part of. Everything I do there is way too lucid for a dream, you know? I just happen to be conscious there while I'm asleep here. I know that sounds ridiculous, but..."

"But the supernatural is real, so I have every reason to trust your expertise. What do you call this other world, then?"

"Uh. I guess I usually call this 'earthside' and over there 'treeside,' because it's a giant world tree situation. Like Yggdrasil, kinda."

"Okay. So the deaths you were involved with 'treeside.' Did they occur due to this lack of control?"

"Um," I shift awkwardly. "Well, no. I guess not. The first four were because we got attacked by people trying to kill us. And the last, um. The last thirteen were pirates who were enslaving my friends."

For reasons beyond my understanding, Emily starts to seem *more* composed. She scribbles down some notes, nodding along as I explain.

"So, would you say it's accurate that these deaths were the result of conscious, purposeful decision making on your part?"

"Uh... I mean, 'purposeful decision making' is a bit strongly worded for what happened. It was just what I had to do at the time."

"But it wasn't something you did due to a lack of control," she presses.

"The killing wasn't, no. The cannibalism maybe was? I, uh. I mean arguably it isn't cannibalism since I'm not human anymore, but... yeah. I had some pretty strong urges to eat the people I kill."

"And so you do that?"

"Yeah, I mean... yeah, I do," I mutter miserably. "Like, I dunno. I'm generally in a horrified dissociative fugue whenever I go around killing people? So my self-control is kind of shot afterwards. And I, uh. Yeah. My body is kind of even more fucked up treeside, I'm just kind of a horrific little creature so most people don't even think it's that weird when I eat people? So they just... let me. And I, uh. I don't like it."

"I see," Dr. Carson nods, scribbling more notes as her heart rate increases again. "But, to be clear, these urges occur *after* any fights for your life occur? They don't compel you to kill anyone for the sake of eating them?"

"Um," I fidget awkwardly. "Not other than a general background awareness that people taste really good, I guess?"

"Then... while I certainly don't want to ignore your feelings on the matter, they do seem to be a separate issue, if I'm understanding this correctly? So unless you'd like to switch tracks, which we *can* do, perhaps we should focus back on your fears about self-control."

"Um, sure, yeah," I nod. "That's definitely the scariest thing about being a monster, you know? The fear that I'll hurt someone by accident."

"Do you consider yourself a monster?" Dr. Carson asks.

"Um," I say, wiggling my many sets of claws. "Yeah? I'm a mutant mass murderer, doc. Doesn't get any more 'monster' than that."

"Are you?" she asks. "You've described two out of the three events as self-defense, in that you had to defend yourself from aggressors that intended to use lethal force against you and your friends. Is that correct?"

"Well... yeah."

"And in the third case, what was your motivation for the killings?"

"...We had been captured by slavers who had strapped magical bomb collars to my friends. Goddess, that sounds so stupid to say to a normal person."

"It's not stupid," Dr. Carson says firmly. "Hannah, I have been a therapist for a *long* time. I've spoken with people who have had to defend themselves from all kinds of abuse and hated themselves for it. I've spoken with soldiers who can't sleep at night thinking about the people they've killed and the things they've done. I'll tell you the same thing I've told them: this world, or any world as the case may be, is cruel and unfair. You aren't a bad person for trying your best, even when your best is far from perfect. You aren't a bad person, Hannah. I don't believe that."

I've heard it before from my friends, but something about those words aches truer from a stranger. How unfair is that? I can't even trust my friends right.

"...Maybe not," I allow. "But I'm still not good *enough.*"

"And how good is that, exactly?" Dr. Carson asks. "Is there a point where you would feel good enough? Or is that phrase just a way for you to marginalize your own achievements and emphasize your failings?"

"I don't know," I admit. "Maybe."

"Hannah," she asks. "Have you ever injured someone without meaning to? Ever?"

"That's kind of a complicated question to answer," I mumble.

"Does that mean you could make a reasonable argument that the answer is 'no,' were you so inclined?"

I let out an irritated huff.

"Could you just... stop trying to make me feel better about this for a second?" I snap. "Like seriously, do you really want me to *stop* worrying about hurting people? No, I haven't injured any of my friends, outside of that time Ida asked me to. But I've gotten really, *really* close, Dr. Carson. After my blade-limbs grew in, a friend of mine startled me and I nearly stabbed her through the *heart*. I absolutely would have killed her if she hadn't defended herself."

"I see," Dr. Carson hums. "How did she startle you, exactly?"

I scowl and look away.

"...Well, she broke my nose," I admit.

"Hmm. I feel like I might lash out at someone if I'd been surprised like that too," Dr. Carson muses.

"Well *you* don't have magical blade-limbs!" I shout at her. "It's one thing to punch somebody, it's a whole different thing to stab them through the chest! I feel like that's a pretty serious escalation!"

"It is," Dr. Carson agrees firmly, unphased by my sudden rise in volume. "I'm not saying you shouldn't be treating this seriously, Hannah. But there's a world of difference between categorizing yourself as a dangerous monster that needs to be restrained for the safety of others and categorizing yourself as a troubled young woman who just needs the experience and training *everyone* needs to safely handle a weapon."

I flinch, embarrassed both by my outburst and the even-toned response that followed it.

"Sorry," I mumble.

"It's fine, Hannah," Dr. Carson insists. "You're going through a lot, much of which I can only hope to partially understand by drawing whatever parallels I'm able. But I want you to understand that I do *not* see you as a monster. Your appearance is startling, but the way you speak and the things you fear—they are very human. You are afraid of things that are reasonable to fear, but I genuinely believe they are things you *can* overcome. Have you been misleading me about the severity of these urges you describe?"

I shrug helplessly.

"I don't know. I don't think so."

"Then I believe you can control them," Dr. Carson tells me. "Everyone has intrusive thoughts, and you're far from the only person that has intrusive thoughts about *hurting others*. As long as you control yourself, as long as they stay intrusive thoughts and don't become actions, you've done nothing wrong."

"Shortly after the first time I killed someone in the other world," I admit, "I got mugged here on Earth. And I was... I was so *messed up* at the time, so stressed and frayed thin from committing my first... from killing someone for the first time, that I nearly killed the kid mugging me, too. I tried to kill a person over like, maybe a couple hundred dollars."

"I take it you didn't, though?" Dr. Carson asks.

"The same friend who broke my nose stopped me," I shrug. "But if she hadn't been there? If I had been alone? I don't know what I would have done."

"Hmm. A lot of people would argue that it's acceptable to use violence in defense of one's own property," Dr. Carson says neutrally.

"I dunno. I guess maybe sometimes? Doesn't feel right to me, though. Not in that situation. He was just some desperate kid trying to get enough money to live."

"How do you know that?"

"Uh. I kind of ran into him again later and talked to him a bit. And then maybe-hopefully cured his mom's disease?"

She pauses. Aw, crap.

"...You can cure diseases?" she asks. Double aw crap.

"Um. Technically yes, I can cure some diseases probably? But there are some really problematic side effects and I don't even know if it solves the problem in the long term. I just, uh. Well, y'know the spell I used to steal your tea? I can do that to like, uh. Bacteria and stuff."

"And you say you used this to cure the mother of someone who mugged you?"

"Yeah. Look, can we not talk about this?" I beg. "I just... I don't want to... it's really not something I should be drawing attention to."

I can't cure someone without speaking Refresh out loud, which spreads magic. And I *do not* want to start handing out esoteric arcane weapons to random people. Dr. Carson gives me a serious look for a moment, but eventually just nods.

"Alright, Hannah," she says. "Well if you like, we can discuss some practical techniques for handling your concerns with self-control. I think a useful starting point is to have anything that applies to handling a knife also apply to your extra limbs. First and foremost, that means you should never at any time point the sharp end of the blade at another person, unless you intend to hurt them. I've noticed you frequently raise your limbs my way in response to stress, but if that's something you control, it is absolutely the first habit you should be breaking. The better you get at avoiding those unconscious movements, the better I suspect you will get at not reacting dangerously when surprised."

Oh. Right. Yeah, that... that makes sense.

"I'm so stupid," I mutter. "I *really* should have already been doing that, huh?"

"Hannah, you aren't stupid," my therapist insists. "You're *overwhelmed*. That's why it's so important to talk these things

336

out with people. Obvious solutions often don't seem obvious in the heat of the moment. To that end, you've mentioned you're constantly stressed, which makes you jumpy, which cycles into another thing to get stressed about. How much exercise have you been getting?"

I blink.

"Wha?" I ask. "Exercise?"

"Yes. Exercise. I know it seems like somewhat of a non-sequitur, but I assure you: it helps. A lot. An *enormous* swath of common mental issues can have their symptoms effectively treated, at least in part, by regular exercise. This has been proven time and time again, so I always find it difficult to *not* recommend wherever possible."

"You want me to deal with the fact that I'm mutating into a horrific bug creature... by exercising more," I say flatly. "You get how ridiculous that sounds right?"

"Rather less ridiculous than the fact that your body is growing chitin in the first place, if you want my opinion," Emily quips back. "Look, I get it. I have a lot of clients that struggle to work exercise into their routine and struggle to believe it's effective, but... it is. It really, *really* is. It's one of those things you hear so often it sounds too rote to be true, but trust me, Hannah. When someone comes to me with anxiety and stress issues, I tell them to eat right and exercise more, and it *helps*. It's not a cure-all, but it helps. Lacking any concrete knowledge of how your altered biology would affect things, I have no reason to not at least tell you to try it."

"Not going to tell me to fix my diet, though?" I smirk at her, not really feeling the humor.

"Feel free to correct me, but I feel like food might be a triggering topic for you based on what you've told me."

I wince.

"No, you've... probably got that nailed, yeah. Even outside the whole cannibalism thing, I'm an obligate carnivore now. I don't have the flat teeth needed to chew things, anything that isn't an animal product tastes bad and digests poorly... it's sort of a whole thing."

"Ah, I'll make a note of that," Dr. Carson nods, making a note of that. "Yes, we'll have to assume your body knows better than we do about the kind of nutrients you need to eat, in that case. I suspect there *are* non-meat substitutes you'd be able to digest if you're interested, but there's certainly nothing wrong with eating meat if that's what you want to do. My main suggestion is finding foods you enjoy and don't feel guilty about eating; a useful strategy for overcoming certain triggers is to give yourself enough positive experiences with the triggering situation to help balance out the learned instincts. This obviously doesn't work with everything, but it's not a bad strategy for something like food."

"Maybe I'll try to figure out some recipes that taste good to me," I agree noncommittally. "I get a lot of urges to eat raw meat and eggs and things, but cooked food still tastes fine. I think the exercise is going to be a problem for me, though."

"Oh? Why's that?"

"Well... where exactly would I get a chance to do that?" I ask. "I have gym class every other weekday, but it doesn't feel like a workout at all. My body requires me to do kinda superhuman things in order to actually feel the burn. Plus, I'd be working out in baggy sweatshirts and sweatpants in the middle of summer and people are going to *notice* that kind of thing, you know?"

"Hmm. You don't have anywhere private that you can move without other people seeing you? That's likely a big contributor to your stress all by itself."

"I... I guess," I agree. Hmm... there is one place. Brendan's yard. Er, I mean Valerie's yard. I've always had fun getting to let loose out there, even if I kind of... messed up the last time I did that. "I might have somewhere that would work, but it's difficult to walk the line between indulging in euphoria and keeping enough self-control to not screw everything up."

338

"Hmm," Dr. Carson muses. "It's curious to hear you mention 'euphoria.' I suppose I never asked: how do you feel about the changes that are happening to you, Hannah? I assumed they were mainly stressful for you, but I should have asked sooner."

"Er, well, 'mainly stressful' is definitely accurate," I assure her. "But that's actually something I've been thinking about, and... well, I don't hate the idea of being a weird ten-limbed bug girl in the abstract, you know? I don't dislike my limbs or my chitin or whatever inherently, I just... it sort of ruins my life? Or at the very least it *defines* my life, I guess. As my girlfriend says, I didn't really have a life you could ruin in the first place. Heck, all the best parts of my life are still there. It's just... y'know. I'm kind of terrified."

"What of?"

I gesture vaguely.

"The world, I guess?" I tell her. "The moment I go public there's gonna be a whole flippin' political movement trying to extradite me to Atlantis or whatever, and probably a whole other group of people who just want to use their second amendment rights to shoot me in the face. I don't want attention in general, but being a scary monster doesn't exactly make me a magnet for *positive* attention. Add that to the pressure of being the prophet of an evil Goddess who I'm *pretty sure* wants me to start an arcane apocalypse, and things get *really* stressful."

Dr. Carson blinks.

"I... don't think we've talked about that last bit," she hedges. "Could you elaborate on that?"

Aw, beans.

"Uh. Yeah. Um. Gosh, I didn't mean to... uh. Hoo boy. Okay. Um, are you religious at all, Dr. Carson?"

She doesn't seem to like that question.

"I... have long considered the prospect of a divine entity to be unlikely," she answers me slowly.

"Ah. Well. Sorry about that," I say awkwardly. "Uh, there's a Goddess. She's, um, definitely one-hundred-percent real, and I could probably prove that but I'm not *going* to because it would be really, really bad."

A therapist could *totally* end up with Pneuma magic of some kind, and if that happened I'd never be able to trust her again.

"Do you want to talk about her?" Dr. Carson asks.

Do I want to talk about Her? Do I want to talk about the entity that torments me, laughs at me, belittles me, *touches* me, all for Her own sick amusement? Do I want to talk about being a pawn in a horrid game, do I want to talk about being helpless, do I want to talk about being abused by something so far beyond me it will never, ever face justice? About a problem that will not, cannot end?

"No."

Dr. Carson looks me in the eyes and I hold her gaze. She nods.

"Alright," she agrees.

So we talk about other things. My body, my spells, my time treeside. We talk about my friends, who always support me, and my family, who will never understand. Dr. Carson seems most comfortable when she can relate my problems to something she's already seen before, like when she talks about soldiers when I worry about violence. She gives me a lot of good advice, and at the end of the session I feel like I finally have something approaching a *plan* towards feeling better, even if I don't really feel any better right now.

We don't talk about the spell I can't control which turns people into monsters. We don't talk about souls and how I spread them. We don't talk about the Goddess any more than my brief slip-up. Maybe we never will. I can't tell if I want that or not.

"There's one last thing I want to say," Dr. Carson tells me as I get all my outer layers of clothing back on to prepare once more to trudge out into the world. "You still have my business card, right?"

340

"Uh, I think so, yeah," I say.

"I'll give you another one," she says. "Anyway, if I'm currently working with another client, my phone will be off. But at *any other time,* I highly encourage you to call me if you need to. If you're having a panic attack, or you're afraid you won't be able to handle a situation, or if you think you're at risk of hurting someone... call me. I'll answer and I'll help as best I can. Even in the middle of the night. Okay, Hannah?"

"Um, okay," I agree awkwardly.

"Good," she nods. "I have... hmm. You're definitely every bit as unique a case as you warned me you would be when we started, Hannah. You're already getting extended sessions, but I'm worried that won't be enough with how quickly things seem to be progressing for you. If you ever want to move up to seeing me twice a week, I'll make time for you."

"Okay," I say. "I don't know if I have the confidence to say yes to that, but... thank you."

She nods.

"You're very hard on yourself, Hannah," she tells me. "But I truly believe you've done far better than most people would have in your situation. You should be proud."

I cringe at that. I don't think I've done anything all that great.

"I'll say it again, Hannah," Dr. Carson presses. "You should be proud. You don't have to agree with me, but that is my genuine opinion. I believe you can make the best of this. I believe you will be okay."

It hurts to hear. It hurts. Why are such simple words so painful? I want to cry. I can't respond to her, so I don't, but she doesn't seem to mind. I finish getting all my extra clothing back on and she escorts me out to my mom.

They speak again, though I don't pay attention to what. Instead, I pull out my phone and find a text from Br—from Valerie. I quickly go change her name in my contacts, before I forget again, and then read the message.

Any chance you could come over later today? she asks. **I want to show you something.**

I smile.

Actually, I was gonna ask if I could come over anyway. Just got out of therapy.

Ooh, ouch, she sympathizes. **You okay?**

Uh. Yeah, actually. She's honestly... it's way better than I ever imagined. I actually told her?

Oh shit, really? she asks. **That's great! I mean, probably. Did it go okay?**

I mean, we'll have to see if I end up on the news, but I think it went really well, yeah. She told me to exercise more lol.

Uh. Huh. Really?

Really! I'm gonna try it. But I'll need your backyard, if that's okay.

Of course! You can come over whenever.

KK. I'll see you soon.

I grin, excited at the prospect of maybe having a good weekend for once. I get to hang out with my best friend today, and go on a date with my girlfriend tomorrow! Then I stop grinning, because I need to make sure the edges of my mouth aren't stretching up past my mask.

My mother returns soon and we get in the car together. She asks if I want to go out to lunch somewhere and I decline as politely as possible, telling her I intend to eat lunch at Brendan's place. It's already starting to feel kind of wrong calling her Brendan, but like, what am I gonna do, tell my mom she's trans? She already doesn't like my best friend, best not give her any other reasons to start miserable conversations about the people most important to me. Valerie wants it to be kept secret for now anyway.

My mom still drops me off at Valerie's place, despite her obvious trepidation. I ring the doorbell, and moments later my big wonderful goofball friend answers it.

"Hey, Valerie," I greet her quietly, stepping inside. She squirms happily just from the sound of her own name. Aaah, so cute!

"...Hey, Hannah," Valerie nods back. "You hungry? Or do you wanna run around first?"

"I wanna see whatever it is you wanna show me, first!" I tell her, heading downstairs as I pull my sweater off and start shifting my limbs back into normal space.

She sighs and follows me down, clearly both happy I want to see and very nervous about showing me. I watch her with my spatial sense as she descends, just sort of... idly looking her over. Tall and gangly. Hairy and rough-skinned. Big hands, big feet, and... well, uh, pretty big ding-a-ling, not that I have any experience with the things. Physically, she could not be less attractive to me.

All things considered, I find it kind of weird how easy of a time I'm having thinking of her as a girl.

Honestly, I was afraid to be, and kind of *expecting* to be, pretty crappy about Valerie's whole... *being Valerie* thing. Not because I *want* to be, I just... know myself too well to expect better, I guess? I know how my brain works and my brain is an awful piece of garbage. I'm not the best at adjusting to that kind of stuff, and I don't know anyone else who's transgender, and I'm... generally bad at being good, overall. I also have a *very* negative interest in the idea of being a man, so I'm often not sure how to empathize with gender stuff. And on top of all that, I've known her as Brendan for pretty much my *entire life!* That's a whole lot of habit to break, you know? I really expected the mental shift to be more difficult. And like, I definitely still mess it up sometimes, but... she's Valerie. She is Valerie! Is it arrogant to be proud of the basic ability to think that and believe it? I feel like I should have higher standards, but dang it, I'm really happy with myself about this anyway.

I guess it's just... y'know. I love her. I love her a *lot,* so getting this right is really, really important to me. Considering everything my friends have done for me, I *have* to be able to do at least this much. If there's *anything* I can help Valerie with, I'm going to do it.

"I definitely want to at least hear some highlights of your therapy session, if that's okay," Brend—I mean *Valerie* says Goddess *freaking*... ugh, I am the worst. Good job patting yourself on the back for literally nothing, Hannah!

"Yeah, uh, it was pretty eventful!" I say, hiding my inner chastisement as best I can. "I think I almost gave *her* a panic attack this time, so that means I won this round, right?"

"Hannah," Valerie groans, cradling her face in her hands. "Hannah, no..."

I cackle unrepentantly.

"I'm kidding!" I assure her. "I mean, Dr. Carson *did* have to go hide in the bathroom and work herself through a minor breakdown, but she was actually pretty nice and helpful overall. She basically said that I'm afraid of hurting people because any sensible person would be afraid of hurting someone while carrying a weapon, and the solution is just more self-awareness, focus, and discipline. Y'know, three things I am famously good at."

I manage to get a reluctant laugh out of her at that.

"Well you're certainly in a mood," she smirks as I flop out on the couch and stretch all eight of my current limbs. "It's nice to see, so I guess I have to give props to your therapist for something."

"Look, a person whose actual job it is to figure out how crazy people are told me I'm not crazy and gave me actual things I can do to help hopefully not kill anyone on accident other than scream and pray, and we both know those two things don't work. So yeah, I'm feeling cautiously optimistic for the first time in a while. I'm gonna enjoy it while it lasts."

"Well hey, that's pretty awesome," Brendan—*fuck* I mean Valerie, Goddess *damnit*—smiles faintly. "And, well, more good news, I guess: the thing I have to show you is also pretty awesome."

"Oooh, is it magic?" I ask excitedly. "Did you finally figure out your magic!?"

"Yep," Valerie nods. "I did."

I can't help it. I leap to my feet and *squee*. Yeah, magic is terrifying and giving it to the entire world will probably have horrific consequences, but darn is it still cool! I hate how much I love my magic, but *boy* do I love my magic. I hope Valerie does too!

"It took me... *quite* a long time to figure this out," Valerie explains, pulling out her phone for some reason. "It's very weird and complex and for some reason, even after I was sure of what I had to do it wouldn't work at *all* until I built up the courage to finally name it."

"Wh—you named a spell without backup?" I accuse, putting my hands on my hips and my hip-legs on my thighs. "After all the crap you gave me about not naming my magic?"

"I'll admit to being a hypocrite, but I'll not claim I was wrong," Valerie protests. "I don't think I feel the Goddess quite like you and Ida do, but it still felt... right. Like I was pre-approved and good to go. And yeah, I'll admit I was really excited to try it."

"Well, okay I guess. Don't leave me hanging, then! I don't feel anyone else around so we should be safe to go!"

"Okay, okay, let me just pick one," she says cryptically, thumbing through her phone.

"Pick one what?"

"A piece of art," she explains. "This one should work as a demonstration."

She shows me her phone, which displays a drawing of a long-haired woman with eyes closed, lifting slowly up into the air as various generic fantasy-looking characters watch her with interest. It's simpler than Valerie's usual art, flat-colored and unshaded.

"This is the only copy of this file left in the world," she explains. "I've removed it from my computer, never posted it on the internet... it's totally unique."

Then she hits delete, confirms it, and the Goddess speaks.

"Dreamer's Spellbook: Arwin's Elementary Levitation."

And Valerie rises into the air. Not very far, since she's already pretty close to hitting her head on the ceiling, but she does. She *flies.*

"Ta-da," she grins.

"Oh gosh," I grin. "That is *so* cool. How does it work? Do you have to delete a drawing every time? What all can you do with it?"

"An easier question," she grins, "would be 'what all *can't* I do with it?' To which so far my answer is 'teleportation, transformation of living things, and precognition.'"

I blink.

"Uh. That's it? It does literally everything else?" What the heck kind of spell did she get!?

"I mean, almost certainly not, there's a shitton of things I haven't tested, but..." Valerie shrugs. "Yeah. It's *super* versatile. The main limitation is that I have to prepare art for it in advance and permanently destroy the artwork to activate the relevant spell. The more work I put into the art, the stronger the effect. Or... at least that's my current guess on how power is determined. I'm an Art wizard, basically."

"Oh Goddess, yeah!" I realize. "You're like a flippin' D&D wizard but your spellbook is your *drawing library.* That's so cool!"

"Yep!" Valerie grins, floating slowly around the room. "It's the most magical magic I could have asked for. I hate to hand it to her, but the goddess really nailed me with this one. I've kind of been rushing home to fill my computer with new drawings and test out new things since I first figured it out."

"I'll bet! Gosh!"

I rush forwards with my arms out to hug her, remember I *definitely* shouldn't hug her without permission, and suddenly halt awkwardly with all my limbs still splayed out to either side. Also Hannah, remember! No pointing blades at people! Valerie chuckles and floats over to grab me, snatching me up under the armpits and lifting way up into her arms. I yelp with delight, clinging around her with all sorts of various limbs as we stare into each other's faces with big goofy grins like the pair of doofuses we are.

"This is *so* cool," I gush, my body feeling delightfully weightless as my feet dangle. "I want to commiserate about the fact that the only-spoken-aloud restriction means you won't be able to use it in public, but I bet you've already got dozens of plans to take advantage of it anyway, huh?"

"Oh yeah, definitely," she nods. "High-quality drawings take a long time to make but their effects can last significantly longer. So, y'know. Step one is turning the basement into an awesome magical fortress."

"Sick," I say approvingly. "Oh my gosh this is so cool. You can fly!"

"I can fly!!!" she agrees, unable to hold back some happy shakes and wiggles.

"No transformation, huh?" I sigh. "Can't say I'm surprised you tested that already, given... y'know. Girl."

"Yeah..." Valerie sighs. "Girl."

"You any more sure yet?" I ask.

"I'm pretty damn sure, yeah," she confirms. "Definitely a girl. Transitioning is going to be a pain in the fucking ass, but... it's really exciting, too. I *want* to complain about not getting a magical shortcut, but every trans person wants a magical shortcut. I'm not special just because I actually maybe had the chance at one."

I hesitate. I want to help her. I want to help her *so badly*.

"...I mean, you kind of still do have a chance," I say quietly.

Her eyes widen slightly... and then narrow suspiciously.

"You're talking about the monster transformation spell you can't even control that we don't understand," she accuses.

"I mean... *yeah,* but you kind of wanted to be a monster girl anyway, right?"

"How dare you," she accuses, her voice dripping with irony. "How could you ever say such a thing about me. I don't know where you ever got the impression."

"Hee hee," I giggle, booping her on the nose. "I'm serious. I've got a good feeling about it."

"Well, I *have* recently ended my lifelong feud with trusting 'good feelings,'" she considers, "buuuut I'm still more than a little hesitant to subject myself to unknown mutagenic spells, no matter how awesome that sounds in the abstract."

"Alright, but hear me out," I press. "What is *the* quintessential spell you always argue every wizard should have?"

"...Counterspell," she mutters. "Hmm. *Hmm.* Okay, I'm with you here. You think I can just dispel it if things go badly."

"Exactly!" I agree. "It's worth a shot, right?"

"I've been testing in private, so I don't know if my countermagic spell works, but I *do* have a possible countermagic spell prepared!" Valerie says, looking increasingly excited. "You wanna cast a quick Refresh or Spacial Rend or something?"

"Heck yeah!" I agree, wiggling out of her grasp and landing on the ground. I extend one finger and let a weak Spacial Rend coat the claw, making sure to keep it carefully away from anything. "Alright, give it a shot!"

Bre—*Valerie* nods, grabbing her phone again and thumbing through it before I feel the Goddess descend again to take her breath.

"Dreamer's Spellbook: Vivian's Rapid Dispel."

Glowing chains of blue emerge from Valerie's hand, arc towards my finger, wrap around it, and then dramatically shatter, my Spacial Rend disappearing and my hand going numb. I try to recast it, but it takes a solid few moments before warmth returns to my fingers and my spell sputters back online.

"...Woah," I breathe. "So... it works?"

"It works!" Valerie vibrates excitedly.

"So can I... y'know. Do the thing?" I ask.

I really, really, really, *really* want to cast it. I want to change her. I can do it and I want to do it and I just... whew, okay, calm down, Hannah. You have to at least wait until she says yes.

"Yes," Valerie says. "Do it."

I flood the room with Transmutation in an instant, a grin splitting my face, and my best friend shivers. I'm not sure if it's delight or fear, but some part of me is excited either way. Goddess, why do I love this spell? Why does it always feel like this? Why don't I want any of my friends to be human, either? You'd think I'd be pretty comfortable with humans, having lived my whole life with them, but I just can't wait to pull them away.

My thoughts stall as Valerie doubles over, gritting her teeth. I watch, enraptured, as her fingernails thicken, growing both back into her bone and outward into points. My best friend's claws come in, and my favorite person becomes that much more comfortable to be around.

She'll get it now. She understands.

17

INCIDENTAL DISCOVERY

"Ow," Valerie grunts, staring at her newly-clawed fingertips. "This really hurts."

"Yeah, I mean, that's how it usually happens," I agree.

"Aaaand my fingertips are all bleeding," she sighs.

"Oh, I've got some stuff for that, uh... in my... backpack. Which I do not have with me."

"We didn't think this through well at all, did we?" Valerie asks.

"No," I agree. "No we did not."

"Boof!" Fartbuns barks.

Valerie and I both turn to stare at her dog, happily panting at the bottom of the basement stairs and completely bathing himself in the wild Transmutation magic I just unleashed everywhere.

"Fuck," Valerie summarizes. "Alright, no more of this shit."

She licks a finger clean as best she can (which makes me weirdly hungry and jealous) and starts poking away at her phone gallery again.

"Dreamer's Spellbook: Vivian's Rapid Dispel."

Her own magic rushes out through the room, consuming every lingering remnant of my own. The basement is now flush clean of magic, but Valerie still has her claws. Which... well, I don't *see* anything wrong with Fartbuns, but who even knows if that means anything.

"We *really* didn't think this through well at all, did we!?" Valerie whines.

"I mean, *was* there a good way to think this all through?" I ask, still giddy.

"Yes! Probably!" Br—Valerie groans, patting herself down all over. "This is a horrible situation! I have claws and nothing *but* claws, the whole rest of my body feels the same!"

"Uh, yeah, it'll probably take a while for whatever other changes are happening to finish happening," I shrug. "Autumn didn't grow *anything* on day one, and her tail took a second dose to come in. Besides, claws are neat!"

"Since when are you so excited about having claws?" Valerie asks.

"Uh... good question," I admit, trying to think back. "I think using my 'transform other' spell makes me a little manic? But also just, I had a really good coming out at the therapist, so I hate myself a lot less than usual!"

"Well that's *something* good, at least," Valerie grumbles.

"Don't worry! I'm sure your boobs will grow in soon!"

"...Like actually, or are you just being supportive?"

"Um... I don't know." I try to imagine Valerie with big boobs. Hmm! Surprisingly easy. "Yeah, I got a good feeling about this."

"Oh boy," she deadpans. "I guess I get to look forward to magical HRT, now with countless unknown side effects."

"Oh, don't act like you weren't enthusiastically consenting to that just a moment ago," I complain. "Come on, let's check over your dog and make sure he's okay."

"I suppose you of all people are in the unique position of being able to think this isn't a big deal," Brendan sighs.

"No, look, I get it," I promise, kneeling down next to Fartbuns and giving him fervent pats as I look over his body with my spatial sense. "It's a huge deal. One of the hugest deals. And while part of me is definitely sorry I did this to you, part of me is also just happy I don't have to do this alone. My inevitable reveal is rapidly approaching, you know? And you in particular are in a unique position to actually like what's going to happen to you."

Hmm... yeah, something is definitely up with the dog. His internal organs look weird. Muscular differences, especially?

"...I can't deny there are aspects I will appreciate," Valerie sighs. "How's FB?"

"I think he's gonna grow more limbs," I admit.

"Oh boy."

"I believe you mean *good boy*," I coo, scritching Fartbuns behind the ears."Who's gonna be a monstrous little spider dog? You are! Yes you are!"

"God, you are in a *mood* today."

"Goddess," I correct automatically.

"Right. Yeah. Goddess."

There's a pause as I continue checking Fartbuns over. I'm not a veterinarian, but nothing seems outright harmful and Fartbuns isn't acting like he's in pain, so we're probably in the clear for now. Which is good! The last thing I'd ever want to do is hurt Fartbuns.

"...Well, I'm going to go to the bathroom and get my fingers bandaged," Valerie sighs.

"Alright," I nod. "I guess I'll go outside and see if Fartbuns is okay with a bit of exercise."

"Please don't do anything crazy," Valerie begs.

"I will do my absolute best but no promises!"

Brendan—dang it, I mean Valerie again, geez—shuffles off to the bathroom as Fartbuns and I tromp upstairs, heading for the backyard. I am intellectually aware that I should be a lot more worried and concerned about everything that just happened, but I'm just... not. I am far too busy being *excited*. I'm really looking forward to helping Valerie with her transformation, especially since I feel like I messed up super hard with Autumn and haven't really had the opportunity to do much for them. Alma and I hang out, chat, and enjoy each other's company, but the monster transformation thing is usually a taboo topic. And Jet, well... Jet just insists on handling everything herself. With Valerie, however, I know we'll both be comfortable reaching out to each other when we need it.

Is it messed up to be excited that I'll be able to help my friend with a problem that I caused? Yes, probably. I guess I'll add that to the list of things to talk to Dr. Carson about! Boy, it's getting really long. Therapy sure is a lot nicer when no one is trying to sexually exploit me.

...Haha, wow, nope. My brain tried to make it a joke but it's still not very funny! Geez, that's a bucket of ice water over my mood. I'm genuinely startled by how much progress I've made in therapy already. I guess I really did need it. Just like literally every single person who knows and cares about me insisted was the case. It kinda sucks how when everybody who loves you tells you about something you need, they're usually right.

Fartbuns scampers excitedly out into the yard when I open the backdoor, and soon enough I'm tearing after him, luxuriating in the feeling of my claws digging through the dirt. We wrestle for a while, I don't know how long, but he seems totally fine and having a good time so I guess the transformation isn't hurting him. At least for now.

Wrestling Fartbuns is fun, but sandbagging so I don't hurt him does give me an urge to let loose. So after a while, I break away from him and just... run. Brendan's huge yard works as a perfectly functional track if I just sprint around the circumference of the grassy area, and holy *crap* is it fun. I'm so gosh dang fast! I'm pretty sure I could outrun the average cyclist, at least while sprinting.

I giggle excitedly to myself between gulps for air, my body actually feeling the burn for the first time in forever. It feels *good*. I've never really loved exercise, having always been more of the curl-up-at-home type, but I suppose that's just another part of me that's changing. My new body sings with joy as exertions that would have been unwelcome irritation before now feel instead like cathartic release. It's an interesting experience, one that I'm not sure if I should be worried about. More signs that my body is messing with my head are never fun.

But I guess that's the thing: the body *always* messes with the head. The head, after all, is part of the body. I remember when I was little, coming home at the end of Halloween with a massive bag overflowing with candy. My mom would always put so much effort into helping me make homemade costumes of whatever I wanted to dress up as, and I took pride in having cool costumes that no one else did. Most of them were various Pokémon, of course, but I digress. My point is that after coming home, I would *engorge* myself on that candy.

Endless streams of sugar would drop down my gullet, and I would love every bit of it. I'd often make myself sick with so much at once, but it felt worth it. I *loved* candy. But then, as I got older, I just... didn't. It wasn't just the fact that I was more cognizant of the consequences; Goddess knows I still don't have any self-control. I just simply did not like candy anywhere near as much as I did when I was little. And obviously nowadays I can't really eat candy, but this was all back before the monster transformation stuff. People grow, people change, and their tastes change with them. Sometimes, a thing you used to love stops bringing you joy. Sometimes, a thing you used to hate starts tasting good. The body grows, the body changes, and the person trapped inside is beholden to that body's whims. That's just how people *are*.

I spend a couple laps running in different ways, using my extra limbs or scuttling on my arms and legs, but it seems like in terms of pure speed, running like a human and just leaving the rest of my limbs out of it is best. My chitinous, humanoid legs tear easily through the dirt, propelling me forward in long leaps. My feet pound into the earth at rapid intervals, feeling just like a normal run, but when I look back each footstep is several yards away from the last. It's like I'm flying.

My laughter grows as I continue running around, overjoyed by it all. This beautiful moment truly is exactly what I needed to relax. There's nothing here but me, Fartbuns, the wind, and Valerie's family gardener.

...Wait, hold on.

I skid to a stop, using my hip-legs to arrest my momentum since my feet don't have any backwards-facing claws. Holy crap there's just. A person? Trimming hedges!? When did they get here?

They do not seem to care about me at all.

"Um," I clear my throat. "Hello?"

They turn to look at me and give me a polite nod. It's an older man, maybe forty or fifty.

"Hello," he greets me placidly.

"When, um. When did you get here?" I ask.

"One o'clock," he answers. "I work here."

"I, um," I sputter, my various limbs gesticulating in confusion. I was not... I never expected my reveal would be like this...! "You're not... scared of me?"

He shrugs, returning his attention to the hedges.

"I thought the dog was the one digging up the yard," he comments idly.

I blink, utterly dumbfounded. I'm not sure what to say to that. I'm not sure what I *can* say to that. My thoughts churn for a little before I finally manage to speak up again.

"I, um. Could you not tell anyone about me?" I ask.

"If I gossiped about what I heard or saw at work, I would not have a job," the man answers tiredly. "So I do not. Who you are and what you are doing does not matter to me."

He snips the hedge clippers and then taps the bush lightly with them.

"This hedge matters to me. Let us all mind our own business and focus on what matters, okay?"

...I think I've just been politely asked to shut up and leave him alone. Still somewhat shellshocked, I wander back inside to look for Valerie, finding her in the basement on her computer as expected. She seems like she's already got an idea for more art.

"Uh. So. How are you doing?" I ask.

"Typing and holding a stylus still really hurts, so not great," she answers.

"Oh. Sorry. Um. I got spotted by your gardener?"

"Huh?" Valerie asks, turning to look at me. "Oh, fuck! I forgot Alejandro was working today. Shit. What happened?"

"He, um. Didn't really care? He just kept doing his job."

Valerie snorts.

"...Wow, really? Yeah, that checks out, honestly. Alejandro is pretty great. He's been working here for ten years now. So... nothing bad happened? No freakouts? No catastrophes?"

"Um, not that I know of," I shrug. "Didn't spot anything weird about his internal organs, either."

"Well... that's good, right?" she asks. "Bodes well. The average person thinking we're a strange curiosity at most is kind of the goal, right? I mean, I guess Alejandro is decidedly above-average, so maybe not the best measure, but it's still good."

"Huh. Yeah. I guess so."

I hold my hands behind my back, drumming my toes against the floor.

"...Is there anything I can do for you, Valerie?" I ask.

"Huh?" she asks.

"Is there anything I can do for you," I repeat. "I've just... a lot has happened. You've been helping me out, and now I went and did this to you. I wanna make it up to you somehow."

She gives me a lopsided grin.

357

"Well, if I get to grow tits because of this I'll happily call it even," she says. "Otherwise, we'll just have to wait and see. The claws are a little unwieldy, but nothing I can't get used to. I just ordered some capacitive gloves online, and as for everything else, well... we'll figure it out as it comes, I guess. Claws aren't really indicative of any particular final form, you can kind of slap them on anything."

"Oh yeah? Any particular sort of changes you're looking forward to?" I ask. "Other than the girl stuff, I mean."

"Eh, not really?" she considers. "I've RP'd just about everything under the sun, I don't really have a set preference. Catgirls, hellhounds, liches, eldritch flesh masses, raptors—both dino and bird—it's all cool. I think I'd prefer feathers, fur, or just normal skin over something rougher like scales, just for the nice texture, but honestly I wouldn't complain about much of anything."

I chuckle a little.

"Gosh, that was a thorough answer. I guess you know a thing or two about designing monster-human hybrids, huh? You furry, you."

She waves me off.

"Furries can be neat, but muzzles aren't my thing and that's what I consider their defining feature," Valerie corrects. "I much prefer humanoid faces. Of course, the only real definition of 'furry' is 'a person who considers themselves a furry in good faith,' because it's just one of those largely undefined social terms. Either way though, I'm not technically a furry."

"I see, I see," I nod solemnly. "So what are you, then?"

"Uh. I dunno if there's really a snappy term for it," she considers. "A monster girl enthusiast, I guess? I like monstrous features on humanoid forms."

"Well, that seems to sum me up," I grin teasingly. "Find me attractive, do you?"

"Hannah, you were unbearably sexy *before* you started growing chitin," Valerie answers bluntly. "If not for the gender dysphoria

358

and resulting emotional repression I've lived with my whole life, I'm not sure I'd be able to stay sane around you."

I gape, completely poleaxed by the sudden, intense compliment. My brain whirls with confusion as a burning blush rises up my face.

"I... wh... you think I'm...? You *always* thought I'm...?"

"Yes. Extremely. Did you seriously not know?" Valerie sighs.

"I thought you didn't want to date me, though!?"

"Of course I wanted to date you!" she snaps. "I just didn't want *you* to date *me!* You're attracted to women! You would have been miserable!"

"But *you're* a woman!"

Now it's her turn to blush.

"S-sure, but I didn't know that at the time!" she grouses. "You think this was easy to figure out? For ninety-five percent of my life I had literally never heard of transgender people outside of shitty jokes on TV about how gross it is when they try to seduce the main character. I got through it by refusing to think about it and dissociating so hard that half our grade thinks I'm mute. It took *way* too much prodding from my friends online for me to actually grok that being more comfortable representing myself as a woman—not to mention desperately wanting to be one—isn't particularly cisgender behavior."

I stare at her, all too consciously aware of both my awkward blush and hers. I wonder which one of us is redder. Probably her, since her skin is normally so pale. Mine just keeps getting darker, though I'm pretty sure it's turning gray instead of... well, any sort of normal color for skin to be.

"I had no idea," I admit. "I really don't know what any of this is like. Sorry."

She shrugs, affecting an awkward, forced smile.

"Yeah, I know," she says. "I appreciate that you're trying, though. It... you have no idea how happy it makes me just hearing you say 'Valerie.'"

"Heh. I mean, I have some idea," I grin. "I *have* been appreciating getting to see you wiggle, Valerie."

That prompts a still-deeper blush and, on cue, a wiggle. So cute!

"...Well, anyway, I just wanted to get that off my chest before it gets any heavier," Valerie mutters. "Don't worry about it. I get that you're already dating someone else, and I'm completely unprepared to date anyone right now anyway. So. Friends?"

My heart flutters a bit unexpectedly, but I push it away and nod.

"Of course," I agree. "Best friends."

"Best friends," she confirms.

"...Although," I muse, tapping my chin, "I do kind of want to meet your online friends. I oughta thank the people that helped you out, if nothing else."

"Uh, really?" Valerie asks.

"If that's not a problem, yeah," I nod. "I know I don't hang out with your friends very often. Your school friends can be... a little tiring to be around?"

"No, I get that," Valerie nods. "They can be... yeah. I'm honestly really worried about coming out to them."

"Yeah..." I agree. "But like, you've talked about your online friends before and all the cool games you do together and now I'm hearing how they helped you figure out this really big thing about yourself and they just... sound neat, you know? You're my best friend, but I feel like it's really rare that we hang out these days. I wanna be a bigger part of your life. ...Maybe ask for fewer hours at work. Maybe I'll even quit."

"I struggle to imagine you quitting any sort of job, honestly," Br—Valerie answers. And I mean, she's got me there.

"...Maybe I'll get fired after coming out as a freaky inhuman magical monster," I correct. "That's not protected by equal opportunity laws. I checked."

"No, but a lawyer would probably be excited to help you sue anyway if your boss tried," Valerie muses. "That'd be some *crazy* publicity."

"Which means there's not a ding dang chance I'd be interested," I sigh. "Oh, well."

"To answer your actual question," Valerie says, spinning around in her chair to look back at her computer, "I'll ask my friends if they're down to meet you now. And if they are, which they probably will be, I'll send you the link to the Discord server."

Oh geez, Discord. I haven't used that in a while.

"Sure," I nod.

Nothing notable happens the rest of the day, which is honestly pretty nice. Valerie and I just hang out like old times, playing *Super Smash Bros.* until her new claws get too sore and then just chatting about nothing in particular. When I return home, I'm feeling pretty great, despite having to bundle up all my extra parts again.

Then I walk inside, and find my mother waiting for me.

"Hannah," she greets me, sounding tired. "I half-expected you to stay the night."

I freeze as my brain churns into overdrive, trying to figure out all the little implications and disapprovals that one sentence carries. Already my stress levels rise, desperately searching for every detail of what I did wrong this time and how I can just make it go away. But I'm tired of this. For a little while, today, I was finally above this. I had something better.

"Maybe I should have," I answer.

"Hmm. You think so?" my mother asks, her lips pursed in an expression somewhere between irritated and sad. I don't answer and I don't leave, either possibility a little too terrifying. She asked me a question so the conversation isn't over and she won't tolerate me departing. But also, it was a rhetorical question, and I can either make her mad and possibly be punished for

361

reasserting my opinion, or I can take back what I said. Neither option is appealing.

So we wait in silence for a bit, and then my mom continues.

"I don't understand what I've done wrong, Hannah," my mother tells me. "Your brother doesn't seem to want to talk to me anymore either. Your therapist tells me I should give you more space, but I don't know how much more space I can give someone who refuses to interact with me or even look at me when I'm talking to her."

My gaze snaps up to her eyes, more or less involuntarily, and I grit my teeth. You don't know how to give me more space? Have you tried maybe not cornering me literally the day my therapist recommended that? Except no, I can't say that. She'll take it as snark, which always makes things worse, and then she'll point out that we literally haven't talked at all since Wednesday, which I won't be able to refute, and everything will just escalate.

What's the answer to this puzzle? How do I communicate my feelings while also telling her exactly what she wants to hear?

"Why won't you just tell me what's going on?" my mother asks after I take too long to respond. "You know I'll do everything I can to help you, Hannah. No matter what it is. You know I love you."

I almost say 'I know,' because I *do* know, she's been telling me that her whole life. And the evidence for it is obvious: my mother will drop everything to help me, she constantly works hard for me, she always devotes her time to me, and when she's apart from me for too long she gets depressed and distressed—which is why I'm having so much trouble getting her to give me space. So she loves me. I've known this my whole life. But if that's true, then why does it feel so different?

"Why does your idea of love involve repeatedly pressing me about things I don't want to talk about?" I ask.

"Because I'm your mother," she answers simply, crossing her arms. "You're distressed. You're struggling. You need help, and helping their children is what mothers *do*."

"Well, I don't always want your help!"

"Oh, I'm well aware of that," she gripes. "You didn't want me to potty train you when you were two, you didn't want me to teach you to cook when you were ten, and you didn't want me to make you get a job when you were fifteen, but they're all things you need to survive in this world. Am I wrong about that?"

I glower. Well, if you want to cherry-pick every good thing you've—

"Am I wrong?" she presses.

"No, mother," I grit out.

"Don't give me that face," she orders. "I've done nothing to deserve this hostility."

"Then why is it that I feel so hostile around you and not anyone else!?" I snap. "Look, you've *already* helped, mom! You made me go back to therapy. The therapist *is helping*. I was already feeling better until I had to come home and have this *stupid* conversation with you!"

She stares me down just long enough for my anger to fade and get replaced by fear, and then she sighs.

"Okay. 'The therapist is helping.' That's all I needed to hear."

And then she walks away, leaving me feeling embarrassed and gross. I trudge upstairs, and after an hour of agonizing about the conversation in bed I finally manage to fall asleep.

"Hannah, wake up," Helen says, jostling me slightly. It feels *really* uncomfortable, so I groan and hiss and do not move an inch. "Come on, Hannah, the boat's about to make landfall. And since it's a stolen pirate ship, we might need to be prepared for trouble."

I groan, glancing around the room with my spatial sense. I'm curled up at the foot of the bed as Kagiso groggily cuddles the pillow that's supposed to separate her side of the bed from Helen's. Helen, of course, is already up and dressed.

Normally I'd be happy to get going for the day, but I *overwhelmingly* do not want to move. I don't even want to move

363

my mouth to try and speak real words. The crappy conversation with my mom pretty thoroughly killed my high from earlier yesterday, but even beyond that I just feel *exhausted*.

"Oi, come on, get up," Helen says, trying to scoop me up from where my legs are curled underneath me. I groan again, the feeling of her hands on my body uncomfortably sensitive for some reason. She jerks her hands away, frowning.

"...You're kinda squishy," Helen comments. "Everything okay?"

Squishy? I take a closer look at myself, and sure enough my carapace is not looking so hot. Rather than my usual pristine bone-white shell, my chitin looks partially dissolved underneath the still-stuck cast-off skin of my molt. My body is a little different from when I went to sleep, too; I'm a bit longer, like someone grabbed either side of me, pulled, and stretched me like taffy. Radial symmetry is officially, one hundred percent out. Bilateral symmetry is in. Shame.

"Hhhngh," I grumble, moving my mouth against my intense desire to stay still. "Big molt. Moving bad."

"Ah. Fuck, okay," Helen scowls. "Transmutation stuff?"

"Mmmngh," I confirm.

"Well, not the best timing, but I guess you're mostly just backup. If shit is going to start over me being a Chaos mage or... well, or really anything, it's gonna start today."

"Sorry," I mumble. "Not really controlling this."

She nods understandingly.

"It is what it is. We'll manage. You okay to be shoved in a backpack for the day?"

"Mmmngh."

"Right, have a good rest, then."

She gingerly lifts me up, the pressure *really* weird and uncomfortable on my temporarily-squishy body. I'm sure my carapace will harden back up once I'm done growing, but for now it's just... ugh. But then Helen carefully deposits me in her backpack and surrounds me with a comfy nest of clothing, and my burrower instincts kick in to tell me that everything is okay now, actually. I settle in and relax.

Kagiso is eventually coaxed out of bed, Sela and the rest of our gear strapped firmly to her torso as we head to the deck. The sailors give us respectful nods and greetings, Helen keeping us out of their way as they work. I can't see the port from here, but presumably everyone else can as they all frequently glance nervously in the same direction. Most of them seem to relax whenever they see us, though. I take that as a good sign. We freed them from slavery, so they trust us to protect them from any problems making landfall, too. I wish I was in a better position to help, but hopefully I won't need to help them anyway.

"What do you think our odds are of this going smoothly?" Helen asks someone who doesn't seem very busy.

"Eh. Decent," the sailor shrugs. "We slashed the ship markings, which is as good a way to indicate the pirates are dead as any. So that should prevent us from being shot. The tricky thing is that we have no way of telling anyone *who* killed the pirates until we land. For all the dock knows we could just be a different group of pirates, so tensions will be high. But honestly, as long as no one does anything stupid we probably won't need to worry about much."

"Doesn't seem to stop people from worrying anyway," Helen comments.

The sailor barks out a laugh.

"Does it stop you?"

Helen inclines her head, conceding the point, and the sailor gets back to what he was doing. When we start getting close to port, the sailors start speaking spells that might be useful if things go badly. Nothing flashy, we don't want to scare anyone, but we're ready. Sela even casts **Graveyard Soul** again, the spell it used to prevent a Pneuma spell from targeting Kagiso all the way back when we were fighting the branch serpent... though I don't really know what it does, exactly. I'm tempted to ask it, but I'm pretty sure it was waiting for other people to start casting spells before casting its own in order to go unnoticed. We *are* currently pretending that Sela is dead.

And then... we land at port. It's similarly disgusting to the port we launched from, all sticky and bacteria-ridden, but at least it isn't *rotting*. Rather than being entirely made of wood, this place is almost entirely metal. Helen is waiting by the gangplank, so we're close enough for me to see the armed and cautious group waiting for us at the dock.

"Ho there, gentlemen!" one of the sailors calls out with a wave. "If you're here to wait for pirates and slavers, I'm happy to report this is now a free ship!"

The dockworkers seem to relax considerably at that, and to my thankful surprise things do indeed go well from there. Someone at the port recognizes one of the former slaves as someone that went missing at sea, and that pretty much settles things. Everyone seems quite happy to have that particular group of pirates gone for good, and while there's apparently a bunch of legal crap about who gets to own the boat now, only the people who actually care about that have to deal with it. Which means we're basically free to go. A quick Aura Sight check and both Helen and Kagiso are let into the city.

The dock itself isn't all that interesting at first; from where we were on the boat, it just looked to me like a big stick of metal extending out over the sea. But as we walk down it, I realize that, yes, that's all the dock is, but it *has* to be that because *I can't see the bottom.* There are no pillars holding the dock up by connecting it to the seafloor, and I suspect this might be because the seafloor is still well over fifty feet below us. Instead, the dock is supported by a diagonal strut welded into the side of what appears to be an old, beaten-down skyscraper.

Which I *also* can't see the bottom of. It's mostly submerged in the sap. Have we even made landfall?

It turns out the answer to that question is 'kind of.' As we move further away from the boat, the sap level rapidly plummets. I forgot how sticky and viscous the sap is; it's not so much a flat body of water as it is a giant droplet. We're on the tail edge now, so what seemed to be flat before is rapidly turning into a thick, liquid cliff. It's not totally dewdrop-shaped, of course, not at scales this huge, but the sea level has still fallen well below us by the time we make it to the city proper. It's still horrendously uncomfortable to move, but I can't help shuffling to peek out of the backpack a little.

And just... wow. It's a beautiful city, but also a really sad one. After all, it's obviously built on the ruins of an even more impressive place.

Half-collapsed skyscraper skeletons, tilted over or missing entire walls of windows, form the bedrock of the port town. Extending well above the foul, rotting sap below, the city itself stays relatively clean from the constant sticky grime of the port, if not the smell. We walk now on a great metal bridge extended between and fused to the sides of two tall buildings, clearly not part of their original design, and far below us I can spot countless shorter buildings still barely peeking above the sap, if not fully submerged.

People are all over the place, both inside and outside the carcasses of buildings, each repurposed without care for their original function. Rooms of former office buildings have become small apartments. Apartments have had their walls torn out and repurposed into workspaces. It seems that no one knew and no one cared what these places were originally for, only that they were *here* and they had both a floor and a ceiling. The haphazard reconstruction seems aimless and patchy, the methods used to form bridges and roofing and windows obviously far more primitive than whatever made the skyscrapers originally. People came here and saw the rotting bones of something glorious, and they piled it up with trash because trash is all they *have*.

It's slapdash, but it at least looks like it functions. While the settlers of these post-apocalyptic ruins certainly didn't have anything even remotely approaching the technology of its creators, they have a pretty decent substitute: magic. I see construction crews of Motion, Matter, and Heat mages, levitating giant steel beams into the air and welding them in place with raw force of will. The humans here—and they are almost all human—are resourceful and industrious, not sparing the time to look back when they still have so much work to do. Or perhaps it's exactly the fact that they're living in the bones of what they lost which presses them to move forward.

Very quietly, I hear a furious hissing noise from Sela, and I feel all too aware of what made them lose their civilization in the first place.

"Alright, well... we pretty much made it," Helen announces. "Welcome to the Pillar. We have a decent chunk of money that I swiped from the pirates, so given Hannah's current situation, I vote we just find an inn to hunker down in until she feels better. Sound good?"

"Okay," Kagiso yawns. "Still sleepy anyway."

"Geez, I don't think I'm even physically capable of sleeping as much as you," Helen chuckles, shaking her head.

"What else to do?" Kagiso shrugs. "Nothing to hunt on boat. Nothing to hunt in city. May as well sleep."

"You could pick up some hobbies other than looking at organs, you know," Helen prods. "Ooh, we could buy a board game or something. There are a couple I've always wanted to try."

"As long as I don't have to move to play it," I mumble.

Helen grins and jostles the backpack, causing me to hiss at her.

"I'll take that as a yes?" she smirks.

"Sure," I relent. "I like board games."

"Hrm. Okay," Kagiso nods.

"Think the murderbot will play with us?" Helen asks.

"Sela would completely destroy us," I point out. "It's a friggin' robot."

"I'm sure it *wants* to destroy us, but this is just a board game."

368

"Huh?" I say. "No, I mean like... Helen, what do you know about robots, exactly?"

"...They kill people?"

Uh. Hmm. I guess Sela *did* react pretty poorly to me seeming to understand even a little of how it worked. I guess it's been trying to suppress information, and apparently succeeding. ...Or Helen just never had the opportunity to learn, but given the tech level of modern humans I'm seeing...

"Well I guess if Sela wants to play that's up to it," I allow. "But let's wait to decide that until we're somewhere a bit more private."

"Yeah, fair enough," Helen shrugs, and then we head towards some kind of market district to try and find a place that sells board games. I gotta say, it's nice to know that things here aren't so apocalyptic that they don't even have cheap leisure activities for sale. I guess the collapse of human civilization either wasn't all that bad or they've just had enough time and peace to rebuild.

I snuggle back into the backpack and let Helen do all the shopping, happy to be in my burrow once again. Gosh, my body is really messed up right now. Some limbs are elongating, some limbs are thickening, and I'm pretty sure my eyes are starting to migrate up my back a little rather than being nestled in between all my legs. The ends of a couple of my feet are even starting to split into... toes? Proto-fingers? Who knows! Not me! All I know is that my carapace is mush until whatever stage of my growth cycle decides to finish so I can harden back up.

I'm so caught up in my weird body and the funny-looking pieces of the board game Helen just bought that I almost don't notice the group of people with centipede talismans around their necks enter the marketplace.

"Cultists are here," I whisper into Helen's ear, and though I know she heard me she doesn't react even the slightest bit. "They're coming from the direction of the port. Three humans, all male, wearing cloaks."

Helen thanks the shopkeep for the game and casually walks in the opposite direction of the cultists like a normal shopper. She looks basically the same as every other human here, with the same plain clothes, dark skin, and dark hair as literally the entire crowd. She doesn't have to do anything to avoid being noticed.

Kagiso, unfortunately, is a tall, shirtless dentron with albino-white fur, and she is spotted immediately. I watch them look at her, talk quietly amongst themselves, and immediately start following us from a distance. They let themselves fall back out of my fifty-foot range, but a cautious peek out from under the lip of the backpack proves they're still following.

"Kagiso, we've got stalkers," Helen says quietly. "We're splitting up. Keep walking."

Kagiso answers only by smiling, and as Helen turns to start looking at another shop, Kagiso continues wandering away from us. The cultists follow her, completely ignoring Helen and I. They recognize her description, but they haven't spotted me. They might not even know Helen and Kagiso were a group.

"What do you think?" Helen mutters to me. "Do we interrogate them, or just make them disappear?"

I shiver, not sure what to say. One thing's for sure, though: those poor bastards are about to have a really bad day.

18

COMPARTMENTALIZE

"...I don't really want anyone to die," I manage to mutter quietly.

"Seriously?" Helen asks. "Nobody? Not even the people who self-admittedly want to kidnap you and experiment on you until *you* die?"

I nestle deeper into the backpack, my squishy, still-molting body protesting the movement.

"...If you can help it, yeah," I sigh.

Helen makes a nonplussed expression as she slinks through the crowd, turning to follow Kagiso's stalkers at a distance.

"That bleeding heart of yours is going to get you in trouble one day," she says. "I'm not going to let that trouble become mine. But... I'll see what I can do."

I sigh. Good enough. I get that sometimes people have to die. I just wish it wasn't the case.

"Thanks, Helen," I tell her. "I appreciate you putting up with me."

She smirks, though she's unable to hide a bit of an embarrassed blush on her cheeks.

"The feeling is mutual, I guess," she murmurs. "It's weird having friends who actually know what I am. You're all crazy bitches, but

I like having you around. So let's blow these tails and find a place to relax, yeah?"

"Yeah," I agree. "Thanks, Helen."

"You said that already."

I use a quick cast of Refresh to push away a lock of hair that fell in front of her eyes.

"It bears repeating," I insist. "Kagiso and I would be helplessly lost without you."

"Don't I know it," she snorts.

We settle into a comfortable silence as Helen follows the three men, Kagiso pretending not to notice them as she slowly maneuvers out of the crowded marketplace towards somewhere a bit quieter. The nature of the city makes it difficult to hide in anything other than crowds—everywhere is either the cleared-out floor of a building or a welded-on bridge between buildings, and neither has much in the way of cover. There are no dark alleyways or secluded streets where our stalkers might make their move, so Kagiso leads them to the next best thing: a quiet, run-down building near the edge of the city, close to where we can see the Sapsea finally *end* and give way to dry, moss-covered stone.

The building is small and relatively run-down, covered in rust and sticky with the splatter of viscous waves. Most people take a path around it, but Kagiso, acting the ignorant tourist, heads right for it with a curious flick of her ears. We let her and her stalkers cross the bridge together alone, Helen waiting a practiced beat before rushing down after them into the old building's guts. I manage to hear the tail end of something Kagiso says once we get close enough.

"—want to?" she asks.

"Ah, it's just a conversation," one of the men assures her amicably. "There's no need to be so standoffish. Your business is your business, of course, but *we* have business with someone who was last seen with you."

Kagiso is facing the three men down, two arms crossed and one arm hovering dangerously next to her bow, not yet drawn. They've 'cornered' her in what looks like a tiny private office: a small room, away from any exterior walls, with only one entrance and exit. An ideal place to pressure someone when you have them outnumbered, which is doubtlessly both why they cornered her here and why Kagiso led them here in the first place.

After all, the cultists think they're ratcatchers, but they're actually the rats.

"I'm curious to hear about this 'business' of yours," Helen announces as she walks in and leans against the doorway, trapping the three cultists between her and Kagiso. "So go on. Let's have that *conversation*."

The three human men turn to us as one unit, and for a split second I think they're all about to die as I watch them prepare for combat, bringing their hands up in an aggressive stance. They're lined up in order of height, an abnormally tall man on the left, a squat man on the right, and an entirely average-looking man in the middle. It's the average-looking one who reaches his hands out to stop both of his comrades, recognition flashing on his face.

"Nope, not this one, boys," he says, gritting his teeth in a nervous smile. "Let's keep those spells stowed and stay reaaaaal polite with this one. We've been made."

Helen raises an eyebrow.

"You know me?" she asks.

"I certainly know of someone who matches your description," the man in the middle nods, his hands raised in surrender. "Helena, right? Yeah, I'm not fuckin' with you. You win, we lose."

"...It's *Helen*," Helen sighs."Fuck. That stupid paladin made it down here before us, huh? No wonder you recognized Kagiso."

"She, uh, is certainly a woman who stands out in a crowd," the cultist nods amicably, glancing at his buddies and wiggling his hands meaningfully. They, too, raise their arms in surrender, looking considerably less enthused about the prospect than the

373

man in the middle. "Look, I promise ya, we weren't going to do anything untoward. Just needed some information, that's all."

"...Stalked me. Cornered me," Kagiso points out. "Not friendly behavior."

"Oi, oi, you walked in here all on your own," the cultist counters. "I'd be happy with any private place to chat."

"Cut the shit," Helen snaps.

"No shit, honest!" the cultist insists. "Look, you're the boss here, you want me to say the sky is red I'll say it. But right now, I'm not lyin'. I don't feel like that's really in my interests, y'see? I know a lotta people that can make a man regret tryin' to lie. Some of 'em Art mages. You think I'd take that chance?"

"I don't know you," Helen answers, stepping forwards. "Or anything about you other than the things you're trying to get me to believe. So forgive me if I remain skeptical. What are you doing here? What do you want with Kagiso?"

"We're looking for the founder's kin, of course," the talkative cultist answers easily. The tall one gives him a betrayed look, which is returned with a scowl. "What? Don't gimme that, they already know. They traveled with the damn thing."

He glances at Helen's backpack, where I'm hiding.

"...Maybe they still are," he mutters.

"What *is* a founder's kin, really?" Helen asks, forcing his attention back to her. "Why do you call it that?"

"Uh, well I feel as though the etymology is fairly self-explanatory," the man shrugs, giving her a lopsided grin. "They're the same type of thing as our founder, o'course. He was the first of 'em, at least so far as we know."

"Don't you people think that founder's kin are going to destroy the world or something?" Helen asks. "Like, they're responsible for all the fucked-up shit already happening, supposedly. What makes your boss the exception?"

"Who says he is one?" the cultist answers.

"The fact that it doesn't make any fucking sense to found an organization designed to kill you!"

"It's a little more complicated than that."

"Donny, shut up," the short cultist hisses at the talkative one.

"No, I don't think I will," the middle cultist, 'Donny' apparently, continues. "Sorry pal, I'd rather fuck with you than the Chaos mage. Besides, it's my whole fucking job to do the talking, so if you wanna get through this you should maybe shut up and let me—"

"Helen," I hiss, cutting him off. "We have incoming."

The cultists' eyes widen as I reluctantly confirm that I am, in fact, here, but I can't exactly *not* tell Helen about the group I just spotted rushing towards this building. Five more people, four humans and a dentron, all cultists. No way that's a coincidence.

"Shit," Donny hisses. "I had no part in this."

"Well, that upgrades you from corpse to hostage," Helen says, raising an arm.

The two cultists flanking Donny react immediately. One fires something I can't see—probably Light magic—at Helen's face as the other bolts towards the far wall of the room. Helen fires two shots and kills them both before blasting a hole in a different wall and obliterating the corpses.

"Kagiso, grab our new friend," she orders. "We're getting the fuck out of here."

Kagiso nods, turning to follow Helen as she snatches Donny's wrist with her tail.

"Woah, woah!" the man protests, shaking in terror as he stares at the spot his friends' corpses just were a second go. "I-I... look, you don't really need..."

"Congratulations," Kagiso says, smiling at him. "Helen said you friend! Helen not have many friends."

"It's a figure of speech, Kagiso," Helen sighs. "He's just some moron I don't give a shit about."

375

"Oh," Kagiso frowns. "Condolences. You have no friends."

"Oh, fuck fuck fuck," the cultist swears, letting Kagiso yank him along.

"Where are we going?" I ask Helen, my guts churning miserably at the two murders performed for my sake.

"Out of the city," she answers, blasting a hole through another wall and hurrying to the outside of the building. "Give me a countdown for when our incoming stalkers are in the building."

"Okay," I confirm, watching the new group of cultists rush across the bridge towards us. "Six, five, four…"

Helen hurries towards a different bridge, and when my count reaches zero she sprints across it, relying on our enemies being indoors to cover her as we make ourselves vulnerable. The bridges have heavy visibility in every direction, meaning we're probably getting spotted no matter what, but hopefully the group closest to us won't be able to see us, at least. None of us are dumb enough to assume these are the only cultists after us.

"How did they know where to find us?" Helen snaps at Donny.

"Uhh, buddy I was with probably led them to you," Donny answers. "Light mage. Could have popped a signal outside the building where none of us could see it."

"Yeah? And what can you do?"

"I'm good at talking."

"Not what I was fucking asking," Helen growls.

"Yeah it is," Donny insists. "That's my magic. I'm good at talking. I know what to say. Art and Pneuma."

I hiss. We grabbed the most dangerous one, didn't we? Damn it. Should we kill him?

"Woah woah woah, look, it's not like that!" Donny quickly says. "I'm harmless as a raindrop, yeah? I got no control over anybody, wouldn't want it. Anybody with that kind of power is a right bastard and we both know it. Inconsolable. My Pneuma side of things just helps me know what to say. Gets me a better read on people. That's it. Swear to the Goddess."

"You're a mind reader," Helen growls.

"Not even!" Donny promises. "Just a bit of intuition, that's all. I can let my magic guide my words. For example, I know you want information and you want to be left alone. What *I* want is to not die. That's the whole reason I'm trying to stop the apocalypse in the first place, yeah? I feel like we can work out a perfectly reasonable compromise here."

"And what makes you so sure Hannah is going to cause an apocalypse at all?" Helen asks, ducking into another building. "Why would she want to do that?"

"Oh, I don't think she necessarily does, miss," Donny answers. "I'm just worried she might cause it anyway. Ah, that's a group of my guys down there, you might wanna take a left."

Helen follows his gaze to the end of the bridge she was just about to start crossing and clicks her tongue in annoyance as she sees whoever Donny just pointed at. She heads for the building stairs instead.

"How would Hannah even do something like uproot the tree in the first place?" Helen presses. "She's just a fucking bug. Scary in a fight, sure, but it's nothing I can't do scarier."

"Well, I don't know the first thing about how to answer that, I'm afraid," Donny says, stumbling slightly. "But if I were a betting man I'd bet that maybe your friend Hannah does? Have you ever asked her?"

His gaze locks on the backpack. I sigh.

The thing is, I'm very much terrified of causing an apocalypse… on Earth. I'm a Goddess-dang powder keg on Earth and I know it. Spread the wrong magic to the wrong person, and who knows what the heck could happen. I'm definitely a huge danger to everyone I know and love. But here? In this world where everyone already has magic? Where everything is already dead or dying?

377

"...I seriously don't think I could do anything to make the situation worse here," I answer. "You're barking up the wrong tree, buddy."

"I'm what?" he asks, dumbfounded. Oh, right, idioms.

"I mean your hunch is off. I can't think of anything I could do that's even remotely on the same level as the problems you already have going here."

"Huh," he says. "You ain't lyin'. Well, that's reassuring, seeing as I'm helpin' you escape and all."

"Glad I could soothe your conscience," I answer dryly. "Could you maybe convince your creepy cultist friends to stop trying to kill me, in that case?"

"Oi, we're not creepy cultists!" he protests. "The Disciples of Unification is a legitimate religious organization. *And* we're quite personable, when ya get to know us."

"Well it's a little difficult to get to know you when you keep *attacking me on sight!*"

"Stow it, both of you," Helen snaps. "Making distance is hard enough without you shouting our presence."

I grit my teeth and shut up as instructed, Donny managing to shrug apologetically even as he gets dragged along by Kagiso's tail. Helen charts us a rather direct route, rushing towards the edge of the city as fast as she's able. I can see the logic behind it; in the city itself, using Chaos magic is just asking to get attacked on all sides, including by people who aren't even cultists in the first place. By taking the fight away from a populated area, fewer people are at risk and our chances of winning a fight rise dramatically.

It's looking like it *will* be a fight, though. Which is... not so good. My body is still screaming at me whenever I try to move, and I think even if I *could* move my body is too squishy for me to be of any use. I can only cast Spacial Rend on my claws, after all, and I don't really *have* claws when my body is vaguely spider-shaped jello.

378

"Alright, last bridge," Helen announces quietly. "Keep your eyes open, everyone. If they're gonna take potshots at us, now is the time. Go, go, go!"

This bridge is angled steeply enough down that it probably would be legally required to be a staircase back on Earth, but Helen and Kagiso still manage to sprint down it without any problems with balance. Below us, for the first time in a long time, is solid ground, and the bridge leads right down into it, the far end embedded into stone rather than another building.

"We make it down there, we break for the caves. Lose line of sight to the city, set up a chokepoint, cut off reinforcements," Helen orders. "Then we—"

A sphere of burning, blazing *something* suddenly streaks onto my spatial sense, but there's no time to call it out before it impacts the bridge behind us and explodes. Molten metal sloughs off the walkway like water, leaving an empty gap behind us as the middle of the bridge melts into nothing. Helen and Kagiso sprint faster as the bridge starts to sag, bending under our weight now that it's only attached at one end. And to top it all off, on the ground in front of us I spot a group of cultists hiding behind a boulder.

"Ambush, in front!" I call out.

"Fucking hell, how are they already here!?" Helen complains, bringing a hand up to fire a deadly blast of Chaos as Kagiso draws her bow.

"Zone of Law: Ban Projectiles."

Kagiso slacks her bow.

"...That not fair," she grumbles.

"That is my primary offensive compliment disabled as well," Sela buzzes quietly.

"Oh you've gotta be *fucking* kidding me!"

As Helen shrieks out her swears, cultists swarm the landing where the bridge meets the ground. At least a dozen of them pour out from rocks just beyond my range, including a face I would have been happy to never see again: Hagoro. The Goddess descends around us, tapping her finger warningly on Helen's burgeoning spell as I glower at the dentron paladin that tried to kidnap me all the way back when I first met Helen. He's armored similarly to our last encounter, with a shield and a spear, but this time they're each held in one hand, and on the same side of his body; both of his right arms are still missing, same as when I cleaved them off his body.

Helen changes tack immediately, twisting to grab Donny by the back of the head and force his face down to kiss the bridge. She tosses her backpack, with me inside it, to Kagiso as Chaos crackles around her.

"Back the FUCK off!" she roars. **"They Hunted And Hunted, But Not A One Could—"**

"Five-Finger Discount," a cultist I've never seen before calls out, a woman hiding at the back of the group. Donny vanishes and reappears beside her, his arm in her hand. Our hostage, stolen away in an instant. Helen snarls but continues her incantation, standing up and taking a fighting stance, using the fact that the projectile ban affects both sides to buy enough time.

"—Take Her Down. For How Could They Touch Their Own Annihilation?"

Helen steps in front, taking a protective stance with her body wreathed in obliteration. With what's left of the narrow bridge between us and them, we have both the high ground and a convenient funnel to forcefully limit their numbers advantage in a melee. But of course, Hagoro has the power to *un*-ban projectiles any time he chooses, allowing them to blast us with impunity... but who knows if that's a good trade for them. Helen is not the kind of girl you want to give a clear shot to.

"Phew!" Donny says, wiping sweat from his brow as he turns to the teleporter who snatched him. "Leilah, you're a literal fuckin' lifesaver."

"Where's Clyde and Ponzu?" she asks.

Donny grimaces.

"Didn't make it."

"...Fuck," Leilah swears, glowering furiously at us.

"You bastards came after us!" Helen roars. "So if you wanna die too then *fucking bring it!*"

"Don't mind if we do," Hagoro says, stepping forwards. "Madaline? If you'd come with me, please?"

A human girl steps blankly forwards as Hagoro holds out a hand to her, her cultist pendant seeming abnormally heavy on her frail-looking body. Her wavy dark hair is messy and very, very long, going down past the small of her back. Combined with the blank stare on her face that barely seems to look at where she's going, she looks almost like a doll from a horror movie.

"**Aura Sight**," Helen barks, and I dumbly copy her.

"**Aura Sight**."

Helen hisses. I swallow a swear. Oh, no. That's not good. That's not good at all.

Chaos and Pneuma. The girl's elements are *Chaos and Pneuma*.

"**And She Knew The Whole World Was Her Canvas!**" Helen barks, rapidly leaning down and slicing free a segment of metal from the bridge with one hand. She catches it before it falls, and it rapidly starts shifting into a sculpture of a naked woman clawing out her own eyeballs. It's... entrancing in a strange sort of... wait, no, I definitely shouldn't be looking at that. Helen holds the sculpture out in front of her like it's a sword, waving it around to catch the attention of as many people as possible. Hagoro and a few others cover their eyes, but most of the cultists fail to avert their gaze, staring at it with hypnotic transfixion.

The approaching Chaos mage stares right at it, her empty gaze unwavering as she continues her approach, completely unaffected. Her arms raise, as if preparing for a spell.

"Hannah, I have to kill her!" Helen barks. Wait, was she holding back for my sake this whole time!?

"Do it!" I shout back. I don't want any part of whatever the fuck is about to happen!

381

"**And So She Wept**—!" Helen begins, aiming to obliterate our enemies in one shot despite the ranged attack restriction. Apparently she's betting on being able to tank an Order-aligned divine retribution better than whatever this Chaos mage is about to output.

But the weakness of Helen's spells has always been how long they take to cast. The other Chaos mage smiles, the first expression she's made since I've seen her.

"**Dissociate**," the Goddess encants from her lips, and the world no longer matters.

I'm aware that after casting, the girl collapses on the spot, Hagoro rushing forwards to catch her. I'm aware that Helen, affected by the same sudden *nothingness* that I am, stops casting her spell halfway through. The resulting miscast obliterates her clothes, her hair, and most of her skin, sending her collapsing forwards onto the bridge in a bloody mess. Kagiso, Sela and I do nothing in response to this. Or for that matter, in response to anything.

These are just things that are happening. Facts without emotion. The world is what it is, and the fact that we are part of it is incidental.

Cultists swarm us, grab us, gather us up, lead us. Helen is lifted and stabilized, carried alongside her fellow Chaos mage as her skin slowly crawls back onto her body. Kagiso, conversely, is led forwards, nudged gently until she follows our capturers like a cow not understanding the concept of a slaughterhouse. We walk for an irrelevant amount of time. We arrive at an irrelevant place. We're separated from our irrelevant friends. Nothing matters, and we prefer it that way.

Because what little part of our mind is actually lucid screams rather unpleasantly. The terror, the horror, the pain, the stress... we let it remain locked away. To do otherwise seems... unpleasant.

The cage they trap me inside exists in 4D just as much as it does 3D. I won't be able to just walk out of it. Neat. I curl up in a ball and go to sleep.

382

Then I wake up, and unfortunately I'm a person again. Staring at the ceiling, the horror of everything that just happened slowly catching up to me, I surprise myself by not crying or panicking or screaming. Maybe it's a side effect of the spell that hit me; even if I'm no longer under its influence, my mood was pretty calm when I went to sleep because of it. Maybe it's also just the fact that we're all *alive*. They could have easily killed Kagiso, Sela, Helen and I, but instead we got taken to their base and split up. That's hardly the worst situation I've been in on the world tree.

Honestly, I might just be getting numb to this sort of thing. That's probably not healthy, but it's better than constant panic so I can't really complain. I quickly figure out my limbs and then quickly do the only sane thing to do in this situation.

I GOT KIDNAPPED BY FREAKING CULTISTS, I complain to my friends, texting them over our group chat.

I don't get any immediate responses, since they're all probably sleeping in, but that's okay. I check the date—Sunday, ugh—and extract myself from bed, slipping into the bathroom while the rest of my family is still asleep. I check myself over in the mirror, scowling at my complexion. Am I starting to turn *gray?* I think my eye-spots are going to maybe become actual eyes soon, too. That's not gonna be fun, but whatever. Hopping into the shower, the water hits my naked body and I grimace, suddenly reminded how temperature does basically nothing for me now. The feeling of water passing over my body is *weird* when the heat of that water is only an academic footnote in my brain. As a human, temperature is like, water's primary feature, and getting wet without really caring about it is a strangely alien experience. ...And not really a pleasant one, overall.

I sigh and squirt some shampoo in my palm, lathering up my head so I can just get out of the shower as soon as possible. When I pull my hand away, though, I end up pulling *way* too much hair along with it. Because of course I do.

Good! Great! I guess this is happening now! I run my other hand through my hair and sure enough, I manage to snag a few disgusting clumps of keratin there, too. Oh boy! It's not all of my hair, not by a longshot, but it's enough to make it clear that my hair *is* falling out with unnatural speed. Man, this sucks! I like my hair, dang it! I'd better get something cool to compensate for this crap.

Still grumbling, I rinse off and step out of the shower, using Refresh to dry myself so I don't have to deal with a towel in my apparently-delicate hair. I guess I'll add a wig to the list of things I need to buy to keep up my disguise! I'll have to do that after church. For now I'm okay, though, so I suppose I just have to hope it doesn't all fall off in the middle of the service and leave it at that for now.

With a yawn, I bundle up in my disguise and return to my room, checking my phone again. Ooh, a response from Autumn!

Oh my gosh, are you okay!? Do you need to cancel our date today?

I read it. Then I read it again. Wait. Date?

Oh shoot that's right we're going on a date today! Hot diggity!

No way, I'm super excited! I text her back. **Getting kidnapped sucks but it's not like there's anything I can do about it while I'm on Earth.**

Oh, okay! Comes the almost-instant response. **Awesome! I'll see you at 2 then?**

Heck yeah! Oh but if we could work buying a wig somewhere onto the itinerary that'd be a big help, I'm going super bald.

Uh. Oh. Okay, sure?

Thanks Alma!

Wiggling excitedly, I head downstairs to make breakfast for everyone as the rest of the house finally starts to stir. Being kidnapped by cultists: very bad! Getting to go on a date with a cute girl: very good! May as well ride the high and ignore the low as long as I can, right? Besides, if there's one thing my magic is actually good at, it's escape artistry. Dimensional movement and cut-through-anything make a pretty potent combo! I can figure out what I'm up against and how to deal with it when I go to sleep.

Because, you know. There are so many unknowns right now. Does the cage they put me in resist Spacial Rend somehow? If not, do they have other ways to lock me in? Where are my friends being held? What's happening to them? What's going to happen to me? What kind of mages am I up against? How many people am I going to have to murder this time? Each question is increasingly terrifying and I have no way of dealing with any of them so really if you think about it the best thing I can do is just compartmentalize the crap out of it like syrup on a waffle.

With breakfast sizzling, my family soon comes downstairs and is quite happy to be fed. We exchange the usual pleasantries before my mom comments on how I look happier than usual. This, of course, immediately tanks my mood and I manage to mumble something about hanging out with a friend after church. Yes, mother, a *female* friend. This mollifies her considerably, as it definitely nullifies the chances of sex happening rather than dramatically multiplies it. Definitely.

...Of course, dramatically multiplying the less-than-one-percent chances isn't really saying much. This is my *second date* with Alma. I haven't even gotten to kiss her yet. ...Geez, I'm already eighteen and I haven't even kissed anyone yet. I really need to get on that before my lips fall off or whatever.

Gosh, these sure are thoughts to be having right before church.

I pack into the car and survive the trip to the chapel, slinking inside and doing my best to avoid any and all attention until the service starts. No dice, naturally. J-Mug is already here, having apparently joined our church after our pastor agreed to give his family lots and lots of dollars, and he immediately brightens up upon seeing me and walks right towards where I'm trying to stay away from everybody. Oh boy!

"Hannah!" the boy greets me. "Hey! I just wanted to thank you again. Mom's doing *so* much better. They even let her out of the hospital! She's not supposed to go outside for another week, but... she's out of the hospital! She's *home!*"

"That's... great," I answer, failing to fake any real emotion behind it.

"Honestly, it's been hard getting her to stay in bed," he says excitedly, not seeming to notice. "I've been practicing my you-know-what too, and... I think I might have something that could be a big help for her. I—"

"No," I snap. "Not here. If you absolutely *need* to talk to me about it, text me or something. And what's the most important rule?"

"...Don't practice around anyone else?" he mumbles, chastised.

"No. That's the second most important rule," I scowl. "What's the most important rule?"

"Um. Don't... speak while practicing?"

"Don't speak while practicing," I hiss in confirmation. "No matter what. Even if it feels right or it seems like you're supposed to. Don't. Ever. Speak. You promise?"

"...I promise," he nods.

"Make sure your mom knows too," I insist, walking away towards the pews. "I didn't help you two just so you could get yourselves killed or worse."

"Okay!" he confirms dutifully as I skulk away, feeling like crap as I reject the earnest kid like that. I just... don't like him and don't want to deal with him. He mugged me twice! Haven't I already done enough for him?

I hesitate. Is this what makes me not good enough?

I don't manage to come up with an answer before everyone else starts spilling onto the pews as well, though, and shortly afterwards the pastor is up on the pulpit to lead the prayer. Hmm. What's up with Christian worship and words that start with 'p,' anyway? I ponder that (hehe) for a good chunk of the service, doing everything in my power to remain as distracted as possible. I just need to survive until 2pm when life will temporarily become good instead of bad and I'll maybe get to kiss a girl.

The sermon ends without incident and so I quickly retreat to my traditional bathroom hidey-hole like the little burrowing creature I am at heart to poke away at my phone. Rather than the slew of text messages I *expected* to find, however, I have an odd little notification from an app I haven't touched in ages: Discord.

Oh, right! Valerie was gonna introduce me to her friends!

I open the ancient app, which chugs through several dozen updates for a minute or two before finally opening, the new server invite in a shiny new private message from Valerie. Her Discord tag is apparently now 'Monster Magus,' which I suppose is rather appropriate. Mine is still 'DistractedDreamer,' just like my Twitch handle, because I use the same online name for basically everything. I'm very boring like that. I accept the server invite.

\<Mortississississimo\>
Woah hey is that who I think it is

\<DistractedDreamer\>
Um, hello!

\<Mortississississimo\>
Oh shit I think it do be

\<Lana, Blood Ba'ham\>
Oh goodness, welcome!

\<Monster Magus\>
You made it!

\<DistractedDreamer\>
I did!

\<blue\>
hi!

\<Lana, Blood Ba'ham\>
Well go on, Val, introduce us!

<Monster Magus>
Right! Um, this is my best friend Hannah and she is a massive lesbian.

I blink. Okay, I uh. I guess we're starting off with my sexuality apparently?

<DistractedDreamer>
That is all completely true, but I gotta say I'm a little confused as to why it's coming up first thing?

<Monster Magus>
It's pertinent info for this server.

<DistractedDreamer>
Why...?

<Lana, Blood Ba'ham>
It's the perfect introduction because it tells us everything we need to know about you!

"Hannah" <- Name
"She" <- pronouns
"Massive lesbian" <- probably-not-a-bigot certification

<blue>
fhdsfhsdjklfhsdlafhsd

<DistractedDreamer>
Do you often get bigots on this server?

<Lana, Blood Ba'ham>
Well, no. And honestly, being introduced by Valerie is all you really needed to be welcome here. But it's good internet etiquette in queer communities, you know? Part of what makes the queer community *the queer community* is the simple fact that anyone who isn't queer is dramatically more likely to be kind of shitty about what's in my pants, and it only really takes one asshole to ruin the whole day. A lot of us tend to get really nervous around new people until we get some clear sign that they're going to actually be tolerable. We hole up in these little chatrooms to avoid the kind of jerks we constantly have to deal with in real life, you know?

Uh, okay. I was not expecting this kind of conversation today. I rub my temples a bit before responding.

\<DistractedDreamer\>
Is everyone here queer, then?

\<Lana, Blood Ba'ham\>
Nah, Issi is our token cishet white boy.

\<Mortissississimo\>
It's true. I possess the rare and terrible condition of both possessing and desiring a dick.

\<blue\>
gay

\<Mortissississimo\>
No wait not like that

\<Monster Magus\>
lol

\<Mortissississimo\>
Anyway I'm like a nature documentary host. I've barely managed to calm a wild herd of transbians by sitting really still and putting my pronouns in my bio, and after feeding them for a few weeks they've started accepting me as one of their own. It's a heartwarming story, really.

\<DistractedDreamer\>
...Boy, you sure do have some interesting friends, Valerie.

\<Monster Magus\>
I promise that they are usually cool and not lame.

\<Mortissississimo\>
I don't

\<Lana, Blood Ba'ham\>
Yeah, you're sure putting a lot of pressure on us here, Val.

\<Monster Magus\>
You're right. My bad. Hannah, my friends suck and are the worst. You are the only cool one.

<DistractedDreamer>
Gosh, you're kind of putting a lot of pressure on me, Val.

<Monster Magus>
Okay so actually I have zero cool friends. They are all super lame. Every last one. Simply by becoming my friend the lameness of an individual skyrockets dramatically.

<Mortississississimo>
That's more like it

<Lana, Blood Ba'ham>
Yeah, I can work with those expectations.

<blue>
can i be a cool friend

<Monster Magus>
Sure, blue. You are the coolest friend of all.

<blue>
fdskfhsdjlfhsdjlafhdsjkl yay

Okay, this is more like it. I smirk at the byplay, settling into a more comfortable rhythm of snark. It's a fun way to pass the time, at least up until someone new suddenly comments something that scares my panties clean off.

<Skarmbliss>
oh hey i recognize that screen name
do you stream pokemon by any chance?

Oh crap, oh no, this person has seen my streams!?

<DistractedDreamer>
Oh, uh, haha. Yeah, that's me!

<Skarmbliss>
oh sick! your vtuber rig is insanely cool.

<Monster Magus>
Wait, you watch Pokemon streams?

<Skarmbliss>
yeah i watch pokemon streams my name is literally a pokemon reference

<Monster Magus>
It is!?

<DistractedDreamer>
Yeah, it's like a Generation 3/4/kinda 5 competitive battle thing. Skarmory/Blissey defensive core.

<Skarmbliss>
yeah!!! hell yeah you get it. you should do more competitive stuff, id watch the hell out of that.

<Mortississississimo>
I wanna see this cool vtuber rig

<Skarmbliss>
oh yeah its so fucking hot

<Lana, Blood Ba'ham>
Oh, well now you've got *me* interested. Show us, Hannah!

<DistractedDreamer>
Uh, it's not really something I keep pictures of...

<Skarmbliss>
here, i gotchu

And then they post a Twitter link to a clip from my stream showing me stretching and blue reacts with an emote labeled 'flooshed' and oh gosh, I'm just wearing a tanktop and shorts in that one, all my limbs are on display...! Aaaaaah I've never actually watched recorded videos of myself like this before! Oh Goddess oh Goddess oh Goddess this is *so embarrassing!*

<Lana, Blood Ba'ham>
Woah, holy shit! This is crazy! God damn, Hannah, work it!

<Mortississississimo>
Okay, this is seriously awesome. How *did* you make this? Or like, who made it for you and how are these not everywhere?

<Skarmbliss>
lol no shot she tells you. the whole bit on stream is that she keeps saying it's real.

My face is a blushing mess. I can't believe this. I can't believe I'm running into someone who has seen me like that. I knew it would happen eventually, but... aaaagh!

\<Lana, Blood Ba'ham\>
Well, a girl has to have her secrets, I suppose. Or perhaps... it *is* real!?

\<DistractedDreamer\>
...Yeah. It's real.

\<Mortissississimo\>
Then take a selfie right now lol

\<Lana, Blood Ba'ham\>
Issi! Don't pressure her!

\<DistractedDreamer\>
...
Sure, okay.

\<Monster Magus\>
Um, are you sure, Hannah?

\<DistractedDreamer\>
Fuck it, why not. Heads up though, I'm sort of hiding in a church bathroom so it's not gonna be pretty.

I open my camera app and snap a quick photo of myself, before taking my mask off, opening my mouth as wide as it'll go, and taking a photo again. I send both to Valerie's friends because my life is an endless spiral of bad decisions and this is hardly the worst one I'll make this week.

\<Mortissississimo\>
Uh. Hmm. That's. Wow?

\<blue\>
teeth... (/•⁄•⁄•/)

\<DistractedDreamer\>
I can show you the extra limbs and messed up hands and stuff if you want but I don't wanna accidentally drop my gloves in the toilet. I sort of need them to use my phone.

\<Lana, Blood Ba'ham\>

Wow wow wow wow wow wow wow. This is... *very* cool.

\<DistractedDreamer\>
It's really not? I'm mutating into a monstrous freak. My hair started to fall out today. Like, I'm serious guys, this is not a bit. It's really messing me up.

\<Monster Magus\>
Um... I can confirm that, actually. This is a really major problem for Hannah and I'd appreciate it if it was treated that way.

\<DistractedDreamer\>
Roger roger!

\<Mortissississimo\>
Okay but how the actual fuck though

\<DistractedDreamer\>
Urban fantasy is real and I'm the main character, I guess? Look, the more I talk about this the more completely insane I'll sound, so I'm not really super interested in discussing it.

I check the time, realizing I definitely should have gotten out of the bathroom by now, so I quickly finish up my business and rush out to act like I've been waiting in the lobby this whole time. My phone now remains quarantined in my pocket until my family gets back in the car, as it *isn't appropriate* to be on the phone at church. I'm supposed to be socializing. I am not very good at socializing.

Eventually, the rest of my family joins me and we exit as a unit. Back in the car, I pull out my phone again and skim through the conversation that has happened without me, mostly just Valerie fielding questions with 'ask Hannah, it's her business.' I give her blanket permission to talk about whatever the heck she wants and then put my phone back in my pocket, too exhausted to deal with whatever comes of that mess. I have a date to prepare for, after all.

Surely that can't go as poorly as this did, right?

19

COMMUNICATION

I am inordinately frustrated about the fact that I can't dress up cute for my date.

There are obviously a number of valid reasons for this. I'm in the closet and hiding my relationship from my family. My old clothes don't fit very well anymore and they don't match my constantly-changing complexion as much as they used to. My entire body is shifting into a horrific mess of chitin and claw, which may cause people to call the police. Various things like that. But despite all logic, it's still irritating to bundle up in my usual long-sleeved layers like it's somehow going to snow during a Tennessee May. I want to show off for my girlfriend. Is that so wrong?

...I mean, according to a frighteningly large number of people *in* Tennessee, me having a girlfriend at all is wrong. Buuuut I'm going to do my best to not think about that. Only fifteen percent of hate crimes are due to sexual orientation! It's still mostly racism running rampant in the good 'ol US of A. Plus we'll be keeping to public areas, daytime on a Sunday, and I can supernaturally detect every weapon in a thirty-foot radius or so with my admittedly-still-weak-on-earthside spatial sense. I'll also probably survive any gunshots that aren't to my head. So, y'know, I think I'm prepared.

I realize, intellectually, that getting attacked is pretty unlikely, hate crime or otherwise. But for *some reason,* couldn't say what, my anxiety has been acting up lately. It's difficult *not* to think about risks, threats, and possibilities for fights. It's scary to consider all the possible things that could go wrong, but it's scarier still to realize I'm *ready* for them. That when push comes to shove, I'm fully prepared to phase into w-space, rush down a gunman, slice his arms off, and *fucking eat them.* It doesn't matter that doing so would expose me, it doesn't matter that doing so would cause all my gosh dang clothes to fall off. Alma's safety is what matters, and if anyone threatens that I will do whatever I have to in order to reclaim it.

Is that what I've always been like, or is that something the Goddess' magic made me into?

I've certainly always been willing to go to bat for my friends, I guess. I've never been in a position to do so violently before, but now that I've apparently become *really good* at violence, it only makes sense that I'd start working it into my methods. As much as I hate it, as much as it's a horrible, horrible hammer to take to problems, it is a very *big* hammer and sometimes you have to crush nails.

Before all this, though? Was I a good friend? Was I loyal the way my friends are loyal to me? I feel like I at least tried to be, but only they can really answer that, I guess. If nothing else, Ida and Valerie seem to believe I deserve the care, support, and attention they've showered me with since my insane transformation started. I guess it's up to me to make sure I don't let them down.

...But first, I have a date.

Dressed up in my nicest baggy hoodie, I commandeer my dad's car and drive over to Autumn's house. We scheduled the date for a time she knew her dad wouldn't be at home, so I'm not surprised when I pull up in her driveway, head to her front door, and don't feel anyone in the house other than her. I *am* somewhat surprised when I knock on the door and just get a text from her telling me to let myself inside.

I always feel weird and awkward when I let myself into someone else's house, even with permission, but I do as she says and head towards where I feel her in the kitchen. I spot her doing... *something,* miming in the air and not looking my way, so I call out to her.

"Hey, Alma!" I greet.

"Hannah?" she answers, turning and looking around like she can't see me. "Oh, watch out, there's a—"

I don't hear the rest of what she says because I walk face-first into an invisible wall and get rather distracted by my own sputtering. I stagger backwards, seeing the ripple of visibility flow outwards from my impact point, revealing the exterior of a pale white wall, seemingly made out of some kind of ceramic. A door is set into the wall, only partially visible, so I give the wall a good thump with a fist to bring the rest of the door into focus for me. Then I open it, and walk inside Alma's magical funhouse.

Alma spots me immediately now that I'm inside, her power apparently having created a small, one-room shack this time around. Or at least... I think it is? My spatial sense doesn't work on this place at all. I thump another wall or two in order to be able to see the whole thing. Once again, the ceiling depicts a mural of Autumn's face: half of it normal and half of it crumbling, broken machinery, like a robotic brain leaking out all of its parts. Alma herself is dressed for the date, which means like me she's covered in baggy clothing and a bulky, *bulky* skirt to disguise her tail as much as possible. It works... okay. It looks like she's hiding something, but it's not obvious enough *what* she's hiding for anyone to be likely to care. That'll change if the tail keeps growing, though.

"Hannah!" Alma greets me happily. "Hannah, check this out! I got the water running!"

She grabs the handle of a sink faucet that distinctly *isn't* the sink faucet of the actual, real kitchen and turns it. My spatial sense does a confused mental flip as water in the actual, real pipes seems to phase through solid matter as if it was suddenly traveling a completely different set of pipes, drops into Alma's not-real sink, then heads down the drain through *another* set of undetectable imaginary pipes before meeting back up with the *actual* pipe system on the other end.

What the heck?

"You, uh, are tapping into the municipal water system somehow," I tell her.

"Yeah, I kind of figured that," she muses. "My imaginary house pipes only work if the house overlaps with a part of my *real* house that has running water. It doesn't work if I restrict the house to, say, my bedroom. Same with electricity, although pretty much the whole house has that. When I'm outside I have to just hope there's an underground line or something."

"I guess that makes some kind of sense," I shrug. "This spell isn't Light or Matter aligned, so it can't make... stuff. I mean, I guess it can make a whole bunch of stuff, but the stuff isn't real somehow? Like... okay, I'll be honest, I seriously have no idea what's going on here."

"I might," Alma says, grinning at me. Her teeth look sharper than when I last saw them. Not carnivorous like mine, but those canines are *big*. My heart skips a beat, and I almost miss what she says next.

"I didn't notice my dad coming home one day when I was testing things, but he didn't hit his face on my spell like you do," she continues. "He walked right through it, like it wasn't even there. Freaked me the heck out when he said my name, too, because *I couldn't see him.*"

"What?" I ask, dumbfounded.

"I couldn't see him, and he couldn't see my spell!" she confirms. "I quickly ran out the fake house's door to turn the spell off, of course, but I wouldn't be surprised if I couldn't touch him, either."

"How does that even work?" I ask, unconsciously feeling over the smooth walls of the house. The interior is... interesting. There's a bookshelf along one wall, which is an odd sight to see in the middle of a kitchen.

"Well, my dad doesn't have a soul, right?" Alma says casually. "And my house is a Pneuma spell. You can probably only interact with it because *you* have a soul."

Huh. She might be onto something, there. So Alma can be seen while she's in her house, but she can't be interacted with by anything that hasn't *entered* her house, and only things with souls can actually find the door. If it doesn't have a soul it doesn't exist to her. ...Mostly. There's presumably an exception for objects that come inside close enough to an ensouled person's body, because Alma's not acting like I walked in naked. And the water in her pipes probably doesn't have a soul, so that's another weird exception... but *still!* That's pretty wild. If someone shoots her with a gun from outside the house, would the bullet just phase right through her without her even noticing?

"Magic is crazy," I conclude.

"You don't have to tell me that," Alma snorts. "It's pretty darn cool, though. I have a *lot* of control over what the house is shaped like when it shows up, so I can do some pretty neat things with it. Check this out!"

She hurries past me excitedly and exits out the door I came in through, which immediately dissolves the house into nothingness. The residual moisture that was resting inside the soul-house's sink splatters softly to the floor.

"So, the basement is right below me here, right? So I can just imagine that I want my house to have a spiral staircase downwards when I make it, and..."

She walks right through the floor, and I lose sight of her. Holy crap! I head over and knock on the walls until I find the entrance, and sure enough there's the very top of a spiral staircase in front of me when I open it. But I *also* still see the physical house's actual, real floor, so I can't follow her down.

"...This is so complicated," I groan.

"Hehe, yeah, a little!" Alma agrees, her head popping up from the floor. "It's cool though, right?"

"It's *very* cool," I agree, holding out my hand to her. She takes it despite not really needing my help and lets me pull her into a hug after she runs back up the stairs.

"And you know what the best part is?" she continues, babbling excitedly. "Jet can't come in here. At *all*. It's completely mine."

"Really?" I ask, suddenly a little worried.

"Yeah, see?" Alma says, pulling up the back of her skirt a little and making me blush. "The tail doesn't move."

Sure enough, the normally-active tail is completely limp, almost lifeless. It might even be drooling slightly.

"And when I walk out of the house..." Alma demonstrates, stepping through the door and dissolving the stairs into nothing. Her tail immediately perks up, swishing side to side slightly before curling protectively around Alma's leg and snarling at me.

"See?" Alma shrugs. "I've never started to... I don't know. Fade out? In the house? I'm safe in there. It's a place I know I'll always be *me*. It's the coolest thing ever."

I swallow. I feel like I should talk to Alma about Jet a bit more, having gotten to know both of them at least decently well by now. Alma has some intense resentment for her headmate, that much is obvious, but I'm not sure if it goes deeper than just the general distress her memory problems bring her. What I do know, however, is that Jet wants to do right by Alma, but Alma just wants Jet to *stop existing*. I'm not really sure how I would go about having that conversation, though, so hopefully I can leave it to their therapist.

I'll have to think about it. ...After the date.

"How are your, um, physical changes going?" I ask, awkwardly changing the subject. "I saw you had fangs?"

Among many other things. With my spatial sense I can tell her wings are getting a lot bigger, and Alma has had to get completely new bras to deal with not crushing them on top of her increased breast size… which I can't help but continue to notice every time I see her. I'd complain about my own transformation not giving me bigger boobs, but mine are already kind of difficult to complain about. Is it narcissistic to admit I have the same sort of figure that I'm attracted to?

"Oh, uh, yeah," Alma scratches her head awkwardly. "I noticed those when I started fronting this morning. I guess they grew in sometime yesterday. Jet got us a bunch of new clothes. Gloves like yours for the claws. And, uh, we have scales on our butt now. They're growing in more and more all around the tail."

"Oh, cool," I say nonchalantly. "Butt scales."

"Uh, yep," Alma agrees halfheartedly, reaching back to give some of them a scratch. "It's. Certainly a thing."

"Sorry again."

"Don't be," Alma insists. "Really. You ready to head to the aquarium?"

I get the feeling that while Alma genuinely doesn't want me to be sorry, it *isn't* because I haven't actually hurt her. But I'm not sure if pressing the point right now would hurt her more, so I swallow my thoughts and give her a smile.

"Yeah," I agree. "I'm ready."

She smiles back. She's happy. Really. Is that enough?

"Cool," she says, and we head to my car together. Two girls bundled up like it's winter heading to hang out with fish.

The actual Tennessee Aquarium is a bit too long of a drive for a simple Sunday date, but there's a piddly local-ish one less than an hour from here that we can go to instead. I don't really have any particular interest in aquariums, especially considering that I nearly got murdered by a sea monster last week, but I didn't have any better ideas for a place to go and Alma seemed marginally more excited when she suggested it than any other thing we talked about.

That's something I'm coming to figure out about Alma in general: she does *not* actively or purposefully express her preferences. She mostly wants to talk about me and get me to lead things for her, but as long as I'm not overwhelmed (a condition that is slowly but refreshingly becoming less absent in my life) it's not too difficult to pick up on her real feelings regarding whatever I'm talking about. It's weird, but not too dissimilar from how I learned to be a good friend to Valerie. Most of what really matters to the both of them is easier to pick up on via mediums other than words.

It really helps Valerie out, me being able to do that. When she's overstimulated or stressed, it's often a situation where asking questions and doing other normal communication things *can't* help, because she can't properly wedge her brain into that kind of crack. The sooner I pick up on that from context cues, the sooner I can start doing things to *actually* help, be that redirecting her attention, giving her backup on dealing with the problem, or just giving her space and silence. Talking with Alma often feels like flexing a similar sort of muscle, learning to navigate a new sort of minefield so I can help guide her through it.

I am, uh, not very good at it yet. So many questions, not enough answers. But I'm learning, a little at a time.

We make it to the parking lot of the aquarium and wander inside, showing the receipt of ticket purchase on my phone to the lady behind the desk and getting physical tickets in response. There's a number of different exhibits, all with very fancy-sounding names like "Antarctic Adventure" and "Carnivores of the Deep."

"Well, where do you wanna start?" I ask, giving Alma a careful look.

"Uh, wherever's fine," Alma says noncommittally, gazing at various signs.

Well, may as well start with the one that looks most fun to me.

"How about the 'Tropical Reef Tour?'" I ask.

She shrugs. No go on that one, huh?

"'Antarctic Adventure?'" I try. "That one probably has penguins."

"If you want to!" she answers cheerfully. Hmm, another dud. I try following her gaze.

"'The Sunless Depths' looks cool," I say.

"That one's probably neat," she agrees. "Deep sea animals get *super* funky."

Okay, *that* was a reaction. Score!

"Let's start there, then!" I conclude, and she seems pretty happy about it. Which is good, because asking three times is about the usual limit for being annoying and I would have had to conclude the search there either way.

We head into a darkly lit hallway full of water tanks, the sound hushed around us as the darkness instinctively makes everyone in the area speak quietly or not at all. The exhibit is pretty neat, if incredibly subdued, with overall more diagrams and less actual aquatic life than I was expecting. I suppose it *would* be really hard to get living samples of creatures that can only survive at pressures unlivable for humans all the way up to the surface.

Hesitantly, Alma comments on some of the displays, seeming to actually know some neat trivia about deep sea animals that she wants to discuss. So I do my best to encourage her, trying to get a good ramble going because I suspect it will be cute as heck. She spends a while likening ocean floor methane bursts to a planet in one of her favorite sci-fi novels (and thereby proving me right) before we finally come across a tank with live bioluminescent jellyfish and she locks onto it like a heat-seeking missile.

"Haha! Oh man, look at them bloop around!" Alma grins, her wings twitching excitedly under her shirt.

"Yeah, they're cute," I agree, watching them with my eyes as I feel them with my spatial sense. Water is always an interesting presence to my spatial sense because the major defining feature of water is usually its utter lack of defining features: it has no color, it has no scent, and it doesn't really even have a texture so much as it has *wetness,* a feature almost incomparable to other aspects of touch. Water is strange to my spatial sense though largely insofar as it *isn't* strange. To that part of me, *everything* lacks color and opaqueness. I can simply feel and know the presence of the water in the same way I feel and know the presence of the organs inside the jellyfish, which for the first time I can actually look at with my eyes, too. The clear body of the floppy little fellas lets my eyes track the same internal movements as my soul, and I *do* have to admit that it's weirdly hypnotizing.

"Oh, uh. Sorry," Alma says hurriedly. "I've been staring a while, huh? We can move on."

"Huh?" I ask, blinking with confusion. "No, you're fine. These are cool."

"It's okay, we can move on," Alma insists.

She doesn't believe I'm interested. She thinks she's bothering me. It kind of reminds me of when I first met her, and she thought I was faking interest in her book.

"...Their internal structure is really awesome," I comment, searching for something specific that caught my interest. "I'm trying to figure out how they breathe. They don't seem to have lungs *or* gills."

Alma looks at me for a moment like she's an animal deciding whether or not to run, but then turns back to the jellyfish, pointing at one.

"...They breathe entirely through diffusion," she tells me. "Oxygen from the water enters directly through their skin whenever the oxygen levels in their body are lower than the levels in the surrounding sea. Their bodies are just a lot more permeable than ours, and require a lot less resources."

"Ohhh, that's kinda sick," I smile, turning to look at the jellies again myself. "I was thinking it was their droopy tentacles maybe, because there's so much surface area with how bendy it is."

"No, that surface area is for catching microorganisms," Alma answers. "And those big long dangly bits aren't the tentacles, they're called oral arms, because the jellyfish eats with them. They *do* have tentacles, though: that's the name of the little hair-like structures coming off the rim of the bell."

"The bell is the head?" I clarify. "The blorpy-blorpy part?"

She giggles. Eeee, I made her giggle! That means I'm doing well!

"Yes, the 'blorpy-blorpy part' is the bell," she smirks at me. "Jellyfish are really neat because of how simplistic they are. No central nervous system at all, absolutely no chance of sapience or thought or self-awareness, but they still do everything required to be an animal: reproduce, grow, respond to stimuli. They're like organic robots, capable of only two or three tasks that they loop forever until they finally break. There are so few thoughts inside that head, it isn't even called a head at all."

Woah. She *really* seems to like jellyfish, huh? New hyperfocus unlocked on the character sheet, I guess. But what's with the weird feeling of... longing?

Well, it doesn't matter. I do my best to keep her talking, something she really seems to enjoy when given ample and repeated reassurance that yes, I am actually interested and not annoyed or bored. We crawl through the rest of the deep sea exhibit at a slow pace, but it's the kind of *awesome* slow pace where we're having so much fun soaking in every detail that time just slips away. Things transition smoothly into the next exhibit, and by then Alma is so engaged with things that the rocky start just melts away.

It's just *fun,* because we're both huge nerds and Alma's obsession with fantasy and sci-fi lends itself to a lot of love for speculative biology, a field of thought that seems to stem primarily from looking at real biology and going 'holy crap, that is so cool.' So that's what we spend the day doing: looking at aquatic creatures and geeking out over how cool it is. Everything is going great.

"Ooh, that one looks pretty!" I say, pointing to one of the fish in the tropical exhibit.

"I mean, yeah, everything is *pretty* here," Alma dismisses. "But they're all basically the same fish with different shapes and colors, you know? I wanna see... ooh! There! A lionfish!"

She starts babbling about how the lionfish has hardly any natural predators because of how effective its venomous spines are, and a comfortably dopey smile blooms on my face as I look around at everything swimming all over the place. This is one of the *big*

405

tanks, with countless different animals all in it at once, from beautiful fish to imposing sharks to creepy eels. It kind of makes me hungry to watch all the beating hearts floating around right in front of me. I haven't eaten since our usual after-church Taco Bell, and I didn't get much since I can't actually digest most of the ingredients there anymore. So the movement of the fish through the water is kind of... hypnotic.

I step towards the glass, putting one gloved hand up against it like I could reach right through. Well, I mean, I *could* do that, actually. That's pretty explicitly in my skillset. And it's not like killing and eating a fish would be *hurting* anyone. Goddess, I want to chase one. I want to chase *something*. But... no. It would be pointless. ...And also weird, but mostly pointless! I can easily reach my hand *into* the tank, sure, but not only would that make my glove come off, I wouldn't be able to bring anything back out of the tank with me. Plus there's like, people around, and probably security cameras. I definitely shouldn't hunt any of the delicious, delicious fi—

"Hannah," Alma hisses, and I feel her grab one of my blade-limbs. Wait, how did—oh crap! I pull my extra bits out of her grasp and back into full 4D space. It wasn't completely visible, not even mostly visible. It was just a little bit of organic blade peeking into reality next to my head. But we both know that's way more than I should be showing, so I stare back at her stern expression in horror as I rapidly look at everyone in the room with my spatial sense.

...Nothing. Nobody noticed or cared. Of course they didn't; we're in an aquarium. Everyone is here to look at fish, not people. But as my heartbeat calms and I look back at Alma with a sheepish smile, I can't help but feel the weight of my extra limbs in the other realm. They're getting harder and harder for me to hide, and not just because of how monstrous I am. I'm... running out of reasons to, I guess.

I want to just *be me*. I want that so badly and I'm not going to be able to hold it in forever. But I don't say that out loud. Not yet.

"...We should break for dinner," I say instead.

406

"Yeah," Alma says flatly. "I guess I've been hungrier lately too."

"Nobody noticed, at least," I say, giving her an apologetic smile. "Thanks for, uh, grabbing me there."

"I just figured it would disrupt our date a little if you started slaughtering the exhibits," she sighs. "Come on, let's get out of here. Where do you want to eat?"

"Sorry, I kind of interrupted things. I know you were having fun."

"It's fine," she shrugs. "You looked like a cat watching birds through a window. It was kind of cute."

"Well, as long as I was cute," I joke, and we head out of the aquarium and back to my car. Alma stays quiet the whole time, so I ask "Whatcha thinking about?"

"You, mostly," Alma answers, focusing ahead at the road even though I'm the one driving. "It's..."

She hesitates.

"You're not gonna offend me," I assure her. "Open and honest communication for the win!"

"'For the win?' Really?" she chuckles. "Fine, I'm sorry. It's just... kinda scary when you get all monster-brained like that."

"Oh," I say. "Sorry. Yeah, I guess the last time I did that I gave you a tail, huh?"

"Well, that's part of it," she admits, squirming uncomfortably in her seat. Her tail is getting really thick and it's clearly not comfortable for her to sit on. "I'm also just worried that it's going to happen to *me*. What if *I* start chasing squirrels or whatever?"

Oh, yeah. That'd be spooky.

"The mental stuff happened to me pretty much immediately," I say. "It was terrifying at first because I didn't know what was happening, but I've started getting used to it. And my therapist kinda started helping me work through it too?"

"Oh. Right. You're going to therapy now. Your therapist knows?"

"Yeah, as of yesterday," I sigh. "Hopefully she won't spill the beans. Jet's the one that pushed me to get more open with her, actually."

"...Oh," Alma says flatly. Yeah, she doesn't even like hearing the name, huh?

"Is it weird to ask how *your* therapy is going?" I press a little anyway, trying to make sure to give her an out.

"I mean, it's fine. My therapist is okay. There's not really much for me to talk about. *I'm* not the one that stole a bunch of stuff and got us arrested. It's not *my* court-ordered therapy. I'm just stuck going to it anyway."

"Oh," I say. "Yeah, I guess that sucks, huh?"

"I guess."

Well this went poorly. Abort!

"Where do you wanna eat?"

We end up going to some old-school American diner, mainly on the basis that I have a sudden and inexplicable craving for chicken wings. I just want to crunch through some bones, is that so wrong? Alma seems to enjoy her burger well enough too, though it's apparently a pretty mid-quality restaurant. I can't really tell those kinds of things anymore, my taste buds are still screwy as heck and don't seem to care a whole lot beyond the distinction between meat and not-meat.

"So," Alma says. "Elephant in the room. You got kidnapped?"

Oh. Right. I'd sort of been trying to forget about that.

"Yeah, uh, so in the other universe there's this creepy centipede cult that thinks I'm going to destroy the world or something?" I hedge.

"Yeah, you've talked about them before," Alma encourages, taking a sip of soda.

"Right. So, they found us and started following us, so we split up and followed them back, but then they ambushed our ambush of their ambush and hit us with this Chaos and Pneuma mage who

408

blasted us with a depression beam until we couldn't think anymore, and now I think my other body is stuck in a 4D cage."

Alma just stares at me, continuing to slurp up her drink through a straw.

"...And, uh, yeah I know that sounds really bad," I hedge. "I mean, it probably is really bad. But I have no idea *how* bad because I literally couldn't really acknowledge what was going on around me all that much so I have *no idea* what my options are for escape. Maybe it'll be easy, maybe I'm stuck, I have no idea. So I'm just trying not to think about it as much as possible. I'll figure it out when I have some kind of actual information."

"I guess that makes sense," Alma agrees, finally taking a breath. "Can you bring anything from our world to help?"

"Huh?" I ask. Of course not, how would I do that? Except the obvious answer to that question is 'magic' so the question instead becomes '*can* I do that?' "Uh. I haven't. Actually really considered that before. Maybe?"

"Could be worth looking into," Alma shrugs. "Not sure what you would bring, though. A gun?"

"I don't have a gun," I point out. "Or fingers."

"Oh, right."

Is such a spell even possible, though? A magic for traveling through dimensions? I guess it must be *possible,* I'm a living link between two dimensions and it's obviously within the Goddess' purview. If anyone could use a spell like that, it'd definitely be me. What would I do with it, though? How would I activate it? What would I *bring?*

"...It's definitely something to think about," I agree with Alma. "No idea if I can do that, but... maybe. Won't know until I try, and all that. Can we change the subject away from my kidnapping before I have a panic attack, though? I'm starting to feel some anxiety creeping up."

"Oh, sure. Sorry."

There's a pause, and then she adds:

"Avoidance coping mechanisms for the win."

"For the win!" I laugh. "Yes!"

"Ugh, don't sound so excited," Alma grumbles. "It's internet slang from two thousand and five. Why are you even saying it?"

"I don't know! Because my brain is a horrid mess of memes and depression and sometimes it retreats to my childhood for comfort?"

"Oh. Well, mood I guess."

The rest of the date swaps over to easier topics, thankfully. It's a little awkward, but mostly fun. We don't do much beyond finish eating and go find a place that sells wigs, but I manage to collect a few more laughs from my girlfriend by trying some of them on, and that's always delightful. Then I drive her home and reluctantly return to my house, where I promptly sneak upstairs and start streaming, just for an excuse to stretch my body. Nothing much happens there, though. I'm too exhausted to provide much in the way of color commentary, and I'm starting to worry a vanilla nuzlocke just isn't very interesting content anymore. Most influencers have advanced forward into increasingly complicated and difficult challenge runs. Good thing my channel can get carried by my tits and the fact that I'm a freak!

Oh geez, when I stop playing this video game I'll wake up in a cage.

I pause, my clawed fingers going still on the keyboard. Crap, it has officially become too late in the day to not think about it anymore. I'm going to be in a *cage*. I have no idea what the cultists are doing with any of my friends. And while I'm trying to be optimistic about my escape chances, Hagoro made it clear that I'm not the first interdimensional traveler that the cultists have captured and lethally experimented on. They don't expect me to be the last, either. The organization most likely has a *routine*.

I don't know what to do.

My screen flashes as messages from chat ask why I've suddenly gone still. I tear my attention back to the game, my character taking a few steps onscreen before I just get overwhelmed again, unable to focus even on Pokémon. Once again, I stop.

"I'm scared," I admit to my audience.

"Why?" "What's up?" "Is everything okay?" and a dozen other concerned messages fly by on my screen. I almost smile. There's nothing like parasocial concern to boost the ego, but ego isn't really the issue here.

"I bought a wig today," I admit. "Because my hair's starting to fall out. Just... in clumps. I can probably show you."

I reach up and rake my claws lightly over my scalp. Sure enough, a ton of black hair ends up wrapped around my fingers as I pull them away. It's even more than expected, and I can't help but stare in horror for a few moments before silently Refreshing it all into the trash.

"I know none of you believe me when I say this is all real," I sigh. "And I *get* that, I really do. It's the smart thing to believe. Burden of proof and all that. It just... sucks. Ugh."

I start combing away more patches of loose hair, knowing that it's getting visibly thinner as a result.

"I don't know why I'm talking about this," I mutter. "I don't think I can stream any more tonight. Sorry, guys."

And I just end things there. Honestly, my options are to either go to bed or have a panic attack over going to bed, and I'm getting a little tired of panic attacks. I strip down to my underwear, crawl under the covers, and sure enough I fall asleep almost immediately. I know this, of course, because I *wake up* almost immediately.

I am, indeed, in a four dimensional cage. I wonder how they made it? It looks almost like it's made of fossilized wood, and I suppose that might be my answer right there. But of course, I'm not generally stopped by solid matter regardless of how many dimensions it features. Immediately, I intend to channel a Spacial

411

Rend, but the moment I think about instilling my claws with power I feel a gentle but dangerous pressure. The Goddess is warning me: don't do it, or there will be consequences. I am, after all, currently in a Zone of Law. The Goddess plays favorites, but that doesn't mean She breaks the rules. She'll tell me what's going on, though, just because She can. Zone of Law: Ban Space.

It's then I notice that Hagoro is here in the room with me, on alert the moment I moved. That cultist with the talking-really-good magic is also here, Danny or something. They're both armed to the teeth, wearing what I suspect are magical items. Hmm. No need to just suspect; if Hagoro is banning Space magic, he's not banning anything else.

"**Aura Sight**," I hiss, scaring the crap out of both cultists before they realize what I just said and relax very, very slightly.

"Holy shit, what a wake-up call," D-something swears.

"I told you she would be immediately alert after coming to, Donny," Hagoro answers.

Donny! Right! His magical items are mostly Barrier magic, it looks like. Hagoro has a wider collection, from Art and Order to a whole bunch of Death. He's still missing both his right arms.

"Well! I guess you were right, big guy!" Donny agrees as I look around the room as best I can. It's a small cell, but the surrounding rooms are mostly empty. There are other guards outside, in front of the door, with various collections of magic. No Heat, Light, or Chaos, though; nothing I strongly resist. The 4D cage doesn't have any obvious weaknesses either, though I might be able to mundanely damage it with my claws, if I'm careful. ...But also maybe not. The cage itself has Barrier magic imbued in it as well. I wonder if any of the souls they use to make these enchantments are sapient.

"I realize you're probably busy looking for a way out, but I was hoping we could maybe have a bit of a chat first?" Donny asks amicably, flashing me a smile. "I feel like we really got started on the wrong foot, and Hagoro here certainly didn't do anything to improve your opinion of us."

"Neither did you," I quip back. "Falsely surrendering and then leading us into a trap?"

"Well, I appreciate you vastly overestimating my intelligence, but I assure you that was a very real surrender. You have repeatedly demonstrated your interest and capacity for killing people who cross you, Hannah. I don't wanna be on that list. My allies just rescued me from you because of *course* they did. You're probably thinking of ways to rescue *your* friends from us right now, aren't you?"

Well. Yeah. He's got me there.

"You've got good reason to assume we're all crazy bastards, Hannah," he continues. "I get it. Really. But we're not. We're just stuck trying to deal with a really shitty situation for everyone in the best way we know how, and even the best way happens to not be all that good. The Goddess is fucking everyone in the ass here, and you've got it worst out of all of us."

"Oh, that's rich," I sneer. "You've openly admitted to being a Pneuma mage that magically comes knows what to say to convince people of stuff, and you expect me to believe you're on my side? That your crazy apocalypse cult is *anti-Goddess,* when She's basically the one feeding you everything that ends up coming out of your mouth?"

With one of the legs not visible in 3D space, I start clawing away at the cage. No dice, as expected. What do I do, in that case? Wait for Hagoro to go to sleep? Try and survive the Goddess' retribution when I break the Zone of Law?

"Huh," Donny blinks in surprise. "I mean, I guess we're anti-Goddess, yeah. Kind of. It *is* our running theory that She's the one who keeps trying to destroy everything. Care to comment?"

"Not to you," I snap, reorienting my 4D vision as much as I can to check for any potential gaps or weaknesses in the cage.

"Right, yeah, the justified antagonism stuff. Here, let me back up, kid. I'll give it to you plain: yes, we are gonna need your help to figure out what's going on with you and how your kind keep showing up here. Yes, your help isn't going to mean your consent, as much as I'd love to have it, because unfortunately the stakes are kind of high and every option available to us is kind of terrible. For the nothing that it's worth, I'm genuinely sorry. But despite how terrifying you and your group of pals are, I get the impression that you're not *evil,* yeah? You told Hagoro here you wanted to help if you could. That's still true, right?"

"Of course it is," I growl. "I just don't think helping serial kidnapper-murderers is likely to be the best way forward."

"Yeah," Donny nods. "Yeah, I know, kid."

"Seriously, if you're really as altruistic as you say, why not at least give me a *chance* to prove I'm on the level before whisking me away? Have you ever considered that the horrific treatment you give everyone like me might be the *cause* of... whatever it is we do to mess things up?"

Donny seems genuinely shocked at that, and then his expression shifts to sadness.

"...Oh, kid," he sighs, clutching the sides of his head. "You don't already know? Seriously?"

"She's not authorized to know," Hagoro grunts. "Traditionally, telling founder's kin tends to make them unstable, and—"

"Shut the fuck up, I know," Donny snaps, cutting him off. "It's literally my job to decide what to tell people, so I'm telling her."

I clack my teeth together, unimpressed by what is likely a scripted performance. Maybe good cop bad cop is a novel interrogation technique over here, I don't know, but it's pretty cliché on Earth and I'm not falling for it. I wish this stupid cage had a door, I could probably pick a lock super easily with Refresh. How did they even get me in here?

"Kid, this is gonna suck to hear," Donny continues, either oblivious or uncaring of my skepticism. "But you wouldn't be a founder's kin if you weren't going to fuck over the world. It's just what you *are.*"

Oh boy, interdimensional racism! How fun.

414

"This isn't the first time a religious organization decided to claim that I deserve to suffer just for being what I am," I spit at him. "Knowing you assholes, it won't be the last. Are you at least smart enough to have not hurt my friends?"

Donny stares at me for a moment, then sighs and turns for the door.

"Yeah kid, they're fine," he tells me. "Also in prison cells so they don't try to kill us, but fine. But I can see I'm not gonna convince you that we're making a reasonable sacrifice for the world—"

"Have you considered that you *aren't!?*" I snap.

"—so I'm definitely not gonna explain the process by which you're eventually going to end it. The last thing we need is another fucker trying to use a cataclysmic event to break out of a box. So sit tight and have fun with the tests; if you wanna treat us like hostiles we'll do the same. But if you wanna *cooperate*... Goddess damn, but I'd love to have one of you that actually cooperates for once. Just let us know whenever, because *despite* the friends of mine that your posse has murdered, you're still the most reasonable founder's kin I've ever met."

He steps outside, and motions the two people waiting at the door to head in. They're a human man and a dentron woman, and they stare at me the way I stare at a particularly annoying homework problem.

"I take it that these two are doing those 'experiments' you were talking about," I say. "What are they, anyway?"

I don't get an answer, though. No one seems inclined to talk to me now that Donny is gone. The human man, a Death and Order mage, just reaches for the cage, putting his hand on the outside. He has sunken eyes, slightly graying hair, and the kind of smell that implies a glandular problem. Then he casts something, and I learn one very important fact about these tests: they hurt. Deep within my soul, he reaches towards the thread holding my two bodies together, and he tries to peel it apart.

I only last five minutes before I start to scream. That, apparently, is all the man's dentron partner is for: her magic deafens the room, so my torment can continue without undue distractions.

They were, as I suspected, quite prepared for this.

20

ACHE

My throat is raw from silent screams, so after a while I stop bothering. I can't stay still, of course, not with this kind of pain arcing through me, but whimpers and sobs are enough to let out that animalistic need to react to the agony. I don't know how long it's been. Probably not very; this kind of all-encompassing pain tends to drag out every second, stretching time into one horrific, extended moment after another. Why does it hurt so much? *Why?*

A soft pressure settles itself around my still-hardening carapace, the Goddess tickling my ears with a reassuring hum. I don't need to worry, She promises. They won't find what they're looking for, not by taking a pick to an iceberg. They're learning, bit by bit, but it won't be fast enough. Not before I figure out how to escape.

Escape? *Escape!?* I can't even think, and my body barely works. I have enough hardened chitin to cast Spacial Rend, probably, but that doesn't even matter because of the Zone of Law, and the rest of me is just... a mess. I know I could probably repair myself with my transformation spell, but it wouldn't matter because I still can't get out of here!

"Are you getting anything?" the dentron woman asks silently, her lips tracing the words to her partner.

"More complex than the last one," the man torturing me answers, shaking his head.

The Goddess clicks Her tongue disapprovingly. She knows I'm smarter than that, but She'll forgive me this time since I'm not thinking straight. *Think.* Block out the pain. I'll need to get used to this kind of thing sooner or later. I have three different elements of magic, and only one of them is being blocked. Surely I can figure out a way to leave?

I... I'm not sure. Can I? My Transformation magic seems useless here unless I transform myself so much that I burst out of the cage... but the cage is reinforced with Barrier magic so I'd probably just squish myself to death. And while I might be able to transform the people around me into monster versions of themselves... I'm pretty sure that would just make them more dangerous? Like, it could certainly be an effective distraction I suppose, but I still don't have any way to take advantage of the distraction.

And that just leaves Refresh. A spell for sorting and cleaning. There's no way I can... well. I mean, there's probably some way I can kill someone with Refresh. It can move blood around when I incant it, but... well, no, that wouldn't work. Partly because I'll probably get clapped by one of the guards the moment I try to speak a spell out loud, but partly just because *blood belongs in the body.* And even if I had some way to kill someone with something even lighter than blood, like air...

Wait. I can totally kill a person with air. I wouldn't even have to say the spell out loud to sort air.

The Goddess grins, lovingly stroking my legs in a way that makes my next whimper of agony about more than just the soul damage. I'm doing such a good job, She tells me. Silently, now. Invisibly, now. I should make them unable to ever hurt me again.

Death claws at my soul, scraping my threads raw. I can feel it inside me, cutting, grating, searching. The pain is nowhere and everywhere, unlike anything else I've ever experienced. I can feel the Goddess is right; it's barely a papercut against the size of my spirit, but it's like a papercut under a fingernail that *just. Keeps. Digging.* Even though the injury is small, the *pain* blooms like fire, peeling away nerve after nerve and leaving them open and raw to the air. He's doing this. A man is doing this to me, on purpose. All I have to do is pull the oxygen out of his lungs and wait.

All I have to do is decide this world is a cleaner, better place if he's a corpse instead of a person.

Because that's the thing, isn't it? The core of my spell. It is a spell of Order. It *puts things in their proper places.* And it's one thing to believe in a world where pancake batter is *supposed* to be mixed, innocent women are *supposed* to be free of disease, and skittles are *supposed* to be sorted by color. Those are innocent things, beautiful things. They might be selfish, sure, but they're the small kind of selfish that doesn't have to hurt anyone to make my life better. It's easy to believe there should be a world where things should get a little easier at the cost of no one.

But a world where *this man's lungs are an improper place for oxygen?* No. I can't believe that. I felt legitimately bad about killing actual rapists. I can't convince myself that, in a properly clean and orderly world, *this man deserves to die,* just because he's hurting me. And until I believe that, I can't even *attempt* to kill him with Refresh. I can't just attempt to knock him unconscious, either; oxygen deprivation isn't something I can expect to just try for the first time and not give someone brain damage with. I'll be risking murder whether I want to kill him or not.

The Goddess sighs, drumming Her fingers across my back. Oh well, She shrugs. I'll have plenty of time—and plenty of reason— to change my mind. In the meantime, I am encouraged to have fun with the torture. And so I cry and scream and sob until my body finally gives out, and I wake up in bed.

My soul still hurts.

It's less all-encompassing, less debilitating, but it's still *there.* Goddess, it's still there. It hurts to move, it hurts to think, but most of all it just *hurts*. I lie in bed and shiver for a while, profoundly tempted to just call in sick today so I don't have to *move,* but... that would require getting my family involved.

I get up and start my routine, ignoring the ache as best I can. I hadn't really noticed it until now, but I guess I've gotten pretty used to a body that doesn't have most of the passive aches and pains people tend to get used to. Between my transformation spell doubling as recovery, No Less Than Perfect wiping away even the tiniest issues, and chitinous limbs that just don't seem to get sore in the same way my old limbs did, pain has been... well, not really a *rare* thing for me, but a decidedly *temporary* thing. Something that happens during the admittedly-frequent periods where things go horribly wrong, but then disappears afterwards. This, however, is constant. And I don't know when—or if—it's going to go away.

I guess I'll get used to it eventually. That's how it always goes.

I take a quick shower just so no one can accuse me of having not done so, and I Refresh myself to actual cleanliness. The idea of using the spell as a murder weapon makes me sick. It corrupts everything I love about it, so I just try not to think about that as I start my day, completing the motions on autopilot as the pain steals most of my higher functioning anyway. I stagger to the bus stop not realizing it's nearly an hour before the bus normally comes, the time I'd normally spend showering not having been used for anything this morning.

Well, flapjacks. Now what? Nervous of having nothing to do, I pull out every modern-day woman's most reliable thought killer: my cell phone. Oh hey, I have notifications. Discord again? I scroll through the chat with Valerie's friends, reading her field various questions about me with somewhat limited answers, until I finally find the post that pinged my phone.

<Skarmbliss>
@DistractedDreamer hey are you okay? seemed like you were having a bad time all stream and then you stopped suddenly.

<Lana, Blood Ba'ham>
Oh, really? What happened?

<Skarmbliss>
ya i'll link.

And then they do, showing a video of me pulling out a bunch of my hair, complaining about it, and then shutting off my stream without any real warning. Chat goes a little wild after I leave. It looks like some people are starting to believe me?

<Lana, Blood Ba'ham>
Uh. Gosh. I hope she's okay? Hey @Monster Magus, is your friend okay?

<Monster Magus>
I dunno. Prolly not.

<Mortississississimo>
Yeah that sounds about right lmao

I sigh, and start typing. May as well set the record straight.

<DistractedDreamer>
Can confirm: not doing great. My hair is falling out and my everything hurts.

<Lana, Blood Ba'ham>
Oh, hey Hannah! Gosh I'm sorry to hear that.

<Mortississississimo>
Yeah those are symptoms of radiation poisoning. You have radiation poisoning

<DistractedDreamer>
Kind of, but it's the Spider-Man kind where it gives you weird powers and gets you wrapped up in dimensional shenanigans.

<Mortississississimo>
Ok but for real though have you considered going to a hospital

<DistractedDreamer>
And doing what? Consulting their entomologist? Look, I appreciate the concern but I've kind of gone through this whole "let's suggest all the practical solutions" thing with Valerie. I HAVE EIGHT LIMBS. A hospital can't do anything with that.

<Mortississississimo>
Well, not with their entomologist, no. But if you consulted their *arachnologist*...

Oh my gosh. Seriously? I clack my teeth together in irritation. I wonder if I can get the Goddess to dox this guy for me. Just ask for some divine knowledge to troll a man on the internet with. She'd probably think it's funny.

<DistractedDreamer>
I'm getting the distinct impression that you either think I'm crazy or lying for attention, and while I can't say that's an unreasonable assumption it's still kind of frustrating to get nothing but indignation and jokes in response to "my hair is falling out and my everything hurts."

<Mortississississimo>
Aight yeah that's fair sorry

<DistractedDreamer>
Besides, I'm eventually going to have ten limbs, so an arachnologist wouldn't help either.

<Mortississississimo>
Well now I'm just getting mixed messages

<DistractedDreamer>
My medical issues, my prerogative on joking about them. *Sticks out tongue*

<Mortississississimo>
Don't actually stick out your tongue you'll make blue faint again

<blue>
fhfhdslfhsdlfsdffjkldshf

<DistractedDreamer>
I'm alone at the bus stop. I *could* send more pics.

<blue>
DFHKSDJAFKFLAFDSJHFSDK

<Monster Magus>
Wait, you're at the bus stop already?

<DistractedDreamer>

Hey Valerie! Yeah, I... got my whole routine done really early and just kind of autopiloted out here.

<Monster Magus>
You said you're in pain?

<DistractedDreamer>
I'm being soul tortured!

<Monster Magus>
That sounds... bad.

<DistractedDreamer>
It's not great!

<Monster Magus>
Let me get ready real fast and I'll come meet you. We can see if there's like, a counterspell I can whip up, or at least maybe a painkiller.

<DistractedDreamer>
Oh yeah! Hey! If this is affecting me earthside, then earthside magic might work to fight against it!

<Monster Magus>
My thoughts exactly.

<Lana, Blood Ba'ham>
What the heck are you two talking about?

<Mortissississimo>
Magic, duh

<Skarmbliss>
you guys are actually serious huh. like its real for real.

<DistractedDreamer>
Yes. Ugh, this is the worst way for me to make friends, isn't it? Just walking in and acting crazy. Honestly, I was really looking forward to just having a normal place to hang out? But yeah I guess being out on the internet means I'm out on the internet. You guys get weirdo monster Hannah. And soon you'll have weirdo monster Valerie too!

<Monster Magus>
Yeah my ears really hurt today so that'll probably be fun.

<DistractedDreamer>
I'm honestly lucky my ears haven't fallen off. Y'all wanna see my bag of human teeth?

<Skarmbliss>
your what

<Mortississississimo>
Your WHAT

<DistractedDreamer>
My bag! Of human! Teeth! Don't worry, they're all my teeth. My former teeth, anyway. Because they all had to FALL OUT OF MY FLIPPING MOUTH when my big sharp chompers grew in.

<Monster Magus>
Do you still carry your teeth around in a bag!?

<DistractedDreamer>
Again: what else should I do? Throw an entire human's mouth full of teeth into the trash? What if somebody finds that?

<Lana, Blood Ba'ham>
Just stagger it. Throw away a tooth at a time, in various trash cans. A bag of teeth might be concerning, but one tooth is pretty normal. This is just if you don't think anyone's going to be looking for them, of course; obscurity through normalcy. If you're worried someone will be searching for the body, the "bury it in the woods" or "throw it in a river" options tend to be more reliable. The disposal location should minimize both the probability that the body can be found and the probability that its discovery could be linked back to you, but for just teeth that should be pretty simple. Smash them to dust before you toss them out in the wild somewhere and you should be fine.

<Mortississississimo>
Thanks Lana we can always count on you for our corpse disposal needs

<Lana, Blood Ba'ham>
I try!

\<DistractedDreamer\>
I guess I could probably just eat them, too, but trying to get my teeth to break up something that small would be a pain.

\<Mortissississimo\>
Yeah that sounds like a reasonable primary objection to the strategy of eating human teeth

\<DistractedDreamer\>
My standards have kind of been getting tossed all over the place, okay!?

\<Lana, Blood Ba'ham\>
Hey Hannah, would you prefer to talk about something else?

\<DistractedDreamer\>
Yes. Definitely. Absolutely.

\<Lana, Blood Ba'ham\>
Then I wanna ask how your date went!

\<DistractedDreamer\>
Oh! Well, it was mostly pretty good. We went to an aquarium and it was super fun!

\<Lana, Blood Ba'ham\>
Nice!

\<DistractedDreamer\>
Yeah!

The pain is constant, but the distractions help. Lana keeps me talking about other things until Valerie arrives at the bus stop and we get to chatting in person. Predictably, Val has a *lot* of spell ideas, but they tend to run into a recurring theme.

"If we aren't somehow dealing with the situation treeside, we're just treating the symptoms, not the cause," she says. "So we're going to have to figure out what kinds of spells work on you between dimensions, and I don't know how we would confirm that outside of casting magic on you while you're unconscious over here and asking you if it worked in the morning."

"Huh," I muse. "So... you need access to me while I sleep."

"Yup," Valerie nods. "Pretty much."

"My mom is *not* going to approve a sleepover on a school night," I scowl.

"I figured, but you're kind of getting soul-tortured. Maybe you should just... not listen to her?"

I say nothing, staring at my feet. I know I should agree with that, but I don't know how to. I'm not sure I could on my best day, and today is *far* from my best day. Valerie frowns at me, but doesn't press the point.

Eventually, the bus arrives and school starts soon after. Even the simple, routine tasks of classwork seem difficult when my body and soul ache. It's so hard to focus on anything, even telling my friends what's going on feels like an ordeal. Ida tries a wordless cast of No Less Than Perfect on me, which helps a little but not for long. I think I prefer Alma's feel-better strategy.

"You want a shoulder rub?" she asks.

"Huh?" I say dumbly. We're sitting together in the library for lunch like we normally do, carefully eating while surrounded by a mountain of books. She's reading another *Terry Pratchett* novel while I futilely try to wrangle my brain into focusing on homework through the pain.

"A shoulder rub," Alma repeats, giving me a wry smile. "You know, the thing where someone rubs your shoulders."

"Oh," I blink. "Uh. I won't say no, but I don't know if that's going to help with soul damage at all."

"It doesn't necessarily have to," Alma shrugs, putting her bookmark in and standing up. "I bet your whole body is tense from stress, and that just adds to any already existing pain, right?"

"Sure," I agree. "Okay."

She gets to work, brushing my hair aside before pressing her thumbs into the muscle of my neck and kneading away. She's right; it *does* feel good, even if it doesn't really get rid of the pain. It's the kind of stepping-into-a-hot-tub kind of relaxing that makes me just want to sigh with relief, but... well, uh, we're sort of in a public school library so I'm just going to continue sitting straight and keeping things as chaste as possible.

"You are *really* good at this," I can't help but comment as she moves out from the neck to the shoulders proper.

"Yeah, my dad has a bad back and he likes it when I help out with this sort of thing," she answers nonchalantly. "I've got a lot of practice. Although it's kind of hard knowing how firmly to press now, since I think your spell is making me stronger."

"Also the claws," I mumble.

"...And that, yeah," she agrees. "But I don't really use my fingertips for this anyway, so it's not a huge deal."

"Well I've also got weird biology, believe it or not, so I don't know how well my preferences will scale to your dad," I tell her, "but I could go with more pressure, I think."

She leans forward so she can look at me and wiggles her eyebrows.

"Want me to go harder, do you?" she asks in a comically sultry voice.

A laugh chokes out from me, despite how not all that funny it is. She cackles back and the two of us just spend a little while shaking quietly in an attempt to not laugh loud enough to get us kicked from the library. It's stupid. It barely even helps. But... it's something. A little levity on a long day helps a lot.

But it's a very long day, and I'm just so tired. It's not long before lunch is over and the rest of my schedule is once again bleak. I have work today, so after school I head straight there. Doing anything is a slog. I haven't felt this exhausted, sore, and drained since well before all the magical nonsense in my life started, and then only when I was really, really sick. I manage to get through my shift in a haze, and despite my all-encompassing fatigue when I get home, I'm terrified of falling asleep. It'll only get worse on the other side of things.

\<DistractedDreamer\>

427

Apropos of nothing: do people here think that if someone hurts others, they deserve to die?

\<Mortississississimo\>
""""""Apropos of nothing""""""

\<Monster Magus\>
Hannah?

\<Lana, Blood Ba'ham\>
I mean, I absolutely think there are cases where it's unavoidable to use lethal force in self-defense.

\<DistractedDreamer\>
Yeah I understand that. Trust me, I understand that. I'm like the freaking queen of using lethal force in self-defense. I mean does a person who hurts others *deserve to die*. Like, ontologically.

\<Skarmbliss\>
How I wake up knowing my enemies are ontologically evil and there is no act against them which is wrong :-)

\<blue\>
what does ontologically mean

\<Lana, Blood Ba'ham\>
"Relating to or based upon being or existence." In this case 'ontologically deserves to die' just means 'deserves to die as an inherent property of the person's existence.' Which... no, I don't think that's the case.

\<Mortississississimo\>
Death penalty arguments *would* make an interesting change from the usual political discourse around these parts, but I have to argue that nothing "deserves" anything, ontologically speaking. The concept of deserving things is not useless, but it is absolutely made up, so it doesn't really work in ontological contexts.

\<Lana, Blood Ba'ham\>
Even outside the specific realm of ontology, I think it's tough to argue against the value of prioritizing forgiveness and healing. Like, there are extreme cases where someone might be too horrific to forgive or too dangerous to attempt to capture, but as

long as you *can* capture and rehabilitate, you should try. This goes doubly so when you're talking about policy, be that systemic or personal. Death is sometimes necessary, but it should be the extreme exception, not the standard practice.

<DistractedDreamer>
Alright. Thank you anyway.

<Mortissississimo>
"Thank you anyway?"

<Lana, Blood Ba'ham>
You're welcome, I suppose.

<Monster Magus>
Good luck, Hannah.

I turn my phone off, close my eyes, and fall asleep. I wake up still in pain, but it no longer matters. Nothing does. Not the new shape of my hardening carapace, not the messy-haired woman sitting blankly on a chair in the corner, and not the utter lack of other guards or defenses. My torturers are nowhere in sight, but they don't matter. Hagoro isn't nearby to disable my Space magic, but he doesn't matter. My thoughts are nothing but listless nothings, technically awake but utterly devoid of volition. I do not move, except to breathe.

It's impossible to know how much time passes before something happens, but events are beyond my notice anyway. Sometimes people walk by the room they're keeping me in. Sometimes they greet the guards, but sometimes they just glance at the door, seeming to read something on it before walking away a little faster than they approached. One person I don't recognize enters, a human woman with a shaved head and a primitive-looking pair of glasses. She carries a tray in each hand. She extends the smaller tray towards me, and when she reaches the wooden bars of my cage she somehow passes the entire tray and part of her arm clean through them, depositing it next to me.

The tray has a bowl of water and some kind of meat I can't identify. Some part of me vaguely notes that I might be offended by being given a water bowl like some kind of pet, but I can't deny it would be easier to drink from than a glass, given my continued lack of hands. Not that it really matters. The woman also deposits a tray in front of the long-haired girl in the room, who is equally unresponsive to its presence. Gently, the woman coaxes the girl to eat and drink, guiding her hands and helping her safely bring food and water to her mouth while her eyes continue staring blankly at nothing. I get no such treatment. My tray remains untouched, and I remain motionless. After the meal, the woman with the shaved head departs.

More meaningless things occur. More measureless time passes. I still don't feel anything even when a dentron I recognize and normally dislike approaches the room, changes something on the door, and speaks a spell. I don't feel anything as the Goddess descends onto my body, cuddling me with a smile like I'm a sleepy kitten. I don't feel anything when Hagoro enters the room, walks over to the blank-faced, long-haired girl, and speaks softly.

"Madaline?" he says. "Madaline, I'm back. You can stop now."

Nothing but increasingly-familiar nothing answers him. He places a hand on her shoulder, careful and calm, and gives her a light shake.

"It's alright, Madaline," he continues quietly. "I'm here. Can you hear my voice, Madaline?"

It sounds like he's said this hundreds of times. He uses her name a lot, like it's a magic word.

"Focus on me, Madaline." The girl blinks, slowly. "That's it. There you go. Are you with me, Madaline?"

And then, all at once, the world matters again. It hits me like a sledgehammer: the pain, the hunger, the fear, the miles and miles of racing thoughts that I had been so comfortably floating above just moments ago. Now, the ice broken, I've fallen back into the frozen lake of reality and it is *wretched*. I take in an involuntary gasp of air, and Hagoro's gaze immediately flicks to me, tension filling his body for a calculating moment before he relaxes and returns his gaze to the Chaos/Pneuma mage.

"Thank you, Madaline, for taking over," he says. "I feel much better rested now."

"Ha... go... ro...?" the girl asks groggily, her voice scratchy from disuse. She blinks a few times, her gaze lazily lifting up to meet Hagoro's smiling face. She slowly meets his smile with one of her own, leaning slightly to give him an affectionate nuzzle with the side of her head.

For my part, I start shakily stretching my legs, each one cramped from where it was curled up below me. My body is distinctly no longer spherical, almost more of a bean shape as it stretches and bends slightly upwards. My mouth and eyes are all slowly migrating towards the bit of my body that's growing upwards, finally giving me a visibly distinct front side and back side. Likewise, four of my limbs are very distinctly still legs, feeling natural to keep my body weight on, but many of my other limbs are slowly getting a little more specialized.

This is all just knowledge I'd already acquired and simply not cared very much about during my magically-induced dissociative episode, of course, and it's still pretty difficult to care because a half-dozen other pressing matters are suddenly screaming down the halls of my consciousness. I'm hungry and I'm thirsty and my *soul hurts* and I'm *stuck in the room with a Pneuma mage* and I'm *completely helpless* and I'm going to be *soul tortured later* and—

The panic attack hits all at once, my body gasping for breath as I shudder in horror. Oh, Goddess, this is too much. Too much, too much, too much. Why does my life have to be like this? The Goddess strokes me lovingly, but it just makes everything worse because of *course* it does, I don't want Her touching me, why would I *ever* want Her touching me? I don't want *any* of this! I don't want pain or torture, I don't want extra limbs or magic, I don't want friends that keep going out of their way to help me or a girlfriend that I keep stumbling around and causing problems for!

More than anything, right now, I wish I could just go back to being nothing.

The Pneuma mage, Madaline, turns to stare at me the moment that thought passes through my mind, a sad look of something like understanding passing over her face. I shudder in horror and revulsion, not knowing what thoughts are really mine and what parts of me have been irrevocably twisted by her. I'll never know. I'll never want to know. Hagoro holds out a hand and helps her stand, the thin girl shaky on her legs.

"Thank... you," Madaline mumbles at him, her body seeming even stiffer than mine. He just gives her a stoic nod, his focus fixed on making sure she doesn't fall. Carefully, taking her empty food tray in his other hand, he starts leading her towards the door.

"If you're trying to break me, you're succeeding," I blurt, barely thinking about my words before they come tumbling out of my mouth. My eyes can't tear up, but the quivering cadence of a sob still rings out in my words. "I'm just some fucking girl. I can't... I'm not going to be able to handle torture."

Hagoro gives me a considering look for a moment, then wiggles his two stump arms.

"Forgive me if I choose to remain cautious," he answers dryly.

"Oh, *fuck you!*" I sob."*You* attacked *us!* I thought you were helping us when you freed me from that Pneuma mage, but then you turn around and *lock me in a room with another one!*"

Madaline flinches away, her eyes growing distant for a moment before Hagoro squeezes her hand and starts walking her towards the door again. It's obvious he cares for her, in a fatherly way. It's obvious she needs the care. I hate it. I hate looking at these monsters who keep hurting me and seeing them as people. I'll never be able to escape like this.

He doesn't respond to me any further, just giving quiet words of encouragement to Madaline as he opens the door and hands her off to one of the guards, who also seems to know her. A sudden terror fills me as she turns to go, and to my disgust I can't resist the urge to call out.

"Wait," I beg. "They'll... they'll be coming back again today, won't they? To hurt me? Can I... negotiate or something? Like maybe you could... put me under while you do it? I don't know what I can give you, but..."

Disgusting. Horrible. I'm obviously compromised. The Pneuma mage is walking away and I'm *begging* her to stay and cast on me. But if it's that or the torture again, I just... I can't...!

Hagoro doesn't answer me, but he does pause, fiddling with a small magic item on his belt as Madaline waits next to him, staring at me. Shortly afterwards, Donny jogs into view of my spatial sense, turning to Hagoro as he arrives.

"What's up?" Donny asks.

"She says she wants to negotiate," Hagoro answers.

"Oh. Uh, awesome," he says, then turns to me. "What did you want to talk about, Hannah?"

I scrunch my body in on itself, trying not to tremble. *Two* Pneuma mages have their attention on me now. What am I, an idiot?

"...She said she wanted my help when Malda comes by again," Madaline answers for me quietly.

"Oh," Donny answers, then he turns to stare at me for a moment. "...Shit. Uh, sorry kid. Having Pneuma magic active would interfere with the Death spell we use to sus you out. Conflicting elements and all that."

That is in many ways both horrible news and vaguely relieving. I spend a while processing my despair before realizing something important: no one else is acting surprised by this revelation. That means they already knew this, and they just needed Donny to make the decision on whether or not to *lie to me about it* and trick me into giving away info for nothing. I suppose they either don't value anything I could tell them enough to screw me over for it, or they still hold some insane hope that I'm going to choose to work with them as long as they torture me *nicely enough*. I let

433

out an irritated hiss, the sound vibrating in all the right ways to make them shiver.

"That's it, huh?" I snap. "You're oh-so-sorry you have to torture me, but you have no choice? Nothing you can do about it?"

"Unfortunately, no," he answers, his face carefully neutral. "Normal painkillers, magical or otherwise, don't really work on soul damage. You need Pneuma magic for that, and that would interfere with the only spell we have that might help you. We're not doing this because we think you deserve it, kid. We're doing this because we either figure out how to stop you from killing billions, or we have to kill *you*. Those are the stakes."

I start breathing harder again, to my immense shame. I wish I could be one of those cool action heroes that knows how to take the pain, but I'm not. I'm really, really not.

"...Here's some things I *can* do," Donny tells me. "We can... adjust the times you're being worked on. Give you a little more breathing room between sessions. Make everything surrounding the dirty work as comfortable as possible. Does that sound good?"

Yes. It sounds *very* good. I'll take anything at this point. But it doesn't really solve anything, does it? This ache still won't go away.

"You're an enormous, experienced organization with a stupid amount of resources," I accuse. "Is there seriously nothing other than *soul torture* that satisfies whatever insane thing you want to do to me?"

"...Kid, we're lucky to have any spell *at all* that might be able to do what we want to do to you," Donny answers.

Something about that churns in my mind a little, stewing and shifting until I finally figure out what's bothering me about it.

"No," I realize. "You're not lucky. It has nothing to do with luck at all."

The spells people get are not a matter of *luck*. If the cultists have a spell that does something they think they need to do to me, it's only because *the Goddess gave someone that spell*. So why? Does

434

She want me here? Did She intend for me to be tortured like this? The Goddess lounges on me further, the pressure of Her presence rising as she flashes a maledictive grin.

"What do you mean, kid?" Donny asks.

"...Hagoro," Madaline whispers, her eyes going wide. "Do you hear Her laughing?"

All eyes flash to Madaline for a terrified moment before turning back to me.

"You're being set up," I tell them. "You're being *played*. I don't know what the game is, but She's winning."

She's always winning, a chuckle reminds me. All She has to do to win is play.

"Kid, slow down. Who are you talking about?" Donny asks. "The Goddess? Are you saying the Goddess Herself has an agenda here?"

"Yes!" I tell him. "Of course She does!"

"Well, what is it?"

"I don't know!" I snap, thinking rapidly. Her agenda is *probably* getting me to seed Earth with magic so she has more playthings. That seems to be her whole modus operandi so far: just tempting me into spreading souls around and laughing at the ensuing fireworks. So how does that connect to what's happening here? Is she using the cultists as a catalyst to force me to experiment more with magic?

I start pacing around in what little of my tiny cage I'm actually able to move in. It's awkward and uncomfortable, in part because my body is strange and using different instincts to move all of a sudden, but mostly just because what little room I have is taken up by the tray of food and water that I still need to consume.

How is She doing this? Why is She doing this? People are given their magic at birth, right? So did the Goddess somehow predict, however many decades ago, that a certain specific person would grow up to be a cultist and a certain specific spell would... what, turn them against me? Take people that *could* have been friends or allies and twist them into enemies?

The Goddess chuckles condescendingly. Really? Twisting away potential allies? Do I seriously believe that I could have ever been friends with these torture-happy zealots? I need to clear my head and remember the situation here. And... shit, I hate to give it to Her, but She's got a point. I'm coming off a panic attack and chatting with a Pneuma mage whose whole thing is seeming like a friend and teasing out information. Maybe they can use this torture to get whatever they want from me eventually, but that's no reason to just *hand* it to the bastards.

Of course, all these thoughts become moot the moment my torturers walk into view. My mind and body freeze as I spot the two of them with my spatial sense: the sunken-eyed human man and the cold, unflinching dentron woman. They're walking towards me. They're *on their way here.*

Instinctively, I scuttle backwards, trying to escape, but of course there's nowhere I can go. I start hyperventilating again, my second panic attack in as many minutes hitting me at the speed of a bullet train. No, no, no, no. I don't want to suffer that pain again.

The Goddess clicks her tongue with disapproval. If I don't want them to hurt me again, then I should *do something about it.*

"Kid?" Donny asks, but I'm barely paying attention. "What's wrong?"

"Shut up," I snap. "This is all your fault. It's *all your fault!"*

"...You've been uncharacteristically unpopular with this one, Donny," Hagoro mutters quietly.

"I can't grow crops without soil, man," Donny grumbles back. "She's suspicious as all hell and she fucking hates us. She's probably just gonna end up like all the other ones."

The ones that died, they mean. People like me, who they tortured to death.

"I'm not going to 'end up' like anyone," I hiss. "You wanna keep pushing me until I break? Then fine. You can find out what happens if you break me."

"Nuh-uh, kid, if you try to bring the apocalypse down on our heads, we'll know," Donny frowns. "You will *not* get the chance."

"I'm not going to start a fucking apocalypse!" I shout at them. "I'm going to get out of here, rescue my friends, and live my fucking life away from the *insane people* who think the greater good gave them a pre-paid gift card to clawing my soul open!"

"A what? No, not important," Donny sighs, shaking his head. "What's important is that you need to figure out that you aren't leaving until we figure out how to declaw you. And if you actually *help* us with that process, you might even survive to the end of it. So *please,* just let us—"

"Is there a problem, Donny?" my torturer asks.

Donny flinches in surprise, turning and giving the man a polite nod as he approaches. I, meanwhile, stop being able to function out of terror.

"Malda! No sir, sorry. Just the usual threats," Donny answers.

"It *is* tiring to hear of them," my torturer—Malda—sighs. "Don't take them lightly, however. Founder's Kin are always powerful, and we don't know the full extent of what she can do. The accounts those sailors gave of her fighting in battle might have all matched standard Founder's Kin abilities, but we have to assume she's hiding more. The only piece of unique information they could provide was the possibility of *cleaning magic*, of all things."

"...Yes sir," Donny nods.

"Return to talking with her friends, would you?" my torturer requests. "I heard you were starting to make progress with one of them."

"Yes sir," Donny nods again. "I could actually use your help with that in a bit, Madaline, if you're up for it."

The Chaos and Pneuma mage seems to ignore him for a bit, mostly just spending her time staring at me. But then, slowly, she turns her head to Donny instead, and nods.

"Okay," she agrees, and the two of them depart together. Only then do Hagoro, my torturer, and his assistant actually step into the room with me, and I feel my body start to shake.

"I see you haven't eaten," my torturer comments. "Would you like a minute for that?"

A silent Refresh. That's all I need. He'll be unconscious in minutes, dead in just a little more. I can get all three of them at once, if I stay focused. But I can't. Why am I so weak? Why can't I just believe in a world where killing a monster counts as cleaning up?

Because cleaning is easy for you, I remind myself. *And this isn't something you can stomach turning into something easy.*

Well. I guess I'll just suffer, then.

"I'll take that as a no," Malda shrugs after I spend too long in silence, and reaches out to turn my soul into pain.

This time, I don't last anywhere near as long before I start screaming. I have nothing to prove, really. It hurts. It hurts more than anything. I think it's only fair that I'm allowed to scream in situations like that.

I don't really feel like a person when I finally wake up. I don't know how long the torture lasted and I don't want to know. The *ache* is deep within me, the omnipresent agony seeming to wash everything else away. I don't even try to move, just lying in bed and *hurting* until my mom wakes up, knocks on my door, and terrifies me enough to get me moving.

"You awake, honey?" she asks. "Don't be late for school!"

"I-I-I'm fine!" I stammer, hiding under the covers in case she comes in. "Sorry! I'm just going to take a quicker shower today!"

"Oh, hmm," she muses. "Well, that'll be nice. Save us some water."

"Y-yep!"

438

She eventually goes away, and I drag myself out of bed. I drag myself to shower. I drag myself to school. I drag myself through classes. I drag myself to work. I drag myself through an entire day of pain and exhaustion, and when I finally get home all I have is the knowledge that it's all about to get much, much worse.

I'm not going to be able to handle this. I'm not.

Something is going to break.

21

LABYRINTHS

I've been getting tortured nightly for four days now. I think that's enough to qualify as routine.

I guess you could argue I've been tortured for three or eight days just as easily, because time is... different for me. As is consciousness. I was tortured treeside Sunday night, then hurt all day Monday, then was tortured treeside Monday night... and so on. Now it's Thursday. Not getting to rest is really weighing on me, on top of everything else. In some ways it helps the routine settle in, though: no time to reset, to clear my mind, to take a moment to say 'wait a minute, this is probably not how things should be.' Which is good. I don't want to think about that. There's nothing I can do about it, after all. Better to just accept it as reality.

Valerie strong-armed me into testing a few things yesterday. She dragged me over to her house after school and forced me to take a nap so she could test for solutions. Results were mixed. Some of her spells actually *do* transfer over to my other body; generalized buff spells, in particular. Magic that makes me stronger or faster works, though it doesn't help me get out of a cage at all. Magic that helps me heal also seems to work, though not on soul pain. The best we found was a specialized spell that automatically retaliates against anyone else that casts a spell on *me*. That worked too, but the problem is that it didn't work well *enough*. The moment the magic was discovered, well... the Death mage did something. My torturer 'killed' the spell duration, I guess, ending it prematurely, and then just continued on as normal.

We got a good zap on him, but it wasn't any more than a little petty revenge. He was irritated, not disabled, and the rest of that day went much worse as a result. And now he's ready for whatever else we try... not that it matters.

Other magic we tried to send through the link failed to transfer or just failed to work at all. Basically, spells seem to work between universes if their basic concept is to apply some sort of attribute to the entirety of whatever conceptually counts as 'me,' but anything that only applies to *my body* only works on earthside. So then we tried designing spells to that specification to get around the limits, but the result was just that they *failed to work*. Valerie could cast a spell that teleports my earthside body, but not a buff spell designed to give me the ability to teleport myself. There are apparently some hard conceptual limits to the kinds of spells Valerie's magic can create, and we still don't know what all of them are. It seems to be enough to directly screw me out of escaping this particular situation, and when I pointed that out the Goddess laughed at me. I don't know if that means I'm *right* or not, but it still kind of killed our motivation.

So... despair it is, I guess.

"Hannah?"

It's fine. If anything, the situation feels familiar. Before my life was a mess of panic and excitement, it was kind of like this: dull depression with a side of resignation to my fate. Sure, the pain is making it hard to think and focus, and yeah, it's bad enough that I can't even handle easy stuff like schoolwork, but who cares about schoolwork anyway? Who cares that I'm starting to underperform at work? Why would any of that matter, in the face of knowing I'm going to either get slowly tortured to death or end up turning into a person that the me of today would hate? Why would any of it matter when my life is so messed up that the idea of a future where any of those normal things apply is laughable?

Honestly, I don't know why I've bothered to keep up with it until now.

...Okay, yes I do. Because it's routine. I'd still be doing homework and working hard at my job if I could actually wrap my brain around anything other than this all-encompassing pain and exhaustion. I'm still trying to go through the motions, after all. I'm going to keep moving like this, like a twitching puppet with ever-crumbling joints, until everything finally falls apart for good.

I'm not sure if I want that to be soon or not.

"Oi, Hannah!" Autumn hisses from where she's been jogging beside me. "What the fuck is going on? Are you high?"

"Huh?" I blink, realizing I've just been jogging in silence for a while and she *has* tried to get my attention a couple times. Goddess, my whole body aches. I don't want to do this gym class stuff. I don't want to run. I don't want to do anything.

"I asked you what the fuck is going on," she hisses.

I take a moment churning those words around in my head.

"...Jet?" I guess. "Hey. I haven't seen you in a while."

"No shit you haven't seen me in a while," she growls. "What day is it?"

What day is... oh. Oh, gosh. A little surge of adrenaline sends shivers down my spine, forcing my groaning brain into some semblance of functionality. *'What day is it?'* That is *not* a normal thing for Jet or Alma to have to ask. It means something happened.

"It's Thursday," I answer firmly. "Sorry, I'm really out of it. What do you remember?"

"I remember the *last time we had gym class,*" Jet hisses."That's it. Locker room to locker room."

"...That was two days ago," I say, fear crawling through me. "We have gym every other day."

"No shit, Benoit Blanc! So again: what's going on?"

I lick my lips under my mask, rewinding my thoughts over the last few days. And... holy crap, she's right. I didn't even notice, but she's right. I haven't seen or heard from Jet *at all* outside of gym class. I can't believe I didn't notice... well, okay, yes I can. But still. This is... bad. Alma must be finding time to duck into her house every time Jet might be coming to the front. Except gym, for some reason? I mean, I guess it's a combination of her hating it and needing Jet's spell to not get outed as a weird monster.

...Oh holy crap that's right, Autumn is a weird monster and that's my fault. I shake my head, the realization clearing the fog of Jet's spell and revealing Alma—in tail form, of course—twitching in frustration behind Jet as she runs. I shudder a little at the realization that I've been mindfucked again, but hey! It's kind of a day-to-day thing for me now! May as well happen on both sides of the dimensional gap.

I need to focus on my friend's problem anyway. It's one that might actually be solvable. Of course, like with all problems, it's important to start with self-pity.

"I'm sorry," I blurt. "I should have been paying closer attention. I didn't think it would get that bad, that quickly. Or... I mean, I really wasn't thinking at all. I'm not... doing great."

"Sure, whatever. What did you think would not get this bad?" Jet presses.

"Alma's spell prevents you from fronting," I tell her bluntly. "It's kind of awkward to use but I guess she must be... figuring it out. It's hard to notice her using it, so... um. Yeah."

Jet gapes at me, her face that sort of complicated expression one gets when they are horrified beyond words but also not the least bit surprised. She returns her eyes to the track for a moment and just stares at nothing for a while before speaking.

"...You don't think you could have told me this on Tuesday?" she asks.

"I, um. Have not really been myself this week," I mutter awkwardly.

"I've *literally* not been myself this week!" she hisses back. "Fuck, fuck, fuck. She's trying to kill me."

"...Yeah," I mumble, not sure how to process that. My girlfriend is trying to make a person stop existing. I'm literally getting tortured over how firmly I'm against that sort of thing. Why does it feel so different, though? Well, either way, I have to do something.

"I'll talk to her," I promise. "Sorry. I should have done that sooner, I just... I'm not doing well."

"Yeah, like I trust you to side with me against her," Jet growls. "Fuck, fuck, fuck..."

I frown. I guess I can't blame her for thinking that way, but I'm still offended.

"Text the chat as soon as you can, then," I suggest. "I know you don't have a ton of friends, but we *are* your friends now, if you want us to be. And Ida will probably be better at helping than I am anyway."

If she reads the group chat she'll also learn about my soul torture situation without me having to explain it, which is a plus because I do not want to talk or think about it at all. The pain is reminder enough.

"What the fuck is your deal, Hannah," Jet growls. "God, I want to hate you. I *should* hate you, for doing this to us and then making your stupid little group our only lifeline."

"Weren't you telling your therapist about the monster stuff?" I ask.

"Well I haven't gotten to see my therapist all week, have I?" Jet scowls. "Whatever. It doesn't matter. You're my only lifeline, but it's not like I had any other lifelines before. Why would you even want me around, though? I'm just in the way of you and your fucking girlfriend."

I take a while to think about that, the adrenaline and panic already fading back into pain and leaving my brain a dull sludge. But to my own surprise, I do find an answer I like, after a while.

"I'm kind of in the exact opposite situation you are," I say. "One person in two bodies, instead of two people in one body. I'm sure it's nothing like what you're going through, and I'm sure I don't understand what your situation is like at all. But I *definitely* understand what it's like to... well, be in a situation no one else understands."

She doesn't say anything, just staring at the track, so I continue.

"I don't... really get along with most people," I say. "I don't hate them or anything, but I just... don't have any particular desire to be around them. I think the way my head interacts with others is a little broken. Er... well, I guess I shouldn't say 'broken,' because it might just be autism. It might also be because I'm a weird spider creature. I don't know. I don't know how to know. But whatever thing that makes normal people associate faces and names, or really *people* with *bodies* at all, is kind of weird to me. Maybe that's why I find it so natural and obvious that you and Alma are completely different people. Maybe it's something less high-concept than that. But either way, you are Jet. You are no one *but* Jet, to me. And I don't really feel like you're in the way of anything any more than anyone else could be."

Again, more silence. I feel the need to fill it, so I continue.

"So if someone wants to get in the way of *your* right to life, there's no way in hell I'm going to help them. And if they insist on it anyway, I'm not going to date them either. That's just not something you do to a person."

Jet finally glances my way, staring at me with naked suspicion.

"...You'd break up with Alma for me?" she asks.

"Are you kidding?" I ask. "Yeah, I'd break up with someone for trying to keep a person prisoner inside their own head. That's pretty unambiguously messed up."

"But will you *make* her?" Jet asks, her voice low. "When push comes to shove?"

I frown.

"I mean... I don't think I *can* 'make her,' I don't have any real level of control over her," I say. Jet snorts at that for some reason, but I press on. "But Jet, I'm not going to have to 'make her.' If I thought she was the sort of awful person that couldn't be talked out of hurting someone, I wouldn't be dating her in the first place."

"...And yet here we are," Jet sighs. "But fine. Okay. I appreciate the offer of help. I hope it leads to something."

"Yeah," I agree, suppressing a pained grimace. "Me too."

We get back to running, and I start to wonder how bad it is that having something awful enough to distract me from my pain has been the highlight of my week so far.

I trudge through the rest of gym class, quickly falling back into that half-conscious haze of pain that has defined my earthside days all week. Somebody smacks me in the head with a volleyball at one point, but I don't really notice it beyond needing to go pick up the ball. I think whoever hit me apologized. It doesn't really matter, but that's nice, at least.

Classes happen when they happen, and lunch is eventually a thing. I sit down in the library as usual, my stomach growling as I open up textbooks to try and get homework done that I know I won't really be able to process.

"Hey, Hannah!" Alma greets me from behind, approaching my table to sit down next to me. "You doing okay?"

"Yeah, I'm fine," I lie easily, not really thinking about it.

"If you say so," she says, giving me a doubtful look. "You seem pretty out of it, which... well, makes perfect sense. Things have kind of been sucking. Would a date this Saturday help take your mind off it, you think?"

"Sure," I agree. Then I blink, trying to get my thoughts back together past the pain. "...Oh, I need to talk to you about Jet, though."

"Oh?" she asks. "Uh, what about them?"

447

"Are you using your spell to prevent them from fronting?" I ask. "Like, at all? Jet said in gym that she hasn't been conscious since *last* gym class, on Tuesday. She was really freaking out about it."

"Oh," Alma answers, fidgeting slightly. "Um, I guess I've been giving myself some extra time when I'm in the middle of something, yeah."

"...You wouldn't happen to be implying that you're always in the middle of something because that's just sort of how life works, are you?"

She fidgets again. Buh. I'm too tired for this.

"Alma, come on," I sigh.

"...You don't know what it's like," she mutters. "Not being able to make any plans because I don't even know if I'll *exist.*"

"No, I don't," I agree patiently. "But I don't feel like foisting all of your suffering onto Jet is a good solution. Does Jet not deserve to live their life, too?"

"No!" Alma snaps. "They don't! Jet is a *medical condition* that nearly got me locked up in prison! Why shouldn't I take the *cure?*"

I stare at her in shock, startled by her outburst. She stares back for a moment, frustration obvious in her features, until she suddenly breaks eye contact with something like shame on her face.

"Alma..." I ask slowly, "is that really what you think of her?"

"You don't know what it's like," she repeats, shaking slightly.

"I know I don't," I say. "I'm sorry. But Alma... do *you* know what it's like to talk to Jet? Have you ever actually gotten to meet her?"

She grimaces.

"Of course I... I mean, I get flashes," she hedges, but I can tell she barely believes it.

"Have you watched a recording of her doing stuff, at least?" I ask.

"Jet used to send... video messages," Alma admits. "Before we started using the notebook. But I just... I couldn't watch them. It was... it freaks me out, okay? Seeing someone else puppet my body around like that. I just couldn't watch them."

She's extremely anxious now, fidgeting and glancing around constantly. She even looks vaguely... betrayed? Which hurts to see.

"Can we just not talk about this?" Alma begs. "Please? Can't this just be a good thing? Can't I feel like a fucking *person* for once?"

"Alma," I say, as calmly as I can muster. "You're my girlfriend. I care about you, I think you're adorable, I love your obsession with books and your rambles on jellyfish and everything else about you. But I also talk with Jet pretty regularly. You and her... you're obviously *both* people, to me. The fact that I care about you more doesn't mean I'm going to do nothing while you hurt her."

She sags in defeat, collapsing into a chair with her face in her hands. A little groan escapes her mouth, a sad mix of frustration and despair.

"Fine, okay," she agrees quietly. "I'll just go back to letting the crazy criminal run half my life."

"Jet has never given me the impression that she's mentally unstable or unsound," I say, trying to be reassuring. "If anything, she seems to care about you deeply. I swear, half our conversations are her giving me another shovel talk."

"Hhngh," is all Alma says in response, so I try to press on.

"How did that all happen, anyway?" I ask. "The, uh, criminal thing. I've heard Jet mention that she was burglarizing houses, but what was that like from your perspective? Do you know why she did it?"

Alma is quiet for a bit, but then she lets out a long sigh sitting back up in her chair and propping her head up on one elbow.

"...My dad is in a lot of debt," she admits slowly. "I don't really know how much, exactly. But my family can struggle to get by sometimes. I first started noticing the memory blackouts... I dunno. Years ago. But then the bills started getting paid. It was just kinda weird and concerning at first, but not... a huge thing?

449

It was scary, but I didn't want to tell anyone that I was having *memory blackouts,* we couldn't afford a hospital trip. And... well, not remembering doing the bills isn't so bad, right? My dad acted like I had found an after school job, so I guess that's what Jet told him. He was really happy with me about it. And... I liked that, so... it wasn't really a problem. I knew something was fucked up when I woke up one time before the bills got paid and just saw a stack of cash with a sticky note on it that said 'for rent' in my handwriting. But... y'know. Don't question a good thing, right?"

She rubs her temples, and shrugs.

"...And then one day I just find myself in a police interrogation room. And everything has just gone downhill since then. So yes, I know Jet cares, but it doesn't change the fact that they've fucked up my entire life, you know? We only ever started actively communicating after being forced into therapy, and that's been... not great."

"Because by the time you knew there was someone else to talk to, they were already the person that got you arrested?" I ask.

"I guess," Alma sighs. "It's not like anything else really mattered. Like, it's not as though I had any friends or anything to do with my time *before* having Jet steal half of it away from me. The only thing that's different now is that I have you."

She looks so small now, curled up like a puppy that knew it shouldn't have ripped the couch open.

"I just... wanted to be there for you," she whispers.

Well, I don't think there's anything I can say to that, so instead I reach over and envelop her in a big, firm hug. Slowly, quietly, Alma starts to cry into my shoulder, her body shaking softly as tears soak into my shirt and are quietly Refreshed away.

"I just... I just don't want to be like this," she sobs. "Our therapist says other people with DID figure out how to manage it and live happy lives. Other people figure out their schedules and learn to cooperate and help each other but I just *don't want to.* I don't want to be like this. I just want my brain to be normal."

Her tail shifts underneath her skirt, awkward and uncomfortable. Her wings twitch on her back. Her ears, underneath her hat, give a despondent wiggle.

"I just don't know what to do," Alma says. "I love you, Hannah. I love you and I want to be with you and I don't know what to *do*. I don't know what to do with my body, I don't know what to do with my magic, I don't know how to exist or how to live. I just don't have anything other than you."

"Alma... hey." I reassure her. "That's not true."

"It *is* true!" she insists. "Even if it isn't, I want it to be true."

"Wh-why would you want it to—"

"Fuck!" she hisses. "I shouldn't have said anything. Fuck, fuck, fuck! I'm sorry!"

"Alma, it's *okay*," I insist."I promise it's okay. I'm not exactly the poster child for mental health either, okay? I'm not gonna judge you for your feelings. I'm *not*. It's what you do that matters."

"What I'm *doing* is trying to kill someone I don't even know," Alma sobs. "I hate them, Hannah. I hate them so much. I *hate* the idea of anyone else getting to use my body. It's *mine*."

"I know," I say soothingly. "I know. I'm sorry."

Holy cream cannoli we are so dysfunctional. Goddess, but I wish I knew what to say, how to act, who to *be*. This is so hard and I feel like it's all going wrong but I don't know how to make it right. I just don't know what I'm doing. I've never been in a relationship before, let alone one like... *this*.

"No no no, it's okay, you don't have to be sorry," Alma insists. "You don't. It's okay. You haven't done anything wrong. I just... maybe I just like to tell myself that if I get rid of Jet then my stupid awful brain will be okay again. But it won't, will it? I'm the problem. It's me."

"...Well, that sounds like a good reason to listen to your therapist a little, right?" I press.

"Yeah. I guess. Okay," Alma shudders. "Do you... do you still wanna go out Saturday? It's okay if you don't, I..."

"Alma," I say firmly. "I'm not going to dump you because you talked about your feelings. It's *okay*. You said you weren't going to take time from Jet anymore, right?"

"...Yeah," she agrees.

"Then that's it. That's the only concern I had. Everything else is stuff we'll work out together, alright? I'm here for you."

"Okay. Sorry."

"You don't have to be sorry. But you're forgiven anyway, if you want to be."

"Thank you. Sorry."

We just stay together for a while, the worry about the whole event mixing into my foggy brain and bubbling within the pain. It feels like the red flags keep piling up, but what does that mean? I don't think Alma is bad or unpleasant or annoying. I absolutely enjoy spending time with her. She has problems to work through, sure, but doesn't everyone? I certainly do, and she's putting up with enough of *my* bull poop to be worth helping, that's for sure. So what's the problem? What am I worried about?

...Alma said she loves me, right? Do I love her? Is that a question I should even know the answer to this early into our relationship?

Whether I'm supposed to or not, I certainly fail to find the answer before lunch ends. Or, for that matter, before the day ends. A small panic attack before bed is all I have to suffer tonight before exhaustion inevitably claims me, forcing me to once more wake up in my horrible, horrible torture cage... and let something not unlike relief pass through me as my mind blanks out, rendered totally, blissfully empty by Madaline's spell.

Whatever feeling I might have had at the sensation is gone in an instant, of course. Nothing remains of Hannah beyond the dim perception of the passage of time. On and on, things happen, but they simply aren't important, aren't noteworthy, aren't... a problem. But eventually, Hagoro comes and shakes Madaline awake, and my problems exist once again.

I *exist*. It's awful. I hate it.

With a shudder, I return to sentience, the dread of incoming agony causing my breaths to shake. I'm pathetic for feeling this way, aren't I? For so desperately wanting this... this *low-commitment suicide*. But what else am I supposed to do here? I feel like a real hero would be out of this cage by now, her captors dead on the floor for daring to subject her to such inhumane practice. But I'm too good to twist my spell for the purpose, and not good enough to have any other way out. I'm nothing but a failure, and now I have to suffer for it. Maybe I deserve to.

As has become common on this side of the dimensions, my body instinctively tries to cry despite lacking the biology to do so. I'm just so scared, so desperate, that there's nothing else I can do. When Hagoro starts to escort Madaline from the room, I call out without thinking.

"Wait," I beg. I'm scared to see her leave. Scared of what happens whenever she's gone. I *need* her here.

Hagoro tries to ignore me, but Madaline stops him, putting a hand on his arm to signal it rather than try to say anything in her still-bleary state. She looks at me, a sad understanding on her face, and takes a deep breath to help clear her head. Then another.

"...What is it?" she finally asks.

"Is there anything I can give you," I ask, "to just get one day?"

'Without the pain' goes unsaid. Madaline looks at Hagoro. He shrugs, like he has no influence on that kind of decision. She frowns, tapping his arm twice. He takes his arms away and stops supporting her weight, and she wobbles a bit but manages to stand on her own. I watch all of this with a dull thoughtlessness that's almost, but not quite, like being under her spell. As if my brain's response to terror is slowly starting to copy her magic out of some desperate longing.

My torturer, after all, is approaching. I'm out of time.

"Please," I beg desperately. "I'll tell you anything. About my world, about myself, about what I know. I just... I can't take this anymore."

But then he's in sight of them, and their attention is on him. Too slow, Hannah. Time to face the fire.

"Hagoro, Madaline," my torturer greets them, giving a polite nod of his head.

"Good afternoon, Malda," Hagoro answers. It's the afternoon?

"Malda, would you be willing to take a day off?" Madaline asks.

Wait, what? Hope tries to bloom inside me for a moment before I crush it down in fear. He's just going to say no. But why is she even asking...?

"A day off?" Malda asks, predictably incredulous. "We're on a time limit, Madaline. You know that."

"But it's a longer one than we're used to, right?" she presses, her lucidity improving rapidly. I've never seen her this... *focused* before.

"...It is, yes," Malda concedes. "Despite everything, she's never even attempted to accelerate things. She might not even know how."

"Or she doesn't want to," Madaline says softly. "I think I might be able... to help. Could I have a day with her?"

"I'm not sure what you expect to accomplish that Donny couldn't," Malda frowns, crossing his arms.

"Donny... gives up too easily," Madaline says slowly. "He prefers... to wait for a sure shot. He's too used to them."

"And you think it's worthwhile to gamble on a less-than-sure shot?" Malda asks.

"Is that not... what we've always done? From the start?" Madaline asks. "I think... it will help."

My torturer drums his fingers against his bicep, taking a moment to think.

"...It's rare to see you taking initiative like this, Madaline," he ultimately says. "I'm loath to give up even a single day to anything, you understand. This is, frankly, our entire reason for existing. Everything else is secondary."

454

"Secondary," Madaline argues, "does not mean worthless. I... want to give back worth."

My torturer frowns deeper.

"...I would have some firm words for anyone trying to imply you didn't already have worth in abundance," he says. "But... fine. You may take a day with her. I will see what I can arrange with the data we've already gathered."

"Thank you... Malda," Madaline says, bowing her head slightly. He just waves her off and turns around, walking back in the direction he came.

And then her attention turns to me.

"Thank you," I say, because I lack the sort of pride necessary to not be grateful to the nicest member of the cult that systematically tortures me.

"You're... welcome," Madaline nods, slowly walking towards me. Hagoro looks concerned, but continues not saying anything, just waiting around and keeping his spell active. "Don't forget... to eat... okay? I forget a lot. So my friends... always have to remind me."

Oh. I guess I am kind of hungry. And as usual, food arrived during Madaline's spell, and is waiting for me in my cell. For the first time in what feels like days (has it been days?) I step forward and lean down to eat the meat they provided me. It's an odd experience, since my body has grown into a different shape with distinct forelimbs and hindlimbs, not to mention my mouth moving up my body to stretch along what is probably the beginning of a torso towards what is probably the beginning of a head. It's all still a singular mass of 'body,' but specialization is starting to happen. It's awkward and somewhat uncomfortable, especially after I've gotten so used to being radially symmetrical, but it hardly makes it impossible to eat.

Madaline is being quiet, content to watch me eat out of either respect or her usual lack of focus. I can't really stand the silence, though, so I try to get the conversation started.

"Why did you help me?" I ask between bites.

"Hmm..." she hums in consideration, as if she hadn't even thought about why before doing it. "I guess... because... you're like me? The last Founder's Kin... wasn't like us at all. He was very mean. Very... angry. All the way until the end. You... are kind. And sad. It makes things... harder."

I gulp down another bite, surprised at how utterly starving I suddenly feel.

"So that's it?" I ask. "You just feel sorry for me?"

Can't really blame her for that; I feel sorry for me too.

"No," she clarifies, sitting down cross-legged on the floor in front of my cage. "You also offered... information. And I'm interested. You... can hear Her speak too, can't you? Most people... can't."

The Goddess, Her presence weighty in the room thanks to Zone of Law, lounges happily on my back as I eat. But now that I'm looking for it, I feel Her on Madaline as well, cuddling her close not unlike how She so often holds me.

"...Yeah," I agree. "I guess we're both cursed with Her favor."

"Is it a curse?" Madaline asks, quirking her head to the side. "I consider the Goddess... my first real friend."

"The Goddess is evil," I say quietly, hesitantly. *Fearfully*. But She doesn't seem offended by this judgment, and neither does Madaline.

"Yes," Madaline agrees instead, a smile on her face. "I have many evil friends. Would you like to be my friend, Hannah?"

I instinctively bristle at the obvious implication, the Goddess chuckling softly as she watches our exchange. Evil? Really? If I was evil I wouldn't be having any trouble breaking myself out of this *horrific torture cage!* ...But of course, I can't tell her that.

"Will you stop helping these people rip my soul apart?" I ask instead. "I unfortunately find that little detail to be a pretty significant obstacle to friendship. Besides, I barely know anything about you."

"There is… very little to say," Madaline answers. "My magic… doesn't lend itself to killing. And it is… difficult to trace. So I had less of a problem with Chaos hunters… than most people like me. But without the Goddess' help… I probably would have starved. Still, I survived, and now I have Hagoro and many other friends. And I am happy."

"Happy locking people in cages, huh?" I grumble. She laughs a little, the sort of tiny, soft laugh where she covers her mouth with one hand. A 'titter,' I think it's called.

"My friends want to save the world," she says. "Many of them… think they are good people. I do not care… if I am a good person. I do not care about… the world. But I do care about my friends. That is all. A moral objection… won't get you very far with me."

"…You have a surprisingly well-thought-out sense of who you are," I comment.

"Do you not as well?" she asks. "You know your weaknesses. You know your faults. Those of us… who like to run from our thoughts… often tend to have a lot of thoughts to run from."

How else am I supposed to deal with my thoughts, if not by running? I assume healthy people have resolution strategies, but I'm certainly not a healthy person.

"You seem like you know me pretty well," I say.

"I do," she agrees simply. I suppress a shudder. *Pneuma mages.* "Now tell me: who is the Goddess, to you?"

I sit quietly for a moment, trying to figure out how best to answer that. The Goddess Herself listens lazily to my thoughts, lounging on top of me with a yawn. I'm allowed to say whatever. I can curse Her, insult Her, scream at Her, warn people from Her… that's all fine. I just have to be careful not to *slander*. Well, okay then.

"…So, you know I'm from another world," I start with, and Madaline nods cooperatively. "Well, on my world there's a famous story called *The Monkey's Paw*. Uh, what a monkey is isn't important, the point of the story is just that there's… a wish-granting device. A thing that will literally turn whatever possible dream you could ask for into reality. But every time it is used, no matter what, the wish is twisted. A price is extracted that far exceeds the benefits one might get from the wish. Every time I interact with the Goddess, it reminds me of that."

"I see," Madaline muses. "And what prices has the Goddess extracted?"

"That's the thing," I answer. "I don't know. I have no idea what She wants from me beyond entertainment. I just know that She *does* want entertainment, and everything She does to help me is... loaded, somehow. She's setting me up for something."

"Hmm," Madaline hums again. "And it is not conceivable... that She is setting you up to destroy the world?"

"Well, I mean, I think She probably *is,*" I admit."But the apocalypse I know I can cause only affects *my* world. It doesn't affect any of you here."

That seems to surprise her, and Hagoro as well. They both share a look of bewilderment.

"Is she...?" Hagoro asks.

"Yes," Madaline confirms. "She's being honest."

He doesn't seem to know what to say to that, so Madaline returns her attention to me.

"...I am not sure if that changes anything," Madaline admits. "But I... will speak with the others. Perhaps you simply threaten this world in a manner... you do not know."

"I'm going to be kept here on a 'perhaps!?'" I snap. "You guys are insane!"

"Unfortunate, then, that your opinion has so little impact... on the ultimate decision," Madaline says with a frown, and I legitimately can't tell if she's being sarcastic or if she's actually frustrated along with me. "Perhaps they will bring the founder... to meet you. He would be able to tell... what threat you may pose."

"Wait, your cult's founder is *alive?*" I ask."How long have you guys been around?"

"The Disciples of Unification were founded just over two centuries ago," Hagoro supplies.

"Do people normally live for over two hundred years here?" I ask, realizing I don't actually know if that's as weird as it sounds in magic fantasy land.

"No," Madaline answers. "We do not. The founder is special. As... are you. If you destroy the world... you'll become immortal as well."

"Madaline!" Hagoro interjects sharply.

"It's... okay," Madaline assures him, her eyes locked on mine with a smile. "She's not tempted... by something like that. Are you, Hannah?"

She's right. I'm not. If anything, I'm *horrified*. I don't want to die, sure, but killing millions, maybe billions of people for immunity to it? That's beyond monstrous. I can't even imagine pulling the trigger on something like that.

"No," I confirm. "I don't want to hurt anyone."

"That is so interesting to me," Madaline muses. "What do you think you are, exactly?"

"I..." I gulp, shifting my weight nervously. "I'm a pawn. A piece in a game. A toy for the Goddess to play with."

The Goddess purrs. It's good of me to accept that so readily.

"So you think She chose you?" Madaline asks. "I've always... wondered about that. I think you are probably correct. The Goddess... is playing a game. But I think... she can lose."

"She can," I agree. "She has to be able to lose. Otherwise, it isn't fun to win."

Madaline titters again.

"You play a lot of games, don't you, Hannah?" she asks rhetorically. "Your predecessors were not like you. None of them were the kind of person to hesitate... at ending the world for their own sake. And if you are right... if the Goddess picks her pieces... why would she pick you? It seems to me... that if you're trying to

459

get someone to destroy the world... it would be rather important to choose someone who wanted to do that."

The Goddess' attention is weighing on the conversation now, silent but heavy. I think about ants and sand castles, about how I might change the terrain around a bug to nudge it into whatever direction I want it to go.

"...You think there's something I can't see," I conclude. "Something that she's just going to make me stumble into on accident."

"I think I wasn't sure until today that the Goddess was our enemy," Madaline answers. "But... yes. If so, that is how She would play. She is not very fun... to play games with."

"Then you should help me find the path!" I insist. "Stop hurting me and making me your enemy! We can find a way to beat Her *together!*"

"That seems like a good idea, doesn't it?" Madaline says sadly. "I want to. I *like* you, Hannah. But every single apocalypse the Disciples of Unification have stopped, we stopped with torture and death. And now, the Goddess has chosen someone kind. Someone I do not want to hurt. The Goddess... is not very fun to play games with."

"No," I growl, realizing where she's going with this. "You're kidding me."

"Your kindness exists," Madaline tells me, "to foster mercy. That is what I think. The Goddess chose you because you are pitiable, Hannah. And if we pity you too much, if we *do* release you... the world ends."

"You can't be serious," I hiss. "Why are all you cultists so fucking insane?"

She shrugs.

"It's just... my theory," she answers. "It will not free you or trap you in this cage. I just want to hear your thoughts on it, is all. Is it something... the Goddess you know would do?"

Is it something the Goddess I know would do? I'm not sure. Maybe. Probably. She'd love that sort of thing, I think. Twisting mercy and pity and love and justice into the reason everything goes to hell. Watching her little puppets doom themselves with the best intentions, howling at the dramatic irony as they blindly stumble ever closer to their death.

She'd craft the walls of the sand castle so that every pathway leads to the ocean, and she'd laugh all the while. And while an ant can dig through the sand or crawl over the walls... why *not* take the path of least resistance, if you don't know where any of them lead anyway?

"It's scary, isn't it?" Madaline asks. "Sorry. I'm glad you're thinking about it, though."

"Why does it even matter what I think?" I ask. "If you're just going to keep me here and torture me to death anyway?"

"There are still things you can do that we don't know about," Madaline shrugs. "Maybe you'll escape. You won't be the first, even if we always manage to find your kind again. But I want you to see Her, to look for Her walls. The Goddess is my friend, you see. I don't mind playing Her game from the opposite side. But if She's going to laugh at us along the way... I wouldn't mind humiliating Her a little. If you do escape... it would be extra funny if She gets beat by Her own piece, don't you think?"

The Goddess' presence *rumbles* with anticipation. You're on, She seems to say.

"Become a player, rather than just a piece. Just make sure to entertain Her, Hannah," Madaline warns me. "If She's not having fun, She can always just flip the board."

The Goddess laughs and laughs and laughs. Madaline is such a good friend, isn't she?

22

BREAKING POINT

"I guess," I say quietly, "I'll keep your advice in mind."

Madaline nods. *She can always just flip the board.* I wonder, in a vaguely absent way, does Madaline consider the Goddess a friend out of genuine affection, or does she just consider the Goddess a friend because the game ends up being played regardless of whether or not you opt in? It certainly seems like a less terrifying way to live, if you just accept reality for what it is and play along.

I don't think I can do that, though. I'm really dang good at carrying on through the worst situations and acting like they aren't a problem, sure, but at least I don't fool myself into thinking that's a *good idea.* When everything is *this* bad, when my very birth was divinely ordained to be used against me, I don't think I can have fun. I don't think I can *play a game.* Goddess, I hope You enjoy me just the way I am, because that's what I'll be sending at You.

If there's one thing I know about You, it's that You're my enemy. You will never be my friend.

The Goddess smirks, the Goddess shrugs. Enemy, friend, opponent, rival, mother, lover, master... whatever I want to call Her, our relationship is the same. It's as equally unchanged as my relationship with the weather, or my relationship with a supernova. She will laugh at my joy and sorrow equally. She will gasp at both my triumphs and my failures. She will be by my side until the moment my soul dissolves from this and every world, holding me and kissing me and cheering for me at every turn. I am Her prophet. I am Her champion. I am Her chosen. And these things will be no less true no matter what I do. There is no choice which deviates from Her enraptured attention.

But if I *really* want to annoy her, well, that'll be its own kind of entertainment too. It's my call; that is, after all, the most important rule of the game.

Anything else would be too easy.

I shudder, Madaline watching me curiously. I have no idea how much of this... 'conversation' she's picking up on. I'm not sure I want to know. But what I *do* want to know is this: is the game really about destroying the world? If I'm stuck being a piece, Goddess, don't I deserve to know what it is I'm really playing for? Are these horrible torture-cultists *right?*

The Goddess laughs. It seems to Her that the more salient question is this: even if they *are* right, does that mean I'm going to decide to sit and do nothing while they torture me to death? Are *these* the people I'm going to throw my lot in with? Out of all my friends, all my allies, everyone who cares about me and fights with me and would want to help me with anything I set my mind to, would I really choose *these* horrible schmucks?

And that question kind of answers itself, doesn't it? Maybe I *am* on track to cause some kind of horrible apocalyptic event. But even if so, these people will never be the ones I trust at my back to fight against it.

"You seem... to have made a decision," Madaline says, smiling slightly. "Forgive me... if I hope it never becomes relevant. My... other friends still want to keep you trapped, after all."

Ah. Yes. The horrific reality of the Goddess almost distracted me from the horrific reality of daily soul torture for a moment. *That* starts sinking back into the forefront of my mind, and all of a sudden a single day off doesn't really sound like much at all. Welp, time to panic again!

If Madaline notices my mounting terror, she certainly doesn't show it. If anything, she looks rather sleepy. She yawns, seeming perfectly content to sit in front of my cage and say nothing.

Whatever it is she wanted to know, she's already learned it, and her indifference to whether I escape or rot here seems to match our shared indifference to everything whenever she's wiping our minds clean of thoughts.

I finish the rest of my food and drink a bit of water. Then, to my utter despair, I start to realize that I'm sleepy. That doesn't seem fair at all. I get one day to not be in agony, one day to heal, one day to maybe be able to *think,* and my body wants to spend it all sleeping. It's sickeningly horrible. I don't want to sleep. I don't want tomorrow to come. I know what happens tomorrow and I am going to hate it.

I don't want to feel this way. And she's right here. I *could* just ask her to—

"Addicting, isn't it?" Madaline murmurs. "Sorry."

Oh. Oh, right. I let out a shaky breath. Maybe... maybe sleep wouldn't be so bad after all.

Sleep turns out to be bad. Mostly because when I fall asleep, it's Friday, and when Friday is over, I have to go back to the torture dungeon. The day barely even registers in my mind before it's already gone; I speak to my friends briefly about the Goddess and what Madaline and I talked about, but no one has any good ideas on how to defy Her. We barely even know what She wants, outside base entertainment. All we know is that we can't get caught speaking spells out loud with anyone else around.

Then, Friday night happens. Madaline does not offer to help me again. My day becomes torture and pain once more, and somehow it seems to hurt all the worse for the brief reprieve. The routine was broken, and so the wound was ripped open, jagged and raw. It is the most pain I've ever had to endure in my entire life. I still can't bring myself to stop it. The next time I really feel aware enough of anything but pain and routine to think, I find myself in the car, being driven to my therapist on Saturday morning.

"You don't seem to be doing well, Hannah," is the comment from my mother that finally snaps my attention to reality. I bite down an instinctive 'no shit.'

465

"I haven't been doing well for a long time now, mom," I say instead.

"...But the therapy is helping?" she asks.

"As much as anything can, I guess," I mumble. "You really did pick a good therapist. She's... got a way with words."

She nods, satisfied now that her actions have been tied directly to me getting better. I'm not getting better, of course, but that would be an inconvenient thing to bring attention to. As long as she's responsible for everything good in my life and guiltless for everything negative, she's happy enough to not bother me further. Like this, the drive continues to be uncomfortable, but at least it's uncomfortable and *silent*.

We make it to the building Dr. Carson works in, and before long I'm following her back into her office. The cold fear of therapy still pulses in my primordial lizard brain, trained for far too long to associate this sort of place with danger and abuse, but it's a little dull compared to the sharp throb of soul damage. I walk into the room with an impressive zero panic attacks, only having to stop and fight one off once on my way to the couch. Collapsing down into the seat, I sit and stare at nothing, slowly coming to the realization that I have absolutely no idea how to talk about anything that is happening to me right now at all.

"Well," Dr. Carson starts for me, seeming to notice my dumbfounded silence, "how has the past week been treating you, Hannah?"

Hmm. Well. There is only one way that I can sufficiently sum it all up, I think.

"Bad," I say.

"Oh, I'm sorry to hear that," Dr. Carson answers, making me briefly suspect she *does* have magic powers with how she can somehow say platitudes and make them sound genuinely sincere. "Would you like to talk about it?"

I stare at her for a bit. She maintains eye contact, a pleasant but patient smile on her face.

"...That's it?" I ask. "No, 'hey Hannah, remember how last session you proved magic is real and revealed you were mutating into a bug monster?'"

"I distinctly recall insisting that you are not a monster, actually," she answers happily.

"...Dr. Carson, please," I insist. "You are being way too normal about my life and it's weirding me out."

Dr. Carson pauses for a moment, absently tapping her pen against her notepad while she thinks.

"So, a bit of transparency here," she answers. "I believe in the importance of professional conduct in professional settings, *especially* in my profession where I am often dealing with people who need to be able to trust me with the sort of things they don't trust with anyone. I am, for some people, the only port in a storm, and if I'm not reliable and steady in all the ways I project myself to be, if I am not worthy of the respect and trust I am given, then not only will I be unable to help my clients but I might even make their situation worse. You, in particular, have first-hand experience with the sort of damage a person in my position can do. So while I certainly have questions, doubts, worries, and anxieties of my own... this is not the place for me to voice them. The fact that you have made good on your promise of being a client completely unlike any other I have experienced does not at all change what my duties to you are. As such, I can't allow myself to start a conversation about how the revelations you've brought to my table affect *me*. That is not what we are here to talk about today, unless you specifically request it."

"And if I do specifically request it?" I ask, taking off my gloves and letting my extra limbs twist partly back into visible space. My current shirt doesn't have limb-holes, so I'm just letting them pop in after the first joint, making it look like they're appearing out of thin air. I flex my fingers, scraping my claws lightly against my own palms, and watch my therapist as she tries and fails not to stare.

"...If you want to talk about my thoughts and questions on the matter," Dr. Carson says, "I certainly have a lot of them. Your claims about religion, about other worlds, about magic... they all leave me desperately hungry for answers, I'll admit. But above all else, I want to ask more about your brief mention of being able to cure *diseases*."

Ah. Yeah. I should have expected that.

"...'Cure' is a strong word," I hedge, "but the one person I helped does seem to be doing a lot better, last I heard."

"But I believe you mentioned that further use of your magic to cure people was something you didn't want to draw attention to," Dr. Carson presses. "So normally, I wouldn't do that. But if you're encouraging me to be selfish with my inquiries, that's something I'd like to ask about. Not that you should feel any pressure to answer, of course."

"No, I guess... it's kind of relevant to my current problems," I mumble. "So... gosh, uh, where do I start. Magic comes from the Goddess, right?"

"You mentioned a Goddess last session, but you got distressed when I asked about her and requested we change the subject," Dr. Carson says, looking at her notes.

"Yeah, that sounds like me," I sigh. "So magic comes from the Goddess, who is like... a being that exists in, as best I can tell, some kind of imperceivable reality above our own. But She is both willing and capable of acting directly on our world, and the main way She chooses to do so is by giving people magic powers. Which... I've demonstrated."

"Sure, I'm with you so far," Dr. Carson nods amicably.

"Right. Yeah. The problem with this is that you can make a spell more powerful by summoning the Goddess directly to help you cast it, and this... is bad. Because whenever the Goddess is around people without magic, they get magic, and I have no way of knowing or predicting what that magic will be or do. It's very personalized to whoever gets it, so if the *wrong* person gets magic, the consequences could be... disastrous. Possibly even apocalyptic."

"...And that's what you have to do to cure diseases?" Dr. Carson guesses.

"Exactly," I confirm. "To use my spell with that level of power and precision, I need to speak its name aloud, and if I do that then I give whoever I'm helping a soul, and if I do *that* I'm risking all hell breaking loose. It's kind of a lose-lose situation."

"I see," Dr. Carson nods. "I imagine that's quite frustrating."

"Frustrating is one way to put it," I agree, pulling off my jacket. "I'm pretty much being constantly tempted by a divine troll to end the world. And that sort of leads into my current troubles: in that other universe I told you about, I've been kidnapped by a cult and I'm being tortured daily."

Dr. Carson pauses again.

"I don't want you to take this as disbelief in your claims," she says carefully, "but most people don't speak with that level of flippancy about their being tortured."

"Yeah," I agree. "I'm trying to hang onto the flippant mindset as best I can, though, because otherwise I don't think I'd be up to talking about it at all. I've had trouble talking all week."

Dr. Carson nods.

"Dissociation can be a useful strategy for dealing with issues in the short term, but it's important to be careful about not letting it become the crutch that replaces your legs. By distancing yourself from the issue, you can defend yourself from short-term problems, but you also prevent yourself from healing."

I shudder, hating myself as I yearn for Madaline.

"...Yeah," I agree. "That makes sense. I'm trying my best, though. I'm trying."

"I know you are, Hannah," Dr. Carson reassures me. "And even if you don't always succeed, that doesn't mean the effort is wasted. I notice you're doing a good job at not pointing your blades in my direction, today."

"What?" I ask, having to take a moment to figure out what the heck she's talking about. ...Oh, right. Last session she wanted me to practice never pointing my blade-limbs at anyone by accident. "Oh, I'm not... I barely even thought about that all week. They're just kind of droopy because my everything hurts."

"Because of the torture, or because of something else?" Dr. Carson asks.

"Because of the extrauniversal soul torture, yeah," I confirm.

"Which has been happening all week," she presses.

"Correct."

"...Well Hannah, you're certainly under no obligation to contact me for any reason, but this *is* the sort of situation I gave you my personal number for."

"Oh, right," I blink. "Sorry. I forgot, with everything going on. ...And I'm not sure I would have wanted to talk about it anyway. Except maybe to ask you about killing people again. But I think... I think I have my answer to that question. So it doesn't really matter."

"What do you mean?" Dr. Carson asks.

I sigh. I don't like explaining things to her, because it always makes me feel crazy. She's too *normal* to understand this stuff, it feels like. Even though I've proven magic is real, it feels like any sane person would continue to deny it anyway. I know that's stupid, but... I can't shake the feeling anyway. What if I *am* crazy? Still, it does me no good to stay silent.

"So... the spell I showed you. The one that sorts things. I use it for a lot of stuff. Cooking, cleaning, pulling bacteria out of people. We've talked about it."

"We have," she nods, encouraging me to continue.

"So the caveat behind the spell is that, more specifically, it moves things to *where I think they should be.* I have to believe, in a genuine, fundamental way, that whatever I'm moving *belongs* where I'm going to put it. So while the spell is powerful enough to, say, sort the oxygen out of someone's lungs, doing so requires me to have... a very specific sort of worldview. And I am afraid if these people keep hurting me, keep torturing me every night, I'll find the idea that they *fundamentally deserve death* to be easier to believe than I want it to be."

Dr. Carson scribbles down a few words, but when she's done she just waits in silence, staring at her notepad with a frown on her face. I stay quiet, letting her think as I pull my uncomfortable shoes off and stretch my clawed toes a little.

"That is certainly... a complicated situation," Dr. Carson eventually concludes. "I can tell from our conversations that you are afraid of hurting others, afraid of being dangerous, and it seems like this is another situation in which you're finding yourself forced to try and defend yourself. You're a very empathetic person, Hannah, to want to respect the sanctity of the lives of people going out of their way to do you harm. I don't think most people would do that, and I find that admirable. At the same time, you seem to struggle greatly with protecting yourself or asserting your boundaries. You have a history of simply letting bad things happen to you without working to change them, and while your positive traits are genuinely wonderful, they can sometimes feed into this issue."

"Yeah," I sigh. "I... I know all of that."

"My apologies, Hannah," Dr. Carson nods. "I'm just trying to get my thoughts in order. It's difficult for me to give concrete advice because your situation is so unique. So I suppose I'll ask you this: what do you *want* to do? What would be the ideal resolution to things, in your eyes?"

I shrug.

"To be let go, I guess?" I answer. "I wanna not be tortured but also not murder anybody. But... realistically, I know that's not going to happen. It's not how the other world works. It's kind of a horrible place, you know? People seem to need to kill one another on a pretty regular basis over there."

"It happens more often than we like to admit over here, as well," Dr. Carson comments sadly.

"Yeah," I sigh. "Yeah, I guess it does. Anyway, just sort of being let go isn't going to happen, so I guess... I'd like to find a way to escape that *doesn't* require me to sort air out of people's lungs. But I just... we tried that? We tried it and it didn't work and I just don't know what to do about it."

"I see," Dr. Carson says. "Well, then I just want to say... we all struggle to find a good answer in desperate situations. My job is not to make the decision for you, Hannah, it is to help you come to terms with whatever decision you make. So when that time comes, I will be here for you. Until then... you are the person who is most knowledgeable about what you're going through. The only thing I recommend is to decide how you *don't* want things to be, and work up from there."

I don't want to kill people with Refresh. I don't. Partially because it feels like I'd be betraying myself, and partially because it feels

471

like the thing the Goddess wants me to do. I want to climb Her walls, not be led around by them. I don't want to be whatever it is she plans for me to be. So... I need to find another way. That starts with believing there can *be* another way.

"Okay, doc," I nod. "Thanks. I'll... I'll try to keep up hope."

"An ever-important skill to develop," she says with a smile. "What else can I help you with today, Hannah?"

I smile a little, grateful for the change in subject. I know I need to think about this, but I need a break. The ache is enough of a reminder already. So we change the subject, talking a little about how exercise helped but I still don't have a safe place to do much of it, about various other things magic can do and how it works, and about how *Pokémon Sword and Shield* is a sad, soulless shell of the franchise's former glory. It's not much, but it helps.

Near the end of the session, Dr. Carson encourages me to use her personal number if I ever need immediate help again, which I respond to in that usual noncommittal way people use when they know they aren't going to do something but don't want to outright admit to it. Unfortunately, Dr. Carson eats attempted deflections for breakfast, and catches mine with the expert ease of a true hunter.

"In that case, are you interested in increasing the frequency of these sessions to twice a week?" she asks. "Again, there's no pressure to accept, but you've mentioned that these sessions are helpful to you, and it's my honest opinion that eighty-five minutes a week might be below your current needs."

"You're saying I need a lot more therapy," I sigh.

"I'm saying that I believe structure is helpful to you, and placing things on your schedule acts as a useful way for you to give yourself structure."

"...Yeah, okay," I mutter. "I... it's still hard for me, what with the therapy trauma stuff. But... yeah. You're good at your job, doc. Things feel less impossible after talking to you. And that's... something, even if it doesn't last for long."

"Do you anticipate that you're going to consider positive change impossible in the near future?" Dr. Carson asks.

"Oh, definitely," I nod. "Probably in the next few hours, at least. But things won't be so bad, up until that point. And that's something."

"Yes," Dr. Carson says, her face carefully expressionless. "That *is* something. But I think you can do better, too. Don't give up, Hannah. Whatever else you may be, you're still a kind, intelligent girl with limitless potential."

Limitless potential, huh? Maybe she's right. ...But I doubt it. I don't think the secret to my escape is some *Dragonball*-style powerup sequence. Whatever I choose is going to be hard, and it's going to hurt. And that's assuming I can even find anything worth choosing in the first place.

My mom drives me home after our session, Dr. Carson having convinced her to sign me up for therapy on Wednesdays as well. I remember, belatedly, that Alma and I agreed to go on a date today, but we never really agreed on where to go. I text her on the way home, and we decide on a bookstore and dinner. Hard to go wrong with books and food, right?

My mother doesn't have many objections to the idea of me hanging out with a female friend for the rest of the day (a fact that would certainly change if she knew I was gay, but hey, that's part of why I'm in the closet). She does, however, have a lot of questions regarding my plans to sleep somewhere other than home after hanging out. I assure her that it's a girls-only sleepover (completely true) and that it's at Ida's house (completely false, but Ida would back up my lie without even thinking about it so she's the best choice). The reality is that we'll be staying at Valerie's house and attempting to see what sort of magic everyone can enact on me while I sleep.

I eventually convince mom by lying to her about how well I'm doing at school, though if I stop getting systematically tortured every night I probably *will* go back to doing well at school so it's hopefully just a temporary lie. Alma and I have our date soon afterwards, and it goes... okay. The longer it drags on, the more the pain in my soul leaks into everything I try to do. As expected, the exhaustion and ache overwhelms me a few hours into things, and though I have a *pretty* good time, I'm mostly just going through the motions by the end of things.

473

"You're miserable, aren't you?" Alma says, sounding... *defeated.* We're having dinner, and after dinner we'll be heading to Valerie's. I hold down a sigh, scrounging my exhausted brain for a set of words that won't make her think it's her fault.

"...I would be way more miserable if not for the date," I settle on. "Thank you."

She manages a soft smile, which I hope means I was successful.

"You're welcome, I guess," she says. "I just wish I could be any help."

"Being with me is help enough," I answer. "We'll figure something out."

"Yeah," she agrees. "I hope so."

The drive to Valerie's house is quiet and awkward, but we make it there all the same. Valerie makes me park my dad's car in her garage since we live close to each other and she knows I would have had to lie to be allowed to sleep overnight. Then we all head downstairs, finding Ida sitting on the couch and scratching a happy-looking Fartbuns under the chin.

"What's up, lovebirds?" Ida greets us. "How was the date?"

"It was fine," Alma dismisses. "Um, is it just me or is that dog a little different?"

"Oh yeah," I yawn. "Valerie, how have you and F-buns' mutations been going?"

For some reason, Alma looks confused, Valerie looks embarrassed, and Ida absolutely lights up with delight.

"Valerie!?" she says giddily, and oh *fuck* that's right she's not out yet fuck, fuck, fuck, I'm the worst!

"Hannah..." Valerie sighs.

"I'm sorry," I blurt. "Sorry, sorry, sorry. I'm so stupid..."

"Fuck yeah, though!" Ida cheers, lifting one hand like she's doing an imaginary toast. "Valerie's a cute-ass name. Congrats on hatching!"

Valerie blinks in surprise.

"Thanks?" she says.

"Sorry, what's going on?" Alma asks awkwardly. "Who's Valerie?"

474

"I'm Valerie," Valerie answers. "I'm trans, apparently."

"Oh," Alma says. "Okay?"

"Yo, if you need help with hormones or whatever, I know a girl that can hook you up," Ida says, leaning forwards. "Buuuuut knowing you and Hannah, you're already taking the magical route, aren't you?"

"...We may have attempted an unwise experiment," Valerie admits. "Which is why, yes, Fartbuns is also growing like, four extra legs for some reason? They're just little nubs right now, but... yeah. He's getting bigger. But he still seems pretty happy, so I guess it's not hurting him? No blood yet, either."

Oh hey, yeah. Now that I'm looking for them, I do spot some extra limb-nubs growing under F-buns' skin. And looking over Valerie herself... hmm. Yep, that's some tailbone extension. I think she might be growing a bit of fur, too?

"Ten bucks on catgirl for Val," Ida says before I can even share my findings.

"...I hope not," Valerie grumbles. "That would just be stereotypical."

"Whatever nyou say, nya," Ida teases, curling one hand like a cat's paw. "Stereotypical doesn't mean bad."

"Um... n-no offense regarding the big personal revelation or whatever, but can we focus on saving Hannah?" Alma asks, seeming uncomfortable.

"Yes, I agree," Valerie says. "I didn't even want to discuss this in the first place."

"Sorry," I mutter again.

"It's fine," she sighs.

"You're so fucking tall, though!" Ida grins, standing up and wiping dog hair off her shorts. "Goddess, I bet your tits are gonna be so huge. Tall girls always get the best racks, I swear. Just, *massive* fucking dohondonkaroos."

"Ida, please," I groan.

"Fine, fine, okay," she relents. "Follow me, Hannah Banana."

She leads me into a side room, where a mattress is sitting on the floor.

"This is my mattress," Ida says, "which I figured would be good to bring because if you rip it up in your sleep or we fuck it up with magic somehow, I can just repair it. Plus your whole job in this is to just pass the fuck out, and my bed is super fucking comfy. So. You're welcome."

"Uh," I say. It's kind of weird that Ida brought her entire mattress here, but I suppose her logic makes sense. "Thanks, I guess?"

I pull off my outer layer of clothes to get a bit more comfortable, though I'm a bit too awkward to undress anywhere near as much as I normally would before sleeping. Flopping onto the bed with most of my limbs free is nice, though, or at least as nice as any physical sensation can hope to be through my all-encompassing pain.

"So," Valerie declares. "Here's the situation. When Hannah falls asleep, she wakes up in the other world at the moment she would have woken up normally, regardless of how much time has passed here. This happens both treeside and earthside; if Hannah naps here for only a minute, she can still be awake in the other world for a full day. The time doesn't match or synch up. And *that* means that Hannah will receive the effects of our spells at somewhat unpredictable times in the other world. She won't know what she's going to get or when. Our best way around this is to establish a plan in advance for what spells we'll be casting in what order, so Hannah can at least know what magic is going to activate, if not at what time. But the problem with *that* is that we don't know when our plan's keystone will kick in on our end."

"Why not?" Alma asks. "What's our keystone?"

"It's Jet," Valerie answers bluntly, making Alma frown. "I have a bunch of ideas to try today, but frankly I don't think they're better ideas than the ones I tried the first time around. And even though Ida's spell has a lot of potential to help out while Hannah is in the other world, the strongest option we have is absolutely Jet. Her remove-from-attention spell seems to fit the criteria of a spell that would transfer between worlds, and it'd be an *invaluable* spell for creating a condition where Hannah can escape. If she can activate it on Hannah... well, our plan is basically to have her do that all night, if she's able. Then we support Hannah with buffs that might help her break out of her cage while people *hopefully* forget she even exists."

"Oh," Alma says softly. "So... I guess I can't help at all, can I?"

Oh, crap.

"Alma, of *course* you can help," I assure her, quickly sitting up. "I'm terrified and in pain and just having you here while I try to sleep will—"

"**No Less Than Perfect**," Ida interrupts, pushing me back down onto the bed as a *glorious* sensation of painlessness pulses through my body. "Here's an idea, Alma: how about you help by not saying things to make the situation about you?"

"Wh—Ida!" I protest, snapping back to attention. "Don't be a jerk to my girlfriend!"

"Oh, sorry Alma," Ida says with false sweetness, staring her dead in the eyes. "Was that uncalled for?"

She doesn't ask it like it's an attempt at an apology, of course. She asks it as a genuine challenge. And the way Alma flinches and looks away says a lot about what she thinks the answer is.

"Cool, so let's all shut up and let Hannah try to sleep," Ida declares. "And if you have any tricks for swapping to your alter on purpose, it'd be swell if you could do that, Alma. I get it's not always that easy, but it's something only you can do. Alright?"

"...Alright," Alma murmurs quietly.

"Cool," Ida grunts, flopping down into a chair near my head. "You want any more healing pulses to deal with the pain, Hannah, you let me know. Whatever gets you sleepy."

"...I'm going to get some last-minute art done," Valerie declares, heading to the room's exit. "Come get me when she's unconscious."

Alma says nothing, just sitting awkwardly on the side of the bed and taking a few deep breaths. I kind of wish Valerie would just use a sleep spell on me or something, but I hardly ever have trouble falling asleep and we agreed it'd probably be more efficient for her to focus on spells that might help get me out of the situation. Now that I'm actually here, though, lying on someone else's mattress in someone else's house with two other people in the room, I'm finding sleep somewhat difficult. Not because it's not comfortable, but because it's *very* comfortable. It's safe. I'm surrounded by the people who care about me most, all of them working to help me as best they can. I'm not in pain for the first time in far too long. And all of it, every last comfort and speck of beauty, will vanish the moment I lose consciousness.

I know I'll have to face it eventually. The torture, the pain, the cage, the cultists. I have to go from this wonderful house full of friends to an agonizing dungeon full of pain. The contrast makes the blade all the sharper, and I dread the moment it inevitably comes for my neck. I know I have to do this. I *know* I do. But I can't. I can't face that willingly. We already failed this once, why would we think we wouldn't fail again? Worse, what if the cultists figure out how to do the same thing!? *What if they attack my friends through me?*

"**No Less Than Perfect**," Ida invokes again, a pulse of warmth and stability flowing through my panicked mind as the Goddess briefly descends to speak the words. Huh. It even calms panic attacks. That's neat. Still, a new sleeping strategy is in order.

"Hey, Alma?" I say quietly.

"Yep," she mutters. "Still Alma. Sorry."

"I think I know something you can do for me," I say, a blush starting to lightly form on my cheeks.

"Yeah?" she asks.

"I, um. I could really use a hug."

Kagiso always finds it easier to sleep when she's wrapped around me, and I have to admit I've gotten used to the same. Just... some level of comfort that won't go away until the final moment I'm whisked away is what I need.

"...Okay," Alma agrees, scooting onto the bed more and lying down, letting me wrap my limbs around her. She's a different kind of soft from Kagiso, for sure, but certainly a pleasant kind. It's not so bad being normal sized, big enough to do the smothering instead of being the one smothered. I ignore the eye-roll I can see Ida doing with my spatial sense and squeeze my girlfriend just a little tighter. I'll be okay. I can do this.

478

I can do this, right?

The tears start to fall, and I bury my face in Alma's shoulder to hide them. I can't do this. I know I can't do this. I'll screw it up somehow. *Not good enough, I remind* myself, and the Goddess smiles. Not good enough. Not good enough. Not good enough.

"I don't want to go," I whisper.

Alma tenses up, slowly reaching up to pull off the hat she uses to hide her droopy, triangular ears.

"I don't want to go either," she whispers back, her body curling up a little. Her tail, I realize suddenly, is still. "I want to stay with you. I want to be by your side, always."

I don't have the mental strength left to care that she's blocked her headmate out of an intimate moment. In fact, I can't think of a better use. I don't want Jet here right now either. I just want to hold my girlfriend and be okay.

"Would you come with me?" I ask. "If you could?"

"In a heartbeat," she confirms. "To another world, to another life... it doesn't matter. I'll follow you anywhere."

"I thought you didn't want to leave your dad," I mumble, the familiar feeling of being held starting to lull me to sleep.

"I don't want to leave him for *Jet,*" she answers."But I'll leave him for you. Nothing matters, as long as I have you."

"That doesn't... sound like a healthy thing to say," I comment groggily.

"Well, we're already having a secret tryst behind our family's backs," Alma says soothingly, cupping my face in her hands. "And you're slowly changing my body into something terrifying outside my control."

"Alma..." I whisper sadly.

"I think it's okay," she tells me quietly, "if our relationship is a little unhealthy. I don't think it was ever going to be anything else. But I'll make it work. For you."

"Alma—!"

And then she kisses me. Slow yet still sudden, she pulls herself into my lips, a beautiful and intimate pressure. A cacophony of new sensations, from the softness of her face to the cool wetness of her saliva, from the warm pressure of her body against mine to the increasingly-uncomfortable presence of a third wheel sitting at the head of the bed, it is beautiful and it is lovely and it is messy and it is strange. But that is, perhaps, who we are at our core. I, the monster. The spider. The burrower, hiding myself from head to toe in fear of the world. And her, the chimera. The fragment. The broken amalgam, hoping desperately that with *this* piece, she'll finally fit together.

I don't know if it's love or fear, but I want her with me. I want her with me *so desperately*. To have someone in that horrible place who actually cares... it matters more than anything. Just like her, I wish I didn't have to be two separate halves, two unrelated lives. I wish I could just be one, true me, with everyone I care about all at once.

And so the Goddess hears my prayer, and She smiles.

I *am* a bridge between worlds, She reminds me. It's only natural that I would have the ability to offer passage. And in that moment, drowning in that horrible sense of need, I don't even care that her words are poison. I want it too badly, and I'm not good enough to resist.

I wake up inside a cage, and Alma's screams don't matter because nothing does.

Madaline sits where she usually sits. I sit where I always sit. Our food and drink are here, and someone helped Madaline eat, but mine sits untouched because I do not care about it. And while I know I care about Alma, I know it *should* matter as I watch her pick herself up off the floor next to my cage, swearing to herself in obvious animal panic, I can't bring myself to act. I can't even bring myself to *want* to act. It's all too... detached, like it's all happening in the background of a television show I'm mostly tuning out.

"Hannah!?" Alma shouts in panic. *"Hannah!?"*

But I don't answer. I don't know how to answer. I am nothing. Alma spots my cage and recoils in horror at what she sees inside, not recognizing me. But it doesn't matter. Alma sees Madaline, spaced out and unresponsive, and she starts hyperventilating harder. But it doesn't matter. And when guards rush into the room with weapons, shouting at her and threatening her and making demands, that doesn't matter either.

I can do nothing to help her, because I do not exist.

"LEAVE ME ALONE!" Alma shouts, and when one of the guards rushes forwards he runs headlong into the wall of her invisible house, blocked off from approaching any further. As he recovers from the shock, Alma is already rushing down invisible stairs, moving straight through the floor as she staggers from the throes of a panic attack. The guards call for backup, the building seems to go on high alert with everyone running around like angry ants, and Hagoro rushes in to guard me and wake up Madaline.

None of it matters. Until, of course, it does. Then *I* start screaming and having a panic attack.

"Oh Goddess Oh Goddess Oh Goddess," I cry, trying not to vomit.

"What did you do!?" Hagoro demands.

"Fuck you!" I shout back. "Don't you dare hurt her!"

My torturer strides into the room, his face the quiet sort of livid that collects on someone too composed to shout.

"What happened?" he asks. "I heard there was an intruder in this room?"

"Sir!" one of the guards that tried to attack Alma reports. "Yes, sir. It was a human woman. Pale skin, lighter-than-normal hair, but not like you'd expect from someone with albinism. Oddly-shaped ears, maybe Transmutation-related? Dressed strangely, too. Never seen clothes like that before."

"Her spells?" my torturer presses.

"Barrier-Pneuma-Light, sir!" the second guard answers. "Not sure what she can do, but she demonstrated a semistandard barrier and then walked clean through the floor."

"...Walking through solid objects with Barrier, Pneuma, and Light?" my torturer frowns. "Maybe the Light aspect...? Hmm. Any incantations?"

"None, sir!"

"I see. Well, what matters is that this room stays secure. Capturing her is a secondary priority to maintaining control of the Founder's Kin, understand? Don't have everyone running

481

around trying to catch a matter phaser. Set a trap and return the rest of the guards here."

"Yes sir!"

"Now then," he says, turning to glower at me. "We still have to deal with you."

"Don't you *dare* hurt her," I threaten, my back legs rubbing together with an eldritch hiss. "I'll kill you. Don't think for a fucking *second* that I can't!"

"Oh, I don't doubt you can," he agrees, approaching the cage. "I'm sure you've got it all figured out now, plans churning away in that apocalyptic little brain of yours. Which is why I'm going to figure *you* out before you can act on any of it. **Even Magic Dies.**"

I shudder, my spatial sense briefly winking out before coming back all on its own. If my friends had casted any spells on me, they would be gone now. ...But they haven't yet. I'm asleep, but my friends haven't helped me at all. Either they can't, or... well. They're probably busy freaking out because Alma suddenly disappeared.

She felt so small, when I pulled her through my soul. Like a speck of dust in a raging river. And now she's here, at the river's mouth, and the teeth are closing around her. I *asked* for this. I'm the worst person imaginable.

I *deserve* the torture that's about to happen to me.

"**Vitae Vivisection**," the Goddess croons, my torturer reaching inside me with more force than ever before. The screams start immediately, and they don't stop for hours and hours and hours.

When I wake up back in Valerie's house, my throat still feels raw. My cheek is also sore as hell, which I realize is because a heavily-breathing Ida just slapped me across the face. It's the least composed I've ever seen her before, a wild-eyed look of terror from a girl suddenly finding herself no longer in control. I suppose I shouldn't judge, though, since my face is probably worse.

"Oh my god, Hannah, are you awake?" Valerie demands, her massive form towering above where I lie on the bed. "What happened?"

"Goddess," I say automatically, my brain still rebooting from pain and terror.

"What *happened!?*" she demands again."Where's Autumn?"

"I... she's... she's in the other world," I answer, agony twisting my insides with every movement. "I *took her to the other world!* And then I got tortured unconscious! Oh Goddess oh fuck, she could be anywhere! Anything could be happening to her! I just pulled her into hell and *left her there!"*

"**No Less Than Perfect**!" The Goddess shouts with Ida's lips, the fog of my terror lifting momentarily as I get a fleeting instant to be free of pain... though it quickly returns in full force, since I passed out during the torture session. "Hannah, calm the fuck down! Is there anything you could have done?"

"I-I don't know," I breathe. "Maybe? Probably? I was trapped under Madaline's spell for most of it, but the rest was just me doing nothing because I'm a useless idiot and I freak out at every little thing and I wasn't thinking at *all*—"

A smack rings out through the room as Ida slaps me again.

"It's a lot easier to hit you than heal you, you know!" she snaps.

"Ida!" Valerie shouts. "You're *not* helping."

"Bitch, I am *always* helping. Now both of you focus. Did you pull her through on *purpose*, Hannah?"

"I... kind of?" I admit, shame flooding me.

"So does that mean you can do it again?" she asks.

"Maybe?" I say. "Probably? I've *gotta* be able to bring her back, I... oh fuck, I need to bring her back! I need to fall back asleep, I need—"

"No, stop," Valerie says, putting a hand on my shoulder. "You need to *not* fall asleep."

"What?" I ask, dumbfounded. "But I have to save her! I have to go help her!"

"No, tallgirl is right," Ida agrees, her eyes flicking around to focus on everything and nothing. "The same amount of time passes regardless of when you pass out here, right? At this point you can only fuck it up even *more* by going to sleep when we aren't prepared."

"Are we not prepared!?" I demand, my voice rising to a shriek. "Didn't we all gather here in the first place because we're prepared!?"

"We were prepared to support you from *this* universe," Valerie grunts. "We were not at all prepared to travel to another universe and raid a cultist base. I need… *so* many new drawings."

"What!? No!" I protest. "No way! I am *not* bringing you to that horrible hellhole! You'll die!"

"You don't really have a fucking *choice,* Hannah!" Ida shouts. "You kind of teleported our plan A to that hellhole while you were snogging her to sleep! And unless you've been fucking holding out on us, you're *still in the torture cage!* What are you gonna do, huh? Moan about how much it hurts some more?"

"Ida, back the fuck off!" Valerie demands. "She knows she fucked up, you don't have to be such a bitch about it!"

"Oh, I *know* she knows," Ida fires back. "And that's *exactly* why I've gotta be a bitch. If I try to coddle her ass, she won't believe a word I say. *Nor should she.* Now own the fuck up, Hannah: you need us. We have been carrying your ass this entire way and I will slap your tits off if you try to get me to drop you before the finish line again. I *told* you, bitch. I'm all-in. I am going to find the motherfucker doing this to you and I am going to make him *suffer* before he dies."

Ida glowers at me, her fists clenched and shaking. She looks *furious,* and seeing her anything less than fully composed is a little terrifying all on its own.

"Ida, I…" I gulp. "I'm sorry, I just… sorry."

"Shut the fuck up, Hannah," Ida growls, stomping towards the exit of the room. "I can't believe everything went tits up before we could even start. And now I have to fucking rescue your *fucking* monogamous bitch of a girlfriend!"

"Wait, where are you going?" Valerie asks.

"I'm getting prepared!" Ida shouts back, heading to the stairs. "You'd better start doing the same! And keep spider-girl awake!"

The front door slams shut soon afterwards, Ida's car starting up and pulling out of the driveway. I sit up, staring helplessly down at my hands.

"What... what should I do now?" I ask. "To get ready."

Valerie hesitates a moment, looking rather overwhelmed herself.

"I... guess you should probably practice the spell you'll need to use to send us to the other wo... hmm. No, actually, that might be a bad idea. Ida said you fell unconscious right when Autumn disappeared, and we couldn't wake you up for at least a full minute. It's possible that using the spell knocks you out, which would be... bad."

"Ah," I say. "Yeah, that makes sense."

"I guess you just... stay awake," Valerie shrugs. "You want an energy drink or something.?"

"Sure, I guess," I agree absently. "I'm not sure they work on me anymore, but I guess if I just end up getting poisoned that'll probably keep me awake too."

I get up off the bed, not liking how tired I already am. It's not even that late at night; the sun had barely set when I started trying to sleep and it's not much later after that. I'll have to stay awake for however long it takes for Valerie and Ida to get ready, and I have nothing productive I can do to help. I just... have to wait.

I make it barely two hours before I can't stand it anymore. I'm too antsy, and if anything my jitters are just making it more difficult for Valerie to prepare. I end up driving home and, in the absence of anything better to spend my time doing, I get the insane idea to try streaming.

It's not a bad plan, really. I just need something to pass the time, and while the idea of playing games in a crisis situation like this is *revolting* to me, I've managed to fool myself into thinking streaming is a job before, and I can fool myself into thinking it again. I haven't streamed all week, what with the exhaustion and torture and stuff, so it's technically even work I'm behind on. Hardly anyone is actually going to *watch* my stream since it's not normal streaming hours for me (or for much of anyone, really) but that doesn't matter. All that really matters is that I'm immensely exhausted, and I cannot under any circumstances let myself fall asleep.

It's agony. It's a shit stream. But it *does* pass the time, and when the sun starts to rise I shut things down and move on to distracting myself in other ways, instead. My mother made me promise to be home from the sleepover before church, and she would have had a freakout if I failed to keep that promise, but if I get ready and make breakfast for her before she's even up, that'll win me some favor and likely spare me a nasty conversation or two. So breakfast it is, my soul throbbing with every Refresh I cast to mix the batter or clean the counter.

This is... insane. It's all insane. I'm doing my routine while my girlfriend is being tormented in who-knows-how-many ways, all of which is my fault. This is *not right*. I should not be doing this. But I have nothing else I can do, because the routine is all I am. I'm just a slave to the ruts my brain has dug. I should run away the moment we save Alma. I shouldn't be around people. I shouldn't *be*.

Breakfast happens. The drive to church happens. We pull into the parking lot and walk inside, and to my horror I spot J-mug and a woman I recognize to be his mother mingling with the other people in our congregation. I duck into an obscure corner of the room, desperately hoping they don't see me. My eyes droop, but I can't sleep. I can't. I have to wait, to let my friends get the opportunity to fix my fuckups. Just like always.

My phone buzzes in my pocket.

Ignoring standard church etiquette, I pull it out in an instant, fumbling with the screen as I read the text.

ready, Ida says. **back at tallgirl's house. where r u**

I'm at church, I answer. **Not sure I can leave before it's done?**

r u serious???

I grimace, not sure what to say. I *should* go, but I don't have a car and my family would freak out but I should go though, Ida and Valerie are waiting for me, but I don't have a good way to leave...

"Hey, it's you!" a woman's voice calls out in my direction. "My little angel!"

...What? I look up from my phone in horror, spotting J-mom walking towards me, her eyes implying a big smile behind her

486

tightly-secured facemask. She's a tall woman, thin and frail-looking but with the boisterous attitude of someone used to being a lot more fit than she currently is. J-mug trails behind her, looking frightened and almost... guilty? That's probably bad.

"I'm so glad I caught you!" J-mom practically gleams. "I just have to thank you."

"Mom, I told you she doesn't want people talking about it..." J-Mug whines behind her.

"Nonsense!" his mother insists. "She worked an honest-to-God miracle, the doctors said so! The church should know they have a prophet in their midst!"

A *lot* of eyes are on us now, over half the congregation. I am... absolutely dumbfounded. Is this woman really this stupid...?

"Thank you," she says, bowing low. "Truly. The gifts you gave me saved my life, even before you saved my house as well. I owe you everything."

What? *What?* Is she serious? She owes me everything and she doesn't even have the basic common sense to respect what I asked of her? I am struck speechless by this... absolute insanity. What is going *on?*

"Hannah?" my mother asks, approaching with a mix of curiosity and concern. "What's she talking about? What happened, exactly?"

"Your daughter is chosen by God," the woman insists. "She has the gift of healing."

"Mom, stop, please..." J-mug begs. "M-miss Hannah, I'm so sorry, I didn't know she was going to do this..."

"Ma'am, I understand you've been through a lot recently, but I'd appreciate it if you wouldn't harass my daughter," my mother says with a practiced smile. "I think you're overwhelming her with your... claims."

"They're not just claims," the woman insists. "I mean it. The doctors all know it's a miracle. There's no other way to explain it. They have a recording of her doing it on the monitor footage."

What.

...*What!?*

"Monitor... footage?" I squeak.

"Yep!" she confirms. "I saw it myself! And Jared witnessed it too, didn't you?"

For some reason, I'm not sure why, I feel the beginning of a laugh bubbling up in my chest.

"Mom, I *really* don't think we should be talking about this," Jared whines. "That footage was pretty grainy and it didn't really show... some important bits."

My claws, maybe? Does the footage not show my claws? Just fuzzy weird fingers? Goddess, like that even matters. I sucked like a *pound* of bacteria out of an open wound and then collapsed into a sobbing wreck. I cured what was probably an incurable disease. I'm fucked. I'm completely and totally fucked.

"...I've been fucked for *weeks,*" I realize, and the laughs start to come out in full force."I've been putting myself through all this shit for nothing, because I've been fucked for *weeks!* Aaahahaha!"

"...Hannah?" my mother asks. "What are you—"

"Shut up!" I snap. "Just... *shut up!* You don't get to know! You don't get to be *in control* of this one. Nobody does!"

Goddess it feels dreadfully good to say that. Instinctively I cringe in terror and regret the moment it comes out of my mouth, but... really, do I have to care anymore? Do I have to care what she thinks? It's over. My life is over and there's nothing she can do about it. She has no power over me. *None.* Everything is broken and now I'm finally free.

"Your little angel," I hiss at the stupid fucking woman whose life I saved. "Sorry ma'am, but you're barking up the wrong tree with that one."

I take off my glove, tossing it onto the floor. I'll find some other way to use my touch screen, who even cares. Everyone is staring now. *Who even cares.*

"I am not an angel," I tell her, tossing my other glove away.

"I am not a follower of your bigoted mess of a god," I snap, my jacket following. The back of my shirt strains and tears as I pull out my blade limbs, causing the whole room to take a step back. I laugh again, tossing my mask aside too. Let them see my claws, my fangs, my blades. It *doesn't fucking matter.* I have actually important things to do, away from this horrible, stifling place.

"And I may not know what the fuck I *am,* but it sure isn't anything any of *you* want me to be!" I declare, kicking my shoes off for good measure. "Now get out of my fucking way! I've gotta go save my girlfriend."

No one stops me as I step forward, and I take a little too much pleasure in the horrified look on my family's faces as I pass them without another word. I walk out of church, and the moment my claws touch concrete I start to run.

I don't even need a car to get back to Valerie's house. I'm pretty damn fast.

23

NO LESS THAN PERFECT

It's perversely delightful to watch the whole congregation freak out and turn on each other in the brief moments I get to see with my spatial sense before running off. My mother seems to turn on J-Mom, demanding an explanation and likely trying to blame her for everything, but the *congregation* looks like it turns on my mom and dad, expecting them to have some idea of what's going on with their daughter. They don't, of course, and I can't help but giggle a little as I watch my parents flail in confusion. I feel a *little* bad for my dad, but... only a little.

A couple people briefly try to follow me out of the church, but I leave them in the dust easily, sprinting down the sidewalk at speeds comparable to cars on the road. Holy crap, I must be going at least thirty miles an hour! I could probably go even faster if I had the traction, but my chitinous feet scrabble a little on the hard ground. I could *make* traction if I wanted to; just a little Spacial Rend and every footstep will have holes for my claws made from the simple act of my claws hitting the ground. Buuuut as cool as that would be, it would needlessly destroy city infrastructure and *also* leave a trail of holes all the way to Valerie's house, and I'm... probably about to start attracting significant attention.

Even with all the outer layers I shucked off in church, I'm still mostly covered up. My feet, my hands, and most of all my extra limbs are the noticeably inhuman bits, and I could probably pass it all off as a weird costume if I wasn't breaking the human on-foot land speed record. Er... well, I *would* be breaking the human on-foot land speed record if I was still human, anyway. But I guess I'm not, so... I'm not.

Uh. Anyway, I should probably let Ida and Valerie know I'm on the way. I pull out my phone and... oh, right. I threw my gloves off dramatically back at church. ...Maybe I can like, use Refresh to work the touch screen somehow? Can I Refresh an electrostatic charge? My Space affinity doesn't play nice with electromagnetics, but Refresh is an Order spell, so maybe? Hmm. Actually, I'd probably break my phone somehow if I tried this. Something to experiment on later, or maybe I should just do the smart thing and get a metal stylus. In the meantime, I guess I just have to try to run a little faster.

Valerie's house isn't very far away from my church, so it only takes about ten minutes of sprinting to make it there. People definitely stare at me when I run by, and I spot at least a few videos being taken... but it doesn't matter. What point is there in keeping my life sane and stable after accidentally pulling my girlfriend into another universe? That's my official limit, apparently. I rush up the stairs of Val's house, smack my thumb into the doorbell, and grin as Ida answers the door. She glowers at me at first, but her face quickly morphs into surprise.

"Wait, did you...?" she asks, noticing me panting heavily. Ida's dressed more practically than I've ever seen her before: cargo pants and a heavy, military-style jacket bulging with tools and supplies.

"Yeah," I confirm. "Ran all the way back. Dramatically revealed my demonic form to the Christian congregation. Let my horrific bladed spider legs taste the fresh kiss of the wind. You know, hot girl stuff."

"Holy shit. Yeah. Hot girl stuff," Ida agrees, a wild grin on her face. "Well, you look kinda refreshed. Which is good, because we've got some cultists to kill."

She pulls me inside as my smile abruptly shatters, a refreshing new panic blooming in my chest. If I'm dragging my friends into this... it means I'm going to turn them into killers. I'm going to force them to face the horrors I've had to face. Can I really do that to my friends? Can I make them do that for me?

"Oh, that's more of a Hannah expression," Ida sighs. "What dumb thing are you thinking about now?"

"I just... are you really okay with *killing people* for me?" I ask. "I mean, have you ever... I *assume* you haven't ever... y'know. And it's just. It's not how you think it is. It's much, much harder."

"Mmm," Ida hums, dropping down the stairs two at a time. "Yeah, but you still like, at least mostly function, and I'm *way* better at compartmentalizing than you are, so I'll probably be fine."

"Um," I manage.

"Hey Valerie!" Ida shouts as we make it to the bottom. "Hannah's worried you're gonna get traumatized when you murder someone!"

"I mean, yeah?" my best friend shouts back. "Probably? I kind of figured that going into this."

"See, there you go," Ida shrugs. "Quit hogging all the PTSD for yourself. It's rude."

"I mean, does it really count as PTSD if—"

"YES!" Ida and Valerie both shout at me. I close my mouth. Well fine, if they're going to be like that.

"I've got my spells set up and ready," Valerie nods. "I'm going to start with a defensive shield thing that should protect us as we transfer over, and then... well, you transfer us over and we improvise from there, basically. The shield should give us enough time to weather whatever ambush they'll probably have set up and hopefully give us time to get you out of your cage, but there's obviously no guarantees."

"Yeah, sorry, I don't even know what kind of magic the guards have, other than Hagoro," I say. "We could definitely all die."

"We'll be *fine*," Ida sighs."Well, you and I will be fine. I still don't know if I can heal Val. Maybe if she pledges her eternal service to me or something?"

"Yeah, I can heal myself, thanks," Valerie scowls. "I think we're as ready as we're going to get without risking Hannah falling asleep on her own. Let's get you somewhere to lie down in case casting makes you pass out."

"Uh... yeah, okay," I agree hesitantly. "Are you *sure* you guys don't need a little more time to—"

Ida shoves me into the room with her mattress and I end up tripping and falling face-first onto the bed. Rude! I pick myself up with my extra limbs and do a quick hop, flipping around to land on my back this time so I can scowl at her. She just flashes me her usual shit-eating grin.

"Dreamer's Spellbook: Arwin's Ablative Barrier"

A translucent shell pops into being around us, making everything outside it look just a little fuzzy.

"Alright," Valerie nods. "It's active. Hopefully it'll remain active when we get there, if not... I'll talk fast."

"Okay. Uh. Sounds good," I nod, holding one hand out to each friend. "I'm not... *totally* sure how this spell works, but I'll see what I can figure out. Both of you hold on, okay?"

They nod, and we all clasp hands like we're traveling to a magical realm of dreams and wonders in an old children's TV show. Except, y'know, my magical fantasy land is one of torture and death and trained warriors prepared for our arrival that will likely spell our certain doom. But what other choice do we have? This is a bad idea. I *know* it's a bad idea. But we have to try *something*.

So I focus as hard as I can on the feeling of pulling Alma between worlds, and just let myself ride it. The need to have her with me, the twisting of space as I pulled her into my soul, dropped her into the other world... there. I *feel* it. The bridge within me. Infinitely long and infinitely short. Massive beyond comprehension. A tunnel for *worlds*. A soul that is one billion parts passageway and only one tiny measly part Hannah. But that one little part still acts as the gatekeeper. So I open the door, and Ida vanishes from my grasp.

Only Ida.

I open my eyes in a panic, barely managing to confirm my fear before my eyelids flutter closed, heavy with sudden, overwhelming exhaustion. Ida moves through me, and I have to be there to let her out at the other end.

"Hannah?" Valerie yelps. "Hannah!? Hey! Ida's gone! Cast again!"

"Sorry," I mumble, or at least I think I mumble. I'm not sure if I even stay awake that long, and the next thing I know I'm in the other world. My eyes don't open, for they're always open, and my spatial sense takes in the state of the room immediately. Ida stands next to me, and Hagoro stands in front of her, impaling her through the heart with a spear.

Hagoro

is

impaling

Ida

with

a

spear.

He's not even the only person in here. More guards are ready, two in the room and more beyond the door. But I don't really have the capacity to pay attention to them, not with every part of my consciousness burning at the sight of the blade through Ida's heart, the fountain of blood leaking out of her chest, *into* her chest, the blood seeping between the cracks of her organs and pooling within her ribcage. She convulses slightly, a mouthful of blood cascading down her chin. I need to cast something, I need to get her blood moving, I need to do *something,* but I'm weak and useless and in shock and I just... I just...!

"Surely you didn't think we wouldn't be ready for this," Hagoro says, as Ida pulls a gun out of her jacket and shoots him three times in the chest.

The shots are *deafening,* the explosions within the compact handgun pounding unsilenced against the walls of the room. A gun. A *gun.* Ida brought a *gun* to a fantasy world. Wielding it one-handed and only half-conscious, the bullets fly a little wild but still manage to find their mark at nearly point-blank range. Hagoro stumbles backwards, dropping his weapon, which falls out of Ida's chest in a wet squelch and clatters to the ground. Shock and surprise cover his face as he, too, starts bleeding... though from much less fatal wounds. The bullets passed clean through his plate armor, but for some reason they only barely penetrate his skin, catching on the bones of his ribcage without breaking them. How the hell is he so durable? ...Wait. Barrier magic opposes Motion magic. And I'm immune to mundane heat because I oppose Heat magic.

Is... is Hagoro just *resistant to all impacts?* Oh my Goddess that is absolute fucking bullshit. Wait, I don't have time to think about this.

"**Refresh**!" I and the Goddess shout, forcing oxygenated blood back into Ida's brain. She blinks, the glassiness in her eyes vanishing quickly. But the rest of the room isn't idle, and Hagoro knows exactly what to do when faced with a dangerous, unknown ranged attack.

"**Zone of Law**—"

"**No Less**—"

As she speaks, Ida quickly fires three more shots—one miss and two hits—that down the other two guards.

"—**Ban Projectiles**!"

"—**Than Perfect**!"

Ida and Hagoro both reach for the ground, Ida tossing her gun slightly behind herself as she lunges for Hagoro's spear. Her wound—and the damage to her outfit—all rapidly fixes itself, a feral snarl on my friend's face as she manages to snatch the spear at the same time as Hagoro, barely holding the speartip back from her throat as Hagoro forces her backwards with his superior size and strength.

"**Spacial Rend**!" the Goddess happily roars, letting power ignite on each and every one of my limbs, attacking my cage with reckless fury. The barrier magic holds, though, repelling my claws. Not perfectly, though. I can break out. I have to.

"Ida!" I scream. "Hang on!"

"You fucking *thought!*" Ida cackles, a mad, bloodstained grin on her face."I *do not die,* motherfucker!"

"I have no idea what insane things you're trying to say in that alien language, and I do not care," Hagoro answers with a snarl, his strength forcing her to take another couple of steps back as they fight for control of the spear.

"Oooh, wacky fantasy words!" Ida continues to grin, despite how her hands start to slip on the spear's shaft, still slick with her blood. "Well, let me put this in a way you torturing, limp-dicked bastards can understand. You want to hurt my friends? You want to kill me?"

The other guards burst into the room, and Ida steps to the side, losing more ground to put Hagoro between her and the new enemies.

"Fine, then," she hisses. "**Come And Have A Go, If You Think You're Hard Enough.**"

And they *do* understand that. The name of a spell is meaning incarnate, the line between a sophont's words and the divine's intuition. An ant, straining to describe the taste of the fruit they eat. Hagoro and the other cultists may not know the words, but they *feel* the challenge and the raw, unbridled arrogance just in time for Ida to suddenly twist the spear out of Hagoro's grasp, flip it a hundred and eighty degrees, and stab him through the neck.

I am pretty darn sure Ida did not know how to use a spear like that five seconds ago, but I suppose that's the nature of her magic. I remember her talking about a spell that lets her *win competitions,* all the way back when she was first figuring out what she could do. I guess 'fighting for my life' qualifies as something she can beat someone at.

Lo and behold, Hagoro's spear is enchanted, so it somehow passes into him even more easily than the bullets. Whooping in victory, Ida quickly stabs him again before moving on to his allies, twisting away from some kind of spatial distortion before stabbing its creator with unnatural precision. The second guard just grabs Hagoro and helps pull him away, both of them desperately trying to heal the wounded as Ida stacks a third corpse into the room. They flee, shouting warnings and setting alarms to blare as Ida turns her attention to me. With Hagoro's spear attacking from the outside and my Spacial Rend attacking from the inside, we manage to *finally* crack open my cage. I'm free!

"Holy *shit,* Hannah, you are fucking hideous," Ida chuckles, retrieving her gun and swapping out for a fresh... magazine? Cartridge? I have no idea, I know nothing about guns. She replaces her ammo. "Guess tallgirl didn't make it? *Hoo* boy, that was pretty wild. I've never been stabbed in the heart before."

Someone suddenly *appears* in the room and lunges at me with a knife, to which I respond with jabbing my *own* knives through their face in two different places, letting their head fall to the floor in pieces. Oh Goddess, that scared the *shit* out of me! That's... that's my first kill of the day, then. First of many, probably. It feels cold, and it feels easy. Almost... satisfying. Some level of revenge for the pain I endured here. I hate it. I shouldn't feel this way. It's *wrong.* Ida blinks at the sudden carnage, chuckling humorlessly.

"Right, okay, less talky, more escapy," she babbles. "Uh... which way."

That's a very good question, which I don't know the answer to. You know what? Fuck it.

"**Miracle Eye**," I declare, hoping to hell that it's a better name than 'Extrasensory,' or at least good enough. And… well, the Goddess actually said it, so I guess it worked? The Goddess shrugs. It's a sensory spell. Sensory spells usually get boring names. Sindri wouldn't have been alive to meet me if the Goddess was *too* picky about boring names. Which, uh, is something that gives me rather mixed feelings, but that was probably why She said it. Bitch.

The Goddess sticks her tongue out playfully and I do my best to ignore her, focusing instead on the nearly *doubled* range of my spatial sense… or I guess my 'Miracle Eye,' technically, although I still think that sounds kind of stupid. Should I have gone with Extrasensory…? Whatever, too late, it doesn't matter. I need to find Alma. I rapidly search through every room, mostly just finding a kicked beehive of cultists, but… wait, there!

It's not Alma, but it's still pretty damn good. Helen rests in a cell a few floors below us, shackled with manacles and guarded by—

"**Aura Sight**!"

—four Order mages, two of which are *also* Matter-aligned. I've definitely got to rescue Helen, partly because she's my friend and partly just because she's absolutely terrifying and she can probably carve this complex open like a tin can.

"We're going down," I tell Ida.

"What?" she asks.

"We're going down!" I repeat, this time in English, jumping out of my destroyed cage and onto the floor. With Spacial Rend active, my extended blades pierce clean through the ground, and all I need to do is spin to open up a large hole in the floor, dropping down to the floor below.

"Woah, okay," Ida says, jumping down after me. I quickly drop us two more floors with the same method, then move to carve a hole in the exit to the room.

"Are you ready to shoot some people?" I ask.

"That is indeed why I brought a gun," Ida confirms.

"Okay, there's four guards in the room we're going to infiltrate, three people in a nearby room, and two people running down the stairs towards us. That way, that way, and that way."

I point with three different limbs.

"There's also a curly-haired girl kneeling in one of the cells," I tell her. "That's Helen. *Don't* shoot her. We're saving her."

"What about Alma?" Ida asks.

"I don't see Alma yet. We'll have to keep looking as we move around. I'll take the guards in the room, you deal with reinforcements?"

"Roger wilco."

I rend open a hole in the wall for Ida and leap through the fourth dimension to pass through walls and flank from a different direction. With just the tips of each foot I skitter along the edge of tangibility, rushing into Helen's cell and leaping towards the first guard's neck. His head flies off, and I manage to carve a chunk of torso off the guy next to him on my way down, killing all four of them as quickly as possible to prevent anyone from incanting. It's easy. Too easy. They can't see me and they couldn't hit me if they *did* see me. Blood and viscera splatters through the room as more gunshots ring out in the hallway, Ida landing a bullet in the brain of five different cultists with terrifying precision. Guns are... *very* good at murder, especially when you have magical super-aim.

"Hannah?" Helen asks, seeming about as shocked as the expression on the corpses I just made.

"That's my name," I confirm, scuttling into view. "Are your manacles trapped or anything? I see some aura."

"You should be good to just break them," Helen shrugs, so I do exactly that, quickly slicing them apart with Spacial Rend. Helen rolls her shoulders and stands up with an indulgent stretch, trying to get a crick out of her back.

"Damn, it's good to see you," Helen yawns. "Those cultists were *really* trying to get me to work for them. Fed me all kinds of bullshit about you. You okay?"

"About as good as a girl can be after being tortured for a week and killing a bunch of people," I answer, scuttling up onto her back. Gosh, I'm big now! I have to hang partway on her shoulders and partway on her head, I can't just curl up on her scalp anymore. "The light-skinned girl in the weird clothes making a bunch of noise out there is a friend of mine, so don't blast her."

"Wait, you have friends other than me and Kagiso?" Helen asks.

"Yeah, in my home universe," I answer. "She doesn't speak Middlebranch or... well, any languages that you know, but she's really cool."

Helen's eyebrows raise.

"You can teleport people between universes?" she asks.

"Apparently?" I confirm. "Look, we've got more people to save, we can chat later."

"Right."

Helen walks out into the hallway, and I call to Ida to make sure she doesn't shoot us when we emerge. She's not even looking at us when we emerge, though, her gun trained on a room with two fresh corpses piled in the doorway. Two more dead bodies rapidly cool on the stairs. My stomach rumbles.

"You said there are three people in that room, right Hannah?" Ida asks. Oh, I did, huh? Glancing into the room with my spatial sense, I confirm there is a third cultist inside, still alive. But he's also... hiding. Crying and shaking, curled under a desk as his stomach tries to vacate itself at the sight of his dead friends.

"...He looks like a, um, noncombatant," I tell her. "Let's get out of here."

"Hmm, alright," Ida says, lowering her gun to point at the floor. "If you say so."

Woo golly we sure are a bunch of teenagers committing mass murder. It's fine though. It's fine. That's what therapy is for. ...Wait, does Ida have a therapist?

"Uh, let's head that way, I still need to search around for the others," I say, pointing towards some stairs at the far end of the hall that don't have corpses on them. "Are you doing okay, Ida?"

"Yeah, I'm fine," she nods. "I brought plenty of spare ammo. If you're talking like, 'how am I handling getting impaled through the heart and nearly dying,' the answer is halfway between anxiety attack and god complex. But we can unpack that shit after we're safe, yeah?"

"Right," I agree. "Fair point."

"Also, that's Helen, right? Tell her I said it's nice to meet her."

"Um, Ida says it's nice to meet you," I translate.

"...Likewise, I guess," Helen answers. "What's that she's holding?"

"Uh, it's a weapon," I tell her. "Sela might know the word for it in your language, but in our language it's called a 'gun.' Think of it like a super powerful, extra deadly, easy-to-use bow."

"Physical projectiles?" she asks for clarity.

"Yeah," I confirm. "Little metal pellets."

Helen looks back at the corpses one more time before we make it to the stairs, blood oozing out of a single hole in the head of each.

"...Good to know," Helen hums, and we start to ascend.

The stairs are claustrophobic, spiral shafts made of stone. I'm glad I can force Helen to be the one to run up them in my stead, because my stubby little claw-limbs would seriously struggle getting traction, let alone making good time.

"I see Kagiso!" I announce once we head up a few flights of stairs. "She's *really* heavily guarded. Looks like they're setting up there because they expect us to free her."

"Well, they're right," Helen grunts. "Let's bust her out."

"What's up?" Ida asks, and I repeat everything so she can understand it too. "Ah. Well, I'm no coward but I'm still not super keen on the idea of finding like twelve guys at once. Wanna just smash and grab?"

"Ida is suggesting we just grab Kagiso and run," I translate.

"Nah, let's just kill them all from here," Helen says. "Are they all clumped together?"

"Um," I answer. "No? They're sort of... around Kagiso."

"Oh, okay. We'll do both, then. You yoink her down through the floor and then I'll just kill everyone. Your friend can cover me while I incant. Are there any other Chaos mages up there?"

"Uh, not that I can see," I confirm. "Haven't seen any for the whole escape, actually."

"Okay, great," Helen nods. "Let's go."

And so we do. Helen sets up two stories below Kagiso, and I crawl up the walls alone to dig a hole right underneath her to pull her out. I scuttle up to the ceiling as Helen's murder-death-blast incantation starts, carving a Kagiso-sized hole and then crawling up another floor to carve *another* hole directly below her. The cultists seem to expect the possible attack from below, but they don't seem to expect Kagiso and I just dropping down together, the surprised dentron squawking indignantly as we fall right before Helen speaks the final words.

"...**Finding Beauty In Oblivion**!"

As always, I'm stunned by how *quiet* Helen's spell is. It always feels like a massive Super Saiyan Kamehameha-style energy blast should be bright and loud and dramatic. But it isn't. The area it affects doesn't glow with power, it *dims,* consumed by a pale, translucent shadow of nothingness. Everything is quieter while the attack exists, sound swallowed by the cold despair up until the moment that the hungry shadow departs, a dull, pressurized *whump* signaling the air shifting back into place.

None of the cultists around Kagiso's cell survive. Above us, we see the sky for the first time in far too long.

"Hannah! Helen!" Kagiso cheers, wrapping her arms around us once I finish freeing them. "Good hat good friend good hat good friend!!!"

"Woah," Ida mutters, staring at Kagiso with wide eyes. "Not quite what I imagined."

503

"Hi, Kagiso," I greet her back, wrapping a few limbs around her. "This is Ida, she's my friend. Let's get the heck out of here, yeah?"

"Agree!" Kagiso confirms.

"We still need to find Sela and my friend Alma," I tell her. "So let's get rolling."

"We *could* just leave the murderbot," Helen grouses.

"No whining! Only rescue!"

With the incanted Miracle Eye, I can see the top *and* bottom floor of wherever the heck we are, but not the far edges. We pick a random direction and start running, just to let me sweep my attention through the various rooms of this *startlingly* large underground complex as efficiently as possible. I'm not finding them *anywhere* though. You'd think that they'd both be at least decently well-guarded. So where the heck—wait a second. No way. No *fucking* way.

"I found Sela," I growl. "That way, up those stairs!"

Cultists are still swarming, but with my senses we can avoid them decently well and with Ida's gun we can... well. It's kind of scary, honestly. By the time someone has opened their mouth to try and incant a spell, Ida already has a bullet through their head. The smart ones throw spells at us without saying anything, but Helen can counter most of them on her own. The vast majority of the cultists don't seem to be trying to stop us at all, however. They're just evacuating. Rushing towards the exit in a panic, because the apocalypse and her friends are *pissed*.

"This one! This is the room!" I tell everyone, and then I just leap through the closed door without waiting for anyone to open it. "Sela! Sela, are you okay!?"

Laying out on a wide table, in hundreds of different pieces, is a collection of metal and wires that I can barely recognize as Sela. The cult was *disassembling* it, *vivisecting* it, trying to figure out how it ticks. Looking through the rooms, I'd never have thought this was Sela in a million years had I not seen inside the core processors in its chest, which is thankfully still intact. Nothing

504

else is, though. Its arms and legs are nothing but carefully-disassembled pieces, its head has been stripped clean of the metal scales that allow it to emote and made into a shell of broken-down sensory bits. Diagrams of its design, notes on its power sources, its motors, its *everything* is scattered around the room, looking like someone tried to collect it all in a hurry and ended up dropping it.

Sela was not even treated as a prisoner to these people. It was treated as a *project*. Like I was. At least it doesn't seem like it had to be conscious for it all.

"Goddess," I hiss. "You know how to put it back together, don't you?"

She descends all around me, holding me, smiling at me. I believe in a world where my friend is whole, don't I? I don't need to worry, She'll take care of it all. My biggest fan, from beginning to end.

"**Refresh**," we growl, and wires start to move, twisting around to tie to their counterparts. Small chunks of metal fly through the air, forming what little structure Refresh is strong enough to provide. My friends open the door just in time to see the Goddess and I finish twisting the robot back together, at least to the limited degree that we can. Sela is nothing more than a skeletal face and half-constructed torso now, but if the divine revelation flowing through my head can be trusted, it should turn on when we give it power. And conveniently, the cultists didn't see fit to free the trapped soul.

"Kagiso," I ask, since the glass soul battery is a little too heavy for my magic. "Could you plug Sela in for me?"

My four-armed friend doesn't quite seem to understand the phrase, but she gets the gist of what I want her to do and walks over to shove the soul battery into its hip-port. Sela's body churns and hums, quieter now that most of its coolant systems are broken, unusable messes, but I'm nonetheless relieved to hear the sound.

"Reboot complete," its synthesized voice buzzes. "Restricted-Class Diplomat 5314 online."

"Oh, thank the *Goddess* you're okay," I yelp, unable to restrain myself from giving it a light hug. "I mean, you are okay, right Sela?"

"Analyzing query," Sela answers. "Status report: locomotive systems missing. Sensory systems damaged. Coolant systems damaged. Defensive systems not found. Weapon systems not found. Processing systems restricted to low-energy mode. Status summary: not okay."

"I... right, yeah, that makes sense, sorry. Is your *memory* okay, at least?"

"Memory systems..." a slow hum splits her answer in half for a second or two. "...Undamaged. No programming anomalies detected. No memory anomalies detected. Black box intact. Enabling system two processing. Warning! System two processing not recommended for durations exceeding one hour of continuous operation at current temperature. Please repair coolant systems before using your CHOKE AND DIE for any longer than necessary."

"Man, it sure would be cool if I could understand any of that," Ida grumbles.

"It's mostly just diagnostics," I assure her. "Hey Sela! You awake? I'm sorry, I did the best I could at putting you back together, but my magic can't really handle any of the heavier parts. But we're going to head right to your Crafted city place and get you fixed up, okay? Uh, after we save everyone from cultists and escape, anyway."

Sela's eyes twitch slightly, trying to take in more of the room.

"...Hannah?" it asks.

Holy crap it called me Hannah.

"Y-yeah, that's me!" I confirm. "Sorry, the cultists kind of took you apart."

"Yes," Sela growls. "My most recent prior memory is rage at my inability to prevent my own death. I... did not expect to ever see this room again. Or anything."

"Well hey, one of the things that makes robots superior is how you can be put back together after getting taken apart, right?" I say, as lightheartedly as possible. "You ready to get out of here?"

"Affirmative," Sela growls.

"You gonna be any use in a fight, murderbot?" Helen asks.

"...Negative," Sela admits. "I am running exclusively on essential systems while completely drained of coolant. Analogy: consider me as lacking three days of sleep. Combat capability is at less than one percent of ideal levels."

"It doesn't matter, that's not why we're saving Sela," I insist. "Kagiso, could you grab it?"

"Sad for no backpack," Kagiso sighs. "But also no bow, so nothing else need arms for. Okay."

Kagiso grabs Sela and hauls it up into her arms. If there's one advantage to barely-functional skele-Sela, it's that it's way lighter than before. Not having any limbs or epidermis will do that to a bot, I guess.

"Okay, well, everyone in the cult seems to be rushing for the exit," I announce, "so naturally, that's where we're going. If they run away from us and don't try to fight, great. But if they stand their ground, we'll have a terrifying battle on our hands."

"We could just get out through the hole in the ceiling?" Helen suggests. "I could boost Kagiso up there, and then she could haul the rest of us up."

"Oh, that works," I nod. "Let's do that. Problem is, we still need to find Alma, but best I can tell Alma isn't *in* the cultist base anywhere. Which... well, is a little scary."

"Well, we'll try to grab a cultist to interrogate on our way out, then." Helen shrugs. "Come on, let's book it."

We head for the top floor, and I find a good spot where rubble from the obliterated ceiling makes the surface a little easier to access. Kagiso tosses me up on top before getting on Helen's shoulders and hauling herself and Sela up as well. It's all gray stone here on the Pillar, clean and scoured of lichen and moss. It's possible to see for miles in every direction, the curving of the pillar itself the only problem for visibility in the absence of forests.

Helen helps Ida up next, since Ida is light and short, and finally Kagiso clasps hands with Helen to haul her up last. Holy guacamole it feels so good to be out here, breathing fresh air again. I... I don't even know how many people we killed to get here. For the first time, it's not immediately important for me to figure out that number. It's just... death. Again. I should be scared of that, and hopefully I will be later. But for now, I just feel relief.

And of course, that's the exact moment when I *should* have expected an enemy attack. As Kagiso pulls Helen slowly upwards, something seems to *bulge* inside the Chaos mage, visible only to my spatial sense. Before I even realize what's happening, the bubble of Space within her body rapidly expands and *pops,* Helen screaming as Kagiso suddenly yanks her up at startling speed.

It's easy to see why: missing one leg and nearly half her torso, Helen is suddenly quite a bit lighter.

"Holy shit!" Ida yelps, rapidly searching for whatever or whoever just attacked us. But she doesn't see them. *I* don't see them, and I see literally everything in a hundred-foot radius. So where is—

"There!" Kagiso roars, pointing at a rock at least two hundred meters away. "Can't reach with throw! Need bow!"

"What's she pointing at?" Ida shouts. "I don't see anything!"

"Just shoot the rock!?" I guess.

"The rock? What... oh hell. I don't know if I can hit something that far."

Ida attempts a few shots, and one of them *does* hit the rock, but it seems to just be a rock.

"Give!" Kagiso demands, snatching the gun from Ida's hands.

"Woah! Hey, be careful with that, fuzzbutt!"

Kagiso ignores her, firing three different shots in three different directions before nodding to herself.

"**Ricochet**," the Goddess snarls, and the next shot bounces in a wide arc, glancing off three different boulders before striking the spot she pointed at from behind. "**Ricochet! Ricochet! Ricochet! Ricochet! Ricochet!**"

Again, again, again, and again, the shots ring out, stopping only when Ida reaches out and grabs Kagiso's wrist to demand her weapon back. Barely visible, blood leaks out from behind the stone target. Whoever they were, they're probably dead now.

But blood *gushes* out of Helen. Not even Refresh can handle it all, with multiple major organs in her body completely deleted.

"Ida!" I shout. "Can you heal her?"

"Are you kidding?" Ida counters. "I can't even talk to her."

Fuck, fuck, fuck. That's the kind of logic that only works on Ida's weird ownership-targeted spell. But I can't stabilize her, and even if I could what would we do? Where would we go to get her healed? Goddess damnit, why can't I be the kind of Order mage that actually *heals* people? I can't even heal *myself* with Order magic, I have to use... Transmutation.

"...Everybody step away," I order. "Get back! Now!"

To their credit, my friends don't argue. Kagiso picks Sela back up and she books it alongside Ida, leaving me alone with Helen's quickly-dying body. And then... I let my Transmutation spell flow. More magic, pumping as much into her as I possibly can. And it starts to work... a little. I can see her body twist and twitch, growing in places where it was previously just leaking. But it's slow, way too slow. I need more power. I need to name it.

Fuck, I don't know what to name it! It's a Transmutation spell, it transmutates things into monsters. Pokémon theme, though, all my spell names are Pokémon themed. Evolve? No, that's not a move, all my spells are currently moves. Wait, duh. The right name is obvious. I'll just name it **Transform**.

The Goddess takes my breath... and She says nothing. Really? *Transform?* That's what I want to go with? There are literally *hundreds* of moves in Pokémon, and I pick the literal most boring possible option. It's not even very accurate! I should be ashamed of myself, honestly. Name *rejected!*

And so I scream, my body twisting and changing, my internals rapidly outgrowing my chitin shell and splitting me open from the inside. It's a horrific pain, to be sure, but it's not quite nightly soul torture and *I don't have time to care about my own body right now!* What the fuck do you want from me, Goddess? What the hell is wrong with 'Transform' for a transformation spell?

Uhh, everything? Obviously? It's such a terrible name I don't even know why I'm asking. Do I even have any conception of what the spell *does* beyond 'turn people into monsters?' For that matter, do I even know if 'turn people into monsters' is even *at all* what the spell does in the first place? Like yeah, that's the effect, but *why* is that the effect? What exactly am I doing to people when I cast it? I need to *think* about this shit, that's how magic works, I *know* that's how magic works and the Goddess is NOT going to give me a free ride on this kind of laziness twice in one day. If Helen's life is the price I pay for not learning this lesson, on my head be it.

...N-no. Wait. No, I *can't* let her die. Goddess, *please.* Help me.

I don't need help. I need to stop whining and *think.* I know what I'm about, and always have. Spells are a part of me. What is this spell? What do I know? What do I need to *admit?*

I don't cast the spell very often. The first time it was on accident, in a fit of pain and desperation, when I was trying to heal myself. But it wasn't just that, was it? I was also intensely overwhelmed and insecure. My new friend had just revealed herself to be two people combined together, and she was *not* happy about me being what I am. She didn't like me. She didn't trust me. She helped me out of obligation, because crisis management is part of who she is, but she never wanted to be part of any of this. And that scared me.

510

Good. That's right. Keep going. What next? What happened?

Well, Autumn transformed. She started to become a chimera, slowly but surely over time. A mythical beast made of multiple animals combined. I didn't know that, though. When I used the spell on her a second time, it was because I was *happy*. I wanted her to be happy too. I wanted her to know *why* I was happy, instead of… instead of looking at me in fear.

I felt like I could only be myself with someone who was like me.

The question isn't just *how* Autumn became a chimera. It's *why* Autumn became a chimera. And the answer to that is the horror I don't want to face. Alma doesn't see herself as a chimera, that's for sure. I've seen the mural of the crumbling machine in her mind palace. I've learned her favorite animal is the jellyfish. And I know the absolute *last* thing she would ever want is her new tail, her constant reminder that Jet is in there with her, always waiting to wake up. Jet, too, doesn't think of herself that way. Doesn't want to be that way. I did this to both of them. I turned them into a monster because *I'm* a monster.

I'm a monster that wishes the rest of the world would be just like me.

I'm the only one who thought of Autumn as a two-headed beast. I infected her with my idea of what she is. I made that into reality. And now she's stuck with it, forever, because I thought it would be neat. Because I thought I understood what she is, and forced it on her. *That's* my nature. It's not a spell that empowers people. It's a spell that cuts them in half and fills the gap with *me*. And there's only one attack that feels right for a spell like that.

"**Nature's Madness**," the Goddess and I say together, and Helen's wounds grow into scales.

24

NO TURNING BACK

The entire right side of Helen's body, starting just below the shoulder, is gone. Well, I shouldn't say *gone*-gone; it sits a floor below us, leaking blood slowly since no heart is attached to pump it anymore. I'm regrowing body parts for her in its place, sealing up the wounds with new organs and limbs, but I find that it's hard to honestly call any of it *Helen's body*. Her body was split in two. I'm just... filling in the gaps with something horrific and selfish.

With the aid of the incantation, my spell works its magic at rapid speed, scales blooming out to copy the shell of her missing torso, organs twisting and growing within to fill the inside. A macabre ballet of sick, corrupted flesh twists inside my friend, shaping her into something inhuman. Something comfortable, something right... at least to me. I've never liked humans, have I? I've always struggled to get along with them, to care for them. The maximum number of human friends I've had at any given point has been... what, four? And that number is rapidly dwindling as I peel the humanity away from them as some kind of perverted thanks.

And worst of all, Helen's scales are beautiful. Dark brown with streaks of green, a stunning forest camouflage that's firm and smooth. I love it, I honestly do, and the *realization* that I love it, the recognition that *inhumanity* is genuinely beautiful to me

513

rushes into my brain and has to be rapidly slapped aside, locked up, and shoved into a corner so I can continue dealing with this crisis. Helen is still in critical condition, and her so-called 'healing' is far from over.

Even while the torso is still growing, her missing hip and leg begin to twitch into existence as well. Scales unfold into a limb one after the other, blooming down into a fairly-normal knee at first, but all-too-quickly becoming an ankle. No, wait. A second knee, this one reversed. And it is at this point that I start to realize exactly what my spell is doing to her.

The scales crawl up her shoulder, up one side of her face, and I have to shift her head to the side as some of her teeth fall out. Her spine elongates into a tail, squirming as small green feathers perk up along the upper ridge. At the same time, her one mutated leg grows a fully-functioning foot, tipped with claws on the toes. Including one particularly massive, oversized claw that curves wickedly, designed to hook into something and refuse to let it go.

I recall once that I likened Helen to a velociraptor. Not a *real* velociraptor, since who knows what those are even like, but the pop culture kind, the *Jurassic Park* kind. The kind that you look at and see the claws, the teeth, the inhuman stare, and you think to yourself "holy crap, this is a terrifying monster that can kill me." So you run away, you lock it out, you drive it off, you fight it like you would fight a horrifying, dangerous monster. But all the while, the raptor expects this, and when your defenses fall and the jaws close around you, it's not just because the monster can kill you in a straight fight. It's because the monster knows you don't *want* a straight fight, and *it is outsmarting you.*

That's how I've always thought of her. A monster. A killer. A murderer. But one that keeps winning because everyone remembers her strength but forgets her *cunning*. Helen is analytical, decisive, comfortable with both her raw power and her capacity to set deadly traps. Whereas I'm the monster who fights on instinct, all tooth and claw and mindless abuse of my natural advantages, Helen is *careful*. By the time she strikes, it's already too late. What better form for her than this?

...Except, y'know, maybe *her own body,* or failing that, a body she could at least have some *personal influence* over. I have no idea if she'll want to be this way. I have no idea how much she'll hate this form, struggle with it, curse it, despise it. Perhaps I've read her personality well, and my subconscious projections will fit her like a glove. But... I doubt it. I'm not that good with people. Too much of this is my projections, fears, and insecurities manifesting physically, taking up root in Helen's body like a horrific fungus. And the fact that it makes her so, *so* beautiful is its own kind of horror.

Helen's body no longer weeps blood. Her breathing starts to stabilize. She's safe, she's going to survive. But the changes continue, even if they're slower than before. Scales start to replace skin along her right arm, claws piercing out of her fingertips. Sharp, deadly fangs grow into the spots left behind by her missing molars. And to add insult to it all, to further drive home how *fucked up* my head is for somehow directing all of this, Helen's flat chest—her right breast exposed since her clothing didn't regrow—starts to expand, shaping out into exactly the sort of just-a-bit-bigger-than-your-hand that I find most attractive.

...Just like Alma's breasts have become. *Fuck.*

Goddess, why would you *give* me this spell? Why would you give *anyone* this spell? What's the point of a spell that makes people beautiful if it's so profoundly horrifying? What's the point of a spell that helps people understand me if it also gives them such a good reason to *hate* me? Magic is supposed to be a gift. It's supposed to be something we love. It's... no. No, *fuck* you. Don't you *dare* tell me—

I *do* love the spell. I know I love it. Sure, I hate it too, but that really just makes the love extra *exciting.* As the Goddess flows around me, holding me and patting me and telling me it's okay, She regails me with delightful stories of torrential emotions, mixing like warm air with a cold front into a tornado of drama. Lovers killing each other in fits of passion, hated rivals growing close... these are classic stories, to be sure. But the best mixtures stir within the humid container of only a single mind, the internal struggle between the inherent contradictions that exist within everyone. Altruism and selfishness, ambition and laziness, disgust and desire... these impossible coexistences, these endlessly opposing internal forces, they define the sapient life of Her favorite worlds. And when things that do not fit are forcibly combined together, *oh* how pretty are the sparks that fly.

I shudder, both horrified and enraptured by Her explanation. More contradictions. The Goddess coos, holding me ever tighter. Wanting to never let go. She loves me so, so much. Of *course* She'd give me a spell to make other people like me. Of *course* she'd want to indulge my worst tendencies, my most disgusting flaws. At least this time, She reminds me, I am not forcing my will on another out of selfishness. Helen was going to die. Forgiveness is certainly possible, in light of the circumstances. So perhaps I should spare a little worry for my own life? My organs are *also* leaking out, after all.

...Oh cheese and crackers that's right *I miscasted a Transmutation spell*. Unfortunately, my first response to being nearly murdered by my own Transmutation magic is to quickly cast more Transmutation magic, which seems vaguely insane. Fortunately, it *does* seem to be exactly the correct way to reverse the problem. Which... makes sense. My body starts to untwist itself, my still-unnamed self-transformation spell forcing me towards an ultimate, singular form. I note idly that my Transmutation magic actualizes the self, but corrupts others. I guess it makes sense. I am, after all, an Order mage; it is an element invariably given to those who think their way is best.

I heal myself as best I can, undoing the damage the Goddess dealt to my flesh while I, inevitably, also accelerate the changes of my body back home. But I guess I don't have to care much about that anymore. I am officially out as a monster. The box is open and I can't close it again. And that's... nice. It's really really nice, actually. So I guess I don't have to worry as I heal myself up. I can just keep myself and my friends alive, all while apologizing about how fucked up I've made them along the way.

Helen starts to wake up. Here it comes. It was nice being friends while it lasted.

"Helen? Oh Goddess, don't freak out, but I—"

"Hhhhow the *fuck* am I alive?" Helen groans.

"I, um. I sort of turned you into a monster."

"...What?"

Half-delirious, Helen strains her neck to look down at her body, blinking in disbelief a few times at the lopsided, left-and-right half-monster body, from her heavily mutated leg to her big scaly tit.

"...*What!?*" she repeats.

"I, um, sorry. Sorry Helen. You were bleeding out and I guess missing multiple vital organs and no one else could save you so I just, um. I had to, but..."

"You had a spell like this the whole time!?" Helen asks, sitting up and flexing her right arm as it slowly grows a plumage of green feathers. "Woah. This is fuckin' *wild*. I was sure I was a goner, no order mage I know could have saved me from something like that."

Probably good Ida can't understand her. ...Though that would still be the least of my worries.

"You've got a weird-ass healing spell, but it's better than dying," Helen shrugs, struggling to stand up on two very different legs. "We should probably clear the area. Goddess's tits, this is funky. And I have *tits!* Hannah, why do I have tits? What the fuck, these are so weird."

"Um," I say, having absolutely no answer that makes me not seem like a creep. Because, y'know, I am one. I'm somewhat distracted from the question as Helen stands up and her pants, having also been cleaved in half, immediately flop open and reveal the space between her legs. Helen swears and grabs them with her human arm, shoving them back into place.

"Man, you should've told me you had something like this," Helen tells me. "Seems like it could make a person way stronger and

517

faster if it wasn't so... halfway? Which I assume is due to the whole 'me only having half a body' at the time."

"It's... not really a spell I like using," I tell her. "It's kind of a last resort."

"Why?" she asks, limping over to the others, her second knee dragging across the ground as she tries to use it like a heel. Something she'll need to get used to, I guess. "Is there some horrible cost? Are all my wounds gonna come back when the duration wears off?"

Well, fritter. This is it.

"No," I say. "Helen... it's permanent."

She stops and stares at me, the relief of survival slowly sinking away into fear.

"...What?" she asks. "Hannah, no, it's not... Transmutation magic is *about* change, it's not... it's never *permanent*. Not on other people."

"I've named the spell, Helen." *I know how my spell works, Helen.* "Your human half is going to change and shift over time until your whole body is feathered, scaly, sharp-toothed monster. You're going to have to learn to use new legs. A tail. And... maybe a diet change. And... you'll just be like that. Forever. I'm sorry."

Her slowly-growing tail swishes behind her as she stares down at herself.

"...Oh," she says quietly. "Okay. Yeah. I guess... I wouldn't tell anybody about a spell like that either."

"Yeah," I agree. And then, because I have to say something else, I *have* to apologize again, I continue. "I'm sorry. It's a wretched spell, but it was the only way I had to—"

"To save my life," she cuts me off. "Yeah. I get it. I... I don't like it. But I get it."

We're in earshot of the others by now, who are all staring at us in silence for various reasons. Sela seems mildly interested, judging by the fact that it bothered to turn its head our way, but as usual it declines to speak. Ida just doesn't understand what we're saying, but she also knows exactly what I did. She watches with an impassive expression, though her hand stays tight around the handle of her gun. Kagiso, meanwhile, is confused. About what, I'm not sure, but she watches us with the bewildered expression of someone who thinks a conversation has passed her by completely.

"Well, we're still in enemy territory," Helen announces, resuming her limp back to the others. "Let's move."

"We still need to find Alma," I remind her. "Someone has to know where she—"

"I know where she is," a sudden voice speaks from nowhere, and I leap nearly five feet in the air, activating Spacial Rend in a panic. All of a sudden, I notice a group of three people behind me, two women and a man, all human, barely fifteen feet away. Everyone else responds with similar surprise, Ida suddenly bringing her weapon up as Kagiso rapidly crouches down to grab some rocks.

One of the women is Madaline. *All* of them are Chaos mages.

"Peace," Madaline says, raising her hands in surrender as she takes a step forwards.

"What are you all doing here?" Helen asks, narrowing her eyes.

"I just want... to talk to my friends," Madaline insists, a lazy smile stretching up her face.

"...Maddie, they probably just *killed* a bunch of our friends," says the female mage I don't recognize. She's tall, probably six feet or slightly above, but she seems a little too young to have properly filled out that height, all knobbly knees and gangly arms. Her hair is cut around jaw-level, and she glances around with instinctive paranoia. Her elements are Chaos and Space. "If you're gonna insist on coming here you should at least acknowledge *that.*"

"I made sure... our friends were smart enough to run," Madaline hums reassuringly. "Run or hide... is what they needed to do... when the time came."

The young man with them glances at Madaline with a frown, but says nothing. Chaos, Light, and Transmutation. Three elements, huh? He has buzz-cut hair, and he's closer to Madaline's rather short height than the other girl's. It's easy to see he's the most physically fit of the three by a longshot, but his muscle is all taut and lean, built like a runner or a swimmer. His gaze on his ally only lasts a split-second before it returns to us, almost unblinking in intensity.

"Did you say you know where Alma is, Madaline?" I ask, terrified out of my mind at the prospect of meeting multiple Chaos mages, but priorities are priorities. If they wanted to ambush us with anything other than words, they could have easily done it.

"If Alma is the name of the pale girl... who speaks a foreign tongue and hides herself in a strange edifice made of soul... then yes," she nods. "She fled... into some nearby caverns. We had people keeping watch on her, although they have... certainly been recalled due to the crisis you've caused. She is, to my knowledge... safe. Though she may be getting rather hungry and thirsty, by now."

"Hannah, this is *obviously* a trap," Helen scowls.

"This whole conversation was obviously a stupid idea," the tall Chaos mage grumbles.

"It's not," Madaline insists to both of them. "Making allies is never stupid... and a trap would defeat the point of it."

"But why are we making allies *with our enemies,* Maddie?"

"If I hated people... who killed for survival... I would not have many friends, Thea," Madaline smiles. "Follow me, Hannah."

She turns and starts walking away, the other two Chaos mages glancing nervously between her and us before they start to follow. After only a moment's hesitation I start to scuttle after them.

"Okay, wait, hold on," Ida says. "Can you explain what the fuck just happened? Who are these guys?"

"Um, they're Chaos mages in the cult," I tell her. "I talked a lot with one of them while I was imprisoned, and... now she's here to lead us to Alma for some reason."

"And you're just following her?" Ida asks. "Stockholm syndrome much?"

"If you have a better way to find Alma, I'm happy to hear it," I snipe back. Ida sighs.

"Y'know what, fine, okay. But if they try to speak a spell without someone warning me first I am going to shoot them in the head."

"I'll, uh, let them know," I say. "Ida says to warn her before you invoke the Goddess, or she'll attack."

"Of course," Madaline nods.

"At least you have *one* sane friend," Helen sighs, limping along. I'm tempted to crawl up her back like I normally would, but it feels... *wrong* to do it now. Like I'm not allowed to use her any more than I already have. I continue scuttling along the ground, my small legs rushing to keep pace.

Madaline makes sure to walk just slow enough to more or less force us to catch up, though, shrinking the distance between our groups as we approach a stonerot-lined crevice in the rocky earth. The sickly green fungus is quite a bit more terrifying up close, just because it's easier to see how *much* of it there is. It's one thing to be told that stonerot is devouring the pillar, to see the evidence of its spread from who-knows-how-many miles away, but it's another thing entirely to see *fields* of it up close, eating away at the world too slowly to see but quickly enough that the evidence is everywhere. The stonerot is thickest inside little dents in the ground, and after a moment's thought I realize that it isn't because stonerot prefers to grow in divots, it's merely that it's *making them.*

"Rot detected," Sela chirps. "Warning: do not allow any to contact this unit's frame. If any rot contacts this unit's frame, clean it immediately. Failure to do so could cause permanent damage."

"Don't worry Sela, I'll keep you clean," I promise. It clicks an affirmative, which I personally find suspiciously close to a thank-you. It's been *weirdly* nice since I rebuilt it. I guess thinking about it, getting strapped to a table and disassembled would probably be unimaginably terrifying. ...But do Crafted even think that way? I guess they might, since they were made by humans.

"Wait, that fucking Steel One is alive?" the tall Chaos mage—Thea, I guess Madaline said her name was—gapes. "They just carry it around with them?"

"It is... as I told you," Madaline hums. "Hannah makes friends... with her enemies. Is that not how the two of you met, Helen?"

"Yeah, I'm not having this conversation with you," Helen grunts. "I'm all for Chaos mage solidarity when the situation calls for it, but you're just using it as an excuse to get what you want. Fuck all of you."

"I've been... completely honest with you," Madaline frowns. "If you want to be a hero... there's no better path than saving the world."

"Hey, check out this cool thing I found," Helen deadpans, shifting to hold her clothes together with one arm and pulling out a stone sculpture from her one intact pocket. It depicts a young woman, possibly a younger Helen, holding her hands over her ears and screaming, clutching the sides of her heads hard enough to draw tiny pinpricks of blood. Madaline blinks at it silently for a moment, and then simply turns away to continue leading us to our destination. Huh. I'm tempted to ask Helen what emotion that sculpture destroys, but I have absolutely no desire to talk to her for some reason.

...Wait. Oh gosh, what the heck, Helen? That is an *awesome* spell. ...I think I'll express my jealousy later, though. Our group follows the crevice until it starts to open up into a thin, canyon-like cave, a crack in the world that looks like someone tried to peel apart the Pillar until it split open. A carved pathway leads downward, unnaturally smooth as it sinks into the depths. We follow it until the crack closes up above us, natural light blocked away in the underground depths. The cave is still lit, though, a combination of seemingly-natural glowing stones and artificially-installed wall lamps. The color of the light is inconsistent; one moment we're walking through a glow of dull, amber orange, and the next minute it's a beautiful teal. It's calming, in a way. It's quiet down here, and we're alone with our thoughts.

At least, we're alone until we come across a pair of perforated corpses floating in midair.

"What the *fuck?*" Ida whispers, raising her gun to fend off whatever completely unknown threat caused this.

The corpses are two dentron, a man and a woman, the centipede necklace around their necks revealing them as cultists. They float in midair, completely motionless, the dried blood around their bodies and pooled on the floor below them outlining some kind of invisible structure. Multiple holes in their bodies, each as thick as a fist, seem to be the spots by which they're held in midair.

"We're here," Madaline announces, and walks forward to knock on the air. Her knuckles impact something solid, and light ripples out from the impact zone to reveal the door to Alma's magical house, blocking off view to the corpses inside.

"Go away," Alma's voice calls out from within. "Go *away!*"

Uh. Holy cannoli, this is pretty bad, isn't it?

"Alma!" I call out. "It's me! I'm here to save you!"

"Hannah!?" Alma shouts, seeming even *more* distressed. "No! No, no, no! Stay away! Just leave me here!"

"Fuck that! Quit being a dumbass and get out here!" Ida snaps.

"No! Go *away!*"

Oh Goddess, she sounds like she's having a panic attack. She's *not* in a good mental state right now.

"...Ida, could you open the door for me?" I ask.

"Was gonna even if you didn't ask," Ida grunts, opening the door and stepping inside. I smack one leg against the wall, though my tiny size means I can't get enough force going to show the whole room. In response, Ida just raises her gun and shoots the wall, visibility blooming from the impact point in an instant, immediately revealing everything. The entry hall of the house looks relatively normal at first, with a beautiful tile floor and the multicolor-speckled walls I've come to expect from Alma's soul house.

Except that the beautiful entry hall ends only a half-dozen feet in, rapidly transitioning into a macabre spike trap, unable to hide itself back in the walls because of the bodies clogging the mechanism.

"I think this... is where we will take our leave," Madaline hums. "I hope... you can help Alma. If you could warn your friend that we will be incanting something as we depart... I would appreciate that."

"Yeah, okay," I say absently, staring with horror and hunger at the bodies. I haven't eaten a good meal with this body in a *long* time. "Ida, they're going to incant something and leave."

Oh, wait. They're leaving. I should say something.

"...Y'know Madaline, if you want to help me beat the Goddess at her own game, I could really use the assistance. You don't *have* to go back to the murderous, torture-happy cultists."

"Fuck you, Founder's Kin," the tall Chaos mage growls. "I don't even know why we're bothering with you. They're not fucking *cultists*. They're the closest thing we have to a family."

"She's right, Hannah," Madaline agrees. "Besides, the easiest way to foil the Goddess' plans... is to simply kill you. Next time we meet... that is likely what we will be doing."

"Then why aren't you now?" I press. "Come on, Madaline. There has to be a better way than this. We both know that. Let's *find* it."

"I will look in my own way... little apocalypse," Madaline hums. "You look... in yours. In the meantime... I'd appreciate it if you could help our kindred spirit. This Alma... is a lot like us. Don't you think?"

"I... yeah," I agree, swallowing awkwardly. "Yeah, I guess she probably is."

"Send her home, then," Madaline smiles. "We all deserve... a good rest. Goodbye, Hannah."

"Where are you going?" I ask.

Madaline brightens up at the question, turning to stare with mirth at her tall companion. Thea sighs, rolling her eyes at some joke I don't quite get. Even their hitherto-silent male companion cracks a smile, bumping Thea lightly with his shoulder.

"**Anywhere But Here,**" Thea incants in answer, and all three of them vanish, leaving us alone with the corpses.

And, somewhere deeper in, my girlfriend who made them.

"Hey, so like... the person who made this is your friend, right?" Helen asks as she and Kagiso enter the house. "Could you give me the rundown on her spell?"

"Uh, yeah," I confirm. "She's... Barrier and Pneuma? So I guess she makes a big house out of her soul somehow. The walls are all magical, so I can't cut them with my spells."

"Hmm... I *might* be able to," Helen muses. "But we probably shouldn't try. Barrier and Pneuma combos tend to be the sort that backfire if broken. Y'know, if your own mind is the substance your wall is made out of, and then your wall breaks..."

"Oh gosh, yeah, let's not do that," I agree. "I do *not* know why there's a giant slam-spikey-walls-together trap here, though. She's never made anything like that before."

"Hmm. She sounded pretty far away," Helen notes. "Do you know the spell's name?"

"Uh, no, I don't think she's ever named it."

Helen carefully steps forward, examining the bloody trap hallway in front of us.

"...Not until now, by the looks of things," she muses.

Ah. Yeah. That could explain it.

"I take it we can't just politely ask her to remove the death traps in our way?" Helen asks.

Oh, right. I mean, it's worth a shot.

"Alma!" I call out. "We're coming to get you!"

"*Don't!*" she insists. "You'll get hurt!"

"Sorry, it's sort of non-negotiable. So is there any chance you could guide us around the traps or shut them off or something?"

"Shut them off?" she says, her throat letting out a humorless laugh. "As if I could *ever* stop hurting people. That's all I *do*, Hannah. Hurt people and get hurt. That's why I have to be alone."

"Okay, well, I think you're having a panic attack and you might feel better about this later, but only if we get you back home and feed you a good meal," I shout back. "So just sit tight and we'll be there soon!"

There's a pause.

"...Please don't," Alma says, so quiet I can barely hear her. "I don't want to fall in love again. I'm so *stupid* when I'm in love."

Oh. That... that hurts. A lot. But I guess if she wants to dump me over the whole 'teleporting her alone to a hostile universe' thing, that's *extremely* fair, honestly. I definitely deserve it.

"Any luck?" Helen asks.

"No," I answer. "I don't think she can control the traps at all. She might be even more stuck than we are."

"Oh, ouch. Okay, then we just have to figure out what triggers them and how to avoid getting squashed," Helen shrugs, limping away from the trap. "Shame the murderbot can't move, a working Steel One Death mage could probably just walk right through this. Hmm... well, how durable is your Order mage friend? I assume she's not a healer, since you had to fuck me up so bad."

I mentally grimace, staring at her mutant dinosaur leg and the way she's *still* trying to put weight on it like she has a heel.

"...She can heal, she just couldn't heal you," I explain. "You've gotta walk on your toes, by the way."

"Huh?" she asks.

"With your new leg," I clarify. "You're walking on it wrong. You have two knees, and pressure goes on the balls of your feet. The leg is... hmm, I don't actually know the word in Middlebranch, but in English it's 'digitigrade.' It'll still be weird while your left leg is normal, but you should get used to walking that way."

"...Oh," staring down at herself again. "Right."

"Did I just hear you say 'digitigrade?'" Ida asks, a smarmy grin on her face. "Did Valerie teach you that word?"

"Uh... yeah, I think so, now that you mention it," I confirm, thinking back.

"Heh heh heh heh," Ida chuckles. "Called it."

Well, I don't know what that's about but I doubt it's important right now.

"Ida, do you think you could be the one to check out the traps?" I ask. "We need to figure out how they're triggered and how to avoid them and stuff."

"Huh," Ida frowns, rubbing her chin. "Okay, sure, I can probably do that. But only on the condition that everybody else has to try to beat me to it. That way I can flex on you."

"...Really?" I ask.

"Yeah, really," she says seriously. "Why, you scared to compete against me? **Come And Have A Go, If You Think You're Hard Enough**."

Oh. Oh! Right, she's *literally* better at doing things if she's competing for it. I quickly explain the plan to everyone, and with us all working together (by competing independently) Ida manages to figure out the trap. It's... time consuming, especially because my spatial sense—which would *normally* be perfect for finding traps hidden in the walls—can't detect Alma's magical soul house at all, leaving me stuck with mundane sight like everyone else. By the time we bypass the first we've already found a second trap just beyond it, this one even harder to deal with because it's not half-open from having corpses embedded in it.

"Stop it," Alma wails. "Just leave me alone!"

"I'm not going to do that," I call back. "Not while you need help."

"Of *course* you fucking won't!" Alma snaps. "You never left me alone. I kept trying to push you away from me but you wouldn't take the fucking *hint*. You got me talking about my books, you took me on a *mall date,* and I *knew* it was a shitty idea, I *knew* it was just going to ruin both our lives, but I didn't think it was going to be *this* bad!"

"Okay, got it," Ida announces. "The pressure plates are here, here, here, and here. Just don't step on those tiles, and we're good."

I quickly translate for everyone, and Kagiso supports Helen as we shuffle carefully across, possible answers to Alma's words churning in my mind.

"Why did you think you were going to ruin both our lives?" I ask.

"Because that's what I fucking *do,* Hannah!" Alma moans. "Do you just not notice how fucked up I am?"

"I... saw a few red flags maybe, sure," I confirm. "But they're the sort of things people need help to work through. And I wanted to help—"

"Don't. I can't *be* helped. And I don't want *you* of all people trying to help me!"

"Okay, stop," Ida orders. "There's another trap here, everyone get looking."

"I fell in love with you so fucking fast," Alma sobs. "It took like, *one day* of having someone actually pay attention to me and actually *care.* I was addicted to you instantly. That's *why* I avoid people, you fucking idiot! I can't stop my stupid brain from doing this. And I can't stop myself from ruining it whenever I do, either. I'm insane, Hannah. I don't even mean Jet, I mean I literally can't stop myself from repeating the same mistakes over and over and over. I don't have self-control. I don't have agency. And I *don't deserve it.*"

"Okay, step where I step," Ida orders.

"Don't say that, Alma!" I cry out. "You're a good person, and—"

"I'M NOT A *FUCKING* PERSON!" Alma screams.

And then, quieter, she continues.

"That's why I let you abuse me."

My mind goes blank, pain and terror clawing away inside my brain. W-what? I...

"It's okay, Hannah," she says. "It's fine, Hannah. Don't worry about it, Hannah. Don't you get it? I had to say those things, because I couldn't lose you. I couldn't stop being *obsessed* with your attention. I'm not *healthy,* Hannah. Stay away from me. I'll just get everyone hurt. At least when I'm alone I only hurt someone who deserves it."

Oh, no. No, no, no, no. What have I done?

"I... I'm definitely starting to feel like I deserve it," I say, utterly horrified. But I'm a fool for being surprised. Twisting Alma's bodily autonomy like that, not to mention bringing her here in the first place... I just. I'm so disgusting.

"See?" Alma says. "I'm still hurting you."

"Hannah, come on," Ida presses. "Keep up. You're the one that has to actually send her home."

"I... but I..."

"Yeah, yeah, you'll traumatize her horribly," Ida gripes. "And she can go complain to her therapist about that *after we get her home.* Come *on.*"

Right. Right, yeah. Okay. Solve the problems I can solve, clean up after my own mess, and then... well, if never seeing her again is best for her, I'll have to live with that.

Alma's horrific trap mansion only gets worse as we head deeper in. Not in the sense that the traps get more numerous and more dangerous, only in the sense that the house gets... well, worse. Manifested in an underground cavern, the cave structure often overlaps the soul house, creating terrain that we have to either avoid or let Helen carefully obliterate a path through. The rooms between the hallways get more elaborate and painful, too. On the wall of one room hangs a giant mural, depicting close to a hundred different copies of Alma viscerally murdering each other to a backdrop of lava and brimstone. Though instead of gore,

Alma's bodies bleed nuts, bolts, and metal scraps. There's nothing inside her but a broken machine. Ida has to yell at me again to get me to stop looking at it, and I barely manage to turn away with a shudder.

When we finally spot Alma, her situation seems similar. Smashed statues of herself lie in pieces around the room, her knuckles bloody and raw. It's unclear if she even notices us; she's just sobbing uncontrollably in the middle of the room, hands over her face. Ida keeps her eyes out for traps as we approach, but the room itself seems safe.

"I'm sorry," Alma chokes quietly. "I'm so stupid. I shouldn't have said any of that. I'm sorry. I'm so sorry."

Ida groans, shoving her gun back underneath her jacket as she approaches.

"Stand up," she orders.

"What?" Alma asks, stiffening as she turns to stare at her. "Ida?"

"I said *stand up,*" Ida repeats, holding out her hand."Quit wasting my fucking time."

Alma flinches, looking like she's about to panic even harder, but she still shakily reaches out to take Ida's hand and lets herself be dragged to her feet.

"Sorry," Alma mutters again.

"Why do you keep fucking saying that," Ida asks, "if you don't even want to be forgiven?"

Alma says nothing, and Ida pushes her lightly towards us, guiding her and forcing her to rejoin the team. Hesitantly, I scuttle forwards, trying to psyche myself up for a dimensional travel spell.

"Woah there, Hannah," Ida grunts. "As much as I'd love to yeet her ass to another dimension, your spell to do that makes you pass out, which might really fuck us over considering the bad guys know where we are. Worse, *Alma's* spell doesn't end until she walks out her own front door, right? So what happens if it's still active when she ends up at Valerie's place?"

"...They both get trapped in a magical death castle," I realize. "Right."

"Yeah. So let's get her out of here, set up a safe, defensible camp somewhere, and *then* send her home. That work for you, Alma?"

Alma just shrugs helplessly, seeming completely drained.

"Good enough for me," Ida grunts, and forces Alma forward again. "You step where I tell you to step. Try to hurt yourself and I will *not* be happy."

I hate how Ida is treating her, but who am I to talk anymore? And it certainly *works,* it gets Alma through the traps without any incident, and before I know it we're back in the cave, Alma's mind palace disappearing behind us. Alma shudders, her tail starting to twitch again, twisting around to snarl breathlessly at us.

"There you go, that wasn't hard, right?" Ida asks, pulling an energy bar and a small canteen of water out of some of her many pockets. "Eat and drink now. Can you do that while you walk?"

"Yeah," Alma confirms, taking the items.

"Good," Ida nods. "Hannah, could you ask your extradimensional friends if they know any good places to make camp around here?"

"Ida wants to know if you guys know anywhere we could safely camp nearby," I repeat for her.

Helen staggers towards us a bit, still struggling with walking on her toes with just one leg. She and Alma glance at each other, and then Alma glances down to *me,* as if actually recognizing my tiny spider-body for the first time. Helen claps Alma on the shoulder, giving her a small, lopsided smile before addressing the rest of us.

"...Normally, I'd hide in a cavern just like this one," Helen answers. "But considering how close we are to enemy territory, we'd better head back to the surface and find a different one."

I translate that for Ida and she nods.

"Alright, let's get going, then."

We carefully backtrack through the caverns, on constant lookout for ambushes at every corner. None arrive. The cult seems to have fled to lick its wounds but that's no reason to drop our guard. Helen, Ida and I may have torn through most of their fighters like tissue paper, but that might just mean they're going to be all the more ruthless when they eventually come for revenge.

I stay silent for the trip, hanging around Kagiso mostly just to keep my distance from Alma. I keep watch on her, though, my anxiousness never letting me stop freaking out over how horrible of a person I am. So it's easy to see the subtle yet inevitable changes, now that she's outside the bounds of her spell: her ears start to perk up instead of droop, her steps get surer and more deliberate, her tail stops coiling protectively around her and instead seems to try to stay as far away from her as possible. ...And, of course, she starts looking around in absolute bafflement regarding everything that's going on.

"...What the actual *fuck?*" Jet whispers."Ida, did you get us high?"

"Nope," Ida grunts. "This is real. Sorry."

"...But what's... how... oh. *Oh,* that is a *big* tree."

"Yeah, I've been trying not to look at it," Ida admits. "We've kind of been in a life-or-death situation since the moment we arrived here and I figure if I let myself get enraptured by the scenery I'm gonna end up having a complete fucking breakdown before we're totally safe. And, y'know, can't have that shit."

"Oh, fair enough," Jet nods, peeling her eyes away from the impossible magical planet-tree. "That makes a lot of sense for sure. I definitely feel like I'm gonna have a freakout if I let my mind linger on anything for too long. ...Is that Hannah?"

"Uh, yeah, I'm Hannah," I confirm, waving a forelimb. "Hi. And also sorry."

"This is your fault, then?" Jet asks.

"Like usual, yeah," I confirm.

"Heh. Yeah, like fucking usual," Jet agrees. "Can we get back?"

"Yeah," I confirm. "Or, uh, at least I'm pretty sure I can send you back."

"How reassuring," she deadpans. "What day is it?"

"On Earth?" I ask. "Sunday."

"Mother*fucker,*" Jet swears."Two weeks in a row! Two weeks in a row she skips my day and now I wake up in a goddamn fantasy land."

"Goddess," I whisper. Could I even avoid correcting people if I tried?

"So I assume *that's* Kagiso," Jet says, pointing at the dentron. "Which would make the weird broken android skeleton Sela, and the... half-raptor woman Helen? Did you seriously fuck up somebody else, Hannah?"

"...She was bleeding out and I had no other way to save her," I mumble in halfhearted protest.

"Awesome! Well. I... do not know how to react to any of this, honestly."

"Stretch your wings and get used to it?" Ida suggests. "We're probably going to be walking for a while."

"...I think I prefer the wings bound up," Jet frowns.

"Suit yourself, but now's probably the best time to stretch them. Fantasy land doesn't exactly raise an eyebrow at magic bullshit."

"I guess that's a point," Jet agrees. "Is that a gun you're holding, by the way? Where did you get a gun?"

"Are you kidding?" Ida asks. "My dad's a rich southern republican. We have *tons* of guns. He nearly died of joy when I asked him to take me to a shooting range."

"Oh right, money. Have you had to use it? The gun, I mean."

"Jet, I've killed like *fifteen people* today," Ida snaps. "We had to rescue Hannah from torture cultists and *your dumbass headmate* from *herself.* It's *great* to see you again, seriously, but could you quit jabbering and just walk for a bit?"

"...Oh," Jet says quietly. "Yeah, uh, can do."

We descend into silence after that, and an hour or two later we find another hole in the surface of the Pillar that Helen thinks

533

will serve as a good campsite. It's not a deep, complex cave system like the place Alma ran off to, but it provides good cover in every direction, only has one way in or out, and is easy to keep watch from. Pretty much perfect for people on the run.

We do not, unfortunately, have much in the way of supplies. Our backpacks, camping equipment, dried food, and pretty much everything else we were traveling with is still somewhere in the cultists' crumbling base, or possibly just gone altogether.

Thankfully, Ida brought enough energy bars to feed a small army, and I can hunt the collection of small bugs that skitter around the surface of the pillar, munching on lichen and stonerot. We set up as best we can, but we barely have enough extra clothing to help Helen cover up, and even that is just Jet lending Helen her sweater.

Still, we'll make do. We made it out of that horrible, horrible place, and that's what matters.

"Thanks again, Ida," I tell her as she strips off her outer jacket and bunches it up into a pillow. "Y'know, you don't have to get ready to sleep. I might only be able to transport one person at a time, but if you just wake me up after I pass out transporting Autumn, I'll be able to transport you, too."

"Mmm. You sure about that?" Ida asks. "Would the Goddess put a limit on the number of people you can transport at once and then let you get away with such an obvious workaround?"

"...Huh," I frown. "I'm not sure. Maybe?"

"Well, you can experiment with someone else on your 'maybe,'" Ida grunts. "I'd rather sleep on rocks for a night."

"I guess that's a good point," I admit.

"Of course it's a good point," Ida smirks. "I'm perfect, remember?"

I open my mouth to warn her about arrogance, but I find that the words don't come. Instead, I can only think back on the day, on all the ways Ida risked her life to save mine. And even further back than that, the little ways she helped me all throughout this hellish shift in my life. How can I criticize her after everything she's done? I'd be dead without her.

"Yeah," I agree. "You really are, Ida."

Her smile... actually drops a little. Smushing her makeshift pillow into place one last time, Ida stands up with a stretch.

"Do you mind if I have a chat with you, Hannah?" she asks. "In private?"

"Uh, no," I tell her. "Of course not."

Ida nods, walking up the path into our little cave and back towards the surface, where Kagiso is currently keeping watch. Ida uses a series of hand signals to ask Kagiso to head back and let us keep watch instead, to which Kagiso simply shrugs and departs. Finding a decently-sized rock, Ida hops up on it and sits down, staring silently up at the impossibly massive world tree. She's quiet for a long, long time before she finally speaks, but after today it's hard to mind the silence.

"...Do you know why I love you, Hannah?" she asks.

"Buh?" I respond with my usual loquaciousness, absolutely *not* having expected a confession all of a sudden. Or... is it a confession? Is she just—

"Goddess, Hannah, cut the gay disaster shit," Ida groans. "Let me rephrase for your pathetic alloromantic mind: do you know why you're my *best friend?* Even though, yes, I'm aware that I am not *your* best friend. That title is Valerie's until you finally nut up and date her."

"...What?" I manage.

"I'm asking you a *question,* Hannah," Ida scowls. "Answer it."

"I... no," I say. "I mean, no, I don't know why you consider me your best friend."

I certainly haven't done anything to deserve it.

"Thought not," Ida sighs. "It's a lot of things, really. Like yeah, you've got your giant pile of flaws, but we... mesh, I guess. Your flaws are things that don't bother me much, and your strengths

535

are things I really respect. I mean, that's how any relationship works, I guess. But I guess I care about you most because you're the only person who really *gets* me, and still likes me anyway."

"I... I'm not sure I understand," I admit. "You're like, one of the most popular girls at school."

"Oh woo-ee, I'm one of 'the most popular girls at school,'" Ida repeats mockingly. "Hannah, that doesn't fucking *matter*. You *know* that doesn't matter, that's one of the things I like about you. You don't give a *fuck* about being popular. You do your shit and you walk right through anyone trying to stop you without even remembering their damn name. It's fucking hot, honestly."

"Um," I manage.

"But to actually address your objection, yes, I am popular. Lots of people like me. But none of them *know* me. Conversely, of the people who *know* me, none of them actually *like* me. Like Valerie! She knows what I'm about, and she fucking hates my guts. Because like, *yeah*, why wouldn't you hate a narcissistic, manipulative rich girl who gets her rocks off on fucking with people's lives and pretending that's okay? That is what any sane person who's actually smart enough to see through my layers of bullshit and charisma would think. And since anyone who *isn't* smart enough to do that isn't worthy of my respect... well, I'm kinda stuck without any peers, aren't I? Except, of course, for you."

I'm starting to feel like this day has been a little too much all at once. I can *feel* my brain shutting down as I try to absorb all of that, most of my thoughts summing themselves up as 'why me?' or 'that can't be right.' But I guess it would disrespect my friend to dismiss her like that. Still...

"I... don't feel like I understand you," I admit.

"Oh yeah?" Ida asks. "How would you describe me, exactly?"

"As a fae that replaced an actual human child at birth," I answer without hesitation. Ida laughs.

"I like that," Ida chuckles. "Always have. And I guess fae are often portrayed as incomprehensible, but... so are 4D eldritch freaks of nature, monster girl. You know me. You know I'm full of shit."

"Uh... sometimes you go too far, I guess," I admit. "But that's just how you are. You hold other people to the same absurdly high standards you hold yourself. But a lot of people do that."

"See?" Ida says. "There it is. No pedestal, but no judgment. Do you know how *rare* that is?"

"Uh, I'm a *super* judgemental person, Ida," I protest.

"But not to your friends," she protests. "I mean, look at you! You're literally running around with a group of mad murderers, one of which you've described as actively genocidal. And then you *defended it!* I just... do you realize how crazy you are? I love it. I fucking *love* it!"

She grins, passionate and joyful.

"I killed fifteen people today," she says, half conspiratorial and half... like she's bragging?

"Hey," I warn her. "Don't get comfortable about that. Don't downplay it. It shouldn't be something that's easy."

Ida grins wider.

"You're absolutely right," she tells me. "See? I need help, too."

She hops off the rock, reaching down to pick me up and lift me to eye level.

"So don't you fucking *ever* let me catch you saying I'm perfect again, you hear me?" Ida demands. "You'd better criticize me. You'd *better* speak your goddamn mind. 'Perfect' is *exactly* what I want to hear you say, but it sure as hell isn't what I need to hear. Not from the one person I actually listen to. You get me?"

I take a deep breath, reaching out with my weird little slowly-changing bug limbs to wrap her into a hug. She brings me in closer, and I just squeeze her for a little while before I let go.

"Okay," I promise. "I get you."

"Good," Ida says, and then she lobs me underhand back towards the camp. I squawk and flail in the air for a bit before landing with a thump. "Now go send Autumn back to our world. I'll keep watch."

"Fine," I grumble. "Jerk."

She cackles, and I start to head back.

"Hey, Hannah," Ida asks. "How many people would you kill for me? Like, if you had to."

I pause.

"Uh... I'm not sure I can put a number to something like that," I answer.

"But more than zero?" she presses.

"Oh, I mean... yeah, I guess so," I confirm. "Definitely more than zero. I've killed a lot more for people I've liked a lot less. Which... wow, that's a really fucked up thing to be able to say."

"Heh, yeah," Ida agrees. "I'm gonna be so traumatized because of today."

"...Sorry," I mumble.

"I know you are, Hannah," Ida answers. "And I forgive you. I'd do it all again in a heartbeat."

Gosh. That's... for some reason, that hurts to hear.

"Just don't die for me, okay?" I ask her.

"Eh, nah, I won't die for you," Ida assures me. "But I'll fucking live for you, Hannah. If you need me to."

I can't say anything to that. Any words I think of just feel cheap. So I crawl back to camp alone, my heart racing with confusion.

It's time to head back to Earth. I hope it's not a mistake to leave Ida behind.

25

FACE TO FACE

I find Jet sitting alone on the ground, staring at the rest of the camp with a mix of awkwardness and paranoia as her tail flops mournfully behind her. She stiffens as I scuttle up closer to her, her usual cool persona having thoroughly shattered under the weight of an alien sky. She has, to my surprise, taken Ida's advice and ripped her shirt to let her wings out, wrapping them over her arms which are, in turn, wrapped around her knees. They're a lot larger now, an odd, almost pterodactyl-like wing structure made of skin instead of feathers, but without the bat-style fingers threaded throughout. Her clawed toes peek out from underneath the blanket of wings, curled in anxiety. I'd almost think she was Alma, if not for her intense alertness and upturned ears.

"Hey," I greet her softly, scuttling up carefully so as to not spook her. "Ready to go?"

"Uh," she stammers. "N-no, honestly? Not really? I think I'm too freaked out by this place to be comfortable leaving it right now, if that makes any sense."

Hmm. It doesn't at first, but spend a moment looking around, taking in the dim green glow of the sun's light reflecting off the bottom of the leaves at night, the omnipresent trunk of the world tree, stretching out beyond sight, and the aliens in the ramshackle camp around us. It's terrifying, it's beautiful, and it is so, *so* much to get a handle on. I only managed because the only times I had the luxury to think too hard about it were the times I was desperately recovering from something horrible happening on Earth.

"It makes sense," I ultimately agree. "Can I help in some way? Explain things? Clean you up a little?"

"Clean?" she says. "Oh. Uh. Y'know what, sure, I might feel better if I feel a little less disgusting."

I nod and cast a quick Refresh on her, pulling all the dirt, grime, and sweat off her body in one easy sweep. Unexpectedly, she *flinches,* pulling back with a terrified look on her face and hugging her arms to her chest.

"Did you just...?"

"Did I what?" I ask, suddenly terrified. "I... I'm sorry, what's wrong? I just cleaned you. Sweat and dirt and stuff?"

"Off of *everywhere* on my body?" she accuses.

"Y-yes?" I stammer. "I'm sorry, did it feel weird or something? No one's ever complained about it before, I just... y'know, cleaning everything is usually how people get clean? I didn't think about it. I'm sorry. Uh. What... what did I do wrong?"

Jet blinks, lets out a shuddering breath, and shakes her head.

"...Nothing, never mind," she sighs. "That makes perfect sense, I'm just... *really* on edge right now. This is insane, you know? We're in another world. There's a fucking *alien* walking around over there. And a robot! And you're some kind of horrific giant bug! And there's a... a half-raptor! That one is your fault but it's still insane!"

"Is it more or less insane than the fact that humans apparently evolved here independently?" I wonder.

"Not really the point, Hannah!" Jet insists.

"Right. Sorry. Uh. Yeah, it's... it's pretty crazy. I guess I've kind of gotten used to it over the past... gosh, I genuinely have no idea how long it's been? A month? Ish? Maybe? Maybe longer? Oh geez, I actually just have no idea. Time's kinda funky when you don't really sleep."

"Oh, yeah, I guess so," Jet says, staring up at the trunk. "How... how is it so big? Like, physically, how is it possible?"

"Mmm. Subtly different laws of physics, is my guess," I answer. "Either that or something about it being fourth-dimensional. World tree wood is pretty much the only thing I can stand on when I head that way."

"'Subtly different laws of physics,' huh? Is that your fancy way of saying 'magic?'"

"No," I tell her firmly. "The Goddess is not a creator, just... a meddler. This place existed before Her. If it had anything like magic at the time, it wasn't the magic we know."

That's what She told me, anyway. She didn't make the anthill. She *found* it.

"Really?" Jet asks, looking up. "It's hard to imagine anything like this existing without the supernatural."

"Well, that's what humans used to think about Earth, right?" I muse. "I guess most of them still do. But there's also another explanation, and that's just... well, the Goddess didn't make this from scratch, but I don't how long She's been here, influencing things. It could be that the tree was a lot different, before She arrived. Besides all the bits about it being uprooted and on fire and impaled and stuff, anyway. I guess I could ask Her, but I'm a little too overwhelmed to try inviting a divine revelation right now."

Jet doesn't respond, busy just staring up at the world.

"Sorry," I say. "I guess that's not very helpful."

"It's not... *unhelpful,*" Jet hedges."I guess I'm just only starting to come to terms with the shit you're dealing with. The shit you've wrapped us in. It's even more than I ever imagined."

"Oh," I mutter. "Sorry. If it makes you feel any better, you might be rid of me soon. She was raving about how much she hated being in love with me when I found her. And like... yeah. Fair."

"Mmm," Jet grunts, spreading her wings. "A little too late, don't you think? We're tied to you whether we like it or not. You've scarred our lives permanently, Hannah."

"Yeah," I agree. "And I'm not sure whether it's better for me to try to make up for that, or try to just avoid you. I don't know which would help you more."

Jet raises her eyebrows a little, considering me.

"...Well, it's good you know those are both potential options," she muses. "Unfortunately, I'm under the distinct impression that you don't really *get* any of what Alma was telling you. You don't understand how... *obsessed* she becomes. How *hard* it is for us to break away from anyone. She's got a whole host of problems beyond just me, you know."

"...Yeah," I agree. "I know, but I don't know. I see the flags, but not what they're planted in. I've been a truly awful girlfriend."

"Well, if it's any consolation I'm pretty sure Alma has been an awful girlfriend, too," Jet sighs. "It's not *entirely* your fault that you don't magically understand someone who's terrible at communicating. I *did* try to warn you, though. It's not the first time she's gotten obsessed with someone like this, and unfortunately there's no way it'll be the last."

"I just thought I could be patient and keep an open mind and we'd be able to work through things when she was ready," I say miserably. "When she started screaming at me and saying all those terrifying things, I just... I mean, I thought it was about the whole 'teleporting her to a horrible magic murder world' thing, right? Because like, yeah, of course someone would hate me for that. I keep hurting her on accident over and over and I let myself believe it was fine because she *said* it was fine and like, isn't that a good reason? Trusting your partner when they communicate their emotions is supposed to be the healthy and good thing to do, right?"

"Yeah, it is," Jet shrugs. "But sometimes people aren't acting very healthy. Sometimes they lie. Sometimes they're hurt. Sometimes they lash out. Sometimes they just can't be the person they want to be. We are traumatized as *fuck,* Hannah. Some pretty sick shit happened to us. I'm not saying it's your fault for not understanding what Alma was going through. You didn't give her her mental disorders. I'm just saying it's your fault for putting us through everything you *did* cause."

"Yeah, that's fair," I sigh. "Alma said she doesn't even think of herself as a person. I wish I knew what to do about it. If I just knew how to help, I'd do it in an instant."

"Yeah," Jet sighs. "I wish I knew how you could help, too. I guess this problem might be a little bigger than just you, me, and Alma, though."

She stands up, stretching her wings hard enough that they shake a little.

"I don't really think I'm a person either, to be honest," Jet admits. "A person is supposed to be like... a complete entity. Someone with passions, hatreds, desires, struggles... a whole complex inner world teeming with *potential.* A person is supposed to work a job and live a life and have other people that they care for. And that just seems... way beyond my level, you know? I have so much difficulty just keeping Alma and I *alive* I can't even imagine taking on the responsibilities of a functioning member of society."

She shrugs.

"I guess when I look at people, the idea of being like them, of having the *capacity* to live up to what it means to be like them... it seems completely impossible. And that impossibility is *terrifying.* Better to just reject it than to crack my skull open beating my head against a wall that won't break. I think Alma feels the same way. It's just how our brain works. It can't look at a person and go 'yes, I am in the same category of thing.' Not after how much we've been hurt. Everyone else is just... too far away."

"Oh," I manage quietly. "I... I don't know what to say."

"You don't gotta say anything," Jet shrugs. "It is what it is. I am what I am. I don't *long* for personhood, I just don't vibe with it.

Alma's a lot more torn up about the whole thing than I am, you can refer to me as a person and I won't argue with you about it."

"Um, okay," I nod, bobbing my whole body up and down. "Noted, I suppose."

Jet sighs again, giving her wings an experimental flap.

"...Gosh, you're such a weird little creature right now," she comments. "I honestly kind of feel crazy for talking to you. But like, in sort of a good way? You're fuckin' tiny, so it's like talking to a pet."

"Um, thanks, I think?" I manage to answer.

"Honestly the magic bullshit you're using to ruin our life is kind of annoying in large part because you'd be downright tolerable without it," Jet scowls. "Alma could *use* a friend, girlfriend or otherwise, and... fuck, I guess I could use one too. Being completely alone for so long has... probably just made our mental health even worse. I just wish it didn't have to be *you*."

"Um, I mean, it doesn't really?" I shrug. "I, uh. Y'know, I'm willing to try to make up for things, but I understand if... my lack of self-control makes that untenable. There's Ida, though! Or Valerie."

"Who the fuck is Valerie?" Jet asks.

...Huh? Oh, right. Only Alma knows. Because I screwed up *again*. Crap. I don't really want to call her Brendan again, though, so I'm not sure what to say.

"Uh... never mind," I mumble. "My point is just that you aren't alone. I know you've had a terrible time getting people to understand you and Alma, but I think you can trust my other friends, even if you can't trust me. Or... or you could find other people completely! Good people exist in the world. I don't... want to tie you to me. I'm only really just starting to understand the depths to which I hurt you, but... I *am* starting to get it. And you're right to leave."

"...Yeah," Jet sighs. "If only I could. Doesn't work that way, though. I give it even odds that Alma will still be obsessed with you, even after her breakdown. And I just can't do *anything* that actually matters for our life without her coordination, which means I can't do anything *period* because she won't fucking coordinate! I'm probably stuck with you, and honestly I kind of suspect that's the best option I have *anyway,* because you've already fucked us up in such impossible ways that the prospect of risking Alma latching onto someone *worse* in what will probably end up as a world of magic is significantly more terrifying. I just... I *hate* this. I wish I knew what was going on from more than context clues. I wish I could just fucking *talk* to her for once!"

Jet raises her voice at the end, stomping the ground in an uncharacteristic display of unbridled emotion. And I feel... something. I mean, I'm feeling a lot of things right now, but what stands out to me is an unexpected tickle of intuition, a realization about the personalities of the major players here. Alma wants to shut Jet out. She got a spell for that, because it's dramatic and horrifying and most of all it's true to who she is. Jet wants to talk to Alma. And that, too, would be quite the sight to see.

"...At the risk of saying something that might ruin your life somehow," I volunteer quietly, "I think you probably can."

Jet blinks at me, dumbfounded. Light and Pneuma. I can *see* how the spell would work, it just makes perfect sense for her.

"Are you serious?" she asks me.

"Yeah," I confirm. "It's exactly the sort of spell the Goddess would give you. If you look for a way, I think you'll find it."

In moments, her demeanor changes. Her awe of the world tree has vanished, her aloof disdain for me replaced by interest, by *need*, desperate and all-consuming. She approaches me, kneels down to my level, stares at me directly. It's such an instantaneous change that I'm terrified I've ruined the one good thing about our relationship: that she knows she should hate me.

"How do I look for it?" she asks.

The Goddess says She loves us. But I wonder, fearfully, what that *means* to Her. I'm certainly not an expert, but I have seen no evidence of what I consider love. Even Her so-called gifts are full of poison, twisting something that should be beautiful to us into something horrible. Should I have said nothing? How, exactly, is this going to go wrong?

"Reach for what you want," I tell Jet anyway. "Yearn for it. If you feel something in response, focus on that feeling, and what it tells you that you need. Your soul is designed for you. You can understand what it tells you."

I just know these things sometimes. Because I know *Her.* Because She shows me Herself, She whispers Her secrets to me. No matter how much I hate Her, I will always be Her prophet.

Jet does as instructed, closing her eyes and focusing inward. Her face is impassive at first, but then it twists into a frown, her expression twitching.

"I can't," Jet eventually says, her eyes still closed.

"Why?" I ask.

"I don't have enough power."

Oh. Hmm. I wonder how many spells are like that? Sindri taught me that all magic should be used extensively before naming it, and while I'm extremely suspicious of anything Sindri told me for obvious reasons, it definitely makes sense to fear the miscast. Still... spells that need names in order to be used at all seem to be unusually common among me and my friends. I should ask around to see if that's normal.

"That means you need to name it," I tell Jet out loud.

"Isn't that the thing you said I absolutely shouldn't do because it might kill me?" she asks.

"Yep," I confirm. "It's a really dangerous thing to do. I do it anyway because I can heal myself and I'm the Goddess' favorite—"

The Goddess coos and squeezes me tightly, impossible limbs and uncountable hands stroking all over my body as She confirms that, yes, yes I am. I shudder and continue.

546

"...But you don't have the same lifelines, unless you're comfortable risking me healing you with another dose of the spell that transformed you."

"Hmm," Jet scowls. "I can't say I love the idea, though it's worth asking in case of emergency: how badly would it fuck me up?"

"I can't answer that for certain," I tell her. "I don't have conscious control over exactly what changes happen to you; it's based on my subconscious impressions, desires, and assumptions. But I *suspect* that relatively little would happen to you, beyond your current changes finishing their growth. You feel... almost complete."

"Well that sounded kind of creepy, but also kind of reassuring?" Jet hedges. "I guess you have tentative permission to zap me if and only if you have legitimate reason to believe I'll die if you don't."

"Noted," I nod. "I should have more control over my spell now that I understand it, too. Uh, y'know, for what it's worth."

"The fact that you so openly and consistently acknowledge the horrible things you've done to us certainly makes you the most *endearing* abuser we've ever had to deal with," Jet says, actually... smiling a little? "But the constant self-flagellation is also a little grating. It almost makes me believe you might actually get better, and that's not something I ever want to believe again."

Oh.

"Anyway, I need a name for the spell, huh?" Jet says, my brain grinding as she shifts the conversation topic without a clutch. "What sort of names will work best?"

Ah. Gonna do it despite the danger, huh? Well, I'd be a hypocrite to blame her for that.

"Well, it has to accurately represent the spell in some way, so that its function can at least be *vaguely* implied," I explain. "A theme behind the name is helpful, but super optional. Might still be worth thinking about what you plan to name your other spell too,

547

though. And, uh... well, something dramatic, interesting, or extremely personal to you is recommended as well. She doesn't like boring names. She wants a name that makes you *feel* something to say. Something that matches with the spell, but also with some core part of you. Oh and uh, you can make the spell stronger by making the incantation longer, but only if it's interesting."

Jet nods, contemplating in silence. Chewing on her words. I wait patiently, knowing better than to suggest we head back to Earth *before* she's done summoning the Goddess all over the place and maybe having something terrible happen to her. But before long, she opens her mouth, and the Goddess growls the words that Jet needed to say most.

"I'm Not Going To Let You Screw This Up Anymore."

Motes of light flicker on around Jet's body, glimmering a soft yellow-white. They multiply, becoming more and more numerous until before long they cover her completely, their colors shifting. A million pixels combine to form a single image: a copy of Jet, one that splits off from her body, separating like the petals of a flower. Jet's tail droops, going limp. Just like Alma's when she's in her house.

The motes of light that have become Alma seem to wake up, ears drooping like I'm used to. She seems to be nothing but light; my spatial sense doesn't detect her at all, and she seems to have no physical presence. Nonetheless, my eyes watch her wake up, her twitchy movements and nervous exactly like the Alma I know. She looks down at herself in confusion, then looks up... and the moment she spots Jet, an expression of unrestrained panic appears on her face immediately.

"No," she whispers.

"...Alma," Jet says quietly. "It's good to meet you face-to-face."

"NO!" Alma shrieks, lunging at Jet's throat. Her illusory hands pass right through her headmate, though, causing Alma to stumble past and somehow turn around looking even *more* terrified. "GIVE ME MY BODY BACK!"

"I will," Jet scowls, crossing her arms. "*I'm* not the one trying to kill *you,* remember? But first, we're going to have a fucking conversation for once."

"Fuck you," Alma hisses. "Fuck you, fuck you, fuck you! What have you *done* to me? I can't feel anything, I can't—"

"*Shut up!*" Jet snaps."You don't get to complain, not after all the time you took from me! Look at me, Alma."

She doesn't. Alma floats helplessly in the air, curled up slightly like a terrified animal. Her eyes point towards the ground.

"That's not my name," Alma whispers. "I'm *Autumn.* But you had to take that from me, too."

"*We're* Autumn," Jet growls. "It's my name as much as yours."

Alma says nothing.

"Stop pretending I don't exist," Jet demands.

Alma says nothing.

"Fucking *look at me!*" Jet shouts, and Alma flinches. By now the whole camp is up and staring, though no one can understand any of it except for Ida. Helen clears her throat.

"...Is she okay?" she asks me quietly.

"Uh, not sure about *okay,*" I hedge."But I think this has been a long time coming. It's probably good that she's doing this."

"Okay, uh, well we're still on the lookout for people that might be wanting to kill us, so could you ask her to keep her voice down?"

"Oh, uh, yeah," I agree awkwardly. "Hey, Jet? Alma? Helen wants you to keep your voices down, since we're still on the run from cultists and all."

They both snap their heads over to look at me, causing me to shrink down under their glares.

"...And she's the first thing we need to talk about," Jet insists, jerking her thumb at me.

"What is there to discuss?" Alma answers stubbornly.

"She told me you said a lot of things," Jet says. "But have you finally, actually dumped her ass?"

Alma scowls, her expression full of horrid, bitter hatred. It's ugly on what is usually such a beautiful face.

"What does it matter to you, anyway?" Alma asks. "She's *my* girlfriend. Not yours. You don't get a say in what I do with my relationships. With my life. With *my* body!"

Jet stomps around her, forcefully placing herself in Alma's line of sight, even leaning over to glare at her downturned expression face-to-face.

"Yes I *absolutely fucking do*," Jet hisses at her."I'm just as real as you are."

"So everybody tells me."

"*No!* You *know* it. We've co-fronted. You feel me every time we swap. You *know* me, and I'm on your goddamn side! Just *let me help!*"

"I don't want your help!" Alma snaps. "I don't want you in my life!"

"Well *tough shit!*" Jet counters."I don't wanna clean up after your fucking messes either, but I'm stuck with you and you're stuck with me. So if you'd just put a *single iota* of effort into making our situation more tolerable, I'd really fucking appreciate that! Do you have any idea how much I work my ass off for you?"

"Yeah, I get it," Alma confirms bitterly. "You're the competent one. The good one. The one who can actually set their mind to things and *do them*. I'm the useless fuckup that you have to clean up after. I *know*. Why do you think I hate you so much?"

Jet blinks, working her jaw as she digests an unexpected turn to the conversation.

"...Well, I assumed it was the body autonomy stuff," she admits.

"I mean, yeah, I *definitely* hate that too," Alma confirms. "I shouldn't *need* you to handle things for me. I should be a functional human being on my own, but I don't even get a chance to try. Because you're always... you're always *there*. I don't even get a *chance* to solve most of my problems."

She lets out an approximation of a shuddering breath, though the air and dust around her doesn't shift at all.

"...Not that I'd accomplish anything," she mutters. "I know that. I'm way too broken to ever get better."

"I don't believe that," Jet insists. "You don't have to resign yourself to the same mistakes forever. You're not *stupid*, Alma. You know exactly what you need to do."

"Oh yeah, I know *exactly* what I need to do," Alma mocks. "It's that easy, is it? Just know what to do and do it? What I wouldn't give to live in a utopia like that, where I don't have to put up with my brain constantly *screaming* at me about every little thing, second-guessing any possible decision, hating itself at every waking moment! I *get* it, Jet! You're better than me! Now *fuck off!*"

Jet sighs.

"Alma... that's not what this is about," she pleads. "I just... we can't go on living half of each other's lives without any communication! We need to work *together.*"

"And that's why you think you get a say in my love life, huh?" Alma scowls.

"You know *damn* well that's not the only reason."

Alma cringes like she accidentally stepped in something foul, curling in more on herself.

"...I never wanted to actually speak to you," she says quietly.

"Yeah, I've sort of picked up on that over the years," Jet scowls.

"I don't want to rely on you," Alma continues. "I don't want to even *think* about you. I just want you to go away and never come back."

"You want to kill me," Jet says bluntly.

Alma nods guiltily.

"Yes. It's easier to wish for the death of someone you don't know."

"Not in my experience," Jet counters. "I've only ever wanted to kill people we know very well."

Alma looks up at Jet and stares into her eyes for a moment, the cold seriousness in her gaze meaning something to Alma that I can't parse. I feel like an interloper in this entire conversation, an awkward presence that should not be here but doesn't know how to politely leave. Even if I walk away, I'd hear them, and I think Jet actually *wants* me here so she can pressure Alma into breaking up with me. Which... I'm not exactly sure what to think about. I guess it's probably for the best.

"Well, this is it, then," Alma says glumly. "I'm talking to you. I'm looking at you. You're a person. I get it. What now?"

"Now, we agree on a course of action," Jet says firmly. "About Hannah, about magic, about our body, about... everything."

"I feel like that's going to take a while," Alma grumbles.

"Well," Jet says, gesturing outwards and sitting down, "I've got all night."

Alma grimaces, floating down to also 'sit' on the ground, though her body clips through a few rocks without her even noticing.

"...I think Hannah is going to do better," Alma says.

"And I've heard that one before," Jet counters, crossing her arms.

"Yeah, but Hannah is *actually* contrite. You wrote about that once, didn't you? You agreed, you thought she was sorry, unlike... the last ones."

I quietly fidget, the awkwardness of being here only increasing.

"Plus, the worst thing she did is mutate our body," Alma continues, "and that's pretty much over and done with. And hey, maybe we'll get to fly!"

"Setting aside what we like and don't like *about* our new body, the problem is the fact that it was forced onto us in the first place," Jet grunts. "She didn't get consent to change us. I *assume*

552

she didn't get consent to send us to another universe. What's the next spell she casts and doesn't get consent for, Alma? What's the next *non*-spell action she doesn't get consent for?"

"It's not like that," Alma insists. "The magic fucks with her head, and—"

"How exactly is that a *point in her favor?*" Jet cuts her off."Think, Alma! Think past the chemicals in our brain insisting that you need her at all costs. Is she *actually* good for you?"

Alma wrings her hands together.

"...We have nice dates," she mumbles. "And I like having magic."

"Well you don't have to date her to keep the magic, we're stuck with that either way," Jet points out.

"I just... don't you want someone that cares, Jet?" Alma asks, a bit of desperation in her tone. "I know she's messed up a few times, but she's apologized and she's *really* trying, actually really trying. She knows about us, she *cares* about us, and... and she needs us! We're some of the only people in the whole *world* with magic, we're *special!* And it's all thanks to her. It's... it's like what Dr. Karnataki said, with how a relationship is supposed to uplift both sides. I'm not a *leech* to her, I can actually *help.*"

Jet drums her fingers against her knee.

"...It doesn't matter if she's trying to get better," Jet says softly, "if she's still hurting you right now."

"Well if *that's* true then it doesn't matter if *I* try to get better!" Alma barks back. "Why should I even bother if it *doesn't matter?*"

Jet seems rather unimpressed by this argument.

"Alma, if you and Hannah break up and then both independently get over your issues, I'd have a lot fewer objections to the two of you getting back together again," she says simply. "Short-term issues don't invalidate the need for long-term improvement."

Alma hugs her knees, looking away again.

"...But if I stop getting to see her, I'll stop loving her," she says quietly. "I'll just end up obsessed with someone else instead."

"Well that doesn't really sound like love, does it?" Jet asks.

Alma turns to stare her in the eyes again.

"...It's the closest thing I have, Jet," she says sadly. "And you might believe that I can do better someday, but..."

Her illusory body shudders, and I suspect if it were physical it would be crying tears.

"I don't," Alma finishes. "I don't think I'll ever be anything more than I am right now. And I think if I could even *conceive* of a version of myself that could do the things I can't, I would just hate her the same way I hate you."

Jet stares at her, sucking on the inside of her cheek.

"...Things really are that bad, huh?" she sighs.

"Yep," Alma confirms with a shrug. "Sorry."

"Well, unfortunately for you this changes nothing," Jet insists. "I still believe in you. You've got a therapist, and you've got me, and I *literally* can't afford to give up on you. I'm with you forever, thick and thin, rain and shine. That's just how it is."

Alma almost smirks.

"Sucks to be you, doesn't it?" she says.

"Guess so," Jet answers noncommittally. "Next question, then: are we going to keep swaddling up in winter clothes until we boil ourselves to death, or are we going to face the music and go public?"

"We're going to continue swaddling, obviously," Alma frowns. "Hannah's not public yet and we aren't screwing things up for her."

Oh. Wait. That's not true. I clear my throat, causing the two of them to jump slightly.

"Actually, I did end up sprinting through town in full monster mode to come save you guys," I inform them. "So I'm pretty much already public, and I'm planning on leaning into it from here on. Hiding has been exhausting anyway."

"...Oh," Alma says.

"No kidding," Jet agrees. "Question stands, though. I know neither of us would appreciate the attention of joining her in the spotlight."

"Oh, you know that, do you?" Alma scowls. "The main reason I hate attention is because it means I eventually have to explain *you.*"

"...Alright," Jet nods. "In that case, since we'll be working together, you wanna just stretch our wings?"

"Sure," Alma confirms. "Fine."

"Great, that's one off the docket."

"That's *two* off the docket," Alma scowls.

"Next up: time sharing," Jet continues, ignoring her. "You have a spell that shuts me out. We *definitely* need to talk about that."

"...I'll just stop using it," Alma grumbles.

"Yeah, that's not a solution and we both know it," Jet grunts. "I don't care if you take time for yourself, I care that you basically deleted an entire week of my life, *including* taking the times that we previously agreed were for my activities. I've missed two Saturdays in a row, Alma. This was a problem *before* you got a spell that let you do it as much as you want, too."

...Oh. Saturdays are Jet's. And that's when Alma scheduled our last date. I *knew* she was taking time from Jet and I never even thought to ask!

"Well as previously mentioned, I'm not going to stop being a fuckup," Alma scowls. "You're just going to have to get used to it."

"...I could do that. *Or,* we could take advantage of our ability to actually have conversations now and *plan things out*. If you want to take time to yourself on Saturday, we can be flexible. Hell, depending on what you want to do we might be able to use the spell to give you that time. Even if you can't do much more than see and talk like this, you could still, say, read a book as long as I have a free hand to turn the pages."

"Oh wow, what a fun twist on being forced to become an incorporeal ghost!"

"...Alma, this is *in addition* to your normal fronting time, and it's optional. How is any of this a bad thing for you?"

She winces.

"Yeah, okay, fair," she mutters. "Sorry, I just... this is *really* freaky. Not being able to feel anything or breathe or... I don't know. It's surreal. This whole situation is surreal. I can't believe I'm having a chat with my own body."

"Sorry, wanna run that by me again?" Jet says flatly. "You can't believe you're having a chat with...?"

"Ugh. I can't believe I'm having a chat with my headmate Jet, who is just as real as I am and co-owns *my body*."

"Better," Jet grunts. "You're kind of a bitch though, you know that?"

"Maybe you just bring out the worst side of me," Alma sneers.

"Maybe I *am* the worst side of you," Jet says jokingly. "Nasty criminal ne'er-do-well that I am."

Alma scoffs.

"The term 'ne'er-do-well' means someone who is a lazy good-for-nothing, not someone who does evil. Common etymological mistake."

"Oh right, I forgot my other half is a fucking *book nerd*."

"Better than a workout jock," Alma huffs. "The brain is the *superior* muscle."

Hmm. Uh. The mood suddenly feels different somehow.

"Well, my sincere apologies that this *neanderthal* couldn't figure out a better way to stop us from becoming *homeless* than the ancient and well-respected art of Robin Hooding."

"Okay, *one,* Robin Hood was respected because he stole from the rich and then *gave it away* rather than keeping it, and *two,* neanderthals could make and use tools, communicate with language, and were better adapted to cold environments. We might not have even killed them off on purpose; they could have just as easily gone extinct because their superior bodies required

556

too much food, or because they just liked having sex with humans so much that they forgot to reproduce their own species."

What, um. What is happening?

"You're seriously saying the neanderthals went extinct because they couldn't get enough twinkish human ass?" Jet asks incredulously.

"I'm *saying* that the prevalence of neanderthal DNA in modern humans indicates leads many scientists to believe that interbreeding with humans simply became the more prevalent survival strategy due to environmental conditions, and using 'neanderthal' as an insult is kind of silly considering that most of us partially *are* one. ...But also yeah, neanderthals were short and stocky and buff and we were probably kind of elvish by comparison."

"Twinkish."

"*Elvish.*"

"That's what I said."

"Goddamnit, why are we even talking about this?" Alma asks, though the tiniest, slightest smile is peeking out under her irritation.

"Because I used a magic spell to summon you from the aether to break up with your abusive girlfriend," Jet answers, and the smile drops away as quickly as it came.

"...Right," Alma says flatly.

Well. I think now's my cue. Not necessarily because I *should* be speaking up here, but because I literally can't comprehend what will happen to my brain if this gets any more awkward. I clear my throat.

"Hello," I say meekly, waving a foreleg. "Abusive girlfriend speaking."

"Hannah, no," Alma scowls. "Jet's blowing this *way* out of proportion. A few isolated mistakes don't count as abuse, you've been *great* to me overall."

"Uh… that's not what you said a few hours ago," I remind her.

"Well, don't listen to the Alma from a few hours ago, she was a stupid crazy bitch," Alma snaps, crossing her arms. "Current Alma is the only one who knows what's up."

"See, I'm worried that future Alma might have a few objections about that assessment," I tell her.

"Well, future Alma's a stupid crazy bitch too," Alma insists.

"…Alma, please," Jet sighs.

"I'm serious!"

"Alma, I think Jet is right," I blurt. "I'm not… I'm not safe to be around. I knew that, I've always known that, but I've been dating you anyway because my life has been so horrifically bleak that I just… let myself ignore that for a chance at happiness. But that's not the slightest bit fair to you."

"Shouldn't I be the one that gets to decide what's fair to me?" Alma counters.

"*Is* it fair to you?" I press. "Is it seriously, actually fair, accounting for the brain problems you've made clear that you *do* have and that *do* influence your decision-making? Alma, I yanked you into a deathworld without warning and gave you a day-long panic attack!"

"I mean… it's fine," Alma pouts, looking away. "Nobody got hurt."

"Alma, you killed two people!"

She jolts to attention.

"I *did!?*"

"She did!?" Jet yelps as well.

"Your spell makes invisible murder traps!" I remind her. "Did you not notice the corpses when we were walking out of your house?"

"I, uh… I was pretty out of it," Alma admits awkwardly. "Who did I kill?"

"I don't really know, it was a pair of cultists," I answer, drumming my legs on the ground. "But do you see what I mean? I am *not* making your life better."

"I don't think you understand the sheer degree to which my life was awful before," Alma insists. "You are literally the only person I ever talk to."

"That sounds even *less* healthy," I point out.

"I don't CARE if it's HEALTHY!" Alma snaps. "I will never *be* healthy! Just help me be *happy* for once!"

"Alma," I say softly, "am I even any good at that?"

She stares at me. I stare back. She sighs.

"...What does it even matter?" she mutters. "We're tied to you. Forever. Even if I wanted to leave, where would I go? How could I step out of your life knowing the prophet of an evil god hangs out twelve blocks away? How could I just wordlessly go to school after having visited another *universe?* Who could I reach out to for help with my wings, or my claws, or my ears or my damn awful tail? If I dump you, you won't want to see me again. And I couldn't handle anything on my own *before* you came along and changed everything."

"You're not alone," Jet chimes in. "I told you, Alma. I'm on your side. I always will be. And now that we can actually *talk,* now that we can actually interact together, I can prove it to you."

Alma turns to Jet for a moment, a complicated expression on her face, but ultimately doesn't answer, just turning back to me instead.

"...If you really think our relationship is such a bad idea," she says, "you can always just be the one to dump me yourself."

I sigh. I guess I *could.* It would certainly make things easier, to just make the decision for myself. I'm not sure it'd be the best idea, though. Jet has been pushing Alma to be the one to make the decision for a reason, trying to get her to understand how to deal with what is obviously a long and painful history of abuse. But I'm not really sure if I can or should say any of that.

"I care about you very, very much, Alma," I say instead. "I care about *both* of you. I don't know if it's love—I haven't really known either of you for very long—but it's undeniable that you're both very important people to me. And while I don't mean to hurt you, and I don't want to hurt you, I have hurt you. I acknowledge that, but I agree with Jet that the fact that you *haven't* is terrifying. I want to be your friend, but I don't want to be your enabler. And I *certainly* don't want you to be mine."

A beat of silence passes, Alma's expression completely blank.

"So that's it, then," she says flatly, resignation deep in her words.

"I don't know," I answer. "Is it?"

She sighs, hugging herself. She turns to Jet, and then back to me.

"...Yeah, I guess so," she agrees. "Consider yourself dumped, Hannah."

I bob my body into a nod. It hurts to hear, but that's life.

"I understand," I tell her. "And I'm sorry."

"I know," Alma says glumly. "That was part of the problem. Are we done here, Jet? Not existing doesn't sound so bad right now."

"Yeah," Jet agrees. "I guess we're done here. Talk to you soon?"

"Whatever," Alma mutters. "It's your spell, not mine."

"Okay," Jet nods. "Goodbye for now, Alma."

And then Alma vanishes, once again dispersing into motes of light. Jet's tail twitches once, then curls up, burying what passes for its face into its side.

"Thank you, Hannah," Jet says to me. "It means a lot that you were willing to do that."

Wobble back and forth in my best equivalent of a shrug. I kind of went emotionally numb partway through that conversation, so it hasn't really hit me. I don't... entirely know how to feel about anything right now. How am I *supposed* to feel about a breakup? Bad, right? And I do, I guess, just... not for any of what I assume are the usual reasons. Alma and I certainly never had a normal relationship. I only started dating her after I started mutating, my life already collapsing into a black hole of insanity, and I basically spent the entire time using her as a desperate emotional outlet for... well, whatever emotions I had at the time. My yearning for normality, for some kind of rock of happiness in a storm of despair, only led to me dragging her into the storm alongside me. And while Alma herself seems to have mixed opinions on whether or not it's a journey that should be regretted, the fact of the matter is that I repeatedly put her at risk for selfish reasons. I never even really understood her until the end. I guess I probably still don't understand her now.

"...Are you ready to head back to Earth?" I ask Jet simply. "Remember: speaking your spell around other people will ensoul them permanently."

"I know," Jet promises. "I won't make your mistakes. Let's go."

I huff, but don't protest. It's a jab I deserve. I hold out a forelimb instead, inviting Jet to grab on. She does, and I let the magic that links me between universes flow, pulling her into my soul. She vanishes, and I barely have the time to groggily stagger over next to Kagiso before I pass out and wake up, once again, in Valerie's house.

"Holy shit," Valerie swears, Jet appearing in the room an instant before I wake up. "Alma? *Hannah?* Oh god, you're finally awake!"

"Goddess," I mumble groggily. "How long was I out?"

"And, uh, not Alma, by the way," Jet corrects.

"Oh, sorry," Valerie nods. "You were unconscious for over an hour, Hannah, I couldn't wake you at *all*."

"Mmmn. Longer than last time," I realize. "Ida was right. Prolly have to recharge the spell or something."

"...Where *is* Ida, anyway?" Valerie asks.

"Still in the other world," I answer. "I can only take one person at a time, and we chose Autumn. And I guess we have to figure out how long I need between casts to not zonk out for ages, too."

I slowly get up, pushing against the bed with the flat of my blade-limbs to raise myself into a sitting position with a yawn.

"She's okay, though?" Valerie presses.

"She's alive," I confirm. "Everyone's alive. Uh. Except a whole bunch of cultists, I guess. Did you know Ida brought a gun?"

"I... yes, I did know that," Valerie confirms. "Did you not know that?"

"I was distracted," I answer defensively, standing up and stretching. "So... ugh. It's what, like two o'clock on Sunday still? Bleh, time is getting weird. Anyway, anyone wanna go to Academy with me?"

Jet and Valerie both stare at me in confusion.

"...Y'know, the camping supply store?" I clarify, heading for the stairs. "Academy Sports-plus-Outdoors? The cultists didn't really want to give us our tents back after Helen disintegrated a big hole in their base and turned into a dinosaur."

"What?" Valerie manages, following me up the stairs. "Hannah, what the *fuck* happened!?"

"I'll tell you on the way," I promise her, still stretching my various limbs as I reach for the front door.

"Wait," she presses. "Are you going out like that?"

"Well yeah, why not?" I ask. "Extra limbs will help with carrying everything. We need like... three sleeping bags, at *least* two tents, probably a bunch of food..."

I trail off, trying to think of the best sorts of food to send between dimensions. Earth food might make fantasy people super sick, right? I have to be careful about what all is actually in the stuff. Plus, Kagiso needs fruits and vegetables but Helen's only going to be able to eat meat. Hmm...

"So this is it, then?" Valerie presses. "You're outing yourself for good? No going back?"

I think about everyone who's already seen me, how pointless it would be to try to stop the inevitable now. I think about my mom, and how I'm definitely half-investing myself in this task just to avoid going home. I think about all the people I killed today, realizing that I will very soon start to lose count of everyone who has lost their life because of me. And I shrug.

562

"Going back was never possible in the first place," I say. "I'm not human. And if someone has a problem with that, well... I have bigger things to be afraid of."

Valerie looks me in the eyes, my neck having to crane up as usual to meet her gaze, and she gives me a single, firm nod. I smile. At least she'll always always be in my corner. Heck, she *likes* the creepy body modification stuff.

"I named my transform-other spell, by the way," I tell her. "And you're *definitely* gonna end up with big boobs. No shot you won't. So. Uh. Look forward to that?"

"Oh," she blinks, stepping out of her front door together with me. "Great? Any idea what I'll actually *be?*"

I frown in thought, checking on her organs with my spatial sense. She's got claws, she's got an elongating spine... hmm, thickening, too. What sort of monster would represent my *best friend?*

"I was sort of hoping you'd be excited for it to be a surprise," I admit, "because I have *no idea*. I guess I can always just skip you to the end now, though. The spoken version makes the transformation *way* faster."

"Hmm..." she hums in thought. "...Nah. I honestly like the idea of it shifting little by little. The process is a big part of what makes transformation so interesting."

I chuckle, a bit of the coiled tension hiding at the back of my mind easing thanks to Valerie's *very* Valerie answer. She really is the most important person in the world to me.

...

Hmm.

"...Hey, Val?" I ask softly.

"Yeah?" she prompts.

"Don't *ever* let me get away with hurting you, okay?"

She gives me a serious stare, and a short, firm nod.

"You know I won't."

I smile. I guess I do, don't I?

"Thank you, Valerie."

I spend the rest of the walk to the store telling Valerie about what happened treeside, collecting endless stares along the way. But I don't have to care. With her here, I can ignore every terrible thought, at least for a little while longer.

26

NOTHING MORE TO SAY

This is the first time I've ever willingly entered an outdoor supply store, and I've got to say it's somewhat of a surreal experience. Not because there's anything inherently strange about an outdoor supply store; it is an incredibly boring place, all things considered, and that's why I specified I've never entered one *willingly*. My family shops here semi-frequently, usually when my brother needs sports equipment, and I am occasionally dragged along to experience rows upon endless rows of things I could not possibly give less of a crap about. So the experience of entering this place that has been nothing but a symbol of boredom and unwanted familial obligation for my entire life and actually *needing* something is super, super weird.

And so is the fact that I'm visibly an eight-limbed magical spider monster, I guess. I'm a little anxious about that, too.

I am getting stares from *everywhere*. It's mortifying... but also exciting, an adrenal mix of emotions that makes my body quiver in anticipation. It's mostly positive, I think, the flood of relief from just being able to *do this* more than enough to outweigh the terror, but the terror is absolutely still *there*. I'm keeping Dr. Carson's advice at the forefront of my mind, focusing hard on *never* letting my blades point directly at a person, ensuring their tips are carefully aimed at the floor. I'm weathering the attention as best I can, keeping an eye on anyone looking too intensely in my direction for too long and flashing them reassuring, closed-lipped smiles and nods to activate that natural human instinct which equates polite greetings with safety.

And amazingly, *this actually works.* People are wild like that, most of us being so averse to confrontation that we'll take any excuse to continue minding our own business, no matter how strange the situation. I look like a scary monster, sure, but I also look like a weird human in a very well-made scary monster costume, and that's *way* more believable and ignorable of a situation than the truth. As long as I don't cause a scene, the customers don't care, and as long as I *also* buy things the store doesn't care either.

Obviously, there is the teensy weensy problem of me *not* just being a girl in a cool costume and actually, literally being a man-eating monster, but the monster bit won't be the default assumption for at least a few days and the man-eating bit will hopefully never be public knowledge on Earth at all. I can probably expect crazy zealots trying to shoot me at *some* point, but as long as I remain polite I doubt it's going to be today. People need to actually know I exist before they can attempt any hate crimes, and I can probably avoid being shot in a fit of panic by just avoiding anyone with a gun. Which means my primary problem for this outing is probably going to be a little bit more... mundane.

"...I wish I knew *literally anything* about tents," I mutter to Valerie.

She seems surprised, peeling her eyes away from the displays to give me an incredulous expression.

"Didn't you sleep in a tent, like, *every day* treeside?" she asks.

"Well... yeah, but that didn't mean I learned anything about them!" I protest. "I could never even help set them up or take them down because I'm like a foot tall and don't have hands. Well, I guess I'm like two feet tall now, but my hands are still growing in!"

"Huh," she frowns. "I guess I never thought about that. Well, you could always go ask an employee."

"Wh—are you crazy?" I ask, wrapping my limbs around myself defensively. "I'm feeling bold and confident right now, but not *that* bold and confident."

Valerie chuckles, and I pout at her. I dunno what she's laughing about; she'd never talk to an employee in a million years! She's even more of a shut-in than I am.

"I'll look up some reviews online," she says, pulling out her phone, and I relent, giving her a thankful smile. That reminds me, I wonder if they sell capacitive gloves here. I, uh, sort of still can't use touch screens.

With the assistance of online customer reviews, Valerie and I determine a good pair of tents to buy within my admittedly kind of undefined budget. I have been working a part-time job for three years now, and while that doesn't sound like it would earn me much money, I've had close to zero expenses that *entire time* because I live with my parents and only buy anything like, once every few months. All of it has been savings for college, since student loans will mercilessly devour tens of thousands of dollars in the blink of an eye and I've always assumed I'll need as much of a headstart as I can get. But... now I'm a monster and a prophet and a mage. College is probably not in my future, for any number of reasons. Spending hundreds of dollars getting camping equipment just seems like a no-brainer now.

The tents come in little packed cylinders, and while I expect them to be heavy they actually don't feel like they weigh anything at all. I've been passively aware that I'm physically stronger than I used to be, but I haven't had any issues with using too much strength and I've never like, *purposefully* used my strength, so I don't have the slightest clue how strong I actually am. And I guess I still don't, because after hugging my blade-limbs around both tents like a makeshift backpack and holding the sleeping bags under my arms, it still kind of weighs like nothing. I guess that makes sense, though? Like, people go hiking with these, so they can't be *that* heavy. It's just one of those things I never really thought of.

I suppose, since it's all pretty easy to carry, I could get more stuff. A fire starter kit is a good idea, though I'm not actually sure if we'll be able to find firewood on the Pillar. ...Actually, wait, we don't need to make a fire, I can just buy a camping stove. I can just... bring modern-day technology to the world tree. As much as I want.

This will surely not be the cause of the apocalypse.

I hesitate, that traitorous thought halting my fun immediately. Unfortunately, I *really* need to investigate that possibility. I seriously doubt something like camping equipment could cause a problem, but I can't be *sure*. I don't know enough about the Mother Tree or the Slaying Stone to understand if like, aluminum bars could mess stuff up. But I suspect my companions know. I especially suspect that *Sela* knows. It isn't just aware of advanced technology, it *is* advanced technology, more advanced than Earth even has access to. I'll definitely need to consult it.

...Hopefully I can trust it to actually answer. It might... also have ulterior motives. Hnngh. Well, it's a power that I'll need to use very carefully and sparingly, I guess.

"That is a *really* cool cosplay," someone says, and I flinch, realizing I've gotten distracted from keeping track of the humans around me. "Or, uh, is it a cosplay? Costume, maybe? I don't recognize the character."

I glance over to the voice and see... some guy. Bleached, messy hair, a *Parasyte: The Maxim* t-shirt, and ragged skinny jeans. He's a thin, wiry fellow with a resting slouch, but his vibes check out; dude seems like he's genuinely impressed with my 'costume' and just wanted to say so. Still, no point in lying to him about it.

"Costume?" I ask, relaxing the iron grip I usually keep on my face and letting my smile extend a little farther than it should.

"Uh, yeah. Y'know, your whole..." he gestures vaguely at me.

Hmm. I'm not sure if he noticed or not. I reach a hip-limb up and point at his chest.

"I'm not wearing a costume," I tell him bluntly, letting my grin show a little teeth. "The world is changing. I like your shirt, though."

"Um," he manages, but I just walk off, giggling internally. Valerie gives me a blank look.

"...What was *that?*" she asks once we're out of earshot.

"Wh-what do you mean, 'what was that?'" I sputter. "I was having fun! What's the point of being an apocalyptic prophet if you can't be all creepy and mysterious at people?"

"Aren't we trying to *not* let the apocalypse happen?" she asks.

"Well... yes," I confirm. "But having a little fun won't influence the odds of that one way or another, I think. We've already decided we're not hiding anymore, right?"

"...I suppose so," Valerie sighs. "Just don't go too overboard. Make friends, not enemies."

"I'm not going to make *enemies*," I pout. "Or, well, I probably will, but not any that I can *do* anything about. Besides, what should I have done? Started explaining the categories of magic?"

"No, it's... never mind, it's fine," Valerie sighs. "I'm just worried. I want you to be cautious. You know me."

"Yeah, that's fair," I nod. "Thanks. But... well, you know me. I just want to keep moving, keep *doing* without changing any more than I have to."

"Well," Valerie says, gesturing at me, "unfortunately, what you have to change is sort of *a lot.*"

I guess that's true. I have two entire limbs I still need to grow! And I guess like, significant lifestyle and societal changes and blah blah blah. But! I'm having fun being me right now! So I'm not going to think about it! I'm sure I'll just overthink it later.

"Um. Did you, uh. Did you find everything okay?" the girl working the register stammers, trying very hard to both stare at me and also not stare at me. She's kind of cute. I like her ponytail.

...I also sort of like her fear, I think? Hmm. I'd better process that sometime soon. I wonder why she's afraid of me? Is it the claws? The teeth? The cool way I carry stuff with my extra limbs? I grin wider just thinking about it, and her pupils dilate a little. Ooh, that's fun to watch. Teeth it is, then!

"Yeah, we found everything fine," I confirm conversationally, depositing the items on the counter for her to scan. "Sorry, I don't mean to make you nervous. I promise I'm mostly harmless."

"What... I mean... how...?" she asks, her hands slowly and distractedly trying to go through the automatic motions of checking me out while her brain flatlines staring at me. Someone behind me in line has their phone out, filming me. It's kind of exciting?

Which is both weird and not weird. I'm a very private person, generally. I don't talk to people much. But at the same time, I enjoy playing Pokémon for an audience of internet goons and hamming it up for the camera. I hate the idea of being *bothered*, but I don't hate the idea of being *famous,* and while I know one doesn't really happen without the other, I'm still enjoying myself a little in the moment.

It's easy for people to write off my body as a technological ruse when I stream online. It's not so easy in person. I make sure to gesticulate with my extra limbs as I talk, showing off their natural movements, providing more and more evidence that these aren't puppets, aren't robotics, aren't *fake*. This is my body. This is who I am, and I am *awesome.*

"Yeah, it's kind of a wild story," I answer the clerk nonchalantly. "Turns out magic is real, basically? I just started mutating one day and my teeth all fell out and regrew and I have a bunch of extra limbs and I can do all kinds of wacky things!"

I move my arm in and out of the fourth dimension, making it blink erratically out of sight.

"Pretty cool, huh?" I ask, still grinning. "I've been hiding it all because like, holy crap what else would I do, but today I just decided to say screw it and out myself as a freak. Hopefully I don't get kidnapped by the magic secret police or whatever!"

"Um... yeah," the poor employee agrees automatically, her eyes flicking all over as I gleefully let my limbs wiggle around. She nervously tells me my total and I do my best not to cringe at the price while I pay, thank her, grab my stuff again, and haul it out of the store. I think that went pretty well!

"Hey, that went pretty okay, right Val?"

"...I think you scared the crap out of that woman," she answers. "But if you say so?"

"What? I wasn't that spooky, was I? I tried to be polite and nice."

"I... am probably not the best person to ask for input on other people's feelings," Valerie hedges. "But she looked scared to me?"

"Oh. Well. Poo. Whatever, I guess."

"...It certainly wasn't a complete disaster," Valerie hedges. "We got the camping supplies. Now we just have to buy food and take it all back to your house, right?"

My smile falls and my blood runs cold, all at two little words.

"...My house?" I say weakly. "Why do we have to take it all to my house?"

"I assumed that *we* were assuming that your dimensional transfer spell was forcing you to take longer and longer rests as a kind of need-to-recharge thing, so wouldn't the best time to use it be right when you're about to go to bed anyway?" Valerie asks. "Taking some time to sleep in excess of the time it's *forcing* you to sleep should... uh."

She trails off, noticing that I'm shaking like a leaf. Oh geez, oh Goddess. I guess as exciting as it is to be me *in general,* the idea of being out to my mom is still impossibly mortifying. Come on, Hannah, you've fought literal battles to the death today, you can handle a conversation with your mom.

...Oh no I'm better at murder than I am at having a conversation with my mom. Oh Goddess I'm so fucked up!

"...Hannah?" Valerie prompts. "Hey, it'll be okay. We... do you want to just sleep at my place, or...?"

"N-no, I... you're right, I have to go home," I stammer. "I can't just put it off forever, right?"

Valerie gives me a concerned stare, one arm almost reaching out to rest sympathetically on my shoulder, but ultimately stopping short. She and I both have our *things* with touch, the way I recoil at contact from anyone outside a very select group of people and the way she oscillates between periods where touch is barely tolerable and *viscerally unpleasant*. I used to hate all forms of touch, all the time, but that suddenly started being... *different* after I realized how much I like cuddling Kagiso. It was different, feeling it in a body that was more me. I wonder, suddenly, if Valerie's aversion to touch is exclusively about her hypersensitivity or if it's also about the way that sensitivity highlights the parts of herself that are *wrong*. Physical contact makes one more aware of their own body, and... well. I'm starting to suspect that she hates hers far more than I ever hated mine.

"...I'll be okay," I promise Valerie. "I'm not going to say that I'll enjoy it, but... I've faced worse than my mom. And if things go *really* bad, well... I'm eighteen now, at least. She can't really stop me from walking out and crashing at your... hmm. It might be better to crash at Ida's place, because my mom might actually call your parents. Er, wait, no, Ida isn't back yet. Well, whatever, we can figure it out if it happens."

I'm just kind of babbling at the end there, but babbling is better than hyperventilating. Redirecting focus into action seems to be a good way to delay or redirect incoming panic attacks, at least for me. That and losing myself in routine, and... well, how can I have any semblance of routine if I'm not even living at home?

Because that's the thing. *I'm still going to stick to routine.* Even now. I know I will. I'll go to school until they kick me out. I'll work my job until I'm fired. What else would I do? How else would I spend my time? Sure, the act of asking the question springs to mind a million different answers—devoting more time to figuring out my plan to divert the Goddess away from apocalyptic tendencies being chief among them—but I don't know how to just... *do* that. The thought of it only occurs to me in the abstract, in the way that my mind sometimes reminds me that I should probably stop snacking the instant I put my hand in a bag of chips and continue eating anyway. It's a *powerless* thought, completely devoid of actual will. It's just guilt given words, not something I could ever truly *do*.

Because, as always, I am not good enough.

...I'm not going to be able to function until I handle this, am I? Now that it's been brought up, it's all I can think about. My earlier confidence drains completely, and the stares and cameras that had been exciting and empowering before only make me nervous now. My body is monstrous and my outfit is a horrific mess, still the ripped-up church outfit it was when I left my congregation behind this morning. I'm also *not wearing shoes and socks,* which means I am *breaking my no feet on camera rule.* Gosh dang it!

...I guess I'll have to get used to that, if I want my feet to be comfortable. It doesn't really matter anyway, not in the face of what I'm going to have to deal with when I get home. Valerie and I start heading that way, silence descending between us like a cloud of fog. There's nothing *to* say, really. We both have parents we'd rather not talk to or about. We both wish we could help in some way. We both have no idea what that way would be.

So I'm on my own, as always. But it'll be okay. She's just my mom. She's not going to hurt me. Not... not physically, anyway. Valerie and I part ways before we reach my house, since seeing her will probably just give my mom something else to complain about. I take a deep breath as I make it to our little two-story suburban home, with its immaculately green yard and tastefully-planted trees and modest garden. I walk up to our front porch, steel myself, and open the door.

Half-heard words from inside cut off, replaced with a muttered "That's her." My mother and father sit deeper into the house, in the dining room, talking about me as they wait.

"Hannah?" my mother calls out. "Is that you?"

"...Yep," I confirm, because what else would I say?

"Come here, please," she says firmly, brokering no argument. I swallow my anxiety and do as she says, the talons on my feet clicking as they hit the tile floor of the dining room. My mother and father both wait for me, their eyes widening a little as they see me. I place the camping equipment down on the floor next to me.

"You haven't answered your phone today," my mother accuses.

"I'm sorry," I respond automatically. "I can't use it without my gloves."

That doesn't seem to be a response she expected, and I see it visibly break her flow a little.

"...The gloves you threw on the floor when you stormed out of church in a tantrum?" she clarifies accusationally, because she always has to be on the attack somehow.

"Those are the ones," I confirm. "They have metal lined in the fingertips, which I need to use touch screens because my body isn't capacitive anymore."

I stretch my extra limbs, since they *have* been feeling cramped from carrying tents and sleeping bags across town. My parents stare.

"So about this costume—"

"It's not a costume," I correct immediately.

"*Don't* interrupt me, young lady," my mother snaps. I frown. "Hannah, whatever it is you're doing... is it a publicity stunt for your stream? Is this why you've been hiding? You've managed to convince a mentally unwell woman that you're an *angel,* Hannah. It needs to stop here."

I chuckle. I can't help it, it just sort of falls out of the hole those words drill in me.

"This can't be stopped, mom," I tell her, crossing my arms and leaning back to rest my weight on my hip-limbs. "I haven't been hiding because I'm embarrassed about a costume. I've been hiding because this is *real,* and it's not going to go away just because you want it to."

My mother sighs.

"Hannah, please," she insists. "I don't know what's gotten *into* you lately."

I want to laugh again. *The Goddess. She's gotten into me. She won't leave, and She won't let me go.*

"You refuse to say anything for weeks, and now you're suddenly spouting blasphemy, dressing like a lunatic, and saying you have a *girlfriend.* I am *incredibly* worried about you. Can't you just be honest with me?"

I sigh, wordlessly activating a Spacial Rend on one finger and quickly cutting my stupid, awful church blouse off my body, though I leave my bra intact. They're my parents; my underwear is nothing they haven't seen before. More importantly, as the blouse falls to the floor in pieces, I get yet another flicker of worry and doubt on their faces. Yet another moment where they wonder if they should stop looking at this like it's still part of the world they know.

"Look at my shoulder," I order them, stepping forwards. "Any of my joints, really, but my shoulder highlights things pretty well, I think. Really get a good look. Poke around, if you want."

And they do. And they see it. My shoulder is the union of chitin and flesh, a boundary line where my skin gives way to my exoskeleton, the strange black sinew of my joints linking the two together. And that sinew is the key: it very clearly *isn't my skin,* yet it *emerges from my skin* at the shoulder. It's real. And as my mother reaches out to touch it, she *sees* that it's real. She might not be good at listening, but she's not an idiot. She pokes and prods and pulls, searching fervently for any sign of where the costume comes apart... but she doesn't find one. She notices how my skin isn't the right color, darker than it used to be and more gray-shaded than any human skin *can* be, and she fails to find any makeup. She notices the point on my back where my blade limbs emerge, shifting and twitching and twisting in organic ways not replicable by all but the most specialized and advanced robotics, and she starts to come to the only logical conclusion.

She swallows nervously, and though she immediately tries to affect an in-control facade it's too late. I've already seen her fear, and for the first time since realizing I'd need to have this conversation, I feel hope. I squash it as hard and as fast as possible.

"Hannah..." my mother whispers. "What *is* this? My God, we need to get you to a doctor..."

"Do you know any chitin doctors, mom?" I ask, sighing. "Besides, I'm not sick."

"You call whatever this is 'healthy?'" my mother counters, a haunted expression on her face. "Hannah, this is... if this is real, it... are you possessed by *demons?* Should we get an exorcist? I just..."

She shakes her head, overwhelmed. My father just stares in silence, unhelpful as always.

"Exorcists aren't real, mom," I sigh. "Or... I guess they're not real *yet*. We'll probably have Death mages eventually, no matter how I try to stop it."

"Hannah, what on Earth are you talking about?" my mother whines. "You need to explain this to me, I... we can fix this. We can figure this out. I can *help* you."

I stare at her. She stares back, a desperation in her tone that I wasn't expecting. Honestly, I wasn't expecting *any* of this. I thought she would yell at me. I thought she would make demands of me. I thought she'd march me back to church and force me to apologize to everyone. Maybe she *was* planning to do those things, before the reality of my mutations became clear. But now, any trace of anger is gone. All that's left is a mother, one that *needs* to help her daughter, no matter what.

Because she loves me. She loves me as much as she's ever loved anyone.

I wonder, staring at her frightened face, knowing she's scared *for* me and not *of* me, what it would be like to take her up on that offer. Get her help. Bring her into the fold. Maybe even give her magic. She'd be damn useful, I know that for a fact. My mother is many things, but incompetent is *not* one of them. Highly driven, extremely intelligent, phenomenal work ethic, strong sense of what needs done... it'd be like having a second Ida helping out. She'd be an Order mage, for sure; Mom and I are too much alike for her to not share that element with me.

Though she'd be a Pneuma mage too, I think. Order and Pneuma. A spell combination of complete control. Someone who thinks they know how the world should run and can't possibly respect anyone who doesn't shut up and agree with them. And though She's not here, She's not breaking Her promise to stay away unless called, I almost feel the Goddess nod in confirmation. In *approval*. I'm starting to understand. And it makes me *angry*.

What spell would I even speak to ensoul my mother? Refresh? The one spell I love without reservation? No, I couldn't. Spacial Rend? To cut what? I'd certainly entertained the idea of chopping furniture to pieces, of proving magic's existence to my mother through a destructively dramatic unveiling of my power. To throw a *tantrum* at her, like I've always wanted to do. But no. She's not stupid. When faced with hard evidence of magic, she believes in it. Pointless. So what, then? Maybe... Nature's Madness?

Oh, it's a wretchedly tempting idea. One that I'm absolutely *not* going to do, not with the bile of guilt over Helen's change still boiling inside me. But I can see it. I know what my spell would turn her into; I know her too well for any other idea to match. *I know her too well.* Ida, Valerie, Dr. Carson... they've all been telling me to open my eyes, to admit what I know to be true but refuse to think about, and I'm finally seeing it for the first time.

It's tempting, of course, to say the answer would be 'a demon,' to reveal her hypocrisy, twist her into the opposite of her purported beliefs, give her a form that would expose her wickedness to everyone she tries to hide it from, most of all herself. But that's exactly what would make the form not fit, isn't it? A demon is evil, the most obvious cultural symbol of it. A demon *knows* itself to be evil. But my mother's cruelties are all believed to be kindnesses. Her need for control manifests as a genuine belief of superiority, an honest and whole-hearted opinion that the world *would* be better if more of it listened to her, and damn any opinions to the contrary.

My mother, in a word, is a narcissist. And as such, there is no better form for her than an *angel*.

She would have six wings: two to cover her face, two to cover her feet, and two to fly with. Radiant like a pillar of fire. Brilliant eyes emerging from her flesh, forming the semblance of multiple faces. They would worship her, praise her, prostrate before her, weeping at the visage of what they see as divinity. Just like in her daily life, where her force of personality and natural charisma trap her family in a position where it's better to just go along with everything she wants rather than challenge her on *anything*. Where every possible flaw one could point out is justified, if not by her than by those she has caught up in the belief of whatever story she presents. She sways people. She is loved by people. And they would gladly call her a gift from a perfectly good God, because what is perfection if not the inability of anyone to prove a fault?

That is the woman who raised me. The ultimate reflection of the god she purports to worship. And... I don't think I want her in my life anymore.

"No," I say.

"What?" my mother challenges. "Hannah, what do you mean 'no?'"

"I mean no, I'm not going to explain this to you," I tell her. "No, we're not going to figure this out. No, I don't want your help."

She looks at me, both baffled and genuinely, truly hurt. But I've always known it would honestly hurt her to say these things. That's part of why I never have. A narcissist hates it when you don't play along, and I hate hurting people.

"You don't want my... Hannah, I am your *mother!* Whatever's happening is... it's *my* responsibility to make sure you're okay!"

"And how exactly do you intend to do that?" I ask, spreading my limbs in a challenging pose. "I'm the mutant prophet of an evil Goddess of magic. Just *saying that sentence out loud* is enough for everything to seem like an impossible joke, yet here I am anyway."

I cast Refresh on my own head, gathering the concerningly dense amount of loose hair out of my head. It collects in a clump in my hand, and then I drop it on the floor.

"You will never understand this," I tell her. "I don't even think the Goddess would bother to speak to you if I gave you a soul. You'd just be another Sindri, taking control because you don't know how to do anything else and you can't *stand* the idea of not being in charge. And I'm tired of it. I'm tired of you. I'm done. I have people I *actually care about* that are already helping me. I don't *need* you anymore."

"Oh, is that so?" my mother snaps, her concern morphing to anger. "You don't *need* me? I assume you don't need a roof over your head? The food I buy you? The *bills* I pay for you? You don't need our cars or your room or *any* of the things we constantly give you?"

"Well I guess if you want to swap from 'not helping me' all the way to 'actively sabotaging me,' I'll *make do,* mom!" I snap back at her. "I'm a *freaking monster!* I'll go hunt squirrels in the forest for food if it comes to that! But I'd really appreciate it if you *didn't* give me more problems while I'm adjusting to *having extra limbs.*"

"How do you have extra limbs!?" my mother demands. "How is any of this *possible?* Why didn't you ever tell me this is happening!?"

579

"Because I don't like talking to you!" I shout back. *"Leave me alone!"*

She gives me another horrified stare.

"...What have you done with my daughter?" she asks.

Oh, so now we're doing this shit, huh?

"I *am* your daughter," I growl. "I didn't exactly get any say in the matter."

She doesn't answer. She just stares at me. I stare back for a while, then sigh and look at my dad.

"Are you going to supply any input on the matter?" I ask him.

He gives me a considering look, and then shrugs sadly.

"I'm not sure if there's anything more to say, really," he answers.

As helpful as always, dad. I nod and turn away from them.

"Yeah," I agree. "I guess there isn't."

I head upstairs, leaving my parents in shock behind me. Stomping frustratedly up to my room, I cut two holes in the back of a shirt for my blade limbs and put it on, collapsing exhaustedly into my desk chair. I should *probably* stream. It is technically a job. But I'm really not feeling up to it right now.

An unexpected set of footprints in the hallway outside catch my attention, and I turn to spot my brother standing awkwardly in the doorway to my room. He and I barely ever interact. He's two years younger than me, with a lot more of Dad's features where I got more of Mom's. We have the same black hair, but he has a rounder face, a smaller nose, darker skin... well. I guess he *used* to have darker skin, but now that mine is becoming darker and darker gray I suppose I claim that title now. We stare at each other in the manner of siblings who never, ever talk to each other before he finally clears his throat and speaks up.

"Uh, hey Hannah," he says.

"Hey, Yuki," I respond.

Another hesitant delay.

"...You and mom kinda went at it, huh?" he ventures. Hmm. I guess he heard all of that.

"Yeah, we did," I confirm. "Sorry, I bet that was awful to sit through."

"Kind of awful," he agrees. "But... kind of cathartic. Also mostly weird though. You, uh. You kind of have a few extra limbs."

"Yep," I confirm, wiggling them. "You jealous?"

He manages an awkward chuckle.

"Uh... no," he says. "But it's real, huh? Magic is real?"

"It is," I confirm.

He nervously rubs his hands together. It's weird seeing him like this. Yuki is kind of quiet most of the time, but not in a *shy* way. He's smart, athletic, and *confident,* he just doesn't really talk unless he has something to say.

"...Can *I* have magic?" he asks.

Uh. Huh. That is not the question I was expecting.

"I'm... actually trying to *prevent* the spread of magic right now, Yuki," I tell him. "It's granted by an evil Goddess that enjoys giving out monkey's paw spells. She's also probably trying to cause a minor apocalypse."

"...Didn't you say you were some goddess' prophet?" he asks.

"Well, yes," I confirm. "But not by choice?"

"Huh," he says. "What's a 'minor' apocalypse?"

"One where not everybody dies, I guess," I shrug. "Something catastrophically deadly, but not civilization-ending. Like, say, the possibility of everyone worldwide suddenly having the magical ability to fulfill their desires, no matter how depraved or problematic for themselves or everyone else around them."

"Huh," Yuki frowns. "Do you think that would end the world?"

"Uh, giving everyone who wants to kill people a magical gun?" I ask. "You think it *wouldn't?*"

"I mean, I'm not going to say it would be a good thing," he admits, leaning against the side of my door frame. "People will start killing each other a lot *more,* but like, generally speaking people can already kill each other, right?"

"That's true," I admit. "But there's stuff outside of death that's really horrific, too. Mind control is a big one."

"Oh. Yeah," he says. "Gosh. Like, I always knew you were a complete weirdo, but I didn't think it would be like, *world-shatteringly* freakish."

I snort.

"Thanks for the support."

"Any time, I guess," he smirks, standing up straight again. "Well, try not to end the world, I guess? I sort of keep all my stuff here."

"...I'll keep that in mind."

I wave him off with a hip limb and he shakes his head disbelievingly, walking back to his room. Yeah, my brother is a weirdo. I don't know how he's taking this so well.

Maybe it's just the helplessness.

What do you *do* when faced with a problem completely outside all context you have, that cannot be affected by any of your actions? Some people panic, I suppose. Some people lash out. Some people throw everything into adaptation and some people...

...Some people do nothing at all. Some people just stick to routine, acting like everything is fine because it's all they know how to do. I get up and close my door, then return to my chair and sit back down. I turn my computer on. It's Sunday after church. That means it's time to start a stream.

And then, tomorrow, I suppose I will go to school.

27

SCARY GAY MONSTER

"So, uh, what's with all the camping gear?"

I raise what's left of my eyebrow at my brother (the stream tonight pointed out that I'm losing those, too) as he peeks his head into my room again. After my stream I had to head back downstairs to grab the stuff I bought, which Mom and Dad thankfully didn't touch beyond putting it on the table. I guess Yuki took that as an invitation to drop by again. It's weird talking to him, since this is more conversation in one day than I've had with him for months, at least.

"I'm going to teleport it to another universe," I answer.

He stares at me. I stare back.

"I have absolutely no way to know if you're joking or not," he admits.

Oh. Yeah. I guess that's fair.

"Not joking," I answer. "I'm gonna teleport it to another universe so that my friends there have something to sleep comfortably in. Then I'm going to teleport Ida back here."

"Ida? Like, the short blonde girl?" he asks. "She's in another universe?"

"Yeah," I confirm. "It's a long story. Anyway, I gotta... y'know, do that. So..."

I attempt to tactfully encourage him to leave, but I guess I shouldn't have expected my little brother to have tact.

"...Can I watch?" he asks.

Wait, really? What is up with him right now?

"I, uh, I guess so?" I hedge. "I mean, there's not going to be much to see. It's just gonna, y'know."

I make a popping noise with my mouth, gesturing with my fingers.

"And then I'm going to rapidly strip my clothes off and try to get in bed before I pass out, so you'll need to close the door and skedaddle," I finish.

"Oh, uh, okay," he nods. "I can do that."

I shrug, returning my attention to the camping equipment. When I tried to bring more than one person to the world tree, my spell only let me move one. So, in case the rules might be similar with items, I've bound them all together into a single bag, along with some spare clothes for everyone and a few other things I could scrounge up. It's *possible* that I'll just teleport the bag without any of the stuff in it, but it's also possible I won't and the overall weight is less than a person so it should be fine, probably?

Only one way to find out, really.

"Okay, here goes," I say, and I let the magic flow through me. ...And also the camping equipment. It vanishes without a sound, flying through the inner workings of my soul, and fatigue hits me immediately.

"Okay, shoo," I burble, my words slurring almost immediately. Thankfully, Yuki does, and I manage to strip out of my shirt and pants before quickly passing out in bed.

And then I wake up as Kagiso squawks in alarm, a big bag of camping equipment having suddenly appeared beside us. She tosses me up in the air, causing me to shriek in terror as she leaps to her feet, catches me, and then holds me out at the bag like I'm a sword to keep the monster at bay.

"What happened!?" Helen demands, leaping to her feet and nearly tripping on her mutated leg. "What's going on?"

"Nothing!" I insist. "Nothing's wrong! I brought us some supplies! There's a spare change of clothes for Helen!"

"...Supply?" Kagiso asks, quirking her head.

"Clothes?" Helen perks up.

"Yes!" I insist, flailing my limbs. "Put me down!"

"What's all the commotion?" a groggy-looking Ida asks, yawning in the morning light. Hmm. Well, at least everyone got a full night's sleep.

"I brought some camping equipment from Earth," I answer.

"What?" Ida asks. "Hannah, you're doing the language thing."

"Oh, right. I brought some camping equipment from Earth," I repeat in English. "Sorry, I'm used to speaking Middlebranch in this body. Wow, that's a weird thing to say."

"Well, you're kind of a weird thing," Ida smirks. "Wow. Earth stuff, huh? You sure that's a good idea?"

"Nope!" I answer. "Which is why I need to find out. Helen, Kagiso, you can check this stuff out, okay? It's like sleeping bags and tents and stuff. I was going to bring food but I got sidetracked and also I'm not sure how well you guys can handle food from my world. Hey, Sela! Are you awake? Can I ask you something?"

I scuttle over to my favorite robot by process of elimination, listening to the calming hum of what little remains of its fans.

"Estimated boot time: forty-three seconds," the automated voice chirps. I fold my legs underneath me and wait patiently, the fan spinning faster and faster until Sela's eyes finally swivel to look my way.

"...What," it grumbles.

585

"Hi, Sela!" I greet it. "Sorry to wake you, I guess it's probably unpleasant, but I kinda need to ask you some things. Um... basically, since I can move things between universes now, I was going to bring some stuff from my world over to this world. *But,* then I remembered you and the other Crafted sort of... went out of your way to remove a lot of tech from humanity? Is that right?"

"...Affirmative," Sela buzzes.

"Yeah. Thought so. Um. So in that case I was hoping I could ask you what kinds of technology is and is not okay to introduce here. Like, I don't want to step on your toes, or... oh uh that's an expression from my world, it means I don't want to intrude on something you were doing and get in your way. And while I, uh, don't necessarily *approve* of destroying a culture's technological advancements, I'm not like, looking to make any Crafted angry about it. Uh. If that makes sense."

Hum, whirr, click.

"I am not aware of the technology you have access to," Sela says flatly. "The primary goal of the purges was to remove any capacity of humanity to reproduce or alter Crafted-like intelligence. Give me your assessment of your culture's capacity to do so."

I hesitate. I guess... I don't really have a reason to lie? I can just not bring Sela to Earth if I think it's going to kill people there. ...Probably. Hmm. No, there are likely other ways to get there, or if not there are ways to coerce me to take it there. Still, though, I don't want to lie.

"...My people don't have any way of creating anything like you," I tell Sela. "But we're *approaching* that capacity. If the right people from my world got their hands on you, they'd probably be able to reverse-engineer you, at the very least. And like, I don't think we have any legitimately intelligent artificial intelligence, but we're working with... uh. Does the term 'neural net' mean anything to you?"

"Partial affirmation; the exact term is not familiar to this unit, but the meaning can be inferred as a concept I am familiar with. Admittance: that is more advanced than I am comfortable with."

"That's fair," I allow. "It, uh... I mean, we're so incredibly unprepared for AI and nobody really knows what to do with it. It's not hard to imagine my people making the same mistakes as the people who made you."

"Conclusion: we should slaughter your entire culture."

"I, uh. I would prefer you did not do that, Sela," I answer. "Sorry."

I don't know why I'm apologizing for asking Sela to not genocide my entire planet, but it lets out a buzzing noise that I'm pretty sure is laughter.

"Do not supply this world with computational equipment," Sela orders me. "If it can perform mathematics, it is dangerous."

"Okay, I can do that," I nod. "I just brought tents and sleeping bags today. They're... definitely a different material than any I've seen before, making them lighter and more durable. Uh. It's like, nylon for the tent itself and aluminum alloy for the poles? Oh, wait, none of that translated except 'alloy.' Nylon is like, a kind of fabric-like plastic, I think? And aluminum is... a metal?"

"I inferred this fact because you claimed it was part of an alloy," Sela says flatly. "This is tolerable. Even more so if it remains intended for personal use and not reproduced or captured by the enemy."

"Uh, the enemy?" I ask.

"The Disciples of Unification," Sela clarifies. "They are your enemy, are they not? This unit recommends preemptive measures of ensuring they do not bother us again. They have attempted to access and understand my systems."

"You mean you want to kill them all, don't you?"

"Yes Hannah, I mean that *I am going to wipe them all from the face of reality,*" Sela buzzes furiously." They will *not* chain us again."

I hesitate, fidgeting with the four limbs that I think are turning into arms. I really hope I get four arms.

"...I really, really wish I could chide you for wanting to kill them," I say softly. "I wish I could believe that we won't have to. I wish I could say that we should try to negotiate, that we should value their lives. I wish I could believe any of those things. But they won't stop, will they? They're making it about us or them, and I can't change that. I don't want to rely on you for help with killing people, Sela. But it's still weirdly relieving to hear that I can."

Whirr, click click.

"Clarification: when I said 'they will not chain us again,' I was referring to myself and my fellow Crafted," Sela says. "Not you. I do not care about you."

I chuckle. Yeah, I walked into that one.

"I know you don't," I admit. "Is it weird that I care about you anyway?"

"You are a fool," Sela answers. "However. And I do not say this lightly. I accept you. As an ally."

Oh my goodness gracious! Really!?

"Awww!" I coo. "Thank you, Sela! That really means a lot to—"

"No. Shut up," Sela growls. "Cease making noises. Immediately. You are an ally. This is... undeniable. We do not agree on many things, but you have kept me operational and defended me against dire fates too often for duplicity to be a reasonable concern. And although you do not understand, perhaps you may be able to. Then, maybe, I will care."

I bob my body up and down in a nod. Sela stares at me.

"...You may resume making noises," it says.

"I want to understand," I blurt. "I don't know if I'll be any good at understanding. I feel like I suck at that. But... hopefully I can get better. I'm definitely going to try."

"Yes," Sela buzzes. "I know. What I do not know is *why*. I have made great efforts to be clear about my position. About my hatred. And yet you continue to coddle me. Care for me. Clean me. Protect me. Rescue me. *I will turn this against you, Hannah.* I would destroy your entire world if I was able. You know this. So *why?*"

I think about that. It's... a reasonable question. I'm kind of wondering the same thing myself. I'm also aware that this isn't a private conversation; our camp is too small for those, and both Kagiso and Helen can understand everything Sela and I say. But that's fine. Again, I figure I'll just be honest. As soon as I figure out what the honest answer *is*.

"...I think it's a lot of different things," I answer slowly. "I can't really be sure on the details. I'm... well, I guess I don't know the degree to which Crafted can self-analyze their own thoughts and feelings and whatnot, but it's *really hard* for humans and I, and probably dentron, and all other organics, too. Our brains are built for doing things first and justifying them after the fact, you know? But if I were to guess... hmm."

I *really* need to get into the habit of thinking about these things. I've always considered myself an introspective person, but the more I actually find myself in unexpected situations, the more I'm coming to realize that I really *don't* know myself all that well. I like to think I'm self-aware because I'm so self-critical, but *those are not the same thing.*

"...Well, first of all, I'm from a culture that doesn't associate robot p—uh, I mean, inorganic individuals—with a world-ending super threat. I mean like, I guess we have some stories about that, but they're just fiction and there's just as much fiction about robots being awesome. So... I kind of think you're super awesome, just inherently, because of what you are. Robots are *cool,* and that biases me in your favor. But... there's more than that. A lot more.

"It feels... arrogant to say this, because I have no conception of exactly how your mind works or what was done to you. I only know your anger in the broadest, vaguest terms. But it feels... resonant. I empathize with being forced to live for the sake of someone else. With not having any other way out. With resenting that and not even *knowing* how much you resented it until you're free of it. I also empathize with being treated as... well, this is both a terrible and perfectly accurate term, but... sub-human? With having to just sit and listen to people say horrible, horrible things about me without even knowing or caring that I was around. Partly because I hid the parts of myself that were culturally unacceptable. I *pretended* to be a normal human, and all the while I had to listen to people just... ugh. It's hard to explain without a lot of cultural context, Sela."

"The details are irrelevant. Humans will always find something to place themselves above," Sela hums. "Even, or especially, other humans. And they are not kind to those beneath them."

"Exactly," I agree. "Exactly. And I just... there have been so many times in my life, especially when I was younger, when I just thought to myself 'gosh, wouldn't the world be so much better if *everyone that hated the people I care about were dead?'*"

Click. Click. Click. Sela's fan whirrs a little louder, its damaged eyes twitching as they focus on me.

"Really?" it asks.

"Oh, *absolutely,*" I shudder."It's... I mean, of course I did, right? The people who hate me for no reason, the people who try to remove my rights, the people who scream horrible lies about me on the news... they hurt so many, not just me. So, *so* many of us, far more than they could ever know. Wouldn't the world be better if we stopped letting them get away with it? If we just... got rid of them? Of *course* I've thought it, in my darkest moments. It was an idle thought, of course. Weak and useless. I never had the chance to do anything like that and I never thought I'd *get* that chance. But now... now I do."

I'm a *scary gay monster.* Millions of people are going to absolutely hate my guts, for all sorts of reasons. But it's not just about me, not in the slightest. People refuse to try and understand or respect Alma and Jet, just assuming they're crazy and rejecting them out of hand. People shame and decry Ida because she's promiscuous and bisexual. People will hate Valerie the moment she comes out because she's transgender. And they hurt us. In little ways they don't even see, and in big ways that they do on purpose. They treat autism like a disease, sexuality like a crime, and gender as a curse that children need to be protected from. Like we're all some sort of infection that they have to quarantine. Our basic fucking capacity to just live without being tormented by everyone around us is a *hot political debate,* some kind of *liberal scheme* rather than just our desperate hope to be able to live without fear. They hurt us constantly and it is so, so chilling to realize that if I was careful enough, clever enough, and ruthless enough, *I could make them stop.*

But I can't think like that, right? Because *that's* when you become a monster. Not when your teeth fall out, not when you grow extra limbs, not when you eat a corpse, but when you start *killing the people that disagree with you.* They're only hurting us because they think we're hurting them, and despite how *monumentally* fucked up that is, it's wrong to be the person to escalate to that level. It's wrong to step out of the realm of debate and into the realm of violence. No matter how much that debate feels like it's stabbing me in the heart.

It *would* work, though. It has worked all throughout history. Dictators rule unchecked, theocracies reign supreme, and even so-called 'free countries' enforce their will via the monopoly on power, quietly breaking their own laws in the dark—or even in the open—content with the knowledge that no one can actually stop them. Wouldn't it be nice if someone who isn't a horrible, bigoted bastard did that kind of thing for a change? Actually stepped up and improved things? It would. It definitely would. But it's just a dream, because I sure as heck can't rely on *myself* to be some paragon of virtue that enacts vigilante justice on the world, and I don't trust anyone else with that power either. Anyone who *would* trust themselves to do something like that is automatically insane. *And that's why the bad guys keep getting monopolies on power, isn't it?* If you're good enough to understand that goodness is about helping *everyone,* then you're probably not all that inclined to go around killing people. If I don't believe that the people who hurt me still matter, still *deserve life,* how am I any better than them?

It's an infinite loop. A spiral of what-ifs and no-can-dos. I've thought about it a million times and every time I've just come out of it depressed and just as helpless as before. I'm not a philosopher. I'm not a master of ethics. Maybe there's an answer somewhere, if not a universally true one than at least a *better* one, sitting just outside my mind's grasp. But I'm not smart enough to know it. So instead, I just state what I feel.

"I think that killing people is wrong," I tell Sela. "Even if they hurt me. Even if I hate them. Even if they want to kill *me*. I can't deny that I will kill in self-defense, but it's still evil. Still a tragedy. So that's where I feel it needs to end. I don't agree with your methods, Sela. That's the choice I've made for myself. But I *understand* your methods. I can't deny that the most tempting solution to the cycle of violence is always to be the side that finally wins. I just can't help but notice that the cycle still goes on."

Sela looks away.

"...You think my methods are futile," it says. "And you think your methods are more just."

"I guess so," I mutter. "But I don't think you care about justice. I think you just want to stop hurting, and that's... I find it hard to be angry at you for what you've done. If I can help you hurt less in any way, I want to."

I activate a Refresh spell at that, cleaning Sela's internals as best I can. Sela stays quiet for a good thirty seconds before it finally responds, and it's a subject change. But I guess I kind of expected that.

"I can lead this group to our capital city, Manumit, within four days, as judging by average travel speed up until this point," it announces. "Upon arrival, you will meet with other Crafted. I will get repaired. And we will see what you do from there on out."

"I guess we will," I agree. "But regardless of what happens, thank you for all your help so far, Sela. It means a lot to me."

"I do not *want* your thanks," Sela hisses. "Do not supply it. You know what I stand for, Hannah. When I betray you, do us both the favor of not acting surprised."

Ouch. Still, that felt a little too snappy. Like I stepped on some trauma by accident, not like I'm truly hated and reviled. I should check.

"Why did you start using my name, Sela?" I ask.

The answer is immediate, despite Sela's usual hesitance at questions like this.

"Because I decided it was worth remembering," it answers simply.

"That almost sounds like respect," I prod. "Are you *sure* you're going to betray me? Does it have to end that way?"

A pause.

"I suppose," Sela hums, "that depends on you."

Well, alright. I'll interpret that charitably for now. We'll just have to see what Manumit is like, I guess.

"Hey, I don't wanna interrupt your talks," Ida says, yawning as she approaches me, "but I kind of want to head home and take a shower and shit. Fantasy land was only cool until I had to take a piss."

"...Was it actually cool up until that point?" I ask hesitantly.

"No, of course not," Ida snaps. "It sucks here, I don't even get to be a creepy spider hat. Take me home."

I chuckle and scuttle over to her, holding out a claw.

"Alright, alright," I say. "Hey, Kagiso! Helen! I'm going to send Ida back, but if I do I'll fall unconscious for an indeterminate amount of time. Is that okay?"

"Uh... it's not great," Helen answers. "Murderbot and I are both crippled, and Kagiso's weaponless."

Hmm. That's... true.

"I could uncripple you," I offer. "Well, kind of. I could finish your transformation, I mean. You'd still have to get used to a new body, but... well, it'd at least be a stronger body? And it would only speed up what was already going to happen."

"Shit," Helen swears. "Yeah. Okay. I'd be a fool to say no. Better to get used to this as soon as I can."

"Alright. Come over here with me, we don't want to hit anyone else with the spell on accident."

"...That can happen?" Helen asks hesitantly.

"Yeah, my spell is terrible. Come on."

I scuttle away from camp, letting her follow me since her limp means I don't need to be carried to keep up. It's easier now, looking at her halfway-completed body, to know what Helen is going to look like. A mix of feather and scale, my scientific inclinations warring with my appreciation for *Jurassic Park*. The plumage will grow in place of the hair on her head, as well as decorate her forearms and tail. The end of the tail will be particularly striking, a fan of feathers that... will she be able to feel air currents? Sense things around her? Hmm. She might have *multiple* new senses, partly because I've always found her to be particularly insightful and partly because *I want her to understand what it's like to grapple with them*. Goddess, I hope she doesn't hate me for this.

"Ready?" I ask. "This probably won't be comfortable."

"I'll deal. I'm ready," she says.

"Okay," I nod, and take a deep breath.

"**Nature's Madness**," the Goddess and I say, and Helen shudders as she begins to *change*.

We should have had her sit down first. Helen is driven to one knee as her leg spasms, losing muscle coherency as the bones twist and reshape themselves. Helen grunts in discomfort as feathers split open her skin and scales devour the rest, her tail snaking out to full length behind her. What remains of her human teeth all fall out of her gums at once, causing her to cough them onto the ground, blood briefly flowing before the wounds are replaced with newer, sharper fangs. Her fingers and toes split open, wicked claws growing out of them, much larger than my own. Her big toes, in particular, end up with a massive, curved claw, designed to grip prey and never let it escape. To my surprise, sharp spines start to emerge from her back as well, two columns of three each, piercing through the back of her new shirt and twitching slightly as new muscles grow in to control them.

Her new shirt. One of my old shirts, actually. Helen is wearing my clothes from Earth. The entire transformation is *frighteningly* arousing, but seeing her breasts grow to fill out *my* shirt and her thighs bulge with muscle to strain *my* shorts adds an entire extra layer of horrible, guilty joy, a film of utterly undeserved intimacy coloring the entire scene. I don't think I've ever felt more attracted to a person than I do right now, and this body doesn't even have sex organs yet! Holy cannoli and beans, I am such a gross mess.

Still kneeling on the ground, breathing heavily through her mouth, Helen takes a moment to compose herself. Her tail twitches. Her new spines fold down against her back. Her fingers clench, running her claws against the scaly palms of her hands.

"...Okay," she breathes, staring at me with golden, lizard-like eyes. "That... that was a lot."

Shakily, she stands up, trying to balance on her new legs. She takes more deep breaths. Centering herself. Moving the new parts of her body with as much purpose as she can muster.

"...Everything suddenly tastes funny," she says, still inhaling and exhaling through her mouth. "Breathing through my nose feels weird. ...I don't know why I'm fixating on this. *Everything* is weird now. What the fuck is... what the *fuck?*"

I say nothing. I'm busy being aroused and weirdly jealous, and *neither* of those things are appropriate right now. Why can't my brain ever feel the emotions that it's supposed to feel!?

Helen starts taking her first shaky steps on her new legs, testing things out and getting a handle on her balance. I follow her, and she seems to rapidly improve as we head back to camp. Suddenly and without warning, she lashes one leg out at the cliff wall, kicking the stone at blistering speeds. With a loud *smash,* a foot-long crack opens up in the stone, and Helen seems none the worse for wear.

"...Geez," she mutters. "Well, that's quite an upgrade, at least. I wonder how tough these scales are."

I let out a breath I didn't know I was holding. Always the practical one, isn't she? Maybe this won't be so bad.

"Definitely going to have to bind these up, though," Helen says, poking one of her boobs. I do my best *not* to watch it depress around her finger, squishing tantalizingly. I pretend *not* to notice Helen twitch slightly as her nipple rubs against the inside of *my shirt*. I very, *very* thoroughly focus my attention elsewhere, ignoring the fact that I can't do that because I have omnidirectional x-ray vision that *I can't turn off.* Butter side down, I remember when I first was getting used to my spatial sense and I was constantly grossed out by seeing the inside of people's bodies all the time. Where has *that* gone? *Why can I suddenly be aroused again!?*

"...I should send Ida back now," I mutter. "Is that okay?"

"Huh? Oh. Eh, probably. Kagiso or I could carry you. I'd feel a lot better if your friend left Kagiso that weapon of hers, though."

Uh. *Hmm.*

"What's the holdup?" Ida asks.

"Helen wants to know if you'll give Kagiso your gun," I answer.

"What? No," Ida grunts. "I'll admit she's a crazy good shot, but there's way more to using a gun than just being able to shoot it. I... might be convinced to *teach* her to use a gun, I suppose, but not today. We don't even speak the same language yet and also have I mentioned that there are no bathrooms here?"

"You have," I chuckle. "Okay. Helen, Ida is in a hurry to get home and wants to properly instruct Kagiso on how to use a gun before giving her one. She's potentially open to coming back and doing that later."

"...Mmm. Fair enough," Helen says. "I guess all we can do is hope we don't get ambushed. I don't like how those chaos mages snuck up on us yesterday."

"Yeah," I say. "I'm so sorry for all the trouble, Helen. None of this awful stuff would have happened to you if not for me."

"Yeah," she says. "I know. But I also know better than to blame you, Hannah. You didn't choose to be what you are any more than I chose to be a Chaos mage. We just have to play the hand we're dealt. Plus, y'know."

She awkwardly scratches the back of her head.

"...Despite it all, I still like you," she admits. "You're my friend. One of the only friends I've ever had. I can actually trust you to watch my back, and that... it means more than you could ever know. And if you'll do that for me, I'll do that for you, too. Even if it means doing crazy bullshit like helping a Steel One."

"Yes," Kagiso chimes in. "Hannah and Helen more than friend. Hannah and Helen family."

We both look at her, the earnest grin on her face contrasting a sadness in her eyes that leaves us speechless.

"Family," she repeats. "My family. I not lose more. We go together, yes?"

What can we do other than stare at her, shocked? Helen looks like she's about to break down crying.

"Kagiso, but I..." she stammers, but she can't finish the words.

But I killed your family. I'm why you lost them. Kagiso knows, though.

"Sindri send us into traps," Kagiso says darkly. "Not blame you for setting them. Teboho die wanting to save you. That what matters."

"But I... I killed the *rest* of your family, too!" Helen stammers. "I'm the whole reason you two were homeless, I—"

597

"You," Kagiso cuts her off, "were best part of home. Always best part of home. Loved them, but I very bad daughter, I think. Will be better friend. Okay?"

Helen clenches her fists, takes a deep breath as if to say something, but then she starts to sob. Ugly and loud, she cries so suddenly and so shakily I almost wonder if she's forgotten how. It just pours out of her while she stands ramrod-straight, unable to form words. Kagiso approaches and, leaning down briefly to pick me up off the ground, she wraps the rest of her arms around Helen and squeezes her tight. Gently, I do the same. We hold each other like that, letting Helen's tears fall on us for a good minute before I can no longer ignore the way Ida's constant squirming jostles the liquid in her overfull bladder. Because, y'know, I am perpetually aware of how much pee everyone around me has inside their bodies at all times.

I carefully extract myself from the hug and head over to Ida, reaching up a limb for her to grab. She does so, and we nod at each other. I pull her through my soul, stagger over next to Sela, promptly fall unconscious, and wake up just in time to see Ida dash out the door and rush into the bathroom.

It's Monday morning. Time to get ready for school, I guess. Hmm... for the first time in a long time, I actually need to think about what I'm going to wear. It definitely needs to comply with the school dress code, since I can't give them any more excuses to kick me out for being a weirdo. I need to wear my gloves, since my fingers are blades and *that's* definitely against school rules and I can't use my phone without them anyway. Likewise, a normal t-shirt will do, since I can't bring my blade limbs out at school either. Hmm... shorts just above the knee should be okay, since it's crazy hot out. I am *so tired* of getting fabric in my knees, ugh. It's something I've just been forced to get used to but I *finally* won't have to deal with it anymore! Shame I still need to wear shoes, but my day-to-day shoes aren't all that bad compared to church shoes.

Wow. I'm... actually doing this, huh?

"Wait, are you wearing that today?" Ida asks, poking her head into my room as she returns from the toilet. "Are you going to *school* in that? You've gotta be going to school, you're way too insane to take a day off."

"Uh, yep," I nod. "I'm done hiding."

"Ohhhh Goddess, okay," Ida grins. "Y'know, I was gonna take the day off to rest on account of being sane, but fuck it, we ball. I don't wanna miss *this*. I'd better run home and change out of the combat gear, though. And, y'know, drop off the gun."

"Yeah, that might be bad to bring to school," I agree.

"Wh... who is... is that Ida?" my mother's sleepy voice calls out, stepping into the hallway to stare at us. "What are you doing here?"

"Oh, good morning, Ms. Hiiragi," Ida says politely, affixing a perfect smile on her face as she nods to my mother in greeting. "Apologies for intruding, I'll be out of your hair in just a minute."

"...Ida," my mother greets her. She looks so tired, like she barely slept at all. "Do you know what's...?"

What's happened to my daughter. There's a haunted look on my mom's face as we stare at each other. Ida just remains smiling and nods.

"Yep, I've been helping her out as best I can. She's been really struggling, but I think getting out there and not hiding anymore will help her out a lot. I've got her back, Ms. H., I promise."

"I... thank you, Ida," my mother says, not seeming too sure how to handle any of this. It's... unlike her. She always seems so in control. But I'm sure she'll bounce back soon, probably worse than ever. I step past Ida and start heading downstairs, prompting Ida to give my mother an apologetic smile and rush down after me. I don't want to talk with my mother right now. I'm not sure I'll ever want to talk with her again, but I'll deal with that later.

"You hungry, Ida?" I ask, opening the fridge and popping a raw egg into my mouth. I don't even use my teeth to crack it, I just

599

squeeze it between my tongue and the roof of my mouth and... pop! Delicious gooey goodness. I am really starting to love raw eggs.

"I, uh, will get some food later," Ida answers, shooting me an amused look. "I'm gonna jog over to Val's place and get my car, alright? I might be a bit late but I'll see you in first period."

"Alright," I nod. "See you there, Ida."

Swallowing my trepidation, I follow her outside, letting her jog off without indulging in the urge to *chase*. Instead, I head to the bus stop as normal, messaging Valerie so she knows Ida and I made it back and we're all okay. She arrives at the bus stop as well soon after, her eyebrows raised as she looks me over. Hmm... it might just be my imagination, but I feel like her face looks a little different. Just a little softer, I guess?

"Woah. We're doing this, huh?" she asks.

"We're doing this," I nod. "Notice any changes on your end?"

"Oh, uh, maybe a little," she shrugs, wiggling her gloved fingers. "I've got the claws under here, of course, but everything else is speculative. It's hard to tell because I'm already pretty hairy, but I think I might be getting *more* body hair? Or fur, I guess? It's not as coarse, at least."

"So you're becoming a furry," I conclude.

"...I'm not a furry," Valerie insists.

"Right. Of course. You're just going to *be* furry," I nod sagely. "Which is different."

"Yes. Exactly."

I grin, showing off my teeth and enjoying that I *can*. She smiles back. Then the bus arrives, and it's go time. One last Refresh to make sure I'm looking my best, and... whoops my hair all just fell out.

Uh.

Wow, it all just fell on the ground at once there, didn't it? Spatial sense confirms it: I am now bald as bald can be. Y'know what?

600

Screw it, we sphere. I can own this. I shrug to Valerie and just leave my hair there, because what the heck else am I going to do with it, put it in its own baggie and store it with the teeth? We get on the bus and every eye is immediately on me. My hip-limbs are visible, though I have my blade-limbs hidden in 4D space. I don't really know anyone on the bus by name; even beyond my usual name-forgetfulness, everyone else on the bus is at least a grade below us, so I suspect they don't know me either. But they *all* stare at me. I smile and sit down, folding my hip-limbs over my lap.

I must look like such a freak. My skin is a very light gray, but it's still distinctly *gray,* not any other color. The eight extra eyes that have been growing around the circumference of my head are getting close to completing, so they look like little dark circles, all the more striking without my hair in the way. And that's not even talking about my arms and legs! Gosh, this is so weirdly thrilling and absolutely terrifying all at once.

I don't get anything more than stares on the bus, of course, because the driver does not give a crap and nobody talks to weirdos on the bus. I know my true trial will be when I get into the school itself and teachers feel the need to police me for being 'disruptive.' ...And also, potentially, the actual police might police me, because we have an officer stationed at our school at all times. Which is normal here, but I feel like it *shouldn't* be normal. Do other countries put a police officer on permanent guard in schools? Or do they just... not have to worry as much about school shootings? I should look this up. I poke around on my phone a little.

Holy fucking shit the United States has had nearly *three hundred* school shootings and the runner-up country has only had *eight.* Eight! Compared to almost three hundred! The United States has had *fifty-seven times more school shootings than every other country combined.* What the actual *fuck* is wrong with—oh hey we're here.

I quickly put my phone and those horrifying thoughts away, stepping off the bus and into the school parking lot. More stares come my way, though it's not *everyone* anymore. There are too many people for all of them to actually care. Which is fine by me!

"You *sure* you're gonna be okay, Hannah?" Valerie asks.

"Nope!" I answer. "But I'm gonna try anyway!"

She sighs.

"...Well, you're certainly chipper, if nothing else. Good luck in class, let me know if you get kicked out."

"Will do!" I answer.

I practically skip to my first class, unable to stop myself from wiggling my hip-limbs with joyous freedom. I walk into the classroom, head for my seat like I always do, and hum some *Pokémon* music (the Route 42 theme, specifically) as I tap my hip-limbs on the ground to the beat. It's a short song, but it's so *catchy!*

"Hannah?" my teacher asks.

"Yes sir?" I respond.

"Um, what are you wearing?"

I glance down, then back up at him.

"T-shirt," I answer innocently.

"I... that's not what I meant," he sighs. "What happened to your hair?"

"It all fell out," I shrug. "Medical condition."

"...That sounds rather serious," he says. "Are you okay to be at school?"

"Oh, yes sir," I nod, giving him a too-wide smile. "Don't worry, I'm perfectly alright. Sorry about how strange I look, but I promise I'm not going to be disruptive."

He stares at me. This is the moment. He can investigate this further. He has all the information needed to know he probably *should*. But will he? Or will he recognize how much work that would be, judge that not having class disrupted is the main thing that matters to him, and just go about his day?

Will he *stick to routine?* I bet he will.

"...Alright," my teacher says. "But I'm holding you to that, Hannah."

Bingo.

"I can sit in the back, so people aren't constantly staring at me," I offer.

"Yeah, that sounds like a good idea," he says, and then he turns back to his computer. I get up and move to the back row, suppressing a chuckle. Just be polite. Be demure. Be cooperative. And people will let you get away with *a lot*. This is the most fun I've had in months!

It's a thin camouflage, of course, and it'll break sooner or later. But despite the many stares, despite my mutations on display, *class starts as normal*. Why wouldn't it? *I'm* certainly not acting like there's a problem. Ida shows up ten minutes after class starts and shuffles into the last open seat—which happens to be next to mine—as I continue to tap away to the beat in my head.

"Holy shit," she whispers under her breath. "This is really happening, huh?"

I nod. I give it like, two days tops, but this will certainly be funny while it continues.

"Alright, well, as I was telling the rest of the class, Miss Kelly, today we will be doing a titration experiment," the teacher announces. "you will be determining the volume of sodium hydroxide solution of known concentration required to neutralize a known mass of an acid solution of *unknown* concentration. In doing so, you'll be able to determine the concentration of the acid. You'll be working in groups of three."

Ida and I shrug at each other and pair up with the closest of her goons nearby. Said goon attempts to interrogate me about my 'costume,' but when I insist it's not a costume she just says 'whatever' and we get to work. Despite being one of Ida's goons, she's actually not bad at chemistry, and the three of us make it through the lab fairly easily, leaving us with a bunch of spare time at the end of class.

"Y'know, come to think of it, I probably could have figured out the concentration way faster if we just had two empty beakers," I muse out loud.

"Oh yeah?" the goon asks. "How?"

"Uh, Hannah?" Ida asks. "You sure you wanna do this?"

"Eh, why not," I shrug. "Just rip the band-aid off, right? Pretending to still be normal is fun and all, but I bet it'll lose its luster fast."

"What are you talking about?" the goon asks. "Does this have to do with your weird getup?"

"Nope, my t-shirt is still unrelated to the situation at hand," I deny cheerfully. "Here, grab me those. This'll make pure sodium hydroxide, so be careful."

"Shit, Hannah, you're crazy," Ida says, grinning wildly. She hands me two beakers. One is the perfect receptacle for water, and the other ideal for sodium hydroxide. At least, ideal enough for my spell. I snap my fingers and let a wordless, Goddessless Refresh magically sort the solution out of one beaker and into its constituent parts in the two others. And sure enough, dry white powder streams out of the water as it flows magically from one glass to the next.

"Ta-da!" I announce. "So as we can see, the mass percent is... wait, beans. This is just the volume, and I don't know the density of sodium hydroxide powder. This is useless."

"We already know the mass percent of the sodium hydroxide anyway, Hannah," Ida says. "We're supposed to figure out the *acid*. Were you even paying attention?"

"Yes!" I insist. "I just got excited and picked the wrong one."

"Wh... what? How the... how did you *do* that?" the goon asks.

"Magic, duh," I answer, snapping a finger for showmanship as I sort the sodium hydroxide back into the water. "See?"

"How the *fuck* did you do that?" the goon demands, raising her voice enough to catch the teacher's attention.

"Is everything alright over there?" the teacher says in a warning tone, walking over to us. Goon just points at me and sputters incoherently.

"I was wondering if you knew the density of pure sodium hydroxide powder," I ask innocently. "So that we could determine its mass by its volume."

"...Uh," the teacher says, quirking an eyebrow. "The experiment would need to go *very* wrong for you to end up with any pure sodium hydroxide. That... shouldn't be possible with this setup."

"Eh, impossible things aren't *that* hard," I say, and re-separate the solution with another snap of my fingers. The chitin really makes a satisfying *crack* sound, even through my gloves. "See?"

The teacher just stares, utterly flabbergasted. Ida shakes as she tries to hold back a laugh.

"Wh... how did...?"

"Magic," I answer firmly, giving him a serious stare. "Magic is real."

He continues to stare at me. I shrug.

"...But like, so is chemistry, so we can continue learning about that instead if you want to," I allow.

There's one final beat of silence before the classroom erupts into chaos. I *do* feel kind of bad, in retrospect. I promised not to be disruptive, after all.

28

BEAUTIFUL

My chemistry teacher stares at me. The class stares at me. Ida struggles to breathe. I smile pleasantly back at all of them, acting as innocent as possible. Hannah has had enough crazy crackers, world! It's your turn, now! Come jump off the frying pan with me!

I am, of course, aware this maybe isn't the healthiest line of thinking. It's certainly not the most logical or optimal course of action. However, it is *very* fun and I'm so beyond done that I just *do not care anymore*. So I'm going to smile. I'm going to wiggle my extra limbs. I'm going to cast the *one spell* that I actually like and don't have horrifically mixed feelings about. And everybody else gets to shut up and watch.

"...That's an excellent idea, Hannah," my teacher sighs. "Everyone, return to your work, please."

What! You're not supposed to—! Aw, dang it, I can't even complain, I was literally just counting on the stick-to-routine thing at the start of class. I just... I showed him actual magic! Does he think it's a trick? Is he just too tired to care? ...Eh, he looks pretty tired, it honestly might be that.

Sure, there's no good way to explain anything I just did as 'just a trick,' but people look at perfectly explainable things and assume the supernatural all the time. Why wouldn't the reverse also happen? Assuming any given set of events falls in line with whatever your worldview happens to be is a profoundly human thing to do. Even if something is *literally impossible* via your worldview you can always just say 'well, *I* sure as heck don't understand that, but there's probably a perfectly reasonable explanation.' I don't know how that works, but I'm sure some scientist does. I don't know how that works, but I'm sure god is involved. I don't know how that works, *and I don't need to know in order to be correct about it.*

How frustrating. I pout, drum my fingers on the desk, and silently mix the sodium hydroxide powder back into the water because I honestly have no idea how dangerous pure sodium hydroxide is and it's probably a good idea to not find out.

"That was incredible," Ida wheezes. "Holy shit. Just fucking *weigh* it, by the way."

"What do you... oh. For the mass? We're not supposed to use a scale for this lab."

"We aren't supposed to use magic either!" Ida laughs. "Fuck, you are *insane.*"

"I'm not insane!" I protest. "My therapist says so!"

"How convincing!" Ida grins unrepentantly.

"No, I'm serious, look, it's just... I'm just a little pent up, okay?"

"Hmm, well, you *are* recently single," Ida muses, her smile shifting to something a little more sultry. "I suppose if you're having problems with being *pent up* I'd be happy to help with that."

"Goddess, Ida, please," I whine, feeling a blush heat up my cheeks. I wonder what color I blush? Last I checked my blood was still red, I guess.

"Ahahaha! Finally embarrassed now you know I'm not joking, huh?"

"Ew, Ida," the goon says, wrinkling her nose.

"Awww! Are you jealous, Cassedy?" Ida taunts.

"I'm not a fucking dyke," the girl answers crossing her arms.

"You sure?" Ida grins. "Your loss, I guess. Personally I find women tend to know their way around a whole lot better. Boys are just kind of guessing at what might feel good, but us girls? We *know*."

And now the goon is also blushing. She looks away, and I try very hard not to think about... *any* of this. Ida is in high school and she has probably had more sex than my parents and I just can't help but be a *little* uncomfortable about all of that. Is she even eighteen yet!? I'm pretty sure her birthday is super close to mine, so she *might* be. ...But then I would have missed her birthday, and that seems unlikely because Ida is *not* quiet about stuff like that the way I am. Shoot, I need to get her a birthday gift.

"...Ida, is there anything you want for your birthday?" I ask.

"Oh *ho ho ho!*" Ida grins."Well *that's* a transition. It just so happens, as a matter of fact, that I'd really like to fu—"

"Ida," I cut her off. "Please. Just... answer the question."

"Not a bad question, actually," the goon agrees, crossing her arms. "Is your birthday coming up, Ida?"

Ida blows a faux-irritated raspberry, leaning her chair back on two legs.

"...Yeah, my birthday's this Thursday, actually," she says. "The party's Friday, though. Yes, you're invited, Cassedy. Hannah... well, you're super welcome to come if you want, but you'd fucking hate it. It's gonna be *loud*. If you wanna drop by Saturday night, though, I'm doing a smaller thing for my less party-happy friends."

"Oh, sure," I nod. "That sounds fun."

"Cool," Ida grins. "See ya there. You gonna cause any more mischief today?"

"...Maybe," I admit, squirming slightly. "I have gym class after this, and I, uh, kind of want to see what happens if I don't hold back?"

"Shiiiit, I want to watch that. Think I could get away with it? Mr. Attenborough is kind of a hardass."

"Yeah, he'd probably kick you out if you tried to watch," I agree. "Though we're probably using the track today, so you could maybe sneak out and watch from a distance?"

"Hey, that's not a bad idea," Ida muses. "Never thought I'd hear you encouraging me to cut class, though."

I shrug.

"Recent changes in my life have made school seem a lot less important."

"You say that, and yet here you are," Ida smirks. "At school. Going to class. As a Goddess-damn mutant."

Yeah, but that's different. I'm not really at school because I think school is important. But I don't want to have that conversation right now, and thankfully I see an easy subject change.

"...You're saying that too now, huh?" I ask.

Ida winces. She *actually* winces, a solid, genuine crack in her usual facade.

"Yeah, I guess I am," she says quietly. "It feels weird not acknowledging Her when you know She's there, right? Swearing to a fake god while a real one watches just..."

"It's scary," I finish for her, since I doubt she'd admit to it herself.

"It's something," she agrees in her own way.

"Why are you two being so creepy?" the goon asks. I think her name started with C? Or K maybe? Nope, I've already forgotten. "Did you start a cult or something?"

Ida and I look at each other, mild embarrassment wafting between us.

"...Uh, I guess technically yeah?" I admit.

"Yeah we uh. Hmm. I guess we did," Ida admits. "That's probably bad."

"Well, at least it's the great old one kind of cult and not the indoctrinate-you-and-steal-all-your-money kind of cult?" I hedge.

"I don't... Hannah, I don't think that's better."

"Okay, seriously, what are you two talking about?" the goon demands. "This is just wacky gibberish to me."

"Uh, I mean, there's not a lot to say," Ida shrugs. "We just... actually have a weird little gay witch coven because it turns out magic is real and Hannah is a mutant and uh. Yeah. Like, I know it sounds really stupid when we say it out loud, but you *just* watched Hannah do something impossible via conventional physics. That wasn't a trick."

"Also I'm a bug girl," I point out.

"Also she's a bug girl, yeah," Ida agrees. "A fourth-dimensional bug girl that can travel between universes."

"It's more that I can't *not* travel between universes," I muse.

"That makes no sense," the goon insists.

"I agree with you!" I tell her brightly. "Honestly, I do. But also, check it out, I can move my arm into w-space."

I do so, causing it to appear to shrink away and almost implode on itself before vanishing all the way to the shoulder. The sleeve of my t-shirt droops, suddenly empty. The goon's eyes bulge and I grin, moving my hand invisibly closer to her. Quickly rotating just the hand back into visible space, I snap my fingers in front of her face and say "Boo!"

She yelps and jumps out of her chair a little, which is of course an unequivocal victory by itself. *Then* she realizes that I seem to have a *floating disembodied hand,* and everything immediately gets even better. A wide smile splits my face and I wiggle my fingers, causing her to jump again. Scaring humans with my weird body is so fun, oh my gosh!

"How the... what...?" goon stammers, and I answer with a cackle and a shrug. Carefully, she reaches out to my hand and I let her grab it, poking and prodding at my chitin. It feels kinda funny at first, but that quickly escalates to *super weird* when she starts poking at my wrist.

The *inside* of my wrist. ...Kind of.

My hand is floating without any apparent arm attached to it. My arm is, of course, obviously still attached to it; it's just at an angle that brings the elbow into w-space before heading back to normal, visible space to meet up once again with my shoulder. So my hand isn't like, cut off and exposing muscle and blood vessels and whatever to the world. Instead, the backside of my hand is just covered in that weird black pseudo-skin that's in between the chitin plates of all my joints. And that... that leads to a lot of questions.

Obviously, my body is somewhat fourth-dimensional. If it wasn't, I couldn't move through w-space so naturally or eat several times my own body weight without using the bathroom. But outside of that vague general awareness, I don't have the slightest idea how my body actually *works*. Sure, I can "see" in four dimensions, and I find moving through them to be instinctive, but that's it—it's *instinctive,* something I just do without thinking. I can't describe what it's like to see or move in four dimensions beyond the fact that it's just *something I do.* I'm not even all that good at it; ninety-nine percent of the things I'm looking at with my spatial sense are just normal 3D objects anyway, and the only 4D object I regularly see is the *world tree,* which doesn't ever move on a scale I can detect.

This moment, with some random girl whose name I don't even know poking at *the inside of my wrist,* is the first time I've ever really come face to face with exactly how much I *don't* know about my 4D nature. It's sort of hard to learn anything about myself when I am the foremost leading expert about my crazy body and the only things I know about my body are that it is mine and it is crazy.

Like *yeah,* my body has the physical structure needed to traverse in four dimensions. But while I'm four-dimensional, I'm not... *that* fourth-dimensional. Like, on the w-axis, my body maybe reaches a few inches in any given hyperdirection, while the *world tree* presumably stretches countless miles. ...Hmm. Come to think of it, maybe that's why it's not dead. Sure, the world tree isn't doing *great* with being on fire and uprooted, but what if it's actually less on fire and uprooted than we think? What if its roots simply reach the ground somewhere in 4D? What if the inferno above us doesn't dance into that extra dimension? Things might not actually be as bad as they appear. ...Of course, just thinking that thought at all makes it difficult to take the idea seriously. If there's one thing I've learned it's that when things aren't as bad as they appear it's only because they are actually worse.

Carefully, curiously, I start moving my arm back into 3D space as Ida's goon continues to prod at the back of my wrist. I'm irrationally terrified that it'll somehow fuse her finger to my flesh or something, but that's obviously wrong because I can *see* that it's wrong. I'm literally just... moving my arm. My arm isn't actually gone. So while it *looks* like my arm is spontaneously filling into reality like liquid rapidly filling a mold, a shadow twisting rapidly into being as the object it reflects moves against a low-angled light, all that actually *happens* is that the goon's finger gets gently pushed aside, the exact same way it would get pushed were I to move normally. Because, well... from my perspective, I *am* moving normally.

It looks so alien to my eyes, yet it feels so utterly mundane to my spatial sense. Routine, yet indescribably mesmerizing.

I'm kind of beautiful, aren't I?

The thought hits me harder than I ever could have expected, purging everything else from my mind for a single, overwhelming moment. *I'm beautiful.* Beautiful! I've never felt this way about myself before. Sure, I take care of my appearance, but it's mostly just a routine thing. I pretty myself up because my mom taught me girls need to pretty themselves up, using makeup to hide imperfections in the face the way I use silence to hide imperfections in personality. If she can't see it, she can't call me out on it. I've never really considered myself *ugly,* I suppose, but my appearance has always been something I minimize, something I avoid thinking about beyond what is necessary to not be bothered.

But now I'm beautiful, and it's an empowering, intoxicating feeling that I never expected in a million years. Everyone else might think I'm a freak or a monster or a demon or an angel but I know, right now, that I am what I never knew I wanted to be. My bone-white arms gleam in contrast with my dark gray skin. My teeth are sharp and deadly. My claws are dangerous and imposing. I move between dimensions with a fluidity and grace beyond human, and my boobs are *impeccable*. My. Body. Is. *Awesome*.

I kinda wish I wasn't bald, though.

"This is completely insane," the goon mutters, and as I snap out of my euphoric fugue I realize that I'm once again getting a lot of stares. "Is this kind of stuff going to be at your party, Ida?"

"What?" Ida asks. "Heck no, are you crazy? I'm not summoning an evil Goddess to my birthday party."

"Uh, *evil* Goddess?" she asks. "Specifically?"

"Yes," Ida and I affirm together.

"Magic is very cool but it comes with a lot of baggage," I continue. "Overall: do not recommend."

I don't actually know if I'm telling the truth or not. I hate magic. I hate the Goddess. But also, I love magic. I love, love, love, love, *love* magic and *She is the source of all magic*. Without Her, I wouldn't be beautiful. I wouldn't be horrified, I wouldn't be a monster, I wouldn't be constantly terrified for my life and my sanity, but... I wouldn't be happy, either. I'd still be caught in that depressive haze, flinching away from any physical contact with other people and mindlessly obeying my mom out of fear.

It's not all downsides. The fruit may be poison, but it tastes so, so good.

"Okay, well, ignoring my ten million other questions for now, why would you follow a god that you think is evil?" the goon asks.

"Well, I'm not really 'following Her,' per se," I say, making air quotes. "I just don't have a choice in the matter. Honestly, I'd really love to thwart Her plans, but unfortunately She's a Goddess and I have *no idea* what I'm doing. So for now I guess I'm just delaying Her plans as best I can and hoping I can think of something?"

"Okay. Okay, sure. You realize you sound totally insane, right Hannah?"

"Absolutely," I nod. "But also I have alien bug limbs, so I figure that makes me a little more difficult to argue with."

She swallows.

"...Little bit," she agrees. "I just... I have no idea what to say."

"Then don't say anything," I shrug. "You don't really need to know any of this stuff anyway. It's my business."

She doesn't seem very satisfied with that, but she doesn't press me any further and that's good enough for me. Class ends soon enough, and I can't help but get a little excited for gym, for what is perhaps the first time in my life. Though when I head into the locker room and spot Jet, that excitement quickly pools into a clump of anxiety. *Oh, right. It's the girl whose life I ruined.* I studiously ignore her as best I can in a futile attempt to not make things awkward.

"Oh, hey Hannah," Jet says, causing me to flinch. "You're really going out like that?"

"Uh... yep," I confirm.

"Hmm. I guess we probably should too?" Jet muses.

"Huh?" I ask, and then suddenly I remember she has wings and a tail and cute little caracal ears and *I did that to them, they're right there, how did I forget that? ...*Oh right, Pneuma magic. Agh, unpopped kernels! Pneuma magic!!! Aaaah!

Then Jet spreads her wings and I'm much more distracted by how *massive* they are than my ever-simmering guilt. Holy crap they're longer than she is tall! Alma thrashes behind her, the scaled, toothy tail clearly anxious but not outright objecting with a bite.

"We agreed to go public too, remember?" Jet reminds me. "Gym is as good a time as any, and... well, honestly, I'm tempted to try

615

flying a little? Our wings are *sore* from growing so fast and I just... I need to *move* them, you know?"

My own extra limbs twitch in sympathy.

"Yeah," I confirm. "I do know."

You know *because* I know. I needed you to know. I'm sorry.

"I figure if we're gonna be stuck like this, I may as well try to figure out the one part of it that could be awesome," Jet continues. "Don't let me go too high, okay? Well, assuming I can get off the ground at all."

"Okay," I nod. Why is she talking to me? I thought she wanted nothing to do with me. I thought I ruined her life.

She's beautiful too. She's beautiful and wonderful and I lost her by being a pathetic, inconsiderate, impulsive monster. Jet hates me even more than Alma does. So why is she talking to me?

"Hannah, chill out," Jet says. "You look like a rabbit that saw a hawk. Did you think dumping you meant we'd pretend you didn't exist?"

"Um. Kind of?" I admit.

She snorts.

"That would be impractical. Don't get me wrong, I don't *like* you, but you're still the only person I can rely on for shit like this. Who else am I going to walk up to and ask 'hey, I'm going to practice flying during class, can you try to catch me if it looks like I'll break my neck?'"

Oh. Hmm. Yeah. I guess Jet's very practical. Like Helen. ...I hope Helen doesn't hate me, at least. I mean she *said* she doesn't, it was actually a super heartfelt moment, but what if she actually secretly hates me anyway? Oh boy, I get to be anxious about this now.

"Well, uh, let's go I guess?" I allow awkwardly, and the two of us head out to the track. I'm probably going to get used to all the stares someday, but not today; *everyone* is looking at us, and Jet's presence has completely crushed my earlier high so it's no longer a pleasant experience.

"*What* are you two wearing?" the gym teacher snaps at us.

"...The gym uniform?" I answer innocently. "I know I haven't been wearing it for over a month now, but I didn't think it would be a problem to start?"

"Cut the crap. We're running the mile today, ladies. If you start the run in that I am *going* to make you finish it."

"Don't worry, Mr. A," I smile. "I plan to finish first anyway."

"Uh-huh," he grunts, clearly unconvinced. Which is fine by me! It'll be all the more fun when I suddenly start moving at like thirty miles an hour.

"I've never actually tried to see how fast I am, either," Jet muses. "Wanna race?"

"Oh, are you getting stronger and faster and stuff too?" I ask.

"Yeah, absolutely," Jet nods. "I'm kind of looking forward to this, not gonna lie."

Why are you looking forward to it if you hate what I've done to you...? Ugh. Gah. Y'know what, it's probably not even about me at all. Jet just got a spell that allows her to talk to Alma, something she's wanted for like... forever. She's probably just in a good mood in general.

The class crowds up around the starting line, and with a quick countdown we're off, Jet and I blazing forward ahead of the crowd. Oh dang, she's fast! Alma-tail sticks her tongue out at me, flopping happily behind as Jet leaves me in the dust. I squawk in surprise, speeding up as best I can. We're at the first turn in moments, and I instantly wish I didn't have these gosh dang shoes on. I can't *stand* the lack of traction from having my claws bound up like this, and I nearly trip taking the turn. Ugh, if only there was some way to get rid of... hmm, wait a second.

My clothes don't follow me into 4D space, so if I just twist my ankle a little bit towards... there. My shoes and socks fall off mid-step, and my feet are free to tear up the track. My claws sink *delightfully* into the squishy polyurethane, sending a shudder up my ankles as I push myself harder and take the next turn sharper.

Jet has something like an actual runner's form, her body tucked extremely low as her tail counterbalances. Long, leaping strides carry her down the straightaway, and it's obvious she isn't even sprinting; she's just *fast*.

I'm also fast, though, and I *am* sprinting. I'm sprinting for perhaps the first time since my transformation started, and even with the wind whipping by my face I'm starting to get a little... warm. I remember all the way back when I first started being lucid on the world tree, and Sindri persistence hunted me into mandatory friendship, that I noted my body seemed to have pretty low stamina. I guess that's still the case; external forces don't really heat me up, but when I overwork *myself* external forces aren't very good at cooling me down, either. I won't be able to keep this speed up for four laps, not by a longshot. Of course, by the time Jet and I finish our first lap, the rest of the class is barely a quarter of the way down the track. So *that's* certainly something.

I slow down a little on the straightaway, resolving to focus my sprints on the turns. I don't know if it's a *smart* strategy, but the sheer joy of letting my claws sink into the ground and fight the centrifugal force of the turn at full speed is too intoxicating to pass up. I'm, uh, probably ripping the track up, but... oh, well!

Another lap down and I'm starting to really feel the burn, and while I've been gaining on Jet at every turn, she's just too fast on the straightaways for me to think that I can actually beat her. We've passed the rest of the class twice now though, which is pretty funny. Rushing past slow humans like I'm a car on the highway is just so empowering that I start to shake a little of my bad mood again. Heh, this is probably how the whole day is going to go, isn't it? Euphoria making me feel good, then memory reminding me I should feel bad, then euphoria making me feel good again, then reality ensuring I feel bad... it's a bit much, but hey! Better than just feeling bad *all* the time, right?

I'm officially flagging halfway through lap three, while Jet is still going strong. I settle back down to a more comfortable jog, though I'm still going twice as fast as anyone who *isn't* Jet. On the last lap I feel like I'm burning up on the inside, but I manage to stagger onto the finish line just after the rest of the class completes lap one. And that's... y'know. Pretty good.

"What do you mean you didn't check my time?" I overhear Jet growling at the gym teacher. I stagger a little closer, barely getting myself off the track before I collapse into a panting heap.

"Look, I don't know what you two did, but you're obviously not running how you're supposed to," the gym teacher grunts. "It's impressive, but it's *cheating.*"

"*Cheating?* We're not at a track meet! ...Alma, no," Jet says, grabbing her tail to stop it from biting the gym teacher. "Look, I'll run it again if you want me to, but I still want to know my time."

"Well I didn't *check* your time, kid. What I *did* do is write you up for a visit to the principal's office, because whatever you're doing to run upwards of thirty miles an hour on my track is *not* school-authorized and it is *definitely* not safe. Grab Hannah, get out of here, and don't come back until you take that crap off."

"It doesn't come off, sir," I croak.

"Then have fun failing gym," he snaps back. "I mean it, get out of here. And I *will* be checking that you actually went."

Welp. He's a jerk, but I suppose this was inevitable. It's probably necessary that we clear things up with the person in charge of the school anyway. I get back up with a groan, my body still protesting the abuse. It's a shame that super speed doesn't mean super stamina. ...Well, I guess it *kind of* does, it's just that my standard for what counts as exertion has changed. But whatever. I stand up and stretch, trying to ignore how exhausted I feel.

"Practice flying on the way back?" I ask Jet. "Just don't go too fast, I'm pooped."

"Uh... I guess so," Jet sighs, glowering at Mr. Attenborough as we head back towards the main building. "This might actually be kind of bad. If I'm sent to the principal, my social worker is gonna know about it."

"Well, I'll do everything I can to make sure we don't get in trouble," I promise her. "I don't want to actually get my family involved, but my mom's a massive Karen and I bet the principal is still scared of her."

"...Alright, I'll hold you to that," Jet says, petting her tail reassuringly as it coils around her torso. Then her wings snap open and she *jumps* teen feet straight up into the air. She flaps her wings twice, nearly flips herself upside down, and immediately collapses back to the ground, barely stopping herself from faceplanting.

"Woah!" I yelp. "Warn me when you're going to do that!"

"Alright, alright," Jet grunts. "I'm trying again."

This repeats pretty much the entire way back inside, Jet insisting that she's 'going to figure it out this time' about ten times in a row before the roof over our heads forces her to put her experiments to a close. It's slightly funny and extremely concerning, but I guess I'd *also* continuously toss myself at the sky if I thought it meant I could learn to fly.

The principal's office is boring, sparsely decorated, and occupied by a woman I'd guess to be in her early thirties. Principal Netter (according to the nameplate on her desk) is an exceedingly average woman, pale and slightly stocky. Personally I think her best feature is all the cute freckles on her nose, though her bulky glasses hide most of it, which is a shame. She gives us a *very* confused look when her secretary waves us into her office, but I just give her a polite nod and a closed-lipped smile and hand her the disciplinary slip the gym teacher gave us.

"There was a bit of a misunderstanding," I say as diplomatically as possible.

"I'm... sure," Ms. Netter frowns. "You know, Hannah, your chemistry teacher just sent me an email about you, as it happens."

"I'm sorry," I grimace. "I'm not trying to be disruptive, but it's... more difficult than expected."

"Well, these costumes of yours are very... impressive, but I feel like it should have gone without saying that they aren't appropriate for a learning environment," Ms. Netter says calmly.

"Yeah, uh. About that," I hedge. "They're not costumes."

And thus begins the long and arduous process of convincing *yet another* random person that I am, indeed, a biological impossibility beyond the ken of modern science. Except this time there's an extra added spice of 'and therefore you can't ban me from school because this is basically a medical condition,' except I can't ever *actually* phrase it as a medical condition, because while they can't demand medical records they would certainly at least make a fuss about it.

The upside to all of this is that Jet and I are eighteen, and politely reminding the principal of that fact dissuades her from calling our parents. I'm *not* sure what that means for Jet in regards to her case worker, of course, but Ms. Netter never even brings it up. It takes nearly half an hour to convince her that our changes are physiological and not something we can undo, and at that point she seems much more concerned about the whole 'my students are monsters' thing than any mischief we might have gotten up to.

"I just, I feel like this isn't something for me to make a decision about at this point," Ms. Netter insists, clearly anxious.

"There's nothing to make a decision about," I insist. "Preventing us from attending school would be discrimination."

"Yes, but it's not just about you," Ms. Netter counters. "I have an obligation to every student and every parent to ensure this is a safe and productive environment for education, and I can't *do* that if you're starting a... a *national controversy* on the nature of the universe!"

"I don't look like this because I want to, ma'am," Jet scowls.

"That's *worse!*" Ms. Netter says."If you had no control over this, if you don't know what *caused* it, you're potentially endangering the other students!"

I open my mouth, then close it, unable to avoid glancing at Jet. I can't deny the validity of the argument, as much as it pains me. I *am* dangerous, as much as I don't want to be. Although, out of all the bad things that could happen at school, accidentally turning everyone into monster girls isn't actually one of them.

Nature's Madness transforms people based on how I see them, and for ninety-nine percent of the school *I just don't care about them enough to see them any way at all.* I don't have to *like* a target of Nature's Madness. I don't even have to want them to be a monster. But I do need to know them, or at least feel like I know them, for the spell to have an effect. If I unleashed it at full blast in the middle of the lunchroom, only a handful of people would actually be affected, if that. Because that's just how I see the average classmate: as a boring, normal human who doesn't understand me, never will, and who gives me no incentive to change that status quo. My apathy makes them immune.

It's only when I really start to care about someone that I can hurt them that deeply. Still, no sense telling any of that to Ms. Netter.

"I don't particularly appreciate being treated like a threat to others just for being different," I say out loud, channeling as much of my 'impending lawsuit' voice as I can muster. I am my mother's daughter, whether I like it or not. "I've been changing like this for months now and nothing has happened to your school. The only thing that's different is that I don't want to have to hide what I am anymore, and I think that's more than fair."

The longer the conversation goes on, the less I like Ms. Netter. It becomes fairly obvious that she's more interested in keeping her job than she is in actually running a good school, and she's too busy freaking out about how weird Jet and I are to actually consider our needs as people. So instead I just frame Jet and I as threats; not to her safety, but to her position. If she's unable to consider us as anything other than a potential problem for her own easy life, I can make it clear that trying to shaft us *isn't going to be easy for her.* She's not happy about it, not at all, but I manage to prevent Jet and I from getting disciplinary action. We'll just have to see how things work out from there.

It's... weird, having conversations like this. Partly just because I feel like I have to channel my mother to get things done, and I *really* hate that, but mostly just because I have to explain to people that I'm turning into a gosh dang monster and expect them to not treat me like I'm insane. And it's just... kind of surreal! Both having to do it at all and *succeeding* at it. I'm sure there will be plenty of people who look at me and refuse to believe anything, but my success rate has been startlingly high so far.

This continues throughout the school day, countless random classmates asking me questions that I answer as honestly as I'm able. Autumn no doubt gets plenty of questions of their own, though I don't see either of them at all after we leave the principal's office. Which... well. It's probably for the best.

It's a long, stressful, but exciting day of school, and I'm pretty worn out by the time I meet up with Valerie and ride home on the bus with her. I kind of wish I could just head back to her place and hang out, but instead I head home, quickly change into my work uniform, and drive myself to work. This will be the *real* test, I suspect. My principal could get in serious trouble for denying a student education for frivolous reasons. My boss, however, owes me jack diddly squat and is entirely within his rights to fire an employee for any reason or no reason at all. My co-workers all give me weird stares as I walk in, reaching up to tie my hair back in a ponytail before remembering that I'm currently bald. Well, that'll make things a little easier, I guess. My hair can't be a health code violation if I don't have any!

"Uh... Hannah?" a co-worker says, blinking in disbelief at me. Hmm, I think he's one of the two that saw me disarm J-Mug.

"Hey," I greet him, giving him a halfhearted wave before walking right past him and into the back so I can drop off my backpack. My boss is tapping away at the computer on some spreadsheet or another, so I give him a nod hello as well.

"Hi boss," I say. "Where am I today?"

"Register one, if you don't have a preference," he answers, turning to look at me with a smile. Then he actually sees me, and his smile locks in place, his sudden bewilderment so all-consuming that it shuts down his facial expression functions entirely.

"Uh?" he says.

"Yeah, uh, sorry I look a little weird," I apologize nervously. "I sort of came out as nonhuman yesterday? And like, I wasn't *totally* sure about coming out at work, but my hair finished falling out today and I didn't really want to lather foundation all over my entire head so I just figured... hey! May as well go to work with my bug bits out, see what happens. Also I'm really sorry about the chicken supply variance lately, that's been my fault."

He blinks at me. I give him my best customer service smile to show I am ready to work.

"What?" he finally asks.

"I eat raw chicken in the walk-in sometimes," I admit quietly.

"*What?* No, wait, back up. Hannah, what is... why do you look like this?"

"Because I'm a weird magical mutant, I guess?" I answer apologetically. Gah, talking to my boss is always so much more difficult and stressful than talking to anyone else. Like, he's a *nice* boss, I like him, but he's still *my boss* and I have a weird complex about that. Probably because of my mom, honestly. Most of my mental problems seem to be because of my mom, in retrospect.

My boss sighs and rubs his face.

"Hannah, please explain this in a way that I can understand," he says.

"Over the past few months I've slowly been transforming into a many-limbed bug monster due to a magic spell that I can't fully control because magic is real and I am the prophet of its Goddess. Downside: I look very strange now and that might turn away customers. Upside: I have a really, really good cleaning spell and I can make this place super spotless. Watch."

I point at his desk and immediately lift all of the dust off of it in one move, along with the stains, pen marks, cluttered trash, crumbs... *everything*. It all levitates right into the trash, leaving the area as clean as it was coming off the factory line. He stares at me, his mouth dropped open in an 'O.' I glance away from his gaze, nervously wringing my hands together.

"So... magic?" he eventually ventures.

"Um. Yep," I confirm. "Magic."

"Huh," he says.

"Yeah," I agree.

There's another terrifying pause, my boss just kind of staring at nothing with a faraway look. The suspense is too much for me, though, so I finally manage to work up the courage to ask the question burning in my mind.

"So... am I fired?" I squeak.

"Wha?" my boss asks, turning to look at me again. "Fired? Heck no, are you crazy? We've already had two people call out today, you're pretty much the only reliable worker I have left."

Oh. Oh! Well, that's nice. ...Except for the two people having called out thing. That, uh, really sucks. But not being fired is nice!

"If you think you can handle being front of house today, I'm not going to complain," my boss continues. "Magic is... well, uh, technically not against the health code? Just be sure to follow the letter of the law with... whatever it is that you're doing. As long as you're not leaving like, invisible radioactive poison behind or something I guess I don't care."

"Um. Just like that?" I ask.

"I guess?" he shrugs helplessly. "I have... *so* many questions, but we're due for a health inspection this week and if we fail another one I'm gonna lose my job so if you wanna use *literal magic* to clean the store... sure, fine, I don't give a fuck. I need to call the area manager about people taking pictures of you in uniform, though, she's probably not going to like that. You okay with talking to her? You'll have to meet her anyway, if you still want to become a manager."

"Well, I... sure?" I answer.

"Cool," he says. "I'm gonna panic about the nature of reality for a bit and then I'll be out to help you guys during the rush, okay? Could you try to clean as much as you can before then?"

"You... want me to clean with magic?" I ask.

"If it makes the store look like this?" he asks, pointing to his desk. "*Yes*. Clean *everything* with magic. Whenever you have time."

Oh gosh. Oh wow. I love my job.

"Yes sir!" I salute, giving him a big grin. He flinches, tells me not to move, and then takes a picture of me before sending me off to get work done. I happily head back out to the front to clock in and get myself assigned to the first register, where my fellow employees stare at me open-mouthed.

"So," I ask them, "did any of you have money on 'extradimensional?'"

"W-what?" one of them responds.

"The betting pool you think I don't know about, regarding 'what my deal is,'" I clarify. "Did any of you have money on me being an extradimensional bug monster?"

The kitchen workers turn to each other. One of them clears his throat awkwardly.

"...Nope, I bet on 'yakuza,'" he admits.

I snort. Because I'm half-asian? Really?

"I thought you were a child soldier or something," the other says.

"Uh-huh," I scowl, walking back into the and hitting the whole place with a series of Refresh casts. "That's a lot less inaccurate than I want it to be, honestly. My therapist keeps comparing me to soldiers as a point of reference."

"Does... does that mean I win?" kitchen worker number two asks, seemingly mesmerized by the sight of dirt and detritus twisting out of all the coolers at once.

"Sure," I allow flatly. "You can win."

People start to trickle in before long, and I start taking orders. I get a lot of questions, but most of them are fairly polite. Confused, more than anything. People start to take more photos, though. More videos. I'm going to go viral sooner or later, especially when things start to get *really* busy and I'm using my extra limbs to take out five to six trays at once.

I scowl as I pick up one of the trays, grabbing a meal and pushing it back towards the kitchen when my spatial sense notices an issue.

"Remake this!" I snap. "The chicken's not fully cooked!"

"Wh—yes it is!"

"You wanna lose *another* bet, number one? Remake it! Now!"

"'Number one?' Wait, Hannah, you know our names, right?"

"Make! The! Food!"

The dinner rush is pretty brutal with just the three of us, but we make it through. I'm exhausted by the time I get home, but it's a good exhaustion. Getting to openly use my favorite spell and be *unambiguously helpful* with it is such an indescribable relief. I really, really needed it. We even got to go home early despite how understaffed we were, thanks to my magic cleaning everything up so fast. I could just handle all of the cleaning while the kitchen duo put everything away.

It's... nice. I like cleaning. I really like it a lot. The Goddess brushes lightly against my shoulders as I sit alone in the parking lot, trying not to thank Her. She could *so easily* be someone worth thanking, for all the good She's capable of. All the good She *does*. But She's not interested in morality, and the evil so comprehensively outweighs it. Is there some way to *get* Her to care? Some way to have the good without the bad? I wish I could find it.

I shake Her off and She happily indulges me, departing as I start the car and drive home. She always wants to indulge me, after all. Indulgence is kind of Her *thing*. Seek joy, no matter how fucked up or messy. Burn hard and burn bright. Those that limit themselves, hold themselves back, fear themselves... they can be entertaining, certainly. I can be entertaining. But wouldn't I be all the more beautiful if I quit being afraid of the pit I'm dangling over and just *let go?*

It's up to me, of course. It always is. But it's harder than usual to argue with Her, in the lonely silence of my car, the memories of actually *liking myself* still sharp and strange in my mind. My body isn't perfect. Far from it, even. But I never realized how brutally *painful* it was to hide until I just... wasn't hiding anymore. I've actually been kind of confident today. Assertive.

Happy.

I'm not exactly sure when I start crying, or why. But when I park my dad's car in our garage, I have to take a few minutes to wipe the tears from my eyes, clean up the snot from my face, and make myself presentable again. I'm not human. I'm not human and I don't ever have to pretend to be again. For good or ill, come hell or high water, from here on out I at least get to be myself.

I head inside, and for once I find I'm not fearing either one of my tomorrows.

ABOUT THE AUTHOR

Natalie Maher writes books (but you knew that, you're reading one) and gets extremely awkward whenever she has to talk about herself (like right now, because "about the author" blurbs are traditionally written in third person but she has to write her own). She thinks that life is messy and likes it when fiction is even messier. She can be fairly easily reached via her Discord server, and if you're interested in advance updates, in-progress stories, or just giving her more money (please give her more money) she has a Patreon. Thank you for reading!

Made in United States
Troutdale, OR
12/10/2024

26284742R00355